Collected Works of the Wingmakers

Volume 1

Also by the author

The Ancient Arrow Project
The Dohrman Prophecy
Quantusum
Collected Works of the WingMakers Volume II
The Weather Composer: Rise of the Mahdi

Collected Works of the Wingmakers

Volume I

by

James Mahu

Edited by
John Berges

 Planetwork Press

Library of Congress Control Number: 2013901992

ISBN 0-9641549-6-x
ISBN 978-0-9641549-6-4

Manufactured in the United States
First Paperback Edition, 2013
Printed on acid free paper

This Ancient Arrow Project novel and Dr. Jamisson Neruda interviews contained in this book are works of fiction. Names, characters, organizations, events and incidents either are the product of the author's imagination or are used factiously. Any resemblance to actual persons, living or dead or actual organizations is entirely coincidental.

 Planetwork Press

403 Gravel Bend Road, Egg Harbor Township, NJ 08234
planetworkpress.com

Dedicated to all seekers
Of true equality and oneness.

Epigraph

Rely not on the teacher, but on the teaching. Rely not on the words of the teaching, but on the spirit of the words. Rely not on theory, but on experience. Do not believe in anything simply because you have heard it. Do not believe in traditions because they have been handed down for many generations. Do not believe anything because it is spoken and rumored by many. Do not believe in anything because it is written in your religious books. Do not believe in anything merely on the authority of your teachers and elders. But after observation and analysis, when you find that anything agrees with reason and is conducive to the good and the benefit of one and all, then accept it and live up to it.

—The Buddha

Contents Vol. One

Preface by the Editor

In September 2009, I unexpectedly received a telephone call from Mark Hempel, the webmaster for the WingMakers, Event Temples, Lyricus, and SpiritState websites. He was calling on behalf of James, the anonymous source of the websites linked to WingMakers.

James wanted to know if I would be interested in being the editor and introductory commentator for all his written works. James had been writing prolifically since 1998, so his writings comprised many pages, as you can see from the size of these volumes.

Call me crazy, but I readily accepted his offer within minutes of the phone call. Now, this wasn't the first time I had accepted a project from James, but it was certainly, the most ambitious one, for in 2007, he approached me with the idea of writing a guide to practicing the six virtues of the heart.

Earlier that year James wrote an e-book called *Living from the Heart* that explained the basic essentials for living a heart-centered life. As an extension of the e-book, the proposed guide would be a handbook of sorts for applying the techniques of the heart that were laid down in *Living from the Heart*.

Well, at the time, I was quite surprised by the mere fact that James thought enough of my understanding of his work to offer me this responsibility. (I should mention here, that I had been in email correspondence with him from early 2001 when I first discovered the WingMakers website.)

So, I slept on his proposal and the next day I emailed him my acceptance of the project. Thus, after several months of concentrated writing, I produced what is now titled *When-Which-How Practice: A Guide for Everyday Use*.

Another, smaller project followed in 2008 when James asked me if I would be interested in writing an interpretive guide to the second Event Temple meditation located at the EventTemples website.

So, despite challenges of these earlier projects, the offer in 2009 struck me as an even greater one because of the sheer magnitude of the materials that would be contained in a collection of James' written works. Nonetheless, as Mark explained, some of the details of the project to me that day, I felt that this was something I wanted to do.

Now, more than a year later, as I write this preface, I realize how much I have learned from this experience, and I also realize how much more I don't know about the expansive vision of the multiverse that James is steadily unfolding before our eyes. It is a humbling experience, but one filled with tremendous hope and confidence in the future of humanity.

With all this in mind, I want to thank James from the deepest feelings of my heart for his trust in me and for the great opportunity he has given me to serve others in some small way at this critical juncture of history. It has truly been an honor and a privilege to edit and comment on this *Collected Works of the WingMakers*.

John Berges, Editor

Preface by the Author

What is within is without equal,
it arises from the smallest space
where the First Vibration of the Unmanifest
surges in the splendor of One World's Grace.

- Hakomi Chamber Four Poem

The WingMakers materials reach outward to open the heart and mind of the reader who seeks to understand what is within that is without equal in our world, and yet, paradoxically, is perfectly equal to what is inside everyone else.

*   *   *   *

Whenever one is asked to explain something as vast as the cosmos and its relation to the individual entity, one is tempted to throw up their hands and expel a deep breath of resistance. Why me? Why now? Haven't people more capable than I done it a thousand times before? The answer to those questions is sometimes hard to understand, and other times hard to ignore. In my case, it was the latter.

I have said before that this was a commissioned work. That is to say, I was asked to produce these materials by an energy field I met when I was a young child. I call it an energy field because I had, at the time, no other way to describe the WingMakers. Over the years, I grew to understand their intelligence and creativity, and ultimately their purpose and how it was linked to my own, and by extension, to each of you who are reading this.

I was given visions of this work when I was yet in my early teens and I could see that its trajectory was not concerned with the production of a text-based treatise. It would require multiple forms of content and technology to include visual art, mythological storytelling, music, poetry, video, philosophy, and ultimately a global community that could embellish these works with its own perspectives and insights.

However, regardless of the many layers, complexity, and scope of these works, there remains a core essence, and this essence is spiritual equality. This is the equality that is found in the deepest layers of the human heart, living free like a mountain stream—uncrystallized and unconformable by social programming or even human experience. You could call this quality of equality many different names. In my own work I've endeavored, and in some cases, struggled, to name it, define it, describe it, compose it or paint it.

This quality of wordlessness and imagelessness is its real essence. How it has survived over thousands of years of persecution by those who would try to own it, enslave it and make it into something it is not, is proof of how carefully it is protected by those who would have you enlightened by its existence. In part, because it is unseen and unspoken, this spiritual equality runs through the DNA of all life as its template of existence—its distillation or quantum essence. It is what survives all time-forms and though it is hidden in the mundane, it is expressible. It can live in our actions. It can have force in our lives. It can become us.

The beauty of this inexhaustible essence is that we—living as human beings—orbit around it like planets to their solar centers. It is this essence that activates us to live a love-centered life and to express the virtues of the heart into our local universe just as the sun expresses its light and energy outward without condition. Spiritual equality is the activator of the highest frequencies of love on earth.

This essence or quality of equality is what is coming to this planet. We are all evolving into it, and it into us, and not necessarily because we are consciously trying or because some all-powerful force is orchestrating it. It is simply a natural outcome of the process that is designed into life. It is the design of an intelligence that arises from our collective sovereign essence. We are all a piece of the design whether we are conscious of it or not.

Part of this design is a clearing of energetic densities that have accumulated since humanity first stepped upon this planet, and this clearing is necessary for all life that composes earth, for all life is connected with earth and to draw distinctions is like trying to dissect the universe with a scalpel.

It may appear that humanity struggles to find its way to a spiritual platform where it can become itself amid the battle of good and evil, but this struggle, even when it takes the form of wars and bitter conflicts, is part of this meshing of domains where the human density is fitted with a spiritual consciousness. For the species as a whole, this is an enormously complex and time-consuming process, but the outcome is that humanity forges a new identity as an interconnected force of unconditional love that explores the multiverse and uplifts all creations that are besieged in darkness.

Darkness is the absence of light and the diminishment of the higher frequencies of love. This darkness is the crucible of change for it draws the light to itself and enables the chemistry of spiritual consciousness to seep into nascent parts of the universe. It is the catalyst and womb of new variations of love and light. While the time-forms of the human instrument come and go, the essence that is within you is unvarying in its will to radiate love into all places of darkness.

The term *human* derives from the Latin conjunction of "homo" (man) and "humus" (earth). Thus a human is an earthly being—descended from earth, as opposed to God or some heavenly abode. The term *WingMakers* is encoded: "wing" is derived from the term wind or blow. It is the active force of setting new states into motion. "Makers" is the plurality of the co-creators—that being the collective essence of humanity. Thus, WingMakers means that from the collective essence of humanity new states of consciousness come into being. This is the meaning of the term WingMakers, and it confers to humanity a new identity.

I have posited that humanity is transitioning to become WingMakers. I realize it is a bold assertion, and some of you will undoubtedly question that humanity is evolving into something that will no longer be called human, and yet it is the case. Many futurists agree that humanity will evolve into something quite different from what it is now, but generally this in the context of machine intelligence and the integration of advanced technology with the physical body and brain system. However, these visions are not far-reaching enough to clearly delineate the human of today from the WingMaker of a thousand years from now—which you who are reading these words, in the flow of time, will become.

And so the human instrument, that which comprises the physical body, emotions and mind, will evolve into a new instrument, even more extreme in its differences as man is to the ape, and this instrument will house the spiritual consciousness in such a way as to allow that essence of spiritual equality I spoke of earlier to truly shine through. This new instrument will not resonate with greed, manipulation, or separation. It will enable the human consciousness to include the spiritual consciousness in its decisions and objectives. This new instrument is what is waiting to be created on this planet.

✳   ✳   ✳   ✳

These works are about the timeless essence and the dynamic changes that occur in the time-based realms that surround it, but more importantly, how the individual can bring a sense of coherence to these seemingly divergent worlds of experience and expression. For those of you who wish to peel the onion skin of the spiritual domains and look underneath the surface, you will find new worlds in these collected works. You will notice a new perspective forming within you as you let the words, images, and sounds dance within you, but remain assured of one thing—you are the practitioner of your own spirituality. There are no rules or laws but one: to express the authentic nature of your heart by living a love-centered life.

It sounds easy doesn't it? It is not. What is easy is to be an automaton and operate like a wind-up toy that is pointed in the direction of consumption. This is the path of least resistance. In order to assert your heart's nature, to express spiritual equality in your behaviors, requires a new sense of individuality—not existential, but connected to all life. A genuine and grounded feeling of spiritual equality, not something held in the head as a concept, but practiced from the heart as a way of life.

For those of you who desire this new sense of individuality, I encourage you to study these works attentive to what resonates with you. Be mindful of the meanings that warm your heart and be especially conscientious to those passages that feel as if you could have written them. Remember, we are in this together. The journey is not yours and mine. It is ours. These collected works could have been just as easily (and rightly) entitled the *Collective Works of the WingMakers*. They originate from all of us, and while I have delineated the words, images, and music differently than what you may have chosen to do, they are nonetheless expressions of our collective state; our spiritual equality in this world and time.

✳   ✳   ✳   ✳

I extend my wholehearted appreciation to John Berges for his contributions in organizing this body of work. John has worked diligently to add his clarifying perspective to these writings with the singular purpose of helping the reader see a deeper meaning and broader perspective to the overall works of the WingMakers. John has been an avid student, researcher, and teacher of these works for more than a decade. He has proven his ability to understand the deeper meanings and subtle persuasions of the WingMakers writings, and to share his interpretations with others. Thank you, John, for your assistance.

The assembled writings in the *Collected Works of the WingMakers Volumes I & II* span approximately twelve years of development and provide a diversity of perspective that can be, at times, overwhelming and even confusing in its sheer variety of definitions and perspectives. One might ask why so many words, images, and music compositions are required to express the simple concept of spiritual equality and living a love-centered life. This variety exists in these writings for one reason: to paint the broadest picture possible so that almost anyone can find a portion that resonates with their personal orientation—the journey that is behind them.

Thus, you are well advised to skim, browse, and search these works for those areas that appeal and resonate with your current beliefs. Some of these writings will seem far-fetched, bordering on science fiction, and if you feel some discomfort in reading these sections, try the poetry or the Lyricus Discourses.

The important thing to bear in mind as you review these materials is that you are composed of a human instrument that consists of your physical body, emotions and mind. The human instrument is equipped with a portal that enables it to receive and transmit from and to the higher dimensions that supersede our three-dimensional reality—the reality of everyday life. These materials are designed to assist your development of this portal so as you read and experience these works, you are interacting with this portal, widening its view and receptivity.

It is this portal that brings the body consciousness, the heart's compassion and love, and the mind's discrimination and insight to a new harmony. And it is this harmony that fuels spiritual equality, anchoring its perspective into this world.

✳   ✳   ✳   ✳

Despite the diversity of the human family and its separation into various races and cultural preferences, the human race is like a tapestry that is morphing into one color, and that color is light. Some will ask how the human memory of separation, injustice, ignorance, racism, genocide, and manipulation can ever be healed, and yet, behind this collection of memories there is a more powerful and compelling memory, and it is of this light where unity resides as the base of consciousness.

Humanity is on the road that leads to this recollection, but it is an infinite journey, and along the way, members of its collective strength show weakness, cruelty and injustice. Human memory will be re-forged into forgiveness as more and more people widen their perspectives to include the higher dimensions where this spiritual equality exists in its full measure. We are awakening from the dream of separate ego-identities to the reality of our collective self—clothed in a power that is harmonious in spirit, mind and heart. This is the vision of the WingMakers, and while some of you may scratch your heads in disbelief, do not feign indifference, for this is the essence of why you are here as you.

You came to this world as an explorer; a soul unclothed wishing to don the human instrument to experience this world of separation not as an experiment or test, but as a transmitter of spiritual equality. And no matter how much the world is pulled apart, no matter how much those in power claw for more power, no matter how befouled love may become, you are here to transmit your heart's virtues and your mind's original insights.

To some, this world can be likened to a schoolroom and we are its students, but it would be far more accurate to say that we are here to exercise our freewill to receive and transmit the higher currents of spiritual equality. It would be analogous to drawing water from a deep well, and pouring a hundred cups of water for our fellow travelers who are thirsty. There is no schoolroom in this analogy; it is more about the dispersion of hope, of vision, of love, of unity.

Be of this heart and mind, and you are aligned to spiritual equality, and in doing this, you are serving your purpose on this planet at this time.

✳　　✳　　✳　　✳

A few years ago NASA finished a low-resolution map of the night sky as observed from our planet. It provided what was then a comprehensive picture of our spatial landscape, but their scientists had a nagging belief that there was more behind the curtain of blackness, and it called them to go deeper. They chose—somewhat arbitrarily—a tiny fragment of space no larger than a pinhead when held to the sky. It was, in every way, unreservedly trivial, just another vacancy, an inky black spot on the tapestry of space, but they pointed the high-resolution lens of the Hubble Space Telescope at that scrap of space, hoping to see something deeper. Something more.

Hubble orbited the earth hundreds of times, and each time it pointed its lens to that pinhead of darkness for about fifteen minutes, gathering the distant photons like a powerful magnet of light. NASA scientists scrutinized the resulting data, and after several days of compiling the layers of imagery their dreams of finding "more" turned to shock. Behind the curtain was not simply a new neighborhood of stars, or a spiral galaxy to compare with Andromeda, but thousands of galaxies! A thousand trillion stars! And one more thing, a horizon line that continued to vanish, where even the eye of HST could not summon the photons as they were too distant to relay their energy to its lens. Within this pinhead of space, ten thousand galaxies whirled on layers so deeply secreted away that we thought they did not exist.

How many pinheads of space hold a thousand trillion stars in their depths? All of them. Imagine for a just a moment that in that unimaginable vastness we collectively call "space" is but one layer of the multiverse. The energy that flows within that one layer originates from somewhere. Life that emerges from that energy; it originates from somewhere. Where is that somewhere? Is it possible it could be inside each one of us? A single, elegant atom of this "somewhere" is all we would need to carry its presence inside us, and if this atom were to exist within us, where would we find it? How would it express itself?

I believe this is the soul, and the soul is sovereign and it is integral simultaneously, hence the term in the WingMakers literature: Sovereign Integral. It lives separate and united at one time in much the same way that light travels in both particles and waves. The soul expresses itself with unwavering love, simple compassion, noble forgiveness, and an unfaltering will to understand the soul in others. The soul feels this vastness even when it cannot see it through a human instrument.

If you took the atom of this "somewhere" from every form of sentient life in this universe, what would you call this new structure, or identity—God, Jesus, Mohammed, Buddha, Krishna, Yahweh, Universal Spirit, First Source, Soul? It does not matter. Names separate. But I would ask you to hold this concept in your hearts as you read these works. The whole of somewhere is everywhere, and it is not simply of this planet or human history. There is no human name bestowed upon it, for it arises not of this planet, solar system, galaxy, or universe. It is far more encompassing and interlinked.

✳   ✳   ✳   ✳

Since 1998 the WingMakers materials have been presented to the world's population exclusively through the Internet without any flourish or promotion.

The *Collected Works of the WingMakers Volumes I & II* is a constellation of materials that sprawl across the websites I have created over the years, and while they may seem quite comprehensive, I assure you that they are only the forerunners of a larger plan known within these materials as The Grand Portal. The Grand Portal is the convergence of science and spirit, of human and soul, of individual and species, and how humanity will discover its soul and connection to spirit through a scientific understanding—not merely as a religious, or spiritual article of faith.

This irrefutable scientific discovery of the human soul will dramatically impact on human culture, science, technology, and religion. Many people have wondered how the discovery of an extraterrestrial civilization could impact on our society. How it would change our worldviews, religions and even our governance. I suspect few of these people have deliberated on the similar notion of what would happen if science could prove the existence of the human soul, and more importantly, enable its discovery for the individual. What impact would this have on our global society?

Just as the concept of extraterrestrial civilizations has found its way into human culture for centuries, so too has the concept of a human soul been brought forward by humanity's mystics whose innate sensitivity made possible their experience of the higher frequencies that we have termed "soul." If you are a seeker, you will have found dozens of definitions for the concept of soul. It is more than enough to confuse and confound the deepest intellect. Some will simply opt-out and become agnostics or atheists, as faith plays too large a role.

Faith plays a part in all things spiritual because the higher frequencies are not registered by our five senses or the lenses of science and technology. The subtle powers of spiritual equality are felt dimly by the human instrument distracted by the duality of a world driven by achievement, greed, and glamour. To lose faith in the worlds of spirit because they do not conform to our five senses, or that their relevancy seems suspect in the face of making a living, is a shame. It is waste of a life to lose faith in that which cannot be seen. You are better off to simply say, "I don't know, but I'll contemplate the possibilities."

That is what I ask you to do as you read. Remind yourself, I don't know, but I'll contemplate the possibilities. There is no one living on earth now, in the past, or in the future that knows it all. Everyone must ultimately say to themselves, "I don't know, but I will contemplate the possibilities." It is in the contemplation that we feel our way to Oneness, and likewise, it is in our lack of contemplation that we slide back to separation and ego identity.

There are many, many people who have incarnated on this planet that are teachers of the spiritual realms or have in some way, a method to help others gain insight into their unique capacities to heal and understand. Intuitive resonance is a key element in your ability to assess the higher frequencies of a particular path or teaching. WingMakers is neither a path nor a teaching. It is simply a way of living based on spiritual equality, and in this way of living, it proposes not to judge, but rather to distinguish carefully between the lower frequencies of separation and the higher frequencies of unity—one and all.

When you feel someone is not in the frequency of unity, then you can withdraw from them if that is your preference, but you can also interact with them in a non-judgmental way by transmitting your internal messages of spiritual equality. This doesn't require words, only behaviors of non-judgment. This is where valor is important because valor requires generosity in the face of separation. It will make you feel taken advantage of sometimes, or too soft, but in reality, those who are generous with their understanding are the ones who are the real warriors on this planet in service to their missions. It is they who are truly the transformers of our world.

More and more people will be introduced to the frequencies of oneness and unity in the coming years, and many of these will come from a path of separation, and when they first come upon the concepts of spiritual equality they may be awkward in their expressions. We are all learning to live in these new frequencies of spiritual equality and unity, and some take to it quickly and effortlessly, while others, perhaps less prepared, navigate into these new waters with caution and a little fear.

It can be difficult to move from the "real" world of material concerns and achievement, to the invisible world of spiritual equality where everything is reduced to an intuitive resonance—a mere whisper of the heart's intelligence. Most people will be traversing this bridge between worlds in the coming decades, and it will be a challenging journey for many, and they will require both generous understanding and compassion.

WingMakers simply aspires to activate people to a higher understanding of spiritual equality through the experience of widening, deepening, and broadening the portal between the individual and their spiritual center. This requires practice. It requires the individual to see themselves as a practitioner of their own spirituality, not someone else's.

You can borrow whatever works for you, whatever resonates with your spiritual center, and you can take these seeds and scatter them around you, and perhaps they will grow into something that supports your journey. However, these seeds are already inside you. Do not deny the spiritual ground you walk on every moment of your life. Do not pretend that you are an automaton of a system that is designed by human or even extraterrestrial hands. You are free to believe and contemplate the highest frequencies of unity regardless of where you live, what your work is, how old you are, how educated you are or what your state of health is. If you practice this contemplation, if you bring self-responsibility to your spiritual life, and you express the messages of unity in your behaviors, what is it that you can possibly lack?

✳   ✳   ✳   ✳

Finally, I want to thank you for your openness in reading these works. It is my heartfelt hope that you will find them stimulating to the part of you that is underserved in this world. You have been educated in the ways of this world and have been told a thousand stories of what you are and what you are not, and here, within these two volumes, is another person—anonymous no less—explaining not so much what *you are*, but what *we will become*.

There is no key to turn. There is no holy mantra to sing. There is no formula to recite to become enlightened. There is instead, the human aspiration to express a genuine spiritual equality without fanfare. Perhaps, even without notice, for it is not seen with the eyes or heard with the ears. It is felt deep within each of us, and in those moments—only those moments—do we draw the truest of our self into this world and share. When we share this part of ourselves, we are doing much more than learning about the cosmos or who we are or why we are here. We bring the vision of our new identity into this world. We become Makers of new states of consciousness for all of us.

From my heart to yours,

James

Acknowledgments

I would like to thank the following individuals for their help and advice in bringing this book to fruition.

First, my heartfelt gratitude is extended to James for trusting me with the responsibility of editing and commenting on his collected works.

To Mark Hempel, for his time, patience, advice, and technical design skills. To Richard Abrams for his early counsel and recommendations. To our weekly WingMakers/Lyricus study group for reading and checking my introductions and commentaries for clarity of content and typographical errors.

Finally, my love and appreciation goes out to my wife, Darlene, for her many hours of patience, care, and wise guidance during these many months. Without her intuitive insights and sage practical advice on various parts of this collection, this book would not be the same. She has truly been a loving friend and partner in this endeavor.

John Berges

List of Abbreviations

AAP	Ancient Arrow Project
ACIO	Advanced Contact Intelligence Organization
ATI	All That IS
ASAP	As Soon As Possible
ATM	Asynchronous Transfer Model (broadband switching & transmission technology)
BP	Resonance broadcast technology
BST	Bland Slate technology
CAL	Computer Analysis Laboratory
CD	Compact disc
CEO	Chief Operating Officer
CI	Complexity Interlocks
CIA	Central Intelligence Agency
CIAT	Cortuem Intelligence Accelerator Technologies
CNS	Central Nervous System
CR	Central Race
DARPA	Defense Advance Research Project Agency
DNA	deoxyribonucleic acid - hereditary material
DOD	Department of Defense
DVD	Digital video disk
EDSS	Encoded Sensory Streams
EITS	Eye in the Sky
ETA	Estimated time of arrival
ET	Extraterrestrial
ETC	Extraterrestrial Time Capsule
FBI	Federal Bureau of Investigation - a US government agency
GMIC	Global Military Industrial Complex
GM	Genetic Mind
HVAC	Heating Ventilation & Air Conditioning
HDMI	High Definition Multimedia Interface
HFO	Holographic Fractals Objects
HST	Hubble Space Telescope
I-steps	Internal Sanitaire Process
ILN	Intra-Laminar nucli
IMF	International Monetary Fund
IM	Invited Members
INS	Immigration and Naturalization Service
IT	Internet Technology
IQ	Intelligence Quotient
KGB	Russian Intelligence Agency
LAN	Local Area Network
LPH	Knots per hour

LERM	Light-Encoded Reality Matrix
LTO	Lyricus Teaching Order
MI6	Military Intelligence 6 - United Kingdom Secret Service
M51	The most famous galaxy in the sky. It is a spiral galaxy, discovered in 1773 by Messier.
MEST	Matter, Energy, Space, Time
MIC	Military Industrial Complex
MIDI	Musical Instrumental Digital Interface
MiG-29	Russian military fighter jet
MJ12	Secret Intelligence Organization
M.O.	Mode of Operations
MRP	Memory Restructure Program
NASA	National Aeronautics and Space Administration
NDRC	National Defense Research Council
NRA	National Rifle Association
NSA	National Security Agency
nRt	reticular thalamic nulci
OSS	Office of Strategic Services
OLIN	One Language Intelligent Network
PGTS	Pattern Grid Detection Systems
PM	Personal Mole
POV	Point of Viewing
PV	Panso Vision - Network's security system
R & D	Research and Development
RICH	Reality Inference Coessential Hologram
RV	Remote Viewing
SL	Security Level
SMT	Surface Mapping Topographer
SLB	Sensory Bi-Location
S & R	Search and Rescue
SPL	Special Projects Laboratory
TTP	Technology Transfer Program
TOP	Triad of Power
TOV	Target of Viewing
UET	Unidentified Extraterrestrial
UFO	Unidentified Flying Object
U.N.	United Nations
U.S.	United States
UIS	Underivatived Information Structure
UV	Ultraviolet
VC	Video Camera
WAN	Wide Area Network
WMM	WingMakers Materials
ZEMI	Sentient Computer

Editor's Notes

Grammatical and punctuation corrections have been made to the contents of this collection in accordance to the Chicago Manual of Style. This has been done for consistency across all of the materials. Importantly, however, no wording has been modified that alters the meaning of the original writings.

On the use of the word "soul" in this collection, please read the following explanation.

Because of the twenty-first century shift in our understanding of consciousness, my introductions and commentaries use the term Sovereign Integral in place of the more familiar word "soul." An explanation follows:

As you read the articles written by James, you will notice that his terminology gradually changes over time. Most of these changes regard the word "soul." His replacements of the word soul are generally prompted by the new psychology and metaphysics that Lyricus is introducing to earth as we transition through the current 2012 dimensional shift. It is also in anticipation of the scientific study of consciousness that will accelerate as the twenty-first century proceeds.

As a result, James' terminology evolves through such terms as the Soul, the Higher Self, the Entity, the Individuated Consciousness, the Wholeness Navigator, the Spiritual Center, the Quantum Self, the Quantum Presence, and the Sovereign Integral. (Often, James does not capitalize these terms, but I do so here for emphasis.)

Although there is a chronological flow to the use of these terms, sometimes he reverts to the term "soul" for papers written as primers to more advanced papers. In other words, sometimes it depends on the target audience. An example of this usage is in one of the latter papers (actually an e-book) written in 2007 called *Living from the Heart*. Here he uses the term soul almost exclusively because this paper is an introductory piece.

Compared to his previous writings, a text interview he gave for the Project Camelot website in 2008 breaks new ground in several areas. One of those areas is in James' use of the term "Sovereign Integral" in place of the term soul. Essentially, Sovereign Integral is the WingMakers/Lyricus term for what humanity has generally come to know as the soul through several thousand years of religious and philosophical texts.

Due in part to the coming shift in our planetary life, an entirely new psychology will emerge that will greatly expand our understanding of consciousness, and especially its core nature—the Sovereign Integral. According to James' body of work, our understanding of the ancient and traditional concept of the soul will prove to be inadequate as new discoveries are made in the fields of psychology, physics, and genetics. Our traditional concepts of the soul are not necessarily wrong, but they are basically rooted in theology and philosophy, not science.

Coming discoveries, will redefine, expand, and alter our traditional concepts of the soul by scientifically proving it to be a real and tangible aspect of our human nature—the core consciousness from which our thoughts, emotions, and actions spring. Thus, we are being weaned from the traditional soul paradigm to a new Sovereign Integral paradigm. This new paradigm has been slowly brought forward in James' writings since 1998.

Further evidence of this expanded paradigm appeared on the final page of the Project Camelot Interview, where a link to James' new website—Sovereignintegral. org was placed. This will probably be the source for future instructional material about the Sovereign Integral.

Below are three definitions of the Sovereign Integral by James from the Project Camelot Interview:

> *The Sovereign Integral is the re-conceptualized expression of the human soul during the era of transparency and expansion. . . . This is the era whose shoreline we have just touched, and those tools, techniques, mental models, and methods of the previous age, well, they are not relevant, just as the abacus is not relevant in the age of computers.*[1]

> *The Sovereign Integral is the transparent Being of expansion, uniquely fit for the era in which we have begun to enter. It is the portal through which the individual can experience First Source in unconditional oneness, equality and truthfulness. It is not the soul or spirit. It is not God. It is not affiliated with the God-Spirit-Soul Complex. It is outside of this construct of the Human Mind System.*[2]

> *If you feel your behaviors reflect a state of oneness, equality and truthfulness, then you are in resonance with the Sovereign Integral.*[3]

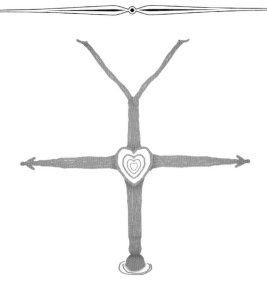

1. *Collected Works of the WingMakers Volume II*, Part IV, Section One, Project Camelot Interview
2. Ibid
3. Ibid

Publisher's Note:

It is rare that a Publisher writes a note for the book or books they are publishing. However, it is felt by this Publisher that a couple of short notes are necessary for these works.

James is a talented neologist. A neologist is a person who creates new words or a new meaning for established words, and those words are called neologism. As you read the Collected Works of the WingMakers Volume I & II, you will come across a word you may not recognize, then go to look it up in the dictionary, only to see that it is not there. When you cannot find the word in the dictionary, you know that James is presenting you with another neologism.

✳   ✳   ✳   ✳

The editor of the Collected Works of the WingMakers Volume I & II, John Berges, wrote a brief autobiography that we felt worthwhile of inclusion:

"Attracted at an early age to all things metaphysical and mysterious, my life has been characterized by a search for a larger reality, a world of meaning and a significance beyond the third dimensional world of human living."

"In all the books read, the esoteric schools attended, the workshops encountered, the study groups engaged, the meditations entered, and the service activities performed, none have been able to quench the thirst of my seeking without the presence of the heart. At the end of the day it is supremely obvious that **heart matters.**"

- John Berges 2008

Event Strings

Before you read further, ask yourself the following question:
"Did I—on my own merits—arrive at this position of reading these words I now read?"

Think carefully. Remember the string of events that led you to this very place in time.

Remember how you found this book and then this specific page? It was not an accident. It was an *orchestrated event-string*. Event-strings are engineered from multiple sets of consciousness, and thus, the answer to the question posed above is, "no." It was not on your own merits, but in cooperation with other forms of consciousness that you are here now.

Consider the planet's population of 6.2 billion people[*]. How many will be reading these same words as you are now? One hundred? One thousand? Ten thousand? One hundred thousand? One million? It depends on the power of an event-string. It depends on the power of the consciousnesses that co-create the event-string. It depends on the resonance of the consciousnesses that activate the event-string. But mostly, it depends on the alignment of the event-string with the will of First Source.

Truly, we tell you, it does not matter as to the numbers. The calculus of spirit is not numeric in nature, but instead, it is the quality of feeling clear and connected with First Source. This is the nature of this specific event-string. It is designed to have this effect, and to enable those who achieve this feeling to broadcast it to the entire planet's population in methods that we are woefully inadequate to describe in words. However, it is accurate to say that this event-string will touch the planet at a more comprehensive level than you can now imagine.

There are many different varieties of event-strings. Some are more dependent on external forces than an intermingling of cooperatively functioning consciousnesses. Some are more personal in nature as in the case of a soul's birth or passing, while others are designed for universal functions. Some are designed to be catalytic while others are preventative in nature.

We want to assure you that as you read these words there are changes in your consciousness that are occurring that will clarify your connection to First Source, and enable you to broadcast this clarity. The broadcasting of this enhanced clarity is not through words or even actions; so much as it is in the vision that you hold within your mind and heart.

This vision is assisted in the paintings associated with this book. They are symbols you can hold in your mind's eye. There will be one image or symbol that will beckon you. Take this image into your mind as if it were a key to the locked door that has stood between you and First Source. Similarly, there will be

---

[*]. This paper was originally written in 2003.

a word or phrase that will beckon you, hold this in your heart. These will activate the event-string contained in this experience that was designed in small part by you, and in large part by a collective of consciousnesses that you may refer to as the WingMakers.

Commentary on Event Strings

Event strings are an interesting concept introduced by James. As indicated in the article, there are various types of event strings. Those given are:

- Externally dependent
- Personal
- Universal
- Catalytic

An *external* event string may involve circumstances that are not dependent on "cooperatively functioning consciousnesses." For example, an earthquake or a flood generates a string of negative effects. Those persons caught in such disasters are the victims of nature. In such cases, there was no cooperation between a group of individuals that caused these events.

A *personal* event string is set in motion by an individual making a decision that generates a series of events, which alter the direction or circumstances of their family, friends or co-workers. Depending on the strength of a personal event string, these can also be classified as *catalytic*.

A *universal* event string might be a string of events caused by global or cosmic occurrences. Economic downturns that affect the world's economy, climate change or a meteor strike, such as the one that science suggests killed off the dinosaurs sixty-five million years ago, are possible examples.

Catalytic event strings effect critical shifts at personal, local, national or global levels. For instance, the invention of the printing press generated a major shift in European society. As a result, writings formerly only available in hand-written manuscripts and mostly in the possession of theologians, royalty, and the rich, could now be printed and distributed to a wider literate population.

Another obvious example is the invention of the personal computer and the development of the Internet. These two technological advances, along with a global telecommunications system, have resulted in a catalytic change of global significance.

If we examine the particular event string associated with coming into contact with these collected works of the WingMakers, the article states that this is the result of your "cooperation with other forms of consciousness." Because the event string concept is being introduced by the WingMakers, the implication is that these other forms of consciousness are the WingMakers themselves. Additionally, the article goes on to explain that the *numbers of people* who interact with the WingMakers Event String is not an issue.

> *The calculus of spirit is not numeric in nature, but instead, it is the quality of feeling clear and connected to First Source. This is the nature of this event string.*

As you delve further into the *Collected Works of the WingMakers*, you will discover that the WingMakers materials are catalytic in nature. Consequently, the event string that brought you to this work is catalytic in nature. All the materials in this collection are designed to catalyze your consciousness and, as a result, expand your view of the world and the multiverse.

If you can accept the event string concept as a working hypothesis, this has interesting implications. For instance, how is it that you are somehow cooperating with other "forms of consciousness," namely the WingMakers? In most cases, one would simply believe that it was just a random event that could have a significant affect on one's beliefs, or not.

If you feel that this catalytic information of the WingMakers has merit, you will probably immerse yourself in it, and you will naturally want to interest others in it also. At this point, you may very well experience what others have—that those who you would fully expect to be interested in this material feel absolutely no resonance with it. And most importantly, these individuals often have grounding in spiritual and metaphysical concepts and writings. The question then arises as to whether this particular event string is directed toward a particular group of individuals scattered across the globe. The answer to this question is yes, but only indirectly, as you will see in the next quotation.

But first, this progression of possible implications now suggests that there may be some kind of continuity attached to all this. In other words, is your contact with this material somehow related to your Sovereign Integral's blueprint? This supposition might sound too far-fetched to consider, but if we do possess individuated Sovereign Integrals, and if our consciousness survives physical death intact, then this opens up the real possibility that all humans have a role to play in the development of our civilization, as well as in the development and expansion of our consciousness. At the physical level, this may appear obvious, but we are expanding the framework to include the possibility of specific Sovereign Integral groups that have roles to play in our planet's future. Further, we are suggesting that these Sovereign Integral groups incarnate at critical junctures in history and effect catalytic changes in society.

Amplifying this point we have the following:

> The WingMakers Materials are not being aimed at any one group. It is more the reverse that there are certain groups and individuals that are being directed to the catalytic material you refer to as WMM. Events strings are like mathematical algorithms that possess a resonance point that, when affected by a certain frequency, can induce a select individual, or to a lesser extent, an entire group, to unconsciously seek out the WMM. This inducement is like a subtle fragrance that draws you to a destination of a flower-covered field without your conscious desire to experience a flower.[4]

4. *Collected Works of the WingMakers Volume II*, Part IV, Section Two, Topical Arrangement of Questions and Answers, Question 1-S3

There are entities incarnated now who will be returning in human embodiment in the next one hundred years who will play a significant role in the unveiling and dissemination of the Grand Portal. Their involvement with these materials now will help them navigate to these roles because it will recalibrate their internal value system, and in some instances, literally recast their destinies.[5]

More information about the Grand Portal will be provided later, but for now, it means the scientific discovery of the Sovereign Integral (soul or greater self). This discovery is the bedrock of the WingMakers mission to earth, and its discovery is described as the single most important event in a planet's history.

Summing up, as the above quotation states, no one has to have a *conscious* awareness of their Sovereign Integral's innate connection to these materials and their implications. It is enough for now—*for all of us*—that we have found this material and that we resonate to it and study it for a deeper understanding of a new metaphysics, a new psychology of the Sovereign Integral, and a new cosmology of our role in the multiverse. Thus, this is an opportunity for expansion at many levels, for if you resonate with what all that is written here, a new possibility opens up for you—the possibility that your immersion in the Event String of the WingMakers is part of your Sovereign Integral's blueprint for contributing to a monumental shift in humanity's understanding of reality and its place on a cosmic scale.

INTRODUCTION

Even as we introduce ourselves to Earth,
it is done under the guise of mythology and story.[6]
- James

Myth—A metaphor for what lies behind the visible world.
- Joseph Campbell, The Power of Myth

What would you think if someone claimed that the world was now on the cusp of a renaissance of spirit incorporating art and science; that within seventy years, a human lifetime, irrefutable evidence of the immortal human soul (Sovereign Integral, see Editor's Note) would be discovered, leading to a new science of consciousness and our interaction with human populations of other planets in our galaxy and beyond? Well, this is exactly what the anonymous author and creator of this collection of writing (and other media) maintains regarding humanity's future in this century.

This individual identifies himself as James (who at the time had not revealed his surname). Over the past ten to twelve years he has produced writings, art, and music to support his assertion. These writings and other artistic elements appeared on the Internet over that span of time and are spread across three main websites: WingMakers.com, Lyricus.org, and Eventtemples.com. While his work continues to unfold and evolve, this book brings together the first ten years of his writings in one collection. (Since that time two websites have been created. These are sovereignintegral.org and spiritstate.com.)

Readers familiar with James' work will most likely come to the *Collected Works of the WingMakers* with a different perspective than will new readers. Early followers have been exposed to a gradually unfolding series of writings (and other media) that have expanded into new directions over the years. In a real sense, this slow release of writing, music, and imagery has been an advantage for those who discovered James' work early on because they learned to adapt to the expanding nature of the information.

Those of you who have recently discovered the materials, either through the websites or through this book, are in a more challenging situation because you are confronted with ten years of writing and may well be bewildered by the amount and diversity of the information.

Hopefully, this introduction and the pieces preceding the various sections of the book will help everyone gain a better comprehension of the purpose of these writings and how the various parts fit together.

The WingMakers—*I am creating a mythological story that contains a philosophical system that is being externalized at this time for the next three generations of humanity.*[7]

---

6. *Collected Works of the WingMakers Vol. II*, Part IV, Sec. Two, Top. Arr. of Qs and As, Ques. 6-S2
7. *Collected Works of the WingMakers Vol. II*, Part IV, Sec. Two, Top. Arr. of Qs and As, Ques. 5-0

The WingMakers focuses on the written works associated with wingmakers. com, and even though this collection concentrates on the written material, it must be pointed out that the WingMakers material also includes paintings and music. As will be explained in more detail in the Part I introduction, the WingMakers offering is a metaphysical presentation of human existence in the multiverse[8] couched in a mythological framework containing the various artistic components. These varied elements can be thought of as a tree. James' novel, *The Ancient Arrow Project* represents the roots and trunk; the paintings, images, music, poetry, and philosophy are the branches.

The name WingMakers is actually a euphemism for what James describes as the Central Race. These were the first humans created by First Source and they were responsible for creating all the human forms that inhabit the space-time worlds (more details on this later).

Although the WingMakers material is presented as a mythological story designed to stir our imaginations, stories of this genre are not necessarily pure fantasy, but often contain elements of truth, and this is also the case with WingMakers. Recall George Lucas' many hours of conversation with Joseph Campbell, probably the greatest student and scholar of mythology in the past one hundred years, as he conceived the Star Wars epic. In his tale, Lucas brings the forces of good and evil into clear focus, but underlying these two exterior forces is the power of the Force. The power of the Force is the bedrock of the mythological world of Star Wars, it being the essential underlying foundation connecting all life. The WingMakers mythos takes the Force concept one step further, making it more specific by placing the presence of the Force within us as—*the Force of the Sovereign Integral*.

So the success of mythical tales, both ancient and modern, lies in their ability to touch our hearts, our feelings, and our deep intuitive sense of connection to one another and to the universe. It's all about how they make us feel through the information they provide. The WingMakers materials follow this tradition.

Hence, the entire WingMakers' presentation, with its array of artistic expressions, is designed to trigger the primal memories of our spiritual origin and nature—long lost and forgotten—as we have journeyed through the worlds of space and time. The material challenges us to feel and think deeply about who we are as a species, where we came from, where we are going, and why we are here.

The intriguing aspect of the WingMakers material is that James urges us to consider the core principles and concepts of this mythological story as true. The following bullet points give a general idea of these concepts and are far from detailed explanations.

- We are immortal, discrete, spiritual entities—individuated beings created by God or First Source. We are God fragments.
- As spiritual entities (or Sovereign Integrals), we inhabit a domain of

---

8. James often employs the term multiverse because universe commonly refers to the physical space-time dimension only, and according to the metaphysics of the WingMakers, intelligent life forms exist in multiple dimensions besides the physical.

unity lying outside the space-time, three-dimensional universe.

- Only a small portion of this entity consciousness is embedded within our human forms, which are designed to live in and explore the space-time universe. WingMakers refers to these forms as Human Instruments. They are designed for physical, emotional, and mental functioning.
- The Human Instruments inhabiting the space-time worlds have been genetically engineered by the first individuated entities created by First Source, identified as the WingMakers.
- As incarnated human beings, we experience life as individuals, separated from our core essences, or Sovereign Integrals.
- This experience generates uniqueness in the human species and leads to enormous creative diversity across the universe of populated worlds.
- This universal activity not only evolves the consciousness of the incarnated entities, but also contributes to the evolutionary development of the multiverse.
- The goal of the human species is to expand consciousness to the stage of the Sovereign Integral[9] in which the certainty of "I am an individual within the species" fuses with the certainty of "I am the species within the individual." In a sense, the human *particle* is also the human *wave*.
- The WingMakers exhort each one of us to strive to live the life of the Sovereign Integral.
- At a particular threshold of consciousness evolution, the human species of any given planet is considered ready for a major transformation and transition from an isolated planetary-based civilization to a connected inter-planetary civilization.
- Earth's humanity has reached this threshold, and consequently, the WingMakers have come forth to guide us to our destiny.

Before we move on, the Human Instrument mentioned above consists of the physical body, the emotions, and the mind. However, there is one more component in addition to these three. This is the Genetic Mind. Our bodies, emotions, and minds are unique to each one of us, but the Genetic Mind is different. The Genetic Mind is that part of the Human Instrument we share with all other human beings on our planet. It is the collective unconscious of humanity, and each of us can access it through our Human Instruments. As you will discover as you read further, the Genetic Mind holds an important place in humanity's future in this century. Much more about the Genetic Mind's importance can be found in my introduction to the Lyricus Discourses—The Interface Zone, as well as in The Interface Zone discourse itself. Following is a brief description of the Genetic Mind. For further descriptions,

---

9. See WingMakers Glossary p.665 and Manifesto of the Sovereign Integral p.590.

refer to the WingMakers glossary and the supplemental glossary in the appendix.

> The genetic mind is different from the subconscious, or universal
> mind as it is sometimes referred to in your psychology texts, in that
> the genetic mind has a peculiar focus on the accumulated beliefs of all
> the people on a planet from its most distant past to its present time.[10]

The story, poetry, art, music, and philosophy of the WingMakers are vehicles for delivering these concepts (and others) to a world population facing unprecedented change at every level of society. And yet, the music, image, poetry, story, and philosophy are more than meets the eye and ear, for James describes them in a peculiar way. He calls these components "encoded sensory data streams."

In simple terms, these encoded components are specifically designed to activate unused and undiscovered portions of our DNA that open our awareness and sensitivity to dimensions of reality beyond the three-dimensional world we currently experience.

Consequently, there will be major shifts in the consciousness of humanity as this century proceeds. The WingMakers are now active on our planet to offer us guidance in this transformation. The millions of people who shift their consciousness to a more refined level will eventually lead to what the WingMakers call the Grand Portal. This will be a scientific discovery that will prove the existence of the human soul; more on this shortly.

So who is James to claim that he has this capability and knowledge? And even if he has such knowledge and expertise, is this a task that one individual can perform successfully? His claim implies knowledge of biology, genetics, and DNA far beyond our current science. Interestingly, in the story, the WingMakers are experts in the science of genetics, and yet here is James implying his knowledge of genetic restructuring through the orchestration of sound and light by means of music, images, poetry, and prose.

To be clear, James is not channeling information from some other-dimensional entity; he states that he has direct access to the information and knowledge he displays. He is not claiming exclusive ownership of this information, but simply as the individual initially responsible for passing this information on to us. But from where does his information come?

The Lyricus Teaching Order—*The exportation of the teachings called WingMakers is in fact the work assembled by Lyricus.*[11]

According to James, he is a member of an ancient group of advanced humans that he calls the Lyricus Teaching Order (LTO). The LTO is not earth-based. Their home world, or origin point is unknown to us at this time, and even if their point of origin were known it would be meaningless to us in the context of the vastness of space.

---

10. WingMakers Glossary, p. 666.
11. *Collected Works of the WingMakers Vol. II*, Part IV, Sec. Two, Top. Arr. of Qs and As, Ques. 52-S3

Just to be clear, and thus avoid any confusion, the great majority of the members of the LTO are part of the WingMakers, but apparently, not all WingMakers are part of Lyricus. What role the non-LTO WingMakers play in the grand scheme of things is not known at this time. The particular WingMakers that are described in the WingMakers material are members of the LTO. We know this because of the following quotation from the Lyricus.org website: "Lyricus is aligned with the Central Race or WingMakers, and the great majority of its members are from the Central Race."[12] In another passage we find this:

> They are a specialized training faction of the Central Race that— for the most part—is not incarnate in a physical form. They are amply described in the WingMakers material that has been released. This part of the story is factually presented. . . . The WingMakers have been communicating with humans for approximately eleven thousand years preparing them for the discovery of the Grand Portal. They are quite capable of contacting people with or without an intervening technology. You will know them by the balance they exhibit between art, science, and philosophy, as well as emotions, mind, and soul. They are particularly focused on training and supporting individuals who are instrumental to the discovery of the Grand Portal.[13]

At the beginning of 2004, the site of the Lyricus Teaching Order (lyricus.org) appeared on the Internet. The nature of the Lyricus documents is quite different from those found at the WingMakers site. Part II of volume II contains the written materials associated with the Lyricus Teaching Order. At the time of this writing there is an article addressing the Grand Portal discovery and its effects on humanity, along with two sets of FAQs on the LTO's relationship to humanity and the methods that Lyricus teachers employ for guiding the human species to the Grand Portal.

Following these background information pieces, the website includes the Lyricus Discourses. These are dialogues between a student and a teacher on various themes. As explained by James in various writings, the Lyricus teachers emphasize teaching through stories because the information conveyed through stories and myths is more easily absorbed through a story-telling style than exclusively through philosophical texts and intellectual activities.

Metaphorically, the WingMakers presentation can be likened to the film or the play that captivates our senses, that draws us into its world of imagery and music, its story and poetry. WingMakers entertains us, informs us, and affects us. But more importantly, it is designed to *prepare* us for the presentation of new concepts and theories related to the nature of life in the multiverse and the role of earth's humanity beyond the confines of our planetary nest. The WingMakers tableau seeks

---

12. WingMakers and the Lyricus Teaching Order, p. 19
13. *Collected Works of the WingMakers Vol. II*, Part IV, Sec. Two, Top. Arr. of Qs and As, Ques. 6-S1

to accomplish this through its art, music, and written materials.

As of this writing, the content of the Lyricus website is scant compared to the WingMakers site. Also, unlike the WingMakers website, the content of the Lyricus site is primarily comprised of documents, with music, and graphic imagery serving supportive roles. The few documents are written, however, in textbook-like style— direct and to the point. There are no metaphorical and symbolic art forms here. The layer of subjective interpretation is not present.

On the surface, this difference in stylistic presentation appears to be a dichotomy, but closer study reveals an integrated and systematic approach to educating individuals attracted to the Lyricus materials. It's really easy to understand and not out of the ordinary at all. It's generally the same as a classroom environment in which students read a short story or novel and then discuss the plot, characters, cultural, and historical settings. In effect, the story becomes the vehicle for delivering the author's message to the reader. So the WingMakers presentation seeds and fertilizes our feelings and thoughts along cosmic, metaphysical, and psychological themes, but the Lyricus teachers step forward and encourage discussion about how the story relates to the life of the "readers." Does the story engender new insights into life in terms of meaning and relationship? What can the story and its symbols teach us about ourselves and the world in which we live?

Just as the life and background of J.R.R. Tolkien, author of *The Lord of the Rings*, may disclose the roots of his Middle Earth, the Lyricus documents, and by extension, James' explanations of his identity and background, disclose the roots of the WingMakers story. In a manner of speaking, the existence and presence of Lyricus here on earth is the story behind the story. A short quotation from the Lyricus site explains:

> WingMakers is part of the mythological expression of Lyricus that typically accompanies its first external expression within a species. It is the "calling card," announcing its initial approach as it treads softly among the species to which it serves. WingMakers is the mythological expression of the underlying structure of the Lyricus Teaching Order. It is symbolic of how Lyricus is brought to the planet.[14]

A team of these teachers (about twelve) is now present in our world, and James is the first member of this team to make himself known through his writing, music, paintings, and communication with those attracted to his work. James and the other members of his team have access to a database, a knowledge repository accumulated over millions of years of Lyricus interaction with human populations spread across the universe and extending into the psychological dimensions of human activity.

Interestingly, the Lyricus mission to earth is more comprehensive and wide-ranging than indicated by the writings of the last ten years. There are at least three categories of Lyricus teachers associated with our planet, and are here to prepare

---

14. WingMakers and the Lyricus Teaching Order, p.19.

humanity for the discovery of the Grand Portal. James revealed this to me in an email that I received while working on these collected works. His comments follow:

> There are three kinds of Lyricus teachers in terms of incarnational presence on a sentient-bearing planet: Transmissioners, Catalysts and Continuers.
>
> Transmissioners are concerned with the transmission of the Genetic Mind to all soul carriers, so that soul carriers can access the Genetic Mind despite the third-dimensional realities of survival, sustenance and the culture of conformity that it begets. Transmissioners connect the soul carriers of early civilization to the collective wisdom pool of the Genetic Mind, which in turn positions the species on the road to The Grand Portal. They allow the stored, collective wisdom of the human family to seep into the evolving soul carriers so that the inventions that ultimately lead to the global communication networks can be discovered.
>
> The Catalysts are focused on The Grand Portal preparation and induction of the prepared members of the human family therein. The Continuers ensure The Grand Portal endures well beyond its discovery.
>
> The Transmissioners incarnate as civilization begins, the Catalysts come much later when the communication networks are in place to support propagation channels that can lead to The Grand Portal. The Continuers incarnate in the generation in which The Grand Portal is discovered and often continue to incarnate twenty or more generations after its discovery. There are no more incarnations once the Final Continuer decrees a planet is a fifth-dimensional entity.[15]

Simply put, this new information from James regarding these three categories of Lyricus teachers reveals the extensive preparations that Lyricus sets in motion once they know that a human species is advancing to the point of reaching the Grand Portal. This extended effort, probably spanning thousands of years at least, testifies to the knowledge base, ancient teaching experience, and well-defined protocols of this cosmic order. As you read further into the collected works, these factors will become obvious to you in the context of the various documents.

Lyricus is not a religious organization, but focuses on science and culture building. Through the documents released by James on the Lyricus website, the LTO's expertise consists of seven disciplines. These are:

- Genetics
- Neo-sciences
- Metaphysics

---

15. Email from James to John Berges.

- Sensory data streams
- Psycho-coherence
- Cultural evolution
- The Sovereign Integral

Lyricus is responsible for shepherding human populations of planets to the scientific discovery of the Sovereign Integral. As mentioned earlier, the LTO calls this discovery the Grand Portal. This is its primary mission. According to Lyricus, genetics holds a central position relative to the other six disciplines due to the requirements of the Sovereign Integral's discovery. What these requirements are is unknown to us at this time and must await future scientific research projects as they evolve through the course of this century. James and the Lyricus team are stepping forward now because humanity has reached a point in its development in which the Grand Portal discovery process can proceed through scientific research.

From the information given so far, particle physics and biology (especially DNA research) are the key sciences necessary for proving the Sovereign Integral's existence. Lyricus estimates that the Grand Portal's discovery will most likely occur about 2080. Generally speaking, this is the LTO's projected estimate based on its extensive knowledge base and the factor of humanity's free will. The implications of what this discovery means for the human race will be addressed in more detail when we introduce the Lyricus material.

Further, the assertion that genetics lies at the heart of the Sovereign Integral's scientific discovery brings us back to James' encoding of the materials related to the WingMakers website, for as you can see from the previous bulleted items, one of the other disciplines of the LTO is sensory data streams. Consequently, James has already begun a process of activating our DNA through the encoding of the WingMakers music, images, poetry, story, and philosophy.

The Lyricus documents inform us that the Grand Portal event is the most important discovery of a human species because it establishes that planetary population on an inter-dimensional, inter-planetary network of human populations on hundreds, if not thousands of worlds. In other words, it enables us to contact and participate in a network of post Grand Portal civilizations. This network is called the Sovereign Integral Network.[16] In effect, and at the risk of over-simplifying the concept, the discovery of the Grand Portal is the birth of a human species from its life in its planetary womb and into the greater universal life it was destined to live. Our species' gestation period is rapidly coming to an end. The Lyricus Teaching Order is here as midwife to this cosmic birthing.

Before moving on to the next phase of James' work, let's chronicle how James gradually released information about himself between 2001 and 2008.

James—*I am not someone to worship, and I am purposely intangible to ensure*

---

16. See WingMakers Glossary p.670.

this will not occur because it will only stand in the way of our mission.[17]

Although James has been careful to maintain his anonymity, the few background details he has provided are just as fascinating as the stories, philosophies, music, and metaphysics he presents. As individuals attracted to his work, it is natural for us to inquire about James' identity and background. Despite his desire for anonymity, James has respected our curiosity by responding to private and public inquiries.

The following few extracts in this section represent a chronological snapshot of James' gradual release of information about himself and his role as a member of the team of Lyricus teachers here on earth who are preparing us for the Grand Portal.

The original WingMakers' website appeared on the Internet on November 23rd, 1998. For all intents and purposes, it was a static website, with no updates, and no one to whom inquiries could be sent until the site underwent an update in the period of February to March 2001. It was at this time that a CD-ROM entitled, "The First Source Disc" became available for sale at the WingMakers site. This CD-ROM contained a letter from James.

As you read excerpts from his letter, keep in mind that James' references to this disc (and future discs) as a platform for delivering his teachings has been overtaken by advances in Internet technology. Without going into needless detail, content beyond the First Source Disc is now delivered via the Web. So, whenever he refers to the discs, also include all the materials that have followed since its production in 2001. Following are excerpts from his letter.

> I am a simple man who lives for a singular mission, and the *First Source* discs are the fruits of this mission. . . . For reasons I'm certain you understand, my identity will be purposely clouded, and I encourage you to not worry about who I am, who I have been or what my role is.
>
> I have been here many times before with names you would recognize, but this incarnation is different, and I vow to remain unknown, even fictional. My soul is no different in nature than yours. I have a body, and therefore, I have my frailties—in some ways, just like you. I am not someone to worship, and I am purposely intangible to ensure this will not occur because it will only stand in the way of our mission.
>
> The *First Source* discs will impact on all people; even those who will never read, look or listen, and these will be in the majority I assure you. These teachings are designed for the entire planet despite the relatively small number who will actively immerse within the story and utilize this portal.
>
> While my personality will always seem intangible, know that I am in this disc more vividly than any teacher that has come before

---

17. *Collected Works of the WingMakers Vol. II*, Appendix III, James' Disclosure Letter

to your planet. It is my nature to live in the universal mystery and personal clarity of my Self. When you are in accord, you will find me with you.[18]

Toward the middle of 2001, the original WingMakers' public Internet forum members assembled a number of questions and sent them to the website's webmaster, Mark Hempel, so that he could forward them to James.

Nobody was sure if the questions would be answered, but to everyone's delight, James answered back. Among the various questions, were several asking James about his work with the WingMakers material and his identity. Note that at that time (May 2001) wingmakers.com was the only website containing James' work.

> **Question 3:** Do you think that something akin to "The WingMakers" inspired you to create this Myth, or are you just lonely and a little bored?
>
> **Answer:** I was not inspired to create the WingMakers mythology; I was commissioned to perform this specific task. No one requires inspiration to carry out a task required of them by the very nature of their purpose as a life form. . . . I refer to it as a mythology only because I must convey—in good conscience—that the material is not completely factual.[19]

Not only does James confirm the mythological nature of the WingMakers material, but also he tells us that he has been commissioned to perform the task. Commissioned by whom? James was not more specific until he answered a second series of forum questions several months later. In this first session, however, he did answer two more questions about his identity.

> **Question 5:** Are you a 'Master' as some proclaim?
>
> **Answer:** There are so many definitions of the term "master" that I am not willing to say I am this, or I am not this, unless a definition accompanies the word. Since you did not provide a definition with your question, I will not provide an answer. I will, however, acknowledge the spirit of your question, which is: what am I?
>
> In this regard I am as you are. I am a multidimensional being who lives simultaneously in a spectrum of realities. My dominant reality is different than yours. Because of this difference, I am able to process this human reality at a different frequency rate, which enables me to perceive behind and beyond the three-dimensional "surface" of this reality.
>
> As a result of this ability, I am able to translate art, music, poetry, philosophy, and scientific insights that are from my dominant reality

---

18. Ibid.
19. *Collected Works of the WingMakers Vol. II*, Part IV, Sec. Two, Top. Arr. of Qs and As, Ques. 3-S3

into yours. In so doing, I have translated sensory data that will catalyze future discoveries that will redefine the human soul.

Now, does this mean I am a master? I am simply performing the exact function I was created to perform.[20]

Question 11: Who/what are you James? Where do you get your information from?

Answer: In my dominant reality, I am known as Mahu Nahi. I am a member of a teaching organization whose roots are very ancient, but paradoxically, very connected with humanity's future. This teaching organization is concerned with transporting a sensory data stream to earth in order to catalyze select individuals of the next three generations to bring innovations to the fields of science, art, and philosophy. These innovations will enable the discovery and establishment of the Grand Portal on earth.[21]

In these two answers, James clearly establishes himself as a human entity from beyond earth, from a different "reality." He says that he is very much like us, but that he is a multidimensional being who *consciously* lives in these different dimensions simultaneously. In the second answer he tells us that in his *dominant* reality he is known as Mahu Nahi. Briefly put, he has a dominant, or home reality and temporal realities where he works as a Lyricus teacher, among other activities that we can only imagine, if that. It appears that at least one of his temporary realities is now on our planet, where he is known as James. As we now know, his task in our reality is to translate and create multimedia encoded resources that will aid us in the scientific discovery of the Sovereign Integral—the Grand Portal.

About two months later, forum members submitted more questions for James and he answered these also. With this additional set of answers, James revealed more details about himself.

Question 6: How did the WingMakers reveal themselves to you and place a profound calling upon your life?

Answer: I am a member of a teaching order that has existed before the creation of the planet Earth. I realize this may seem like an impossible reality, but it is my reality nonetheless. This teaching order is allied with the esoteric teaching orders of earth. The teaching order of which I represent is not known in your world because it has chosen to remain hidden until the Grand Portal discovery process is made public.

You may refer to my teaching order as Lyricus. It is the closest name that resembles the vibration of its true name in your native language. Lyricus is aligned with the Central Race or WingMakers,

---

20. *Collected Works of the WingMakers Vol. II*, Part IV, Sec. Two, Top. Arr. of Qs and As, Ques. 5-S1
21. *Collected Works of the WingMakers Vol. II*, Part IV, Sec. Two, Top. Arr. of Qs and As, Ques. 9-S1

and the great majority of its members are from the Central Race. Within Lyricus, expertise is centered on seven disciplines. These include the fields of genetics, cosmological sciences, metaphysics, sensory data streams, psycho-coherence, and cultural evolution. We are not, as you can see, focused exclusively on philosophy or spiritual teachings. Our central purpose is the irrefutable discovery of the humanoid soul upon three-dimensional, life-bearing planets.[22]

With this answer, James explained that he is a member of Lyricus, an order so ancient that it has existed before the creation of our planet. This is quite a statement, indeed. It is, however, not so far-fetched when we consider that the known universe is now believed to be at least 13.5 billion years old, while the age of our planet is now estimated to be about 4.5 billion years old or roughly one-third the age of the cosmos. Accordingly, the existence of intelligent beings in older parts of the universe is a real possibility, since these beings would have had at least two times longer to evolve.

Question 47: Why did you think it necessary to make yourself known as the creator of the WM Materials, rather than leave the materials first presented as being a creation of Humans from the future, called "WingMakers?"

Answer: I have always been consistent on this issue. I am not the creator of the WingMakers materials, I am the translator. The materials existed before I incarnated on earth. I have taken the original content and transduced it (for lack of a better term) into a form (music, art, words, symbols) that would resonate to the human senses and mind. The original materials, of which only a small fraction has been translated and published on the Internet, are created by a subset of the WingMakers called Lyricus (my term). Lyricus teachers assembled the materials and have exported them to the various life-bearing planets like Earth. At the appropriate time, a lineage of teachers incarnate and begin the rigorous process of translating the materials into "human form." I am merely the first of this lineage to begin the process of translation. As to your question, the lineage of teachers I speak of do—in a real sense—represent humanity's future.[23]

This extract provides more details about James' work of translating the WingMakers material (also see volume II, Topical Arrangement of Qs and As, Translation Methods). Especially interesting here, is that our planet is not unique in this process of guiding humanity to the discovery of the Sovereign Integral and its interactions with multi-dimensional realities, including those associated with other life-bearing planets.

It was not until April 2008 that we learned a little bit more about James' personal

---

22. *Collected Works of the WingMakers Vol. II*, Part IV, Sec. Two, Top. Arr. of Qs and As, Ques. 6-S2
23. *Collected Works of the WingMakers Vol. II*, Part IV, Sec. Two, Top. Arr. of Qs and As, Ques. 47-S3

life. At that time, James offered to give an audio interview to Mark Hempel, at Mark's home in Minneapolis, Minnesota, USA. This was the first time the public had heard James speak. In the third and final segment of the interview, released in early 2009, James gave a few details of his early personal life.

In it, he explains that he was born in Spain, outside Barcelona, where he lived a normal childhood. His father was a government scientist and his mother was a "stay-at-home mom." He has an older brother and a younger sister.

As he grew up, James had access to scientific texts through his father's career and interests. At various times, his family lived in other countries of northern Europe and also in India for a while. As an adult, James eventually came to live permanently in the United States sometime in the mid-nineties. As of this writing, this is about all we know about James personal life on earth.

Interestingly, as James has gradually released information about himself, his story ends at the most mundane, most easily acceptable point—as a human child born on earth, just like the rest of us. But, as we know from the foregoing information, this is where "the rest of us" are left behind, for beyond our parental origins we don't know where we have come from, where we are going, nor why we are here. Do we exist prior to human birth? Do we survive death and live after our biological bodies die? Do we live on other planets and in other dimensions besides earth? From James' remarks and the enormous body of writing contained here, James claims to know these answers (and many more) and he is here, along with other Lyricus teachers, and in alliance with the "esoteric teaching orders of earth," to help us discover these greater truths for ourselves.

If we are open to following these existential questions into metaphysical and cosmological territory, then James' story of his trans-earth existence is—in and of itself—a broad and deep view of a greater reality, a reality lying beyond our earth-based sciences, philosophies, and theologies. It is a cosmic-centered view fraught with enormous implications about the nature of human consciousness and our place in the multiverse.

If your mind is open to this possibility, then you may agree that James is offering us a truly sweeping vision of the human experience that radically decentralizes our earth-identified sense of reality. This reorientation and expansion of human consciousness is, according to the LTO knowledge base, the next step in our consciousness evolution as a species. As disclosed earlier, Lyricus has guided humans on other planets through this process many times, and now—in this century—our time has come to take a major step in cosmic-spiritual evolution. And as the next section explains, one of the steps before us involves a psychological approach.

A Shift in Focus—*The heart is the hub in the grand network of souls who are incarnated, regardless of space or time.*[24]

In 2005 James' work expanded into new territory with the release of his paper

24. *Collected Works of the WingMakers Vol. II*, Part III, Sec. One, "The Energetic Heart: Its Purpose in Human Destiny"

"The Energetic Heart: Its Purpose in Human Destiny." This was soon followed by another paper in early 2006, entitled "The Art of the Genuine: A Spiritual Imperative." (The written materials pertaining to the heart are collected in volume II of the collected works.)

These two papers signaled a shift from the "big picture" themes of WingMakers and Lyricus, to a focus on the individual through a form of spiritual psychology that concentrates on the heart and a set of virtues that come through it from the Sovereign Integral. These virtues are appreciation, compassion, forgiveness, humility, understanding, and valor.

Taken alone, this turn toward individual personal development and behavior does not seem to fit into the cosmology and metaphysics of the WingMakers and Lyricus materials. But upon closer examination, these two papers accentuate the long-term Lyricus goal of guiding humanity to the Grand Portal. This is because the development and consequent expansion of human consciousness is an essential element of the Grand Portal discovery. Scientific knowledge and technology are the other key factors for sure, but without a new stage of psychology that bores deeply into the nature of consciousness, and its physical, emotional, and mental attributes, the discovery of the Grand Portal cannot take place.

In 2007 a new website was launched by James called EventTemples. This site continues the psychological work initiated by the two earlier papers on the role of the Sovereign Integral and heart in today's stressful world. To be clear, the word heart refers to the emotional aspect of human psychology, especially as opposed to the mind.

The foundational e-book *Living from the Heart,* first published at EventTemples.com, is a comprehensive primer on the value of the heart for establishing a life expression balanced between the spiritual and material realms of living. These are not mutually exclusive, as often historically exemplified by the withdrawal from everyday living by individuals who wanted to live a life cloistered in a monastery or isolated in a cave awaiting enlightenment. By contrast, the coming time is one in which we remain in everyday life and achieve enlightenment through contacting the teacher within.

As first noted by James in his 2005 paper on the energetic heart, a major contributing factor to this rapid change in world conditions is a global "dimensional shift" that will further refine the quality of energies of our planet. Many refer to this shift simply as 2012 because this is the year when the Mayan calendar ends (specifically December 21, 2012).

Some believe this marks the end of the world, while many others feel that this time marks the end of a world era of strife and the beginning of an era of harmony. Although he has not given specific details at the time of this writing, James describes the coming time as an era of transparency and expansion. The effects will be more subjective and subtle and less objective and physical (such as catastrophic earth changes). Thus, a great proportion of the earth's population will feel increasingly nervous, anxious, and uncomfortable in the more refined psychological atmosphere of the planet. And this is the primary short term reason for James' introduction of the heart-oriented material. It is especially brought to focus in his second paper's title, "The Art of the Genuine: A Spiritual Imperative." Bluntly speaking, in the coming new era following 2012—*it will be imperative to live a life of the genuine.* In this increased, more refined energy there will be no nowhere to hide, especially relative to our greater Self, the Sovereign Integral. How this will translate into physical behavior and world events is unclear and probably unpredictable, but generally speaking the times will be challenging to all established institutions that evolved prior to the shift.

The other component of the EventTemples site is the event temple meditation sessions. These are specifically timed daily meditation events that anyone can participate in. They are designed to encourage people to send loving energy to others, as well as to give individuals the opportunity to practice activating, receiving, and transmitting the heart virtues in a practical way. If nothing else, James' initial two papers along with the EventTemples materials represent the practical application of the more theoretical foundation laid down by the WingMakers and Lyricus writings.

So, taking the WingMakers, Lyricus, and EventTemples materials as a whole, this volume along with volume II can be thought of as a well-planned psycho-spiritual and metaphysical curriculum in the beginning stages of its presentation to humanity.

Clarification of a Few Terms

Spiritual. The term "spiritual" as used throughout this collection, applies to any activity, religious or secular, that contributes to the wellbeing of humanity and the natural world. Spiritual also includes subjective states such as emotions, thoughts, and intuitions that result in feelings of joy, unity, understanding, compassion, etc. These states, and the practices or conditions that induce them, transcend any particular religion.

Metaphysical. Related to all matters lying beyond the range of the five senses.

Consciousness. Awareness of one's self as distinct from others. Self-awareness.

Soul. The term "soul" especially adopted by the religions of the West is roughly the same as self-awareness, or consciousness, excluding any dogmas attached to it. James' use of soul can usually be interpreted as individuated consciousness. As explained in the Editor's Note, James is now identifying the soul, or individuated consciousness as the Sovereign Integral, and therefore this term is used for the most part in all the introductions and commentaries.

Reading the Material

The purpose of bringing all the written materials together in these volumes is to provide a source for reading, studying, and cross-referencing the enormous amount of information contained in the separate documents. These *Collected Works of the*

WingMakers Volumes I & II can thus be read at whatever level of depth desired.

There is no specific order in which the material should be read. The idea is to allow your inner voice to guide you and when questions arise you may want to search through the collection for related topics that can increase your understanding. For instance, if you are reading about the Grand Portal and you want to review what else James has written about it, you can perform a search and explore other documents containing references to the Grand Portal.

Another suggestion is to hold the idea of the big picture in your mind. Keeping oneself open to the many concepts set forth in these writings and accepting them as a working hypothesis, will help to avoid "not seeing the forest for the trees."

It is often the case with materials such as these, which provide a large cosmological worldview, for readers to get stuck on minute details that don't make sense to the left-brain, logical aspect of the mind. In such cases, it is helpful to release what doesn't seem to make sense at the time and simply proceed to absorb the overall concept. Often the details fit into the larger scheme as our understanding matures.

As James explains in his interview with Mark Hempel, it is not so important where one begins to explore the materials, as long as one begins. Having said that, he proceeds to suggest that we not limit ourselves to just one aspect of his work, but to examine other areas as well. In James' own words, here is that section of the interview:

> **James:** You will notice that the first floor of the structure that Lyricus built consists of the WingMakers materials. When you design a building, the main floor is where people enter the building even if that building has one hundred or more stories. Everyone enters through the ground floors. Now, if that skyscraper is sitting in a busy intersection, it has entrances from all four sides of the building. Some on the main level, some underground, perhaps. In the same way the WingMakers materials have many different access points because some people will resonate to the materials in the Neruda interviews, that speak of government conspiracy and extraterrestrial influences, others will find the philosophy particularly meaningful, perhaps others will find the art or music to draw from. However they enter the structure, from which entrance—it doesn't really matter—so long as they enter the building and proceed to higher levels of the structure.
>
> Now the matter of feeling fear or frustration is a common side effect once people better understand the dark forces and learn how they try to manipulate the systems of culture and government in their favor. But this is also part of the activation, because the individual must again choose to be led by these forces or disengage from them and discern their subtle influence. We don't turn a blind eye to these forces, nor do we fear them. Instead we see them as part of our

family that have lost their connection to the higher frequencies of love and we send our compassion to them.

I would suggest to readers of WingMakers: Do not stop your exploration of these materials in the Neruda interviews or the Ancient Arrow book, but continue your investigation into the Lyricus and EventTemples materials, as these will acquaint you with the higher levels of the Lyricus structure.

Mark: And what are these higher levels, James?

James: Well, the highest level is the Grand Portal itself, and perhaps later I will add some textures and details to the meaning of the Grand Portal. For now I will just say that it is the ultimate goal of the structure. After WingMakers came the disclosure of the Lyricus Teaching Order or LTO. This was the next level of the structure that was built out so as to make clear that the mind behind the WingMakers was not affiliated with the subject of its writings, namely the ACIO or Incunabula—the alpha organization of the Illuminati. So, the LTO was disclosed in its role, seeding the human understanding of its purposeful journey to the Grand Portal. This was done to clarify the purpose of the WingMakers materials. The next level after Lyricus was more recently launched, and it is the EventTemples.

EventTemples is the activity-based level of transitioning from the instructions of philosophy or mythology, and placing the focus on living a love-centered life through the expression of the six heart virtues.

These three levels—WingMakers, Lyricus, and EventTemples— are aligned and coherent expressions of the one goal of our human family uniting in the behaviors of love and collectively knocking on the door of the fifth dimension, and meshing these energetics of the fifth dimension with the human domain. That is the Grand Portal.[25]

Keeping James' advice in mind, may your reading experience lead you to consider and ponder another view of what it means to be human in a multiverse of unimaginable livingness, limitless opportunities for growth, and countless exploration possibilities.

PART I

The WingMakers—

The real import of the WingMakers materials is to, in effect, dislodge the person from the historical mind and move them into a sense of connection to their higher Self and the Spirit that supports it.

Collected Works of the WingMakers Vol. II, Part IV, Sec. One,
Mark Hempel Interview with James, Session One

WingMakers and the Lyricus Teaching Order

Lyricus is aligned with the Central Race or WingMakers, and the great majority of its members are from the Central Race. Within Lyricus, expertise is centered on seven disciplines: the fields of genetics, neo-sciences, metaphysics, sensory data streams, psycho-coherence, cultural evolution, and the Sovereign Integral. Lyricus is not focused exclusively on philosophy or spiritual teachings. Its central purpose is the irrefutable discovery of the humanoid soul upon three-dimensional, life-bearing planets.

Lyricus could be likened to the Jesuits or Tibetan monks of the Central Race, except that the teachers of Lyricus place a much more significant emphasis on the nexus of the integrated sciences and arts. Nonetheless, they are a faction of the Central Race and bear responsibility for shepherding a species to the Grand Portal, and thereby indoctrinating the species, as a whole, into the broader network of the intelligent, interconnected universe.

This task requires a very broad agenda, encompassing genetics at its core, and the other six disciplines mentioned above as integral, but peripheral forces that propel a humanoid species to discover its own animating life force and the subtle vibratory fields in which it operates. Lyricus employs a variety of sensory data streams to awaken a species, ranging from music, books, art, science, culture, and mythology. Generally, these are isolated expressions, but as the species draws closer to the Grand Portal, the sensory data streams are increasingly integrated, encoded, and represent potent forces for the expansion of consciousness.

WingMakers is an expression of an encoded sensory data stream that is designed to help in the awakening process of those individuals incarnating in ever increasing numbers over the next three generations. The WingMakers sites—each of the seven—will be translated in a specific order. Each site carries a central theme that is connected to the seven disciplines of Lyricus. These seven disciplines—collectively—are the triggers for those incarnating in approximately thirty-five to forty years who will be the scientists, scholars, psychologists, and artists who will uncover and disseminate the Grand Portal.

WingMakers is part of the mythological expression of Lyricus that typically accompanies its first external expression within a species. It is the "calling card," announcing its initial approach as it treads softly among the species to which it serves. WingMakers is the mythological expression of the underlying structure of the Lyricus Teaching Order. It is symbolic of how Lyricus is brought to the planet.[26]

---

26. Source: Lyricus.org

SECTION ONE

The *Ancient Arrow Project* Novel and Dr. Neruda Interviews

On a level that you have never seen, you are a holographic entity that is woven throughout all things, and when you touch into this feeling, you awaken a frequency of your consciousness that will guide you into our world. You have no reason to believe us, yet you know our words have no other purpose than to awaken a part of you long dormant. We are the WingMakers. We leave you in the Light that is One.

The Ancient Arrow Project, p. 69.

Dr. Neruda:

"The best way to conceptualize who these beings are, is to consider them as geneticists who were the first born of First Source. The galaxies in which the Central Race resides are approximately eighteen billion years old and their genetics are immeasurably more developed than our own. They are the optimal soul carrier in that they can co-exist in the material world and the nonmaterial dimensions simultaneously. This is because their genetic blueprint has been fully activated."

The First Interview of Dr. Jamisson Neruda, p. 266.

Introduction to The Ancient Arrow Project Novel

"We are here to assist beings like yourself to first conceptualize and then experience the multidimensional universe as it truly is—not only through the language of your world, but through the Language of Unity."[27]

The *Ancient Arrow Project* novel is the centerpiece of the content at the WingMakers website. The paintings, music, poetry, and symbolic language have their origins in the novel and are extensions of it.

The story's plot involves shadowy global power forces, top-secret government agencies, extraterrestrials, time travel, secret advanced technologies, and remote viewing. If all of these were not enough, there is the unexpected intrusion of a highly advanced, enigmatic group of beings called the WingMakers.

The WingMakers are the catalytic force of the novel's plot. In the eyes of Fifteen (signifying the level of his security clearance), the head of the of the Advanced Contact Intelligence Organization (ACIO), the WingMakers are a potential threat to his own secret agenda.

Here the plot thickens as we learn that Fifteen, unbeknownst to his supervising agency, the National Security Agency (NSA), has formed an even more clandestine research team called the Labyrinth Group. Even though the ACIO's mission is to investigate and reverse engineer alien technologies (collected from crashed UFOs), Fifteen is primarily interested in time travel research, and this is the primary task of the Labyrinth Group team.

Fifteen's top scientist is Jamisson Neruda. He is an expert in linguistics, encryption, and decoding technologies. Neruda's father, Paulo, was a high level director of the ACIO and thus Jamisson's interaction with the secret agency began at an early age. Following his father's death, Jamisson became fully involved with the ACIO and Fifteen became a mentor to the young Neruda. As a consequence of these circumstances, Fifteen, the ACIO mission, and the Labyrinth Group's secret time travel research are the focus of Neruda's entire life—until the WingMakers arrive on the scene and turn his world upside down.

Is this story true? Yes and no. One of the most controversial aspects of the WingMakers material is whether it is based on actual events in the life of Jamisson Neruda. Because the WingMakers site and its original content were on the Internet for a little more than two years prior to when James came forward to claim responsibility for all the content, a sizable number of visitors to the site became convinced that the material was a true account by a government scientist turned whistleblower. Even now after more than ten years of an ever-evolving and more encompassing array of topics created by James; topics that extend beyond those of the novel into psycho-spiritual areas, there are those who cannot accept the original WingMakers material as a mythology created by James. They believe there are super-secret government agencies in contact with extraterrestrials and that they

---

27. The *Ancient Arrow Project*, p. 40.

are developing technologies from such contacts. They believe there is an agenda for global dominance by a clandestine group of financial power elites. In fact, many believe that the individuals, events, and technologies contained in the *Ancient Arrow Project* are real.

As the years have gone by since the novel's final version and official release on the First Source disc in 2001, James himself has admitted that his story is generally based on facts, real events, real individuals, real organizations, and most importantly—a real race of advanced human beings called the WingMakers. He tells us, however, that the story and its characters are fiction, but *based on these hidden realities*.

James briefly comments on this controversy in an excerpt from his disclosure letter on the *First Source* disc.

> The WingMakers website created controversy and debate, and many have delighted in debunking its authenticity. Those who debate whether it is true or not, have diminished their sight of the truth that is woven into its structure.[28]

He offers further comments on this fact or fiction controversy in answer to an interested inquirer.

> There were elements of the story that were purposely under-developed in order to keep the story in the realm of a mythology, and not a real-life series of events. These would include the place photographs, artifacts, and some of the storyline itself. I was well aware that these elements would be discovered for what they are. And I am aware that there are some who feel a disappointment in this reality, but it is only because the real light of the WingMakers has not fallen on the ground and illumined it. It still hangs in the air, traveling to a destination that is yet unseen.

> Question. For what reason is the material a mixture of truth and disinformation? What purpose does it serve to do this?
> Answer. Remember that I am creating a mythological story that contains a philosophical system that is being externalized at this time for the next three generations of humanity. This mythology is a Tributary Zone (which you are well aware of), and it must be encapsulated in multiple media in order to attract the new generations who will require it. Because it has multiple media, and the original content from whence it comes is not of this earth, it requires augmentation. This augmentation is a storyline that threads together the real Transition Zone characteristics (e.g., philosophy, metaphysics, glyph language, poetry, music, and art), with the mythological elements of the ACIO and Ancient Arrow mystery.

---

28. *Collected Works of the WingMakers Vol. II*, Appendix III, James' Disclosure Letter.

It was considered eons ago that a philosophical, text-based treatise was not the appropriate catalyst for the generations of the twenty-first century.

Question. Is the story factually correct, apart from places, names and dates?

Answer. The story I assume you're referring to is the ACIO and Ancient Arrow site. This part of the story is based on fact. I won't divulge how I know these things, but it certainly isn't difficult to ascertain if you've studied the story in any detail. There are techniques that can be applied to secure the information.[29]

What James has created in his novel is not much different than what other authors have done with their creative writing, namely they have taken actual historical events, individuals, and organizations, and built fictional stories around them. One recent example is Dan Brown's novel, *The Lost Symbol*. Brown states that the story has a basis in Freemasonry and other organizations, which he researched for the novel. He simply created his story around these. James has done the same thing, except for one huge difference. He claims that he gathered his information, not from on-the-ground investigation and research, but rather through what he calls sensory bi-location, a much more advanced form of remote viewing.

In answer to a question asked by a public forum member about how he obtained the information for his novel, James states:

The information is based on factual data secured through a form of remote viewing, referred to by my teaching organization as sensory bi-location. SBL is different from classic RV because it is associated with the higher mind rather than the psychic channels of astral vision. Because of this distinction, SBL permits one to analyze motive and intent, in addition to the sensory/action environment that RV technology acknowledges. SBL is also more focused on active sensory channel selection, rather than reactive selection as in the case of RV.[30]

Therefore, although James' story is a fictionalized rendering of real behind-the-scenes activities, he gathered this information in a manner that is beyond the known capabilities of remote viewing as reported by various researchers and investigators. Presumably, his ability to utilize SBL is a result of his affiliation with the Lyricus Teaching Order, or has he says "my teaching organization."

For those unsure of James' claims and the true nature of the *Ancient Arrow Project* story, the proof of validity may never come because James is not interested in proving anything, including his identity. He is primarily interested in stimulating

---

29. *Collected Works of the WingMakers Vol. II*, Part IV, Sec. Two, Top. Arr. of Qs and As, Ques. 6-0
30. *Collected Works of the WingMakers Vol. II*, Part IV, Sec. Two, Top. Arr. of Qs and As, Ques. 2-S2

our imaginations and opening our minds to a trans-materialistic paradigm of human existence culminating in the discovery of the Grand Portal and the science of multidimensional reality in the latter part of this century. The *Ancient Arrow Project* novel represents the initial stage of this process—a process holding enormous implications for what it means to be human. This quantum leap in human evolution is too important for a one-track approach and therefore numerous tracks besides the specific Lyricus mission exist for its eventual success. And this success is dependent on all seekers of truth tapping into their inmost selves through whatever path they resonate to, for that is where the truth lies. As an old adage says, "Many true paths lead to the same summit." As James states:

> I am appreciative of your interest and desire to understand more about these works. To those of you who are studying these materials, please be attentive to the path you have chosen to walk. This path is not for dabbling or mental exercise. It is a journey into your personal wisdom. If there were anything else you seek, I would encourage you to set these materials aside in favor of another path, or even no path at all.[31]

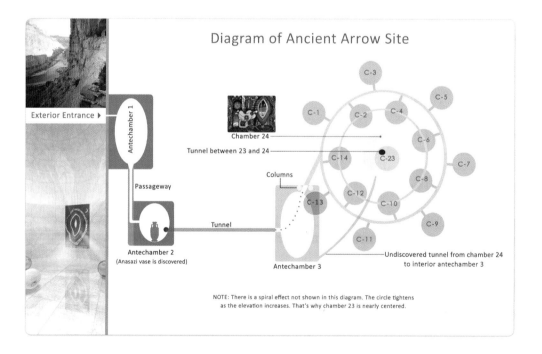

Diagram of Ancient Arrow Site

Exterior Entrance ▶

Antechamber 1

Chamber 24

Tunnel between 23 and 24

C-1   C-2   C-4

C-3

C-5

C-6

C-7

C-14   C-23

C-8

Columns

Passageway

C-13   C-12   C-10

Tunnel

C-9

Antechamber 2
(Anasazi vase is discovered)

C-11

Antechamber 3

Undiscovered tunnel from chamber 24
to interior antechamber 3

NOTE: There is a spiral effect not shown in this diagram. The circle tightens
as the elevation increases. That's why chamber 23 is nearly centered.

31. *Collected Works of the WingMakers Vol. II*, Part IV, Sec. Two, Top. Arr. of Qs and As, Concl. Remarks by James

THE
Ancient Arrow
PROJECT

James Mahu

PROLOGUE
CRUCIBLE 826 A.D.

Traveler of the Sky entered the steep canyon in a dreamlike fog, drawn by a towering rock structure that seemed to clutch the sky. Never had anyone from her tribe ventured so far into the mountains. She was from the Chakobsa tribe, whose genetic origins were Mayan and whose progeny would later become known as the Anasazi Indians of Northern New Mexico. Her lean, bronze skinned body bore the ritual tattoos signifying her as leader of the Self-Knowers.

The Self-Knowers focused on the spiritual development of the Chakobsa tribe. They created the various rituals, rites of passage, meditation chambers or kivas, and were responsible for the tribe's record keeping with regard to its origins, history, and belief system.

Traveler of the Sky was thirty-four years old, dressed in tanned deer hide cut just below her knees, with turquoise beads adorning her neckline and hemline. Over her heart was an ink print of her right hand in blue-violet ink with tiny white beads attached, signifying a starlit sky—a reference to her name. Her straight, black hair fell below her shoulders to the small of her back, held in place by a headband made of rabbit fur. Her youthful face framed the eyes of an elder of great wisdom.

She continued her deliberate descent into the canyon where, from the deep shadows, a towering, needle-like rock structure twisted into the pale blue sky like an impertinent finger dipped in red paint, pointing to the unseen stars. It had drawn her attention the day before.

As she walked toward the red tower of sandstone, a flash of light alarmed her. The sun had just crested the ridge of the canyon and it had sparked a luring reflection from an object only twenty feet from her side. She suddenly felt like a trespasser. Her body froze, eyes glued to the shining object, no larger than a human head, half buried in pine needles between two, gnarled pinion trees that stood like steadfast guardians.

At first she thought it might be a stone of silver, but as she neared the object, she noticed it was covered in unusual markings, like thin snakes twisting over its surface, frozen, embedded into its surface as if they were claw marks from a bear. As she squatted to get closer she noticed its color was both gold and silver, something she had never seen before. She edged nearer to its lustrous surface. It was an unnatural object. She was certain of that. It was not from nature, and it was not from her tribe.

Intrigued and entranced by its unusual color, she stared at it for several minutes trying to decide how, or whether, to approach it. If it was supernatural, it was her task to make it sensible to her people. If it was a threat, it was her task to discharge it from their land. As a shaman in her ancestral homeland, it was her duty to be inquisitive, even forceful.

Traveler of the Sky raised her hand over the object as if blessing it. Her thin lips recited an ancient verse of her people, "You are known to me in the great mystery. I am honored in your presence." Her hand began to tremble, and then her body shuddered as a current of electricity flowed through her like a tidal wave. Her hand was drawn to the object and involuntarily clasped it as if it were a powerful magnet. Her fingers, clenching in an irrepressible reflex, grasped the object and pulled it to her chest, cradling it as though it were a baby. Her entire body vibrated uncontrollably as she held the object.

Everything she knew—every experience she had to draw from—was purged. Her mind emptied like a sack of butterflies released to the wind, and she felt completely free of her past and future. There was only the fleeting vastness of the now. Minutes passed as she held the object to her chest, completely unaware of her actions. She gradually became aware of the weight she held. It was heavy, about the weight of a young child, despite its small size.

With some effort, she placed it back on the ground. As she did, it began to vibrate almost imperceptibly. The distinct lines on the surface of the object began to blur. Traveler of the Sky rubbed her eyes in distrust of what she saw. Her face bore a mixture of confusion and foreboding fear, but she couldn't move. Everything became dreamlike and she felt that she had been cast into a haze—into the Great Mystery of her ancestors.

The canyon's light shimmered and pulsed in the unmistakable rhythm of a hypnotic dancer. Before her were three, tall, odd-looking, but handsome men. Their eyes, variegated in blue, green, and violet, were serene yet radiant. Long beards of pure white hair touched their chests. They were dressed in emerald-colored robes that were strangely transparent, and they were standing in front of her like majestic trees. She felt no fear because she knew she had only one course of action: surrender.

"We are your future, not only your past as you now believe," one of the beings in the middle spoke. She nodded, trying to acknowledge that she understood them, but her body was somewhere else—in some other world that she was rapidly forgetting.

She noticed that although she heard his words, his lips did not move. He was speaking directly into her mind. And he spoke perfect Chakobsan, something unknown for an outsider.

"You have been chosen. The time has come to lift your gaze from the fire's brightness and cast shadows of your own. You are our messenger into your world. As you are the Traveler of the Sky, we are the Makers of Your Wings. Together we redefine what has been taught. We recast what has become truth. We defend what has always been, and will always be, ours."

She could only observe. Reverence towards these Makers of Wings filled her heart without effort. The beings before her drew it from her by their mere presence. It poured from her as though an infinite, secret reservoir had been tapped.

"There is no thing more divine than another," the being said. "There is no pathway to First Source or the Great Mystery. All beings are intimate with First Source at this very moment!"

Somewhere from far away she felt her will to speak return. "Who are you?" the phrase formed in her mind.

"I am from the Tribe of Light, as are you. Only our bodies are different. All else remains in the clear light of permanence. You have come to this planet forgetful of who you are and why you are here. Now you will remember. Now you will assist us as you agreed. Now you will awaken to the reason for your being."

A whirring sound above her head sounded like the beating of a thousand pairs of shapeless wings, and a spiral of light descended from the sky. Within the light, shapes similar to those she had seen on the object twisted, merged and separated. Intelligent lines—a language of light. The light slowly entered her and she could feel the surge of energy, tremorous yet deep, unsheathe her like a sculptor's chisel. There was no struggle. No obstruction to overcome. And then she saw it.

A cacophony of images released within her and revealed her future. She was one of them—the makers of this object. She was not Chakobsan, it was a mask she wore, but her true lineage was from the stars. From a place so far away that its light would never truly touch earth.

When she came to, her vision quickly began to evaporate, as if her mind were a sieve and could not hold the images of her future. She picked up the object, caressing it with her hand, knowing that she was its keeper; aware that it would lead her to something that was not yet ready to be discovered. But she knew her time would come. A time when she would wear a different mask—the mask of a woman with red hair and curiously white skin. It was the final image that passed away.

INTRODUCTION

In 1940, several recoveries of crashed UFOs justified a special government budget to establish a new organization within its top-secret, Government Services Special Projects Laboratory responsible for securing, protecting, and analyzing technologies recovered from extraterrestrial spacecraft. It had the dubious honor of being the most secret of all the research labs within the U.S. government.

Based in the high desert near Palm Springs, California, this heavily fortified and secretive compound housed top scientists from government laboratories with pre-existing, security clearances.

The ET Imperative, as it was called in the 1950s, was considered to be of vast importance to the national security of the United States and, indeed, the entire planet. The Advanced Contact Intelligence Organization (ACIO) was charged with analyzing recovered alien technology—in whatever form it was found—and discovering ways to apply it to missile technology, guidance systems, radar, warplanes, surveillance, and communications in order to dominate the arenas of war and espionage.

In the mid 1950s, several alien spacecraft were recovered with aliens inside, still alive. These incidents occurred not only in the United States but also in the Soviet Union and South America. In one such incident in Bolivia, a brilliant electronics expert, Paulo Neruda, removed some navigational equipment from a crashed UFO and bargained successfully to join the ACIO in exchange for its return and the use of his services.

Paulo Neruda and his four-year old son, Jamisson, became United States citizens in 1955. The elder Neruda became a high-level director of the ACIO before he died in 1977. His son, Jamisson, joined the ACIO shortly after his father's death and became its primary expert in linguistics, encryption, and decoding technologies.

Young Neruda was a genius at languages—computer, alien, human, it didn't matter. His gift was considered essential to the ACIO in its interaction with extraterrestrial intelligence.

The recoveries of live aliens in the 1950s had created a new agenda for the ACIO. A Technology Transfer Program (TTP) grew out of the recovery of extraterrestrials from two distinct alien races known as the Zeta Reticuli and the Corteum. Selected technologies from these races were provided to the ACIO in exchange for various services and privileges extended by the U.S. and other governments.

The ACIO was the repository and clearinghouse for the technologies that grew out of the TTP with the Zetas and Corteum. The ACIO's agenda was broadened to develop these technologies into useful, nonmilitary technologies that were seeded into both the private and public sector. Before their time technologies such as integrated circuits and lasers were among the progeny of the ACIO's TTP with the Zetas and Corteum.

CHAPTER 1
DISCOVERY IN THE DESERT

> Your theories of evolution are simply layered upon an existing paradigm of a mechanical universe that consists of molecular machines operating in an objective reality that is knowable with the right instruments. We tell you a truth of the universe when we say that reality is unknowable with any instrument save your own sense of unity and wholeness. Your perception of wholeness is unfolding because the culture of the multidimensional universe is rooted in unity. As your wholeness navigator reveals itself in the coming shift, you will dismantle and restructure your perceptions of who you are, and in this process humanity will emerge like a river of light from what was once an impenetrable fog.

An Excerpt from *The Wholeness Navigator*, Decoded from Chamber Twelve

WingMakers

There were times when Jamisson Neruda marveled at his job. Beneath the cone of light from his desk lamp lay a certified mystery. It had been found a week earlier in the high desert near Chaco Canyon in northern New Mexico and now, after three, exhaustive days of research, he was convinced the artifact was unearthly.

Neruda had already compiled notes about the unusual artifact. The main characteristic, according to the students who found it, was that it induced hallucinogenic images when held or touched. But, no matter how hard he tried, he couldn't induce anything resembling a hallucination. Maybe, he speculated, the two students had been under the influence of drugs. That would explain the hallucinogenic property. Nevertheless, no one could dispute that the artifact projected an exotic, otherworldly presence.

It was two o'clock in the morning and Neruda's dark eyes were gritty with sleep deprivation. After comparing the hieroglyphic markings on the Chaco Canyon object to similar markings from ancient Sumerian and Linear B script, nothing really matched. After three days of comparative analysis, he could only conclude one thing: they were not of this earth.

His report bore the same words on the title page.

Neruda rubbed his eyes and looked through his microscope again, examining the metallic surface of the textured silver casing and copper colored markings. The artifact contained thousands of ridges, tiny spinal cords that coalesced, like nerve ganglia, every eight to ten centimeters into one of the twenty-three distinct glyphs on the object.

Though it was the size of a toddler's shoebox, the artifact weighed more than a blue-ribbon watermelon and had a density similar to lead. But, unlike lead, the surface was completely impenetrable to every probe Neruda or his colleagues employed.

Maybe it was the sculptured quality of the glyphs that fascinated him. Or maybe it was the subtle variations in the lines. He had never seen such sophisticated depictions of a cryptographic alphabet before. Somehow it only compounded the irony that the artifact remained silent.

"I think we found something."

Emily Dawson poked her head into Neruda's office, cradling a cup of coffee as if to keep her hands from freezing. Her long, brown hair, normally in a tidy bun, fell to her shoulders, looking more tired than her sad, soulful eyes.

"Doesn't anybody ever sleep in this place?" Neruda shot back with a boyish grin.

"Of course, if you're not interested in what we found…" Her voice trailed off to a whisper.

Neruda smiled knowingly. He liked Emily's quiet manner; it was almost irresistible. He loved the way she was so unobtrusive.

"Okay, what exactly did you find?"

"You'll need to follow me. Andrews is still checking his computations, but my instincts are certain that he'll confirm our original findings."

"And they are?"

"Andrews told me not to tell you until you were in the lab—"

"Andrews forgets I'm his supervisor. He also forgets it's two in the morning and I'm unusually irritable when I'm tired and hungry."

"It'll only take a few minutes. Come on." She casually took another sip of coffee. "I'll get you a fresh cup of coffee and a cinnamon bagel." She let her irresistible offer dangle in the quiet of his office.

Neruda could only push back from his cluttered desk and smile.

"Oh, and bring the artifact," she added. "Andrews needs it."

Neruda's hair, tussled from his restless hands, covered his right eye almost entirely as he bent down and carefully tucked the object under his arm like a football. He staggered just a bit while the weight of the object found a point of balance.

Neruda was Bolivian and had the great fortune to own one of the most distinguished looking faces ever to grace the human body. Everything about him was intense. His hair was as straight as it was black. His eyes resembled mysterious wells in moonlight, dodging the question of how deep or how full they were. Nose and lips were formed from Michelangelo's chisel.

As he walked by her in the doorway, Emily swept his hair to the side. "I'll bring the coffee to the lab."

"I'll take cream cheese on my bagel," Neruda said, walking begrudgingly to the lab to confer with Andrews, one of his most demanding but brilliant assistants.

The hallways of the ACIO were quiet and antiseptically clean at this late hour. White stucco walls and white marble floors gleamed beneath the overhead halogen lights. The odor of various cleaning formulas sterilized the air. Neruda heard his stomach growl in the deep silence of the hallway. It, too, was sterile. He'd forgotten dinner. Again.

"Finally!" Andrews said as Neruda entered. He had the unnerving habit of never leveling his eyes with his human counterpart. Neruda sort of liked it; it made him feel comfortable in a strange sort of way. "This shit is unbelievable."

"And what are you referring to, exactly?" Neruda asked.

Andrews kept his eyes on the charts in front of him. "I mean the way the surface analytics show how precisely this thing's been designed. What looks like chaos is actually a precisely executed pattern. You see these subtle variations? They aren't arbitrary. We screwed up; we didn't build our plot diagrams with enough granularity to see the pattern before."

"And what pattern is that, exactly?" Neruda's voice betrayed a growing degree of impatience.

Andrews positioned a large chart on the table before him. It looked like a topographical map of a mountain range.

Neruda instantly saw the pattern. "Is this the complete surface of the object?"

"Yes."

"Are you sure?"

"I've double-checked everything and my replication data is an exact match."

Neruda set the artifact on the table beside Andrews' chart with a thud.

"There's no way this could be an anomaly?"

"No way."

"And what's the plot granularity?"

".0025 microns."

"Is it visible at any other granularity?"

"I'm not sure. That's why I asked you to bring the little monster here. I'll do some more tests and we'll see what else shows up."

"Any idea what it means?"

"Yeah, it's not from around here," Andrews laughed and struggled with the artifact to move it onto a metal platform for testing.

The measurement device was called a Surface Mapping Topographer (SMT) and it made an extremely detailed topographical map of the surface of objects. Similar to that of fingerprint analysis, the ACIO's version was three-dimensional and could be utilized microscopically.

Neruda leaned closer to the poster-sized chart while Andrews positioned the artifact exactly to his requirements.

"It's definitely not Zeta or Corteum."

"And it's definitely not human—past or present accounted for," Andrews said.

"But this pattern… it's unmistakable. It's… it's got to be a topographical map. It might even represent the discovery site."

"Okay, let's say it's ET, but not the friendly ETs we send Christmas cards to,"

Andrews flashed a smile, "and these ETs visited us in our distant past. They happened to be cartographer freaks and decided to make a map of their settlement on earth. Then they got bored with New Mexico—an easy thing to do, I might add—and had no need of the map anymore, so they left it behind."

"This artifact was found above ground," Neruda reminded him. "Someone or something placed it there and did so recently, or else our little monster would've been buried."

"Maybe it unburied itself." Andrews' voice was nearly a whisper.

Neruda backed away, feeling a sudden wave of exhaustion for the first time. He slumped into a nearby chair, ran his hands through his hair, and then stretched his body with a long sigh. Rubbing his neck, he laughed low in his throat. "You know, maybe they just have a sense of humor."

"Or they like to torture their victims with misdirects," Andrews offered. "You do remember our experience with the Zetas?"

"This is entirely different. The language structure of this race is so dimensional that it must lack telepathic abilities. Why else would they construct such a complex language?"

"Maybe it's not a language or a map. Maybe it's just an artistic expression of some kind."

"Not likely. It's more probable that they've created a multi-dimensional language that integrates their mathematics with their alphabet as a way of communicating a deeper meaning. It's not misdirection. I can feel misdirection in my bones."

"Yeah, but we're too shit-faced stupid to figure it out."

"We've only had three days."

"Okay, but we're almost as clueless as we were on the first day."

The door of the lab swung open and Emily walked in with a tray of coffee cups and bagels. "Anything else you gentlemen need before I retire?"

"A million thanks," Neruda replied.

"You're very welcome. So what do you think about our little picture?"

"Everything just got a lot more complicated."

"So you're happy," Emily quipped.

"Either they have a mathematical structure encoded within their alphabet or this object portrays a very detailed topographical map."

Emily set the tray next to the artifact, careful to avoid touching it. "I prefer the map hypothesis. I was never very good with math." She flashed her most innocent smile. For an instant Neruda saw her as a young girl, complete with braids, braces, and training bra.

Emily was relatively new to the ACIO. She had come to the attention of Neruda after he read her seminal book on the Sumerian culture, which she had written as an Associate Professor at Cambridge University.

Forced to leave her post at Cambridge, due to an illness rumored as some form of cancer, she had fallen into a deep depression during her convalescence that had left her body and spirit ravaged. Two years ago, the ACIO recruited her, at Neruda's urging, and he had taken her under his wing as her mentor.

"You *are* happy about this aren't you?" Emily asked, half-serious.

"Come on, boss," Andrews chimed, "burning the midnight oil, drinking coffee and eating donuts every meal, never having to wear sunglasses… what could be better?"

Andrews was the prototypical nerd engineer. Appearances last, mental acuity first. Not that he was a bad looking man. He just preferred to analyze complex problems and solve them, instead of laboring with time-consuming tasks like brushing his teeth or combing his hair.

Neruda sipped his coffee and stared at the chart without response. Something bothered him about the pattern. It was too perfect. If someone wanted to encode a language within a language, they would make it less obvious. Otherwise, what's the purpose of encoding?

"I think we should take granularity plots at .001 variance down to .0005 microns. Also, ask Henderson if he'd get us a set of twenty topographical maps of the discovery site up to a hundred kilometers radius at increments of five kilometers. Okay with you, Andrews?"

"No problem, but at least tell me what you're hoping to find."

"I don't know," he replied, looking suspiciously at the chart. "I don't know, but maybe it's not a language so much as a map."

"This *can* wait until the morning, can't it?"

"What, and waste a good cup of coffee?" With that, Neruda smiled broadly and told them to get a good night's rest. He was closing up shop, too.

On his way out, Neruda noticed a thin blade of light beneath Fifteen's office door. The Executive Director of the ACIO was known as both a night owl and workaholic, but 3 a.m. was late, even by his standards.

Neruda knocked softly and opened the door a crack. Fifteen was at his computer terminal, lost in thought. Absentmindedly, his hand motioned Neruda in, but in a halting gesture, motioned him to wait a moment before speaking. A few more keystrokes and Fifteen turned around to face Neruda.

In his early sixties, Fifteen had been the reclusive and revered leader of the ACIO for more than thirty years. The scientists privileged to work at the ACIO considered him the most brilliant mind on or off the planet.

Fifteen got his name by virtue of his security clearance. The ACIO had fifteen distinct levels of information distribution and he was at the top of the information chain.

The ACIO had developed the most powerful knowledge management and information systems on the planet. And because of its unique access to the world's most powerful technologies, its information databases were more carefully secured than the gold in Fort Knox. Fifteen was the only person in the world who had a Level Fifteen security clearance, which gave him unfettered access to all the sectors of the ACIO data warehouse.

Neruda sat in a leather chair opposite Fifteen, waiting for some sign to speak.

Fifteen took a sip of tea, closed his eyes for a moment as if to clear his mind, and brought his dark eyes squarely on Neruda's face. "You want to go to New Mexico, don't you?"

"Yes, but I want to tell you why—"

"Don't you think I already know?"

"Perhaps, but I want to tell you in my own words."

Fifteen shifted in his comfortable chair, as if his back gave him problems. Spanish by descent, Fifteen often reminded Neruda of Pablo Picasso, with long silver hair. He had the same stout body style as Picasso but was probably a bit taller.

"So tell me."

"This artifact is more sophisticated than either the Zeta or Corteum. It can't be probed. It's entirely seamless. And tonight we've confirmed that it has a multi-tiered alphabet that migrates from a two-dimensional cryptographic code to a three-dimensional fractal pattern that looks a lot like a topographical map.

"Combine these factors with the report from the kids who discovered it, that the artifact projects some form of a hallucination when held, and I think there's probable evidence that this thing isn't an isolated artifact."

Fifteen breathed a long, weary sigh. "You're well aware that I've already dispatched a team to the area where the artifact was found. We used our best people in search and rescue and they found no additional debris—"

"But that's just it! It's not from a crash site. The artifact is perfectly intact. Nothing but microscopic scratches—"

"Then explain how this most sophisticated alien technology was found by two kids above the ground. We both read the report from Collin that estimated an object of that weight and size would become at least partially buried in that environment within six to eight months."

"It's possible it was left behind recently."

"You're suggesting an alien race left it behind as their calling card?"

"Perhaps."

"Speculate. Why?" Fifteen asked.

"What if they had left behind something important in that area and wanted to be sure they could return to the exact same location years later."

"A homing beacon?"

"Yes."

"Are you aware that there's been absolutely no anomalous radar activity in that area in the past twelve months?"

"No."

Fifteen swiveled in his chair, hit a few keys on his keyboard, and began to read:

"ZONE NM1257 HAD THREE INCIDENTS OF ZETA FLY-OVERS DURING THE REQUESTED ANALYSIS PERIOD. THEY WERE: 0311 HOURS, MAY 7; 0445 HOURS, MAY 10; AND

0332 HOURS, MAY 21. FLIGHT PATHS WERE ESTIMATED AT
SPEEDS IN EXCESS OF 1,800 KPH – NO SIGNIFICANT SPEED
VARIATIONS."

The implacable expression on Fifteen's face softened slightly as he turned to face
Neruda. "You see? This object wasn't left behind, it unburied itself."

Goose bumps stippled Neruda's neck at the recognition that he'd heard this
twice in the last hour. "Or it was left behind by time travelers," Neruda said.

Fifteen paused to reflect on the conversation. He took a quick sip of tea and
shifted in his chair, this time with a grimace. "You mentioned a three-dimensional
fractal pattern that looked like a map?"

"Yes," Neruda said, his voice gaining in intensity. "And the precision is at least
.0025 in the granularity plots. It could be even higher. We'll find out tomorrow."

In a drawn out, somewhat irritable voice, Fifteen asked, "So what do you
propose?"

"I'd like to assemble a small team tomorrow afternoon and take the artifact
with us. The artifact may be a compass or a map of some kind that's only operational
in the local environment it was found. It's worth a test before we put this thing
into storage."

"And you really think it's more sophisticated than Corteum?"

"There's no doubt in my mind."

"You have my approval, but if the artifact goes with you, so do Evans and anyone
else he thinks is pertinent. Understood?"

"Yes, but this is my mission and I presume I'll be leading all operations." He
hoped his words sounded more like a statement than a question.

"And the plot charts from the object," Fifteen wondered aloud, "did they have
any markings as to a strategic position?"

"That's just it, when the twenty-three glyphs are laid out in the SMT analogue,
with a little imagination one can define at least two or three strategic positions. I'm
ordering topographical maps of the entire region within a hundred kilometers of the
point of discovery. We'll see if there's any correlation when we do an overlay analysis."

Fifteen stood up and glanced at his wristwatch. "Before you leave tomorrow, I'd
like a mission briefing for the directors. I'll schedule it at fourteen hundred hours in
my office. I assume you'll come prepared to show the SMT results, the topographical
map correlations—assuming they exist—and any other relevant findings pertaining
to the glyphs."

Neruda rose to his feet and nodded affirmatively. Thanking Fifteen for his time,
he left the sprawling, Zen-like office with a peculiar sense of apprehension. Why
would Evans need to come along? Fifteen must sense something peculiar here.

James Evans, Director of Security for the ACIO, had been a Navy Seal commander
for six years before his training methods became a little too extreme, even for the
Navy Seal program. He was removed from his post through a conspiratorial set of

circumstances that ended in an Honorable Discharge.

Afterwards, the NSA secretly recruited him. He worked there for three years until he came to the attention of Fifteen through a collaborative project between the NSA and the ACIO, code-named AdamSon. To scientists within the ACIO, Evans and his security department were a necessary evil, but evil nonetheless. Their tactics introduced to the scientific core, a sense of paranoia which Fifteen seemed oblivious to.

Evans was a likable person. His position was one of high prestige: Director of ACIO Security and Admissions. In his role, he enjoyed a Level Fourteen security clearance, along with six other Directors. These seven people were the most elite team surrounding Fifteen, and were consulted by Fifteen on every major initiative.

To Neruda, Evans was a well-trained thug. His intellect was superior to the average person only because of mind-enhancement technology that the ACIO had obtained from the Corteum. Without the aid of the Minyaur Technology, as it was called, Neruda often thought Evans would make a fine State Representative for Wyoming, or perhaps an NRA lobbyist.

Since his arrival twelve years ago, and his rapid rise through the ranks of the ACIO, Evans had implemented many new security technologies, such as the subcutaneous tracking beacon all ACIO staff had implanted in their neck. To Evans' credit, there had been no security leaks or defections during his tenure, but Neruda hated the very existence of internal security and Evans was an easy target for his disdain.

Neruda entered the elevator, paying particular attention to the Status and Forecast reports displayed on the embedded monitor just above the doors. It was 0317 hours, 7°C, no wind, moon at 12 percent luminosity, 120 kilometer visibility, barometric pressure steady at 29.98, and humidity 16.4 percent.

The elevator doors swung open before he could catch the forecast but he knew he'd be underground all day tomorrow. Besides, the weather wasn't exactly volatile in southern California.

ACIO "Topside" was forty-five meters, or twelve stories above the executive offices and laboratories of the ACIO. Topside was also a completely different facade: long, one-story, stucco building with antenna-like protrusions and satellite dishes on the roof. At its gated entrance, a simple sign said, UNITED STATES GOVERNMENT EXPERIMENTAL WEATHER CENTER. RESTRICTED ACCESS.

The ACIO was, to anyone who might wander by, a government weather center responsible for developing sophisticated, weather instruments to help the U.S. military and intelligence communities to better predict, and even control, weather conditions across the globe. This was part of the ACIO's mission. But only a fraction of its budget and project plan went to these endeavors.

Of its 226 scientists, eleven were deployed in the development of weather-related technologies. The majority were involved in the development of complex technologies devoted to financial market manipulation and encryption technologies that enabled the algorithms to operate without detection.

The ACIO had a long history of working with the secretive powers behind the throne. The highest powers within the intelligence community and private industry revered the ACIO's brainpower and innovations. It was widely rumored within the intelligence community that such an organization existed to reverse-engineer extraterrestrial technologies, but only a handful of the most elite actually knew of the ACIO.

Neruda reached Topside with a queasy stomach stoked from too much caffeine. He thought a warm glass of milk and a banana before bed would soothe him. Sleep and little else drew him home. He had never married and now, at forty-six, the prospects seemed remote. His entire adult life was absorbed by the ACIO. Since the age of sixteen when he began to work as an intern with his father, the ACIO was his shelter and sanctuary, workplace, and social venue.

Starlight always caught him by surprise when he left the compound. The velvet night air was indeed clear; 120 kilometers visibility seemed understated. He drove the six kilometers to his home in a new subdivision of mostly ACIO personnel.

His head hit the pillow before the warm milk found his stomach. The unpeeled banana slept beside him on the night table. As tired as he was, his mind's eye kept looking at the strange markings that encircled the artifact's exterior casing. In thirty years of studying ancient scripts he had never seen such intricately carved glyphs.

Suddenly he noticed a soft, diffuse light penetrate his eyelids. His eyes flew open as if hinged on high-tension springs. The room was silent and dark. He closed his eyes again, figuring that he must have slipped into a lucid dream of some kind. Turning on his side he adjusted the covers tightly around his neck and let out a long, tired sigh.

In a moment the light returned. This time he kept his eyes closed, watching in amazement as the light began to form into the same glyphs he had seen on the artifact. They wavered over his head like a mirage of shimmering gold light: serpentine, sculptural. He looked at them with all his intensity, and to his surprise they began to move, not the glyphs, but something inside the glyphs. Something was circulating within them like blood coursing inside an artery.

Whatever it was, it began to speed up. Faster and faster, and then Neruda noticed a whirring sound, similar to the hum of electricity but infinitely smoother. It began as a low humming sound and then started to rise in pitch to a near-inaudible state, and just when Neruda thought he would lose it, it began to oscillate. At first, the sound was a wavering of electrical rhythms pulsing like a massive heartbeat a million miles away, but then something changed and he could hear words forming. Nothing intelligible, he told himself, but it was definitely a language pattern. His whole body and mind leaned towards the sound, trying desperately to make out the words.

Then it happened. English. Words he could understand. "You are among friends. Feel no fear. Relax and simply listen to our words." The words were spoken with perfect diction, articulated like a Shakespearean actor. "What we will impart to you, will be stored inside your mind for later recollection. Upon awakening you will have no recall of our meeting. We regret this, but it is necessary at this time."

Neruda could feel his mind forming a protestation but it dissolved before it could be given voice.

"What you desire is to activate our technology," the voice intoned. "But you do not yet understand the context in which our technology is placed upon your planet. This insight will come, but it will take time. Rest assured that we are watching, waiting, and ever vigilant to protect your interests and those of our mission."

Neruda could feel his body, but was unable to move his limbs or even open his eyelids. He was completely entranced by the voice. He swallowed hard and tried to speak—whether with his mind or vocal cords he wasn't sure. "Who are you?"

"We are what you will become. You are what we have been. Together, we are what define the human soul. Our name, translated to your language, is WingMakers. We are interpenetrated in the light of First Source. You live in the weaker light that has been stepped down to receive you. We bring the Language of Unity into this weaker light so you may see how you will become unified to a new cosmological structure the architecture and grandeur of which you cannot even imagine."

Neruda's mind flashed to his father's voice: "...the new spirituality will have as its foundation a cosmological substrate so profound that the mind will not contain it."

He smiled inwardly at the recollection of his father's voice. "Why? Why can't we imagine it?"

"You have not been able to understand the Language of Unity because you do not understand wholeness. You do not understand the grand universe in which you live and breathe.

"Your plants have root systems that penetrate earth and drink of her substance. In this way, all plants are linked. Now, imagine that each plant had a secret root that was invisible but was nonetheless connected to the very center of the planet. At this point of convergence, every plant was indeed unified and aware that its real identity was this core system of interconnected roots and that this secret root was the lifeline through which individual expression was brought to the surface of earth and its unified consciousness released. In this same way, humanity has a secret root that spirals into the uncharted realm of the Central Universe of First Source. It is like an umbilical cord that connects the human entity with the nurturing essence of its creator. The secret root is the carrier of the Language of Unity. And it is this language that we have come to teach.

"All life is embedded with what we will term a Wholeness Navigator. This is your core wisdom. It draws you to perceive fragmentary existence as a passageway into wholeness and unity. It is eternal and knows that the secret root exists even though it may seem intangible to your human senses. The Wholeness Navigator is the tireless engine that drives fragmentary, life experience into unified life expression. It is the immutable bridge over which all life will surely pass.

"The Age of Enlightenment is the age of living in the multidimensional universe and appreciating its wholeness, structure, and perfection and then expressing this appreciation through your mind and body into the world of time and space. This is the seed vision of the Wholeness Navigator. The imprint of its purpose. We are here to assist beings like yourself to first conceptualize and then experience the multidimensional universe as it truly is—not only through the language of your world, but through the Language of Unity; as you see it in these glyphs. As this experience flows through you, you will transform. The Wholeness Navigator will be able to deposit a new perception of your Self that is aligned with the image of First Source. It is this new image, emerging through your Wholeness Navigator, that will change the course of this planetary system. We are here to accelerate the formation of this image in the mind of humanity."

Neruda continued to listen even as the sound of the voice subsided back into the pulsing of the glyphs. A part of him lurched forward, trying to explain what was happening as a mental construction—a dream and nothing more. But somewhere deep inside himself, beneath all the layers of his education, a faint remembrance was re-kindled; a sense that reality was upon him with the intensity of a jaguar capturing its prey; a sense that everything in his universe was focused on this event. All eyes were watching.

He felt a question bubble to the surface. "Why do you care if this experience is achieved by humans—myself, or anyone else? What's so important that this new image, as you call it, is accelerated in humanity?"

"If humanity understands that this secret root exists and that it is the carrier of the Language of Unity, then humanity can become responsible stewards of more than the

Earth, its solar system, its galaxy and its universe. Humanity can be stewards of the human soul and transform into what we are. We are all, regardless of our position on the evolutionary timeline, encoded to re-ascend the stairs of the universe. It is our migratory path. Some start and end sooner than others, but all will make the journey."

"So, now what?" Neruda managed to ask.

"Follow what you have found. It will lead you to us."

The voice faded back into the pulsing sound of the glyphs. The low humming returned and his mind relaxed into a deep, forgetful sleep.

CHAPTER 2
RECONNAISSANCE

There is no supplication that stirs me. No prayer that invites
me further into your world unless it is attended with the feeling
of unity and wholeness. There is no temple or sacred object that
touches me. They do not, nor have they ever brought you closer to
my outstretched hand. My presence in your world is unalterable for
I am the sanctuary of both the cosmos and the one soul inside you.

An Excerpt from *First Source*, Decoded from Chamber Twenty-three
WingMakers

Neruda was always a little nervous when he had to make a presentation
to the Directors, especially when he was late. The lab results had taken
longer than he had expected, as usual. Damn replication data, he thought.
Nevertheless, he was pleased with the results and could hardly wait to present their
findings. Andrews was right: this shit was unbelievable.

His stomach was both hungry and queasy. He grabbed a drink of water from the
hallway fountain outside the lab and made his way to Fifteen's office. He reminded
himself that he was a member of the Labyrinth Group, just as they were. They were
no more intelligent than he was; in fact, on the subject of language, he was the
world's authority—even if no one outside of the ACIO knew it.

The Labyrinth Group was a secret subgroup of the ACIO. When Fifteen took
over control of the ACIO in 1967, he felt the National Security Agency (NSA)
was trivializing the agenda of the ACIO. He wanted to harness the technologies
that resulted from the TTP with the Zetas and Corteum and apply them to the
development of Blank Slate Technology (BST), an elaborate technology for altering
time-based events without detection. Fifteen wanted to develop the ultimate
defensive weapon, or *Freedom Key* as he called it, in the event of a long-prophesied
extraterrestrial invasion. He was convinced that the ACIO should focus on this
scientific pursuit.

Partly to achieve this mission and partly as an outgrowth of new ACIO
technologies, Fifteen established a secret organization within the ACIO composed
of only his innermost circle of loyal associates. Established in 1969, this elite group
called itself the Labyrinth Group. All personnel with a security clearance of twelve
or higher were automatically inducted into this small but powerful organization.

With a membership of only sixty-six, everyone had undergone a variety of
enhancements that amplified their natural intelligence and innate abilities—including
psychic abilities—and that was exactly what made Neruda's stomach queasy.

"Good afternoon," Neruda recited to the assembled group of Directors.

"I apologize for being a little late, but the replication data and the correlation analysis took longer than we thought." He smiled charmingly, brushed his hair back, sat down, and looked at Fifteen, who stood at the end of the long rosewood conference table; since back spasms had begun to assail him several months earlier, he rarely sat for too long.

Around the conference table were Fifteen's direct reports: Li-Ching, Director of Communications and Protocol; James Louden, Director of Operations; William Branson, Director of Information Systems; Leonard Ortmann, Director of Research and Development; Lee Whitman, who managed all TTP relationships, both to and from the ACIO; and James Evans, who managed security. Jeremy Sauthers, Neruda's supervisor and Director of Special Projects, was on holiday and absent from the meeting.

With this group, it was impossible to go through a meeting, no matter how short, and not make a mistake. The only question was how large the mistake would be. Neruda knew this better than most and fidgeted in his chair, wondering what he'd overlooked. He found himself wishing he had asked to leave later in the week so he'd have had more time to prepare. His stomach grew wings.

"I asked Jamisson to present his findings," Fifteen began, "because it seems we have a technology in our presence that our best personnel, using our best technology, cannot probe. We have an alloy that is undoubtedly extraterrestrial or possibly time-shifted, we're not sure." He turned to look directly at Neruda. "Are we?"

"Probability is that it's off-planetary, but because we're not able to probe it, no, we're not sure."

"Neruda came to me last night or, I guess it was this morning, and asked me if he could lead an exploratory team to New Mexico with the artifact in tow. He gave a reasonable rationale, and I simply want each of you to be updated."

Fifteen narrowed his eyes, as if squinting at a window of light. "We know the object was above ground when it was discovered. We also know it was not left behind in the last twelve months by an ET source. According to Jamisson, the object is quite possibly a map or homing device of some kind. He's here to explain his hypothesis. I've already given him permission to go to the site, but I wanted you to have an opportunity to ask questions and formulate your own opinions."

Fifteen nodded to Neruda and sat down gingerly.

Neruda stood and walked over to the large whiteboard adjacent to the conference table. Grabbing a red marker, he wrote the word, *MAP*. He shuffled a few short paces and wrote, *HOMING DEVICE*. He then drew a vertical line between the two words. Above the words, in the middle, he wrote *EVIDENCE* in capital letters.

He turned around and faced the austere group, all of whom were watching with interest. They knew Neruda wasn't prone to rash pronouncements or wasteful rhetoric.

"We're convinced that the object is one, or possibly both, of these," he said, pointing with his thumb behind him. "Which means it's probably not an isolated artifact. It's also clear that this is a technology, not an inert art form or organic object. The technology is superior to anything we've investigated to date. It's completely concealed. Buttoned-up, seamless, and silent in all respects."

He walked back to his chair and distributed copies of a poster-sized scan document. "Except one," he said. "In this SMT analysis you'll notice the obvious similarity to a topographical map of something resembling a mountainous environment. These lines are invisible to the human eye, but with a .0025 granularity plot, the lines become visible and, more importantly, reveal a pattern.

"We also downloaded satellite pictures of the discovery site and reduced them to simple, three-dimensional topographical maps. We conducted a correlation analysis this morning and concluded that the object's surface is indeed a map."

Neruda distributed another large document to each of the directors. "Once our computers matched scale and orientation, we found a 96.5 percent correlation. Clearly, a map is embedded in the surface of the object—"

"And this map is of the discovery site?" Evans asked.

"Actually, the discovery site is on the periphery of the map."

"Tell them about the reference point," Fifteen urged.

"As you can see, twenty-three glyphs surround the periphery of the map area. These glyphs may be pointing to a central area right here." Neruda held his marker at the position that was approximately equidistant from the twenty-three glyphs.

"How large an area does this map reference?" Ortmann asked.

"It's about twenty square kilometers."

"Why would an alien race leave behind such an object and include a map if not to identify a point of clear, specific reference? Seems improbable, doesn't it?" Ortmann folded his arms and leaned back further in his chair as if to emphasize his frustration at having to waste his time speculating.

"Not if the object were both a homing device and a map," Fifteen answered. "Perhaps the map is designed to lead you to the general area that activates the homing device. From there, the homing device supplants the map's function."

"If we can't probe the object, what evidence do we have that it's a homing device?" Ortmann pointed to the whiteboard where the word *EVIDENCE* seemed to stand alone as an island.

"We don't really have any hard evidence," Neruda replied, "However, the students who discovered this—"

"If you're going to mention the hallucinatory state of these students as evidence that this object is a homing device," Ortmann said, "then you may be a bit naive about college students and their penchant for altered states and drug experimentation."

"I personally subjected these students to a full debrief," Evans said. "They weren't, in my opinion, lying about the hallucinations. They were clean kids; they weren't druggies."

Evans was rarely so outspoken with Fifteen present unless he was certain of his convictions. Everyone knew this about him. It was enough for Ortmann to stop his line of inquiry.

"Let's allow Neruda some latitude here," Fifteen interjected. "I happen to have my own hypothesis, based on informed intuition mostly. I'm sure we all do. But no one's better informed about this particular set of issues than Neruda is. So let's give him an opportunity to show us his working hypothesis."

The directors nodded support for Fifteen's suggestion and turned with robotic precision to Neruda. He preferred to let others talk and wished that Fifteen would explain his hypothesis.

"I wrote the words on the whiteboard because I wanted you to know the facts about this finding," Neruda began. "There's very little in the way of physical evidence in support of my hypothesis."

He walked back to the white board and wrote underneath the word *MAP: SMT FINDINGS (.0025) TOPOGRAPHICAL CORRELATIONS 96%.*

Under *HOMING DEVICE*, he wrote, *SITE-SPECIFIC HALLUCINATIONS REPORTED BY RELIABLE SOURCES.*

"This is the extent of the evidence, as we know it today, that explains the probable purpose of this artifact. Moreover, we know from our language analysis that the glyphs are not referenced in our Cyrus database. They are, for the most part, unique and significantly more intricate than anything we've ever seen before.

"What's particularly unsettling is the fact that the object was found above ground, as if someone or something had placed it there to be found. There was no attempt to conceal it, other than the fact that it was in a very remote section of northern New Mexico.

"Our hypothesis is that the object's primary purpose is a homing device. The map holds a secondary purpose that could be used by someone should the artifact be dislocated from its intended drop site. The object is site sensitive and when held within a certain proximity—what we presume to be the area depicted on this map—it somehow projects an image in the mind of the holder as to its home base—"

"And you're suggesting its home base is a location within the center of this map?" Evans asked.

"Yes."

"And that this home base," Evans continued, "is either an ancient, abandoned ET settlement or an active site?"

"More likely the former than the latter."

"Why?" Branson asked.

"Even though we've been unable to carbon date the object or use the Geon Probe, we've analyzed the map correlations. The tiny variations in the correlations consistently pointed to erosion factors and, having done a regression analysis of the probable erosion patterns of the map area, we concluded that the object is at least six hundred years old. It could be twice as old." Neruda paused, expecting someone to interject. He was met with silence.

"We believe our best course of action is to take the artifact to the central region depicted on the map and test the hypothesis." Again Neruda paused, fishing for questions.

"Let's back up," Li-Ching offered. "We know the object is authentic, right?"

"Yes. There's no hoax here," Neruda said.

"We also know that it's UET."

"Or time-shifted," Neruda added.

"The most vexing issue to me is that the object is some six hundred years old and just showed up one day without a trace. Are we sure it poses no threat?" Li-Ching asked, her forehead slightly crinkled.

"That probability is low, according to ZEMI. Well below ten percent."

"We do have some enemies," Li-Ching reminded the group, "and this type of object would naturally find its way to the ACIO. How can we be sure it's not a weapon of some kind if we can't probe it? Remember the dimensional probes our Remote Viewers found last year, courtesy of Zeta Rogue Twelve? Our technology couldn't probe those, either."

"Speaking of RVs, has anyone performed an RV on this object yet?" Ortmann asked.

"Yes," Neruda replied, "but again, with no results—other than to confirm the object's incredible resistance to probes."

"Were you planning to include RVs on your exploration team?"

Neruda sighed internally, knowing his oversight had been found. "No. But it's an excellent idea." Neruda couldn't lie to this group. Their bullshit detectors were so sensitive they could spot a lie, no matter how small or benign, in deep sleep.

"By the way, do we have any further reports on Professor Stevens?" Ortmann turned to Evans.

"We've been monitoring the good professor since we secured the artifact. He's sent a few emails to colleagues and had a few phone calls, but he's followed our story to the letter—"

"I wasn't referring to his compliance," Ortmann said. "I was interested in the content of his e-mails or phone calls. Does he have a hypothesis?"

Professor Stevens taught archeology at the University of New Mexico. When students from the University stumbled upon the artifact during a hiking trip, they had taken it to Stevens for identification. Stevens immediately considered it an extraterrestrial artifact of some kind and sent several e-mails to colleagues, all of which were flagged by Echelon, a secret intelligence unit of the NSA. Since one of the keywords that caused e-mails to be flagged was "extraterrestrial," the e-mails were forwarded to the ACIO.

When the ACIO arrived in Stevens' office thirty-six hours after the artifact had been discovered, it delivered a powerful message: The "artifact" was a stolen, highly classified, experimental weapon. It could be very dangerous in the wrong hands. Professor Stevens, under these circumstances, was only a little reluctant, and somewhat relieved, to turn the object over to Evans, who posed as a NSA agent.

Evans punched on an embedded keypad in the conference table and brought up a screen on the overhead projector. He darkened the room slightly and hit a few keys. "We put a Level Five Listening Fence around Stevens," Evans told the group. "Our post-ops analysis is that this guy believed the object was alien. And he believed it was a weapon. He also believed it was best suited for the NSA to figure out disposition and care."

"In this file," Evans clicked open a file object, "are all of his relevant e-mails and phone transcripts since Tuesday, nine hundred hours. If you search on the words, *hypothesis*, *theory*, *supposal*, or *conjecture*, you'll find only one context."

Evans finished typing the words and hit the ENTER key. Instantly text from a phone transcript, entitled OUTBOUND 602-355-6217/SINGLE TRANSMISSION/OFFICE/0722/1207/ 12.478 MINUTES popped up. He selected 30 percent in a window entitled CONTEXT FRAME, clicked the AUDIO AND TEXT button, and hit ENTER again. The room filled with the audio recording of a phone conversation between Stevens and a colleague. As the audio played, the text automatically scrolled synchronized with the audio:

Stevens: I know this thing was hot. For Christ sake, the fucking NSA was all over me.

Jordan: Why would you let this thing get away? They took everything, didn't they? You know the government can't just walk in to your office and steal your goddamn rights, let alone your personal property or the property of the University.

Stevens: There was no choice. This thing could be a weapon.

Jordan: Why? Because some agent told you so?

Stevens: Look, I know one of the students who found this thing and they claimed it induced some sort of hallucinatory experience when they held it, or even came within a close proximity of the thing.

Jordan: And it was just sitting out, in plain view?

Stevens: Yes.

Jordan: What was the NSA's explanation that this top-secret weapon was just laying out in the middle of nowhere?

Stevens: They said one of their operatives had defected and stolen the weapon several months ago and was still missing. They claimed the weapon was a mind control device that was designed to fuck with someone's mind until they went crazy. They assume the defector went crazy and left the weapon behind.

Jordan: Shit. It probably is an experimental weapon. But then why all the strange hieroglyphs? Why wouldn't it say U.S. Government on it?

Stevens: My theory is that this thing was so secretive they wanted it to look alien. Again, I remind you, it was the fucking NSA that came knocking on my door. Not the local police or FBI. It took them only twenty-four hours to find me. And it wasn't because the students tipped them off. They knew because this thing, this fucking weapon, had a homing signal that led them right to me.

Jordan: Whoa. If this thing has a homing signal, why didn't they find it before? If it was just sitting out in the middle of Chaco Canyon, it's got to be easier to find there than sitting in your cluttered office.

Stevens: Very funny. Apparently, the students activated the homing signal somehow.

Jordan: So that's it? That's all you can do?

Stevens: All I can do? What else can I do? (shouting)

Jordan: Talk with your Chair or Board. Tell them exactly what happened and ask them to approach the NSA.

Stevens: You're not listening. I signed papers from the fucking government saying I wouldn't do anything that could possibly incite interest in this thing. If I did, they'd haul my ass off to jail for espionage or terrorism.

Jordan: All right, all right. Fuck the government and their weapons. Just cool down. Maybe you're right. I'd hate to have to spend any of my precious time visiting you in jail. (Laughter) Maybe you should take the weekend off; I mean, get out of the office, you idiot, and go fishing or something. Let's see what happens in the next few days. If nothing happens, maybe you're right. Let the thing go.

Evans hit a few more keystrokes, the lights came up, and the projector screen disappeared into the ceiling. "That's the extent of his theories," Evans said.

Neruda watched with some admiration as Evans settled back into his chair and crossed his legs like an English gentleman. His body was not the stereotypical, muscle-clad, bar-bouncer Navy Seal. Nevertheless, even in his loose-fitting clothes, there was no mistaking his athletic build and imposing, six and a half-foot presence.

Fifteen stood up slowly. His shoulder-length, silver hair was tied back in a meticulously braided ponytail, no doubt the handiwork of Li-Ching. There were persistent rumors that he and Li-Ching were romantically inclined, though no one had absolute proof. If the rumors were true, they were amazingly discrete. No one ever asked and neither Fifteen nor Li-Ching ever said or did anything that would definitely confirm or deny the gossip.

"I think we all support your exploratory trip," Fifteen said, "and we all understand the urgency to test your hypothesis. Perhaps it would be helpful if we spent a few minutes discussing your mission agenda. Have you had a chance to define it yet?"

Neruda made a conscious decision not to swallow. He wanted his second oversight to be minimized. Taking one direct hit was enough. Now he had to admit gracefully that he hadn't defined his mission agenda. Damn!

"I've been so busy working on the SMT analysis, map correlations, and mission planning," he said, "that I've admittedly overlooked the mission agenda, at least in terms of writing it down in a presentation format—"

"Well, for now, why don't you simply tell us what you plan to do when you arrive at Chaco Canyon. We'll add some of our own ideas if we think of anything. Okay?"

Fifteen was too civil. He was the best psychologist Neruda had ever seen, but usually he lost his gentleness after two mistakes.

"Yes. That's fine," Neruda said with a nervous smile. "We've selected six sites to test and we've ranked these sites in priority order based on our map correlations and best estimates of where we believe the glyphs indicate site preference—as said earlier, mostly in this center section of the map.

"At each site, we'll have RVs initially test the artifact's hallucinogenic effects and determine its home base. Assuming we're successful in activating the homing device, we'll follow its signal to home base. At home base, we'll secure the area first, assess supply and manpower requirements, and then return for supplies and mission planning."

He looked briefly at his wristwatch, hoping to send the not-so-subtle message that he was finished and hurried for time.

"Comments?" Fifteen asked.

"Who's on the exploratory team?"

"Dawson, Collin, Andrews, Evans, and myself."

"And who's the RV, then?" Ortmann asked.

"Yes, well, I haven't had a chance to review that as yet. Does anyone have a recommendation?"

Remote Viewers were very specialized personnel within the ACIO who were trained to be able to remotely view an environment across distance, and even time. But unlike other intelligence organizations that used RV, the ACIO also used a technology to enhance their natural psychic abilities. The technology, called RePlay, enabled RVs to capture their observations more accurately.

RVs were often attached to ACIO reconnaissance missions with the purpose of locating an object, person, or specific space/time coordinate. Their accuracy was startling. They could "see" the place where a subject was and if there were landmarks, they could pinpoint the exact location.

Branson cleared his throat. "Given the nature of your mission, I'd recommend Samantha Folten. She's relatively new, but her focus is the best we've ever seen in external, unpredictable environments. Walt Andersen is also a good bet, but I'd take Samantha because of her unusual focus. If these hallucinations proved to be powerful, her concentration could be a real asset."

"What's Samantha's clearance?" Evans asked.

"She's SL-Five as of last June."

"I think we should limit personnel on this mission to SL-Nine," Neruda said. "We don't know yet what we'll find and the memory restructure with RVs is seldom effective."

"Walt, then, is your man. He's SL-Ten."

"I agree with Evans," Fifteen asserted. "Take Andersen and let him know that he needs to be ready to leave at eighteen hundred hours. Speaking of having to leave, I'll bid you all adieu, as I have another meeting awaiting me. Thanks to Neruda and his team for their breakthrough on the map correlations. It's the first thing we've found that might unlock this mystery. Good luck to your team."

Neruda and the Directors all stood up in unison and, with an anxious movement to the door, filed out of Fifteen's office. Li-Ching remained behind, presumably the waiting "meeting" Fifteen had referred to.

Neruda had exactly three hours before the birds would fly. The Q-11 choppers were the preferred transport system for the ACIO, particularly for classified missions.

He and his team would be sleeping in New Mexico tonight. He couldn't wait to see the stars. Working underground for so many years made this particular mission all the more exciting. His appetite for fieldwork had never been that strong, but right now the grass looked much greener in Chaco Canyon.

CHAPTER 3
THE ARTIFACT

All beliefs have energy systems that act like birthing rooms for the manifestation of the belief. Within these energy systems are currents that direct your life experience. You are aware of these currents either consciously or subconsciously, and you allow them to carry you into the realm of experience that best exemplifies your true belief system. When you believe, "I am a fragment of First Source imbued with ITS capabilities," you are engaging the energy inherent within the feeling of connectedness. You are pulling into your reality a sense of connection to your Source and all the attributes therein. The belief is inseparable from you because its energy system is assimilated within your own energy system and is woven into your spirit like a thread of light.

An Excerpt from *Beliefs and Their Energy Systems*, Decoded from Chamber Four

WingMakers

The desert at night was a magical world steeped in silence and clarity. Neruda was reminded of this as he and Andrews set up their tent.

Neruda needed a good night's sleep. During the two-hour, chopper ride he had stolen a few minutes of shuteye, but most of his time was spent reviewing the mission agenda with Evans; selecting a site to make camp; and bringing Samantha Folten up to speed on the mission objectives and the artifact.

Walt Andersen hadn't been available for the trip on three-hour notice due to an illness in his family. Evans relented, allowing Samantha to join the exploration team despite her relatively low security clearance. Neruda was secretly pleased, partly because Samantha was new and enthusiastic, and partly because she was so highly recommended by Branson.

"You know tomorrow's gonna be one kick-ass day, boss."

Neruda smiled at Andrews' unconventional choice of words. Among the scientific core, Andrews was the only one who spoke with such guttural spontaneity. Over the years, it had become a comfort to Neruda. Oddly enough, it was even a source of admiration. Neruda often wished he could recite these same words with Andrews' natural ease.

"As long as you're around to provide colorful commentary, I'm sure it will be." When Neruda was alone with Andrews, sarcasm was an involuntary reflex.

Emily poked her head inside the sloping tent. "You boys still playing with your tent?" she lightly prodded.

Neruda and Andrews answered in unison. "Get out!"

"A little sensitive, aren't we?" Even in the dim light of the lantern, her smile was contagious.

"Samantha and I finished our set-up, brewed some decaf, and we're just about ready for a little walk before bed. We thought we'd see if you *gentlemen* wanted to join us." She put just enough of an English accent on the word "gentlemen" to remind them both of her Cambridge education.

"Yeah, yeah, yeah, go ahead and brag all you want about your quick set-up, but you didn't have to listen to the bossman explain, in tedious detail, all about our contingency plans."

Neruda could only grunt in disagreement, as he focused on tying the final rope and taking out any slack.

"Is Samantha with you?" he asked.

"She's a little shy around you SL-Twelvers," Emily quipped.

"She's probably heard how you read minds and pick apart alibis. All the RVs are wary of you guys. Everyone else thinks you're just a bunch of pussycats," Andrews said half-seriously.

"Did I hear correctly? You have coffee made, or are you just trying to make us old *gentlemen* feel bad?" Neruda asked.

"Yep."

"Yep to which question?"

"Both actually."

"And were you planning to share some of that coffee?"

"Let me confer with my new roommate." Emily stuck her head outside the tent for a moment.

Whispered voices exchanged a few words.

"Yep, but we have one condition."

"And that would be?"

"Samantha wants to see the artifact."

Neruda paused, trying to feel his reaction rather than think about it. "Okay," was his instinctual reply. "I know it's hard to believe, but we're almost done here. We'll meet you at your tent in a few minutes. I'll bring the artifact along and make the proper introductions.

"Will you two busybodies have enough time to bake some cookies before we arrive?" Neruda smiled as he spoke, darting his mischievous eyes between Emily and the silhouette of Samantha outside the tent.

"Probably will, I reckon." Emily turned and left her fake southern accent floating behind.

"You know, boss, I'm not sure it's such a good idea to let Samantha look at this thing," Andrews said, pointing to the aluminum carrying case, custom designed for the artifact.

"Why not?"

"She's an RV. I realize you don't trust RVs, but try to be a little less paranoid if you can."

"Lookit, I'm paranoid because we have Evans and an RV on our mission. The combination's shit. You know that. Anything that happens out of the ordinary will immediately fall out of your hands." Andrews was whispering again.

"Well then, let's make sure we keep everything as ordinary as possible," Neruda replied. "And we could start by getting our damn tent set up."

"Relax, boss. We're all done. Ta da." With that he stood up and put his arms out the way a magician does after completing an extraordinary feat of illusion.

✳   ✳   ✳   ✳

"Is your tent still standing?" Emily asked with a smile. She was tending the coffee on the fuel cell heater and organizing some shortbread cookies she had brought for the trip.

"It was when I left it."

"Luckily there's no wind tonight."

"Luckily there's coffee." Neruda's love of coffee was bested only by his zeal for discovery.

"Is Andrews going to join us?"

"I think he wanted to stay away from the combination of RV and artifact," Neruda whispered, leaning towards Emily's ear. "When you strip away his macho facade, he's basically a scared little puppy underneath."

Emily laughed and called Samantha out of the tent.

Samantha was young by ACIO standards, mid-thirties, slightly overweight with a shy smile and strikingly beautiful emerald-colored eyes that dominated her face. She looked Celtic with wavy red hair that was nearly waist-length. She was the kind of person who looked half enchantress, half wistful introvert.

Neruda gave her his most relaxed smile. He placed the case on the ground. "I think you'll find this fascinating," he began. "As I told you on the chopper, the object was found about nine kilometers from here. I want to wait until tomorrow morning before we proceed with full-blown RV and RePlay, but you can take a quick look at it now."

As he flicked open the latches and raised the top of the aluminum case, the artifact, half-buried in foam rubber, immediately began to hum in an eerie, pulsing manner. Samantha peered over the edge of the case. The light from the fire and nearby lantern seemed to pool in her face.

A look of worry replaced her excitement. Her eyes narrowed to focus exclusively on the object, and her lips tightened as if they'd been forbidden to speak.

Sensing something was wrong, Neruda hurriedly closed the lid over the artifact. Samantha crumpled to the ground, her head falling directly on top of the case. Emily shrieked. Neruda grabbed Samantha and held her head up lightly patting her cheeks with his hand. "Samantha. Samantha. It's okay. It's okay."

Samantha opened her eyes almost instantly. She looked at Neruda who was holding her head in his lap. "It's alive," she whispered as if in fear of being overheard by the object. "It's an intelligence… not a technology."

"Let's get you up," Neruda said as he helped her to her feet slowly.

"Are you okay?" Emily implored.

"Yes. I'm okay, just a little shocked by this—"

"What the hell happened?" asked Evans as he burst on the scene, followed by Collin a few paces behind.

For an instant Neruda wasn't sure what to say.

"What happened?" Evans asked again, this time more insistently.

"Everyone just calm down," Neruda replied softly. "Is there enough coffee for everyone, Emily?"

"Yes, yes, of course."

"Let's sit down then, have a cup of coffee, and we'll tell you what we know. I'm as interested to hear from Samantha as anyone."

Samantha was visibly shaken, and Neruda helped her ease into one of the folding chairs gathered around the fire. Evans and Collin joined the circle of chairs loosely configured around the campfire.

Emily quickly began to pour coffee. Neruda gave the first cup to Samantha. The night air was starting to get cool, and the warm cup reminded Neruda that the desert's stored heat was giving way to the frigid darkness.

"You're sure you're okay?" Neruda asked again, crouching before Samantha. She took a long sip of coffee.

"Yes, I'm fine. Thank you."

"What did you experience? Can you tell us?" Neruda stood up only to sit down opposite Samantha in a folding chair that Evans had set up.

"I heard this humming… it… it immediately entrained my mind. It was an incredibly powerful hypnotic effect. It suggested an image—"

"And what was the image?" blurted Evans.

"It was of a cave or dark structure of some kind."

"On earth?"

"I don't know… maybe. It was designed… not a natural cave… more like an anteroom. Yes, the cave was constructed but disguised as a natural structure."

"By who?" Neruda and Evans asked in harmony.

"I don't know."

"Samantha, you said earlier that the artifact was alive. That it wasn't a technology, but rather an intelligence. What did you mean exactly?"

"I could be wrong, but the object seemed to project itself." Her voice was quivering and her breath was short. She swallowed, looking dazed. "It was reading my mind. I could feel it scan me. It was a little like being eaten alive—only it was my thoughts that it was eating."

"It could still be a technology that did this, couldn't it?" Evans looked briefly at Neruda and then Collin.

"I can't imagine how this object could have organic intelligence," Collin stated. "It's just not practical that something made of metal alloys—"

"I think we should assume this thing is dangerous." Evans stood up and remained silent. He was clearly thinking of alternatives.

"Let's not assume we know anything about this object," Neruda said. "This image you saw, Samantha, was it an entrance?"

"Yes, I think so."

"And all you saw was a dark structure of some kind?"

"Yes."

"Did you get a feel for distance or direction from our camp?"

"No. Not really. Though, just when you asked that now, it seems that it was nearby. I don't know for sure. It all happened in a few seconds. I was overwhelmed. It was a feeling of… of mental rape." She began to cry, her eyes dropping tears at every blink.

Emily squeezed her hand in support, and Evans, pacing around the fire pit assembling chairs, suddenly stopped. "You know this could be a probe. I don't know why you didn't consider this before. Homing device, compass, map. You thought of everything but a probe. Why?"

"Before we conclude our investigation, let's begin it," Neruda said with a hint of sarcasm.

"With all due respect to Samantha, she could be misinterpreting the true intentions of the artifact."

"How so?" Evans demanded.

"It's possible the device was activated by her psychic abilities. Perhaps my own. I don't know. But the device was activated somehow, and it could be that its primary action is to try to connect with whatever activated it and deliver a message or image."

Neruda turned to Samantha again. "Did you hear what I just said?"

She nodded.

"Is it possible that the device was simply trying to connect with you? That it wasn't trying to hurt you?"

Samantha didn't move her head. Her face was withdrawn. Her eyes closed like ponderous doors, and everyone waited.

"Samantha, did you hear me?"

She remained unmoving as if she were sleeping.

Neruda intuited that the artifact was again probing her, or trying to connect in some way.

"I think she's communicating right now with the object."

"Shouldn't we snap her out of it?" Evans demanded. "She could be in some danger."

"She looks composed. Even peaceful." Neruda whispered. "Let's just observe for a while." He unlatched the aluminum case and slowly opened the top. The object was emitting an unmistakable vibration. It wasn't the hum from an electrical device. This hum was very subtle, almost unnoticeable, even in the silence of the desert. It was felt more than heard.

Samantha continued to look withdrawn, trance-like, in total rapport with the artifact. Neruda leaned closer to her and touched her forehead with the back of his hand as if he were trying to determine if she had a fever. He checked her pulse. He was satisfied that Samantha was okay.

As he sat back down, Neruda became a little woozy and disoriented.

"Are you okay?" Emily asked.

Neruda nodded slowly, but there was uncertainty in his eyes.

"I feel like I'm being dragged into unconsciousness," Neruda said faintly. "It's not easy to resist this thing—"

Evans stood up and began pacing again. "Does anyone else feel this… this hypnosis?"

Collin and Emily both shook their heads and mumbled "no."

"Damn it, I thought we agreed to wait until the morning to start this investigation." Evans' voice was raised in pitch and intensity.

"I forgot to tell the object we were going to wait until the morning," Neruda confided, showing his sense of humor was intact. "Don't worry, I don't feel any danger. It's just trying to wire itself to its home base and to my mind at the same time. It's as if this thing were making an introduction." Neruda mouthed the words like he were talking in his sleep. He rubbed the corner of his eyes with his forefinger. Every movement was strained as if gravity were suddenly intensified and time was stretched into the realm of slow motion.

"I understand." Samantha stirred. Her whole body shot out of her chair and she knelt before the artifact. She picked it up with great strain on her face, her arms struggling with the weight. She touched certain glyphs in a specific order with her fingers. The humming ceased.

"It's been designed to ward off intruders," Samantha explained. "It's protecting itself. It probes to determine your intent, and while it's probing, it discombobulates your thoughts. It essentially renders you helpless as it assesses your intentions."

Neruda snapped back to reality when Samantha turned the device off. "Did you see the site?"

"Yes," she said excitedly. "It's nearby. It's well-hidden, but I think we can find it."

"What site? Where?" Evans asked, slightly bewildered.

"I saw something, too," Neruda said. "I think I'd recognize it if I saw it again."

"Fine, but do you know where we should begin looking?"

"No," Neruda replied as if distracted by something.

"I think I can locate it by a landmark I saw." Samantha set the object back into its foam nest within the case, struggled to her feet a bit, and plopped herself back into her chair with a long sigh.

"You were about to tell us about a landmark," Evans reminded her.

"It's a thin, pointed rock formation, like a chimney stack. It's maybe thirty meters high, ten in circumference at its base, but only about five meters at its top.

There can't be too many of these rock formations around here. Can there?"

"Did you see this, too?" Evans turned to Neruda ignoring Samantha's question.

Neruda shook his head. "For some reason I didn't see anything I could identify as a landmark, it was more of an assemblage of images, like a mosaic. And most of these were of a cavern or something subterranean."

"So what is it," Emily asked, "technology or a living intelligence?"

"Maybe both." Neruda smiled. "Whatever it is, it knows us a lot better than we know it."

"I don't know how it could be a living intelligence," Samantha began slowly, "but every bone in my body screams that it's alive. It's not an inanimate, programmed technology. It's a vital intelligence that is somehow stored inside or projected through this object."

Then, in frustration, she added. "Oh, I don't know what I'm talking about. I'm speaking in gibberish tonight. Excuse me."

"Under the circumstances, gibberish may be the only language of choice." Neruda smiled disarmingly and poured himself another cup of coffee. "You know, if it weren't for your coffee, Emily, I might've been dragged into unconsciousness by that thing." He laughed, and pointed with his free hand to the artifact. It looked tranquil like a baby bird asleep in its nest.

"It's decaf," Emily replied with a deadpan expression.

"So you're to blame for my lapse of concentration——"

"I wish you'd take this a bit more seriously," Evans interjected. "We've just seen a technology render you two helpless, mentally rape you, as Samantha put it, and you're joking about the coffee."

Neruda calmly turned to Emily. "Can you bring me the SMT chart… number 2507?" Turning to Samantha. "How long before you could have RePlay set up and operable?"

"Ten minutes," she answered.

"Fine, go ahead and get set up." Neruda turned to Evans with sudden impatience etched on his face. "And what did you want to do?"

"Just observe… for now." Evans turned his gaze to the fire, detaching from Neruda's authoritative stare. Evans knew his presence on exploratory missions was always resented. He knew he put his colleagues on edge. He also knew it was his job to do so.

Emily returned from her tent holding a large sheet of paper and a flashlight. She handed both to Neruda, who spread the chart out on the ground about two meters from the fire.

The flashlight illuminated the center of the chart, which was covered in lines of various colors. Evans, Collin, and Emily all moved behind him, standing hunched over with hands on knees. Neruda was crouched with one knee on the ground.

"Here's Samantha's landmark," Neruda pointed with both the flashlight beam and his index finger. There was a small point of tightly formed circles, almost concentric, in a rainbow of colors near the center of the topographical map. "It's isolated, the right proportions, and about thirty meters tall," he continued. "And it's about three kilometers due east from our camp."

"Let's wait on RePlay until morning," Evans said. "It's late, we know where we need to go. Let's all get some rest." His voice sounded clipped like a machine gun.

Samantha came out of the tent with her monitor and a headpiece that looked a little like a wire cage for her head. No matter how many times Neruda saw it, he always thought it looked like the silliest technology he'd ever seen. Most of the technologies that the ACIO developed were never mass-produced or designed with a consumer perspective. They were built by hand, one at a time. How they looked was never considered important.

"We're going to wait until morning, Samantha," Neruda said. "I'm sorry I wasted your time getting set up. But I think Jim's right, we should all get a good night's sleep and concentrate our energies on finding the site during the day."

Samantha nodded, somewhat relieved that she wouldn't have to make further contact with the artifact that night. She was feeling drained of energy, and sleep sounded like the perfect prescription.

"By the way," Neruda turned to Samantha, "how'd you know how to turn off the artifact?"

"What do you mean?" Samantha replied.

"Don't you remember getting up and shutting this thing down?" Neruda asked.

"No..." Samantha's eyes thinned to a line of fluttering eyelashes. She was concentrating her mind like a laser, and Neruda could see why Branson liked her so much.

"I have absolutely no recollection of getting up and turning anything off. Are you sure?" She looked from Neruda to Emily.

"I saw it, too," Emily confirmed. "You got up from your chair as quickly as if your pants were on fire. You picked up the artifact and began turning it in your... your left hand while your right hand was touching glyphs, in what at least looked like a specific order. You seemed to know exactly what you were doing."

"If I did that, I don't remember."

"Maybe your mind was a bit traumatized," Emily offered, "and you've got a mild case of amnesia."

"That doesn't explain how she knew how to de-activate the artifact." Neruda glanced at Emily. "The artifact somehow planted this knowledge inside you without you remembering. You acted without knowing your actions."

"So what're you saying?" Samantha asked. A nervous smile spread across her face, and her concentration scattered like smoke in the wind.

"I think we should stop speculating," Neruda closed the case and buckled its latches with a loud, synchronized click. "The only thing I know for sure is that this thing is not an only child. It has brothers and sisters that're nearby. And I can't wait to find them."

"How will you sleep tonight?" Emily asked with her southern accent fully lathered.

Neruda just laughed and picked up the case. "I'll see you both in the morning. Good night."

Neruda could hear Samantha's and Emily's muffled voices as he walked to his tent about twenty meters away. There was no movement in the desert air. It hung so perfectly still; Neruda felt its presence all the more.

Andrews was asleep. His headphones were still on and a book was draped across his chest, face down, spread out like a wounded bird of prey. From the sound of his breathing, Neruda knew he was in deep sleep. A place he wanted to be also, but he knew too much about the day's events awaiting them. He couldn't sleep. At least not yet.

CHAPTER 4
INITIAL CONTACT

The blueprint of exploration has an overarching intention; you are not the recipients of divine labor and meticulous training only to ensure that you may enjoy endless bliss and eternal ease. There is a purpose of transcendent service concealed beyond the horizon of the present universe age. If I designed you to take you on an eternal excursion into nirvana, I certainly would not construct your entire universe into one vast and intricate training school, requisition a substantial branch of my creation as teachers and instructors, and then spend ages upon ages piloting you, one by one, through this enormous universe school of experiential learning. The furtherance of the system of human progression is cultivated by my will for the explicit purpose to merge the human species with other species from different universes.

An Excerpt from *Tributary Zones*, Decoded from Chamber Twenty-two

WingMakers

Though Neruda lacked the infrared equipment, he did have a compass. It was still fairly early by his standards—about 2300 hours. He took a few supplies with him in a small pack, selected a standard issue ACIO jacket that said *DOD Weather Research Center* in small block letters, and began walking in an easterly direction.

He took a wide berth around the campsite careful to avoid detection by Evans. Neruda coveted his privacy such as it was. He knew very well that Evans or anyone associated with the security team could track his whereabouts. All ACIO personnel had embedded tracking devices that the ACIO satellite network could follow. No one liked it, but the Labyrinth Group conceded that it was necessary when the technology was developed in the mid '60s. It *managed paranoia*, as Fifteen explained.

The implants were only the size of a grain of rice and inserted just below the neckline to the right of the spine. They transmitted an individual's unique body frequency. The ACIO discovered in 1959 that every person emitted a relatively stable and totally unique vibratory pattern. The bodyprint, as it was called within the ACIO, was every bit as reliable as a fingerprint. This discovery led to a technology that isolated a person's bodyprint and transmitted it to a satellite network jointly owned and operated by the NSA and ACIO.

Defections within the ACIO were considered the greatest risk to its ongoing success and future. The body print implant technology was the primary method through which ACIO employees were restrained from defecting. There were other technologies—both in development and fully deployed—that also minimized the risk. It was the one thing about the ACIO that Neruda had never been able to accept.

A coyote's mournful howl brought Neruda to a full stop to get his bearings.

He had cleared the campsite and was picking his way through the sparse Pinion trees and sagebrush. The moon was a thin, florescent sickle, its light as faint as a tired whisper despite the clear night air. In contrast, the stars almost glared at the desert landscape and managed to reveal enough desert flora and rocks so Neruda could pick his way at a comfortable pace.

He felt more confident as he went out of visual range of the campsite so he turned on his flashlight and picked up his pace. His flashlight seemed uncomfortably powerful against the dark desert, and he felt like he was intruding into a restricted world.

He made it to the top of the ridge he had pointed out to Emily only fifteen minutes earlier. He could see it, even without infrared. It looked just as Samantha said. A lonely, phallic-shaped sandstone formation looming over its neighborhood of gnarled trees, intricate sagebrush, and stunted rock outcroppings.

When the binoculars came down from his eyes he could tell the site was less than two kilometers away. Neruda assessed his situation. He wasn't particularly tired. Maybe a little winded from the climb, but otherwise his body and mind were wide-awake. The air temperature was cool, but the climb up the ridge left him feeling warm.

Without hesitation, he walked towards the rock structure like it was home.

❋   ❋   ❋   ❋

The smell of coffee and bacon woke Andrews even before the morning light seeped through the dark, green skin of the tent. He rolled over in his sleeping bag and heard the book crash as it found the red, rocky floor. It brought his eyes open with a start. No Neruda. His sleeping bag was empty and undisturbed.

"Are you guys awake yet?" It was Emily radiating her cheerful voice outside the tent.

"Yeah, we're up," Andrews replied through an unconcealed yawn, "but I haven't seen anything of Neruda. He must've gotten up early."

"It's *early* right now. It's only six," Emily retorted, her voice less cheerful.

"Well, if you haven't seen him and he's not in here, then he's probably with Collin or Evans."

"No, they're eating breakfast, and they never mentioned seeing Neruda."

Andrews unzipped his sleeping bag and stood up. "Maybe he liked the walk so much last night that he took another this morning. Shit, I don't know."

"We never went for a walk last night."

"Well, I'm sure he'll turn up soon. For one thing, the smell of coffee should draw him out if anything will. It's working on me."

"If you see him, tell'um we have eggs, bacon, and coffee ready."

Andrews could hear her footsteps fade as she walked away.

Evans was reviewing maps when he looked up, "Any sign of Jamisson yet?" He took a sip of coffee.

"None that I've seen," Andrews replied, "but then I've hardly been looking for him either."

"Maybe we should…"

"I can't believe he'd just leave the camp," Emily said. "Did you see him at all last night?"

Andrews was heaping eggs and bacon on his plate. "I don't know… I don't remember seeing him at all last night. But when I sleep, I'm out cold."

"He went to the site," Evans said with incredulity in his voice. "He broke protocol again. He couldn't wait until the morning. I'll bet he went last night after we went to bed."

Evans pulled out a small black box about the size of a pack of cigarettes. The ACIO only used secure lines when communicating, and the black box was a digital paging device. His large hand, resembling tanned leather, completely smothered the object as his thumb pressed a green button. He turned his back, and in a hushed voiced, spoke into its transmitter, "Immediately perform a bodyprint scan for Neruda. Send exact coordinates. Determine movement boundaries within one meter." He pushed the *send* button and waited for message confirmation. An amber-colored light blinked and Evans put the pager back into his vest pocket.

The ACIO preferred single-loop, or non-real-time communication. It was much harder to decode because encryption was changed every time a message was sent; thus the context was nearly impossible to derive. But it frustrated Evans sometimes because it took longer to get an answer.

"Is the artifact still in your tent?" Evans asked turning to Andrews.

"Far as I know. The case is there, I assume the artifact is inside."

Emily jumped to Neruda's defense, "Are you implying he'd take the artifact and go to the site without us?"

"He's at the site," Evans replied. "He probably didn't take the artifact only because of its weight. But trust me, he's there."

"And why would he do that?" Andrews asked, his mouth full of food.

"You don't know about last night, do you?" Emily asked.

"No… I was sleeping, remember?"

"Samantha and Jamisson were both communicating with the artifact. It somehow activated and sent them images of where its home base was. We got a pretty good fix on its location… about three kilometers east of our position." Evans stood up from the folding table, and pulled his pager out of his pocket. "What's taking them so damn long?"

"It's very early; maybe they're short-staffed," Emily offered.

"So when will we leave for this site?" Samantha asked.

"As soon as I get verification, I'll call our ride."

Andrews turned to look east for a quick glance. "Looks like a pretty good climb up that ridge. How're we going to carry the artifact?" He shoved more food in his mouth like a parolee's first taste of home cooking.

"We're all being airlifted. Don't worry." Evans' voice revealed that his thoughts were elsewhere. "Damn it, Jenkins! What's taking you so long?"

"So tell me what happened last night with you and the artifact." Andrews stole a quick look at Samantha and then anchored his eyes on the scrambled eggs he was devouring.

Samantha stuttered a bit, unsure of how to describe her experience. "I saw an image of its home base."

"And we know it's three miles east because… because you saw an image of… of what?" Andrews asked.

"An unusual rock formation." Samantha found herself reluctant to talk. Her psychic abilities had been questioned and ridiculed her entire life, and she had become expert at sniffing out what she called, trip-up questions. It had taught her the skill of calculated reticence even among her ACIO colleagues.

"She also saw a cavern—"

"Finally!" Evans exclaimed before Emily could finish her thought. He sat down and scanned the small display screen, cupping his hand to shield it from the awakening sun. His lips moved, but surrendered no sound as he read the message:

> 0527 – 0921: NERUDA BP ID'ED @ NML0237/L0355. 3.27 KILOMETERS ESE FROM YOUR PRESENT POSITION. MOVEMENT BOUNDARIES NEGATIVE. VITAL SIGNS INTACT. EXTREMELY FAINT READINGS. ADVISE.

Evans pursed his lips momentarily and spoke into the pager, "No further actions required. Monitor and update. All is well. End transmission."

"He's at the site, and he's sleeping," Evans made no effort to conceal his frustration. He glanced at his wristwatch. "Let's get ready. Bird'll be here in less than fifteen minutes."

Evans walked away without another word. Emily looked at Samantha as if to read her eyes for an explanation, but Samantha could only stare to the eastern ridge, her mind squarely on the task ahead.

"Did you notice if he took his sleeping bag?" Emily asked.

"He didn't take it," Andrews replied. "It was unused."

"I can't imagine Neruda sleeping out in the desert without a sleeping bag," Emily said, "let alone his morning coffee. Something's wrong."

"You think he's injured?"

"I don't know, but something's wrong." Emily turned to face Samantha. "What do you feel?"

Samantha looked to Emily with a sense of empathy. "He's okay. That's what I feel."

"You don't feel he's in any danger?"

"No."

Emily's face visibly relaxed. "If we're going to keep up with Evans, we'd better get in high gear."

"Shit, if there's one thing you can count on, Neruda's too damn smart to put himself in danger." Andrews' voice was consoling. He rustled a few paper plates into a plastic garbage bag, and handed it to Emily. "Anyway, I have to disassemble a tent in five minutes that took us thirty to put up. I better run. See ya in ten."

✳   ✳   ✳   ✳

"Last chance, do you want to walk it or ride?" Evans' voice was barely audible above the roar of the helicopter. Sand was ripping through her hair and pricking her skin like tiny scythes eager for blood; Emily finally relented to ride.

"I just think we should send someone by foot in case he retraces his steps." She sat down in the seat beside Evans with a scowl on her face.

"The point is," Evans began, "is that he's still sleeping or I would've been updated on his change of position."

"How will we pick up his trail when we land?" Emily asked. "This thing puts out hurricane-force winds." She waved her hands in the air wildly to emphasize her discontent.

"Look, we'll land a half kilometer east of his position and double back. Okay?" Evans dropped his head to peer over his bifocals, which he had donned to look at a map. He knew it gave him an authoritative look.

"Okay." Emily echoed silently with her lips.

It was only seconds later that Collin pointed to the spindly rock tower that loomed ahead. It was an eerie structure. Silhouetted against the rising sun, it looked like a stack of coins ready to fall at a mere breath.

The helicopter reached its position in less than five minutes. Emily kept an eye on the rocky terrain throughout the ride, while Evans was preoccupied with the map. Samantha closed her eyes seemingly troubled by the noisy ride, or perhaps to avoid a conversation with Andrews.

The copilot came back to the passenger chamber and told them that they were going to land directly below, and everyone should get ready to jump out. Samantha held her stomach and grimaced, obviously unsettled by the sudden drop in elevation.

They filed off the chopper quickly, Evans first, assisting everyone else to a safe exit. The copilot handed some backpacks to Evans and Collin, and then the aluminum case was delicately transferred to Evans. "We'll be on standby unless we hear from you, otherwise we'll rendezvous at these coordinates at 1800 hours. Good luck."

Evans acknowledged the copilot with a wave of his hand, and the helicopter sped away like a large beetle. The ensuing silence swallowed them as only the desert can do.

"So where the hell do we pick up his trail?" Andrews asked, a little uncomfortable with how loud his voice suddenly seemed.

"Before we get started, there're a few protocols we all need to bear in mind from this point forward," Evans was pivoting his head to survey the landscape as if he were getting his bearings. "First, base communication is exclusively through me. Second, if we find anything peculiar—like the home base of this artifact—we operate in reconnaissance mode only. We secure the site; we don't explore it. Understood?"

Everyone nodded as Evans swiveled his head to look for a response. "And keep hydrated. We'll stop periodically to rest and take water. If anyone needs more frequent rests, just say so. Otherwise we'll press on."

Evans looked west for a few moments; his nostrils flaring like he was a bloodhound sniffing out its prey. "We have his coordinates, we'll start there and then walk in a westerly, southwesterly direction until we spot his trail. In this mixture of sand and stone, it shouldn't be too hard to see his footprints."

"What about Samantha?" Emily asked. "Couldn't she help?"

"Let's try it the old-fashioned way first," Evans answered. "If we don't pick up his trail in the next twenty minutes, we'll look at other alternatives—including RV."

Andrews looked to Evans after taking a long sip of water from his canteen. "If you really want to try the old-fashioned way, how bout yelling at the top of our lungs?"

"Let's find his trail first. Then we can yell." Evans laughed under his breath as he walked towards the coordinates that disclosed Neruda's bodyprint. Andrews adjusted his backpack and became the thing he hated the most: a follower.

Evans picked a path through two rock arroyos that were about fifty meters across. The rocks were the color of light cinnamon, and as the sun was rising in the east, they bore a reddish tint. The air was completely still and the jackets were beginning to feel a little too warm as they walked their way through the sparse desert underbrush.

✳   ✳   ✳   ✳

Only ten minutes into their trek, Collin found a footprint.

"Neruda!" Evans immediately yelled with his hands cupped around his mouth. He called several times in the direction of the footprints and waited for a response. A slight echo accompanied his call, but nothing resembling Neruda's voice. Emily tried as well, but to the same effect.

"Isn't it reasonable to assume he's hurt?" Emily asked, turning to Evans. "I mean let's face it, Neruda's not prone to sleep in the open desert without a sleeping bag. Something happened to him." Her voice trailed off to a whisper. "And it can't be good."

"We don't know that for certain," Evans argued. "His vitals were fine. I'm sure he's just sleeping."

"Then why isn't he answering us?"

"Let's just follow his trail and find out," Collin replied like a mediator. "No sense standing around speculating." Collin was very thin, mid-forties, with reddish-brown hair revealing a hint of silver over both ears, and a single streak on top to match. He seemed uncomfortable standing in one spot for long, as if his bird-like legs couldn't support his body weight.

"NERUDA!" Evans called one more time, his voice sounding increasingly impatient at the return of silence.

"Let's go wake him up," Evans said.

They followed his tracks easily, until they came to a rock outcropping where his trail became more suspect. They fanned out, scattering themselves like ants in search of food. But his trail had disappeared. No one could find any more footprints.

"He's got to be somewhere in these rocks. Maybe there's a ledge or cave somewhere." It was Evans' voice yelling to the rest of the team. "Look for any signs of a crevice or opening in the rocks."

Emily could sense a growing concern in his voice. She could feel a tension in the air. Everyone was aware that they could be within a few meters of an ET home base. Perhaps an active site. The disappearance of Neruda compounded the strange sense of impending doom or discovery.

"I found a print," shouted Samantha. "It's the same as the others… I… I think." She was kneeling near the print with a stick in her hand pointing it out as everyone arrived.

"Good," remarked Evans. "Now we know which direction he was going." Everyone fan out five meters apart and let's walk slowly."

"NERUDA!" Emily shouted again. A stronger echo sounded now that they were in the depths of a canyon wall. They were approaching a massive wall of rock that towered forty meters in a nearly vertical line. They walked deliberately, their heads pivoting like surveillance cameras.

"I think I found another print," Samantha said, "but I'm not sure."

"It's as if he disappeared into this wall of rock," Andrews said. "Why would he have come here? Isn't that the rock you saw in your vision?" He was pointing, like a hitchhiker, to the slender rock structure directly behind them about one hundred meters away.

"Looks like a print, but it's not a clear one. Unfortunately, there's not much sand or loose rock around here." Evans closed his eyes momentarily as if he were trying to clear his mind to focus on Neruda's whereabouts.

"He's nearby. I can feel him. He's not sleeping. He's awake." Evans' voice sounded distant, as if he was talking to himself. "I think he's in there." His hand was pointing directly ahead to the sheer rock face of the canyon wall.

"If he's in there, how'd he get in?" Emily asked.

"There must be an opening somewhere. Let's examine the rock face carefully. There's an opening somewhere."

"Maybe we should use the artifact," Samantha offered. "If it's a homing device, and we're this close—"

"Let's find Neruda first," Evans snapped, "and worry about the artifact's home base later."

"But maybe they're one and the same location," Samantha said hesitantly.

"I doubt it." Evans looked away, staring with his gunmetal eyes to the wall in front of them. "How the hell would he find the home base without the artifact?

Especially at night."

"I don't know, but then how'd I know how to turn the artifact off last night?" Samantha's words hung weightless in the crisp morning air, surrounded in deep silence like an archipelago in a turquoise sea.

"Okay, we'll look for an opening first… and if we don't find anything in ten minutes, we'll try the artifact."

"Why not let Samantha fiddle with the little monster while we look for a doorway into this fucking mountain?"

Evans sighed. He looked to Emily and Collin to see their reaction to Andrews' suggestion. "Emily, you look over there. Collin, try that side beyond those rocks. Andrews, take that ledge over there, just beyond those small trees. I'll take the center so I can stay close to Samantha in case anything happens. If you see anything that even vaguely resembles an opening, let me know immediately."

"I still don't see why you think he's in there," Andrews was looking disdainfully at the massive rock wall in front of the team. "Maybe he was just fucking lost. One footprint shouldn't—"

"Look," Evans said, barely checking his anger, "I *feel* that he's in there. That's good enough for me. If it's not good enough for you, look elsewhere, but stop arguing with me."

Andrews looked down pretending to examine the footprint.

"Let's go." Evans started to walk away and then stopped abruptly to look at Samantha. "Are you okay with this?"

"Yes, I'm fine. I'm sure I'll be okay." She smiled weakly, resigned to the fact that she'd be alone with the artifact.

"I'm only seconds away. Call if you need anything."

"Good luck," she managed to say under her breath as they dispersed to their assigned search areas. Emily waited while the others walked away.

"Samantha," Emily said quietly, "are you going to RV Neruda?"

"It doesn't sound like I need to. Evans knows he's in there. He's SL-Fourteen. I'm not going to argue with him."

"They're not perfect," Emily said. "I've heard stories about their psychic abilities, too, but I think it'd be a good idea to RV him if for no other reasons than to corroborate Evans' assumptions."

"I can do that," Samantha offered.

"Thanks, you're a sweetheart."

"You're very welcome," Samantha replied, smiling to the ground.

"Oh, by the way," Emily asked, "do you remember how to turn off the artifact if it re-activates?"

"I've no idea, but then that didn't stop me before. Besides, I think we're acquainted now. I have a feeling it will behave differently with me now."

"I hope you're right," Emily patted her lightly on the shoulder as she walked by in pursuit of Neruda's whereabouts. She liked Samantha's shy, sensitive nature. It reminded her of herself some years earlier, before the cancer.

The wall of rock loomed before them, blocking the sun's rays and casting a sense of surreal beauty and mystery. In the shadow of the wall the air was cool, but the absolute calm made it tolerable even without a jacket. The rocks that had fallen from the mammoth wall over the millennium were the size of small houses. It was easy to imagine how it might have looked and sounded when they fell like glacial shards.

Samantha busied herself with the task of setting up RePlay and preparing for her encounter with the artifact. She always preferred to work alone when she was doing RV work. All she required was a data input, which were usually search coordinates and time frame. It was odd, but if she knew too much about the search parameters, she was less likely to be accurate. Branson called the phenomenon Ghost-Knotting, somehow implying that too much knowledge about the search confounded the free flow of psychic energy.

Samantha had experienced this only once before, and it troubled her now because she was in similar circumstances. She knew the subject, location, and the objectives of the search. Consciously, it would be hard to let go of her knowledge and simply see and hear the images that press upon her during a Remote Viewing session. The images are so delicate and fragile. They require complete absorption. Otherwise, they dissipate before they can be understood and made sensible by RePlay.

As she donned her headgear, affectionately called the Brain Shell, she opened the case. The artifact was quiet. She was a little surprised. Maybe she had turned it off permanently. Or maybe its mission was completed last night.

She looked over the object carefully, touching its casing as if it were a newborn babe. She flipped the switch for RePlay, adjusted the capture sensitivity, settled into a sitting position with legs crossed Indian style, and closed her eyes like heavy doors shutting out the noise of a busy street.

At the last second, she had changed her mission objectives from locating Neruda to identifying the location of the artifact's home base. She rationalized that Neruda would be there anyway, and with this strategy, she'd kill two birds with one stone.

Within moments, she began to see an image emerge on the screen of her mind. Her boss referred to this phenomenon as BS Static because the Brain Shell, when it was first turned on, often produced an image of its own in the RV operative. It had something to do with its electrical field and its proximity to the visual cortex. However, this image was unlike anything she'd ever seen before.

Three hazy shapes were forming that looked like green rectangles floating in a gray-brown light. Her mind's eye squinted in reflex to the diffuse shapes, hoping that she could resolve the shape and purpose, but nothing she did made a difference. They looked a little like doorways—though she didn't intuit that that was their purpose.

The rectangles, hovering in space, began to spin—each in different directions. The first remained vertical, spinning counterclockwise; the second rotated forward lengthwise like a windmill; and the third spun clockwise in the vertical plane. Without warning, she became aware that the artifact was humming and that it was somehow connected to the image—the motion—she saw.

She decided to test the door hypothesis and approached the objects. As she came closer they stopped, and the humming from the artifact became silent. She thought about stopping the session, but there was something about the way these rectangular shapes commanded her attention. There was a presence, a power that they exuded, which she had never before encountered. It seemed natural and unnatural at the same time, and it was this paradox that drew her forward.

Samantha reached out to touch the middle object, and as she did, the shape changed. It began to take on characteristics of a human male, elderly, tall, bearded, looking the part of a wizard with eyes that bore into hers with such intensity she could only turn away. "Do not fear us," a voice filled her, reverberating inside. It was as if every cell in her body had suddenly grown ears.

"We are what you seek, what you have always sought," the voice continued. It was authoritative, yet gentle. "You are being led even at this very moment to find what we have left for you. It is already within your grasp, and when you find your fingers reaching for it, close them securely without hesitation. Without fear. We tell you that it is the only way. The only way."

The words gave way to silence. Samantha looked again at the being that was before her. It had reverted to the form of a rectangle. Hovering like a green, featureless door.

She spoke from pure instinct. "What is within our grasp?"

"The way into our world," the voice replied.

"Your world?" She echoed without thinking.

"You will only find our world if you proceed without fear. It is the only barrier into our world that is impenetrable."

"Why do you want us to find your world?" Samantha asked, aware that her voice sounded perplexed.

"We have been within your species since its creation on this planet that you call Earth. We are within your DNA—encoded into the invisible structures that surround and support your DNA. Our world is both within you and more distant than your mind can comprehend. You will find our world because you need our assistance to awaken a part of your nature that is hidden from your view behind the languages of your world."

"Hidden?" Samantha asked. "In what way?"

An image of Earth, encircled in a latticework of light filaments, filled the surface of the center rectangle. It was as if a three-dimensional movie were being projected on its surface. "Your planet is of interest to an extraterrestrial species that you are not aware of at this time. It is a species more advanced and more dangerous than your average citizen can imagine. If humankind is destined to be the stewards of this genetic library called Earth, which we so carefully cultivated and exported to this galaxy, then it will need to defend itself from this predator race."

The image of Earth enlarged as if a camera were slowly zooming in on the diminutive blue sphere, floating in the vastness of an ink-black space. Samantha began to notice several pulsing lights that seemed to mark strategic locations on the planet. Her eyes locked onto the general area of New Mexico, where she saw a location marker.

"What is hidden from you," the voice continued, "is that your planet is part of an interconnected universe that operates in ordered chaos outside the constructs, instruments, technologies, and formulaic inventions of your scientists. There is something beneath the particle and wave, beneath the subconscious, beneath the spiritual resonance of Earth's greatest teachers, and this Language of Unity remains hidden from you. It is encoded in your DNA. We did this. And we placed the triggers within your DNA that would awaken your ability to survive a shift in your genetic makeup."

"Why? Why do we need to make a genetic shift?" She couldn't contain her skepticism, but as she spoke the words she could feel her fear begin to rise. Whatever she was interacting with was an unknown, and she knew that to trust anything or anyone in a self-directed RV session was folly.

"You will find out soon enough," the voice replied. "After this encounter, you will feel a new confidence in your powers of inquiry. It is the one element that will sustain you in the face of doubt and fear that will confront you in the weeks ahead. On a level that you have never seen, you are a holographic entity that is woven throughout all things, and when you touch into this feeling, you awaken a frequency of your consciousness that will guide you into our world. You have no reason to believe us, yet you know our words have no other purpose than to awaken a part of you long dormant. We are the WingMakers. We leave you in the Light that is One."

The rectangles blurred into a greenish-gold light that completely filled her vision. The sound of Andrews' distant voice broke her concentration, and she regained her human composure, faintly aware that she had lost contact with the most amazing force she had ever seen.

CHAPTER 5
THE SEARCH

As it is my nature to be seven-fold, there are seven universes that comprise my body. Within each of these, a species of a particular DNA template is cast forth and is nurtured by Source Intelligence to explore its material universe. Each of these species is sent forth from the Central Race into the universe that was created to unveil its potential and seed vision. Your species will converge with six other species in a distant future that will reunite my body as the living extension of known creation. While this may seem so distant as to have no relevance to your time, it is vital for you to understand the scope of your purpose. You can think of these seven species as the limbs of my body rejoined to enable me/us total functionality within the grand universe. This is my purpose and therefore your own as well.

An Excerpt from *Tributary Zones*, Decoded from Chamber Twenty-two
WingMakers

Very few people in the mysterious world of Fifteen made him uneasy, but Darius McGavin was one of them. McGavin was the director of the NSA's Special Projects Laboratory. Ostensibly, McGavin masqueraded as Fifteen's supervisor because the ACIO had been established as an unacknowledged department of the Special Projects Laboratory when UFO activity became an imperative in the late 1940s. Technically, Fifteen reported to McGavin.

Fifteen's stealth and intellect were so refined that McGavin was completely unaware of the real scope of the ACIO, its true mission and objectives, or the existence of the Labyrinth Group and its TTP with the Corteum. It was truly a masterful cover-up considering the paranoia and technological prowess of the NSA.

But what really disturbed Fifteen was that McGavin was making an unscheduled, short-notice visit, which could only mean one thing: a serious problem was underfoot. Very often these serious problems were rumors about the ACIO's clandestine initiatives with the military industrial complex, or private sector, industry partners.

Fifteen found these short-notice visits a supreme annoyance. McGavin was arrogant, and splendidly ill informed; a combination that Fifteen could only tolerate in small doses. He had already arranged a series of urgent meetings surrounding his obligatory meeting with McGavin. If he were lucky, McGavin would be back in route to Virginia in a mere thirty minutes.

It was 1100 hours when the knock on his door reminded him to look chipper and smile like a party host. His back spasms were attacking him more than usual, but he never used painkillers or any kind of medical aid. He ambled over to the door with his white cane, rehearsing his smile one last time.

"Darius, how good to see you."

"Good to see you as well." McGavin replied. "What's with the cane? You're not actually getting old are you?" He snickered as he walked by Fifteen to seat himself at his small, desk-side table. McGavin set his briefcase down and gathered himself in the waiting chair, running his hands over his hairless head as if some phantom hair still remained.

"I'm just having a few back spasms the past few weeks. The cane, well, it's just for sympathy." He smiled politely, just as he had practiced.

McGavin was a rare combination of technical genius and political astuteness. Graduating from the Air Force Academy in 1975 top in his class, he went on to Massachusetts Institute of Technology (MIT), graduating with a mechanical engineering degree, and then adding an advanced degree in quantum physics from Yale. He was the perfect student, blessed with the ability to study the professor's biases, and reflect them like a newly polished mirror. The NSA recruited him when he was only twenty-three years old and fast-tracked his career into the SPL.

In just eleven years, he became its director. Fifteen had already been the Executive Director of the ACIO for eighteen years when McGavin took the reins at the SPL. Fifteen could barely stomach the charade of being a subordinate to the *indolent youngster*, as he often referred to McGavin within the Labyrinth Group.

"So tell me the nature of your visit," Fifteen intoned as he eased himself into his chair. His voice resonated with such absolute confidence that McGavin instantly shifted in his chair like a schoolboy called into the principal's office.

"Actually, I was hoping you could help me understand what these are?" McGavin opened a small, glass vial, which contained a small electronic device about the size and general shape of a thimble. Fifteen instantly recognized it as one of the ACIO's phone tap technologies they used for setting up their Listening Fences.

Fifteen put his bifocals on, picked up the device with his hand and examined it closely. "Looks like a wiretap to me. I could have one of our electronics people take an internal scan."

"Two curious things have occurred this week that don't add up." McGavin's face took on a serious cast and his voice fell to a whisper.

"First, a professor from the University of New Mexico has sworn in an affidavit that he was intimidated by the NSA to turn over an unusual artifact discovered only days ago by some student hikers. Second, we have evidence that two ACIO missions were launched to New Mexico—only a few miles from the discovery point of this artifact—in the past four days. One as recently as yesterday."

McGavin paused, taking inventory of Fifteen's body language, looking for any clues to embroider his analysis. Fifteen remained motionless in all respects, waiting for McGavin to continue his story.

"And then this morning our agents, in an attempt to corroborate this professor's claim, did a routine sweep of his home and office. We found seven of these devices. They look similar to our own surveillance devices, but they're more sophisticated, according to our electronics people."

"And you thought the coincidence of an ACIO mission to New Mexico and this professor's sworn affidavit were irreconcilable. Right?" Fifteen had a pained expression on his face.

McGavin nodded. "Look, just tell me what's going on. You damn well know that you have to report your activities, or I'm forced to assume you've gone rogue. You know the protocol under those circumstances. So just tell me straight out, what the fuck is going on?"

Fifteen pushed back his chair and stood up awkwardly. With cane in hand, he shuffled over to his desk and took out a large file folder. He plopped it on the table in front of McGavin. "Here's everything I know."

McGavin opened up the file and began to scan several documents. "You can't probe it?"

"We can't get anything out of the damn thing. It's a sealed technology. So tight we're completely perplexed. We sent two scientific teams to the general area hoping to find something else."

"And…?"

"Nothing so far," Fifteen replied.

McGavin's eyes turned again to the file documents. "Why didn't you report this?"

"There was nothing noteworthy to report. We're only four days into our investigation—"

"Four days is a long time my friend. In this business, it can be a lifetime." McGavin set the file down. His fingers were nervously fidgeting with the plastic tab that read, ANCIENT ARROW.

"So you have an alien artifact, a project name, you've sent this professor into major panic, you wiretap his office and home, but you don't think you have anything noteworthy to share with me."

Fifteen listened intently. He restored the concerned look on his face, and painfully gathered himself into his chair. "I know you'd prefer more instant communication, but we have nothing to report—"

"You have a fucking alien technology! Now I'm not the expert about these technologies that you are, but if you can't probe this thing, then it's damn sophisticated. For all you know, it's a weapon or probe of some kind. The operating protocol states that any evidence of an alien technology must *immediately* be communicated with SPL. You know this as clearly as I do."

McGavin lowered his voice. "You know I have to set-up an investigation. It smells like a cover-up. I don't want to waste my time and energy investigating the most productive laboratory in the NSA's holdings. It's a fucking waste. But I have no choice."

"I completely understand," Fifteen said. "While it's an inconvenience, we'll cooperate in every way we can."

"You can start by having Evans contact Denise Shorter and arranging to have a shadow agent assigned to the Ancient Arrow Project. We'll keep the communication loops open if we're involved in the project."

"Of course. He'll contact her tomorrow."

"No, today. I don't want any more delays in communication."

"Evans is on a field assignment until tomorrow. He's without secure communication—"

"Then have Jenkins make the arrangements," McGavin replied. "I don't give a shit who calls Shorter, just get it done immediately.

"Look, I'm well aware of all the rumors surrounding this fiefdom you've built. I know you like to play games, and I know you have powerful allies. But don't fuck with me. Just communicate through standard channels. If you're too busy, then Li-Ching can do it for you. I don't care who performs the communication. I just want to have confidence that when you put a project name on a file folder that you'll send a duplicate file to my office within minutes. Not hours. Minutes. Understood?"

"Completely."

"And one more thing—"

A knock on the door interrupted McGavin.

"Yes," came Fifteen's voice.

The door opened slowly and a man poked his head into the office. "I apologize for the interruption, sir, but your next appointment is here. In which conference room would you like them to await you?"

"We were just finishing up," Fifteen said, "let's use the Hylo Room."

"Thank you, sir."

The door closed without a sound.

"You were saying…?" Fifteen reminded.

"What's so special about this artifact?"

"We don't know if anything is special about it. It may turn out that this thing is truly a sealed technology, which would be a shame, but nonetheless, if we can't probe it, there's not much we can do but place it in storage and wait until we have the technology to probe it.

"I noticed you had nothing in the file about RV analyses. I assume you'll do an RV."

"Yes, of course."

"I'd like to see the RePlay tapes when you have them."

"Of course."

McGavin looked around the spacious office as if he were stalling. Fifteen knew that he was annoyed by the fact that another appointment had been scheduled so close to his own. "I will fry your ass if I find anything that looks even remotely suspicious about this project. You might think that you're well beyond the reach of my powers, but let me remind you that your budget has my signature on it. Don't fuck with me."

With that, McGavin stood up and opened his briefcase. "I assume I can take this with me?" He held the file folder that Fifteen had given him to read.

"Of course."

"I'll call Shorter in thirty minutes," McGavin said. "I trust she'll have spoken with Jenkins by then."

McGavin closed his briefcase, returned his chair to its previous position, and walked to the door, escorted by Fifteen. McGavin put his hand on the doorknob, stopped short of opening the door, and looked directly into Fifteen's eyes. "Octavio, I have doubts about your motives and your operation. And these doubts... they trouble me. And when I'm troubled, I get paranoid. And this paranoia... it makes me ruthless."

"What're you trying to say?" Fifteen asked innocently.

"I can make your life a living hell if I can't trust you."

"You now know as much as I do about the Ancient Arrow Project," Fifteen calmly replied. "We'll all do a better job of keeping you informed. We just didn't think we had anything worthy of distracting you. I see now that we miscalculated. It won't happen again. I assure you."

"Pray that it doesn't."

The two shook hands and bid each other a good day.

Fifteen closed his office door. He laid his cane on the table and sat down in the same chair that McGavin had sat in moments earlier. He closed his eyes. His face completely relaxed. His hands went underneath the table and pulled out a small, black object. Fifteen leaned closer to inspect the device, and slowly smiled. A knock on his door interrupted him.

"Yes."

"Sorry to interrupt, but I was curious to know how your meeting with McGavin went." It was Li-Ching. She was wearing a red wool skirt that draped to her ankles, and a sleeveless white silk blouse. Her raven-black hair was tied back in an exotic ponytail that was held together by a silver lattice of thread.

Fifteen held the tiny black object up for her to see, and smiled broadly like the Cheshire cat.

She sat down on the edge of the table next to Fifteen; a narrow slit in her skirt parted to reveal her ivory legs, perfectly turned as if by a lathe. "Judging from your face, it went pretty well."

"Yes," Fifteen replied, "but it's a pity he doesn't trust us."

Fifteen took his cane and delivered a fatal blow to the electronic listening device that McGavin left behind.

"Only one this time?"

"Only one," Fifteen sighed. "You'd think he'd give up on this pointless effort to wire my office."

"He just wants to remind you that he's watching and listening," Li-Ching said. "You know the strategy, the more paranoid you are, the more mistakes you're bound to make."

"He wants to get rid of me."

"No, he wants to get rid of the ACIO and its separate cover and independence.

He's no dummy. He knows that the only way he'll ever seize control of the SPL agenda is if the ACIO is integrated within his department. That's where he's headed. Everything he does is designed to move him closer to that goal."

"Perhaps if he knew what we really did, his interests would wane."

"What do you have in mind?"

"The damn idiot ordered an investigation—ostensibly to determine whether we went rogue on the Ancient Arrow Project, but I'm sure his real agenda is to snoop into our technologies. They found the Level Five Listening Fence in Steven's home and office."

"Shit!" Li-Ching stood up and started pacing.

"He suspects we're keeping the pure-state technologies and sending them diluted versions. This investigation will center on that. He wants proof. With that in hand, he'll try to remove me."

"God, what a waste of time." Li-Ching said.

"He doesn't know that."

"Well, then he *is* a dumb-ass after all."

"Let's let him have his investigation, shadow agent, and anything else he requires. Evans will take care of the SPL agent and you'll take care of all the communication protocols."

"Did you give him the Ancient Arrow file I prepared?"

"Of course," Fifteen replied. "He seemed satisfied, at least partially."

"Most of it's true anyway. I didn't have to doctor much."

"He wants the RePlay tapes from our RV department related to the artifact." Fifteen sighed. "You'll need to get Branson working on that immediately. I'd like to approve the script before we make the tape."

"Understood." Li-Ching's voice seemed far away as if she were thinking about an entirely unrelated issue. "You implied earlier that you want him to know what we really do around here. What did you mean?"

"Let's give him evidence of what he already believes is true. He doesn't have any clue about Labyrinth or Corteum. He may have heard some disjointed rumors, but nothing more. He believes we're rogue and that we've not shared some of our best technologies."

"You want Ortmann to leak some of our more benign pure-state technologies… like our listening fences?"

"Yes, can you have him put a list together as to which technologies he thinks we can live without?"

"No problem."

"I want McGavin to feel victory. He'll relax then, and get off our collective back."

"Anything else?"

"Stevens is unstable," Fifteen said. "I think he needs a reminder visit and a Level Seven Listening Fence."

"What about memory restructure?"

"The damage's done. If he suddenly forgets, it might only worsen our situation by alarming his colleagues who already know, not to mention McGavin. No, let's have Morrison pay him a reminder visit ASAP. Jenkins can reinstall the listening fence."

"Okay."

Li-Ching sat down again on the table's edge. Her skirt parted as she crossed her legs. Fifteen's hand wandered to the exposed leg and he smiled with his mischievous eyes.

"Damn McGavin!" Fifteen's fist pounded the table. "I can't have my way with you right now… I just remembered that I need to confer with Jenkins on an urgent matter."

He stood up abruptly and Li-Ching understood her time with him was finished. She kissed his cheek and whispered something in his ear. Fifteen's eyes narrowed as he listened attentively. Li-Ching finished as Fifteen's face visibly flushed to a reddish hue.

"Just in case McGavin managed to plant more than one listening device," Li-Ching said. She disappeared before Fifteen could utter a sound of protest. As the door closed, he struggled a moment to remember Jenkins' extension.

✳   ✳   ✳   ✳

Evans saw an indentation in the canyon wall out of the corner of his eye. It was small, only about half a meter high, but it was clearly an opening into the cliff face. He resisted the urge to call his colleagues. Instead he kneeled down and peered into the darkness of the fissure, and in a loud voice called Neruda's name several times. He listened with all his power, and a faint voice returned, "I'm here. I'm in here." There was more, but Evans couldn't understand the rest of it.

There was urgency in the voice that was unsettling. Something was awry. The voice sounded like Neruda's, but lacked his normal vitality. He was hurt. That was the only plausible explanation. Evans yelled with all his force. "We'll be there in just a few minutes. Hang on."

He immediately stood up and yelled to his team. "I found him! Everyone follow my voice and come here!" He continued to yell, "I found him!" every few seconds. In a matter of minutes the entire team was assembled except for Andrews.

"What happened to Andrews?" Evans asked.

"He's carrying the Little Monster as he refers to it," Samantha said. "He offered." She put her arms out, palms up, as if implying a small miracle occurred.

"I can only imagine how long we'll have to wait," Evans said in disgust. "We don't have time. Collin, you and I will go ahead and locate Neruda. He's probably trapped himself in a narrow tunnel. I can't believe he'd do that… at night no less.

"The rest of you wait here for Andrews. We'll be back as soon as possible— hopefully with Neruda."

"Can't I join you?" Emily asked. "We don't both have to wait for Andrews." She looked to Samantha and then Evans.

"Okay, but be extremely careful, and stay right behind us. Samantha, keep yelling every so often so Andrews has something to track."

"Okay," she replied.

"Everyone has their flashlights, I presume," Evans stated like a commandment. "I have a rope, first-aid kit, some food and water. Anything else you can think of?"

Emily and Collin looked at one another and shook their heads.

"Then let's go."

The three disappeared into the open fissure like travelers moving through a portal into a new world. Evans went first and had the most difficulty getting through because of his physical size. Only after contorting his shoulders and head like a magician trying to release from a straight jacket did he find success.

On the other side of the opening was a large chamber or cavern about twenty meters in diameter, with an opening into darkness on the far side of the chamber. Their flashlights sliced effortlessly through the interior darkness, crisscrossing randomly across the brown stone.

"Neruda, where are you?" Evans shouted.

"I'm here," came the faint reply.

"Can you give us directions to where you are," shouted Emily.

"Good to hear your voices…" answered Neruda. "I'm straight ahead. Go to the opening and stay straight for about another twenty meters or so. You'll come to a fork in the tunnel, stay to the right. However, before you take another step, listen carefully.

"This is home base. I don't have any real evidence yet. But as you move deeper into the interior, you'll notice it becomes increasingly sophisticated in its design. And part of this sophistication is in its security system."

"Come again?" Evans shouted.

"There's some form of a security system surrounding this system of tunnels. I fell into one of its traps because I wasn't expecting any such sophistication, but believe me, the entire place could be filled with traps. In other words, be extremely careful."

"Any advice?" Collin asked.

"Go slowly and retrace my steps until you come to a glyph carved in the wall of the tunnel—it's on the right side of the tunnel wall. I'm okay. If it takes you an hour to get here that's fine, just get here safely."

"Are you trapped?" Collin asked.

"Most definitely."

"What happened? Maybe we can learn from your experience."

"The problem is I don't know what I did. I may have touched a pressure-sensitive pad or tripped a wire. I'm not sure. All I know is that it happened so quickly that I couldn't react fast enough to save myself. I fell quite a distance, but nothing's broken."

"Okay, we'll take your advice. Be patient." Evans yelled in return.

"Don't worry, I'm not planning to go anywhere," Neruda replied faintly.

Evans, Collin, and Emily looked like statues anchored to the ground. Their flashlights were scanning the floor of dust, dirt, and rocks looking for any sign of potential danger, and Neruda's tracks. The light beam of their flashlights would occasionally illuminate an animal skull or skeletal carcass of a wayward rabbit stashed against the wall of the chamber like windblown trash collects against a fence.

"I think we have a clear path to the tunnel entrance," Evans remarked.

Evans carefully picked his way toward the tunnel opening at the far end of the chamber. Collin, then Emily, followed close behind, each trying their best to trace the exact same footprints that Evans left behind. As they entered the tunnel, the air became noticeably cooler and they could feel a slight downward slope to the tunnel's path.

"Can you see our lights yet?" Evans asked.

"No, but you'll understand why in a few minutes. Just keep advancing per my instructions."

Emily was comforted by the fact that Neruda's voice was getting louder. He seemed relaxed and in no imminent danger. She could feel his own optimism rise with every footstep.

"I'm trying to trace your steps," Evans yelled.

"That's fine, but try to avoid my last one," Neruda laughed, "it's a real dilly."

"This is the last time I'll ever travel without local communicators," Evans said under his breath.

"This whole trip was planned too quickly. We should've waited," Emily lamented.

Evans cast the beam of his flashlight down the narrow tunnel hoping to see some evidence of Neruda, but the beam blended into darkness before anything distinct could be identified.

Evans turned around to face Collin and Emily. "If this tunnel stays at this rate of slope, it goes down deep. It's going to get cold."

"Can you see our lights yet?"

"No. But turn off your flashlights for a moment," Neruda suggested. "I'll turn mine on and see if you can see anything."

Instant blackness engulfed them as their flashlights were turned off.

"There, I think I saw something about fifteen meters ahead. Yes, I definitely saw a light." Evans flicked his light back on. The walls of the tunnel were only about three meters across and tools had shaped them. Not much precision, but definitely a designed structure.

"Okay, Jamisson, we saw your light. We'll be there as fast as we can. Your voice sounds like it's below us. You said you fell. How far, do you know?"

"I'm not sure. I lost consciousness for some period of time—maybe ten minutes or so. I still have a helleva headache to confirm my fall."

"Okay, just take it easy and we'll get there shortly." Evans turned to Emily and Collin. "Let's stay very tightly packed. I'll keep my flashlight trained on the path ahead of us. Collin, position your beam on the right side of the tunnel, and Emily, you watch the left. Stay alert. If you see anything that looks unusual, say so immediately and freeze your position. Understood?"

Though he had a tendency to be obnoxious, both Collin and Emily were glad that Evans was leading them. He instilled confidence through his every mannerism and movement. He seemed to extract exhilaration from such circumstances where others could only find fear.

As they inched their way down the corridor, Collin's voice broke the silence. "Stop!"

They froze in their positions. "What is it?" Evans asked.

"It's the glyph that Neruda mentioned earlier."

All the flashlight beams converged on a hieroglyph intricately carved upon the rock wall of the tunnel. The wall had been carefully prepped and was relatively smooth in order to accommodate the detailed lines and pattern of the glyph.

"What did you make of the glyph on the wall?" Evans called out to Neruda.

"I've never seen anything quite like it before," he replied. His voice was unmistakably closer, but also coming from some distance below their position. "It's related to the glyphs on the artifact, but it's different in many respects. Keep an eye out for my final step, it wasn't much farther that I tripped something."

Evans' flashlight identified Neruda's final footprint about two minutes later. A skid mark veered off to the right of the tunnel, but there was no sign of a door or exit path.

"Let's position all of our light on this area." Evans used his flashlight beam like a laser pointer to define the area he wanted them to collectively illuminate. "Okay, do you see anything that looks like a seam?"

"Nothing so far," Collin replied.

Emily pointed to the top of the tunnel where her flashlight was positioned. "What's that?"

"It looks like a ventilation duct or small opening of some kind," Evans said. "Maybe that's how we can hear Neruda."

"Jamisson, say something," Evans suggested.

"Something."

"A little more of your usual verbosity would be helpful," Emily said playfully.

"Okay, but I'm warning you, my life story is pretty boring until I hit the age of five or six—"

"You're right, it's the source of his voice," Collin said excitedly.

"Jamisson, this is Evans, we found a ventilation duct or something in the ceiling of the tunnel. It's a small hole, maybe ten centimeters in diameter. We also found your last footprint, but there's no sign as to where you fell. We can't see any seams or edges indicating a door or exit path. Any recommendations?"

"Do you have any rope?"

"Yes, about ten meters in length I suppose."

"Can you fit the rope through the opening?"

"Yeah, I think so," Evans said.

"Try feeding the rope through the opening, as much as you can. With a little luck, I'll see it."

"What kind of a room are you in?" Emily asked.

"It has tall ceilings—maybe ten or twelve meters, it's about three meters in diameter and the ceiling is arched like a dome. It's definitely a construction… an elaborate construction. But I can't see any openings, and like you, I can't find any seams. I don't exactly know how I even got in here."

Evans was on his tiptoes trying to get the rope through the opening. He looked a little like a giant, awkward ballerina. The opening in the ceiling was about half a meter beyond his reach, and the rope was too limp to thread the opening without Evans jumping.

"This may be stupid to jump around here, but it's the only way I'm going to be able to feed this rope through. You two stand back. If I go down, Collin goes back for help. Emily, you stand watch. Here's my base communicator." He handed it to Collin.

"I could boost you into position," Collin said.

"I doubt it. I weigh too much for you. And we can't afford to lose two of us."

Emily agreed. Collin resembled a walking stick.

"Why don't you boost Collin up," Emily suggested. "He'd be like a feather to you."

"I'm not willing to risk two of us, if it can be done with one. Let me try it first myself. If I fail and nothing happens, I'll boost Collins. Get back at least five meters."

Evans waited for them to retrace their steps backwards. He jumped perfectly to the hole like a basketball player dunking the ball. The rope sailed in cleanly. And then fell out. Evans came down hard, but safe.

Ten minutes later they had found an appropriately sized rock to tie to the end of the rope, and Evans once again dunked the rope into the hole. This time it stayed.

"Do you see anything?" Evans shouted as he began feeding the rope through the opening.

"Yes, but you'll need a lot more rope to reach me."

"Any chance you could climb the wall and grab it?"

"None."

"If I could get you a rope, would you be able to make it to the top of the chamber?"

"I think so, but it's not clear to me what we'd do next. Last time I checked, I couldn't fit through a ten centimeter hole."

"We can widen the hole," Evans replied, a little irritated. "But can you make it to the top of the chamber?"

"Yeah, there's something of a ledge that circles the top of the walls before they become the dome ceiling. It could be useful."

Evans turned around to face Emily and Collin. "I need you to go back to the entrance. Contact Jenkins and inform him of our situation. I'll get Jamisson out and we'll meet you back at the entrance in two hours. If we're not there in two hours, have Jenkins send a security detail with search and rescue equipment immediately."

"How are you going to get Neruda out by yourself?" Collin asked in a mystified voice.

"Before we do anything," Emily said, "can I suggest we try to replicate Jamisson's last footstep and see if we might be able to trigger the passage to open without falling into the chamber ourselves?"

"It's too dangerous," Evans interjected.

"It seems to me if it's pressure sensitive, we should be able to touch the same spot and the doorway should open. Maybe we could keep it open."

"I agree, it's worth a try," Collin said. "I don't see how you'd have any chance of getting him out otherwise."

"Neruda, are you listening to this?" Evans asked.

"Yes."

"Opinions?"

"Yeah, Emily and Collin should do as you suggested. The sooner the better."

Evans whispered. "Please, go now. And be careful to retrace our steps exactly as we came in. We'll be out within two hours. Go." His arm waved them on like a sea swell.

Emily and Collin walked away stunned. They could see no reason for Evans' confident posture. It was even more baffling that Neruda would agree with him. Something strange was going on. But they dutifully fulfilled their part of the plan and rejoined Andrews and Samantha, at the entrance. They made good time, requiring only seventeen minutes.

The light hit their eyes hard as they stumbled from the narrow opening into the waiting arms of Andrews and Samantha who helped them ease through the crack.

"What the fuck took you so long?" Andrews asked.

"We found Neruda. He's okay," Emily began. "But he's trapped in some sort of a chamber, and we can't get him out without supplies. Evans stayed behind. They're going to try to get out on their own, but if they're not out in another… hour and a half, we're supposed to have Jenkins send a security team."

"We need to alert Jenkins now," Collin reminded her.

Collin pulled out the base communicator that Evans had given him and fired the RECORD button. He spoke into the microphone haltingly. "Subject found. Search and rescue likely. Update in ninety minutes. Please prepare for immediate dispatch of S&R in ninety minutes. Will send exact coordinates in next communiqué. Please confirm."

Collin played back the recording and then hit the SEND button satisfied with his message's accuracy and brevity. Everyone knew that Jenkins and Evans hated long, detailed messages.

It was a little past ten in the morning, and the warmth of the desert sun was beginning to make itself known. Andrews had set-up a makeshift campsite, and they all settled in to wait out the next ninety minutes. Emily busied herself in the task of making coffee on the solar heating pad. Collin looked over the maps to get the exact coordinates for the search and rescue mission.

"It's the home base isn't it?" Samantha asked Emily.

"Neruda seems to think so."

"Did you see anything… anything unusual?"

"The tunnels are artificial. There's a glyph on the wall of the tunnel similar to the glyphs on the artifact. Somehow Neruda ended up in the equivalent of a jail cell, but we couldn't find any exit path or door in the tunnel. It was as if he was literally dematerialized and placed in holding—"

"For what?"

"We don't know."

"They're protecting something," Samantha said.

"What're they protecting?" Andrews asked as he approached Samantha. "I mean, if it's more artifacts like our little monster here, what's to protect?"

"A genetic technology," she said both as a statement and question.

"How do you know this?" Emily asked.

"I had another experience with the artifact during an RV session just before Evans discovered the opening in the wall. I saw images—"

"Like?"

"Like an image of what these ETs look like."

"Woah…" Andrews started. "How do you know you can believe the image this thing put in your head?" He was pointing to the aluminum case that held the artifact. "These same ETs built the equivalent of a Goddamn mousetrap, which now holds Neruda prisoner. Doesn't exactly engender trust in my little ol' heart."

Samantha started to say something and then stopped.

"Jesus, Andrews," Emily said, "Can we let her tell us what she saw without interruptions and your bloody opinions?"

Andrews kicked the loose rocks beneath him and watched them scatter. His lips danced silently with words that no one could hear.

"All I'm saying," Samantha said slowly, "is that the images I saw were of something altogether different… more advanced… maybe human, maybe something else. It varied from a human-like presence to a geometric shape like… like a rectangle." Samantha stopped for a moment as if she was trying to remember something.

Collin looked up from his maps and listened intently.

Samantha began again, "I can't pretend that I know what or who they are, but this image is as clear to me as you are, and it's not the image of a truant or warring species. My sense is that they're benevolent—even helpful to our species. They've stored something here that was supposed to be discovered by us, and it has something to do with genetics. It's all part of a masterful plan."

"That of course includes Neruda being fucked over." Andrews mumbled.

"I don't know about Neruda," Samantha explained, "but I'm sure of what I've told you. They probably designed a variety of protective mechanisms to ensure that *we* discover this site instead of someone else. There's something here that they want us to have."

"So you think there's something inside this mountain… a gift from these unknown ETs, with our name on it?" Andrews couldn't contain himself. He was one of the few within the ACIO that didn't have a healthy respect for RVs and the job they did, or anything else that went bump in the night. To Andrews, RVs were simply glorified psychics.

"Yes." Samantha answered quietly.

"Collin, did you get any message back from base yet?" Emily asked.

"Yeah, we're confirmed," he glanced at his watch, "sixty-eight minutes and counting."

"So what are they?" Andrews asked. "Friendly ETs who came to earth twelve hundred years ago, played around with the Indians, and then stored something inside a mountain for us to find? I buy that."

"These are just feelings you have, aren't they, Samantha?" Collin asked quietly, trying to mitigate Andrews' sarcasm. "You don't actually have anything on RePlay, do you?"

Samantha shifted her position on a large rock, and brushed back her hair with both of her hands. "No. When I went back to RePlay the images weren't recorded. Somehow they bypassed the capture sensitivity of RePlay. They're probably based on the imagery projected by the artifact, and I wasn't even in RV mode. But these images are powerful. I mean real powerful. I can't overstate that."

"Okay, I'm still confused," Andrews said. "You saw an image of a geometric shape—I believe you said rectangle—and from that you feel that there's something buried inside this mountain, perhaps a form of genetic technology. Is that about it?"

"I saw several images. The other image was of the earth floating in space and there was a grid surrounding it like filaments of light, and at certain cross-sections, I could see a pulsing glow—"

"How many?" Emily asked.

"Maybe three, no, maybe five. I'm not sure."

"Did you notice where they were located?" Collins asked.

"The only one I paid attention to looked like it was here… New Mexico." She squinted her eyes and then closed them completely for a few moments.

"I had an overwhelming impression that the technology was stored in this very place," she added. "It was left here by this race for a very specific reason, but I'm not sure what it is…" Her voice trailed off into silence. Everyone had been listening so intently to her voice that they hadn't noticed Neruda's muffled pleadings, just inside the canyon wall, for coffee.

"My God, you made it!" Emily cried as she saw Neruda break through the crevice opening into the light. The angle of the sun had cleared the wall and was now shining—in all its glory—directly on Neruda. Blinded by the sudden light, he squatted to the ground and shielded his eyes.

"The warmth feels great, but I wish someone could dim the damn lights." Neruda's eyes were thin slits looking for a familiar face. He found Emily first. "I don't suppose you have any coffee made? I have a splitting headache."

Emily laughed with a mixture of relief, joy, and ample surprise.

CHAPTER 6
IN TRANCE

Your consciousness is faceted to express light into multiple systems of existence. There are many, many expressions that comprise your total Selfhood, and each expression is linked to the hub of consciousness that is your core identity. It is here that your ancient voice and eyes can multi-dimensionally observe, express, and experience. This is your food source for expansion and beautification. Place your attention upon your core identity and never release it. With every piece of information that passes your way, discern how it enables you to attune to this voice and perception. This is the only discipline you require. It is the remedy of limitation.

An Excerpt from *Memory Activation*, Decoded from Chamber Seven

WingMakers

Red rocks emphasized the sky's azure blue. The starkness of the high desert was lunar. Immaculately natural. The sun rendered jackets and vests superfluous, leaving the air temperature perfect for cotton T-shirts and shorts.

The excitement of seeing Neruda and Evans emerge from the canyon wall drew the team together as if an invisible web bound them. Emily embraced Neruda, momentarily forgetting her professional distance. Andrews and Collin each shook Neruda's hand and welcomed him back "among the living," while Samantha simply watched with a broad smile.

A flurry of questions erupted about how Neruda got free and the nature of his rescue, but Evans and Neruda fended them off for later, showing more concern about Neruda's physical needs: to get warm and feed his empty stomach.

Once they had all settled down, cross-legged around a small fire that Andrews had managed to craft from dead pinion branches, Neruda began his story. A cup of coffee warmed his hands.

"All I can tell you," he began, his tone becoming introspective, "is that I went on an innocent walk after our experience last night with the artifact. I only wanted to hike to the top of the ridge to see if I could see the rock structure that Samantha had told us about.

"When I got to the top and saw this thing," he pointed to the structure directly behind them, "I had an irresistible urge to see it up close. I wasn't tired; in fact, I felt energized. So I hiked for about fifteen minutes... the whole time knowing I was doing something... something stupid—and yes, I knew it was against protocol. But in my defense," he turned to Evans, "I thought I was following orders."

Evans got up and asked Collin for his communicator. "I've already heard this, so forgive me, but I need to update Jenkins." Evans walked away and began pushing buttons on his communicator.

"Orders from whom?" asked Collin.

"As odd as it may sound, the artifact. I'm certain it planted something into my head," Neruda replied. "There's no other explanation."

No one, including Evans, would dispute, or even question, Neruda's conclusions. He was well known within the ACIO as being scrupulously accurate about his observations and motivations. But his statement drew blank stares from Emily, Andrews, and Collin. Only Samantha nodded knowingly.

"And the *something* you're referring to," Samantha suggested hesitantly, "was an irresistible motivation to find its home base. Right?"

"Yeah, but I'm amazed that anything could compel me to do this. It seems completely implausible…"

Andrews leaned forward to poke the fire into rebirth. While there was no need for more heat, it gave his hands something to do. "How'd you find this hole in the wall in the middle of the fucking night? And more importantly, why'd you go inside alone? That's what I'd like to know."

"I just knew where to go," Neruda said. "I knew exactly what to do once I got near the canyon wall. I had this image stored inside my brain, it… it was like seeing a split image—one inside your head, the other in external reality—and then seeing these two images morph into one image the closer I got.

"When I saw the opening, I looked inside with my flashlight before I entered. I saw on the far side of the cavern a dark hole that looked like a tunnel. It looked artificial… manmade. But of course I was thinking the whole time that it was the artifact's home base.

"I climbed inside," he continued, "and all I could do was to walk toward that tunnel as if my life depended on it somehow."

"Weren't you afraid?" Emily asked.

"No. I was completely calm. I had a mission coded inside my head and everything else was shut out."

"So you followed the tunnel and fell into the chamber?" Collin said.

"Remember the glyph on the tunnel wall?" Neruda asked.

"Yeah," Collin and Emily chimed.

"The instant I saw it, I had verification. The glyph was clearly from the same lineage—though it bore a different design. In my excitement I picked up my pace. A few steps later I slipped on something and fell… must've been nearly seven meters, to a stone floor… into the very same chamber you discovered me in this morning."

"Okay, so tell us how the hell you got out?" Collins inquired.

"I figured out how to climb the wall high enough to grab the rope. Evans pulled me to the top and together we enlarged the ventilation hole large enough that I could crawl through—"

"But that was solid rock, how'd you enlarge the hole… I mean what tools did you have?" Emily asked.

"Evans has a knife large enough to filet a whale. It wasn't that hard to enlarge the hole. The rock is sandstone, the wall wasn't very thick, it breaks apart pretty easy." Neruda replied casually.

Evans walked back to the group and sat down on a large rock opposite Neruda. He had his communicator out and was checking its small display screen and fidgeting with one of its buttons. His face looked expressionless.

Andrews looked puzzled. "Am I the only idiot who doesn't understand what the hell is going on here?"

"None of us know," Samantha said as if she were in a room with sleeping wolves. "We can be sure of one thing, though. The creators of this artifact have brought us to this place, and if they didn't want us here, we wouldn't be here."

"You may be right," Evans swallowed hard, "but we haven't really discovered anything yet. We have an empty chamber and a glyph on a tunnel wall. Seems like a waste if this is the extent of its home base."

"Okay, okay, I'm just denser than the rest of you," Andrews said with a scowl. "But could somebody tell me, what's our working hypothesis? I mean, shit, we do have one… a working hypothesis. Right?"

Evans remained silent.

Neruda looked around at the faces of his team. He knew they were reaching out for leadership right now. And he knew they expected him to provide it. "The artifact's led us to this site for a specific reason that we've not yet determined. But it has something to do with what lies behind this canyon wall, and the sooner we start looking, the sooner we'll find out why we're here."

"But the place is booby-trapped," Andrews exclaimed. "How're we supposed to find anything if we're being trapped in chambers?"

Neruda looked down at his watch, ignoring Andrews' question. "We have exactly seven hours and thirteen minutes before we have to rendezvous with the choppers."

Neruda struggled to his feet, tipping slightly as the blood shifted in his body like pebbles within a rain stick. Emily came to his aid momentarily as he steadied himself.

"You didn't sleep much last night did you?" She asked.

"You know, the thing about a cold stone floor is that it makes for a very long night." He smiled wearily. "But my body is coursing with coffee—It was regular, wasn't it?"

"Sorry, I only brought decaf."

"Shit."

"We have aspirin in the first-aid kit. Do you want me to get some for you?" Emily asked.

"Thanks… make it three." Neruda turned to Andrews who was getting his pack loaded. "The way we avoid getting trapped is to bring the artifact with us. It'll show us what to do."

"Oh, great, boss," Andrews said without looking up, "my arms are already dragging on the ground from carrying the little monster all morning, so if we're bringing it along, find another sherpa. Pahleease."

Neruda could only laugh. The image of Andrews carrying the artifact in the rock-strewn desert, cursing at everything along his way, struck him as funny.

"Maybe it's put something into your head, too." Neruda commented. "I mean carrying it around all morning, I'll bet your head is programmed with God knows what." He laughed again and grabbed the case.

"I'll take it Jamisson," Evans offered. "You didn't get any sleep, and that bruise on your hip can't feel too good either."

"You have an injury?" Emily asked instantly. "I thought you said you were fine after the fall.

"I'm okay," Neruda replied. "Evans is just being kind."

"Let's get going then," Evans said firmly.

They all donned their packs and walked silently to the thin slit of darkness protruding from the canyon wall. Solemn faces wound their way to the opening and stopped short of entering. They gathered around Evans.

"Listen carefully." Evans set the case down on the ground and tucked his sunglasses inside his shirt pocket. "Stay close and trace the footsteps we've already left behind. We'll rest about every five minutes. Don't touch anything. If you see anything that looks suspicious, holler, otherwise, stay quiet. We don't know what we're getting into, so let's keep a low profile."

"And what do we hope to accomplish in six hours?" Andrews asked.

"Stay alive." Evans answered as he took his pack off and tossed it inside the opening as if he were feeding a large, hungry mouth.

Andrews laughed. Nervously.

✳   ✳   ✳   ✳

"Goddamn asshole," McGavin spat, slamming the phone down. The metal and wood cabin echoed his words for a brief second. The Gulfstream V had a lively ambiance, even at 35,000 feet doing one thousand KPH.

"Didn't go well, I take it," Donavin McAlester remarked sitting across the table from McGavin. He was McGavin's newly assigned, shadow agent for the ACIO. Donavin specialized in espionage and security techniques, learned over the years as a field agent in Russia. Most recently, his job had been to direct the NSA's initiatives to monitor and contain the Russian Mafia In this capacity, he'd worked with virtually every branch of the government including the CIA, INS, Justice Department, and FBI.

"Maybe he'd kiss your butt if you'd yank his budget, sir." Donavin said.

"You're not exactly timid are you?" McGavin was still fuming at his recent phone conversation. The veins at his right temple looked like the Mississippi River on a satellite map. "You know that asshole only now called Shorter, three hours late! And it wasn't Jenkins that called, no, it was a subordinate two levels down from Jenkins—a Henry something or other. Shit!"

McGavin stood up and hit the intercom button. "What's our ETA?"

"Local time 1935 hours, sir, or about another two hours and fifteen minutes," came the voice.

McGavin flicked the intercom off, and walked over to the wet bar to get a scotch and water. Mostly scotch.

"What do you know about the ACIO?"

"Only what I read in the briefing you sent me last week," Donavin confided. "I've been in intelligence for twenty-nine years. Not even a rumor about such an organization found its way to my ears." Donavin shifted in his chair and took out a pack of cigarettes. "Do you mind if I smoke?"

"Not if you don't mind if I drink."

They both broke out in smiles, and the tension in the room diminished like smoke in a strong wind.

Donavin had close-cropped, light brown hair with just a tint of auburn. He was tall, but his frame bore about twenty extra pounds, mostly in his belly. He wore trendy glasses, which made him look studious despite his large, athletic build.

"I have to level with you, sir," Donavin said, "extraterrestrials aren't exactly my bag... nor the highfalutin technologies they might spawn. My expertise is in strategic enemy infiltration planning. And that's about it, but I thought—"

"So when you read the briefing," McGavin interrupted callously, "did you think I was interested in your expertise about ETs, technology or infiltration?"

"The latter, sir."

"Good, I'm glad we've established that." McGavin sat back down with his drink, poking at the ice cubes with a plastic straw. He had heard good things about Donavin, and he didn't want this to sound too much like a job interview. He was hired whether he wanted the assignment or not.

"What we want," McGavin asserted, "is to install you as our shadow agent on the Ancient Arrow Project."

"Sir?"

"I only found out the ACIO's official project name this morning. That's why it wasn't in your briefing. It's related to the rogue activities they're engaged in relative to this newly found artifact in New Mexico."

McGavin slid a file folder from his briefcase across the polished cherry wood table. "Make a copy." He pointed to a fax/copy machine in the corner. "This will tell you everything that the ACIO wants us to know. I'm sure it's doctored, but at least you'll know more than you know now."

He took a long drink while Donavin got up from the table and started to make copies.

"This Fifteen character," Donavin asked with his back to McGavin, "does he have any real power outside the NSA?"

McGavin smiled at the naïve question. "His power is completely outside the NSA."

Donavin spun his head around with a look of surprise. "How's that possible?"

"You really don't know anything about the ACIO, do you?"

"I've had my head buried in the Russian Mafia for twenty-odd years, sir."

"Fifteen was a little-shit college drop-out, in fact, he was kicked out of college for smearing the reputation of his professors. He's completely anti-authoritarian, but he's so goddamn smart no one can control him."

"If he was so smart, why'd he get kicked out of college?"

"Like I said, he did a smear campaign. He wrote an article for the school paper—I think it was Princeton—where he defined, with clinical precision, the weaknesses of the teaching faculty. It was a highly regarded article by the student body—not that most could understand it—but it infuriated the faculty. They kicked him out two weeks later after things had calmed down enough to keep his exit relatively low profile."

Donavin continued to feed documents into the copy machine, puffing on the cigarette held tightly by his lips. "So how'd a shit-faced nerd end up the executive director of the ACIO?"

"I don't know," answered McGavin betraying his limits of knowledge. "No one really knows for sure, other than the retired director of the NSA, and he's not the kind of man to blab about such things. All I know is that Bell Labs hired him when he was kicked out of school because of his work in heuristics and computer modeling. He was only eighteen at the time and was only months away from having a doctorate in quantum physics and mathematics.

"At Bell Labs, he worked in one of their think tank engineering groups that was developing black box technologies for the government. As the story goes, while he was there, he developed the homing system for satellite reconnaissance systems to eavesdrop on precise, targeted sites. The ultimate customer was the NSA. That's how we found out about him. That was back in the late 50s."

"You're shittin' me."

"No, I'm not." McGavin tilted the glass of scotch all the way back. The ice cubes rattled in his empty glass as he returned it to the table. "Look, the man's incredibly bright, but he's also a royal prick. Somehow he wormed his way into control of the ACIO and he's creating technologies that he's selling to private industry and world governments… behind our back."

"But how could he get away with that? It doesn't make sense; we have the best intelligence network in the world."

"Reality check," McGavin said. "There're elements of a world government—and I'm not talking about the United Nations here—that are more secretive than any state government including North Korea. And our intelligence network has been designed to overlook these elements."

"So you're not talking about the Mafia?"

"No, no, no." McGavin shook his head for a few seconds and then got up to refill his glass. "The Mafia is organized and secretive, but it's run by relative morons." He poured straight scotch, no ice or water. His taste buds were properly desensitized.

"No, I'm talking about the elite plutocrats who run the world's financial markets. They're the ones Fifteen works with, and they're the ones who have the power. It's not the politicians, Mafia, or the goddamn military. They're essentially pawns of this network—"

"And what're they called… this group of elitists?" Donavin asked.

"They don't have an official name. Some have called them the Illuminati, or the Bilderberg Group, but these are just pseudonyms. We refer to them as the Incunabula. We don't really know how organized they are or what their M.O. is… but we believe they get a significant amount of their technology from the ACIO… specifically their encryption and security technologies. Fifteen's in cahoots with them. I'm certain of it."

"And you want me to infiltrate the ACIO to uncover this link with the Incu… Inculnab… whatever?"

"Incunabula," McGavin corrected.

Finished with copying the file, Donavin returned to his chair to light another cigarette. He pushed the original file back to McGavin with a quick smile and thanks.

"It's a damn shame," McGavin sighed.

"What is, sir?"

"It's a damn shame you can't infiltrate them. But believe me, your experience with the Russian Mafia didn't qualify you for this job. The ACIO is impregnable. We've tried so many times and failed that I'm done with that strategy.

"What I want is for you to turn their top security guy—a guy named James Evans. We need a defector to confirm our suspicions. Armed with the info this guy could supply us, I could topple Fifteen and his little fiefdom."

"What're his pressure points, this guy Evans?" Donavin asked, his voice suddenly cold and calculating.

"First of all, he's an ex-Navy seal."

"So that's it. That's why you want me."

"Only part of the reason my dear boy. He's also half-Irish." McGavin twinkled his eyes and used his Irish accent like a child wearing his father's shoes for the first time.

"Any signs that he'd cooperate or be motivated to turn?"

"About six months ago," McGavin answered, "we recorded a conversation between Evans and his subordinate, Jenkins—what an asshole." He paused long enough to finish his second drink. "Anyway, Evans said some things that led us to conclude he might be convinced to turn if he could get protection—"

"What kind of protection, sir?"

"We don't know all the details, but the higher you advance within the ACIO the more importance they place on your loyalty. They use implants for retention compliance. We're not sure what kind. But the real barrier to defection is their Remote Viewing technology. No one'll defect because they've convinced their employees that they'll be found through their RV technology."

"You lost me there. RV technology, what the hell is that?"

"I'll make it simple," McGavin returned to the wet bar, his voice becoming a little more slurred. "They have trained psychics who can look into a crystal ball and see you—just like the wicked witch in the Wizard of Oz."

"And they got the flying monkeys, too?" Donavin said laughing. "The more you tell me about this group, the more I think I just stepped into the Twilight Zone."

"Are you sure you're not ready to join me yet?" McGavin held his glass up for Donavin to see, wiggling it enticingly in the air. "Up here, it tastes so much better." He smiled, hoping for compliance.

"Sure, what the hell, if you don't mind, sir."

"Not at all. I'd appreciate the company."

McGavin busied himself with making drinks. He looked older than his forty-seven years. He was almost completely bald, and what hair was left was on the way out. He had a mustache that seemed to be his only hope of hair, like the last leaf on a November Oak. Years behind a desk gave him a rounded physique that seemed hell-bound for shuffleboard and bowling.

"I could tell you stories about RV technology that'd scare the shit out of you," McGavin said. "But I won't. The reason is that we've figured out how to block it. It's in operation right now on this airplane. We can install this technology in any size room—even an auditorium.

"We believe Evans might turn if you can convince him that he'd be taken care of financially, protected by our anti-RV technology, and given a completely new identity in a country of his choice."

He handed the drink to Donavin, their glasses meeting in an unspoken toast. "Trust me, you'll like this assignment." McGavin smiled, his eyes wandered to the monitor that flashed a message.

"Hold that thought…" he intoned, and sauntered over to the monitor with his drink in hand. He clicked the mouse and opened up an e-mail file. "Shit!"

"Could you wait for me outside for a few minutes, I need to make a phone call."

Donavin stood up and instinctively hunched over to avoid hitting anything in the cabin, even though there were another two feet of clearance.

"Didn't you forget something?" McGavin was looking down at Donavin's scotch and the Ancient Arrow project file that lay on the table.

"Yes, thanks for the reminder, sir," he scooped up his glass with his talon-like fingers. "You're right, I'm going to like this assignment."

"Good, I'm glad you agree. We'll talk more in a few minutes."

Donavin closed the door behind him. He swirled the scotch in the bottom of his glass and smiled. Then tossed his head back careful to catch every drop.

✳   ✳   ✳   ✳

The smell of damp chalk mixed with copper pervaded the cavern as they shimmied inside, one after another. Evans walked cautiously toward the tunnel. The aluminum case looked like luggage, and Evans looked like a tourist in search of an airport.

"Did you want to take the artifact out now?" Samantha asked quietly to Neruda. Evans was already on his way toward the tunnel.

"I suppose we could," he replied to Samantha. Then he turned to look at Evans' back. "Hey, maybe we should unpack the artifact in the cavern and see what happens.

Maybe the tunnel isn't the right approach inside."

Evans stopped in his tracks and turned around to face them. "There's another way out of here?"

"I don't know," Neruda said, "perhaps. I just think we should check it out. Who knows what this thing might do once it's inside the site."

Evans walked back with childlike reluctance.

Neruda unsnapped the locks and opened the lid. All the flashlight beams converged on the metallic surface of the artifact. It looked completely alien, yet somehow at home in the cavern like a luminescent creature found in the black depths of the ocean.

The artifact was as silent as the cavern.

Samantha bent down with her flashlight locked on the object like her eyes. She touched the artifact tentatively. With barely a whisper, something activated inside the object—it began to vibrate. Its edges blurred. The artifact no longer appeared cylindrical. It was morphing into a spherical, transparent object and its mass seemed to be molting into vaporous light. Like a ghostly apparition, it rose from the case. An intense heat began to fill the chamber, and suddenly a pale green light flashed from the object as it hovered two meters above the aluminum case that had been its surrogate home.

Frozen in their footsteps, everyone watched the tableau spectacle like cavemen may have watched the first flames of domestic fire.

Neruda managed to find his tongue first. "It's unbelievable… it could only mean one thing… it's activating something."

"Or communicating something," offered Samantha.

Andrews stepped back a few paces. "Is it safe? That's all I wanna know. Cause it's scaring the shit out of me."

"Relax," Neruda said, "and observe."

The heat became more intense as did the light. The cavern was completely shrouded in the presence of the object—sound, light, even smells. There was a molecular change occurring within the cavern, brought on by the artifact, and it charged the air with an intense electromagnetic energy field. It was building. The intensity escalated until even Evans couldn't resist the urge to step back a safe distance.

Then the object burst into a kaleidoscope of whirling, spinning colors that washed the walls of the cavern and everything inside it.

"It's going to explode!" Emily yelled. "Can't you feel the surge?"

Neruda could see fear in her eyes as she turned to him.

"What's your hypothesis now?" Andrews asked.

"Maybe we should get out," Evans shouted. "Could be another trap."

"No. It's okay." Neruda shouted back. "Everyone, relax. Just keep an eye out for directional signals. It's trying to tell us where to go… I'm sure of it."

"Fuck, maybe it's telling us to go to hell and leave it alone," Andrews opined.

The energy field continued to build, shedding a static electricity that had everyone's hair standing on end as if gravity vanished. A thin layer of dust from the cavern floor was drawn into the air, swirling to the pattern of the light. Everything in the cavern felt unified by the light and sound.

Samantha stepped toward the object, her arms out as if she were blind and feeling for obstructions in her path. Neruda caught her sleeve. "What are you doing?"

She looked toward the object with a blank stare.

"What are you doing?" Neruda asked again. Samantha returned a blank stare and struggled to continue her advance to the object.

Neruda hesitated for an instant, unsure of whether to let her go. She was obviously mesmerized or being controlled by the object.

"Samantha!" Neruda shouted, his hands firmly holding her arms and blocking her path to the object, "tell me what you're trying to do."

Samantha turned her head to look at him, aware of his presence and hold of her. "I need to turn it off."

Her response was too faint for Neruda to understand.

"What?"

She struggled with him. Neruda yelled to Evans for help, but Samantha fell to the floor, unconscious, before Evans could respond.

"Did anyone hear what she said?" Neruda yelled over the sound of the object.

Everyone shook their heads, no.

"Let's get out of here," Neruda said. He knelt down and started to place his hands underneath her body to lift her. Suddenly the maelstrom ceased, and the darkness and silence returned with an almost welcome eeriness.

Neruda jumped to his feet and whirled around to face the object. His eyes couldn't adjust quick enough to see if the artifact was still there. He squinted hard. Utter blackness mixed with the echo-lights flashing in his mind. He couldn't see any distinctive shapes, including his colleagues.

"Can anyone see anything?" Evans demanded with alarm in his voice.

"I can't even see my own hands right now," Emily lamented. "What happened to our flashlights?" The sound of switches flicking on and off filled the cavern as they tried to re-activate their flashlights. Nothing worked. Gradually, the opening in the cavern wall became visible to Neruda as his eyes began to adjust to the dim light.

Neruda closed his eyes hard hoping to squeeze any remnant light distortions from his mind.

"The damn electromagnetic field must've neutralized our batteries." Andrews said.

"How's Samantha?" Evans asked.

Neruda went to his knees, hoping he'd orient his searching hands so he could take her pulse. He fumbled for her body and found her head. Placing his forefinger on her neck, he sighed in relief as he sensed her pulse, erratic, but clear.

"She's fainted is all," Neruda said. "Let's move her over to the opening where there's more light. She may have hurt herself in the fall."

Evans quickly found Neruda and together they carried Samantha to the narrow crack in the canyon wall, setting her down just underneath the rupture of light.

"Can anyone see the artifact?" Neruda called.

"It's just hovering in place," Emily said. "I can see it, but it's not very clear. It'd help if we could get our flashlights to work."

Andrews began to walk closer to the object. He cocked his head in a strangely submissive position, as if a forty-five degree angle would give him better perspective. "It's barely visible… The thing's changed in to a… fuck, I don't know. It's just different. Maybe half a meter in diameter, mostly round… like a large basketball. It's translucent. Maybe twenty lumens. I don't know what happened to the little monster I've come to love, but it's transmuted into something completely different. Maybe it's gone through the equivalent of puberty."

"Don't touch it," Evans commanded. "We don't know what the thing might do if we touch it again."

Neruda opened the first-aid kit that was stored in Evans' backpack and took out some ammonium carbonate. As he waved it underneath Samantha's nostrils, she coughed and sputtered like old farm machinery in the early spring.

"What happened?" she asked.

"Take it easy," Neruda replied. "We'll get to that in a minute or two. Just catch your breath and relax as much as you can. Everyone's okay. Including you." He gave her a big smile, even though he knew she couldn't see it.

Samantha squinted and blinked her eyes while her right hand grabbed her forehead. "God, I have a headache."

Neruda opened up the aspirin bottle and gave her two aspirins and a water bottle. "Other than that, how do you feel?"

"Okay," she said quietly.

She took both aspirins with a hard swallow. "Is it hot in here, or is it just me?"

"It's hot in here," Neruda said. "We're all feeling it." Emily, Collin, and Andrews had all joined them at the opening like moths huddling near light.

"So what happened?" Samantha asked, propping herself against the cavern wall just below the opening.

"Do you remember anything after you touched the artifact?" Neruda asked.

"I touched the artifact?" Samantha asked slowly mouthing each word, her tone withdrawn.

"You don't remember anything?"

"I guess not."

She closed her eyes and took inventory of her thoughts. Samantha was still dazed by the incident. She knew something had happened to them, but everything in her mind was vague. She wondered if this was what amnesia felt like.

Suddenly a beam of green light shot out from the artifact, as though it were scanning the cavern. The beam was no larger than an inch in diameter, and the light was soft and diffuse, unlike a laser, but equally precise. It scanned the walls of the cavern in a circular, deliberate motion, like it was looking for something.

"Stay calm," Evans ordered. "Do you see the scan pattern?"

"I think so." Neruda answered as if he and Evans were the only ones in the room. "Let's keep a low profile. I'm not sure we want this light to touch us."

"I agree," Evans said.

The beam of green light silently made its way along the cavern wall, kindling dust particles that hung in the air as if they were impertinent obstacles to its goal.

"I'm beginning to think the only way we can avoid contact with this light beam is to leave," Evans said.

Samantha got shakily to her feet. "I think it wants to find us."

"Why?" Neruda asked.

Evans stood up and positioned himself next to Samantha like a bodyguard. "Take it easy. We don't know what it wants. Let's just avoid the beam for now."

With alien precision the beam continued to scan the room undisturbed. Suddenly, a second beam started as if the artifact's patience had come to an end. Together the two beams cut the dark interior of the cavern in a grid-like pattern resembling the lines of a globe.

"This just got a lot more complicated," Andrews said.

"If we're going to leave—" Emily started to say.

"Now! Let's get out now!" Evans was already gathering everyone to the opening in the wall, his arms motioning like a windmill.

"Shit, the scan speed is increasing. There's no way to avoid this thing." Collin argued. "Let's just stay put."

Neruda glanced back at the artifact. Persistence filled its aura of green, ghostly light. "I agree with Collin. Let's see what it wants to show us. Evans, maybe you, Emily, and Andrews should leave in the event this is a trap. The rest of us'll stay."

While they were discussing options, no one noticed that Samantha had been walking toward the object—the source of the green light beams. The beams found her on her third step forward. They instantly stopped.

"They found Samantha," Andrews said. "Now what?"

Everyone turned to look and held their breath, as Samantha was transfixed—frozen as the two beams of light scanned up and down her body.

"How does it do that?" Andrews marveled.

"What?"

"How do the beams go right through her?" Andrews replied, his voice sounding completely mystified.

Neruda was equally amazed. The light was going through Samantha as if she were transparent. The beams were less distinct after passing through her body, but nonetheless they were clearly visible.

"Does everyone see it?" Neruda asked, questioning his own eyes.

His question was answered by silent nods, as though the others didn't want to draw the thing's attention to them.

"What should we do about Samantha?" Evans whispered.

"Wait." Neruda whispered in return.

The beams of light converged on Samantha's forehead. There was a strange sense of gentleness to the process.

As abruptly and as silently as they had come on, the beams suddenly disappeared and the artifact fell to the floor of the cave with a metallic clatter. Samantha stood still for several seconds and then turned to the group behind her. "We won't have any more problems. They've deactivated all the security devices."

Neruda rushed forward to Samantha. "Are you saying you were in communication with them?"

"I guess you could say that," Samantha answered. "They wanted to assure me that we're not perceived as intruders. Whatever they're guarding is for us to find."

"So they perceive you as our leader?" Evans asked, almost shouting.

"No, I don't think so," Samantha answered calmly. "They just chose me because their technology is tuned to my mind. It could have been Neruda. Either one of us can communicate with the artifact."

"So what the hell was the artifact doing these past few minutes?" Andrews demanded.

"It was assessing our intentions, orienting itself, and deactivating the security devices that were designed into this structure when they created it."

"When you say, *they*, who're you referring to exactly?" Neruda asked.

"The creators of this place," she spun slowly around with her arms out and her head back. She seemed uncharacteristically relaxed and carefree.

"But this is a cave—"

"No, it's something amazing that this culture left behind," Samantha said with sudden intensity.

"What culture? Do you have a name?" Emily asked.

Samantha turned silent; her face was without features because of the dim light in the cavern. "WingMakers," she replied too softly for anyone else to hear. "For some reason, they feel like old friends of ours. As… as if we should know them as well as they know us."

"What makes you think they know us?" Neruda asked.

"It's just a feeling, but it's a strong feeling."

"So we can enter the tunnel without concern for deathtraps?" Evans asked, changing the subject.

"Yes."

"You're quite certain of our safety?" he tested one more time.

"Absolutely," came Samantha's confident reply.

"Let's go," Evans said.

The flashlight beam swept across the floor of the cavern and found the deep blackness of the tunnel on the far end. It reminded Neruda of when he was a boy and used to shine his dad's flashlight into the blackness of the Bolivian sky. It somehow made him uneasy when the light trail couldn't outlast the darkness.

CHAPTER 7

ETC

There are, below the surface of your particle existence, energies that connect you to all formats of existence. You are a vast collection of these energies, but they cannot flow through your human instrument as an orchestrated energy until the particles of your existence are aligned and flowing in the direction of unity and wholeness.

An Excerpt from *Particle Alignment*, Decoded from Chamber Ten

WingMakers

"You can come back in," McGavin called from behind the cabin door.

The custom Gulfstream V was made exclusively for top directors of the NSA. It was immaculately designed with every creature comfort known to man. Even the paneling was cut from a single cherry tree to ensure an unwavering consistency in the grain, color, and pattern throughout the cabin interior.

Apart from the view out the small, oval windows, one wasn't even conscious of being on an airplane. It could have been any executive's high-tech office—assuming they liked to drink.

Donavin sat down at the same chair he had previously occupied some twenty minutes ago. McGavin looked solemn, he thought. Whatever he had been discussing on the phone must not have gone his way.

"I was just about ready to freshen up my drink. Would you like another?"

"That'd be great, sir."

Donavin started to light another cigarette. "Can I ask you a question?"

"Anything you like," McGavin shot back.

"You want Evans to believe that the ACIO's RV technology can't harm him, right?"

"Yep."

"How will I prove that the NSA's Special Projects Laboratory has the technology to shield him against RV probes?"

McGavin stopped his ice chopping for a moment, dropped the ice pick, and ran his hands over his near-hairless head. There was a mirror above the wet bar and he looked at Donavin like a taxicab driver talks back to his fare through the rearview mirror. "There's only one way. You'll have to show him the technology at our offices."

"And how will I do that?"

"Invite him. Hell, you're both ex-Navy Seals, he'll trust you."

"What happened to him?"

"What'da mean?"

"*Ex*-Navy?"

"Oh," McGavin said, "he was discharged honorably."

"Yeah, so was I," Donavin replied. "But it wasn't all that honorable as I remember it."

"Exactly why you two will get along so well." McGavin smiled as he went back to his chopping.

Donavin took a long drag on his cigarette. He was feeling very relaxed, even a little tired. Maybe the scotch was working better than he thought. Altitude did have its advantages, he reminded himself.

"The thing that doesn't make sense to me is why would the ACIO—any of the ACIO personnel—trust me with anything? I'm a big fucking nobody. And an outsider."

"I don't care if anyone in the ACIO trusts you other than Evans. He's the only one that matters. Besides, the other elements of your mission don't depend on trust.

"Believe me," McGavin said putting two drinks down carefully on the table, "they don't trust anyone from the NSA."

"So how am I supposed to infiltrate without their trust?"

"You won't gain their trust. You're going to have to be devious." McGavin sat down with a cagey smile and slid one of the drinks across the table to Donavin. "We've sent two agents into the ACIO before with similar missions. Both came back with nothing. We think their memories were wiped. If they discovered anything, they never got a chance to share it with us."

"I'd like to review their files if I could," Donavin said. "Maybe I could learn something from their mistakes."

"I doubt it, but I'll have Francis arrange to get them to you. By the way, you're starting next Monday. I expect updates weekly. We're clear on communication protocols?"

"Yes."

"You get Evans to our Virginia offices. You watch the Ancient Arrow Project like a hawk. And you find out everything you can about any technologies that they're hiding from us. And then you can retire very comfortably. Got it?"

"Got it.

"Just one more thing, sir. What did you mean by *devious*?"

"What do you think I meant?"

"Throw out the rule book," Donavin replied. "Don't worry about standard protocols. Use whatever means necessary to accomplish my mission. That sort of thing."

"I'll put only one restriction on your activities," McGavin said. "Don't kill anyone affiliated with the ACIO unless it's in self-defense. Understood?"

"Understood, sir. But if Fifteen is such a problem to the SPL, why not take him out? There're a hundred ways for him to have an accident."

McGavin took his last gulp and plunked the glass down hard on the table. He looked at Donavin with immediate alarm. "The other two agents thought the same thing. We'd have to take out his top twenty or so underlings as well. It's pretty hard to make that look like a mass suicide." He laughed as if the image had been slumbering in his unconscious. "Besides, the last enemy you ever want to make is the Incunabula."

"Geez," Donavin exclaimed, "I was envisioning a bunch of buttoned-up pinstripes in Switzerland punching calculators—"

"Then your vision is fucked," McGavin said definitively. "The Incunabula is the very definition of power because they have the gold and therefore make the rules." His tone lightened. "They also have the platinum, diamonds, emeralds, sapphires. It's no accident that Fifteen has allied the ACIO with them. They're... they're like his big brother."

"So how did Fifteen endear himself to this group of financiers?" Donavin asked.

"First of all they're not financiers, that's just their hobby. They're elitists who like to control world events; everything from the weather to the stock markets. Of course, their specialty is manipulating the world's governments, shifting borders and the power bases within them.

"They've been around a long time, a helleva lot longer than the NSA, CIA or any government. They arose from the time of kings and royalty, when bloodlines meant something. They still operate in that world—only with high-tech toys instead of moats and guillotines."

McGavin shifted in his chair searching for a more comfortable position. He hated airplanes and their confining spaces and uncomfortable chairs.

"To answer your question," he continued, his voice slurring intermittently, "Fifteen created a variety of technologies—we don't know how many—that the Incunabula use as their high-tech toys. We know for certain that the ACIO has supplied them with some weather-control technology that we call the Pabulum Seed. We have no proof that they've transferred anything more, but once you have an intimate relationship with the Incunabula... well, let's just say it's hard to say no to them."

"Does the NSA have a relationship with this group?"

"The Incunabula?" McGavin asked with surprise in his voice.

Donavin nodded.

"None that I'm aware of," McGavin said, "but it wouldn't surprise me if we did."

"Is there a file I could read about them?"

"No."

McGavin pushed back in his chair with his near-empty glass in his hand. "I think we're about finished then. Any other questions?"

Donavin shook his head.

"Good. Then take your drink with you and leave me alone so I can get some work done." McGavin looked into his empty glass and swirled the ice as Donavin stood up and left the room. The phone rang twice and then stopped. Thank God for voice-mail. He was too tired to answer it. Besides, he hadn't had a good phone conversation all day.

✳   ✳   ✳   ✳

"Well I'll be damned. It's another cavern," Evans said.

The exploration team was thirty meters past the section of the tunnel that had trapped Neruda the night before. The tunnel had suddenly opened into a large, rounded cavern, slightly smaller than the first, about fifteen meters in diameter.

"Hey, there's something here." Evans said as the rest of the team dispersed into the cavern.

"It's pottery," Emily stated, "and it's beautiful."

The flashlight illuminated a large vessel in the middle of the cavern. Around it were various bones, feathers and a few traces of what looked like animal fur or maybe human hair.

"Shit, I wish we could've brought torches instead of a damn flashlight," Andrews complained. "I need something to keep me warm. It's freezing in here."

Ignoring him, Neruda grabbed the flashlight from Evans' hand and shined it inside the vessel, looking over its rim, which stood nearly to his chin.

"Anything?" Evans asked, as the vessel became momentarily translucent in the dark cavern.

"Nothing. It's empty, except for something that looks like melted wax at the bottom."

"Do that again," Emily asked. "Put the flashlight inside."

Neruda followed her suggestion, but this time he stepped away from the vessel as far as his arm would allow so he could see what interested her.

"It's Anasazi," Neruda said. "They were the only one's who integrated turquoise into their pottery—probably Chacoans. Their homes were only about thirty kilometers from here."

The vessel bore three sky blue spirals, surrounding its widest portion. Each was made up of hundreds of tiny turquoise beads like a mosaic.

The rest of the vessel was paper-thin, terra cotta colored clay. It looked incredibly fragile. Neruda couldn't even imagine how such a fragile vessel could have been carried from Chaco Canyon to this site without it breaking.

"So what is it?" Evans asked.

"This isn't it," Samantha said. "This isn't what they want us to find."

"Okay," Evans said. "But what is it?"

Neruda bent to inspect the spiral mosaic. "It's not an ordinary spiral. It's M51."

"How can you tell from a simple pictograph?" Emily asked. "Aren't there about twenty billion spiral galaxies?"

"M51 is distinctive because it has a conjoined galaxy—NGC5197—right here." Neruda pointed with his index finger to a smaller spiral that was attached to one of the rotating arms of the larger spiral.

"The Whirlpool galaxy," Andrews said in fascination. "That's cool. M51 wasn't discovered until the late 1700s. Did the Anasazi buy their telescopes from Popular

Mechanics or just make them from quartz crystals?"

Neruda shrugged. "You know, Andrews, sometimes you can really get irritating."

"I'd like to second that," Emily added.

"Third," Collin offered.

Andrews feigned being offended, pouting his bottom lip and tilting his head down. "I'm just pointing out that you can't reconcile Anasazi pottery—ostensibly created a thousand years ago, and M51 that requires perfect conditions and at least a fifteen centimeter lens to see."

"I really don't care about the origins of the spiral," Evans reported, "I just want to know what this thing is. Obviously, we've gone to a lot of trouble to find it, so I'm interested in definitions—"

"Let's look around a bit more before we adorn it with definitions," Neruda suggested.

"What's your instinct?" Evans queried, frustration showing in his tone. "What's it saying?"

"Maybe it's a sacrificial site," Neruda answered reluctantly. "The Chacoans were very superstitious about the weather, particularly at the turn of the millennium. The serpent deity was in charge of the rain and fertility, so maybe this was a site where they performed animal sacrifices to appease it."

Evans was satisfied with his explanation.

"If it was a sacrificial site—why's there no representation of a deity?" Emily asked. "The spiral, as you've already suggested, doesn't represent a serpent deity. Right?"

"Yes, I agree," Neruda replied, "but let's stop speculating, I don't know what this thing is."

Neruda cast the saber of light to the ceiling and then the floor of the cavern in a pattern. He slowly spun around. The team tracked the beam of light as if it were a predator. Neruda was making a deliberate assessment of whether there were any other tunnels or passageways that might open out from the cavern.

"I don't see any other tunnel out of here. This looks like the end of the road." Neruda commented.

"It can't be," Samantha whispered to herself, but in the quiet of the cave, everyone heard her.

"I agree with Samantha," Collin said, "It'd make no sense that all this would be constructed by ETs just so the Anasazi could appease their serpent deity. I don't buy that theory."

"Does anyone see any habitation debris?" Neruda asked.

"Go back there," Evans directed his arm to the location that the beam of light had just passed. "Yeah, there. What's that?"

Neruda walked towards something that looked like a large, flat stone lying on the ground. "It's a stone, but it looks like it's been shaped. Whoa…" Neruda let out a long sigh. "There're glyphs incised on top—and they look a lot like Mayan." His voice raised in pitch, excited at the prospects of being able to read something.

"What's it say?" Emily asked, well aware that Neruda could read virtually any language.

Blowing on the surface of the stone and brushing debris off with his fingers, Neruda shook his head. "I'm not sure. It's a hybrid."

The entire team had gathered around to see the stone's inscription.

"Can you read it?" Evans asked.

Neruda was tracing one of the glyphs with his index finger and remained silent—deep in thought. He could feel a drilling of energy in his forehead as if something were trying to breakthrough to his awareness, but it remained elusive.

"Looks like the word *temple*," Andrews explained, pointing to a series of strange markings.

"Yes, I know," Neruda said. "Its meaning is something like… *Within this temple… remember light.*"

"Why do I get the feeling they didn't bring an electrician along?" Andrews quipped.

"Is it a cover of some kind?" Collins asked.

"Can we move it?" Evans asked, getting on his knees. He tried to get his fingers underneath it for leverage, but it was too tightly fitted to the ground.

"Time for the whale knife," Andrews said, turning to Evans.

"What?" Evans asked.

"The knife you used to get the bossman out of the hole he fell into. Remember?"

"Unfortunately, I dropped that knife into the chamber," Neruda lamented. "But I have a small pocket knife. Let's see if we can get under it with this. Anyone who has a knife, let's get to work. Emily, could you hold the flashlight?"

"Sure."

She took the flashlight from Neruda and knelt down. She banged the end of the flashlight against the rock several times in different places—starting at the center.

"It sounds like it may be hollow underneath."

"I'm counting on it," Neruda said with an unmistakable eagerness.

After ten minutes of chiseling with their knives, enough space was excavated so their fingers could get a hold on the flat, white flagstone.

"On three," Neruda said, "let's try to move it towards Emily."

On cue, the men strained, but to no effect. The stone was about three feet in diameter and about five inches thick, and heavier than the four men could move.

"How much do you think she weighs?" Evans asked, turning to Neruda.

"Three hundred kilos… possibly more."

"I brought something that could prove useful," Evans said. "I'll be right back."

Evans walked away from the encircled stone into the dark shadows.

"Where the hell's he going?" Andrews whispered to Neruda.

"He's kind of secretive about his backpack." Neruda winked in half seriousness.

Moments later Evans returned with another flashlight. "I forgot I had a spare flashlight in my backpack. I also had these." He held up a pair of blasting caps. "They're small as explosives go, but they may be enough to fracture or break this thing up."

"Why'd you bring blasting caps on this mission?" Andrews asked. "Tell me you weren't expecting something like this?"

"I was a Boy Scout," Evans laughed. "What can I say?"

Using the same holes they had dug for their fingers, Evans affixed the blasting caps on opposite sides of the circle hoping they'd break the stone in half.

"We're set," Evans said. "Might be a good idea to retreat to the tunnel in case we get some flying debris."

"How much wire do you have?" Neruda asked.

"There's enough."

They walked back to the tunnel while Evans reeled out wire from a small spool. "That's as far as I can go."

"Is it okay?" Neruda asked.

"It's a small charge," Evans answered. "I'm sure I'll be okay. Ready?"

"We're set when you are." Neruda replied.

An explosion came moments later kicking up a cloud of dust. The sound made everyone's heart pound a little faster. It was deafening, but only for a few seconds. A series of echoes faintly followed the tunnel's path, six—Neruda mentally counted.

Evans was first to see the stone had cracked. "We should be able to handle half the weight, don't you think?"

"Only if you're really men." Emily's quick-witted response brought laughter to the entire group as they looked down upon their stone nemesis like conquerors.

"Shine your light right here," Neruda commanded pointing to the crack in the center of the stone.

"It's dark underneath. Something's here."

"What do you make of it?" Evans asked.

"It could be an ancient storage pit," Neruda said, "but I hope it's more than a bunch of maize or pinion nuts."

"If that's the case, I'll personally go back and shoot what's left of that horseshit artifact," Andrews said. "All this trouble for a bunch of nuts."

"Can you three help me here?" Neruda asked.

"Okay," Evans agreed. "Ready?"

"Ready."

Evans levied a massive kick with his right leg. The crack grew. His boot came down hard a second time, and the rock split horizontally.

"Let's move this out of the way," Neruda said. "Lift!"

Emily trained her flashlight beam as the bottom half of the stone was removed, revealing an inky void. "It's deeper than a storage pit, more like a shaft," she said excitedly.

Neruda took one of the flashlights and lay on his stomach, reaching his arm as far down the opening as possible. A rush of cool, dry air met his nostrils. "Yes, it's a shaft," Neruda said, "maybe straight down for three meters and then it turns horizontal."

"There's no way this could be active, is there?" Evans asked.

"I doubt it. This thing's been sealed up tight."

"Yeah, assuming this is the only entrance," Andrews added.

"We're not making any assumptions," Neruda replied. "I'll go down first and assess the situation. Once I determine the risks, I'll return and we can decide our course of action together. Agreed?"

The team members nodded.

"This is it," Samantha said. "This is the entrance. This is what I saw. It's like a birth canal. It's like being reborn into their world."

She paused, realizing her comments sounded peculiar. "I don't know how I know this, but I do."

Neruda prepared himself for the descent into the tunnel. He removed his backpack; the diameter of the tunnel would just accommodate his shoulders.

"Whoever these ETs were, they weren't overweight," Neruda said, easing himself into the hole. "I'll see you topside in ten."

"Be careful," Evans said. "Give us voice checks every minute so we know you're okay."

"Will do."

Neruda held the flashlight in his mouth so his arms were free to support his body weight as he descended into the black tube. The air was completely stale, as if there had been no circulation for centuries. It was arid and there was a hint of some chemical substance that he had never smelled before.

"There's an odor—very subtle," Neruda said halfway down the shaft. "Does anyone else smell it?" With the flashlight in his mouth, his speech was reduced to amateur ventriloquism.

"Yeah, I think so. I was wondering what that was," Collin said.

"Any ideas what the smell is from?"

"It's definitely a chemical compound," Collin replied.

"But do you think it's xenobiotic?"

"Smells a little like aromatic hydrocarbon, but it's not that… it's nothing I'm familiar with."

Evans was nervous. "Jamisson, if you feel the slightest nausea, you get out of there immediately. Okay?"

"Understood," Neruda answered, "but I feel fine. Don't worry. It's just an odd smell."

"It's a preservative," Samantha said tentatively. "Just a preservative."

"For what?" Evans asked.

"Something molecular that decays with time," Andrews chuckled, "or am I being too specific?"

Samantha remained straight-lipped, ignoring Andrews' remark. "It preserves something they've left behind. We'll know soon enough."

Neruda climbed down slowly, his legs searching for the bend in the tunnel when he could again use gravity to his advantage. The vertical walls were rough—perfect for handholds. "Okay you can drop the rope down now," Neruda said.

His feet finally had reached solid rock. He took the flashlight out of his mouth, glad to be rid of the taste of metal.

The height of the tunnel ceiling was just over a meter. Neruda sat with his back to the wall of the shaft, staring down the length of the tunnel before him. The flashlight illumined the ancient darkness, and Neruda was surprised to see no dust or dirt in the clear beam. "This place is clean… I mean spotless."

His hand stroked the smooth, pristine surface. "This entire section of the tunnel's been smoothed to a fine finish—not unlike polished marble. It's still the same reddish-brown color, but it's completely polished and smooth. It's amazing."

Evans dropped the rope down the tunnel's shaft and hit Neruda in the shoulder. "You're all set. Let me know if you need more."

"Can you see anything beyond the tunnel?" Collin asked.

"It looks like it opens up into something in about ten meters—maybe another chamber—but I can't tell for sure. The light's reflecting so intensely off the sides of the tunnel that it's hard to see that far ahead. But I'm pretty sure it opens up. Stay tuned."

"Neruda, this is Collin again. Can you tell if the tunnel is polished stone or is it coated with some form of a polymer? Maybe that's where the smell is coming from."

Neruda put his nose directly to the side of the tunnel and took a long, inward breath. "I think it's both. It's definitely polished stone, but I also think it's been sealed with something—maybe a polymer, I can't say for sure."

His knees screamed bloody murder as he began to crawl the length of the tunnel. The rock was as hard as granite, and Neruda's knees were his Achilles' heel. "Okay, I'm coming up to a seam in the tunnel. It looks carved. It circles the complete diameter of the tunnel. There're three sequential seams—maybe five centimeters apart. Very strange."

"Any sign of the far opening yet?" Evans shouted.

Neruda's eyes traveled the length of the light beam, and saw a perfect circle of darkness at the end of the tunnel. "I'm not positive, but it looks like it opens up; I'll know for sure in a minute."

He continued crawling towards the black void at the end of the tunnel, his knees aching against the unyielding stone. "I can see the opening," Neruda exclaimed; his breathing got faster and his heart began to pound louder in his chest.

The lip of the tunnel protruded into a large, oval-shaped chamber. It was about a two-meter drop to the floor from the tunnel. Neruda swept his flashlight across the room in amazement, as he hung his legs over the tunnel's lip.

His heart continued to beat louder. It was the only sound he could hear, a surreal soundtrack to the view into a chamber that was the most intricately designed stone structure that he'd ever seen.

The chamber was about twenty meters at its widest section and then narrowed at both ends in the shape of an oval. At one end of the oval the tunnel emptied into the chamber. On the opposite end of the chamber, a nine-foot-high archway revealed another tunnel leading away into darkness. Two columns framed the archway, each with intricate carvings in a rich assortment of hieroglyphs. The chamber was domed, reaching about twenty feet at its highest ambit. The walls, floor, and ceiling were perfectly smooth, polished to a rich, cream-colored luster.

"Jamisson, what's up?" Evans' voice carried down the tunnel's shaft reminding him of his other world and responsibilities.

"Well," he said, choosing his words carefully, "I found something at the end of the tunnel that substantiates the artifact's existence."

"What?" Evans shouted.

Neruda turned around to face his colleagues, realizing his voice had been lost inside the chamber. "Get down here, you've got to see this!"

Evans immediately sprang into action. "Okay, leave your backpacks here, but bring anything you think is valuable in your pockets. I'll go first. The rest of you follow. Let's go."

The team almost lunged into the shaft with excitement, but they had to move slowly down the vertical tunnel, waiting patiently for the handholds.

"Holy shit!" Evans said as he looked down the tunnel to Neruda's shadowy figure. He was still surveying the chamber from the tunnel's mouth. "This thing's amazing."

Neruda looked back and shined his flashlight signaling his whereabouts. "Wait till you see what I'm looking at," he said smugly.

Like a caterpillar inching its way across a branch, the team crawled obediently to Neruda's perch. The tunnel was too narrow to get a good view for the rest of the team, so Neruda swung his body around like a gymnast readying for a dismount from the high bar.

With the flashlight in his mouth he drawled, "See ya down there," he motioned with his head to the floor of the chamber below, and then jumped. He made a soft landing, but even so, his knees released a shudder of pain through his whole body.

"Damn," Neruda said as he hit the floor.

"You okay?" Evans questioned.

"Yeah, after last night's fall, my knees are feeling a little sore."

"Whoa, what is this place?" Evans blurted.

His flashlight beam was shimmering in the bleached stone interior. "Shit, this place has been carved out. This is no natural cavern."

"No kidding," Neruda answered.

Behind Evans, the rest of the team was struggling to get a view. "Let's go," Andrews said in the very back of the line. "Some of us would like to see, too."

Evans launched himself to the floor of the chamber as had Neruda.

"It's carved out of solid rock," Neruda said, turning to Evans as he landed.

"It's unbelievable," Evans returned in a whisper as his head pivoted like a compass needle in search of its bearings.

"Why the white stone?"

"I don't know, maybe to brighten the interior. It reflects more light."

"How'd they do it?" Evans asked rhetorically.

Neruda ignored the question. "There's another tunnel, do you see it?"

"It must've taken years to create this room…" Evans said, still in awe, unable to respond to Neruda's question.

The rest of the team began to drop out of the tunnel's mouth like drops of water from a faucet, and the chamber filled with an excited buzz.

"Everyone stand perfectly still and stay silent for a few seconds," Neruda commanded. "Just listen."

"I can hear the blood flow in my body," Samantha whispered. "It's amazing."

"There's no ambient noise in here, and yet we're in a perfectly ambient environment," Collin said. "Maybe it's an acoustic chamber of some kind."

"Have you seen any artifacts yet?" Emily asked.

"No, this chamber's empty," replied Neruda. "Notice there's not a speck of dirt or debris. This place is—"

"—Antiseptic," Evans interjected.

"Antiseptic," Neruda echoed.

"So now we know they suffer from obsessive compulsive disorder," Andrews said, chuckling softly. "Maybe they died of cleaning fumes."

Neruda had made his way slowly to the archway and columns, studying them with his flashlight. "Again the M51 spiral," Neruda said tracing his fingers over the incised glyph. "I think we know where they're from anyway."

"That doesn't exactly pinpoint it," Andrews remarked. "M51 is home to about one hundred billion solar systems."

Neruda ignored Andrews' comment and turned to the team members edging to his position. "This corridor's got a pretty steep incline. Be careful."

"Are these glyphs related to those on the artifact?" Evans asked as he was studying the column.

"Definitely," Neruda answered, "but they're not the same glyphs. I didn't see any that were identical to those on the artifact."

As he passed under the archway, Neruda could feel the incline begin, and his knees immediately alerted him to the added pressure of walking uphill. At least he could stand straight up. The ceilings in the corridor were three and half meters high and were domed in a similar manner as the chamber.

"I see another archway ahead," Neruda said.

"Tell me something," Andrews asked, "how does anyone carve this structure into solid rock and leave no debris or signs of their construction?"

"I don't know," Neruda replied. "Maybe we'll get lucky and find out."

"They're certainly good magicians," Andrews said. "The debris pile that this thing must've created would've been enormous. Where the hell do you hide something like that?"

The team filed under the archway, and one by one touched the marble-like columns as if they were sacred prayer wheels.

"It looks like a room juts off from the corridor," Neruda said loudly over his shoulder. He was about twenty feet ahead of Evans and the others who had stopped to examine the graceful glyphs on the archway's columns, which seemed almost alive with movement.

"What's inside?"

There was only silence.

"What do you see?" Evans asked again.

Silence.

Evans picked up his pace, almost running to Neruda's position, followed by the rest of the team. They found Neruda in the middle of a small chamber only twelve feet in diameter. It was perfectly round with a high domed ceiling. Its wall, opposite the entrance, bore an amazing wall painting that Neruda's flashlight beam was illuminating, its colors so bright that the team had to squint, as though it were transmitting light and not just reflecting it.

Below the painting, sitting on a raised platform that was carved from the same stone as the wall, was an object that was of a shape similar to a football, but nearly twice as large. It was completely black except for three silver lines that encircled it at its center. It was without seams, buttons or any exterior opening.

Neruda was busy examining the wall painting, mesmerized by its brilliant colors and abstract form. "This is definitely not Anasazi," he managed to say, his voice cracking slightly. "They've left this behind purposely. These aren't rooms where someone lived. This feels more like a diorama at a natural history museum."

"So an extraterrestrial civilization came to earth a thousand years ago and left behind a museum for the Anasazi Indians to enjoy." Emily wondered aloud. "The Chacoan Anasazi are reputed to have mysteriously disappeared around 1,150 AD so they closed the museum, but left behind a homing device that somehow was recovered nearly 850 years later."

"By us," Andrews added with perfect timing. "Sure, I mean, how could you argue with that hypothesis?"

"I'm not saying I believe that theory," Emily defended. "I'm just thinking out loud."

"Let's keep investigating," Evans suggested, "we only have another three hours and ten minutes before our rendezvous."

"How much time do you think we should allow for travel time to the rendezvous site?" Neruda asked.

"Let's allow forty minutes, we may not need that much time, but I'd just as soon have a few extra minutes in the event anything unforeseen occurs."

"Okay, so that gives us another two and half hours," Neruda said. "Let's check out where this corridor leads."

"It's a helix," Samantha stated matter-of-factly. "Like a spiral staircase. And there'll be more of these small chambers. I saw all of this... I just didn't know the scale of it."

"If you're so informed about what's going on here," Andrews challenged, "then kill the suspense and tell us what the hell it is."

"Look," Samantha said with sudden intensity, "I've seen images that were placed in my head by the artifact. If… if you don't accept that reality, then fine, but at least be civil about it."

"It's okay, Samantha," Neruda said. "Just ignore him, he's actually being civil by his standards. Trust me. I've seen him when he's a loose cannon, and it's not pretty."

"She's been right about everything so far," Emily said. "Let's trust her, okay?" She turned to Andrews and smiled.

"Fine," Andrews quipped.

"Have you looked at the artifact at all?" Emily asked.

"Haven't touched it," Neruda responded. "I'm not sure we should touch anything. Our mission is discovery, not investigation."

"Let's see what else there is," Evans suggested.

"What is it about this painting?" Collin asked. "Why would they go to all this trouble for the Anasazi? Or for us for that matter? It just doesn't make sense."

Neruda walked out of the chamber letting Collin's words hang in the air like dust particles. Speculation irritated him unless it was illuminated by at least a few facts. For now, his only motive was discovery.

"Did anyone bring the VC with them?" Neruda asked as they continued up the corridor.

"Of course," Emily said. She took out a small, silver box, about the size of a cell phone, with several, round, recessed dials on one side and a small lens on the other. "Do you want me to film?"

"Yeah," Neruda said, "but let's wait until we've seen everything this museum has to offer first. Collin, you're in charge of the précis, so start thinking about what you want to say."

"Is this project video going to Fifteen?" Collin asked.

"Who else?" Neruda replied.

"Shit."

"Don't worry," Neruda said, "Fifteen likes your style. It's sagaciously scientific and colorfully eclectic."

Everyone laughed, including Collin.

"You do a good imitation," Evans smiled, turning to Neruda. "Don't worry, I won't say a thing."

Neruda laughed, pleased with how civil Evans had been throughout the expedition. He actually enjoyed his company—something he hadn't expected.

"There's another archway," Neruda pointed his light to the doorway. It was only about ten meters farther up the corridor from the first, but this time the chamber was on the interior side of the corridor. The corridor was indeed like a spiral staircase winding its way in a clockwise motion at a consistent grade.

Neruda walked to the archway and this time waited for everyone to catch up.

The team was breathing a little heavier than before, but looked eager to view the second chamber as one collective body.

"Ready?" Neruda asked.

"Let the light show begin," Andrews said.

Neruda and Evans unleashed their light beams into the chamber. An eerie similarity awaited them when their beams intersected on the far wall of the chamber, which bore another wall painting of similar style, size, and brilliance. Beneath it, glistening in the light, laid another artifact, black and silver with flat panels joined together in a hexagonal pattern. Each panel was about the same size of a playing card, but twice as thick. The exterior of the hexagon was black, and the interior brilliant silver. Again, no buttons, seams, or evidence of an activation switch.

The wall painting appeared to be stylistically similar to the first chamber's painting, but with different glyphs and objects. It was about four feet wide and about six feet high.

The chamber itself was identical in scale and shape. Every nuance was an exact replica. Only the painting and artifact were different.

"I'm open to any thoughts anyone has," Neruda said.

"It's not logical," Evans started. "Why would they leave behind these artifacts in this way?"

"Why not?" Samantha said.

"There're some references in this painting that at least look intelligible," Collin said. "Here, at the bottom, these look a lot like the rock formations from around here."

"We should at least consider the possibility that it's a weapon of some kind," Evans said.

"We will," Neruda replied. "Any other thoughts before we move on?"

Andrews moved closer to inspect the painting. "The star patterns might be worth looking at—assuming they're not arbitrary. Also, the sign of infinity is used. It wasn't invented until the turn of the seventeenth century. And as far as I know, it wasn't invented by an ET from M51."

"Well, if there're no other comments." Neruda said, "let's move on."

The corridor continued upward. Every thirty feet a new chamber would lead off through an archway, alternating from the exterior and interior of the corridor. Each chamber was exactly like all the others, but with a unique wall painting and artifact inside.

Over the next hour, the team found twenty-two chambers, and was beginning to realize the scope of the discovery.

"We found it," Neruda shouted back.

"Found what?" Evans asked, walking up from the twenty-second chamber.

"The last chamber."

Evans poked his head in. "I left my flashlight behind with Collin and the rest. They seemed hypnotized by the wall painting in chamber twenty. I'm no artist, but these are amazing paintings… not exactly your typical cave art is it?"

"Not unless you consider Picasso a caveman."

"This chamber's different," Evans said finally. "It's like they ran out of time in their construction and left it in its natural state."

While the twenty-third chamber was identical in shape and size, its walls, floor, and ceiling were rough and unfinished. The wall painting was the only surface of the chamber that was smoothed and polished like the other chambers. The floor was full of debris, mostly rock chips and what looked like fibers of some kind.

"Very strange," Neruda said shaking his head slowly and rubbing his chin with his hand. "Notice the artifact?"

Evans followed Neruda's light beam to a shiny disc, about three inches in diameter. "It's an optical disc. Let's hope it explains what the hell this thing is."

"It's a time capsule," Neruda said. "It's a set of forty-six artifacts—half art, half technology. It's as if an extraterrestrial civilization planted these artifacts as someone might bury a time capsule for later retrieval."

"For what purpose?" Evans asked.

"An extraterrestrial time capsule is the most logical theory I can conjure for now," Neruda said methodically. "As for its purpose, that I can't explain. Let's hope this disc tells their story."

Neruda picked the disc up and examined it closely. Like a CD, only smaller, both sides had a gold sheen, with a center hole about the width of a pencil. "This could be an alloy of gold... I'm not sure it's an optical disc. It could be currency, or some sort of conductor."

Evans leaned forward to inspect it, taking it from Neruda's hand. "You're right, it might be gold. It's heavy." He waved it in the air judging its weight. "But it sure looks like an optical disc."

"What should we do with the artifacts?" Neruda asked.

"We're not set up to take them back with us," Evans answered. "I brought a level ten security fence, so we can keep this thing under wraps indefinitely."

"Why not bring this back with us?" Neruda asked holding up the disc. "I have a feeling it's the key to this whole mystery. The sooner we can open it, the better."

"It's outside of mission parameters," Evans began, "but I agree with you. I don't think Fifteen would have a problem as long as we both agree."

"Have you seen Samantha?" Emily asked, entering the chamber and looking around.

"No, we assumed she was with you," Evans answered in alarm.

"She was," Collin said, "but then she just walked off—we thought to find you."

"Without a flashlight?" Neruda asked.

"—Holy shit," Andrews exclaimed as he walked inside the twenty-third chamber. "The teenager must've lived in this room, I'd put money on it."

"Yeah, this chamber was left in a mess," Collin added.

Neruda pointed to the wall painting with his flashlight. "If they were in such a hurry, why'd they take the time to polish the wall where the painting is? I think they left the rest unfinished purposely."

"And that purpose would be?" Collin asked.

"I don't know," Neruda said. "But at least we might find some answers in this." He pointed to the gold disc.

"Cool, now we're talking," Andrews said. "They speak my language. Let me see it."

Andrews took the disc, placing it flat in the palm of his left hand. "Shine the light right here at this angle," his right hand was cocked at an odd angle mimicking how he wanted the flashlight to be positioned. Neruda complied.

"It has index lines," Andrews said triumphantly, "But they're as subtle as hell."

He turned it over with great care. "You probably already guessed that this has gold in it."

"Yeah, it looks like an alloy of some kind or possibly a coating," Neruda shrugged, "but who knows without lab results."

"We're taking this with us, aren't we?" Andrews asked, nodding his head.

"Yes," Evans said, "but the rest we'll leave here until we can assemble an excavation team."

"Good," Andrews whispered as he continued to look down on the disc. "It has index lines on both sides throughout the disc. There's probably a shitload of data in this thing." His finger started to move across the disc as though he were counting something. He flipped the disc over again, his finger moving across the surface of the disc subtly.

"There're twenty-four sections—twelve on each side."

"That's interesting," Neruda said, "given that we found twenty-three chambers."

"There're twenty-four if you count the antechamber," Emily reminded him. "Anyway, I'm gonna look for Samantha, anyone care to join me, preferably with a flashlight?"

"I'll go find her," Neruda said. "I'd prefer you and Collin work on the video report, oh, and by the way, the précis, at least as I see it, should include the term ETC, or Extraterrestrial Time Capsule."

Neruda turned to leave amidst a flurry of questions from Emily, Collin, and Andrews. "We're short on time, so I can't explain my theory. Evans will tell you as much as I know. Just do your best, and don't worry."

Neruda walked down the corridor aware of the discussion he'd just stirred up. The acoustics of the structure made eavesdropping effortless.

He made some mental calculations and judged the entire structure—from the antechamber to the twenty-third chamber—to be about 150 feet high and about one hundred feet wide. It was surreal walking down the winding corridor with chambers protruding outward like pods bearing gifts from an ancient, extraterrestrial civilization.

The structure was completely baffling to him. His mind was turning scenarios and theories over and over like a threshing machine, hoping to make some sense out of it.

"Samantha," he called loudly. "Where are you?"

"In chamber two," Samantha's voice filtered up the corridor like a ghost.

"Everything okay?" Neruda kept walking, not sure which chamber he was at.

"I'm fine," Samantha said, her voice quieter even though Neruda was closing in on her position.

Neruda's knees were still stiff and in pain, and he noticed how much they ached when he picked up his speed. He slowed down to a modest pace. She was okay, he reminded himself.

"Samantha?" Neruda called. "I'm not sure which is the second chamber, so talk to me, I must be close."

"Did you find the top?" She asked.

"Yeah, we found it, but it's not what you'd expect."

"It's unfinished isn't it?"

Neruda stopped in his tracks. "Yeah, but how'd you know that?"

"Have you noticed how similar this structure is to a single strand of DNA? There're twenty-three chambers extending from a helix-shaped corridor. Twenty-three pairs of chromosomes in each cell of our body—"

"Yes, but that doesn't answer my question," Neruda said. "How'd you know?"

He resumed his walk down the inclined corridor, following Samantha's voice. The thought of walking down a strand of DNA amused him. He might as well be inside a cell wandering within a chromosome—he was that far removed from the outside world.

"I think they're trying to tell us that our DNA is flawed or unfinished."

Neruda tracked her voice and entered the chamber. She was sitting cross-legged, facing the wall painting in the center of the chamber. In her hand she held a cigarette lighter and the flame flickered as Neruda entered.

"It's an amazing painting," Samantha said quietly. "I couldn't leave it. Sorry."

"It's okay," Neruda sat next to her. "I've been on my feet more than usual today, it feels good to sit."

He bent his knees up and wrapped his arms tightly around his legs. He was a little cold and tired. "What is it about the painting you find so fascinating?" Neruda asked.

"It moves," she replied.

Neruda looked intently at the wall and turned his flashlight off. He wanted to see it in the same light as Samantha had with just the flame of her lighter. "It moves? I'm not sure what you mean," he said. "What moves?"

The painting consisted of a series of interlocking ovals of various colors. In the outermost oval, glyphs were imbedded. The object looked a little like a cross-section of an onion, and it was floating against a starlit sky with a sickle moon.

"I'm not sure," she replied hesitantly, "maybe I'm the one who's moving. All I know is that I find myself being pulled into this painting."

Neruda scrutinized the painting, but sensed no movement. Nonetheless, he had come to respect her intuitions and insights so he continued to watch carefully for any change of perspective or sense of motion.

"So what do you think it is?" Samantha asked.

"This?" Neruda put his arms in the air signifying the total structure.

"Yeah, this." Samantha's eyes looked upwards like a weak echo of Neruda's arms.

"My current hypothesis is that an explorer race, originating somewhere from within the M51 galaxy, came to earth approximately a thousand years ago and interacted with the Chacoan Anasazi Indians. They built this... this structure to house a collection of artifacts that represent their artistic and technical nature. They wanted it to be found at some later time, so they left behind a homing device, which somehow magically appeared and led us to this amazing site." He paused to catch his breath. "I think it's a time capsule left behind by this race."

Samantha let the words dissolve in the air before she spoke. "Does your theory include any speculation as to their motive—this explorer race?"

"No, but we did find an interesting artifact in chamber twenty-three that might shed some light on that."

"What?"

"It's an optical disc—or at least it looks like one. If it is, it might have answers to all our questions."

"It's a good sign," Samantha said. "Everything's been encoded and cryptic up till now, as if they didn't want us to be able to communicate with them immediately. For example, in your theory, you said that they came to earth and interacted with the Anasazi Indians. If so, wouldn't they be able to communicate in the Anasazi language?"

"Probably."

"And yet, their glyphs, paintings, artifacts, are anything but easy to understand... even for you. If some other organization found the homing device, say the CIA or NSA, for example, do you think they'd have even gotten past it?"

"Who knows? Maybe..." Neruda said. "But what's your point?"

"I think this race has cleverly disguised its intentions. This may be a time capsule, I don't know, but it's more than a collection of artifacts that they wanted us to discover. There's a process they want us to go through. I feel we're being led. It's as if this discovery is only a small step on a very long and twisting journey."

Samantha's lighter ran out of fuel and plunged them into total darkness. "That's my point, I guess."

"I understand your reasoning," Neruda said, flicking on his flashlight and standing it on the floor with its beam straight up like a torch. "It's true that any race that had achieved intergalactic travel—especially an explorer race—would have sophisticated language translation technology. It's also true that they'd have multiple points of contact—with more than the Anasazi, unless they were only here for a very short visit, which is unlikely—"

"—So they purposely set barriers and obstacles to ensure their message would require significant time and effort to understand," Samantha said. "I'll bet the optical disc is no cakewalk to access, and when it is, it won't be in English, or any other language known to man."

Neruda stretched his legs out in front of him and leaned back with his arms behind him. "So you think they're very particular about who uncovers their time capsule?"

"That's my sense of it," Samantha replied. "You've seen how we've been tested and probed at each step along the way."

"And the only logical reason for being so particular is that the message is profound, or of significant importance to a large number of people. And they want it to fall into the right hands. Ours."

"That's what I believe," Samantha said, getting to her feet. "I don't pretend to know what's here, but it's part of something massive… more sophisticated…" She paused. "I think there're more of these structures elsewhere on the planet."

She closed her eyes as if remembering her vision. "If there are, they could be inter-connected in some way."

Neruda got up and gave her a quick look as he brushed off his pants out of habit. The floor was perfectly spotless. "I can't help but think you're withholding some information, as if you're afraid to share it. Are you?"

"They call themselves the WingMakers," Samantha said with sudden relief. "They're somehow involved with our genetics. It's as though they live inside us at some level and also live a great distance away. They also said something about our need to defend ourselves against another race of beings. An extraterrestrial race with technology more advanced than we can imagine. These… these WingMakers are wrapped up in this because, according to them, they're the creators of our genetics."

Neruda rubbed the back of his neck and grimaced. "Anything else?"

"No."

The sound of laughter stirred the silent air of the chamber. The team was on its way down the corridor, and Andrews was telling some amusing anecdote.

"Keep this to yourself for now," Neruda directed. "I'll tell you why later. Okay?"

"Sure." Samantha shrugged her shoulders in nervousness.

Neruda motioned to the corridor with his hand. "Let's see how they're doing with their little film project." He took one last glance at the painting in chamber two, feeling a new respect for the intellect of this alien explorer race. Somehow they had already managed to touch him across space and time. He could feel something inside changing, or crumbling. He wasn't sure which.

CHAPTER 8
ZEMI

If the entity is fragmented into its component parts, its comprehension of free will was limited to that which was circumscribed by the Hierarchy. If the entity is a conscious collective, realizing its sovereign wholeness, the principle of free will was a form of structure that was unnecessary like scaffolding on a finished building. When entities are unknowing of their wholeness, structure will occur as a form of self-imposed security. Through this ongoing development of a structured and ordered universe, entities defined their borders – their limits – through the expression of their insecurity. They gradually became pieces of their wholeness, and like shards of glass from a beautiful vase they bear little resemblance to their aggregate beauty.

An Excerpt from *The Shifting Models of Existence*, Chamber Two
WingMakers

Fifteen shifted in his chair a bit uncomfortably. His assembled directors did the same, but without a grimace. "Jamisson, that was one of the best reports I've seen in years."

"I agree," Branson nodded.

Neruda smiled back appreciatively and remained silent. His presentation *had* gone exceptionally well. The directors were attentive and completely reasonable in their line of questions. Neruda was careful not to induce or sway, but to simply report the team's findings. He was well aware that the directors were unforgiving when they smelled persuasive tactics.

"So what're our next steps?" Ortmann asked.

"We need to do a complete restoration and excavation of the site, which'll probably take about seven to ten days," Neruda answered. "So we'll need to set up a perimeter security system and an excavation campsite."

"And what's the status of McGavin's shadow agent?" Ortmann asked, turning to Evans.

Fifteen stirred to action at the sound of McGavin's name. "His name is Donavin McAlester," he interjected. "He'll be joining us Monday. Interestingly, McGavin suggested that he report to Evans, but I thought to comply with any suggestion made by McGavin would be foolhardy. So I'd like him to report to Li-Ching since McGavin complains about our communication."

"Who's heading the Ancient Arrow Project then?" Ortmann asked.

"I'm sorry," Fifteen said apologetically, "I thought I had made that clear. Jamisson will lead the project. Given his fine work to date, I thought it was only fitting that he be permitted to lead the project to its conclusion." He paused for a moment and looked around the table. "Is everyone okay with that?"

Heads nodded silently in affirmation of Fifteen's rhetorical question. Neruda kept his head still, but his dark eyes darted furtively to read the response from the directors. It was unanimous.

"Back to McAlester," Fifteen continued, "I'd like all of us to treat him with utmost care. There's no doubt as to his agenda, which is to find out why we secured this artifact without alerting the SPL. In other words, what are we trying to hide."

"How long will he be here?" Evans asked.

"That depends," Fifteen replied. He looked up briefly and rubbed the back of his neck. "If we can convince him that the information we leak to him is legitimate, he'll be gone within a month. If not, probably two, maybe three, months."

"Let's make it one," Evans remarked to a roomful of nods.

"Agreed," Fifteen said. "Are there any other questions before we break?"

Neruda's heart began to pound, and he could feel his mouth turn cotton dry in a matter of seconds. He caught Fifteen's eye.

"Did you have something else, Jamisson?" Fifteen asked politely.

"I guess... I think it would be a good idea..." Neruda paused and gathered himself as best he could. "Samantha has some interesting observations that I think the Labyrinth Group should at least be aware of. I'm not saying these are factual observations—clearly they're not. But they're interesting—"

"Just tell us," Fifteen interrupted, "and stop worrying about how any of us may react. We'll assume whatever you tell us is speculation and we'll leave it at that. So, what is it?"

"Samantha had several encounters with the homing device," he began. "In one of these, she had a vision of the planet covered in gridlines and there were at least three, maybe four additional areas that were possible ETC sites."

"You're saying that Samantha saw an image of multiple sites?" Fifteen asked. "And that these images were transmitted to her from the artifact?"

Neruda thought Fifteen's eyes brightened and looked more intense. "That's what she's told me."

"But the homing device is destroyed," Whitman remarked. "How would we get verification of multiple sites?"

Fifteen went to his desk and paged his assistant.

"Yes, sir," came the smooth, pleasant voice.

"Please find Samantha Folten and have her come to my office at her earliest possible convenience."

"Certainly, sir."

Neruda's stomach struggled to remain calm.

"Well, let's see what we can learn from Samantha," Fifteen said as he shuffled back to his chair. "No disrespect to you, Jamisson, but the vision is Samantha's and we should talk with her directly. Wouldn't you agree?"

"Of course," Neruda said hesitantly. "It's just that I haven't requested her permission to speak about these matters—"

"I'm sure Samantha will understand," Fifteen replied casually. He turned his head to Branson. "She's SL-Five, correct?"

"Yes."

"Poor girl," Fifteen said smiling, his head downcast to his empty cup of tea. "Let's be on our best behavior and make her feel completely comfortable."

"Are we leaving her on this project?" Evans asked.

"What would you recommend?" Fifteen replied.

"Her contributions were significant. I'd leave her on the project. She's got something I haven't seen before in our other RVs."

"And what's that?" Ortmann asked.

"I'm not sure I can put it into words," Evans said thinking hard. "She just seems to surrender to the situation and somehow wrests more information from it than anyone else."

"I'd agree," Neruda said. "Her ability to develop a psychic rapport with the homing device may allow her to more easily communicate with the other technology artifacts found at the site."

Fifteen leaned back in his chair. His eyes were closed for a few moments while silence overtook the room. "It looks like this meeting will go another twenty minutes or so, if anyone needs a break, this would be a good time to take it." No one made a move to leave.

After a timid knock on the door, Samantha poked her head in hesitantly. "You asked for me, sir?"

"Yes," said Fifteen, getting awkwardly to his feet. "Please come in and join us." He motioned to an empty chair next to Neruda.

"Jamisson was just providing us with an excellent overview of your recent trip to the Ancient Arrow site…" He paused, deep in thought. "Do you want anything to drink before we get started? Some tea perhaps?"

Samantha looked quickly at the table and nodded.

Fifteen poured the teapot and handed an intricate, ivory-colored china cup to Samantha, steam billowing from its surface.

"Thank you," she said, the tremble in her hand betraying her nervousness at being in the same room with the directors.

"A remarkable trip, Samantha. The entire team deserves our highest recognition for its ingenuity and resourcefulness." The directors all nodded in agreement.

"Thank you, sir."

"Jamisson was kind enough to comment on some of the experiences you had with the artifact. He felt we should know about them because of his respect for your insights and abilities. Anyway, I was hoping you'd do us the honor of explaining, in whatever way you're most comfortable, what you saw and what you think it means.

We'd be very grateful to you if you wouldn't mind."

Fifteen paused, looking around the table signifying that he spoke for everyone in the room. Then he returned his gaze to Samantha. "Okay?"

Samantha stole a quick glance at Neruda, who smiled in support. "I'm not sure what you already know, and I don't want to be redundant and waste your time—"

"Jamisson mentioned that you'd seen an image of earth encircled with gridlines that seemed to indicate that there may be multiple ETC sites. Why don't you start there," Fifteen suggested.

Samantha closed her eyes and took a breath. "I can see it clearly," she said, her eyes opening in slow motion. "I'd been getting RePlay ready... everyone had left to look for Neruda, and I was trying to communicate with the artifact. RePlay was cycling through to Alpha... and the next thing I remember was... was seeing three geometric shapes like doors floating in space. Moments later the middle shape displayed an image of earth, which was surrounded in gridlines like filaments of light, and at the intersection of these lines—in certain areas—there were glowing dots."

She paused, closing her eyes again. "I sensed three of these glowing dots... they were like markers. Somehow I just knew they signified areas where there were additional time capsules or artifacts. I remember only seeing one clearly... the one in New Mexico. The others weren't distinct, but I'd say there were three, perhaps four in total."

"Can you specify the general location of the other sites?" Branson asked.

"I think South America, Africa, maybe Eastern Europe," Samantha said slowly. "I'm not sure. For some reason, my focus was on New Mexico."

"Did you see the entire globe, Samantha?" Fifteen asked.

"No, I don't think so," she replied. "It seemed that only four continents were visible... North and South America, Africa, and Europe," she closed her eyes again.

"Did you get a sense that each of the markings on the grid signified another time capsule?" Fifteen asked.

"That was my sense."

"And did you get a feeling that there were more on the other side of the globe?"

"Perhaps... but I don't remember thinking anything about it," she said softly, almost in a whisper.

"Was RePlay on during this session?" Ortmann asked.

"Yes, but it didn't capture anything," Samantha replied. "I had forgotten to adjust the capture sensitivity because I had an image almost instantly and assumed that RePlay was adjusted properly."

"So nothing was recorded?" Fifteen asked.

"No."

"Why don't you tell us about some of the other images you saw?" Fifteen suggested.

Samantha cleared her throat and took another sip of tea. "During this same episode, I saw an image of what looked like a tall, bearded, human-like man. His eyes were certainly unique, but in all other respects, he could have passed on the street as human."

"What was so strange about his eyes?" Fifteen asked.

"They were a mixture of strange colors, and they were very large. Very piercing."

"Did you communicate with this being?"

"Yes."

"Tell us about it," Fifteen said.

"This being told me that they were the geneticists who developed our DNA. They were trying to trigger something within our DNA that would enable us to withstand a shift of some kind—a genetic shift. And that this was all necessary because we needed to defend our planet—"

"From what?" Fifteen almost shouted, sitting up in his chair.

Samantha became tentative. "From an alien race."

The room became chillingly quiet. Samantha wanted to take a sip of tea, but was afraid she might spill it if she did. Her hands were visibly shaking.

"You might want to mention why you think the discovery of the time capsule was an orchestrated event," Neruda ventured, hoping to steer her comments to a new subject.

Samantha turned to Neruda, aware that he was under some pressure to justify her presence in the meeting. "As you've probably already considered," she began, "the artifact was very selective. It probed both of us," she turned to Neruda again, "down to our molecular structure… or at least it felt like it.

"It was like this artifact had been programmed to assess our motives and establish our suitability for the discovery. Fortunately, it decided in our favor… though I'm not sure why." She flashed a quick smile that betrayed her nervousness.

"I kept feeling, and still do, even now, that this time capsule isn't exactly the right description of what we've discovered. It's much larger than that, and its creators have encoded its true purpose behind the glyphs, the art, the artifacts… behind everything. These are gestures, not the real substance of what they're trying to communicate."

"Gestures?" Fifteen repeated.

"I mean they're like facades," Samantha quickly returned, realizing the cryptic nature of her statement. "I don't think we'll be successful in decoding anything here, I think they have a whole different meaning."

"And what do you feel that is?" Fifteen asked.

"My sense is that the artifacts, including the optical disc—if that's what it is—will prove impossible to probe, just like the first artifact. The paintings won't reveal anything significant. And the glyphs will be impossible to decode."

"And the reason you think they did this is?" Fifteen asked.

"Because there's something in the process of trying to understand these artifacts that's more important than what they are or what they do. That's the only thing that makes sense to me."

"Well, you're right about one thing," Fifteen said, "they've chosen to be cryptic for reasons that aren't obvious." He stood to his feet and poured more tea for

Samantha before she could refuse.

"Samantha, you've been very helpful, and we appreciate your candor. Is there any reason why you believe the artifact chose you in the way that it did?"

"How do you mean, sir?"

"It seems to me that you were its primary contact. And yet there're no RePlay tapes or seeming effort on your part to make contact with it. In other words, it seems to have selected you. Why do you think?"

"I assume because of my psychic abilities—"

"That's all?" he asked in a friendly tone.

"I think so."

"But how do you *feel?*"

Samantha paused, editing her words before they were spoken. Her eyes searched the ceiling as if she were looking for help. "I never had a chance to really use RePlay. It contacted me before I had an opportunity... it... maybe it didn't want anyone else to see these images."

"What do you feel *is* the purpose of the ETC?" Fifteen asked, watching her intensely as if he were reading her body and mind simultaneously.

"It's something to do with genetics," Samantha said with sudden conviction. "It's something important and it's something that impacts a large number of people."

"Why a large number of people?" Branson asked.

Samantha looked directly at her supervisor, her green eyes intense and alive. "Why else would they be so careful about who they selected to discover the site?"

Silence filled the room. No one said anything for several seconds, as if reviewing his or her thoughts in light of what Samantha had just said.

Fifteen stared at Samantha. "Is there anything else that you can think of that might be valuable for us to know?"

Samantha shook her head. "No, I don't think so."

Neruda cleared his throat. "Their name?"

"Oh, yes," Samantha said, "They referred to themselves as the WingMakers."

Again, silence filled the room.

Fifteen tapped his fingers on the table. "The WingMakers..." He let the words dangle in the air, and then looked at Samantha. "What do you think it means?"

"I don't know, sir," Samantha replied, looking a bit surprised that he'd ask her opinion.

"Jamisson?"

"It actually sounds familiar to me, but I don't know why."

"Have we done a search?" Fifteen asked.

Neruda shook his head slowly and looked down at his hands. "My thoughts have been on the optical disc and excavation team. Sorry."

Fifteen pulled out his console from underneath the table and hit a few keys. He typed in the word WINGMAKERS with blazing speed and clicked search. Moments later he shook his head and pushed the console back to its position beneath the table.

"Nothing in our database or the net."

Fifteen resumed his tapping on the table. "Jamisson, you have a memory as perfect as anyone I know, how could you have a familiarity with this name and not be able to place it?"

"Maybe it was stored in his subconscious by the artifact," Samantha said, answering on his behalf.

"Hmmm" Fifteen said, nodding slowly. "Nothing else?"

Samantha looked to Neruda quickly and then shook her head. "No, sir."

"Well, we're very appreciative for your time and information, Samantha. You may return to your work. Thank you."

Fifteen motioned to the door as he finished his sentence and watched as she left the room hurriedly.

Fifteen stood and removed his cardigan sweater and carefully secured it to the back of his chair, and then sat down with cautious grace.

"Do you believe her?" Li-Ching asked.

"I believe she's being honest," Fifteen replied, dodging the question slightly. "We're talking about an encounter with what could possibly be an authentic representative of the Central Race."

"You mean because of the reference that they're allegedly the creators of our DNA that they're from the Central Race?" Whitman asked.

"That and the fact that they've deposited a structure within our planet that looks more sophisticated than anything we've ever seen before—by a considerable margin I might add.

"I'd like to have our Corteum counterparts made aware of this discovery," Fifteen said, turning to Whitman.

"Full disclosure?"

"Yes, they're more knowledgeable about the mythology of the Central Race than we are, maybe they can detect something in all of this that corroborates or debunks what we've heard and seen here today."

Fifteen turned to Branson. "I'd like her to have a promotion. Okay?"

"SL-Six?"

"SL-Seven," Fifteen said. "We need her loyalty strengthened. She's very good. I like her… but she has a weakness in her loyalties. She's loyal to her heart, more than to our ideals and mission. What I find interesting is that she's also afraid of her potential disloyalty, and this'll make her more prone to compensate in unsavory ways. Make it retroactive to the first of the month."

"Done."

"Now," Fifteen said, turning to the full group with his teacup in hand, "I'd like to hear your thoughts, theories, and opinions."

The sound of shifting bodies in leather chairs filled the room.

Neruda spoke first. "Whoever they are, they seem to know about the 2011 prophecy. That alone gives some credibility to Samantha's story."

"If Samantha's facts are straight, saying that we need to defend earth from aliens doesn't necessarily mean they're talking about the 2011 invasion prophecy," Ortmann said.

Li-Ching stirred in her chair. "Perhaps an RV session would be in order."

"On the WingMakers?" Evans asked.

"Why not?" she replied.

"I'll leave it to Neruda to decide RV protocols for the project," Fifteen announced. "But let's not jump to any conclusions about the identity of the WingMakers, and let's be certain to keep all RV sessions at levels one or two. I don't want any more contact with this race than is absolutely necessary. Agreed?"

Heads nodded obediently to his question.

"What else?" Fifteen queried.

"If she's right about the wide-ranging importance of this discovery," Li-Ching offered, "then we'll have internal pressure to release this finding to the outside. The implication is that security will need to be tightened and personnel more carefully screened. I'd suggest we limit access to the Ancient Arrow file to LG members."

"Done. Except I want Samantha to continue on this project," Fifteen said. "She'll be allowed into the surrogate file, but not the LG version."

Fifteen took a long sip of tea and swallowed with exuberance. "Whitman, I know you'd like this project under your supervision, but we just don't have a dynamic understanding of this species and its intentions right now to justify TTP leadership. However, I'd like you to supervise all surrogate database management and file creation, including all LAN/WAN knowledge links. Okay?"

"Yes, I understand completely," Whitman replied with no surprise in his voice.

"What else?" Fifteen summoned. "You must have more to offer than security issues."

Ortmann cleared his throat. "Now that we're in a mode to recover an additional twenty-two artifacts of unknown origin, value, and function, wouldn't it make sense to re-evaluate our security measures with Professor Stevens and the students?"

"What are you suggesting?" Evans asked.

"The value of this project, at least in my mind, has gone up by a factor of ten with the discovery of this ETC site. For all we know, this is the technological equivalent of BST... hell, it could be BST. Who knows? All I'm saying is that we should ensure its secrecy, and we have three loose ends in New Mexico that could create problems for us."

"What are you suggesting?" Evans asked again, hoping to force Ortmann to be specific.

"I know we've placed our best security fence around these people, but there're variables that even our best technologies can't control."

"So what do you want us to do?" Evans asked, his frustration starting to show.

"I think an accident cover should be executed for each of the three—I'd leave the specifics to you."

Fifteen had been listening intently. "Leonard, it sounds like you want to be rid of these risks, but by doing away with them wouldn't we also create more risks? Remember McGavin's recent allegations?"

"If I may add," Evans said, "I think the students represent more risk than Stevens. In the case of Stevens, the worst that he can do is already done, and we'll manage the fallout. I'm not worried. The students are another issue altogether."

"How so?" Fifteen asked.

"So far they've cooperated," Evans answered. "But only because of Stevens' influence. And that seems to be increasingly shaky because of his recent interaction with McGavin's goons. I'd say they could blow if they get any reinforcement from Stevens."

"So why not take the students out?" asked Li-Ching. "I can handle all the communication issues with a two-day window."

"The advantage of an accident cover with the students," Evans continued, "is that it would send a good message to Stevens. It also provides us with leverage downstream if we plant subtle evidence of his involvement in their deaths."

Fifteen set his teacup down and closed his eyes; bored or tired, no one could tell. "Can you two have some specific recommendations on my desk by eighteen hundred hours?" he paused only for a quick breath, emphasizing the rhetorical nature of his question. "I'd like a minimum of three scenarios, priority ordered, and I'd like the most probable implications defined. Oh, one more thing. We're not in the business of killing people just for the sake of security—for this project or any other. Am I clear?"

Li-Ching and Evans confirmed their understanding with a silent nod. Everyone else just stared.

"I'll authorize exceptions only as a last resort, and only if it clearly compromises our broader agenda. I'm quite certain of one thing; security on this project won't be our problem. Our problem will be loyalty."

He turned to Neruda as he finished his words. "Please have the excavation team list assembled tomorrow by twelve hundred hours in my office. And I'd like Evans included. Work with Whitaker and Ortmann to choose the rest. Okay?"

"Yes, that'd be fine, sir."

"Very well," Fifteen said standing up. "I assume there're no other questions or comments for now. Thanks once again to Jamisson for a brilliant report, and pass our comments on to the team. They all deserve our praise for an outstanding job."

Neruda fumbled with his presentation materials while everyone filed out of Fifteen's office, including Li-Ching. The sound of the door closing startled Neruda as he snapped the buckles on his briefcase. "I talked with Jeremy this morning," Fifteen said, walking to his desk with an occasional grimace. "He was pleasantly surprised to hear about your discoveries in New Mexico. I told him I wanted you to lead this project to conclusion. I also told him I wanted you to be promoted to SL-Thirteen."

He paused with a warm smile. "If that's okay with you, of course?"

Neruda could only manage to nod, flustered by the sudden honor.

"We'll wait for the official status change until Jeremy returns from holiday, but I'll inform the other directors this afternoon of your acceptance. Evans will have a new password to you later this morning. Okay?"

"Yes… whatever you think is best," Neruda managed to blurt out.

"One last thing, Jamisson. What I said earlier about loyalty… I'd like you to keep Samantha involved with this project, but watch her carefully. We have too much at stake with this project to let her or anyone else, lose sight of our mission objectives."

"I agree, and I will, sir," Neruda said. "I mean I'll keep an eye on her."

"Good. I know you'll do your best," Fifteen said.

"If you don't mind my asking," Neruda said, "what did Jeremy say?"

"About your promotion?"

"Yes."

"Something about you being too young to be an SL-Thirteen. I think he said something about him being fifty-two when he attained that lofty height," Fifteen said with a wink. "But he was all too happy to agree with my suggestion, and you know Jeremy, if he hadn't, he would've said so."

Neruda smiled and nodded in agreement. His supervisor was definitely as independent as he was brilliant. He was the one director that could and would stand up to Fifteen if he genuinely disagreed with him.

"Thank you for your confidence in me," Neruda said as he started for the door. "I truly appreciate it."

"You're very welcome."

Neruda left Fifteen's office with a strange sense that the warning about Samantha had also been meant for him. But despite that intuitive sense, he was buoyant about his promotion. He only wished he had someone other than his staff whom he could tell.

✳   ✳   ✳   ✳

The ACIO laboratory was washed in halogen light from an array of floodlights that hung from the ceiling. Inside each fixture was a miniature, closed circuit video camera. The lights were strategically positioned so that every square centimeter of the laboratory was observable, a reality that always irked Neruda.

Pattern Grid Detection Systems were established in each camera's electronic eye, that were able to distinguish an anomalous activity and alert security. It was why Neruda had to contact Security to enter the lab after 8 p.m.

The lab was sequestered under the tightest security fence that the ACIO had. Under the best of circumstances it took too long to get in, but tonight, Neruda was losing his patience because Security wasn't answering its phone.

After the third try, he decided to give up. He took the laboratory elevator, which was the only way to enter the lab. The security fence could detect body prints and determine the associated security clearance. There were no retina scans or security cards.

As the doors of the elevator opened onto the sixteenth floor, which housed the mammoth lab, Neruda was beginning to question whether he should try to make one more phone call. He decided against it. He was SL-Thirteen. Screw it, he concluded.

The outer perimeter door opened without hesitation so he walked through with similar confidence. Fifteen was a patron of the arts, and had virtually demanded that paintings and sculpture grace every wall and unused nook of the lab. It was a stimulating contrast to see originals by Gauguin, Kandinsky, and Miro as companions to the world's most advanced technologies.

At eleven at night the hallways on the periphery of the lab were quiet. Neruda walked to the main door and it opened with the hushed sound of air-compressed hydraulics. The door itself was fireproof, bulletproof, bombproof, and impervious to lock-picking of even the most sophisticated kind.

Neruda walked briskly through a brightly lit anteroom. He was restless to talk with Andrews and see the results from the initial probes of the artifact found in the twenty-third chamber. Another door awaited him down a short hallway that held the bathrooms and access to the lunchroom.

"Dr. Neruda," a voice sounded in the hallway directly overhead via the PA system, "we have no record of a permission request to visit the lab after hours. Please verify."

Neruda stopped in frustration and gestured impolitely to the speaker in the ceiling. "I tried calling you guys three times only fifteen minutes ago. No one answered the phone. Is there a problem?"

"No problem, sir," the voice replied. "Just verifying entries for the record. Have a good night, sir."

"You, too," Neruda said with a sigh of frustration. He hated the meddlesome nature of security.

Again Neruda was greeted by the sound of an automatic door opening at his approach. A camera scanned the entrance to the lab, but wasn't visible. Neruda couldn't tell where it was hidden, but he knew he was on tape, though he suspected no one was watching.

He entered the Computer Analysis Laboratory (CAL), which was the largest of the rooms off the main lab. CAL was known as home to the ACIO's most powerful computer system ZEMI, which had been developed collaboratively between the ACIO scientific core and the Corteum, an extraterrestrial race that had a secretive technology transfer program with the ACIO for the past twenty-seven years.

The ZEMI processors were approximately four hundred times more powerful than the best supercomputers on earth. Its operating system was custom-fitted to four individuals, each with security clearances of ten or more. These four operators were the exclusive users of ZEMI, and even Fifteen had to rely upon one of these individuals to interface with ZEMI if he chose to use it.

"Hey," Andrews said.

"How're things?"

"Could be better," Andrews replied, fumbling with some papers. "I could be sitting at home watching Golden Eyes, drowning in margaritas, and eating some exotic pizza with red peppers flown in from Chile."

"Sounds boring in comparison," Neruda commented.

"Shit, I can't get anything from this report," Andrews complained. He turned to a monitor panel in front of him. On the screen was the image of a man in his late fifties sitting in a high-back leather chair. The monitor was the only means of communicating with the ZEMI operators, who were isolated in special control rooms that shielded them from electromagnetic frequencies and psychic disruptions.

"David, could you try something a little unconventional?"

"What do you have in mind?" the face on the monitor asked.

"Try varying the angle of the read laser in a random sequence and simultaneously varying the spin rates."

"What're you looking for?"

"A fucking access point! We need to find the angle and speed correlation. It's out of our standard range. So we need to expand our range. Can you do it?"

"Just give me the parameters," the face said.

"Every conceivable angle and spin rate outside of our standard range," Andrews said. "Is that specific enough?"

"No."

"Can you calculate the parameters then?"

"Yes."

"How long will it take?"

"They're on the monitor now," the face said glibly.

"I mean how long will it take for the random tests?"

"Do you want angle and spin rate correlations to be exhaustively or randomly tested?"

"Exhaustively. Is there any other way?"

"Test cycle requirements?"

"This first round, let's try two seconds."

"It'll take at least two hours," the face said.

"Okay, let's get going," Andrews commanded. "I'm tired."

The man on the monitor panel closed his eyes. Seven, thin, glass filaments ran to a black colored headband that went from the back, center part of his neck, to the center of his forehead just above the bridge of his nose. He was completely bald, one of the sacrifices the operators of ZEMI had to make. The headband was called a Neural Bolometer, and it translated the radiant energy of the operator's brain activity to the command structure of ZEMI's operating system—effectively hard-wiring him to ZEMI's computing power through thought and visualization.

"So nothing to report?" Neruda asked, hoping to stir something out of Andrews.

"Zippo."

"I like the approach you're taking," Neruda said. "It's completely logical, oddly enough." He stopped and smiled. "I'm sure something will turn up in the test data."

"I'm not," Andrews shrugged.

"Why the doom and gloom?"

"If it's an optical disc, and they wanted us to read it, you'd think they'd have made it more similar to our standards."

"Remember this thing was left behind a thousand years ago, a bit before—"

"Shit, I know that," Andrews whined. "But I'm tired of these damn artifacts being so impregnable to our probes. I can't help but think they're wasting our time simply because they can."

"We've only had one day in the lab with this thing. Remember it took you three days to make the breakthrough on the homing device. Give yourself another day or two. It'll sing. You'll see."

Andrews hit the com button again. "David, can you do me a favor?"

"Yeah?"

"When you get the results on round one, if they turn up negative, try cycle times of ten seconds. When that's completed, let's add a third variable, laser diameter. Vary it at the smallest possible increments and the widest possible range. Okay?"

"Got it."

Andrews switched the button to its *off* position, and turned to face Neruda. "I'm going home. Sorry I'm in such a foul mood, boss. I'm just frustrated that this thing is so fucking closemouthed."

"Go home and relax," Neruda encouraged. "It'll open its mouth soon enough, and when it does, you'll be among the first to hear it sing."

"I hope you're right, but I have this nagging feeling that this fucker isn't gonna sing anytime soon."

"We'll see," Neruda said. "I'll walk out with you."

CHAPTER 9
LOOSE ENDS

All human life is embedded with a Wholeness Navigator. It is the core wisdom. It draws the human instrument to perceive fragmentary existence as a passageway into wholeness and unity. The Wholeness Navigator pursues wholeness above all else, yet it is often blown off course by the energies of structure, polarity, linear time, and separatist cultures that dominate terra-earth. The Wholeness Navigator is the heart of the entity consciousness, and it knows that the secret root exists even though it may be intangible to the human senses. It is this very condition of accepting the interconnectedness of life that places spiritual growth as a priority in one's life.

An Excerpt from *The Wholeness Navigator*, Decoded from Chamber Twelve

WingMakers

Fifteen studied the report that Li-Ching and Evans had put on his desk three hours earlier. The track lighting was dimmed, and the mood in his office subdued. He and Li-Ching were alone.

He removed his glasses and rubbed his eyelids. "You know what bothers me about this?" He said, holding up the report.

"Yes," she replied. "You have too soft a heart for your own good."

"Perhaps. Or perhaps yours is too hard," Fifteen said with a whisper.

"Octavio, I can assure you that both Evans and I are convinced this is the right thing to do. We're not anxious to take the lives of two youth, but these kids are potentially unstable, and in light of our ETC discovery, we think it's only prudent. There's too much at stake now."

"You don't have to sermonize to me," Fifteen said. "I know how serious the situation is." He put the report down, stared at his hands on the desk, and sighed deeply in resignation. "Maybe you're right and we should eliminate our risks, but then Stevens has already alerted the NSA. If these kids end up dead, McGavin will assume the worst."

"So what if he does?" Li-Ching replied. "He won't be able to prove anything."

"And what proof do we have that these kids are risks?" Fifteen asked, his voice sounding irritated. "Because it's not clear from your report."

"First of all, Stevens has protected the students' identity. He hasn't told the NSA how he came by the artifact. But we know the students know that Stevens has gone to the NSA. We're not sure if they know any details of what he told them, but we've got to assume he's told them something."

"And for this we should have them killed?" Fifteen asked.

"If Stevens wants these kids to remain anonymous to the NSA, he's protecting them for some reason. Octavio, they're just a loose end that could haunt us later. Why not make sure we don't have to deal with that risk."

"Both of you feel strongly about this?"

"Yes," she replied without hesitation.

He looked directly at Li-Ching, his eyes intensely scrutinizing her face. "If we do nothing, how does it hurt us?"

"What if these kids go to the NSA, courtesy of Stevens, and show them where they discovered the artifact? Don't you think McGavin would have his team snooping around the ETC site? It's a risk we shouldn't take. All McGavin knows is that we've dispatched some reconnaissance to New Mexico. He doesn't know where. We made sure that the NSA satellites were out of range when our missions made ground."

Li-Ching adjusted her tone. "If we sanitize the situation, we can ensure the site remains our secret."

Fifteen sighed in resignation. "Okay, but I don't want to hear anything more about this, unless there's a problem. Okay?"

"Understood."

Fifteen's third extension light signaled a caller. "You know who this is," Fifteen said with an air of dread.

Fifteen flicked on his speakerphone. "Yes?"

"Hello, Octavio," McGavin said. "I was hoping you'd still be at your office."

"As you know, I practically live here—"

"I'm on your speakerphone, aren't I?"

"Yes, you are."

"Are you alone?" McGavin asked, suspicion showing in his voice.

"I'm just trying to keep my hands free so I can make some tea. Okay?"

"Where's my RePlay tape? I was expecting it yesterday."

"Oh, I wasn't aware of a proposed delivery time."

"I just want the tape. When can you send it?"

"Tomorrow."

"When tomorrow?"

"Tomorrow afternoon."

"Please overnight it. I want to review this ASAP. Understood?"

"Anything else?"

"No, that's all."

"By the way," Fifteen said, "when you spoke with this professor... I think his name was Stevens... about the artifact he recovered, did he say anything about where he found it or how he obtained it?"

"You don't know?"

"No."

"According to the good professor, an anonymous source sent it to him."

"In the mail?"

"No, it was delivered by messenger, I think," McGavin said. "Why?"

"One of our current theories we're working on is that the object is a homing device. It'd be helpful to know where it was found. It could prove useful."

"Well, if this anonymous source turns up, the good professor is supposed to contact us. If he does, we'll find out what we can."

"Thanks."

"Other than that," McGavin said, "any success in probing the damn thing?"

"No, but we're still trying."

"Good. Well, I've got to run," McGavin said. "I look forward to seeing the RePlay tapes. Oh, and you do remember that Donavin starts tomorrow. You'll be gentle with him I presume—"

"Of course. Of course."

"Good. How's the tea by the way?"

"What?"

"The tea," McGavin said. "You said earlier that you were making tea—"

"It's just fine. Just fine. I'll let you go, Darius, I know you've got to run. Have a good weekend."

"Thanks. You, too."

Fifteen waited to hear the dial tone before he pushed the speaker button off. "Thoughts?"

"He's a jerk," Li-Ching replied. "Anything more I could say would be superfluous."

"Actually, I was referring to his story about the anonymous source."

"It corroborates that Stevens is protecting the students."

"Yes," Fifteen said, "but it also suggests that our professor is telling two different stories. He told us that the students were the source of the discovery. He told McGavin that an anonymous source delivered it to him."

"So he's trying to test whether McGavin would accept his different story," Li-Ching interjected. "If his story was accepted by McGavin, then he knows that we—posing as the NSA—the people who took the artifact, weren't affiliated with the NSA."

"Exactly," Fifteen nodded.

"He's a clever man," Li-Ching observed. "But this whole line of reasoning assumes McGavin is telling us the truth. That's not easy to accept."

"Perhaps not," Fifteen replied. "But I'm sure of one thing, we need to do something about these two students." He picked up the report off his desk and opened it to page four. "Why didn't we do memory restructures on each of them when we discovered this thing?"

"You know the answer," Li-Ching replied calmly. "We didn't think this was anything more than an isolated artifact—possibly a hoax. We didn't think it warranted extreme measures. Besides, our hush documents work ninety-eight percent of the time."

Fifteen scanned the report and turned to the last page of the document and signed his name. "Use scenario two. Alert Branson and keep this out of RV. I don't want Samantha to know about this."

"I understand," Li-Ching said. "Are you ready for a back rub?"

"I think I'm going to make some phone calls and check on the Code Frensel project before I turn in. Thanks anyway."

"What's wrong?" Li-Ching asked, concern showing on her face.

"There are days when I think our mission objectives collide with morality so violently that every atom in my body recoils from the impact. This is one of those days."

He rose from his desk. "I think I'll have that cup of tea now. Damn, that McGavin."

Li-Ching left his office in a diluted state of exuberance. She was elated that she had been able to convince Fifteen how to handle the students, but she was also disturbed by his lack of enthusiasm. His eyes seemed so tired and his mood so solemn. She thought about staying, but Fifteen almost ushered her out of his office, assuring her that he was fine. All she could do, as she walked down the hallway, was to wonder why his eyes glistened so clearly in the dimness of his office.

✳   ✳   ✳   ✳

"I hear that I'm not on the excavation team," Emily stated, her voice betraying mild indignation.

Neruda looked up from his papers. He looked tired. It was too early, at least for him, and he was still waiting for the caffeine to kick in. "Sorry, but I just thought your insights would be more valuable here than in the field," he replied casually.

"And what's more important here?" Emily asked.

"We have reams of new data that's being generated from the optical disc. I just thought you and Andrews should stay here and concentrate on that."

"Is Samantha or Collin going?"

"Samantha is going, but Collin is staying behind pretty much for the same reasons you and Andrews are."

Emily tried to sound unperturbed at the news of Samantha's appointment on the excavation team. "So how long will you be gone?"

"I think two days will be sufficient to excavate the artifacts from the site and pack them for shipment. We'll send a restoration team a few days later and then do final photography of the chamber paintings in about a week."

"Are you staying that whole period?"

Neruda glanced at his watch; he was already late for his meeting with Andrews. The ZEMI data was in, and he was anxious to see it. "No, I'll shuttle back and forth depending on what's happening with the optical disc and if we can open it."

"What's your impression? Can we open it?"

"I'm supposed to meet Andrews," Neruda replied, looking at his watch again, "about ten minutes ago."

"Mind if I tag along?" she asked.

"Not at all."

When they arrived at the Computer Analysis Laboratory, Andrews was flipping through a stack of computer printouts from the overnight testing. "I still haven't seen anything that would indicate an access point or any hint of a data stream that could be transmitted in any conventional means at our disposal. They've buttoned this up as tightly as the damn homing device."

"I'm updating Fifteen at 0900 hours," Neruda said. "Are you telling me there's nothing to go on?"

"Fuck, I don't see anything," Andrews complained. "I've been in here for two hours checking and cross-checking the data records. The access points for the index tracks are encrypted in something ZEMI hasn't seen before. David left the following message this morning at five o'clock, just a few minutes before I got here."

Andrews turned on the message screen, where the face of David, the ZEMI operator, began to materialize like a photograph in a processing tray. He hit the *Play* button and the face lurched into animation.

"Hi, Andrews. I just completed the tests per your specifications. It took us a little longer than I thought, mostly because the disc's in stealth mode. At least to our technology. I tried everything within our technical specs and your parameters, and nothing's been effective. Sorry.

"You might take a look at the ten-second cycle time tests. Reference number, nineteen-zero-five, looks interesting. At least it stands out as producing a resonance to the disc itself.

"And when I say resonance, look at the way the disc's vibratory rate increases. The molecular scans show a speed increase of nearly five hundred forty-two percent. It's really quite unusual. According to ZEMI, the laser is somehow inciting the molecular change, but the data trail dead-ends before ZEMI can lock in on the causative factors.

"The only thing we're certain of is that cycle time and pitch angle aren't the relevant variables. It's the laser beam's diameter as it penetrates the index track that seems to be the key. Ordinarily, I'd say this is a quirk of the alloy this thing's made of, which, incidentally, we still don't have a fix on. But this thing is very sensitive to focused light energy, and it may be intentional. With the right focus of light it awakens something at a molecular level within the disc.

"To us, this is the only interesting finding, other than the fact that no access point can be found from which data can be retrieved.

"If the diameter of the laser is the key variable to eliciting the resonance of the disc, we recommend that you test different wave lengths and beam intensities using the same diameter. Let us know if you'd like us to run these tests. Hope this information is helpful. I'll be back in around sixteen hundred hours. If you have any further requests for probe testing, we can look at it again then. Per Whitaker's request, I've cleared my schedule to concentrate on this. Bye for now."

Andrews flicked his knuckle on the pale-colored *Stop* button, punching the message screen back into blackness. "I love the way he says 'us' and 'we'. I mean it's fucking eerie how married these operators are to ZEMI. I wonder if the four of them ever get into cat fights about who's on more intimate terms with the horseshit computer."

Neruda couldn't contain his laughter and Emily quickly followed like an echo.

"Have you had a chance to do any further analysis of the light resonance of the disc?" Neruda asked.

"No, do you think it's that interesting?"

"Not really, but it's all we've got."

Emily sat down next to Andrews, picked up a stack of data records from the overnight tests, and flipped to the summary page. She seemed disinterested in the conversation between Neruda and Andrews.

"Here's my problem," Andrews said. "Even if the laser, focused at a certain diameter, incites a resonance within the disc itself, how does that move us one fucking micron closer to accessing the data on the disc?"

"I don't know," Neruda replied, "but as I've said before, this may not be a data disc as we think of data discs. So let's not be tied to our definitions. Let's just explore anything that looks unusual with a completely open mind as to how this thing might work. Make no assumptions that it'll behave according to our preconceptions. Okay?"

"Got it," Andrews replied.

Emily looked up from her reading. "Can I make a suggestion?"

"Of course," Neruda replied.

"Isn't it possible that the other artifacts might play a role in accessing this thing?"

"It's possible."

"And if it's possible, then doesn't it make sense that one of those artifacts could be the key… in other words it emits the signature light beam that activates the disc?"

"It's also possible," Andrews interjected, "that the other artifacts hold the data and this thing is just a fucking impostor."

"Unfortunately I'm not finding much that I can use for my briefing with Fifteen," Neruda lamented.

"One thing I'd add," Neruda continued, "is that we should test whether ZEMI can tune the resonance up or down, once it's incited. In other words, can ZEMI affect the resonance and alter it independent of the laser."

"Good idea, boss," Andrews said. "That way we could manipulate the resonance and test an endless variety of activation sequences and access points—assuming resonance is the key."

Neruda exchanged a few more words with Andrews and Emily and then excused himself to prepare for his briefing with Fifteen. For some reason, he couldn't help but feel confident that the access was just a day or two from being discovered. He also couldn't help feeling that it might not be data that was stored on the disc.

✳   ✳   ✳   ✳

Robert didn't even feel the tiny injection as the miniature tranquilizer dart found the back of his neck. He immediately fell asleep, as did his girlfriend, Linda. The TV's black-and-white flicker of Casablanca was the room's only source of light.

A few empty beer bottles stood guard on the coffee table over a near-empty bowl of popcorn.

Two figures dressed in black body suits slipped out of the shadows behind the couch, each carrying a black cloth sack. The taller figure deposited the two sleeping bodies in front of the apartment door, placing them strategically on the floor. The students looked like actors being positioned for a crime scene. The darts were carefully removed from their necks.

One of the figures pulled a gun from his bag and attached a silencer. He aimed at the chest area of Robert and squeezed two rounds into his chest—one hitting his heart, the other purposely off target. He did the same thing to Linda from a different angle. They checked the bodies again. No pulse.

In less than five minutes, the apartment was methodically and silently trashed by the two black-clothed figures. Books and clothing were strewn on the floor, and a planter was deftly tipped over.

One of the figures removed a leather pouch with four glass vials, and placed their contents in specific locations throughout the apartment. There was a clear purpose to the random trail of hair, fabric, dirt, and chewing tobacco.

The figures turned the television off and dragged it closer to a nearby window. The VCR was unplugged and placed at an odd angle on top of the television, its wires dangling in front of the TV screen.

The shorter of the two figures opened a window and skillfully broke its glass with hardly a sound. A laptop computer and some jewelry were placed inside one of the cloth sacks and lowered to the ground just outside the apartment window. The position of the broken glass was assembled just below the window on the cream-colored carpeting by the two figures as if they were constructing a jigsaw puzzle.

One of the figures climbed out the window and collected the bag of stolen goods, walking cautiously to a parked car. The other stayed behind like a sentry scanning the outside neighborhood for any signs of activity.

The figure silently slipped into the car and settled into the driver's seat. He removed his mask and body suit to reveal normal street clothes that did little to soften his hard, chiseled face and close-cropped, military style haircut. Taking a small transmitter from his shirt pocket, he whispered, "Everything clear?"

"Everything's a go on this end," his partner responded, also in a whisper, climbing out the window.

"You have twenty seconds," the driver said. "Go!"

The black-hooded figure placed a strange looking box on the window ledge. His thumb landed hard on a small, silver button, which he pushed four times in rapid succession.

Four loud, piercing gunshots echoed through the neighborhood. Seconds later, the black figure hurled himself into the waiting car, which sped away to the sound of tires screeching and loose gravel flying. Lights in the apartment building came on as residents peeked through curtains and blinds. After several blocks, the car lights snapped on as it climbed up a freeway onramp disappearing into Albuquerque's starlit night.

✳   ✳   ✳   ✳

Neruda knocked softly on the closed door. It was ten minutes after nine. He was late, but the briefing report took longer than he had expected, mostly because he was trying to invent some reasonable hypothesis that would satisfy Fifteen.

Early in his career with the ACIO, Neruda had learned the hard way about the consequences of inadequate preparation when presenting to Fifteen. No one could pick apart presentations better than Fifteen if he sensed poor preparation was at the heart of a feeble presentation.

"Come on in, Jamisson," Fifteen said through the heavy metal doors.

Neruda opened the door, but stopped short of crossing the threshold. A stranger was inside, and he hesitated as to whether he should continue. "If you'd like, I can wait outside until you're finished."

"Nonsense," Fifteen exclaimed. "I want you to meet someone who'll be working with us for a week or so." His arms motioned Neruda inside. "Donavin McAlester, I'd like you to meet our Senior Project Analyst, Jamisson Neruda."

As the two men shook hands, Neruda asked, "I'm sorry, but have we met before?"

"Not that I can recall," Donavin replied. "But then my memory for faces isn't that good. Do you have any Seal or NSA work in your background?"

"No, afraid not. I just have a familiarity with your face I guess. Oh, well. Welcome to our little laboratory."

"I haven't seen everything yet, but *little* isn't exactly the word I'd use to describe this place," Donavin smiled disarmingly. "Until last Wednesday, I'd never even heard of this unit. And now, I think I understand why." He looked around Fifteen's office with wonderment showing in his eyes.

Fifteen cleared his throat. "Donavin's here as an attaché from the SPL—he's essentially here to spy on us," Fifteen flashed a mischievous, but friendly smile.

Donavin looked at his shoes in embarrassment. "It's not spying. I'm simply here for a few weeks to observe and make recommendations to our respective organizations on how we can better cooperate and communicate."

"Is this something you do with the NSA on a regular basis?" Neruda asked.

"Not exactly on a regular basis," Donavin explained, "but often enough to keep me busy."

Neruda turned to Fifteen with a questioning look. "Would you like to reschedule our briefing meeting for later this morning?"

"No," he replied, shaking his head. "Li-Ching will be taking Donavin on a little tour of our facility in a few minutes. I just wanted you two to meet since Donavin's expressed a strong interest in the Ancient Arrow Project. Since you're leading the project, you'll have some contact with him from time-to-time."

Donavin went to his briefcase and retrieved a file folder, which he opened to a document. "Actually, I prepared something of a questionnaire for you," he handed the papers to Neruda. "It's just a few questions about the project and how you'd like to communicate with the SPL in reference to working hypotheses, project briefs, plan modifications, and the like. I'd really appreciate your help if you could take a look at the questions and return it in the next few days... maybe Wednesday if that would work with your schedule."

Neruda looked up from the papers as Donavin stopped. His forehead was furrowed and his eyes slightly squinted. "Can I get back to you on that? My week looks pretty busy right now. And by the way, I counted twenty-seven questions." He paused briefly. "A *few questions* isn't exactly how I'd describe this." He held up the papers and smiled.

"Touché," Donavin said, smiling back.

"I'm sure that Jamisson will do his best to comply," Fifteen offered. "We'll all do our best to make you feel comfortable and welcome here."

Li-Ching entered Fifteen's office in a splash of color and energy. Her straight black hair was untethered by her usual assortment of hairpins and barrettes. "Are you ready for your tour?"

"...Yes," Donavin said, obviously uneasy with her striking beauty.

"Okay, then, follow me... assuming you're done here," Li-Ching said turning to Fifteen for confirmation.

"We're done for now," Fifteen nodded. "We'll see you later for lunch, then. Have a great tour."

"Nice to meet you," Neruda offered as he shook Donavin's hand.

"Likewise," Donavin replied. "Bye for now."

Li-Ching gestured for him to walk in front of her and she turned to look back at Fifteen, disgust showing on her face, the kind a child might show to a parent for having to walk the dog. Neruda thought the door closed a little louder than normal, perhaps another sign of her dissatisfaction with having to babysit the SPL spy.

"It's clean," Fifteen said as he sat down at his desk. "He came in squeaky clean. No bugs, somewhat to my surprise."

"So what's the disposition of this guy relative to the Ancient Arrow Project? Do I give him access to anything?"

"He's already been assigned an SL-Two access code. Treat him accordingly. He knows nothing about the Ancient Arrow project except that we have an artifact that was recovered from Professor Stevens."

"Did you see this questionnaire?"

Fifteen smiled. "No, but he's obviously taking his job too seriously."

"What about the artifact?"

"How do you mean?" Fifteen asked.

"If the one thing Donavin knows about the Ancient Arrow Project is that we have an artifact, we don't exactly have it anymore. Other than a burned out shell, the artifact is gone, vaporized."

"We gave him a file that included three-sixty photos in three light spectrums," Fifteen said. "So he knows what the artifact looked like. Our cover is that the artifact destroyed itself under a UV scan and the shell is what's left of it. We'll show him the shell and convince him that the artifact and the whole project is a dead-end."

"Don't you think McGavin will want to launch his own investigation?" Neruda asked. "What's left of the artifact is not very similar to original pictures he's seen."

"Of course he will," Fifteen said. "But that was inevitable anyway. The fact that the artifact destroyed itself plays perfectly to our hand. The only nuance we can't control is whether McGavin will believe our story or if he'll assume we destroyed the artifact purposely."

"What about the RePlay tape?"

"It's being sent this afternoon," Fifteen replied.

"Has Donavin seen it yet?"

"No. I was thinking that you'd show it to him tomorrow and maybe orally answer his *little* questionnaire. It'll save you the time to write formal responses."

"Okay, I can do that."

"Good. Now tell me about our latest problem child from M51." Fifteen asked.

"We've discovered a way to get into the structure at a molecular level, by using a specific diameter laser beam. We've incited a resonance—a significant resonance. It may be that these artifacts are like shape shifters. Molecularly, the substance that they're made out of reconfigures itself when stimulated by specific light frequencies."

Fifteen leaned back in his chair and put his hands behind his head. He was staring at the ceiling as he often did. "What's the resonant beam's diameter?"

".00475," replied Neruda.

"And the light frequency?"

"UV seven-eighty-four."

"I assume you'll be trying a broad range of frequencies?"

"It's all in place for tests this afternoon when David returns," Neruda said.

"You think this object may transform in a similar way as the homing device?"

"Yes, I think it's possible."

"Tell David to have video on all tests—three frequencies, multiple angles… shit, he'll need some help. Have Whitaker assign a team to get that set up this morning. Okay?"

"Understood."

Fifteen looked at his watch. "I'm going to be in the sunroom the rest of the morning with our friends from Berne. I'll continue to think about probable testing paths and I'll find you should anything else occur to me, but for now I have to run. Anything else of an urgent nature?"

Neruda handed Fifteen a couple of documents. "Here's a progress report on the optical disc, aside from the resonance beam, nothing too exciting. Also, you'll find my excavation team list, role definitions, project strategy, and preliminary supply list. You can look at these at your leisure."

"Thanks," Fifteen said. "I'll do that later this afternoon. Anything else then?"

"No, that's it," Neruda replied.

Neruda wished he could join Fifteen in the sunroom. Of all the rooms in the complex, the sunroom was his favorite. It consisted of an array of floor to ceiling windows in an octagonal shaped structure that was two stories above the ground. It looked a little like an airport control tower.

A private elevator, just outside Fifteen's office, took passengers directly to the sunroom. It was the only way to access it.

"Hope your meeting goes well," Neruda said.

"Thanks, I'm sure it will. They need us a lot more than we need them. It always makes for good odds. Stop up later if you can," Fifteen offered. "I'll be there for at least another two hours."

"Okay. Thanks."

Fifteen turned to his assistant who was sitting attentively at a reception area opposite the elevator. "Just send our guests up when they arrive. If they're more than ten minutes late, make them wait an equivalent time in the Signatory Room."

"Very well, sir," the assistant replied.

The elevator door opened, and Fifteen disappeared into the dark, rosewood interior. Neruda knew that he wouldn't have the time to join Fifteen. He also knew the meeting was with the Nereus Syndicate, one of the most powerful organizations in the world. Neruda had developed their encryption algorithms when he had first started with the ACIO. He knew them well, and was all too glad to let Fifteen handle the meeting.

CHAPTER 10
DISCLOSURES

First Source is the ancestor of all beings and life forms, and in this truth, is the ground of unity upon which we all stand. The journey of unification—of creature finding its creator—is the very heart of the human soul, and in this journey, the unalterable feeling of wholeness is the reward. Every impulse of every electron is correlated to the whole of the universe in its eternal ascent Godward. There is no other direction we can go.

An Excerpt from the *Habitat of Soul*, Chamber Twenty-one
WingMakers

"Did you see it? Did you see the way that fuckin' thing reacted?" Andrews bubbled.

"Unbelievable!" Collin said. "Neruda was right, it's a shape-shifter just like the first one."

The two men were looking at videotape recorded overnight by David, the ZEMI operator assigned to the Ancient Arrow Project. The video showed the optical disc separating into two discs, like a sandwich, with a cloud of light between them. The light was like a prism with thousands of tiny bead-like globes dancing between the two discs, in what appeared to be a random pattern.

"Doesn't exactly look like anything we've seen before, does it?" Collin asked rhetorically.

"Just when you think you've met all the neighbors in the cosmohood," Andrews said, laughing in his halted style. "Mother of pearl, wait until the boss man sees this."

David's head came back on the screen. "As you can see, Fifteen's hypothesis was correct, except that it was twenty-three of the index tracks, not all twenty-four that constituted the magic number."

"Okay, so now what do we do with it?" Andrews asked.

"That's where it gets interesting," David commented. "We managed to catalyze a molecular shift, but we have no more an idea on how to access the data on the tracks than we did yesterday. The data, assuming it exists, is in a format that ZEMI can't read or, for that matter, even analyze."

"Could these lights—I mean between the discs—be reduced to binary code?"

"Negative," David replied. "If you look in the data file I sent you, you'll see a complete analysis of the light structure, but the best we can do is to provide frequency rates, spectrum analyses, and the standard baseline data."

"So all we've managed to do is create a deeper mystery. Great." Andrews lamented.

Collin slapped Andrews on the back. "Don't despair my friend, we have Fifteen's attention. If you can't figure it out, he will."

"Very funny, asshole," Andrews whispered to Collin. He then turned back to the monitor. "So you're telling me that we have absolute chaos in-between these discs? ZEMI can't find anything resembling an ordered pattern?"

"That's correct, at least in the context of our tests thus far."

"How's that possible? What's the longest cycle time ZEMI's analyzed?"

"About thirty minutes."

"We should test longer cycle times."

"We agree," David replied. "ZEMI's been doing that," he looked down at his Rolex, "for the past three hours."

"Good," Andrews said. "Anything else you can show us?"

"One other thing, there's an audio loop occurring between 52 and 195 kilohertz during the time that the shape shift incidence was occurring. It's an extremely complex loop, and we're working on stepping it down to an audible frequency range."

"Whoa, that could be very interesting," Andrews commented. "It's a continuous loop?"

"Yes, there's a discernible pattern that repeats every two minutes, thirty-two seconds. Precisely."

"Maybe this is the break we've been looking for. When will you have the audio file?"

David closed his eyes for a moment. "We're close, maybe another thirty minutes."

"Okay," Andrews said, "just send it to my office when you have something. Oh, and by the way, did you think about testing the audio pattern to see if there's any synchronicity with the light show?"

"We already concluded that there was no synchronicity. It's completely independent in terms of the pattern, but the light globules *are* generating the sound frequency."

"How, then, could they be independent?" Collin asked.

"We don't know."

"Thanks, David. I have to run to another meeting. I assume you've forwarded this to Neruda."

"Actually, I'm meeting with him in Fifteen's office in about an hour."

"Good luck. That's a tough audience, even when you're hooked to ZEMI," Andrews said, laughing.

David smiled politely, his hand reached for something, and the screen went blank.

Andrews turned to Collin with a surge of energy. "This thing's literally gonna sing!"

"We'll see," Collin said. "Don't get your hopes too high. It may be something spurious from the light source."

"Yeah, maybe, but I doubt it. The light is the source of the sound frequencies, and yet there's no relational pattern. Something else is going on here, and it ain't science."

"A light source can't generate audio frequencies independent of its change in frequency," Collin said. "It's not possible, you know that."

"So what're you saying, ZEMI's wrong?" Andrews asked.

"I'm saying that physics is right. ZEMI's another matter entirely, as is this artifact."

"Maybe we're gonna find something here that defies our laws of physics," Andrews offered. "And if we do, it may explain how we deal with the other artifacts we found."

"Perhaps," Collin said, "but I have my doubts."

The two colleagues left CAL and rode the elevator down to their offices in the Special Projects Department. They were excited about the new developments, and hopeful that they would soon know the optical disc's purpose.

✳   ✳   ✳   ✳

As helicopters touched down, their dust clouds obscured the regal sunset. The excavation team poured out of the birds, fosurteen members divided into three subgroups. Handlers were responsible for the safe removal of the remaining twenty-two artifacts. Security was responsible for ensuring that the entire site was hidden behind a level twelve Security Fence. Research made up the third group, responsible for assessing the chamber paintings, glyphs, and architecture for any telltale signs that could help explain the origin and nature of the site.

The team had been delayed by five hours because some hikers had been spotted on satellite reconnaissance pictures and were deemed too close to the site. Subsequent satellite pictures confirmed that they were moving in a westerly direction that would take them eight miles north of the ETC site. Evans was comfortable with the buffer. From the high-resolution satellite pictures, he was also confident that the hikers were not NSA operatives.

Neruda called to his team. "Follow me. We have about a kilometer walk."

The dark gray, unmarked choppers flew off like giant locusts. The team gathered its gear and formed a line behind Neruda. They were going to make camp inside the first cavern in order to remain invisible to any NSA "eye-in-the-sky" searches.

Cold, dry desert winds blustered through the narrow canyons, but fortunately, everyone was dressed for such weather, well aware that the interior chambers of the site were only 42° Fahrenheit.

As they approached the cavern's entrance, Evans pulled out a small, flat box that looked like a remote control with numerous metallic buttons. After fidgeting with the device for a few moments, he pointed it directly at the wall of the canyon where the cavern entrance had been before, but was now completely disguised.

In a matter of seconds, the narrow slit began to open up. The red light from the setting sun cast an eerie glow on the face of the rock wall, and the black entrance of the cavern grew like a wound, as the slit gradually became visible.

The ACIO had developed a technology to cloak physical objects. It was an outgrowth of the Technology Transfer Program (TTP) initiated with the Corteum. The technology was known simply as RICH or Reality Inference Coessential

Hologram. It could be tuned to take on the texture, color, and all material qualities of a desired object—in this case, the sandstone wall of the canyon.

RICH was a perfect technology to hide objects and was used extensively in the ACIO headquarters for Labyrinth Group classified technologies. These pure-state technologies were heavily guarded, and RICH was one of them. Only personnel with SL-Seven clearances and above were allowed to observe the workings of the RICH technology, and most of the other pure-state technologies were reserved for only the Labyrinth Group.

The excavation team climbed inside the cavern, one at a time, and set up their camp. The entrance was again placed in RICH stealth mode, and the team was sealed safely inside the ETC site, completely isolated from the outside world.

✳   ✳   ✳   ✳

Donavin McAlester walked down the long hallway of the sixteenth floor to Li-Ching's office. He was in a bad mood. No one was around to talk with, and Neruda had ignored his questionnaire.

"Can you spare a few minutes," Donavin asked, as he knocked on the open door politely.

"Certainly, Mr. McAlester," Li-Ching replied, looking up from her computer monitor. Her green silk dress was subdued in the modest light of her solitary desk lamp. She preferred low light when she was working on her computer.

"Where is everyone?" he asked. "I tried to talk with Evans and Neruda yesterday afternoon and again this morning, but no one can tell me where they are, let alone when they'll be back."

"They're on assignment," she answered calmly.

"I know that. When are they due back?"

"I believe Friday afternoon or perhaps Saturday, I'm not sure. Is there something I can do for you in their stead?"

Donavin invited himself in her office and slumped in a blue leather chair in front of her desk. "I came here to improve communications between our respective organizations, but I can't seem to find anyone who's interested in talking about it. Everyone's too damn busy. If I filed my report this morning to McGavin, I'm afraid you wouldn't like my conclusions—"

"Mr. McAlester, we're running the most technologically advanced organization on the planet with only a hundred scientists—peanuts compared to any of the government or military labs. We're not as heavily funded as the NSA or any other intelligence organization, so our people are stretched thin. Very thin. No one's deliberately hiding from you. We're all extremely busy. That's all. Don't take it personally."

Donavin looked at Li-Ching with puzzlement. "They're too busy? You do realize the significance of my report?"

"Of course," Li-Ching replied. "But you, unfortunately, don't understand the significance of our work. If you have a problem with our conduct, then I'd advise you to talk directly with Fifteen."

"Hell, he's another one I can't track down. His assistant is the smoothest liar I've ever met in my life. And believe me I've met some good ones in my tenure with the NSA."

"I'm sure you have," she said, smiling.

"Listen, if my report casts a negative light on the ACIO, your funding may be in serious jeopardy, doesn't that make it a priority for your organization? Or am I missing something?"

"In light of the fact that Evans and Neruda are on assignment, what do you want me to do for you?"

Donavin flipped a file on Li-Ching's desk and pointed his finger. "This file has the original blueprints for this structure. It says you have exactly 71,000 square feet of finished space. I'd say our tour provided me with perhaps 20 percent. I'd like to see more."

"And how is that going to improve our communications, Mr. McAlester?"

He looked her squarely in the eye. "Perhaps it will engender more trust."

"Okay, then, follow me, I'll give you a more thorough tour if that's what you want."

Li-Ching stood up and grabbed the file that he'd thrown on her desk. "You can have this back," she said offering it with her arm outstretched.

He took it without reply.

The two walked down the hallway to a metal door that looked like an elevator entrance. As they approached the door, it opened silently to reveal a narrow corridor with elaborate Turkish rugs laid on a parquet wood floor. It looked more like the interior of an expensive home than a government facility. The corridor was about eighty feet long with seven doors—three on each side and one at the end of the hallway. All the doors were closed.

"What's here?"

"This is *our* Special Projects Laboratory," Li-Ching said.

"I thought the lab was on the fourteenth floor," Donavin replied.

"Our main lab is there," Li-Ching explained, "but this is where our most secretive projects are based—what we call our pure-state technologies."

A voice came from overhead and startled Donavin. "Ms. Ching, good morning. Your guest, Mr. McAlester, is not registered for security clearance for this area of the building. Are you overriding Security in this matter?"

"Yes," she replied looking to the ceiling camera hidden in the track lighting fixtures. She touched her right ear with her left hand signaling to the camera that she authorized the clearance and was under no coercion.

"Thank you, have a good visit."

"How high up do you have to be to gain access to this area?" Donavin asked.

"Higher than you," she said deftly, and walked down the corridor to the first door, which immediately opened. She grabbed two surgeon's masks from the wall, shoe covers, and lab coats. "You need to wear these when we go inside. This is a biologically clean room. And don't touch anything, please."

Ahead of them was another door, marked "BioLab Level Seven."

Donavin donned the sterile, white clothes, eager to see what was on the other side. "So what's inside?" his head motioned towards the door, as he was preparing to place the cotton mask over his face.

"It's our laboratory for extraterrestrial studies—of a biological kind. It's one of our highlights on the tour. I think you'll like it."

"You mean you have aliens in there?"

"No, mostly we have parts of aliens in there," she said with a coy smile.

Donavin adjusted the mask and followed Li-Ching through the door. Inside was a row of stainless steel examining tables and what appeared to be a medical emergency room. Metal compartment doors filled one wall from floor to ceiling, and the opposite wall bore strange devices that looked like surgical equipment or examination tools, not unlike a dentist might use.

Li-Ching walked to a large, glass tank where something floated inside. She quickly donned rubber gloves, opened the top, and scooped it from the tank.

"This is something new we got in just a week ago from a remote area in the Gulf of Corinth, from a trolling boat, only about eighty kilometers from Athens."

She turned to face Donavin who had been patiently waiting. In her hands was a fetus, maybe two pounds, mostly brownish-red in color, with immense, blue veins surrounding a disproportionately large head.

Li-Ching checked the clock on the wall and then Donavin's eyes. "Are you okay?"

Donavin was staring at the fetus in Li-Ching's hands and his legs began to wobble. Before he could answer her, his knees collapsed and his body crumpled to the floor in complete surrender to gravity.

"I'll need some help putting him up on the examining table," Li-Ching said to a man in a white lab coat who rushed into the room as if on some predetermined cue.

"Get the mask off of him, now! I don't want him out too long," she ordered, as she replaced the fetus in the tank.

Donavin's surgical mask had been coated in a mild neurotoxin that was odorless and tasteless, yet capable of rendering a man immobile and unconscious for twenty minutes. It had one other redeeming quality: it left no traces in the bloodstream or urine.

The two lifted Donavin to the examining table, laying him on his back. His head was carefully fitted into a concave depression at one end of the examining table. A metal sphere, about the size of an orange, silently fell from the ceiling like a spider descending from a silken thread. Red lights projected from the sphere moving slowly across Donavin's face, mapping his facial features.

The metal sphere retracted, and a long robotic arm positioned itself just above his head. A needle extended from the arm and entered Donavin's nasal cavity, where it implanted a tiny transmitter, no larger than a grain of sand.

Known as Personal Moles or PMs, they had a dual purpose: a listening device that would transmit every word Donavin uttered for up to thirty miles, and a tracking device that could be monitored anywhere on the planet by the ACIO satellite network.

"Verify activation," Li-Ching said.

Her partner, now in a control room adjacent to the examination room, nodded. "We have activation."

"Good," Li-Ching whispered.

"I'll have a keyword list to you within three hours," she said in a louder voice. "You can deliver hard-copy transcripts twice daily, assuming he has something interesting to say. Understood?"

"Understood."

"Let's finish up, then," she said.

She took a small device from a table near the examining table and held it to the bridge of Donavin's nose. She turned a dial and then pressed a small button on the back of the device. It made a small incision, which immediately began to bleed. She sterilized the cut and gently placed a bandage over it. Then Donavin was lifted off the examining table and re-positioned on the floor where he had fainted only eight minutes earlier.

"Are you ready?" Li-Ching asked.

The man nodded, broke open a small packet of smelling salts, and waved it under Donavin's nose.

His body convulsed. He curled up in the fetal position momentarily, and then, as if remembering where he was, struggled to sit up. "What the fuck happened?"

"You fainted," Li-Ching replied.

Donavin shook his head and looked sheepishly to Li-Ching and then her partner. "Who's this?"

"I'm sorry, this is Dr. Stevens. You went down pretty hard, so I asked him to take a look at your nose."

Donavin's hand instantly reached for his nose and felt the bandage. "It's not broken, is it?" vanity showing in his voice.

"No, no," Dr. Stevens assured. "Just a cut and bruise, but you might have some pain or discomfort for a few days. If you need anything, let Li-Ching know, and I'll take care of it for you."

"Thanks. How long was I out?" Donavin mumbled.

"Just a few minutes. Maybe you should get some fresh air," Li-Ching suggested. "Do you want to go topside and get some refreshments?"

Donavin staggered to his feet, leaning against one of the examining tables for support. "Maybe that'd be a good idea."

Li-Ching placed his arm in hers and together they walked out the door, Donavin gingerly testing his balance.

As they removed their lab coats and shoe covers in the anteroom, Donavin looked at Li-Ching like a suffering animal. "What was that thing?"

"An alien fetus—Zeta Reticuli, to be exact. It was jettisoned from one of their submersibles along with a variety of other experimental refuse."

"So they're not exactly pro-lifers then?"

"No, they're more like pro-experimenters."

"It looked part human to me—"

"Please, Mr. McAlester, keep this to yourself. What I showed you in there is highly classified, as high as it can get. I simply wanted you to get a sense of my trust and our willingness to cooperate with you. Let's leave it at that."

"So you won't answer any more of my questions? Which incidentally, number in the thousands."

"No."

"Great," he said bitterly. "You don't really expect someone to see that thing and then clam up, do you?"

Li-Ching adjusted her dress, while Donavin watched discreetly out of the corner of his eye. Her figure was exquisite—petite, taut like a ballerina that Degas may have painted. Having disarmed her prey, she retorted coldly. "What I expect is compliance. I trust you, you trust me. Isn't that what you want, Mr. McAlester? Or did I misjudge you?"

"Okay, okay, no more questions," he agreed, "but at least tell me one thing, these Zeta's, are they here?" he gestured with his arms.

Li-Ching shook her head and smiled. "Mr. McAlester, if they were here, do you think I'd show you a dead fetus?" She took his arm in hers. "I'll escort you topside. How do you feel?"

"Just a little woozy," he complained.

Her right breast settled directly on his left arm as they walked down the corridor, and Donavin began to lose interest in the tour, feeling more important things were beginning to take shape.

✱   ✱   ✱   ✱

"The satellite images are in, sir," the voice over the intercom intoned.

"Have'em bring'em in, then," McGavin said.

Holden was always scared of McGavin's reaction to anything inconclusive, and the satellite photos certainly fell into that category. McGavin's assistant motioned him in with a subtle nod toward the double, oak doors.

He walked into McGavin's office, situated on the top floor of an obscure, five story, office building thirty miles northeast of Richmond, Virginia. The NSA's Special Projects Laboratory was nestled in a cultivated pine forest behind a fortified, perimeter fence with sophisticated, motion-detection sensors above and beneath the ground. It was a beautiful, but isolated setting for a clandestine operation.

To any casual observer, the SPL was a company called *ConnecTech*. To any researcher or journalist, and according to its web site, ConnecTech was a private, tightly held corporation that developed specialized, missile guidance systems for the military. In reality, the SPL was owned and operated by the NSA and developed a wide variety of technologies for surveillance and counter-terrorism, many of which had been initially designed and developed by the ACIO and then transferred to the SPL for further development and modification.

Core technologies were often a result of the ACIO's Technology Transfer Program with either the Zeta Reticuli or Corteum. In other instances, an extraterrestrial technology might be recovered without knowledge of its source, and then reverse-engineered. Regardless of how these technologies were acquired, the ACIO would develop them into pure-state technologies for applications related to the Labyrinth Group's agenda. These pure-state technologies would then be diluted for export to the SPL and other clandestine organizations throughout the world.

"So what do we know now that we didn't know yesterday?" McGavin snapped.

Holden sat straight as a board in his chair while his eyes darted around the room, never fixing on anything for more than a second. "We know that three, Q-Eleven choppers left the ACIO headquarters bearing in an east-southeasterly direction at approximately 1800 hours."

"Destination?"

"We lost radar thirty-two miles from exit site—"

"Why can't we track these idiots?" McGavin screamed, his hairless head, like a chameleon, turning a shade of crimson to match the curtains behind his desk.

Holden began to say something, but McGavin leaned forward in his chair and silenced him with a wave of his hand. "Tell me we have flight path extrapolations."

"We do, sir," Holden assured, his eyes nervously averting McGavin's icy stare. "However, the choppers never returned to ACIO headquarters, so we can't accurately extrapolate distance."

"Just show me what you do have."

Holden opened up a legal-sized file folder and pulled out three maps of the continental United States, each with several, dotted lines radiating from southern California going eastward, but at slightly different angles.

McGavin looked them over quickly. "So they went to southern New Mexico... maybe eighty, ninety miles south of Albuquerque—"

"Sir, we don't know if they actually stopped, they may have continued east or stopped in Arizona even California—"

"I know you don't know squat," McGavin said gruffly. "What's the legend indicate? I can't read a damn thing; the print's so small—"

"The red line represents the highest probability flight path," Holden pointed out.

McGavin leaned back in his chair and stroked his clean-shaven chin. "What's the passenger and cargo capacity of a Q-Eleven?"

"It seats six comfortably and can carry a four-and-half ton cargo load," Holden responded, glad to be reciting facts he was familiar with.

"Why would they fly so many personnel to New Mexico unless they found something big?" McGavin wondered aloud.

Holden waited in silence, aware it was a rhetorical question.

McGavin hit an open phone line; instantly a dial tone filled the room. "Was there anything else?" he asked, looking to Holden.

"No, sir," Holden acknowledged.

"Then you can go," McGavin said, hitting a speed dial button. The staccato tones of a phone number being dialed interrupted the dial tone as Holden got up to leave. He heard McGavin say something about the number "fifteen" just before he closed the door behind him.

"Then find him, I'll wait," McGavin said in a restrained voice.

Silence filled his office as he went over to a secret cabinet door and opened it with a quick, but accurate kick. The door sprung open to reveal several bottles of scotch. He poured himself a drink—straight up—and downed a large belt.

"Mr. McGavin," a voice broke in, "we've located Fifteen and he'll be with you momentarily. Thank you for your patience."

"You're welcome," he replied sarcastically, the scotch beginning to work its magic.

He had just finished pouring his second drink when Fifteen's voice came over the speakerphone. "Hi, Darius, sorry to keep you waiting, but I was in a meeting and I'm afraid my assistant didn't know which conference room I was in. What can I do for you?"

McGavin set his drink down on his desk. "Why did three Q-Elevens leave yesterday for New Mexico?"

"We're doing some reconnaissance with the Ancient Arrow Project, looking for more artifacts—"

"Why three?"

"We broadened our search area, I thought we'd try a triangular search pattern."

"And what've you found?"

"So far as I know, nothing," Fifteen replied. "But they've only been there about eighteen hours—most of which was sleep and set up. The last time I had an update was early this morning. I'll personally call you if anything turns up, though."

McGavin emptied his drink and set it down hard on the desk. It was already having the desired effect. "I don't want a call *after* the fact. I want to know your *plans*... then you can update me on the facts. All I'm getting on this project is some bullshit run-around. And I'm not buying it."

"So what do you recommend?"

"I want to know exactly what's happening," McGavin shouted. "The last report I saw showed the artifact had somehow managed to explode. Our lab confirmed it was alien technology, but to say it was the same artifact you showed me in the Ancient Arrow file... that's a stretch. Even you'd have to admit that."

He paused, wondering whether it made sense to get another drink. He decided it did and repeated his visit to the liquor cabinet. "You've sent three separate missions to the area, and I still don't know the precise location or the logistical plan of these missions. Let's start with that."

"I know you want us to improve our communication, but I can't hire a bigger staff just to perform this type of sensitive communication. I only have Li-Ching, and she's stretched so thin—"

"We have the most sophisticated intranet in the fucking world, all you need to do is to copy me on your e-mails. I'm not asking for proprietary communication. Just copy me."

"You know we don't trust networks. We can't compromise our projects with communication protocols that are open to hackers, espionage, and sloppy receipt handling. It's not an option, Darius."

"Your lack of trust is ridiculous," McGavin said. "Our IT people say it's impossible to hack our system—"

"I'm not going to waste our valuable time arguing about it, Darius, I simply won't compromise our projects by using it. Nothing's unhackable at the right price and with the right motivation, and you know it. If you want proof, give me a day and I'll send you copies of every e-mail you have in your system."

McGavin sighed long and loud. "So we have an impasse," he observed, ignoring Fifteen's boast. "What do we do about it?"

"You need to trust me," Fifteen offered. "It's that simple. It's the only way this can work."

"Do I have a choice?" McGavin asked.

"Of course."

"No I don't," McGavin complained, the scotch now well in control. "You flaunt your fucking power even in the suggestion that I need to trust you. You're my subordinate, Goddamn it! I'll decide who I trust and who I don't. There's something going on with the Ancient Arrow Project that's unusual—every bone in my body tells me that."

"Darius?" Fifteen interrupted.

"What?"

"I need to go into another meeting, right now. Can we finish this discussion tomorrow?"

McGavin tipped his glass back, finishing his third drink. He let the question dangle in the air, hoping it would unnerve Fifteen. "Fine, I'm tired of this whole line of discussion. Just make sure you give Donavin full cooperation on this."

"Thanks for your understanding," Fifteen said, breaking the connection.

"You're welcome," McGavin returned, the dial tone interrupting his words.

"What a fucking jerk," McGavin snarled as he clicked the speakerphone off. He looked once more at the flight path extrapolations and realized how little information he had secured from Fifteen. His anger continued to rise the more he obsessed about it. He, the director of the NSA's Special Projects Laboratory, couldn't even get a straight answer on where the location of this supposed search site was. He poured his fourth drink hoping it would assuage his frustration. It didn't.

CHAPTER 11
THE CENTRAL RACE

In your world, you are taught to believe that your body has a mind and spirit, when indeed, it is your spirit that has a mind and body. Your spirit is the architect, your mind is the builder, and your body is the material embodiment. The architect—your spirit—is only a thought away. Listen to its ancient voice. Perceive with its ancient eyes. Honor these gateways of intelligence as you would your Creator. They are your reality. They are the defining elements of your existence. It is time they yield the information that is the only true source of your liberation. You have only to command it, for we assure you, the teacher you have always sought is awake and waiting.

An Excerpt from *Capacities of Self-Creation*, Chamber Eleven
WingMakers

Alone in the seventh chamber at the ETC site, Neruda was trying to decipher the glyphs in the chamber's paintings. Some of them had familiar structures such as the infinity sign and the spiral, but many were unlike anything he'd ever seen before. The technology artifacts had already been carefully packed up and placed in the outermost cavern for removal to the ACIO laboratory for evaluation and analysis.

The excavation team had made camp in the outer cavern, and Neruda was dimly aware that he was the last one left in the chambers. He glanced at his wristwatch and sighed. Eleven o'clock. No wonder he was tired. He stood and stretched his legs and arms hoping to find new energy to continue his analysis of the glyphs.

"Anyone here?" he shouted, poking his head into the corridor and facing downward toward the entrance.

Silence rejoined the corridor and chambers, the halogen light-pods inside each chamber and at each chamber entrance being his only reassurance of humanity. Other than that, he might as well have been on some other planet in some other galaxy. He collected his notebook of sketches, returned to the center of Chamber Seven, and sat down, cross-legged.

"Jamisson, are you in here?" a faint voice drifted into the chamber.

Emily, he thought. "In here. Chamber Seven."

Emily had volunteered to accompany Neruda's team to help in the laborious cataloging process.

He listened for the approaching footsteps the way he imagined a blind person might focus on an unfamiliar soundscape. Voices revealed that Emily wasn't alone, or else she was talking to herself—something entirely possible, he reminded himself.

"Time for coffee and cookies," Emily's voice promised.

Neruda's heart gladdened at the prospects of coffee and some joy-food, not to mention, company. "You didn't," he exclaimed to the ceiling, knowing that the sound of his voice would find her ears.

"I did," she replied. "You said Chamber Seven, didn't you?"

"You heard right."

A moment later she appeared with Samantha in tow, both wearing blue jeans and carrying backpacks. Samantha had her hair up in a bun and was wearing a green turtleneck sweater that perfectly complemented her striking red hair. Emily wore a white cardigan sweater against the chill in the chambers, which made sweaters and long pants a necessity.

"It's good to have some company," Neruda said. "I was beginning to feel a little too isolated in here. These chambers can get creepy when no one else is around."

"Anything new?" Emily asked as she opened her pack and withdrew a thermos of hot coffee.

Neruda shook his head. "Not really."

"What're you working on tonight?" Samantha asked.

"We're just beginning to analyze the glyphs in the context of the inscriptions. We're looking for clues as to the spelling system and language structure."

"The paintings are so luminous," Samantha said, as if ignoring his explanation. "It's so strange to be looking at paintings by beings from a different galaxy. It's—"

"Unbelievable," Emily added, completing her sentence.

Neruda smiled. "Their application technique defines the word *permanence*. That's why the paintings are so luminous after some twelve hundred years."

"Whatever it is," Samantha remarked, "I've never seen such brilliant colors before. They literally glow as if they emit light, not merely reflect it."

"I agree," Emily said. "They're almost eerie… in an uncomfortable way."

Emily poured three cups of coffee from a vacuum flask and handed one each to Neruda and Samantha. Curls of steam rose up, filling the sterile atmosphere of the chamber with the aroma of coffee. Neruda warmed his hands on his cup and thanked Emily. He leaned back on the floor on one side, propped up with his right elbow, his one leg bent up and the other straight out. He was dressed in khaki pants and a black sweater with a white T-shirt poking out around his neckline. "This'll keep me going for another hour or two. It is regular, isn't it?"

"Yes," Emily assured him.

"Good."

Samantha sat down next to Emily, still staring at the painting. "You know, the people they draw in these paintings don't look that alien. Some could pass as humans, others as angelic."

"They're a bit too abstract for me to judge that," Neruda replied. "Besides, they could represent the Anasazi Indians, and not necessarily themselves."

"What's the chance that a race from another galaxy would look like ourselves?"

Samantha asked, turning from the wall painting to look into Neruda's eyes, her face as open and trusting as a child's.

"Excellent, actually."

"Excellent?" Emily returned in disbelief.

"Well, I'm not suggesting they'd be carbon-copies, but look at the Zetas and Corteum, they certainly bear a resemblance to us. The humanoid genotype varies, but the basic shape and structure is essentially the same."

"Can you tell me something?" Samantha asked. "Why haven't we been given the green light to RV the creators of this site?"

Neruda stared back with a blank expression as if her question completely surprised him. "I don't know. I've been too involved with the optical disc and now the site itself to make it a priority."

"So no one's made a conscious decision *not* to RV the creators?" Samantha ventured.

"No."

"Do you want to?"

"Now?" Neruda asked.

"Yes, now," Samantha replied eagerly.

"I suppose we… we could," he replied hesitantly, his mind calculating all the ramifications. He had monitored dozens of RV sessions in the recent past, so he knew the procedure well.

"I'll need a pad of paper and a pen or pencil," Samantha said.

"Right here? Now?" Emily questioned.

"Might as well," Neruda said, offering his notebook and pen to Samantha.

"You've done this before?" Emily asked turning to Neruda.

"Many times."

"Okay if I watch?" Emily asked. "I've never actually seen one of these sessions live and in person."

Samantha straightened her back and crossed her legs Indian style. "It's fine with me."

"I assume you didn't bring RePlay," Neruda said.

"No, I wasn't planning this. Am I outside protocol?"

"I haven't officially established RV protocol, so we'll make it up as we go. I'll record your findings exactly as you relate them, don't worry."

Samantha closed her eyes. Her face went blank. "Could you move the space heater a little closer? I always get cold when I do this."

Neruda got up and adjusted the heater. "Anything else before we get started? Samantha, are you ready?"

"Yes."

"I'd like you to move to a L-2 survey of the ETC site. Point of creation time frame."

"I'm there," Samantha reported, her voice strangely distant sounding.

"Report."

Samantha's hand began to draw something on the notebook in her lap. "I'm detecting creatures of some kind, tall… no, very tall—"

"Are they corporeal?"

"Yes, but less dense than we, as if they're only partly there," Samantha replied. A rough sketch showed slender, humanoid creatures with long heads. "They seem like angels—"

"Why?" Neruda interrupted, "What makes you say that?"

"Their heads possess a light around them… like angels… or… or saints. Like I've seen in paintings. Their skin is almost translucent, as if light were being cast outward."

"I'll record angels as an analytic," Neruda said. "What're they doing?"

"They're designing something… something of critical importance… to them and to us."

"Okay, Samantha, look at the design," Neruda suggested. "What do you see?"

"They're blueprints that represent a massive construction project that they're going to place on earth—"

"Why earth, Samantha?"

"They're the original planners who genetically seeded earth with higher life-forms like humans, apes, dolphins, whales, dinosaurs, and so on. They wanted to create a genetic library of DNA-related, interdependent life forms. They wanted a repository… or library in the galaxy that they could draw from for their future creations."

She paused and took in a deep breath. "We're like a genetic reference library to them."

"Okay, cue on the design blueprints, but move forward in time one year," Neruda said. "What do you see?"

"A… a huge three-dimensional sphere—maybe fifty meters in circumference. It's suspended from a domed ceiling that's equally vast—like a huge cathedral, but much larger than any cathedral I've ever seen."

"What is this sphere?"

"I'm feeling that it's earth, but it doesn't look like earth exactly. No, it's earth… it's primordial earth. I'm looking at a model of earth maybe a billion years ago."

"Sketch what you see. Pay particular attention to the land masses and where they are."

Neruda paused for a moment, catching Emily's eyes, wide open in amazement. Samantha was busy drawing what she saw. Her eyes remained narrowed slits with an almost imperceptible tremor.

"Cue on the purpose of the sphere," Neruda ordered.

"It's a representation or model… no, it's a holographic photograph of some kind. Wow, there're other planets in this building—"

"For now, keep your focus on the sphere that represents earth," he said. "What's the purpose? Why do they have this on display?"

Samantha was quiet for a few seconds as if she was observing something too immense to put into words. "It's not a cathedral, it's a… a warehouse of some kind… no, I'm getting the analytic that it's a computer database, but that doesn't make sense—"

"Stay in observation mode," Neruda commanded. "Cue on the purpose of the sphere."

"I get a strong sense that this sphere is in a database... like an information catalog of potential life-bearing planets. These beings are like genetic planners, and they're assessing which genetics should go to which planet. Yes, that's the purpose of this place. It's a repository of all life-bearing planets within our galaxy!"

"And what do these planners want to do with these planets?" Neruda asked, striving to maintain an even tone despite his rising excitement.

"They're selecting which planet will be the genetic library for our sector of the galaxy."

"Why?"

"I'm struggling here," Samantha whispered tensely. "Someone is approaching. He... or she... no, it's a he... he knows I'm here. They can sense RV observation. He's contacting me. He wants to know why I'm here."

"Do not respond," Neruda ordered. "Move to point of creation relative to the ETC site in New Mexico."

Samantha's face relaxed noticeably. "I'm in a building of some kind. It reminds me of a large monastery. Everything is quiet. Peaceful. The smell is somewhat salty like it's near an ocean. I can't see anything outside... but it's gotta be near an ocean."

"What do you see inside?"

"I'm in a room—fairly large, like a conference room. There're at least twelve of these same beings. They speak telepathically. I can't understand them, but I know they're talking with one another. There's a large table in the middle of the room, and in the middle of the table is a beam of light coming from some source... from above. It's like a projector. The light is illuminating an image—no, it's creating the image of a three-dimensional helix. It's the ETC site. It's a holographic cross-section of the site. I see it!"

"Good," Neruda said. "Now, look closely at the image, what's its purpose?"

Samantha's face tensed up as furrows suddenly spread across her forehead like ripples in a pond. "Again they sense me. They're trying to ask me something... I'm not sure what I should do, they're probing me... they want to—"

"Do not respond, Samantha! Focus on my voice! What's the purpose of the ETC site?"

"I can't," Samantha whispered. "I can't ignore them. Their minds are too powerful—"

"Samantha, listen to my voice. Do you hear me?"

"Yes," her voice trailing off.

"Okay, go to point of first contact between these beings and humans."

She remained silent.

"Samantha, can you hear me?"

Again, she didn't respond, her face completely relaxed.

"Should we wake her?" Emily asked, concern showing in her voice.

Neruda ignored Emily's question. "Samantha, if you can hear me, acknowledge. Now!"

Neruda stood and shook Samantha's shoulders firmly. "Wake up!" Her eyes flew wide open and she shivered as if she were both cold and afraid.

"Are you okay?" Emily asked.

Neruda moved the space heater closer to Samantha.

"I'm okay," she said, "just a little scared."

"What happened?" Neruda asked.

"I've never done an RV session where my presence was detected. It's a very uncomfortable feeling. These beings just wanted to know why I was there. They didn't feel threatened. They just don't like deception. I feel as though they scolded me."

"Did you communicate with them?" Neruda asked.

"I'm ... I'm not sure," Samantha stuttered, her voice quivering from body chills. "I felt their minds probing me, and then I heard your voice. That's... that's all I remember."

"Do you remember anything else before that?" Neruda asked.

"I remember everything," Samantha said. "It was one of the most vivid RV sessions I've ever had. I saw primordial earth—or at least a holographic model of it. It was incredible! You realize what this means?"

"What?" Emily and Neruda asked in unison.

"It means that earth was seeded by these beings. They're the mythical Life Carriers."

Neruda returned to his original position on the floor. "It's possible, but I wouldn't necessarily assume that that's their identity."

"What else could they be?" Samantha protested, shocked that Neruda could doubt her.

"The Corteum always portrayed Life Carriers as subspace beings. I doubt they exist in corporeal form. Also, your description infers they might be more related to the Shining Ones—also mythical beings—but less obscure."

"Shining Ones?" Samantha thought aloud.

"They're also known as the Virachoca, sometimes the Kukulcan, and more commonly as the Elohim. There are even a few, brave scholars that believe our angel mythology stems from their involvement in our planet's prehistory."

"And what do the Corteum say about the Shining Ones?" Samantha asked.

"Very powerful beings," he replied, "who've mastered how to disguise their influence. They keep a low profile by being incomprehensible."

"They keep a low profile by being incomprehensible?" Emily echoed in frustration. "What does that mean?"

"The Shining Ones, according to the Corteum, are the Central Race, the original race of beings that evolved in the centermost galaxy of the universe. As the universe expanded and created ever-increasing space, energy and matter, these beings expanded into the other galaxies as the creator gods or galactic planners who exported the master DNA templates from the more evolved, ancient galaxies to those that were in development or incubation."

"I've never heard of the Central Race—"

"It's not exactly taught in school," Neruda said, smiling. "They're not unlike the

Central Cell. This is the original cell that comes into existence when the father's sperm unites with the mother's egg. From this Central Cell, all of your other eighty trillion cells spring. Your other cells are differentiated; the Central Cell is not. It holds the master blueprint of your physical, emotional, and mental make-up. It lives in the pineal gland.

"In the case of the Central Race, they're the original humanoid genotype, and everything of a humanoid existence stems from their DNA structure."

"Are you implying these beings are the ancestors of every humanoid life form in the universe?" Emily asked slowly, weighing each word as she spoke.

"According to the Corteum, yes." Neruda replied, "And they're also our Gods."

"Gods?" Emily mirrored.

"That's not necessarily what they are," he explained, "it's what they've been dubbed by individuals who've somehow managed to come in contact with them."

"Like who?" Emily asked.

"Like Jesus, Buddha, Krishna, Mohammed, to name a few."

"So now you're going to tell me that our spiritual leaders were fooled by these beings—our distant genetic forebearers—into thinking they were God?" Samantha looked distraught.

"I'm only relating the Corteum perspective. Their cosmology is much more developed than our own, and they don't distinguish between spirituality and cosmology. To them, cosmology *is* spiritual study."

"But fooled?" Samantha asked again.

"I'm not saying they were fooled by these beings," Neruda replied. "It's not like these beings masquerade as Gods. They make no such claims. According to the Corteum, the Central Race possesses what looks to us as God-like powers only because their evolutionary timeline is so vast."

"So," Emily ventured, "if these beings are the Shining Ones, the Central Race, as you put it, then all the religious references to God or… or Gods… are really about them?"

"Again, according to the Corteum, yes."

Emily let out a long sigh. "So who created *them?*"

"As far as I know, no one knows," he replied.

"It still doesn't make sense to me," Samantha blurted. "Why would such highly evolved beings essentially be in the business of exporting DNA from galaxy to galaxy?"

"There's nothing more important—physically speaking—than DNA structures. The Central Race is essentially charged with the administration of humanoid genotypes. The human genotype of today is dramatically different from that which dominated earth a million years ago. The Corteum view is that this didn't happen due to evolutionary development, but through the intervention of the Central Race—the Shining Ones."

"So our Gods are geneticists?" Emily said. "It leaves me cold." She pulled her legs up and wrapped her arms around them.

Neruda shrugged. "I'm not stating this as the infallible truth. It's the opinion of the Corteum. It's their cosmology. Not mine."

"So you don't believe it?" Samantha asked.

"I try not to think about it too much. But I find it interesting and entirely plausible."

"So you do believe it?"

"I don't know," he answered, picking at the heel of his hiking boot. "We know that the universe started with a relatively small number of galaxies, and has expanded into about a hundred billion galaxies. It seems plausible that somewhere in the center of the universe, a race of humanoids could have evolved or been created. This race could be the progeny of God and the progenitors of humanity—here, everywhere."

Neruda stood and stretched his legs. "It's getting late; maybe we should go."

"I can't leave until you answer one more question," Samantha stated. "If the Central Race constructed this site, then wouldn't it be logical that it has something to do with genetics?"

"It's completely logical," Neruda replied. "I'll update Fifteen tomorrow on our return. We'll see what he thinks. We could be way off base on this. It's too early to extrapolate anything more than alternative hypotheses."

"Will we be doing additional RV sessions?" Samantha asked.

"That'll be up to Fifteen. It's worrisome that they can detect us, especially if they can probe us through our RV inquiry. It makes us vulnerable. We'll see what Fifteen wants to do. Okay?"

"Why the concern about communication?" Emily asked. "I mean why not just ask them who they are, what they want with us, and why they left this site behind?"

"Remember the timeline she was on?"

"Yeah," Emily answered.

"When you move into the past or future with an RV session, protocol dictates that the session remain in observation mode only," he said. Neruda squatted to organize his notebooks and return them to his backpack. "It's dangerous because our interaction could somehow change a past event, which could have a catastrophic impact in our time. So, until we know with some certainty that a change is in our best interest, it's better to remain incommunicado."

"I hope he approves further contact," Samantha said. "I think it's essential to understanding this site and all it contains."

"We'll see," Neruda said. "But don't get your hopes up too high. He's very skittish when it comes to alien communication, particularly if it's with a more advanced race. And I'm hard-pressed to imagine a race more advanced than the Central Race."

"Whatever happened to the notion that the more advanced a race is the more spiritually inclined they are?" Samantha asked.

"The fear has to do with manipulation," Neruda explained. "An advanced race can manipulate the perceptions of a less advanced race. In other words, they could make themselves appear as the Central Race or another benign, spiritually advanced race of beings, and be something altogether different. And we couldn't tell the difference."

"Sounds a little paranoid to me," Samantha said.

"There's good reason to be paranoid, if that's what you wish to call it. Especially when you're dealing with timelines that stretch back a billion years—"

"But that's just it," Emily interrupted. "If this race had holographic databases a billion years ago, wouldn't that make them extremely advanced. Our evolutionary equivalent of a great, great, great grandfather? And if they were so advanced, wouldn't that make them spiritual benefactors, and not potential adversaries?"

"Yes, but only assuming that RV technology is flawless and perfect. And I'm sorry to report, it isn't. The mere fact that they could detect Samantha indicates that they could also be in a position to conceal their identity. In effect, manipulate her perception for their own agenda."

Neruda ran his hands through his hair. "I know this sounds paranoid, but trust me, there are good reasons for caution. Be patient. I'll talk with Fifteen and we'll see what he says. Can we go now?" he asked, with a hint of growing impatience. "I still need to draft a report before I turn in."

They packed up and made their way back down the sloping corridor to the campsite in the outer cavern. The Handlers had already left earlier in the evening with all the artifacts. Most of Security had also left, having finished securing the secrecy of the site. Only the Research team remained with one security attachment.

*   *   *   *

Like a sleek cat, Li-Ching slid out of her car. As she closed the door, Donavin appeared, clothes disheveled, as if he'd dressed in a hurry. His normally neat hair was mussed, victim to the high winds following last night's storm.

"Everything okay?" Li-Ching asked.

"Fine, just fine," he said. "And you?"

"I'm doing well, thank you."

"Thought we should talk," he said. "Can I buy you a cup of coffee on the way down to the office?"

"I'm a little late for a meeting—"

"Please," he pleaded, taking her hand.

Li-Ching quickly glanced around the parking lot, assuring herself that they were alone. "If this is about last night, don't worry about it—"

"I didn't mean to assume anything... I thought you were coming on to me. That's all."

"Trust me, Mr. McAlester, you'll *know* if and when I ever come on to you," she said, walking away.

Donavin stood motionless watching her walk away. Her short, blue skirt revealed her perfectly turned legs, and he momentarily forgot his rehearsed speech. "Look, when you decide what you want, tell me. In the meantime, I'll keep a professional distance."

Li-Ching stopped, turned and walked back to him, stopping with her face just inches from his. "*If* I decide what I want, there'll be no telling. I'll show you. And if you intend to keep your professional distance, you'll need regular cold showers. Do you understand, Mr. McAlester?"

Feeling her warm breath on his face, Donavin swallowed hard, and struggled to regain composure. "Fine, so what do you want me to do?" he asked meekly as Li-Ching spun and walked away.

"I think you can decide that on your own," she said, tossing the words over her shoulder, and continuing her path to the ACIO entrance.

Donavin adjusted his sunglasses and glanced at his watch, trying to look cool despite his discomfort. Why does she have to be so damn complicated, he thought? But he knew full well that this was exactly what attracted him.

✳　　✳　　✳　　✳

Neruda had met briefly with Fifteen the night before and updated him on the RV session at the ETC site. Fifteen had scheduled a priority interrupt meeting for Saturday at 0900 hours. Neruda was early for the meeting because of the location. The sunroom was his favorite, and today was a beautiful one in all respects, as large, billowy clouds waltzed across a royal blue sky. Dressed in navy blue slacks and a white cotton shirt with the sleeves rolled up casually, he relaxed comfortably in a rattan rocking chair. As he scanned his notes in preparation for the meeting, the aroma of fresh coffee permeating the sunroom enhanced his already pleasant, well-rested mood.

Samantha and Branson had also been summoned, and she was the next to arrive. "I was surprised the elevator worked for me," she said, gingerly entering the room. "I've never been in here before."

Her eyes scanned around the room, eager to spy something unusual or secretive.

"You'll be disappointed if you expect to find anything extraordinary here," Neruda commented. "Fifteen was in charge of the decorating and he's a minimalist at heart."

"Actually I like his taste in interior design," she replied. "Besides, the view outside is what counts."

"Did you see Branson or Fifteen downside?" Neruda asked.

"No. Do you think they'll want to do an RV session?"

Neruda put the cap back on his pen and returned it to his shirt pocket. "I met briefly with Fifteen last night and gave him a quick update. He was very interested in our session and asked some good questions—"

"Who does he think they are?" she asked in a flurry.

"Even if he drew any conclusions, he didn't tell me anything."

"Nothing?"

Neruda shook his head.

Samantha walked over to a set of shelves that housed a variety of beautiful and exotic shells and crystals. "He collects these things?"

"Yeah, he'll collect anything as long as it's organic, untouched by human hands, and conveys a uniquely beautiful energy."

"So I shouldn't touch these?"

"I meant *manufactured* by human hands," Neruda laughed. "You can touch them."

Samantha picked up a crystal and examined it with rapt interest. "These are the most unusual things I've ever seen."

"That's because they're gifts from the Corteum," Fifteen said as he came off the elevator with Branson. "When the Corteum built their underground cities, they found pockets of crystals that even they had never seen before. What you're holding is completely uncut, they grow that way like organic fractals."

"They're remarkable," she said.

"Pick one out that you like and it's yours," Fifteen offered.

His eyes held an uncommon brightness that attracted everyone who met him, and Samantha stared at him for a long moment, drawn into those eyes, as she searched for the right thing to say. "Thanks, but ... but I couldn't."

"No, I mean it, take one," Fifteen said. "I might not offer again." He winked and whispered something to Branson, who smiled in return.

Samantha bent over to examine the crystals more closely. She took one of the smallest, and cradled it in her hand like a child might do with a baby bird. "I'll take this one. It's perfect."

"They literally are perfect," Fifteen said. "I mean that in a mathematical sense."

"Thank you so much," Samantha said.

"You're very welcome, but I should tell you one thing about these crystals, there're none on earth except what you see right here, so I need you to keep it in your office if you don't mind."

"I understand," Samantha said.

Fifteen sat down in his favorite chair and stared out the windows at the high desert flora and gray canyon walls that surrounded the east end of the ACIO compound. Branson and Samantha also sat down in the chairs that encircled a round marble coffee.

"Jamisson tells me you made a breakthrough," Fifteen said, suddenly turning to Samantha, catching her off guard.

She fidgeted in her chair with embarrassment. "I'm not sure it was a breakthrough, sir, but we did find it extremely interesting."

"Would you like to try again?" Fifteen asked.

"You mean another RV session on the ETC site?"

"Yes."

Samantha's eyebrows rose slightly and her eyes widened. "You mean communicate with them?"

"Perhaps," Fifteen said, not wanting to get her hopes up too high.

"You'll be the monitor?" she asked.

"Would you prefer someone else?" Fifteen replied.

"No, no," Samantha answered, shaking her head vigorously. "It would be great to have you monitor, sir."

"Good, then we've established our agenda for the morning."

"So … er … you believe the creators of the ETC site are the Central Race?" Samantha asked hesitantly.

"I believe we'll know more after our session," Fifteen replied smoothly. "Perhaps we'll be convinced, perhaps not. We'll see."

Fifteen hit a button on a console next to his chair. "We'll have no interruptions from below. Now, are you ready to get started?"

"One thing before we start," Neruda said. "In the last segment of our RV session, Samantha was probed by these beings. We don't know to what degree, but they may already know something of our activities. Also, I couldn't monitor Samantha during the probe. She was uncommunicative. I would assume she might—"

"We'll handle it a little differently then," Fifteen said. "Everyone ready?"

"Do you still want RePlay on?" Branson said, as he leaned over to open up his briefcase.

"Yes," Fifteen replied, "unless you think it would hinder you in any way, Samantha."

"I don't think so," she said.

Branson unpacked the device and handed it to Samantha. He plugged one of the leads into the console next to Fifteen.

"See if David's ready," Fifteen said, turning to Branson, who flicked a switch. An overhead, computer monitor crackled on. He flicked another switch and window shades silently covered the windows, bringing the room to a comfortable darkness.

"David, this is Branson, we're ready on this end, are you live?"

David's implacable face appeared on the overhead monitor, and nodded. "I'm good to go, sir."

Fifteen turned his attention to Samantha, who looked increasingly uncomfortable. "Samantha, we're going to have ZEMI monitor the RV session through David. It'll prompt me if it sees something that I might miss. Think of it as insurance. Are you comfortable with that?"

"Of course, sir," she replied, trying to sound indifferent.

"Good, let's begin," Fifteen said. "David, I'm going to put ZEMI on text scroll outputs. Bill, can you put the text scroll on the bottom third of the screen?"

The computer monitor went blank except for a thin, blue line, about two-thirds down.

"Samantha, whenever you're ready, we'll begin," Fifteen said.

Samantha made final adjustments on the harness straps of the RePlay headgear, sat back in her chair, and folded her hands in her lap. With a fleeting look at Neruda, she closed her eyes. A minute passed. "I'm ready," she said with a whisper.

The top part of the monitor screen began to flicker as a hazy image began to form.

"Samantha, go to point of creation of the ETC site, L4 survey mode, and cue on the planetary database," Fifteen said. "Report your findings when you're ready."

Samantha's face was expressionless as she began to report what she saw. "I'm in a huge auditorium… its dimensions would measure in kilometers, not meters. Intricate patterns cover the walls, floors, and ceilings—more intricate than I can describe… the colors are browns, yellows, blues, and black.

"I see three beings… similar to the ones I saw before. They're walking inside this huge interior space like tiny ants in a huge field. One of them is carrying a device of some kind. He's pointing it at these spheres or… or what I believe are holographic representations of planets. There're thousands of these things… spheres I mean, but I get the impression that there're many more rooms like this one. This building is unbelievably huge."

The monitor screen showed a blurry depiction of what Samantha saw. It looked like the first images of television, except there were color tones, albeit faint.

"Okay, good, now I want you to look around in this building, but do not stay in any POV for longer than about ten seconds. I'll remind you to switch POV. Report."

"The planets are holograms… I can see through them when I'm up close. From a distance they appear to be solid representations. I'm looking at one that's completely water, no… no there's a small landmass at its southernmost pole—"

"Change POV, Samantha," Fifteen ordered.

"This planet is large, it's also mostly water… I'm getting the analytic that it's a very young planet. It has no life, but it's being cultivated to have life. Its weather is very volatile—"

"Samantha, change POV. Cue on the device that the three beings are using. Report."

Her face showed some strain as she focused her attention on the object. "It appears to be an activation device… yes, they use it to activate the database. As before, I get the strong impression that this entire structure is part of a three-dimensional, holographic database."

"Go to the model representing earth," Fifteen ordered.

"I see it. It's smaller than most of the other planets represented here. It's also bluer in color…"

"Samantha, I want you to go inside the hologram of earth," he said. "Do you understand my directive?"

"Yes," she replied. "I'm there. It's an amazing mixture of colors and patterns."

"Can you locate their source?"

Samantha's face remained expressionless as she paused for a few seconds. "I see a cord of light… something inexplicable… it seems like an umbilical cord…"

"Follow it to its source," Fifteen said.

"I'm inside something—maybe a room… maybe a… computer, I'm not sure. It feels like architecture. I see thousands, no, millions of these cords converging into something… it almost looks like a nebula. I don't know how else to describe it."

"We can see it, too," Fifteen reassured her. "Don't worry about descriptions. Cue on the purpose of this room."

"I'm getting the strong analytic that the room is non-physical. It only appears physical. It's a generator of some kind. It's like the central energy system for this building where the planets are represented. Perhaps it's a holographic generator, but it seems more like an organic computer."

"Good, Samantha," Fifteen said. "Now, cue on the generator into which these cords of light converge. Report."

"I'm not getting anything... oh, wait, these cords... they're like miniature filaments that conduct something... energy or... or maybe a life-giving substance of some kind. I'm not sure—"

"Stay in observation mode," Fifteen directed. "Can you locate their original source of energy?"

"No, everything here seems like a pattern that's been replicated billions of times over. There's no original structure that I can feel. Suddenly, I'm getting the analytic that this room *is* the planet. That I'm inside this planet in which the building is situated."

On the bottom third of the monitor a message began to scroll from ZEMI.

> PROBABLE HYPOTHESIS (10.0 PERCENT CERTAINTY RANGE): THIS PLANET IS A CONSTRUCTED SATELLITE DESIGNED TO HOUSE A LIFE-BEARING PLANETARY DATABASE. INSUFFICIENT DATA TO DETERMINE PURPOSE OF THE DATABASE. PLEASE DIRECT RV TO ESTABLISH THIS PURPOSE. END.

"Samantha, return to the room where the earth hologram is represented. Exterior view. Hover above it ten meters. Are you there?"

"Yes."

"Good, can you see any of the beings you saw before?"

"Yes, there are three of them walking below me, perhaps five hundred meters away."

"Do you sense they have detected you?"

"No."

"Good, now move within several meters of these beings. I'd like to get a close view of them, but return to your present station on my cue. Okay?"

"Yes."

"Go," Fifteen commanded.

Samantha's forehead crinkled up and her closed eyes squinted as if some sand had been blown in her face. "They see me. They're asking me questions about my purpose—"

"Return to your station, now."

The image on the screen remained for a few more seconds. Three ghostly shapes in long, white robes could be seen. They were looking directly in Samantha's direction, so their faces could be seen. Large, oval heads with flowing white hair and beards. All three looked similar in appearance, and projected a diffuse but nonetheless bright light from the top of their heads that seemed to connect them. The image was slowly replaced by a distant view looking down on them from Samantha's previous position above the hologram of earth.

A new message from ZEMI scrolled across the monitor screen.

> INTERPRETATIVE ANALYSIS: 65%+ PROBABILITY THAT THESE BEINGS ARE WHAT THE CORTEUM REFER TO AS THE CENTRAL RACE. FURTHERMORE, DATA FROM THE SAME ARCHIVE STRONGLY SUGGESTS THAT THE THREE BEINGS ARE ACTUALLY ONE PERSONALITY. THE CENTRAL RACE HAS EVOLVED INTO A TRIUNE PERSONALITY WITH MIND, EMOTIONS, AND SPIRIT ESSENCE REPRESENTED EQUALLY IN APPEARANCE. THIS WOULD INDICATE THAT THE PLANETARY DATABASE IS CONNECTED WITH GENETIC ENGINEERING. END.

"Samantha, do you sense they can detect you from your current position?" Fifteen asked.

"Yes," she replied like an automaton. "They know I'm still here. I can feel their minds probing me. They seem impatient to talk with me."

"Samantha, resist their probes," Fifteen ordered, his voice commanding and resolute. "I want you to remain at your present POV but to move your TOV into the future by the equivalent of one year of our time. Report."

"No detectable change," she said.

"Do you see the three beings?" Fifteen inquired.

"I don't sense anyone in the room with me. I feel alone."

"Examine the holographic model of earth carefully. Report your findings."

"The planet appears normal. All the continents—geographically speaking—appear to be in order. I can see location markers on the continents—"

"Cue on the purpose of these markers," Fifteen said.

"I get the sense that they're construction sites—"

"How many?"

"I can't tell, yet," she replied.

"Samantha," Fifteen said. "I need you to slowly circle the planet so we can record the site locations. You don't need to describe anything; RePlay is providing a satisfactory image."

The computer monitor showed North America and a red circle denoting the New Mexico ETC site. Another in South America, near Cusco, Peru. Next, the monitor displayed an area in north central Africa in the vicinity of Lake Chad. An area north of Helsinki, Finland was the next location marker. Another location marker could be seen in southern China, near Canton. The sixth marker could be seen in south central Australia.

All the markers were the same color and size with one exception, the New Mexico site had a yellow dot, blinking in the center of the red location marker.

"Samantha, I need you to provide us with a top and bottom view of the planet as well."

"Understood," she replied.

The monitor picked up a blurry image of Antarctica in Wilkes Land where the final location marker could be seen near Vostok.

"That makes seven location markers," Fifteen said. "Stop for a second, what's that?"

The monitor showed a hieroglyphic string of symbols of some kind at the bottom of the sphere.

"Samantha, I'd like you to cue on this name. What is it?" Fifteen asked.

"I don't have a sense of a name," she answered.

"David, anything?" Fifteen asked.

The monitor began to scroll text.

> INTERPRETATIVE ANALYSIS: THE HIEROGLYPHS ARE NUMERIC VALUES. THERE ARE THIRTEEN DIGITS, AND THE NUMBER IS THEREFORE BETWEEN ONE TRILLION AND 9,999,999,999,999. IT IS HIGHLY PROBABLE THAT THE NUMBER REPRESENTS OUR PLANET'S SERIAL NUMBER IN THEIR DATABASE. END.

"Samantha, I'd like you to once again cue on the purpose of these location markers. Report."

"They're constructing a security system on the planet. They want to protect earth."

"From what?"

She paused. "From… its destruction."

"By whom?"

"I'm… I'm not sure—"

"Human or alien?" Fifteen asked, "Concentrate, Samantha."

"I feel these sites are part of a weapon of some kind. They want to protect their genetic library. They know that they must be vigilant and prepare for all eventualities. It's happened before."

"What's happened before?"

"These beings have deposited their genetics on countless other planets, and something has come along bent on destroying these genetic libraries… it's… it's a very ancient enemy, but not human."

"Okay, Samantha, return to the sunroom. You've done an exemplary job."

Moments later, Samantha opened her eyes, blinking them to adjust to the light. She instinctively removed her RePlay headset.

Fifteen stood and helped her to her feet. "It's good to walk right after an intense session like this. Gets you grounded again." Fifteen held her by her arm, helping her get steadied. He walked her to the elevator, which opened up as they came near. "I think we'll stay awhile and chat about our next steps," he said. "Why don't you get some rest and relax for about twenty minutes and then rejoin us?"

Samantha could only mumble in agreement as she was escorted inside the elevator. The doors closed and Fifteen returned to his chair.

Neruda and Branson were already in a deep discussion. The full-screen version of David was on the computer monitor listening to the conversation.

Neruda leaned forward to pour some coffee as Fifteen sat down. "You stopped pretty abruptly," Neruda said. "Did you sense something was wrong?"

"No, I just wanted Samantha to rest," he replied. "I know how exhausting these sessions are, and when you're tired, you're easier to probe."

"What did you think?" Branson asked, eyeing Fifteen.

"I think we found the Central Race," Fifteen said. "To me, it feels authentic, which puts this discovery on a whole new playing field."

"I agree," Branson offered.

"Why'd you choose not to communicate with them?" Neruda asked.

"I think we did," Fifteen replied. "They've clearly probed Samantha—at least twice. They know something of what we're doing."

Neruda leaned back in his chair and crossed his legs. "Are you opposed to a more direct communication?"

"What do you know about the Central Race?" Fifteen asked, looking over his cup of coffee.

"I know they're purported to be our ancestors," Neruda replied, "at least according to the Corteum—"

"Correction, they're everyone's ancestors—at least those of the humanoid persuasion," Fifteen interjected.

"Right, but doesn't that make them friendly to our cause?"

Fifteen shook his head slowly from side to side. "Our cause is BST, the most powerful technology in the universe, and therefore, the most controlled. Guess who regulates such a technology?"

"The Central Race," Neruda answered.

"Precisely," Fifteen said. "They're well aware that BST can be a powerful defensive weapon, as well as an indefensible offensive weapon if utilized with evil intent. They undoubtedly possess this technology, but they'd never place it on our planet. Too risky. It would assuredly fall into the wrong hands. So, instead, they've installed these seven sites, which somehow constitute our defensive posture against an alien invasion."

"So you think the Central Race would prevent us from developing BST if they knew our agenda?" Neruda asked.

"I have no doubt of it," Fifteen responded. "And I have no doubt of their capability to prevent us should they learn of our agenda."

"How do we know their technology is inferior to BST?" Neruda asked. "If their goal is to protect earth isn't it logical to assume they'd protect it with their best technology?"

"No," Fifteen answered. "It's logical to assume they'd use a benign defensive system like stealth technology. And how do we know this would be sufficient against this alien invasion? Because they say so from their safe perch in the central universe? This is their ancient enemy as Samantha put it. An enemy of the Central Race must be extremely sophisticated, or it would be vanquished. And how many genetic library planets have fallen prey to them, I wonder?"

Fifteen shifted in his chair searching for a comfortable position. "I don't mean to argue with you, Jamisson, but if you believe in the prophecies and our RV reconnaissance, it's hard to dispute that this invasion, if it should take place, will be a ruthless takeover of earth. All we know is that the invading force is from M51— some thirty-seven million light years away, and without doubt, a primeval galaxy. Hubble Space Telescope (HST) pictures have revealed that this galaxy may have star systems that go back fourteen billion years. Do you really think these races will have primitive invasion technology?"

Neruda remained silent knowing the question was rhetorical.

"I don't believe we can afford to rely on anyone, even the Central Race, for our protection and survival." Fifteen set his coffee cup down, and smoothed his pants with his hands, as if signifying his need to remain calm and collected.

Branson hit a button on the console and the shades opened up again, allowing natural light to pour into the room. "Is it possible that the Central Race left behind these sites for more than just defensive purposes? Surely the paintings don't have any defensive purpose," Branson said.

"It's another reason why I believe this defensive system is benign," Fifteen replied. "The ETC structure seems to be the result of competing objectives. This would weaken it."

"But isn't it reasonable to assume that the Central Race would have the ability to protect their genetic warehouses?" Neruda asked.

Fifteen furrowed his brow for a moment and made a quick assessment of Neruda from the corner of his eyes. "The beautiful thing about our predicament," he began, "is that we know so little of the facts. It provides us the luxury of speculation. Speculation and nothing more. As for me, when I find myself in this mode, I always prefer to create the solution rather than wait for some unknown benefactor to present it to me."

"Why?" Neruda asked. "I mean why not evaluate the defensive quality of this system before we write it off as benign and ineffective?"

"I never suggested that we wouldn't evaluate it! We absolutely must examine it and determine its usefulness. I only meant that we wouldn't rely upon it. We won't let it deter us from creating our own solution with BST. We're only weeks away from our first round of preliminary tests of interactive time travel! It's conceivable, if everything goes well, that we'll be ahead of schedule by five to seven years."

Neruda stood up and walked to one of the large windows overlooking the juniper trees, wild flowers, and sagebrush in the garden beneath the sunroom. In order to concentrate, he had to avoid eye contact with Fifteen. "The blinking light inside the red, location marker of the New Mexico site, it could only mean the homing artifact. Right?"

"That's my interpretation," Fifteen said.

"So why aren't other homing devices identified? The homing device for the Chaco Canyon site blew up. We have no way of finding the other sites without a homing device, unless we choose to interact with the Central Race through an RV session."

"I understand," Fifteen said. "You want Samantha to interact with these beings so we can find the location of the other sites—"

"You agree that it's an interconnected system?" Neruda said. "That it'd only operate if all seven sites were online or activated?"

"It would be logical," Fifteen replied.

"So how else would we find the other sites to activate the system?"

Fifteen chuckled. "There may be location markers imbedded in the site, on the optical disc, in every chamber painting. They wanted us to find this site first. There's probably an activation sequence, which would make good sense if it were an integrated technology. Hear me well, Jamisson, I will not authorize any further RV inquiries, especially involving interaction with representatives of the Central Race."

Neruda stared at the landscape, his back the target of Fifteen's eyes. He could feel them. There was something strange about this sparse, desert flora. It reminded him of an alien world for reasons he couldn't sort out. He had vague recollections of his home in Bolivia, surrounded in lush tropical foliage, warm rains, and the smell of earth rising from each footstep he took. The two worlds were so settled in their differences.

Fifteen's voice stirred him from his reverie. "I understand your interest in this race. They're undoubtedly one of the most fascinating discoveries we've encountered, but also the most potentially dangerous to our mission. And there's nothing more important than the creation of BST."

"Then we'll concentrate our efforts on decoding the optical disc," Neruda said as he turned around to face Fifteen and Branson. "We'll keep our focus on trying to discover the other six sites and learning all we can about the purpose of the defensive system."

"Very well," Fifteen said. "And one more thing, Jamisson, this encounter will remain SL-Twelve only. He turned to Branson. "We'll need Samantha to submit to an MRP this morning. I'd like David to personally take care of the matter. Okay with you, David?"

"Of course, sir," David replied without a change in expression. "Did you want to specify time coordinates or event coordinates?"

"We'll use event coordinates," Fifteen answered. "Neruda can provide those."

Neruda looked to Branson, hoping for a more sympathetic audience. "Can we limit our MRP to this singular event, or do you want to erase both sessions?"

Branson opened his mouth, but it was Fifteen who answered. "We need to erase both sessions and any prior or subsequent dialogue related to the event coordinates," Fifteen said. I want the key word, *Central Race*, erased completely. The identity of these beings must be contained within the Labyrinth Group. Understood?" Fifteen looked from Branson to Neruda, searching for compliance. Branson nodded, while

Neruda sighed in restlessness.

"Is something wrong?" Fifteen asked, directing his full attention to Neruda.

"There's one thing I failed to mention to you last night. Emily Dorrian observed the first RV session. She's also aware of the identity of the site creators, or at least she's aware that I thought they might be the Central Race."

"Might?" Fifteen queried.

"I didn't say anything definitively, but I did mention the Central Race and some of the mythology that we've learned from the Corteum. I didn't go into any detail—"

"Emily is SL-Seven," Fifteen said, "she'll need to undergo the same procedure as Samantha. You need to handle the arrangements with David, and I'd like it completed this weekend—this morning if possible."

"I understand," Neruda said.

"I'll have project protocols on your desks Monday morning," Fifteen said, "especially with regard to RV inquiries. In the meantime, nothing, I repeat, nothing, of this project can be shared with anyone outside of the Labyrinth Group. Understood?"

David, Neruda, and Branson nodded in unison.

"Then we're finished here," Fifteen decreed, picking up the crystal that Samantha had selected from his collection, and placing it back on his display shelf. "She would have liked this crystal," he said, mostly to himself.

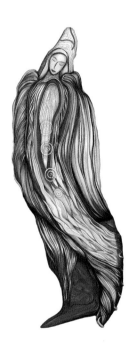

CHAPTER 12

RESTRUCTURE

You are in the infallible process of inward ascension—journeying from the outer reaches of creation to the inner sanctum of the One Creator who is First Source. We, the Central Race, your elder brother, remind you of the journey's purpose so you may understand that the role of the human form is to embody that which unites us all. However, it is only within the centermost universe that the children of time may experience the spokes of identity and the supremacy of their convergence.

An Excerpt from *The Central Race*, Chamber Thirteen

WingMakers

"So what's the emergency?" Emily asked as she walked into Neruda's office. It was Saturday afternoon, and she was dressed in casual, cream-colored shorts and a sleeveless, cotton blouse with flower patterns in navy blue and beige. Her hair was tied back in a single ponytail, and she looked to all the world like a schoolgirl on summer vacation.

"Remember our RV session in the ETC site last Thursday night with the Central Race?"

"Yeah," she replied.

"You need to submit to a single event MRP," Neruda said, trying to sound casual.

"Why? What happened?"

"I wish I could tell you, but I'm not able to explain the exact circumstances. It's in your own best interest to remain uninformed."

"That's an interesting way of putting it," she said with a sigh. "What happened? Come' on, tell me."

"Emily, I can't. Just trust me on this, it's in your best interest. It'll only take a few minutes, David's all set-up and ready to go—"

"Does Samantha have to go through this as well?"

"She's already had her MRP," he replied.

"And?"

"And what?"

"And did everything turn out okay?"

"Of course."

"I've heard that some don't," she said.

Neruda focused his full attention on Emily, turning off his computer monitor and sitting forward in his chair. "In the last nine years, every MRP has been successful and permanent. The fact is that almost seventy percent of personnel have had at least one MRP, they just don't remember it. The procedure is that good."

"What about me?"

"In what respect?" he asked.

"Have I had an MRP before?"

"You know I can't tell you that."

"But you know?"

"Yes."

She sat down with a sudden thud. Her facial expression caught Neruda's attention as he watched for signs of her acceptance level. He knew from experience that this was one of the most difficult procedures to explain to personnel—regardless of their loyalty. It was exceedingly invasive, and he knew from personal experience that it was unpleasant to willingly submit to such an invasion of one's private world of memories.

"Don't take this personally," she said, "but how do I know that the only memory that's being extracted is the RV session?"

"Emily, I'll be there," Neruda reassured her. "I've already determined the event coordinates, the missing time will be explained with our standard illness scenario, and you'll feel absolutely no ill effects. I'll personally see to it."

"Okay, okay," she said. "But isn't there a way to insert a different scenario other than an illness memory? Something like good sex?" she smiled seductively.

Neruda stood from his chair with a chuckle. "I'll see what I can do."

As they walked together to the Memory Restructure Procedure lab, Neruda had a strange sense of déjà vu. He knew this was Emily's third MRP. He wasn't sure how many he had had, but he assumed at least a half dozen. He handed Emily's file to David when they entered the prep room. Emily was immediately escorted to a private room and asked to sit in a comfortable chair with the back tilted at a 45 degree angle. Neruda watched from a glass window in the control room while David carried out the preparations. Emily seemed at ease and was joking with David, something Neruda marveled at, since David wasn't known for his sense of humor. After a few minutes of adjustments to the MRP headset, David joined Neruda in the control room. "What are the margin key words for today?" he asked.

"Central Race," Neruda replied.

"And the time marks?"

"1420 hours and whenever you start the MRP," Neruda said.

David donned his ZEMI interface and flicked the intercom switch. "Emily, we're just about ready. Any questions?"

"Just be gentle," she said with a snicker.

"One more minute," David announced, closing his eyes to mentally access the command structure of the MRP program.

"You still there?" Emily called.

"I'm not going anywhere," Neruda replied. "Don't worry, David's the best MRP operator we have."

"I'm really very calm," Emily said. "I'm surprised."

Neruda knew that part of the prep was to release a relaxation inhalant in the room called Paratodolin. It was so subtle that most never suspected their state of relaxation was artificially induced. David opened his eyes for a moment reading all the various monitoring data. "We're good to go," he said, turning to Neruda. His hand flicked the intercom switch one last time. "Emily, we're ready to start. *Central Race.*"

Emily immediately fell into an unconscious state. Her eyes moved wildly beneath closed eyelids, but otherwise her body seemed relaxed and comfortable.

"We're done," David said moments later.

Neruda flicked on a different intercom switch. "We have about five minutes to move her in position. Let's go."

Within ten seconds, two assistants entered the MRP room, removing Emily's headgear and easing her onto a sleek, stainless steel gurney. David looked on, his face unperturbed. "The seamless activation phrase is, 'Emily, are you okay?'"

"Thanks for everything, David. I really appreciate your help," Neruda said.

"It's no problem."

The assistants wheeled Emily to an examining room inside the health office through a secret hallway that connected the two departments. Neruda followed.

Once inside the examining room, Emily was moved to an examining table, and Dr. Stevens appeared. "This is scenario seven, correct?"

"Correct," Neruda said, shaking his hand.

"And she's never had this scenario before?"

"Correct."

"All the watches have been set back twenty minutes?"

"Shit, I forgot my own," Neruda said. He quickly set his watch back accordingly.

"Are you ready, then?" Dr. Stevens asked.

"I'm ready."

"On your word."

Neruda took Emily's hand in his and looked down at her expressionless face. "Emily, are you okay?"

Her eyes opened, blinking in rapid succession. "What happened?"

"You fainted," Neruda replied.

"How… why… why did I faint?"

Dr. Stevens stepped forward, peering over Neruda's right shoulder. "Emily, your blood sugar level is alarmingly low. I think it's why you fainted. How's your diet been the past few weeks?"

"My diet?"

"Yes?"

"Normal… I think," she said, trying to get up. Neruda helped her sit up. She rubbed her eyes. "I feel so groggy… like I need about another two hours of sleep."

"That's normal for your condition," Stevens said. "Have you ever suffered from hypoglycemia before?"

"I don't think I've ever fainted before in my life," she said.

"No, I mean have you ever been diagnosed with hypoglycemia? It doesn't show up in your medical records."

"No," she replied, still trying to regain her composure.

"Emily, can you try standing?" Dr. Stevens asked. "It may help to move around a bit."

Neruda helped her off the examining table, and she leaned against him for stability for a few moments, then walked around the room on her own for a few seconds, returning to the table next to Neruda. "I feel better." She glanced at her watch, "How long was I out?"

"A short time, but you were really out cold," Neruda said. "We were just lucky that Dr. Stevens was in on a Saturday."

"Thank you," Emily said, looking to Stevens.

"You're very welcome, Emily," he replied. "I'd like you to take a few of these tablets twice daily over the next four days. They'll help you to stabilize your blood sugar levels. Also, eat lots of fruit—apples, pears, grapes, that sort of thing. Okay?"

"You got it," she said, taking the small plastic container of pills.

She and Neruda walked slowly out of the health office. "I vaguely remember you called me into the office, on some emergency. What was it?" she asked.

Neruda stopped dead in his tracks. His face began to light up like a child just before opening a birthday present. "I think I found the access point of the optical disc!"

"You're kidding," she said. "What is it?"

"Each of the chamber paintings has a master symbol. I asked David if he could replicate the symbols in a three-dimensional hologram and input them into the optical disc when it reached its optimal resonance, in the exact same order as the chambers."

"And?"

"We have, as of this morning at 1100 hours, over two thousand pages that have been printed out!"

Emily gave him a big hug and then quickly pulled away. "Wow, what incredible news! What's the format?"

"Mostly hieroglyphs, some star charts, digital artifacts that we can't begin to make sense of, and a sense that the information is organized in the same structure as the chambers, namely twenty-three sections, but we won't know that for sure until we've finished printing. And that'll take another few hours we think."

They began walking again. "Let's go and check on the print-outs. I want to see what they look like. Okay?" Emily asked.

"I was already on my way when you fainted," Neruda grinned. "Do you think you can manage to stay conscious this time?"

"Very funny," she said, a smile curling around her mouth. "By the way, did you actually carry me all the way to the health office?"

"I'm not incapable of heavy lifting, you know," Neruda replied. "Not that you're heavy, mind you."

"Careful," Emily warned. "You're treading on dangerous ground."

"I'm just glad you're okay," he said.

The two walked side-by-side to the Computer Analysis Lab.

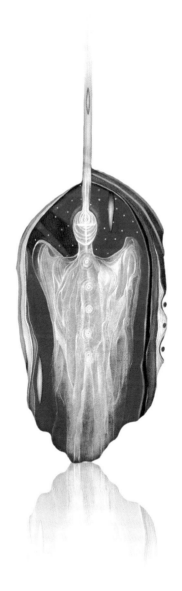

CHAPTER 13

DISSONANCE

Evolution in the material universe has provided you with a life vehicle, your human body. First Source has endowed your body with the purest fragment of ITS reality, your wholeness navigator. It is the mysterious fragment of First Source that acts like the pilot light of the human soul—fusing the mortal and eternal aspects. Can you fathom what it means to have a fragment of the Absolute Source indwelling within your very nature? Can you imagine your destiny when you fuse with an actual fragment of the First Source of the Grand Universe? No limit can be placed upon your powers of Selfhood or your eternal possibility.

An Excerpt from *The Function of the Wholeness Navigator*, Chamber Fifteen
WingMakers

Neruda, Andrews, and Emily had just finished their second pot of coffee. It was a few minutes after midnight, and the day's events had left them wired, even more than the caffeine. They had spent the last few hours analyzing the printouts from the optical disc—8,045 pages in total—and were now convinced that they had found the mother lode.

"Hey, bossman," Andrews said, "does Fifteen know what we've found here?"

"He knows," Neruda replied.

"So where is he?"

"He had meetings all day. He's also aware that I'll brief him Monday morning."

"Shit, man," Andrews said, "if I ran this place, I'd be here."

"If you ran the place, we'd all be designing James Bond's techno toys," Emily quipped. Andrews grunted in disagreement.

"David, I know it's late," Neruda said, turning to the monitor, "but could you try one last time to discern any repetitions in the text that could be construed as a section heading or title?"

"Using what criteria?" David asked.

"Let's try repeating glyph strings of up to thirty signs that repeat twenty-three or twenty-four times over the course of the text, and have a similar number of characters before and/or after them."

"Done."

A moment later David's voice came over the intercom. "We've identified something that meets that criteria. There're twenty-four repetitions and the sign-strings vary from four to twelve characters. It'll be onscreen in just a moment. Hold, please."

Neruda grinned and turned to Andrews. "We may have just found our first clue to their language structure."

The computer monitor flickered for a moment, and then text began to scroll over the screen.

> PRELIMINARY ANALYSIS: THESE SIGNS REPRESENT FULL WRITING, AND ARE NOT PICTOGRAPHIC IN NATURE. THERE ARE A TOTAL OF FORTY-SIX UNIQUE SIGNS, AND 49,721 UNIQUE SIGN-STRINGS, PRESUMABLY WORDS. VARIATIONS SEEM LIMITED TO 210 SIGN-STRINGS.
>
> THE TWENTY-FOUR SIGN STRINGS THAT YOU SPECIFIED HAVE—WITHIN A SEVEN-PERCENT MARGIN—ONE HUNDRED THOUSAND SIGN-STRINGS EITHER BEFORE AND/OR AFTER THEIR APPEARANCE. THIS DENOTES A STRUCTURE WITH HIGH PROBABLE COMPLIANCE TO THE TWENTY-FOUR INDEX TRACKS FOUND ON THE OPTICAL DISC.
>
> A LIST OF THESE TWENTY-FOUR SIGN-STRINGS FOLLOWS WITH PAGE MARKERS. PROBABILITY IS 97.6 PERCENT THAT THESE TWENTY-FOUR SIGN-STRINGS ARE THE EQUIVALENT OF SECTION HEADINGS RELATED TO THE INDEX TRACKS.
>
> THE MASTER SYMBOLS CONTAINED IN THE PAINTINGS, USED TO ACCESS THE OPTICAL DISC, ARE NOT REPLICATED IN THIS TEXT. THEREFORE, IT IS PROBABLE THAT THIS LANGUAGE STRUCTURE USES BOTH PICTOGRAPHS AND FULL WRITING IN SOME INTERACTIVE RELATIONSHIP. THIS RELATIONSHIP SHOULD BE FURTHER STUDIED. IT MAY BE THE KEY TO DECIPHERING THE TEXT. END.

Neruda finished reading before the others. "Thanks, David. Hold one second."

He turned to Andrews and Emily who were still reading from the screen. "I need you to leave for a few minutes."

"Now?" Andrews asked. "I'm not finished reading."

Neruda nodded.

"Should we start a fresh pot of coffee?"

"I think we're done for the night," Neruda said.

"Okay, then, we'll see you in the morning," Emily said, standing to her feet and stretching her arms and legs. "Don't stay up too late. It's almost midnight."

"It's twenty after," Andrews said.

Emily glanced at Neruda, who nodded.

Emily looked at her watch again, thumping it a few times on its crystal. "Must be time for a new battery."

"Rolex is so overrated," Andrews said.

"As much as I like Mickey Mouse," Emily sighed, "I have a hard time trusting a cartoon character for my time."

"Hey, don't knock'um, at least *my* watch works."

"Goodnight," Neruda said in the unmistakable tone of a parent reminding their children to go to bed.

"We're out of here," Andrews said. "I can tell when we're not wanted."

Emily looked over her back and waved. "Goodnight."

Andrews and Emily left the room without another word. As the door closed behind them, Neruda flicked on the intercom. "Have you done any comparative analysis, with the thirteen-digit number Samantha picked up in our last RV session, against this text?"

"No."

"Can you indulge me one last time?"

"Sure," David said. "Analysis is coming online."

Neruda glanced at the display of text as it scrolled across the monitor screen.

> ANALYSIS: EACH SIGN IN THE THIRTEEN-DIGIT SIGN-STRING IS REPLICATED IN THE TEXT (DETAILED ANALYSIS AVAILABLE ON REQUEST). THERE IS ONLY ONE PLACE IN THE TEXT WHERE IT IS REPRESENTED IN EXACTLY THE SAME ORDER, PAGE 121, LINE EIGHT.
>
> INTERPRETATIVE ANALYSIS (34.3 PERCENT CERTAINTY): IF THIS NUMBER DOES REPRESENT THE SERIAL NUMBER OF PLANET EARTH, IT IS LOGICAL THAT IT WOULD BE CONTAINED IN THE FRONT SECTION OF THE TEXT. IT IS PROBABLE THAT THIS SECTION DESCRIBES THE COSMOLOGICAL STRUCTURE OF THE CENTRAL RACE'S BELIEF SYSTEM AND ITS RELATIONSHIP WITH EARTH AND HUMANITY. END.

"David, cross-check the numbers against the twenty-four sign-strings. Let's see what the overlap is," Neruda requested.

"Do you want redundancies filtered?"

"Yes."

"Analysis complete," David said. "Should be on the monitor momentarily."

> ANALYSIS: THERE ARE ELEVEN NUMBERS FROM THE THIRTEEN-DIGIT SIGN-STRING THAT MATCH THE TWENTY-FOUR SIGN-STRINGS FROM THE TEXT, PRESUMED TO BE SECTION HEADINGS. ASSUMING THAT THEIR NUMBER SYSTEM IS HOMOLOGOUS TO OURS, AND BASED ON THE SEQUENCE OF THE THIRTEEN-DIGIT SIGN STRING, THE

SERIAL NUMBER OF OUR PLANET—ACCORDING TO THE
CENTRAL RACE—IS 5,342,482,337,666. END.

Neruda collected his thoughts with a long, drawn-out sigh. His mouth formed
the number again, silently. "David, ask ZEMI what the serial number means."
"Understood."
The screen scrolled a single line of new text.

ANALYSIS: THERE ARE AT LEAST 5,342,482,337,666
INHABITED AND/OR POTENTIALLY INHABITABLE PLANETS
IN THE UNIVERSE. END.

"David, I'd like an interpretative analysis even if it's below ten-percent certainty
levels," Neruda announced.
"Onscreen," David replied.

INTERPRETATIVE ANALYSIS (8.5 PERCENT CERTAINTY):
ACCORDING TO OUR OWN DATA, THERE ARE
APPROXIMATELY 1.2 TRILLION INHABITABLE PLANETS
WITHIN THE UNIVERSE. HOWEVER, THAT ASSUMES THAT
THE UNIVERSE IS SINGULAR. IF EARTH IS PLANET NUMBER
5,342,482,337,666 THEN IT SUGGESTS THAT THERE ARE
MULTIPLE UNIVERSES AS PROPOSED BY THE CORTEUM IN
THEIR MANIFESTO, LIMINAL COSMOGONY. END.

"Just when you thought you had everything figured out," Neruda whispered to
himself. "David, I'll put together some decipherment strategies and send them to
you tomorrow morning around 1100 hours. For now, let's call it a night."
"Agreed," David replied. "Signing off, then. Have a good night."
"You, too."
Neruda electronically pasted the analyses from ZEMI to his personal, knowledge-
management system, and then tidied up the office area, knowing that Fifteen might
wander by in the morning before he got in.
He picked up a section of the text—presumably the first section, which he
assumed was a good place to start the deciphering process. He packed the 341 pages
of alien script into his briefcase, waved at the security camera, and turned off the
lights. His legs ached from sitting all day and it felt good to be walking, even in the
sterile corridors of the lab.

*   *   *   *

Monday morning Neruda was preparing for his briefing meeting with Fifteen. A
knock on his door distracted him.
"Yes?" he said.
The door swung open and Donavin invited himself in. "I can see you were

expecting someone else."

"Actually, I wasn't expecting anyone at this hour," Neruda said. "What can I do for you?"

"I was hoping you'd return my questionnaire," he replied. "Completed of course."

Neruda motioned him to a chair. "Can I get you anything to drink? Some coffee or a soda?"

"Coffee would be good," Donavin answered, his voice warming a bit.

Neruda opened his thermos and poured a cup of coffee into a Styrofoam cup, handing it to Donavin. "I tend to make my morning java a little strong. My apologies."

"Don't worry," Donavin said, "I could use a good jolt this morning." He took a sip and winced. "I see what you mean. Yikes, how do you stand it?"

"Years of practice. And growing up Bolivian," Neruda said, smiling. "How's your project progressing so far?"

"Great, except for one thing. No one's ever around to talk with," Donavin lamented. "Don't you guys ever just sit and chew the fat?"

"We're understaffed, Mr. McAlester—"

"Please, call me Donavin," he interrupted.

"As you wish. But we are," Neruda continued, "we're terribly understaffed and have no time for the pleasantries of a normal office environment. Unfortunately, this must appear to you as if we're avoiding you, but I assure you, we're not. It's just a question of priority."

"Isn't everything," Donavin said, more as a statement than a question.

Neruda smiled. "You want your questionnaire, and you want it today. Right?"

Donavin smiled in return, nodding.

Neruda unlocked a drawer in his desk and pulled out a file folder. "Here's your questionnaire, completely filled out."

Donavin couldn't hide his amazement. "Thanks. I'm a little surprised." He thumbed through the pages quickly, noticing the level of detail in the answers. "This looks great."

"Was there anything else?" Neruda inquired.

"No, no, I think that was the main thing," he said. "Can I take a look at this and get back to you later, just in case something isn't clear to me?"

"Of course."

"Great," Donavin said standing to his feet and taking one last sip of coffee. "But next time, the coffee's on me."

Donavin stopped. "By the way, is Evans back in the office today?"

"I believe so," Neruda said.

"He's harder to catch then you are," Donavin said, closing the door behind him.

Neruda smiled to himself, knowing his responses to the questionnaire would undoubtedly fester in Donavin's mind, and a return visit was certain.

✳   ✳   ✳   ✳

"You've seen these?" Li-Ching said as she placed the transcripts on Fifteen's desk, his office door clicking shut behind her.

"One of the perks of having complete access to ZEMI and the knowledge network," he replied. "Why, is there something wrong?"

"You know I'm just playing with him," she said.

"Naturally."

"He means absolutely nothing to me," Li-Ching said, "I'm just trying to keep him preoccupied with the travails of an office romance. You even suggested it, remember?"

"Do I detect guilt," Fifteen said. "Or are you angry that I take an interest in your affairs?"

"Neither!" she said. "I don't like the insinuation that I'm doing this for any other reason than to protect you!"

Fifteen leaned back in his chair and removed his reading glasses. His desk was scattered with a variety of newspapers including The New York Times, London Times, and The Wall Street Journal. Dressed in a navy blue suit with a satin, white pinpoint shirt, and yellow tie with pastel accent colors, his normally commanding presence was amplified.

"Let's both calm down," he said. "I haven't accused you of anything, nor, as best I can tell, have you done anything worthy of an accusation. Let's start with these assumptions."

He started to clear his desk of the newspapers, stacking them as if he had just noticed the untidy state of his office.

Li-Ching sat down and crossed her legs and then her arms. Her lips were pursed as if she were holding back a torrent of expletives.

"Good, now that we've both calmed down," Fifteen said, "let's try to sort this out. You're angry because I reviewed the transcripts of Donavin's recent… exploits—"

"No! I'm mad because you insinuate that I've chosen this course of action because I have real feelings for him. And you damn well know that I don't."

"And how have I insinuated any such thing?"

"You reviewed the PM transcripts using keywords that clearly indicate a lack of trust."

"And how do you know this?"

"I'm the Director of Communication, have you forgotten?"

Fifteen made a mental note to delete the digital signature requirement to review PM transcripts via key word search. At least for him. "Okay, let's assume what you say is true—"

"No, let's admit that it is."

"Okay, I admit that I reviewed the transcripts, and yes, I did use key words that could be construed as untrusting. But in my defense, I'm not comfortable with Donavin. He could be more troublesome than we think."

"I love the way you can rationalize your irrational actions," she said. "You're not worried about Donavin any more than I am. You just want to spy on me to make sure that I'm not swept away by his rugged good looks and obvious physical charms."

"You find him physically attractive?"

"That's not the point!" Li-Ching said, almost screaming.

"Then what is the point?"

"Your lack of trust in my judgment," she said, softening her voice.

He stood from his chair and sat down next to Li-Ching, putting his arm around her shoulder. "My trust in you has never diminished, it's Donavin I don't trust." He raised his hand to his lips as Li-Ching started to speak, silencing her. "And it's not a rationalization. It's just that I care deeply about you and want to make sure that you're okay."

Li-Ching's pupils were like black holes absorbing light. "That's all this is?" she finally managed to ask. "You want me to believe that that's all this is about?"

"Yes," Fifteen replied.

"You trust me completely? Even if I choose to continue this trumped up affair with Donavin?"

"Yes."

"And do you want me to continue to seduce him and then push him away?"

"If that's what you want," Fifteen said. "It's probably the best way to keep him distracted. I know it'd work on me."

"You want to be distracted?" she said, her tone seductive.

"I already am."

"Good."

They began to kiss one another passionately just as a knock on the door interrupted. "Who is it?" Fifteen asked curtly.

"It's Jamisson," said the muffled voice from behind the door. "We had a meeting scheduled."

"One moment," Fifteen shouted, standing to his feet. He lowered his voice and turned to Li-Ching. "If you like, you can stay and hear his report."

"That's okay, I saw your e-mail this morning. Sounds like we have a whole new project on our hands. Are you going to leave Neruda in charge of it?"

"For now," Fifteen answered. "He's doing an exemplary job."

"You know that Whitman wants this project under him in the worst way. Expect to be lobbied hard, especially now that we've opened up the disc."

"Let's just hope we didn't open Pandora's Box," Fifteen said as he escorted her to the door. With his hand on the doorknob, he kissed her again.

As she pulled away, her thumb wiped across his bottom lip. "Are you too busy tonight with Echelon, or can you spare some time with me? I'll be home all night. Alone."

"Alone? I hardly think so," Fifteen whispered.

✳   ✳   ✳   ✳

"How'd your briefing go with Fifteen?" Emily asked.

"It went well," Neruda answered, joining Emily, Andrews, Samantha, and Collin in the Hylo Conference Room for their ritual project meeting. David was also present—on the monitor screen—tethered as always to ZEMI.

"Any changes to plan?" Emily asked.

"The good news, is that he's very impressed with our progress," Neruda said, pouring himself a glass of water. "A sign that he trusts our team's resourcefulness."

"And the bad news?" Andrews said.

"He changed the security level of the project to SL-Twelve."

"Shit," Andrews exclaimed. "So you and David get all the fun and glory."

"Why?" Samantha asked. "Why'd he decide this?"

"Let me finish my explanation," Neruda said, trying his best to look optimistic. "Everyone will be amply rewarded for their work to date, which will include a fifty-thousand-dollar bonus, and a promotion, one level up, Samantha being the only exception since she's already received her promotion.

"Fifteen's also granted that each of you can take next week off so you have an opportunity to spend and enjoy your bonus."

"That's great," Samantha said, "but what happened that required us to be pulled off the project?"

"He can't tell us," Andrews interrupted. "Give it up. It's time to take the money and run, unless you wanna visit the MRP lab."

Neruda sat down. He was dressed in khaki pants and a denim shirt with the sleeves rolled up just beneath his elbows. He looked well rested, but a little jittery—a combination of the caffeine and having to deliver bad news to his project team. He raked his hand through his straight, black hair. "I know you're disappointed. So am I, but Fifteen feels very strongly that this is in the best interests of the ACIO and each of you individually."

"Now what?" Emily asked.

"You'll each get new assignments after you return from your vacation," Neruda said.

"And in the meantime?" Collin asked.

"In the meantime, you'll be involved in organizing the existing database for the project."

"Geez, it looks like I finally got my wish," Andrews said. "A nine-to-five job."

"You mean semi-retirement," Collin chimed in.

"It's not so bad," Neruda said. "You'll have some downtime, relax. It's not the worst thing that could happen."

"Are we going to have to undergo MRP regarding our involvement to date?" Emily said.

"No MRP will be required," Neruda replied.

Relief could be seen on the faces of the team.

"Your bonus was transferred to your accounts this morning," Neruda said. "I'm sorry the four of you can't remain on the project. I'm truly sorry. Li-Ching and Evans will handle security dispositions. They've scheduled a meeting at 1400 hours in the Literati Room. Should only take an hour, afterwards you can take the rest of the day off and get your heads clear. Any other questions?"

"Will we get updates on the project?"

"According to your security level, yes, you'll get weekly updates."

A knock on the door startled the group, and Fifteen entered with a grave, but friendly look on his face. "I'm sorry to interrupt," he said, "but I wanted to convey my appreciation for your hard work on this project, and extend my personal thanks for all your contributions."

Everyone smiled in return of his praise.

"One thing you can all be assured of is that the directors and I will do everything in our power to provide you with rewarding assignments when you return from your vacations. We have several exciting projects that are ready to commence, and you can be involved at the ground level."

He stopped, looked around the table, assessing each person individually. "I hope you enjoy your well-earned break and return rested and ready for a new project."

Neruda wanted to read Fifteen's eyes, but he was too self-conscious to look. Instead, he kept his eyes focused on his hands before him on the table. He was anxious for Fifteen to leave. "Thank you for stopping by, sir."

A chorus of thanks joined Neruda's, and Fifteen left without another word.

"If there're no further questions, I think we're adjourned here," Neruda said, standing to his feet. "Oh, David, if you could stay a while, I have a few things I need to go over with you."

"No problem," David replied.

The rest of the team picked up their papers and notebooks and filed out of the conference room. The mood was mixed, half-elated and half-depressed. No one wanted off the project, but they understood that Fifteen must have reasons. Good reasons. Everyone within the ACIO respected his intellect and judgment.

Neruda waited for the door to close shut. "David, I have some decipherment strategies that Fifteen and I talked about this morning. I'd like you to try these this afternoon if you can and let me know what you find. Okay?"

"Okay."

"First, let's take their numbering system and apply it across all the text—"

"Actually," David said, "we did that this morning already."

"Good. What's the numeric density across all the text?"

"Fractional, if you want an exact number, I can get it for you in a moment—"

"No, it's okay," Neruda said, "I'm actually more interested in applying the chamber and ETC-site glyphs to the text. I know the master symbols aren't replicated, but what about the others? Have you done any analysis yet in this area?"

"No."

"Let's get that done. Also, several of the technology artifacts have glyphs on their body—including the homing device that blew up. All these glyphs are recorded in file number AAP-787990A. I'd like ZEMI to include these in the analysis."

"Understood," David replied. "Anything else?"

"We have a parent-language archive in the morphology database, file number AAP-1290B. I'd like an exhaustive, comparative analysis performed against this database. Use a ten-percent variant margin to sort matches."

"Understood."

"One last thing," Neruda said. "I was looking through the first section of the text last night. Have you made a note of the digital artifacts that came off the printer?"

"Yes, they're very odd."

"Are they actually artifacts or a separate language structure?" Neruda asked.

"We did our standard quality tests on other printers and replicated the results precisely every time. They're not, technically speaking, digital artifacts, though they sure look like it.

"What does ZEMI make of it?"

"We think it's a different language structure."

"Mathematics?" Neruda asked.

"We have no way of knowing at this time. Mathematics, music, and geometry are at the top of our list, but it's impossible to be any more definitive."

"We need to include these in our language analysis process. The morphology database includes abbreviated music and mathematics tables. I trust that you can locate them."

"We already did," David said with a not too subtle grin on his face.

"Great," Neruda said. "That's all for now, David. Thanks for your help on this. Oh, and I assume you'll contact me as soon as you have the analysis. Any time estimates?"

"I'll have something for you this afternoon."

"Thanks."

"No problem," David said.

The monitor screen returned to its normal, blackish-green color, and Neruda suddenly felt very alone in the conference room. He gathered his papers and tidied up the room a bit.

As he left the conference room, he steered a course by Fifteen's office, hoping that the sunroom wasn't being used for a private meeting. He needed to fill his eyes with the sights of something natural, something curved by the hand of a creator he was all too anxious to find.

∗   ∗   ∗   ∗

"Why are you whispering?" Samantha asked softly.

"It's prudent," Neruda said. "We can take my car, and then I'll drop you off later."

"Okay, but I could follow you if you'd prefer."

"No, that's all right, I'd prefer to go in the same car so we can talk," Neruda replied. "Evans will know anyway."

Neruda and Samantha pushed through the double doors after waving goodnight to the security guards. It was early evening, and Neruda had a dull headache that didn't seem to want to go away. Samantha had left him an urgent voice message earlier in the day, but he had been too busy to meet with her. The comparative analysis had come in from ZEMI, and the data had consumed his entire afternoon and part of his evening as well.

What had troubled him about the message was her tone of voice and the fact that she had found a document that used the term, *Central Race*.

They got into his Honda sedan, feeling oddly conspicuous as they drove through the security gate at the front entrance. An elderly guard named Curtis waved them on from his glass booth, but not before carefully scrutinizing Neruda's passenger. Neruda had known Curtis for almost twenty years, but trust didn't come easy for Evans' security team, who were carefully cultivated to be paranoid. In the worst way.

Once they got past the final security check—a dozen, secret video cameras installed inside a metal arch that overhung the entrance to the compound—Neruda visibly relaxed. "So what's the document you found?"

"I've had an MRP, haven't I?" she stated, ignoring his question.

Neruda took a quick glance at her face and then returned his attention to the road. He hated to lie. "What makes you think you've had an MRP?"

"Please, just answer my question truthfully," she pleaded.

Samantha's red hair was accented by the red glow of the setting sun. She was dressed in a sleeveless, white cotton dress cut just below her knees, and trimmed in iridescent turquoise.

Neruda glanced regularly in his rearview mirror; his paranoia bubbling to the surface of his mind for reasons he couldn't pin down. He blamed it on his concentration, which was waning because of his headache and the ups and downs of the workday.

He forced himself to look relaxed and sound casual, preparing to answer her questions exactly how he had been trained. "If I answer your question... truthfully, I might compromise project security. It would be a blemish on both our records, and could require serious remedies."

He turned to look at her eyes to see what effect his words were having. Her eyes were closed.

"When I was recruited to this place," she said, "one of the things Branson assured me was that I'd never have to worry about anyone misusing or abusing my special abilities. Ethical dilemmas—should they ever arise—would be sorted out with my involvement and cooperation."

She opened her eyes and stared at Neruda. "Someone's lying to me. I was taken off of this project for reasons I don't fully understand," she paused, her hands trembling slightly. "I *know* I was given an MRP."

"What exactly leads you to that conclusion?" Neruda asked.

She sighed at his evasion. "This afternoon I was organizing some of my project notes. In the margins of my project book, I found scribbled—in my handwriting— the phrase; *it was the Central Race who were the creators of the seven ETC sites.*

Neruda felt an adrenaline shot to his gut. He mentally scrambled to recover. "Samantha, maybe you're just reacting to something you wrote as speculation—"

"Speculation?" she exclaimed. "I've never heard of the term Central Race, nor was I aware that there were *seven* ETC sites! How can this be speculation?"

Neruda remained silent, his eyes glued to the staccato white line that divided the gray, endless road.

"There's more," she said, her voice softening. "After reading this, I immediately had an image form in my mind of three beings. The image triggered something... fragments of an RV session that I had with you, Branson, and Fifteen. They're jumbled images to be sure, but I remember enough to know that I interacted with this race. Didn't I?"

Neruda was cornered. He suddenly turned off the two-lane county road onto a gravel road he'd never been on before.

"Where're we going?" Samantha asked, alarm showing in her voice.

"I need to get out of the car," he replied. "I need to feel the sky. I've been cooped up in the office too long."

She nodded with understanding.

Two miles down the gravel road, they came to a washed out gully where Neruda pulled the car over and turned the engine off. "Let's take a walk."

The air held the faint aroma of pine needles from some nearby trees, which hid them from the setting sun. They followed the dry riverbed as their walking path, the setting sun at their back.

Neruda kept his eyes straight ahead, glancing occasionally to the sky in search of emerging stars in the growing twilight. Venus was already casting her silver charms.

"What I said before," Neruda admitted, "wasn't exactly the truth, but I... no, we, have a real dilemma." He stooped to pick up a stone that had caught his eye, tossing it back down after a quick look. "You've stumbled upon the very thing that caused you to have an MRP and be removed from the project."

"What's so secretive about the Central Race or the fact that there're seven ETC sites?" she asked.

Neruda stopped. "I'm not sure how to answer you, Samantha. There's a part of me that sympathizes with you, and wants to tell you everything. But there's also this rational side of me that knows protocol and knows I should follow it."

"And what is protocol in this situation?"

Neruda knew he was talking with the best RV within the ACIO, perhaps since RVs were first used twenty-two years ago. He either had to openly bullshit his way through the situation, or tell the truth. He chose the latter. An indelible instinct from somewhere deep inside told him to protect his credibility. "I'm supposed to sympathize with you, while at the same time deny your claim based on the probable implausibility of the given situation."

"Sounds like something Evans would write," Samantha said, her quiet sarcasm belying her feeling of total helplessness.

Neruda chuckled to himself, glad that for the first time in a long while he was following his instincts and not his training.

"So who's the Central Race and why's their identity so protected by Fifteen?" Samantha asked.

"I know you want to know, but you need to be clear about the consequence of this knowledge."

"Which is?"

"Fifteen has ordered that no one under SL-Twelve know of the Central Race and its creation of the seven ETC sites. If you have this information, you'll be subject to another MRP, and this time he'll probably be inclined to extract your memory of the entire project. I can't, in good conscience, let you have this knowledge and not tell Fifteen."

"I understand," Samantha said, "but maybe we could convince Fifteen that I'm an asset to the project instead of a liability."

"We could try," Neruda said. "But I have to tell you, Samantha, it's a slim possibility that he could be convinced of such a thing unless we had a watertight rationale. Do you have something in mind?"

"I don't know enough of the story," Samantha replied. "Tell me."

"Are you willing to risk a radical memory replacement of eighteen days?"

"It's my only real option… I mean… I *have* to know. It's just the way I'm wired," she said.

"You're quite certain?"

"I'm quite certain," she said, her voice firm.

"This procedure can have residual effects ranging from mild paranoia to fugal depression, which are usually temporary, but can last for months, even years in some sensitive types."

"And you're implying I'm a sensitive type, aren't you?" Samantha said with a hint of bitterness.

"I just want to make sure that you're aware of the consequences of what you're asking." He quickly glanced back at his car. His paranoia was as high as it had been for nearly a decade. "Right now, this very instant, it's quite probable that Evans or Jenkins are aware that we're having this meeting out in the middle of nowhere. Given who you are and the fact that you underwent an MRP yesterday, they'd assume that we're discussing your situation. I'll have to file a report in the morning and you'll fall under Fifteen's scrutiny."

"If you're trying to make me nervous," Samantha said, "you're succeeding in spades."

Neruda saw a large rock outcropping. "Let's sit down over there so we can talk."

They walked to a group of stones that looked like bones of earth bleached white from the desert sun, and sat on opposing boulders, the size of small cars. Neruda faced the final remnants of the setting sun, his dark skin saturated in the blood-red glow that bathed the western sky.

"You know this is an all-or-nothing situation?"

"Yes."

"I tell you all, and if Fifteen decides you retain nothing, you willingly submit to a radical MRP." Neruda paused, looking deep into her eyes. "I have your word?"

"You have my word."

"Okay," he said, shifting his legs to find a more comfortable position. He took a deep breath. "We've had two RV sessions within the last week. In both instances, you were probed by representatives of the Central Race."

Samantha began to interrupt, but Neruda held up his hand to silence her. "The Central Race is the most ancient of all races, their evolutionary timeline being something on the order of twelve billion years. They're considered by the Corteum to be the Creator Gods of all beings in the universe—"

"They're our gods?" her voice quivered.

"No one knows exactly who they are," he replied. "There're a few ancient scripts that refer to them. The Sumerian, Mayan, and Dogon cultures all had interactions with these beings that were recorded. We have the original texts in our database, and there're a few contemporary, channeled manuscripts that refer to them as well.

"But the Central Race has never been described in detail because no one really understands their unique consciousness, way of life, and culture, except presumably *their* creator. They are truly mythic beings. And, yes, they are, according to the Corteum, our gods—at least as it pertains to our physical bodies and minds."

"So what happened to God? *The* God?" Samantha asked.

"The Central Race was created by God as the original humanoid soul carriers. They could be likened to the first version of humanity, who ultimately evolved into the elder race that engineered and refined the DNA of higher life forms or soul carriers. God endowed a fragment of itself into this genetically engineered soul carrier or what we call the physical body; so, you could say it was a joint venture between God and the Central Race. Again, this is according to the Corteum, who seem to have more insight into this race than any other source that we've found."

"Okay, for the moment," she said, "I'll go along with you as to the identity of the Central Race, but why is it such a big problem that I know about this?"

"I'm only relating the background story," Neruda replied. "The real issue is that the Central Race created the ETC sites, which *are* seven in number, to defend the planet against an ancient enemy of theirs that's prophesied to visit earth in 2011 and take it over."

"You mean literally?"

"Yes."

"Okay, I'm still with you," she said. "When do we get to the part that I shouldn't know about? Because I've heard about a dozen doom and gloom prophecies for the turn of the millennium."

Neruda smiled. "Globally, there's not a lot of attention paid to these prophecies of Armageddon and the rise of the Antichrist. The real story's a little too graphic and frightening to convey to the public, but watered down versions are allowed to circulate. And with them the persistent belief that religious prophesy has no real relevance or bearing in today's society."

He paused and swallowed hard. "But the prophecies that we have access to convey a tragic and overwhelming takeover of Earth by a race of synthetic beings from outside our galaxy. We now have confirmation from the ETC site that this galaxy is M51, some thirty-seven million light years away."

"How's that possible?" Samantha asked. "I mean, even traveling at the speed of light, it'd take them thirty-seven million years to get here."

"They're synthetics from an ancient race of beings, not associated with our human genotype," he said. "That's all we know. Even the Corteum haven't encountered them nor anyone who ever has."

"Have we RV'd them?"

"Yes, many times."

"And?"

"I can't tell you," Neruda replied. "But Fifteen's convinced the threat is real and that they have the technology to travel inter-galactically."

"You said you'd tell me all," she reminded him.

"You shouldn't take me literally. I only meant I'd tell you all of what you need to know relative to the Central Race and why you were taken off the project and subjected to an MRP."

Her face wrinkled in frustration.

The sun was now completely below the horizon, and the stars were visible, their pinpricks of light, poignant reminders of the universe's enormous scale.

Samantha tucked her legs under her. She felt a little light-headed, as if she had just come out of a RV session. "So the Antichrist is a synthetic, soulless race from some other galaxy?"

"Yes."

Samantha shook her head from side-to-side and stared at the ground. She had wrapped her arms around her to fend off the chill that suddenly possessed her. Her hands were cold and she blew on them—her warm breath reminding her of her humanity.

"Okay, so back to my problem," she said. "Why was I taken off the project and given an MRP?"

"Fifteen felt that you had been probed by the Central Race, and he doesn't want them to know about our capabilities and objectives relative to the defense of the planet."

"You're telling me that the ACIO has a weapon to guard the planet against these... these synthetic aliens?"

"It's developing such a weapon or defensive system."

"What is it?"

"Again, I can't tell you," Neruda answered, aware of Samantha's building frustration.

"Shit," she whispered under her breath. "Can you at least answer my questions with a yes or no?"

"I'll try."

She closed her eyes for a moment, sorting through the order of her questions. "The Central Race designed seven ETC sites and installed them on earth sometime in our distant past?"

"Yes."

"And they intended these sites to be an integrated force to protect our planet?"

"Yes."

"Earth is important to them because we have human DNA that is unique... or... or perhaps highly valued for some reason?"

"We're not sure, but we think it has something to do with genetics. In one of your RV sessions, you referred to the Earth as a genetic reference library for this sector of our galaxy. We assume they're protecting these libraries by installing a planetary defensive weapon."

"So this weapon conflicts with the weapon that the ACIO is developing?"

"We don't know," Neruda said.

"But it might?"

"Yes."

She stopped and gathered her thoughts. "Representatives from the Central Race detected my presence during an RV session and probed me?"

"Yes."

"Fifteen fears that they'll find out about our weapon... that they're in a position to prevent us from using it?"

"Something like that," he replied.

"That's it! That's it, isn't it?" she exclaimed. "Fifteen doesn't want any of us below SL-Twelve or Thirteen to know of the Central Race and the fact that they've installed a defensive weapon on earth that competes with our own. Right?"

Neruda looked away and sighed.

"Right?" she asked again.

"That's part of it."

"And," she continued like Sherlock Holmes, "he doesn't want us to have any further RV sessions because he's afraid that the Central Race has the capability to intervene in the deployment of our own weapon."

"I'm not sure that I'd use the word afraid. I've never known Fifteen to be fearful. I think he's more concerned that the Central Race wouldn't like our choice of weaponry."

"Why?"

"I can't tell you."

"Because our weapon is so powerful that it could destroy the planet?" she asked.

"In a manner of speaking, but it's a completely defensive weapon as Fifteen envisions it."

"Shit," she said in a whispered voice.

Samantha stood to stretch her legs and arms. Her head arched back to look at the sky. "I'm in over my head," she said.

"Maybe we all are," Neruda said. "We're not infallible in our approach, Samantha, but the ACIO has the best technology on the planet and is quite literally the only organization with knowledge of the 2011 invasion. If anyone is to stop this takeover, it will be us."

"I'd put my dollars on the Central Race, if they are who you say they are. How could we hope to have a more advanced defensive technology than the beings that… that created us?"

"It's not that our technology is more advanced than what the Central Race has because we assume they have this capability as well. It's that the Central Race, at least in Fifteen's opinion, wouldn't place this technology on the planet to be discovered by humans, especially if their ancient enemy could somehow secure it."

"Then wouldn't it make sense that they'd do this for a good reason?"

"No," Neruda replied. "It's assumed that they'd restrict the use of this technology without knowing that the ACIO is in a position to properly utilize it and secure it."

"So, we have this weapon at our disposal right now?"

"No."

She stopped, and sat back down. "Everything you've told me is all based on assumption. For all you know, the seven ETC sites are exactly what we're trying to build. And for all you know, the Central Race would protect its genetic library with its best defensive weapon."

"Samantha, you must know that I can't tell you all the reasons for our assumptions," Neruda said. "Believe me, we arrived at these conclusions by a thorough analysis given the available information."

"Then why doesn't Fifteen desire to interact with the Central Race? What's he afraid of? That they'll dismantle his incomplete and unproven technology?"

"Fifteen is a visionary far beyond what the world has ever seen before," Neruda confided. "He was planning this technology before you were born. When most kids are worried about pimples, he was designing the blueprints of this system. At the time, he didn't know anything about this impending alien invasion. He simply wanted to create this vision… to re-create time—"

Neruda stopped in mid-sentence, aware that he had said too much.

"So that's what this technology is about." Samantha interrupted. "Time travel."

"I can't tell you."

"Why? I'm going to have this memory cleared anyway," she argued.

"I've said enough."

"Great! Now what do we do? I'm caught in the crossfire of the ACIO's secret weapon and the Central Race. How do I save myself? How do I convince Fifteen to spare my memory?"

The desert was morphing from heat to cold, light to dark, and sound to silence. As they paused momentarily, Neruda could hear the muffled and somewhat annoying ring of his cell phone in his car. Apart from that, silence honored the light jewels of the deep, blue-violet sky. Samantha shivered in the evening chill, standing with her back to him as if she were absorbed in the sanctity of something unobservable.

"Maybe we should be getting back," he said.

"You have no ideas?" she pleaded, her voice struggling to find its normal tone.

"My mind is perfectly empty in this regard."

Samantha nodded faintly, her eyes staring deep inside herself.

Neruda admired her more than he ever expected. He had never been that fond of RVs. They spooked him. Maybe his Mayan roots made him fear anything that seemed like magic or sorcery. But he could see that Samantha was authentic and vulnerable at the same time, traits he was attracted to, and this attraction wasn't easy to suppress. He felt a strong moral obligation to help, but he felt equally powerless to protect her. In fact, he may have signed her expulsion papers, if not her death warrant.

"What do you think I should do?"

"I think we should go," he answered. "Let's meet again in the morning—before work—at this very same spot. 0700 hours. Maybe with fresh minds, we'll be able to come up with something."

"I'll bring the coffee," she offered.

"You're from the Midwest, aren't you?"

"Yeah."

"I'll bring the coffee," he smiled. "You bring the pastries. Deal?"

"Deal."

They walked the hundred meters back to Neruda's car and rode back to the compound in silence. They were both tired, and their minds reeled from the decision that awaited them only ten hours away.

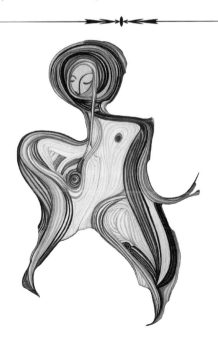

CHAPTER 14
REMINDERS

When a species in the three-dimensional universe discovers irrefutable scientific proof of the multiverse and the innermost topology of the Wholeness Navigator, it impacts on every aspect of the species. It is the most profound shift of consciousness that can be foretold, and it is this event that triggers the Return of the Masters to explicit influence and exoteric roles.

An Excerpt from *Beliefs and Their Energy Systems*, Chamber Four
WingMakers

Evans opened his front door, startled to see Jenkins. "This better be good," he said as he walked away, leaving the door open and Jenkins standing at its threshold. "Yes, you can come in," Evans said over his shoulder.

Jenkins was a tall man, with a lanky build and wiry muscles that seemed ready to snap like a bear trap. He was widely regarded within the ACIO as the heir apparent to Evans, and for good reason. He was extremely competent. His dark eyes always seemed to be searching for clues to a person's weakness or vulnerabilities, a trait that endeared him to Evans.

"I thought you should be aware of something. Can you open up PV?"

PV, or PansoVision, was the Security department's internal network, and was only accessible to SL-Twelve personnel through permission from both Evans and Fifteen. The only ACIO personnel who could use the system were the seven directors, Jenkins, and Fifteen.

"It's open, it's just on standby mode," Evans replied. He was in his robe, barefoot, and his hair was slicked back. "Can I get you anything?" he offered as he walked into his kitchen.

"No thanks," Jenkins replied. "I just wanted you to see this." Jenkins brought PV to operational mode and with a few keystrokes the monitor displayed a video picture of Neruda's profile in the driver's seat, next to him was Samantha. He clicked a button and freeze-framed the image. In the lower right corner was a date and time stamp.

Evans walked into the living room with a glass of white wine. "Are you sure?" he asked, lifting his glass.

"No, really, I'm fine, thanks," Jenkins answered.

"So what do we have here?" Evans asked, looking at the monitor for the first time.

"An anomaly," Jenkins said. "Neruda and Samantha Folten left the office together a little past 1900 hours and drove to this site. A detailed photograph replaced the image of Neruda and Samantha. In the lower right corner was the phrase, *Archived EITS Photograph 091092: 1721 PST.*

"EITS was out of range?" Evans asked.

"Yes, by only twenty minutes," Jenkins replied. "He accessed our scheduling charts."

"Or got lucky," Evans remarked.

Jenkins hit a key and two red lines of code could be seen overlaying the satellite map. "They stopped here and talked for twelve minutes."

"Romance?" Evans asked.

"Can't say for sure, but the terrain was rocky and it was only twelve minutes."

"Not a very likely location for a lovers' tryst, then," Evans said with a grin.

"Samantha had an MRP yesterday per Fifteen's order," Jenkins said. "Since she's an RV, she may have had some memory bleed."

"What's the time-mark on their return?"

Jenkins hit a few keys and an image with Neruda and Samantha in the car displayed on the monitor, returning to the ACIO compound. "They were gone forty-two minutes."

"Current status?" Evans asked.

"They're both in their respective homes."

"Okay, we'll see what he does tomorrow," Evans said. "He knows we know. He's too smart."

"Do you want me to forward anything to Fifteen?" Jenkins asked.

"No, I'll handle it myself. I'm glad you brought it to my attention though. Keep me informed if there's any change. Let's switch to Theca Five for the next forty-eight hours, and watch these two as carefully as we can. He'll probably file a report in the morning and no harm done, but I want to make sure he knows we've turned up the heat, so let's leave no doubt."

"Her, too?"

"She wouldn't know the difference," Evans said.

"But she's an RV."

"Shit, I don't care, Jenkins. I was just trying to save you the time and effort. If you want to fuck with her head, too, be my guest."

"Okay, I'll be on my way," Jenkins said.

"Thanks, again."

"You bet. Goodnight, then."

Jenkins left the image of Neruda and Samantha—frozen in time like Bonnie and Clyde—on the monitor. Evans took one last look before putting his system on standby. He toasted his glass of wine, looking at the monitor screen. "Don't blow it, man. We need you clean."

✳   ✳   ✳   ✳

Samantha heard his footsteps before she saw him. Her heart jumped as he scaled the rock. "You scared the hell out of me!" she exclaimed.

"Sorry," Neruda said, holding up his coffee thermos and two Styrofoam cups. "I wasn't trying to scare you."

"It's okay, I'm just a little wound up."

"Under these circumstances," Neruda said, "you'd have to be tranquilized not to be wound up. My morning brew should relax your jangled nerves."

"I've heard about your morning brew," she laughed. "Does it really come out in lumps?"

"Rumors. Only rumors," he grinned, sitting down next to her.

"Did you notice anything unusual last night when you got home?" Samantha asked, her tone serious and soft.

"Like?"

"Like my phone has a carrier signal now, and my home terminal has a different hum that pulses almost imperceptibly, but I can feel it.

"They've placed us both in Theca Five," Neruda answered matter-of-factly.

"Which is?"

"They know we met yesterday and they want me to know they know. It's their not-so-subtle way of saying either you come forward and report what you know, or we'll assume your loyalty and intelligence are compromised to such a degree that you're no longer useful to our purposes. Something like that."

"How can you manage to joke about this?"

"I'm not joking," Neruda corrected her. "I'm lightening the situation so it's easier to cope." He flashed his smile.

"So they're watching us right now?"

"No. I checked the Eye-in-the-Sky schedule before we met yesterday. We have," he glanced at his watch, "about forty minutes, but to be safe, I'd prefer to be out of here in thirty."

Samantha stared at him. "There's no privacy, is there?"

"You're an RV," Neruda laughed. "You of all people should know that."

"RVs are never used against ACIO personnel," Samantha said.

"True, but every other technology we have is, particularly if the personnel in question are meeting out in the desert the day after an MRP session."

"Have you talked with Evans or anyone yet?" she asked.

"Don't need to," he replied. "They have exception algorithms that monitor our Body Prints and report any anomalous activity like this." His arms stretched out like a priest in communion with the Holy Spirit.

Samantha relaxed her face and let out a long sigh. "Okay, I have an idea to get us both out of this situation." She paused, as if on some dramatic cue. "What if we did an RV session right now, at point of creation of their weapon system?"

Neruda remained silent, his eyes staring at his hands.

Samantha continued, taking his silence as a good sign. "If we could determine the nature of their defensive system, perhaps we could convince Fifteen that they could be allies and not foes."

Neruda rubbed the back of his neck. "I haven't even had my coffee yet. Can we wait a few minutes?"

"There's no time if we have to leave in less than thirty minutes!" she said with an intensity that surprised Neruda.

He stood, surveying the landscape. "I'd be guilty of insubordination. Insubordination of a direct order from Fifteen, I might add. It would only worsen our situation, or at least mine."

"I know it's risky, but without this, how else do we convince him I should stay on the project and keep my memory?"

"Do you have anything to eat in that thing or is it only your RePlay headgear?" Neruda said, pointing to a dark green shopping bag sitting at Samantha's feet.

"I do," she said.

"I'll take whatever you have that isn't RePlay. Please."

Samantha opened the bag, and pulled out a store-bought assortment of pastries, while Neruda opened his thermos and poured coffee.

"Two lumps or one," he asked.

"You're talking sugar aren't you?"

"Sugar?"

"Very funny," Samantha said, "but no lumps of either kind, thanks."

Neruda handed her a cup and they both settled into a quick breakfast. Samantha pointed to the sky with her free hand. "If Evans knows we're already here, why do we need to avoid detection from EITS?"

"The 'e' stands for more than eye," Neruda explained.

"You mean they can hear our conversation… thirty… forty… however many miles up the thing is?"

"When EITS launched in seventy-five, the technology wasn't available for audio transmission… that was added in ninety-one when the system was upgraded."

"They can hear our conversation?" she repeated softly.

"They can," he said.

"How?"

"Remember how you were required to have a security implant when you started?"

"Yes, but I thought these were for tracking purposes—"

"—That's their main purpose, but they also have the ability to transmit audio to EITS. It's one of the most sophisticated technologies in our entire arsenal. And it'll be used on us in some thirty minutes if we're not careful."

"But these things were placed in my neck—"

"They transmit voice resonance, which the computer enhances, and they're so good, they can eavesdrop on a whisper."

"Wish I knew sign language," Samantha lamented under her breath. "I assume that they don't tell personnel about this technology on purpose."

"Correct."

"So, what do you think about my plan?" she asked.

"It's too dangerous to disobey a direct order from Fifteen. But I know another way we could do it."

"What?"

"Our goal is to present the facts to Fifteen. He'd know any deception, so it's not an option to tell anything but the full and complete truth. The facts are that you've had significant memory bleed in the span of twenty-four hours following your MRP. Obviously it wasn't successful. The memories were too powerful."

Samantha nodded while Neruda paused to take a bite of his pastry.

"The problem," he continued, "is that you're the only one who's seen these beings and communicated with them. You were the one who guided the original exploration team to the site. You're somehow connected into their frequency."

"Okay," Samantha asked, "so you're suggesting that I represent myself as a liaison to the Central Race?"

"Sort of," he replied. "We don't know if any other RV can make contact with this race. You've been the sole contact thus far. Perhaps we can convince Fifteen that your memory shouldn't undergo a radical MRP until we've made sure that a different RV can make the same connection. This would buy us time and provide a reason for your continued involvement in the project."

"You're saying that Fifteen will want to retain the option of contact with the Central Race in order to find out certain things in the future?"

"Correct," he replied. "When we first heard about the Central Race from the Corteum, Branson conducted several experiments to see if contact could be made, but nothing worked."

"Give me an example of something he might want to investigate in the future?" she asked.

"We have strong reasons to assume that the seven ETC sites are linked together through some means. We also know that there was only one homing beacon, which has since self-destructed, so we really don't know how to get to the other sites. You could help us determine how to access the other six sites."

"Do you think he'll buy this approach?" Samantha asked.

"I don't know," Neruda said, taking his last bite of pastry. "But it's an honest approach to our dilemma. It's the best option I can think of."

"Okay, then. When do we confront him?"

"I think it's best if I talk with him alone," Neruda answered. "He'd be much more close-lipped if you were in the room. We need him to be candid; he might just come up with a better solution."

Samantha nodded and began to gather up the pastries and put things away. "One more thing before we go," she said. "If you were planning to report the truth to Fifteen all along, why'd you go out of your way to elude EITS?"

"It's intelligent to retain control of your options. Fifteen and Evans respect that. Perhaps more than anything else. You don't want to make a habit of displaying any weakness or error in judgment to either of them."

"I'll keep that in mind," Samantha said.

The two quickly packed up their belongings and walked to their cars. Samantha couldn't stop thinking about EITS coming into position overhead. She could almost feel its prying eyes and ears, and once she settled into her car and watched Neruda pull away, she yelled several times at the top of her lungs, "Screw your EITS!"

She immediately felt better.

＊　　＊　　＊　　＊

"Good morning, Jamisson," Fifteen said. "Are you looking for me?"

Neruda was on his way to Fifteen's office when he almost bumped into him as he turned a corner in the hallway. "Do you have a few minutes you could spare? It's important."

Fifteen motioned with his arm to his office door. "Of course. Go on in. I'll be right there."

Neruda sat down at a small conference table next to Fifteen's desk. The office had a way of making him feel vulnerable. It was so sparse that Neruda felt there was nowhere to hide, particularly when he had to deliver bad news.

The sound of the door closing startled him. Neruda turned to see Fifteen, Li-Ching, and Evans all joining him at the table. "We're all aware of your meeting with Samantha," Fifteen said. "We just want to hear your report. I invited Li-Ching and Evans so I don't have to repeat myself. Okay?"

Neruda nodded, though he'd have preferred to meet alone with Fifteen. He began to feel that his actions might have been a more serious breach of security and protocol than he had thought.

"As you know," Evans began, "We're aware of your actions of yesterday evening and again this morning. You're fully aware that these actions subvert protocol and—"

"Now, now," Fifteen interrupted. "We don't need to be so hard-nosed about this. I'm sure that Jamisson has an excellent reason for his behavior." Fifteen put his hands flat on the table, and paused. "What we have I'm sure is just a misunderstanding. You have the floor, Jamisson. We'll simply listen and ask questions."

Neruda looked with searching eyes to his colleagues, careful not to betray his nervousness. "I had every intention of telling you exactly what happened," he said, looking directly at Evans. "Samantha had some memory bleed. Her memories of the RV sessions were too powerful to suppress."

"What triggered it?" Li-Ching asked.

"She was organizing her project materials and found a notation—in her own handwriting—about the Central Race and the seven ETC sites."

Fifteen pulled on a console that he slid from underneath the table and pushed a button. "I want Branson in here as soon as possible."

"Yes, sir," came his assistant's voice.

Fifteen turned to Neruda, his eyes serious and sympathetic at the same time. "And what did Samantha want from you?"

"She wanted to know whether she had undergone an MRP," he replied. "And she wanted to know who the Central Race is."

"And you told her?" Fifteen inquired.

"Yes."

"Why?" Evans asked.

"Because she's the best RV we have, and my choices were to lie and alienate her, or speak truthfully and secure her trust. I chose the latter."

"What does she want?" Fifteen asked.

"She wants to remain on the project. She feels that her skills may prove valuable later on."

"And you agree with her?" Fifteen asked.

For the first time that morning, Neruda locked eyes with Fifteen. "We don't know if any of our SL-Twelve RVs can contact the Central Race and perform RV reconnaissance, which could prove vital to the project later on. Samantha, I'm convinced, has a special connection with this race."

Evans stirred. "Can you think of a reason we'd want to contact or observe the Central Race?"

"No, Jamisson is right," Fifteen interjected. "We don't know if anyone else could successfully make contact. We tried when the Corteum told us about their existence, and we had no success."

"But that was before we had any physical connection," Li-Ching said. "Samantha had the artifacts and ETC site. It's not a fair comparison."

"But that's the point," Neruda said. "She *has* had an advantage, and her advantage could be—sometime in the future—used to our advantage."

A knock on the door distracted them. Branson stepped into the office, slightly out of breath. "You wanted me?" he asked.

"Yes, come on in and join us," Fifteen said. "Samantha's MRP failed."

"In what way?" Branson asked as he sat down at the table next to Neruda.

"In every way," Fifteen replied.

"Shit," Branson said under his breath. "I'm not completely surprised."

"Let's assume that her memories can't be suppressed by MRP... that... that they're too powerful as Jamisson suggests," Fifteen said. "We have two options. We can perform a radical MRP and eliminate the entire project experience, or we can retain her services for the project and isolate her from sensitive information as best we can."

Fifteen glanced at Neruda out of the corner of his eye. "How much classified information did you provide her—in addition to information about the Central Race and the seven ETC sites?"

Neruda could tell that Fifteen sensed something. His voice tightened as he felt Fifteen's intuitive powers begin to reach inside his mind. "A little bit about EITS... I... I explained our rationale as to why we had to shut down her contact with the Central Race—"

"You told her about BST?" Fifteen asked, alarm showing in his voice.

"No, I didn't explain anything about BST, only that we had a defensive weapon... nothing more of consequence," Neruda answered defensively.

Evans couldn't restrain himself any further. "So now she knows about EITS and BST? We don't know how she'll handle this information. She's too wet behind the ears. I can't imagine how any payoff in this matter could outweigh the risks."

"She *is* the best RV we've ever had," Branson said. "The best. Jamisson couldn't have bullshit her any more than he could bullshit us. At least he managed to retain his credibility with her, which could prove more valuable to us than anything else, at least in dealing with Samantha."

Silence hung over the conference table for a few moments. Neruda kept his eyes cast on the tabletop, wishing the meeting were over, but knowing it may have just begun.

Li-Ching fidgeted with one of the buttons on her blouse. "Why can't we take her off the project and give her a radical MRP?"

"I think Jamisson is implying that we need her," Fifteen replied. "We need her RV skills to accelerate our understanding of the seven ETC sites and how they interrelate… assuming they do."

Evans turned to Branson. "Are you sure we couldn't make contact with the Central Race using one of our SL-Twelve RVs?"

"We didn't have any success in our last attempts eleven years ago, but then we didn't have any artifacts or materials to establish contact either. We might be able to now."

"All I was suggesting," Neruda interjected, "was that we retain Samantha on the project until we know whether she has a unique capability to contact and communicate with the creators of these sites."

"Are you suggesting the creators of these sites are not the Central Race?" Fifteen asked.

"No," Neruda replied. "But we really don't know who they are within the Central Race. I just think we should retain her skills and knowledge base until we've determined that we have a redundant, reconnaissance strategy and equally competent RV."

Fifteen sighed and turned to Branson. "Your succession plan for her is still seven years out. We don't want to do anything to jeopardize her leadership abilities. We want her to be a director. Given that, what's your recommendation?"

"She's retained on the project with full access to the SL-Twelve knowledge base—concerning Ancient Arrow only. She'll remain SL-Seven in all other respects."

"Evans?" Fifteen asked.

"I think the risks are too great to keep her on the project," Evans replied. "Any more contact with the Central Race, or any faction therein, could bring unwanted scrutiny to our own projects, particularly BST. I think a radical MRP and Theca-Five containment for a period of time… perhaps three months thereafter, is the best course of action."

Fifteen turned to Li-Ching. "And you?"

"In general, I agree with Evans," she answered. "The risks do seem to outweigh the rewards. However, I can also see the possible advantage of having an RV reconnaissance strategy that gives us the flexibility to probe the creators of these sites… who knows what we'll want to know in the future."

Fifteen leaned back in his chair, spread his fingers apart and put his hands together fingertip-to-fingertip. "First of all, we know the Central Race or some subset of the Central Race, created the ETC sites, of which we have good reason to believe there are seven in number. These beings can probe Samantha. This means that they may be able to access her entire memory structure, which means that if she knew about BST, they might be able to learn of our plans regarding BST.

"If we want only SL-Twelve personnel involved in this project, no RV reconnaissance can be performed. However, if we kept Samantha on the job, they could only probe to the level of SL-Seven, which may be an acceptable risk so long as she knows nothing about BST."

He turned to Neruda with an intensity that Neruda had only seen once before. "I will only ask this one more time, Jamisson. How much does she know about BST?"

"She knows we have a defensive weapon that the Central Race may not sanction. She's aware that the ACIO—at a high level—is engaged in protecting earth from the 2011 invasion… And she's aware that our weapon may have a connection to time travel."

"Nothing more?" Fifteen asked.

Neruda shook his head and looked down to his hands folded in his lap.

Fifteen took a deep breath and released it slowly. "She knows too much to be our RV. Any of our SL-Twelve RVs have the same dilemma—they know too much. These beings will probe any RV we use and they may very well, as a consequence, know our plans for BST. It's too dangerous to interact any further with representatives of this race. In this matter, I agree with Evans."

He paused long enough to shift positions in his chair; his back continued to bother him, despite the acupuncture that Li-Ching had prescribed. "However, I think that if we performed a radical MRP on Samantha, we would risk both her state of mind and possibly Branson's succession plan. If Samantha wants to stay on the project, I will grant her request, on one condition. She must refrain from any RV sessions with the Central Race."

Fifteen turned to Neruda. "You agree?"

"In what capacity would she operate if not as an RV?" Neruda asked, after nodding agreement.

"Whatever role she desires as long as it doesn't include RVing the Central Race… I don't really care." Fifteen looked to Branson. "We'll do as you say. She'll be permitted SL-Twelve access on the Ancient Arrow project and remain SL-Seven on everything else."

"Okay," Branson replied. "Effective?"

"Now," Fifteen said. "Evans, are you okay with this? I want your support, too."

"You have it," Evans answered, "but I'd like to keep her in Theca Five for another few weeks if you don't mind."

"Done," Fifteen said. "Anything else?"

Silence hung in the air long enough for Fifteen to call the meeting adjourned. "Jamisson, could you stay behind for just a few minutes?"

Neruda nodded and sat back down in his chair while the others filed out of Fifteen's office. At the sound of the closing door, Fifteen sat down, his face solemn. "You're thinking you made the right choice by opening up to Samantha, aren't you?"

"I'm not sure what I think," Neruda replied. "I *feel* like I did the right thing—"

"Rest assured that you did not," Fifteen asserted with finality.

Neruda's internal composure crumbled at the words, though his physical presence was unshaken. "In what way?" The question left his mouth before his mind could censor it.

Fifteen shrugged. "You know. You already know. I just wanted you to be sure that I also know. And if you ever take liberty, as you did in this case, with another subordinate, you will most certainly be without subordinates. Do I make myself clear, Jamisson?"

"Very clear, sir."

"Good."

"One question, though, if… if I may," Neruda said tentatively.

"Go ahead," Fifteen said.

"If we hit an impasse in decoding the material on the optical disc, or the other artifacts prove unyielding to our probes, doesn't it make sense that RV may be our only hope? And if that's true, isn't Samantha our best bet?"

Fifteen's face softened with an eloquent smile. "It's the only reason you weren't taken off the project. It's the silver lining in the breakdown of your behavior. We'll see if your actions pay off in the future, but in the present, they unequivocally do not."

Fifteen stood and looked down on Neruda. "That's all, for now." He walked away without another word, opening his office doors and walking out. Neruda slowly stood from his chair. He felt chilled to his bones, knowing that he'd come as close as he ever had before to being terminated from the ACIO.

He felt like he had betrayed his father, his hero and mentor, as well as his future.

CHAPTER 15

SEALED

Upon the merging of your will with that of First Source, you unconsciously participate with thousands of personality formats devoted to the Great Cause. It is the joined endeavor of all that you are with the perfect unfoldment of all that is and will ever be. It is the suggestive line of evidence that points to your purpose even before you can speak the words or feel the emotion of your gift, and it only requires you to desire the will of First Source to take ascendancy in your life.

An Excerpt from *Personal Purpose*, Chamber Seven

WingMakers

Neruda got to his office and found Samantha waiting in one of his desk-side chairs, her face a collision of worry and hope.

"How'd it go?" she asked, trying to sound calm.

"You're still on the project," he smiled, "but on the condition that we perform no RV with the Central Race."

"Fifteen ordered that?"

"Yes."

"What else?" Samantha asked.

"You need to talk with Branson," he replied. "I'm not sure there's much else I can tell you."

"You got in trouble, didn't you?"

"Yes."

"I'm sorry to have dragged you into this whole mess," she said. "Is there anything I can do?"

Neruda sat down at his desk and turned on a lamp, leaned back in his chair, and finally looked at Samantha. She was wearing white, cotton pants and a sky-blue blouse. Her red hair was tied up tightly behind her head.

"Just talk with Branson and stay away from the Central Race," Neruda replied. "That's all. You can do that, can't you?"

"Yes, but how will the others take this news?"

"Don't worry about them," Neruda answered. "Fifteen's decisions—though there're not always understood—are always respected."

"But will they hate me for being allowed back on the project?"

"No, of course not," Neruda answered. "You're an RV... a specialist. Everyone involved in this project knows that you had some special connection with the creators of the ETC site, so don't worry about it."

"Okay," she said softly. "So how do we know for sure that the Central Race created the ETC sites?"

Neruda could feel his mind being tossed on some inner wave. He felt an invisible tide pulling him farther and farther from the safety of shore. "Please trust me on this, just talk with Branson."

He took out a piece of paper from his notebook, and began writing.

> *You're in theca five for another two weeks. Can't discuss these matters with you—office bugged—they're listening. Sorry.*

He handed the note to Samantha, which she quickly read. A troubled expression came over her face as she recognized the grave situation she was in.

"Okay, then," she said. "I'll talk with Branson. Thanks for all your help."

"You're welcome."

Samantha stood. "I need to talk with you," she mouthed the words silently to Neruda.

Neruda shook his head. "I'll see you later, Samantha."

"Thanks again," she said.

She left his office frustrated at her loss of freedom, but gratified that she'd remain on the project and retain her memory, such as it was.

✳   ✳   ✳   ✳

A banging on his door woke him. Neruda checked his bedside clock, unsure if he was still dreaming or it was real. It was just after 1 a.m., and the alarm clock's luminescent dial assured him it was real. His intuition went on alert, trying to sense who it was.

He quickly put on his bathrobe and trudged downstairs to the front door, where he could see a shadowy figure waiting. "I hear you, Samantha," he hollered. "Just give me a few seconds to turn the security system off."

Neruda pushed a few buttons and then opened the door to the distraught face of Samantha. Her eyes were red from crying. "What's wrong?" he asked, inviting her in with his arm.

As if a damn broke, she wrapped her arms around him and began to cry. Neruda stood still and tried his best to comfort her, eyeing the street and neighborhood for any signs of onlookers. It seemed quiet and he felt safe, so he remained at the doorway, comforting her while she sobbed uncontrollably.

"Tell me what's wrong. Please."

"I'm sorry… I'm… I'm sorry to burst in on you… like this," she said, letting go of him and walking toward a chair in his living room. "Can I sit down for a minute?"

"Of course," he said. "Can I get you anything?"

"Maybe a Kleenex… or two."

"Sure, hold on a moment."

Neruda left for the kitchen and pulled several tissues from the dispenser and poured a glass of water. When he returned to the living room, Samantha was sitting in a chair, staring at the ceiling, tears streaming down her face.

"What's wrong?" Neruda asked as he handed her the tissues and placed a glass of water on the coffee table in front of her chair.

"Thanks," she said, blowing her nose. "I had a visitor tonight."

"Who?" Neruda asked, the news jolting him awake like a shot of caffeine.

"Before I tell you, is... is your home wired—I mean, can we talk?"

"Yes we can talk here. They already know you're here."

"Can EITS pick up on our conversation even inside your home?"

"It can pick up yours, not mine."

"You mean I have a different implant than you?" she asked.

"Mine was installed nineteen years ago, before we had the BP resonance broadcast technology."

"Once again, I'm the problem." Her face looked completely distressed. "So, they can only hear my side of the conversation?"

He nodded. "We're okay, Samantha, but if you don't mind, before you get started with your story, let me quickly change into some clothes and get some coffee on. Okay?"

"Yeah, that's fine. It'd give me some time to compose myself."

Neruda put some fresh coffee on and then changed into a pair of jeans, a white sweater, and quickly donned his Rolex. He splashed some cold water on his face and combed his hair. Five minutes later, he was serving coffee. "It's essentially decaf, so don't worry," he said, handing a cup to Samantha.

"*Essentially decaf?* You mean it's normal coffee, don't you," she said, forcing a smile to her lips.

"You were about to tell me about your visitors..." He commented, ignoring her remark and sitting in a chair opposite hers.

"It's okay? You're sure?" Samantha asked.

"I know the schedule for EITS, we're okay... for at least another ten minutes."

"But you said earlier that they already know we're here, so how can they know this if EITS isn't overhead?"

"The ACIO has twenty-eight satellites that comprise the EITS system, only nine have the updated technology for resonance broadcast, and the closest of those nine satellites is about ten minutes away from intercept range."

"How? I mean how... how do you know this for sure?"

"I have a photographic memory, remember?" Neruda explained.

"Must be nice," she laughed nervously.

"Tell me what happened, Samantha."

She took a sip of coffee and let out a deep breath. "I was in my bedroom tonight... around nine o'clock, and decided to do some meditation because I was so wound up after the day's events."

She closed her eyes as if she was watching something on her inner screen. "I had just started and was trying to drain my body of tension, when a light… a green and yellow colored light passed through my body. It was kind of like when the sun goes behind a cloud, you know, when it passes over you and you feel the difference, but you know the source of the shadow is a long ways away."

Neruda nodded. "You mean you saw it with your eyes, or you felt it within you?"

"Both, actually. The light source felt familiar, but I also knew it came from a great distance away. I watched it interact with my mind. It was a very gentle and peaceful experience."

Samantha leaned forward and set her coffee cup down, and folded her legs underneath her. Her face was slightly swollen and reddish in color. "And then this light somehow took hold of my mind and began to… to reconnect me… or my memory."

"In what way?" Neruda asked, leaning forward.

"The light was like a conduit… or portal. It had a magnetic pull and either I went to it or it came to me… I'm not even sure which—"

"It?" Neruda asked impatiently.

"It was a being," she replied. "An intelligence…"

"Did it have a shape?" Neruda asked.

"Not really, but I felt its presence and it scared the hell out of me."

"Why?"

"I don't know," she replied. "I… I've done meditations before and I've felt… or… or least seen lights, but I've never had the light become something intelligent."

"In what way was it intelligent?"

"It restored my memories of the RV sessions with the Central Race." Samantha let her words hang in the air for a few seconds while she took another sip of coffee. "I have complete recall of my experiences, more now than before the MRP."

"How?" Neruda asked, knowing he sounded incredulous.

"I don't know how, but it happened. I remember everything as if it happened a few moments ago. And there's something more," she said, her voice suddenly quiet. "It activated *all* of my experiences with them, including the time I was scanned inside the first cavern and… and earlier when I lost consciousness trying to communicate with the homing device."

"And?"

"I know more about the plans of the ETC site's creators," Samantha said. "But I don't know if I should tell anyone."

"Why?"

"Because Fifteen'll want to take away all my memories, if not my life," she said, as tears formed in her eyes. She dabbed the corners of her eyes with a Kleenex. "There's no doubt in my mind."

"Why?"

"Because I know too much, and for some reason, the creators of this site embedded something inside me that they use to contact me… or… or activate me to do certain things."

"What?"

"Look," she whispered, "you said that we had ten minutes before EITS would be in range. I'm completely spooked. I don't know who I can trust… other than you."

"EITS can only pick up your voice," he said, glancing at his watch. "Let me ask questions and you can either write the answers down or just nod yes or no. Okay?"

"And you're sure that you have no other listening devices in your house?"

"I'm sure."

"Okay. I'll tell you, but only if you'll agree to keep this conversation strictly between you and me. Okay?"

"Agreed," he replied.

Neruda stood to gather his thoughts. The living room was spacious with a grand piano in one corner silhouetted by a large picture window. A floor-to-ceiling, sand-colored flagstone fireplace dominated the far end of the room where he began to pace back and forth.

He stopped pacing and turned to Samantha. "So, a light entered your body and reconnected all your memories concerning your interactions with the ETC site, RV sessions with the Central Race, and the homing device. Correct?"

Samantha nodded, and then blew her nose.

"It was like being re-wired by a remote source that you took to be a representative technology or force from the creators of the ETC site?"

Samantha's face froze for a few moments as if she were debating Neruda's question inside her own mind. Finally, she nodded again, but motioned for something to write with. Neruda responded with a pen and pad of paper from a nearby desk. She scribbled something and handed the pad back to Neruda, pointing to her comments.

> It wasn't a technology or force; it was an intelligence with the specific purpose of activating my memory.

Neruda nodded. "And this intelligence, it only reconnected your memories… it… it didn't communicate anything of its own?"

Samantha looked at Neruda and nodded.

"However," he continued, "the memories of your experience with the homing device are intact, and they somehow gave you an expanded view of the creator's plans for the ETC site. Correct?"

She nodded.

"Do you know what the purpose of the ETC sites is?"

She shook her head, and began to write something and handed it to Neruda when she was done. Neruda took it and walked away, reading it out loud. "Not sure, but it's not a weapon. It has more to do with raising the consciousness of the planet."

He turned around and locked eyes with Samantha. "Do you know how it will do this?"

She began to write.

> I'm not positive, but somehow the seven etc sites combine to form a data stream that raises the molecular vibration of the planet and everyone on it. This data stream modifies the dna structure, not only of humans, but all life on the planet. It was designed to enable us to make a critical discovery later in the twenty-first century.

His lips moved almost imperceptibly as he read her note. "This light, or intelligence, as you refer to it, is it from the creators of the ETC site?"

Samantha nodded.

"And you know this because it activated your memories. Are there other reasons you feel this way?"

She nodded again, and started to write another note.

> I assume it was implanted in me when i came into contact with the homing device, but it felt like it came from an incredible distance away. It felt ancient. It felt eternal. It felt like god.

Neruda nodded as he read the note. "Do you know how we'll be able to locate the other six ETC sites?"

Samantha nodded, but then shook her hand as if she were erasing something from the air. She wrote in a flurry of motion.

> Don't know how to locate the sites, but i know that we're not the ones who'll find them.

His face instantly looked puzzled as he read the note. "Someone else is going to make the discovery?" Neruda asked, his voice sharp with surprise.

"Yes," she said, her hand moving to her mouth as if she wanted to recapture her word. Neruda waved her inadvertent remark away; assuring her it was no big deal.

"Do you know who?"

She shook her head.

"But you're quite certain that it will *not* be the ACIO who discovers these other sites?"

She nodded.

Neruda sighed and sat down in the chair opposite Samantha.

"You're telling me," he began, sweeping his hand through his hair, "that you know with certainty that the ACIO will not discover the other six sites before someone else does. Correct?"

She nodded, her face showing signs of frustration at not being able to explain with speech. She began writing another note.

> This discovery has been carefully orchestrated dating all the way back to the anasazi indians who first discovered it. We play a very critical role, but there's someone else who'll figure out how to access the other sites. Our role—i mean the acio's role—is to find the others who'll help us find the other six sites.

Neruda lost his patience half way through her writing of the note and stood behind her, reading over her shoulder as she wrote. When she finished the last few words, he walked back to his chair and sat down in frustration.

"We'll never convince Fifteen to take this discovery outside of the ACIO," Neruda lamented. "He won't allow the NSA to know anything substantive about this discovery, let alone publish anything about this discovery in a scientific journal. Do you know anything about who this outsider might be?"

Samantha's face was downcast and showed the telltale signs of uncertainty.

"Do you know if it's a person or an organization?" he asked.

She shook her head from side-to-side, and mouthed the words, "I'm not sure."

"Write down your explanation for why you're convinced that the other six sites will be discovered by someone or... or some group outside of the ACIO?"

Her pen was instantly in motion as Neruda finished his last word. She wrote without hesitation for about a minute, and then handed a sheet of paper to Neruda.

> One of my most vivid, restored memories had to do with a girl—maybe fifteen or sixteen years old—who was able to find these sites and activate them through a means i don't understand. It had to do with her mind. Something she had been born with. She's from the central race. She's one of the original creators of these sites, but now lives inside a

human body. Her face is not familiar to me. But she's the one who'll open this thing up. I don't think she's aware of her role yet. We have to find her. I'm sure of this. Without her, we'll never access the other sites, and without the other sites, this technology will never operate as it was intended.

Neruda read the explanation and looked up. "How do we locate this girl?"

Samantha shrugged.

"You have no idea?"

She shook her head, wrote a quick note, and passed it to Neruda.

It's all orchestrated. It'll happen if we get the word out about the etc site. Somehow this girl will step forward when she hears about the discovery.

It was Neruda's turn to shake his head. He looked up at Samantha. "There's no way this discovery will see the light of day. The chance that Fifteen would authorize such a thing is nil. It won't happen. Is it possible that the girl you recollect from your memory is related to something else?"

Samantha shook her head and frowned at the suggestion that she could be mistaken.

"Explain again the source of this vision or memory," Neruda requested, sitting up in his chair and taking a sip of coffee.

Samantha began writing immediately.

It was a vision that was planted in my mind by the homing device when we were in the first cavern. I saw this girl very clearly, and she looked completely human, but i was told that her soul is very ancient and that she was one of the original planners of the etc sites. She would be the one to activate this system. They needed to have one of their own architects incarnate as a human in order to activate the system. It had to be an inside job, so to speak.

Neruda groped for the right words. "You believe that these beings... the

creators of these seven sites… that they're going to make this discovery public…
a public event?"

She nodded in agreement.

"But nowhere in your memory do you see how they will orchestrate this?"

Samantha formed the word "no" with her lips and shook her head in slow motion.

"Do you have any sense of how far in the future your vision was? I mean months,
years, decades?"

She scribbled something quickly and handed it to Neruda.

> It felt like one, maybe two years in the
> future, but i'm not sure.

"Do you have any sense of what this critical discovery is all about?"

> Not sure, but it has something to do with a
> profound shift in humanity. It was genetic
> and spiritual at the same time. I got the
> strong impression it would revolutionize
> science and religion.

"We have a major dilemma, Samantha. I have to report this to Fifteen first thing
tomorrow. I have no choice—"

Samantha stood up and stormed away to the other side of the room. She
was furious and didn't hide it. She turned around and walked back within a few
feet of Neruda's chair. He watched her as she silently mouthed the words "you
promised!" twice.

"I know," he said, "but I didn't realize the gravity of the situation like I do now.
I'm sorry, Samantha. I'm really sorry, but I don't have any choice."

Samantha sat back down and grabbed her pen and paper and wrote like an
imprisoned martyr to her tormentors.

> If you tell fifteen he'll not only take me off
> the project, he might remove me from the acio
> altogether. You promised not to divulge this to
> anyone else!

"Samantha, I can't stay quiet on this issue," he said. "You pose a security risk to
the project and to the ACIO. You either believe this discovery should be published
and shared with the world, or you don't. There's no middle ground."

She began to write, stopped, and then crossed out what she had written. She
closed her eyes and leaned back in her chair. Her face trembled with confusion. Tears
were beginning to flow from her eyes, but she began to write anyway, brushing her

eyes and cheeks with a tissue.

> I'm not planning to tell anyone other than you. I know the risks i'd be taking if i took this story public. I don't have the courage... all i can tell you is that this is not in my hands. I believe the creators of these seven sites orchestrate this entire series of events. I'm just the messenger, don't shoot me! I need your help, protection, advice. Whatever you can provide. Help me, please!

He looked up at her just as she closed her eyes to blow her nose. Even in her disheveled state of mind, her face held a regal poise and grace that attracted him. He felt a brotherly love for her. Something he couldn't exactly explain, or deny. "If you want my help, you can't expect me to lie on your behalf. I can't do that."

Samantha shook her head, showing her agreement. A flicker of hope crossed her face.

"If I tell Fifteen the truth, our only hope is that he's convinced that we'll not be the ones who take this discovery public. And the only way we could convince him of that is if we're convinced of it ourselves. Are you?"

Samantha froze for a few moments. She looked down at her pad of paper unsure of what to write. Then:

> I'm convinced that someone will make this discovery public, and i'm convinced it won't be me. That's all i can tell you.

"Who? Who would make this public?" Neruda asked in a grave tone of voice. "Not McGavin. Certainly not Fifteen. It'd have to be someone who'd defect. There's no other way. And if we kept this to ourselves, it would have to be you or I. And... and you just said you wouldn't do it. So that leaves me..."

Samantha waved her arms as if motioning him to stop. She began writing again, her intensity rising like a spiraling hawk.

> I have this strong feeling that this discovery is of extreme importance to the planet, even though i can't explain why. It must be shared. There's something hidden in these artifacts that's catalytic to humans. I'm supposed to carry this message. You have

to help me. I can't change fifteen's mind by myself.

Neruda read the note twice, stalling his response. He could only see one road ahead, and it scared the hell out of him. He couldn't champion this public disclosure with the Labyrinth Group's cooperation. He'd have to defect. There was no other way.

"If I bring this dilemma to Fifteen, he'll think I'm crazy if I advocate a public disclosure based on your vision, no matter how revered you are as an RV. The only help I can offer is to explain to Fifteen your experience and the reason for your visit, and downplay the whole thing. It'll buy us some time, and give us an opportunity to decode some of the material from the optical disc. Maybe something'll show up that'll add credibility to your vision."

Samantha had begun writing before Neruda finished his comment. She tossed him her note with a curtness that surprised him. She stood, whispered "goodbye", and walked out the door before Neruda could even object. He read her note with a chord of fear reverberating through his body.

So i'm going to be made to look like an idiot. My credibility will be undermined in order to preserve your own. Thanks for all your help. I was hoping for more.

The sound of her car screeching out of his driveway brought him to his feet. He watched her drive away, while his heart sunk to a depth he'd not felt for many years. His choices unsettled him. He knew he'd have to talk with Fifteen in the morning, and he needed to give careful thought to how much he'd disclose.

Neruda picked up the coffee cup and discarded the tissues that Samantha had carefully placed on her saucer. He could only imagine her frustration and fear. But he felt as trapped as she, perhaps more so, because he was the only one who could take the Ancient Arrow Project public. And somewhere in his heart, beneath all the disquiet he felt, he knew this path lay ahead of him, and that his life had just changed irrevocably.

He hit the "call" button on his phone and heard the telltale carrier signal that told him he was once again in Theca Five. He hated the efficiency of Evans and his technologies. He flicked on his computer terminal to check e-mail. David had left him a message about a breakthrough that they'd made. A ray of light moved over him as he read one of David's comments over and over.

We found an access point consisting of a maximum of twenyty-three characters in what we presume is a fifty-two character alphabet. It's an interactive password. We're on our way.

Neruda's mind couldn't concentrate on the breakthrough, though he felt some relief that progress was being made. He could only think about Samantha and how he'd explain what she had told him to Fifteen. He knew that Samantha was her own worst enemy right now, and was almost capable of anything. Perhaps he was, too.

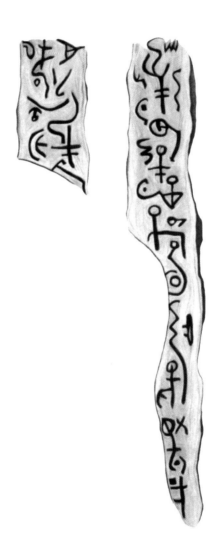

CHAPTER 16

SOVEREIGN INTEGRAL

First Source is not a manifestation, but rather a consciousness that inhabits all time, space, energy, and matter; as well as all non-time, non-space, non-matter, and non-energy. It is the only consciousness that unifies all states of being into one Being, and this Being is First Source. It is a growing, expanding, and inexplicable consciousness that organizes the collective experience of all states of being into a coherent plan of creation; expansion and colonization into the realms of creation; and the inclusion of creation into Source Reality—the home of First Source. This Being pervades the Grand Universe as the sum of experience in time and non-time. It has encoded ITSELF within all life as a vibratory force that is the primus code that creates you as a silken atom in the cosmological web.

An Excerpt from *The Primus Code*, Decoded from Chamber Nine

WingMakers

Neruda looked down the long hallway that led to Fifteen's office. It was empty, and the lights were dimmed. An almost ghostly terror shivered through him as he heard the elevator from the sunroom open. His instinct was to fall back behind the corner's edge and wait.

Fifteen and Evans came off the elevator, and Neruda strained to make out their conversation.

"So you're clear?" Fifteen asked.

"Completely," Evans answered.

"Good, then keep me informed if there's any change. I'm meeting with Jamisson in a few minutes, so I'll handle him myself. You just see to Samantha."

Fifteen began to walk into his office, and then stopped momentarily. "Oh, and by the way, when you deliver the news, do it with sympathy. Put on your long face. Okay?"

"Understood," Evans returned.

"Oh, and remember," Fifteen added, "I want this handled exclusively by you."

"Jenkins knows—"

"No, he doesn't," Fifteen interrupted. "No one knows but you and me, and I want it kept that way. If you need to take Jenkins for MRP, do it. But I want this handled completely SL-Fourteen."

"As you wish," Evans said.

Evans walked down the hallway toward Neruda. Neruda ducked into a conference room, remaining unseen. He was puzzled by what he'd heard. They definitely had a plan in dealing with both him and Samantha. His stomach began to swirl like a horde of butterflies trying to take flight amidst a windstorm.

It was still early, almost 3 a.m. He had sent Fifteen an e-mail message marked "urgent" about an hour earlier and Fifteen had responded immediately, insisting Neruda meet him at the office at 0300 hours. Typical of Fifteen, sleep wasn't a priority. It also served notice of Fifteen's seriousness.

He made the slow, almost painful movement to Fifteen's office. The door was ajar, and the office brightly lit. Neruda knocked gingerly on the door. "Good morning, sir." He didn't try to hide the tiredness in his voice.

"Come on in, Jamisson," Fifteen said without looking up from his computer terminal. "Find something to sit in. I'll be right with you."

Neruda measured Fifteen's voice, looking for any hints of his mood. All he could hear was frustration, and his intuition told him it was more than mild. He sat down in front of Fifteen's desk in a wood chair with a seat of black leather. Its carved wood arms reminded him of a swan's neck—fragile and supple at the same time.

Fifteen hit a keystroke and turned his computer off. Silence filled the room as his hard drive came to a halt. Looking up at Neruda, Fifteen locked his gaze and said, "We know," the words dropping from his mouth with absolute finality.

Neruda looked puzzled. His forehead crinkled like a pond stirred by a sudden gust of wind.

"You know what I mean," Fifteen said, "so don't look at me with those innocent eyes."

Neruda remained quiet, not sure how to respond.

Fifteen leaned back in his chair, waiting with the patience of a fisherman.

"You're referring to Samantha's unexpected visit?" Neruda asked.

Fifteen shook his head. "We know what happened *during* her visit. We know what you discussed and we know what you're considering even at this very hour."

"You spoke with Samantha?" Neruda asked, trying his best to sound casual.

"Yes."

Fifteen shifted in his chair to ease his nagging back. The tips of his fingers joined like beams of a log home, his customary pose when he was preparing to expound on a subject. "For my sixth birthday, my parents took me to the Barcelona Zoo where the marquee attraction was the gorilla exhibit. They had an old timer, named Tumba—maybe twenty-five years old—who had been the signature exhibit for better than two decades. They claimed that Tumba scared people because of how humanly he behaved, which was exactly what attracted the crowds. When we arrived at his cage—thick bars of steel—he was emptying his bowels. When he finished, and with great relish on his face, he heaved his feces into the crowd of people who were watching. It was an intentional, carefully orchestrated event. Unfortunately, some of it fell on my mother's dress and hair."

Neruda leaned forward a bit, drawn by a rare glimpse into Fifteen's childhood.

"My father was enraged," Fifteen continued, smiling at the recollection. "My mother embarrassed. And I... I was hopelessly amused... until I saw the daggers flash from my father's eyes."

Fifteen smoothed his long gray hair behind his ears; his characteristic ponytail was missing. "To my mother's protestations, my father took us to the zoo's administrative offices to complain. We went into the office of the director and listened to a rather lengthy apology. When my father asked why the gorilla would do such a thing, the director explained that Tumba had suddenly begun the odd behavior only a few weeks earlier. The zoo's staff was in something of a panic because their star attraction was quite literally pissing off the patrons of the zoo, and they had no idea how to control Tumba's behavior.

"Now, my father was a gifted engineer, but he couldn't offer any practical suggestions to the zoo director or his bewildered staff that they hadn't already tried. The one thing they'd devised was to mount Plexiglas as a precautionary measure, hoping that Tumba would relent when he saw that his feces couldn't reach his intended victims. But he kept on throwing it anyway, and they had to take down the Plexiglas because of the intolerable appearance. They were left with only one choice. Close down the exhibit.

"The zoo director explained how he'd called upon the best gorilla experts in the world and no one had any viable solutions. So, he was resigned to do what he had to do, particularly in light of my mother's appearance. I asked him what would become of Tumba, and the director explained that he'd be shipped to a new zoo in Africa, closer to his original home. The zoo was going to exchange Tumba for a new gorilla. It seemed so clear to me that Tumba was simply doing what he had to do in order to change his habitat. Change his life. Make something happen—as if twenty-five years in the same cage was enough."

Fifteen lowered his eyes to half-mast and squared them on Neruda. "So, my friend, is this what you want? A change?"

Neruda tried to keep his eyes on Fifteen's, but after a few moments he had to look away, stumbling on his first few words like an awkward schoolboy. "I've... I... I think you're making assumptions that I believe Samantha's conclusions. And I'm not sure why you'd conclude that—"

"I wasn't speaking about conclusions," Fifteen interrupted. "I was asking you the question, do you want to make a change?" He paused and then added, "I believe you'll know when I've made my conclusions."

Neruda felt lost in some surreal dream that wasn't entirely of his own making. So many events of the past three days were whirling around in his mind, and none pressed upon him more intensely than the story he had just heard. He knew what Fifteen was saying. He also knew what Fifteen wanted to hear.

"No," Neruda explained, "I don't want to leave or change my status with the ACIO. You're like a father to me. You know that. I don't have any intention of taking this story to the media or anyone else."

"Are you sure?"

"Absolutely," Neruda found his head nodding well after his word echoed into silence.

Fifteen stood up and walked over to his bookcase. Only his directors and a handful of others were aware of the treasures he kept there. Ancient manuscripts—many that Neruda himself had translated—were bound in humble leather of browns and dirty grays. He took down one of the largest of the books and opened it. Thumbing to a specific page, his eyes smiled like a leprechaun as he began to read aloud. "The Central Race is blessed with the identity of God instilled in them, just as strongly as man is endowed with the identity of an animal humbled by an ego, so compelling as to render him incapable of understanding his creator."

He turned a few pages. "There is no race so advanced as the race of human archetypes known as the Central Race. While there is no one who knows this race in our galaxy, their presence is universal, and all life within our galaxy is interpenetrated by their culture and vision."

He put the book down on his desktop without a sound. On its tan-colored cover was the title, *Liminal Cosmogony* in gold, cursive type. "It was written by the Corteum, but you did the translations. You remember, twenty-five years ago, don't you?" Neruda remained silent, but his head nodded faintly in response. "So, my dear Jamisson, do you want a change?"

Neruda flinched at the unrelenting method that Fifteen used to pull out into the light what he believed was protected or hidden. He could persist like no one else. It was the essence of his power. And Neruda felt the hypnotic persuasion rendering him increasingly vulnerable. He swallowed and reminded himself that he was at war with the most brilliant mind on the planet, and now was not the time to let exhaustion or intimidation get the best of him. "As I said before, Fifteen, I'm not seeking any change. You persist in this line of inquiry for reasons of your own, but I assure you, your suspicions are baseless."

"We'll see," Fifteen intoned. "We'll see very soon."

"I feel like someone who's unwittingly flung themselves in the cross-hairs of a witch hunt," Neruda said. "I've done nothing wrong other than to help Samantha. It's not my fault that she's made contact with the Central Race—"

"What you think may be the Central Race," Fifteen corrected. "We still lack proof of who they are. They call themselves WingMakers, and yet our databases have no reference to this name whatsoever."

"Yes, but we also know that they've implanted a series of technologies on our planet that clearly suggest they're the genetic curators of our species and probably most of the other animal life on this planet. Anything less than this conclusion would be denial. Wouldn't you agree?"

It was Fifteen's turn to avert his eyes. He sat down, fingering the leather cover of the book he had just placed on his desk. "Jamisson, I had a succession plan with your name on it before you even completed this translation. You know that. From the age of seventeen, you were destined to become a member of the Labyrinth Group as its Director of Special Projects. What you don't realize, is that it doesn't end there."

At Fifteen's remark, Neruda felt as though he were rotating above the flames of an invisible fire. He had never considered himself in line for Fifteen's position. He didn't know if he wanted it, much less if he was even capable of performing such an esteemed and complex role. Fifteen would be impossible to replace.

"Seems unlikely, huh?" Fifteen asked, smiling.

"No, seems impossible."

"You're not in the cross-hairs of a witch hunt, you're in the cross-hairs of a succession plan that involves you as my heir."

"Why're you telling me this now?" Neruda asked, his voice suddenly distant and withdrawn.

"I want you to know why I scrutinize your actions so carefully. It's not because I'm your adversary. I'm your future," Fifteen leaned forward, locking eyes with Neruda. "I need you to work with me, not against me. I feel you're being swayed by mythology… or… or at least a set of events that aren't exactly what they seem."

Fifteen paused and leaned back in his chair as if waiting for Neruda to say something.

"I think you expect too much from me," Neruda replied. "I'm not the one to fill your shoes, I don't know how I could possibly lead the development of Blank Slate Technology… let alone the ACIO. Why me?"

"Because I selected you," Fifteen replied. "You'll just have to trust me on this."

Neruda realized he had no choice. And if there was one thing he trusted, it was the soundness of Fifteen's decisions. "Does the rest of the Labyrinth Group agree with you?"

"It's our little secret," Fifteen said with a wink. "No one really knows. I prefer it that way. However, with the intuitive power of this group, there's little doubt in my mind that everyone suspects it."

"Do you really think the WingMakers are not what they appear?" Neruda asked, hoping to steer the conversation off of himself for a moment.

"Assuming the Corteum are right, I believe the Central Race is incapable of deception," Fifteen looked at the book and then spoke in a measured, choppy style. "But - we - don't - know."

Fifteen sat back and slipped his right hand behind his lower back, massaging a tender muscle. "Don't lose sight of the bigger issue," he added. "The so-called WingMakers could be a rogue subgroup of the Central Race or they could be representatives of the M51 synthetics. Who knows for sure? Don't be seduced by the unknown when the *real* world has a higher calling for your talents and skills. That's all I'm saying, Jamisson."

Neruda listened carefully. His mind had recovered from the initial shock of Fifteen's disclosure. "What do you want me to do?"

"I want you to stay on the project and concentrate on decoding what's on the optical disc. We have over eight thousand pages of information, and if you've seen David's e-mail you know that we've found an access point into the disc. The information on this disc could be critical to our understanding of the technologies we've secured from the ETC site. But I need your focus and leadership."

"What's to become of Samantha?" Neruda asked.

Fifteen drummed his fingers on the top of his desk for a moment and then looked at his wristwatch. "She's being taken off the project."

"Entirely?"

"Yes."

"Why?"

"Because she's a security risk," Fifteen replied.

"And she's a distraction to the project?"

"Yes."

"We're not going to perform any more RV sessions, are we?"

"No."

Neruda gathered his courage. "Will she stay in the ACIO?"

Fifteen stole a glance at Neruda out of the corner of his eye. "As I said, she's a security risk. Let's leave it at that, my friend."

"I can't leave it at that."

"Why?"

"Because I believe she's the best RV we've ever had, and this race—whoever they are—is connected to her in some way that none of us truly comprehends. To put her through a radical MRP and send her to... to God knows where is not only cruel and senseless, but stupid."

Neruda folded his arms across his chest, looked to the ceiling and signaled his disgust with a long, drawn out sigh. He could feel his face flush crimson, expressing the telltale signs of anger that he couldn't suppress. He felt responsible for her eviction from the ACIO and he knew the effects of a radical MRP and dislocation program on Samantha. She'd never recover.

He stood and walked over to Fifteen's refrigerator, taking a soda. He needed something to cool him down. Despite everything he felt for Fifteen, he knew he had a battle on his hands. Feverishly, his mind searched for a strategy to restore Samantha's good name. "Are you afraid she'll influence me in some unsavory way?"

"The only thing I fear is that you'll follow her into oblivion."

Neruda paused to take a deep breath before he answered Fifteen's comment. "Are you saying that Samantha will be killed?"

"No."

"Then what *are* you saying, exactly?" Neruda returned to his chair.

"Oblivion is just a metaphor," Fifteen explained. "She's no longer part of the ACIO, and I can't afford to lose your services, Jamisson. It's that simple. You know the magnitude of our work. I shouldn't have to explain to you how vital you are to our plans. We need you to be sharp and focused. The path that Samantha has chosen, while regrettable, doesn't need to affect you. She's young and impressionable, and unable to control her self-interests. Don't make her same mistake. That's all I'm saying."

"We shouldn't do this..." Neruda mumbled.

"We *must* do this," Fifteen announced with strange conviction. "I swear to you, Jamisson, this decision is *not* reversible, so don't waste my time discussing it."

"Who's performing the MRP?"

"David is," Fifteen replied. "Evans will assist."

"When?"

Fifteen looked at his wristwatch. "Within the next hour or so."

Neruda sighed. "Can I talk with her before the MRP?"

"Why?"

"She has information that might be vital to our understanding of the purpose of the ETC site and its technologies. I'd like to get as much of this from her as possible before it's too late."

"As I already told you, we talked with her. We know what she knows."

"She wouldn't tell you everything."

Fifteen picked up his phone and dialed a number. "David, I'm sending Jamisson up. Tell Evans I'd like Jamisson to have some time with Samantha before the MRP." Fifteen put his hand over the phone and whispered to Neruda. "How much time do you think you'll need?"

"Twenty minutes?" Neruda shrugged.

"Jamisson needs about twenty minutes," Fifteen said. He nodded, listening to something David said.

"Good, then I'll send him right up." Fifteen put the phone down gently. "Evans just arrived with Samantha. You should go now."

"Do I have your permission to conduct this interview in private?"

"Why private?"

"If Evans is there, she'll clam up," Neruda explained. "She has insights that we need, and if we don't get them now, we'll never get them." Neruda stood to his feet as if Fifteen had no other choice.

"I'll call Evans."

"Thanks."

Fifteen walked around the desk and held out his hand. "Do we have an understanding?"

"We do," Neruda replied, shaking his hand as if a complicated business transaction had been completed.

"Oh," Fifteen added, "the only thing I require is that this interview with Samantha is recorded. Understood?"

"I assumed as much. I just don't want Evans in the room."

Fifteen nodded and walked Neruda to the door, patting him on the shoulder like a father would his son. "Just so you know, I'm not stepping down anytime soon."

Neruda laughed. "Good, because I won't be ready for about another twenty years."

Fifteen smiled knowingly. "You're more ready than you realize."

They shook hands again, and Neruda left, the office door clicking solidly behind him. On his way to the MRP lab, Neruda's mind focused on Samantha like a laser beam. He needed to help her, but he had no idea how he could do so without contradicting everything he'd just pledged to Fifteen. Something told him that he was through sleeping for the day.

✳   ✳   ✳   ✳

When Neruda arrived at the MRP Lab, Evans eyed him with suspicion. "Looking for Samantha?"

Neruda simply nodded.

"She's in there," Evans said, pointing with his pencil to a closed door. Neruda scanned the security monitors and found the one with Samantha's blurred image sitting by a table with her hands propping her head up. She was staring at a box of white tissues.

"You have twenty minutes," Evans reminded him, pushing a button on his wristwatch.

Neruda opened the door as quietly as he knew how. Samantha didn't look up. She continued to stare, as if she'd lost interest in anything having to do with the outside world.

Neruda placed his hand on her shoulder and kissed her cheek. He could taste salt on his lips. "I'm sorry, Samantha."

"For what?"

Neruda pulled up a chair and sat down. He wasn't sure how to respond to her question, but he was relieved to hear her voice. "Are you okay?"

She turned to look at him. Her eyes were swollen and red, and her hair was tussled like spaghetti. "I'm not sure what I am. I feel like a damn lamb being led to the slaughter, so, no, I'm not okay. I feel like shit. No, absolute shit. Perfectly shitty, that's how I feel. Glad you asked. And how the hell are you?"

Neruda leaned back in his chair. He reminded himself that he'd never seen Samantha angry. It was a new side of her that he hadn't expected for some reason. He could imagine Evans smirking in the next room. "I think your description fits me pretty well, too."

"Are you playing the role of the priest? Here to give me last rites?"

"No one's going to die," Neruda said confidently. "I asked Fifteen if I could have twenty minutes to talk with you—"

"No, you want to get every last piece of information out of my brain before I become a vegetable. That's it, isn't it?"

Neruda looked down at his hands folded on top of the table. Samantha turned away and put her head on her arms. She looked as weary as he felt.

"Samantha, you're right, but I don't have any options. If I could wave my magic wand and release you from this situation, I would in an instant. But I can't. What I can do is preserve some portion of your memory that can help this project."

"Then tell me," she asked, "what's my disposition after the MRP? Am I escorted out of the ACIO to Timbuktu, or do I return to my post as an RV oblivious about the Ancient Arrow Project? Which is it? And don't lie to me."

"I don't know where you'll be taken…" Neruda sighed long and hard. "But you won't be returning to the ACIO."

"Thanks," she whispered.

"What?"

"Thanks."

"For what?"

"For being honest with me."

"I only wish I could do more," he put his hand on her shoulder again.

"What'll happen with my family? I mean, will I remember them? Will I be allowed to see them again?"

"I don't know," Neruda confided. "I haven't been told how deep they're going with the process."

"It's the hardest part—not seeing my family again. Can you make sure they don't do that?"

"You have my word that I'll try my best."

Neruda withdrew his hand and remained silent for a few moments while he collected his thoughts. "Samantha, I only have fifteen minutes. I need to know if there's anything you haven't told me yet that could be used to our advantage in decoding the ETC site. Can you think of anything?"

"Are they recording our conversation?"

Neruda nodded.

"Did you bring a pencil and paper?" she remarked sarcastically.

Neruda shook his head and smiled.

"What would you do in my shoes?"

"I'd walk out of here until they shot me. I'd resist until they forced me to submit. I'd never give them anything they could use. And I'd curse them so intensely they'd never be able to look themselves in the mirror without feeling guilty."

"You make honesty into an art form, don't you?" Samantha snickered. "Are you sure they're recording this?"

Neruda nodded, a thin smile gracing his lips. He knew he was being a bit boastful, but it was, in essence, the truth. "I'm exaggerating, but I wouldn't let them take my memory without a fight."

"So how do I fight them?" she whispered, leaning a little closer to Neruda.

"I don't want to get your hopes up. There's nothing I can do to reverse this decision. If there's something you know that you think could be valuable to our understanding, the best I can do is use it as a bargaining chip to help you negotiate something. But you have to tell me first."

"So, I tell you something that's vital to the project that you don't already know. You tell Fifteen. Fifteen says, wow, this is great stuff! Let's keep her on the project—no, let's promote her to SL-Ten. Is that what you're suggesting?" Her voice raised in both volume and pitch, cynicism dripping from each word.

For the first time, Neruda could fully sense the futility of their situation. It was nearly 4 a.m. They were both tired. Samantha felt her sanity slipping away like someone caught in quicksand without a rope. Neruda's own anger and frustration were beginning to show through, and he didn't know how to contain it.

His heart pounded like a tribal drum. "I'd do anything I could to put everything straight between you and Fifteen, but I don't know how I can do that. His mind is made up. Please, Samantha, if there's anything you know that would be useful to the project, share it with me now."

"I'm no longer a member of the club, so fuck them all. That's how I feel."

"That's it?"

"I think *fuck them all* sums it up pretty well," she said.

"Look, Samantha, I'm just trying to help, but you need to give me something—"

"What I know that you don't wouldn't be helpful to the ACIO anyway."

Neruda looked at his watch. He knew his time with Samantha was rapidly evaporating. "Who'd it be helpful to then?"

"Look, I appreciate everything you're trying to do for me. I really do. But this is all going to happen just the way it's supposed to happen. Do you really think Fifteen, or anyone else for that matter, can change the course of this thing? I could tell you everything I know and it wouldn't change one little thing. This thing is huge, and it's gonna happen exactly as it was planned billions of years ago."

Samantha raised her head and leaned back in her chair, staring at the ceiling. "The forces that're orchestrating this are not human or even extraterrestrial. They're ancient, primordial, fundamental… the very essence of life itself. It's been inside us from the start. The ACIO is kidding itself if it thinks it can hide anything from the WingMakers, or deny the unfolding of their plan. It's too late. Something happened twelve hundred years ago that set all of this in motion, and nothing's going to stop it."

She turned her head to look at Neruda. "Nothing."

At hearing a metallic edge to her voice, Neruda looked into her eyes. The back of his neck stippled with goose bumps and his body shuddered with chills. She was in a trance, and he had the uncomfortable feeling he was no longer talking with Samantha.

"Who are you?" Neruda asked.

Someone or something stared at him through Samantha's eyes. "Your technology will fail you," her lips moved awkwardly. "It is based on the unreality of your physics and your limited understanding of cosmological unity. It will fail you, mark our words."

Neruda could sense a powerful, awe-inspiring presence. His skin crawled as a powerful electrical force pervaded the entire room, raising every hair on his body.

The being using Samantha's body continued; her lips moved almost imperceptibly. "What you seek, what you believe you require, is nothing less than that which is perfected within you. And while this perfected aspect of you is invisible to your senses, it is all we can see of you. To our senses, your animal body and primitive human mind barely register. We see only the core of you, your essential consciousness. You have glimpsed this core as well, but you have seen it through the lens of technology, and not through an organic, natural awakening. You are therefore misguided. Your technology is flawed and will surely fail you."

The voice stopped and Neruda struggled to think of something to say. He didn't want it—whatever it was—to go away. He had the sense that it could answer any question he could imagine. "What do you want?" he managed to ask.

"We desire your awakening. We want only this."

"How?"

"It is not a question of how, it is a question of when."

"Then when?"

"It is soon."

"Soon, in terms of days, weeks, months, years…"

"Soon, in terms of minutes."

Samantha's voice was barely a whisper. Neruda imagined Evans adjusting the gain control on the listening monitor. He looked into her eyes but could feel none of her present, as if she had physically left the room. Her head continued its awkward cant, staring into his eyes while it rested on the back of her chair. Her body was limp and lifeless except for her eyes.

"Come closer before we leave," the voice commanded in a barely audible whisper.

He leaned forward.

"Closer. Put your ear to her lips."

Neruda leaned forward, placing his right ear directly in front of her mouth. He closed his eyes, focusing all his attention on the words coming from Samantha's mouth.

"We are from the centermost point of existence. It is the place of your mythology, and yet we are not myths. We are the eldest of your kind, so ancient that we have been forgotten from your minds. Our presence is being re-established in your race so you can become reacquainted with your future.

"We have placed within you, Neruda, a code that is activated by two words: *Sovereign Integral*. From this point forward, you are awakened to our mission and you will serve this mission even though you do not understand it. The code is now activated and you are awakened. You must leave. You must find the girl, Lea. She will appear to you through her mother, Sarah. You must leave now. Do not worry about Samantha. She is in our care, as are you. Go, and take this secret with you."

Suddenly, the door flew open and Evans entered, his suspicious eyes darting around frantically. "What's going on?" he demanded.

Neruda jerked his head up absentmindedly and spoke without hesitation. "Samantha needs some water. She's not feeling well."

Evans left and returned momentarily with a plastic bottle of water. "It's mine, but she can have it."

"Thanks," Neruda said, handing it to Samantha, now returned and disoriented and groggy. She drank the water and began to cough uncontrollably. Neruda wanted to pick her up like a child and put her to bed, but he knew other plans were in store for her.

"Is she okay?" Evans asked.

"She'll be fine, just give her a few minutes."

"Fifteen wants to see you before you leave," Evans reported, hinting that it was time for Neruda to go.

Neruda knew Fifteen had been watching his meeting with Samantha on closed circuit video. He'd probe him about what had been whispered in the last few minutes of his meeting. Secrecy unnerved Fifteen as few other things could.

Neruda noticed that he felt oddly different—somehow more confident. He knew that something had changed in him, though he couldn't place it. It was the feeling of being right or maybe it was the feeling of being on the right team. He had the sudden sense of conviction that he inherently knew what he needed to do, even though he didn't know what it was. He glanced at Evans and caught his eye. "Take good care of her."

Evans nodded and remained silent, trying to look patient. Neruda leaned over and kissed Samantha on the cheek and whispered in her ear. "You'll be okay. I love you." His finger touched her cheek as tenderly as any lover's could. He felt a new energy coursing through his body, which was causing a tremor in his hand.

Samantha smiled. Her expression relaxed, and the bitterness and anger that had possessed her earlier seemed extinguished. She formed silent words with her lips. "I love you, too."

Neruda turned back to Evans. "Like I said, take good care of her."

"Don't worry," Evans assured him. "You better go."

Neruda took one last look at Samantha, turned and left. He had the uneasy feeling that it would be a long time before he'd see her again—if ever. He wondered what would become of her in her new world. He wondered the same about himself.

✳   ✳   ✳   ✳

"Come on in, Jamisson," Fifteen said. "You could probably use some coffee about now."

"You made coffee?" Neruda asked, his voice incredulous.

"You've had a busy night," Fifteen said, ignoring Neruda's question and pouring a cup of strong, black coffee. "Care to tell me what went on?"

"You watched?"

"Yes."

"Then you heard," Neruda mentioned. "There's not much to add."

"Why don't you start with the part I couldn't hear?" Fifteen asked as he passed a cup of steaming coffee to Neruda.

"She wasn't feeling too good," Neruda began, "and I tried to help her—"

"Don't start down that path. If you do, you'll deeply regret it."

Neruda locked eyes with Fifteen and felt his equal for the first time. He had no fear, and he knew Fifteen sensed this. "What do you want?" Neruda said in a frustrated tone. "If there's something specific that you're looking for, it would save us both a lot of time if you'd just tell me what it is so I can tell you what you want to hear. I'm tired of your suspicions."

Fifteen eyed him as a man does when a lifelong friend suddenly becomes his adversary. Neruda could feel his scrutiny like a throng of emotions pressing in on his heart. He took a long sip of coffee and gathered his thoughts, knowing that Fifteen would assail him for his impudence.

"For such a short conversation, you've changed in a rather dramatic way," Fifteen observed. "Are you sure you're prepared for the consequences?"

"Perhaps more than you're prepared for what I have to say."

"Let's remain civil, Jamisson. You don't want my wrath, I assure you. So, just tell me what was said. This is the last time I will ask."

Neruda knew his threat was real. There were technologies that Fifteen could use—under severe circumstances—to retrieve memories from either an unwilling or forgetful source. It was an unpleasant, invasive, and potentially injurious experience. Neruda had never required it, but everyone in the Labyrinth Group was well aware of the procedure and feared its use. The after-effects were often described as a "simmering paranoia" beyond the mitigating influence of drugs or therapy.

"You heard what she said," Neruda replied. "Our technology will fail us. She said the WingMakers' plan will—"

"Stop! As you well know, I don't give a damn about what *she* said! I'm interested in the conversation you had with the entity that took over her body in the last four minutes of your discussion. You remember? The one that identified itself as *we*."

Fifteen fiddled with the controls on his computer and swiveled his monitor so Neruda could see the screen. A video image of him with his head poised in front of Samantha's face filled the screen. "Even with full gain, I can't make out what is being said, and because you're blocking the view, we can't read her lips. You can understand why I'm suspicious, and you can understand why I'm growing more suspicious as a result of your obvious evasion. Just tell me the truth. It's all I want from you, and you can go home and get some rest. I think we all could use some more sleep."

"I don't know who the entity was. It reiterated what it had said earlier. Our technology would fail. Their plan would prevail. That sort of thing. Evans interrupted before it could finish. That's all."

Neruda took another sip of coffee, well aware that Fifteen was scrutinizing his body language.

"Why is your hand trembling?" Fifteen asked.

"The energy of this being or entity was amazing. The electromagnetic field in the room must have been off the scale, and it's a shielded room, too. I'm still in the throes of it."

Neruda shifted in his chair. "Look, I'm sorry for sounding so damn pissed off, but I really care for Samantha and the thought of her mind being wiped clean... it... it just makes me angry. And then all this suspicion on your part doesn't exactly help my state of mind. I need some time to deal with all this."

"Maybe a few days off—starting right now," Fifteen suggested.

"No, there's too much to do now with the breakthrough David made last night. I want to start on it immediately."

"Okay. Maybe I've been a little too intense about all this," Fifteen said. "Accept my apologies. But in the future, be a little more forthcoming. Trust me. It worked for your father."

Neruda set his coffee cup down on the table next to his chair, and pushed back his chair, standing up too quickly. His head swooned from the sudden rush of blood and he steadied himself with his right hand. "I appreciate your understanding, and I'll take your advice."

"Which one?"

"What?"

"Which piece of advice will you take?" Fifteen asked, his voice clear and precise.

"The one about trust. Being more forthcoming."

"Good," Fifteen remarked. "But consider the other one as well—the one about taking some time off. It might be just what you need."

Fifteen returned his monitor to its original position and hit some keys on his keyboard. "Have a good day, Jamisson. Update me as soon as you have something on the decryption. I'll be around all day."

"I will, sir" Neruda said. "One more thing. Whatever happens with Samantha, I need your assurance that she'll be able to contact her family after this is all over."

"I heard your remark on the video. You have my word."

"Thanks," Neruda said. He walked to the door and turned around just as he reached for the doorknob. "Why do you have such strong suspicions about me?"

"I have suspicions about everyone. You're just my latest target because of the circumstances surrounding your interactions with Samantha. It's quite obvious that she's under the control of forces that are not friendly to our cause. I know how easy it is to be seduced by the forces of change. Especially when that change is from a force like the Central Race."

"Then you do believe the ETC site is their creation?"

"It's the most reasonable hypothesis. But remember, Jamisson, Central Race or not, they're still human, older, by billions of years perhaps, but not necessarily wiser. Remember that."

Neruda nodded. "So experience doesn't amount to much?"

"No, it's damn important, but so is ingenuity and passion, and a hundred other things. No one knows this race. We've encountered extraterrestrial races more ancient than our own, and are they so much wiser than we are? They have a more developed brain system or capacity for assembling data, but are their decisions infallible? No!"

Fifteen stood and retrieved his sweater from the back of his chair, slipping it over his shoulder like a backpack. "We can't afford to rely on anyone for our safety. Let me remind you, the Corteum, with brain systems more than double our own, are now living on their home planet in underground cities, the result of their own undoing. It's not simply a matter of intelligence or experience. It's a matter of orchestrating a hundred variables toward a singular goal. It's what we do. And we do it better than any other organization on this planet. We can't afford to have our top people influenced by the romantic notion that the Central Race is our savior. We will be our own savior. I don't think there's any other way."

He paused for a moment at the sound of his computer alerting him to a new e-mail message. "If Samantha is in rapport with the Central Race somehow, and that entity who was talking through her was indeed a representative from the Central Race or WingMakers, as they call themselves, then they seem convinced we'll fail. How could they know? Just ask yourself that question, Jamisson. How could they know?"

Neruda shrugged.

Fifteen reached for his briefcase and closed its buckles. "The whole notion of life before earth—of our planet being seeded by master geneticists, who were actually ourselves, just billions of years more evolved, may indeed be true. But doesn't it seem odd that they'd be relying on a *junior* RV to whisper something into *your* ear in order to convince us of the perfection of *their* plan and the futility of ours? Think about this the next time you feel them tugging at your conscience. Your life may depend on it."

Neruda could feel the seduction of Fifteen's strategy. Plant seeds of doubt. Employ subtle threats. Hope that his hand-picked heir would step back into line. Neruda understood how Fifteen could believe that his strategy would have worked, except that now something within him was different. A brilliant, resolute, granite-like consciousness had moved over Neruda, enveloping him in its incorruptibility.

"I'll walk out with you," Fifteen said, heading for the door.

"I'm gonna stop by the lab and see if David's still around," Neruda replied. "I'm anxious to have a look at his results. Besides, the coffee's kicked in, I couldn't sleep now if I tried."

"I'll be back by eleven hundred hours. Give me an update then if you can."

"I will. Good night," Neruda said.

"Good night."

Neruda walked down the hallway, opposite the direction that Fifteen walked. He noticed how well the sounds of their footsteps were synchronized until he could only hear his own. His attention shifted to the image of Samantha lying in the MRP lab, her memories being stripped out with surgical precision. Barren of eighteen days and all they held. Memories unlike any other on the planet.

As he took the elevator to the lab he repeated the words, *Sovereign Integral*, in his mind, over and over like a momentum generator perfectly tuned to its source of energy. Each time the words rolled through his mind, he felt a propellant force, something within driving him towards a destiny of which he knew nothing except that it included a girl named Lea. He wondered how he'd ever be able to leave the ACIO to find her. How would this all happen?

He smiled at the recollection of Fifteen's childhood story. Maybe Fifteen was more prescient than he knew.

CHAPTER 17
MOTHER LODE

The potency of the human soul is defined first by the laws of creation, and second, by the awareness that these laws assure cosmic stability and spiritual poise.

An Excerpt from *The Primus Code*, Decoded from Chamber Nine
WingMakers

When Neruda arrived at the computer lab, he noticed a handwritten note posted on his project monitor.

> Jamisson,
> Check out file aap-1220. You'll find everything you need there. I sent fifteen a duplicate file. I'm back in at 1400 hours. Leave me instructions if you want and i'll work on it as soon as i arrive.
> David

Neruda's hands were trembling once again. He slumped in a black leather chair and ran his hands through his hair. The lab was completely deserted. Neruda hit a key and watched his monitor screen come alive with the phosphorescent glow of grays and blues. He clicked on the project file and settled back in his chair. David and ZEMI had found a potential mother lode. They had discovered the first real breakthrough in the decryption process. They had found the access point into the disc. The first opportunity to interact with the content that had been so carefully hidden on its gold, metallic surface.

An alert button drew his attention. He clicked it on. A video window instantly opened up and David's image slurred into motion.

HI, JAMISSON. I ASSUME YOU'LL GET THIS FIRST. WE ASSUME THE ALPHABET IS INTERMIXED WITH MUSIC NOTATIONS OR MATHEMATICS BECAUSE IT HAS SO MANY CHARACTERS. IT COULD BE THAT THE ENTIRE ALPHABET IS MATHEMATICAL. THE GOOD NEWS IS THAT WE KNOW HOW TO ACCESS THE DISC AND IT'S CLEARLY INTERACTIVE. IT HAS THE EQUIVALENT OF A PASSWORD; WE'RE CONVINCED OF THAT, BUT WITH FIFTY-TWO CHARACTERS IT'LL TAKE A LONG TIME TO RUN ALL

COMBINATIONS. LEAVE ME AN INSTRUCTION SET. AS OF
2300, WE'VE BEGUN THE RANDOM GENERATOR PROCESS
OF ASSEMBLING AND PROCESSING PASSWORDS. SEE YOU
THIS AFTERNOON.
        DAVID

Neruda's excitement was irrepressible. He gave out a loud whoop that echoed throughout the lab. They were on the cusp of cracking the safe. He could feel it. An electronic pop jerked him from his euphoria. One of the blank monitors lit up and David's image slowly emerged. He was busy putting on his headband or Neural Bolometer. "I thought you'd be in here," he said.

"I was just going over your report. It's great news." Neruda said, looking up at the monitor image of David. "How'd it go with Samantha?"

"As well as could be expected. She's sleeping in recovery. I'm monitoring her right now—all vitals are strong."

"Can you keep me posted on her recovery?"

"No problem."

David continued to make adjustments to his headband of glass fiber tentacles. He was dressed in a black sweater with thin white lines crisscrossing over his chest in a checkerboard pattern. "Any ideas about access strategies?"

"Not really," Neruda said. "Are you confident that we'll be successful through a random generator process?"

"If it's a mixture or combination of their character set, we've got everything we need. The only problem is time. We can assemble over ten to the thirteenth power password attempts per second, but the disc's validation process slows us down by a factor of two. Unless we get extremely lucky, we won't find it in our lifetime." David shrugged with a slim smile.

"The disc's access entry," Neruda began, "how many characters does the space accommodate?"

"Twenty-three, we think, but we're not absolutely certain."

"So, if we place the right combination of their characters in the password space and input it to the disc, what result do you expect?"

"We'll get a translation index for the disc. The good news is that once we find the correct password, it should only take us less than a minute to decode the entire text. But that's in theory."

"How many passwords have you tested so far?"

David closed his eyes. "As of this time-mark," he snapped his fingers, "approximately 3.65 to the sixteenth power."

"Shit! That's not even scratching the surface," Neruda grumbled.

"We could get lucky," David smiled.

"I'm not interested in luck. Why exactly is it taking so long?" Neruda asked in frustration.

"We're talking fifty-three characters—"

"I thought you said it was fifty-two characters?"

"It is, but we have to include the digital equivalent of an empty space because we don't know if there're multiple words."

Neruda nodded before David had finished his sentence. "So there're twenty-three character positions, each of which could contain one of fifty-three characters. It's an astronomical number—forty some zero's."

"The exact number is 4.5535 to the thirty-ninth power," David said. "Even without the relatively slow process speed of the disc, we'd still need over a trillion trillion years under ideal conditions to exhaustively test every possible password variation."

"It might as well be infinity," Neruda said under his breath. "David, do you have the glyphs from the twenty-three chambers handy in your database?"

"Of course?"

"But you haven't included these?"

"No."

"If we include these, we're now talking seventy-six characters that could potentially create the password string."

"Which adds thirty more zeroes to the number of years."

"I can't believe they'd do that," Neruda lamented.

"What?"

"I can't believe a race this sophisticated would make accessing their data impossible. We're missing something."

"Yeah, but to them, it may not seem very complicated," David asserted. "They may be able to do these computations in their head. Who knows?"

"Except they knew we'd be finding this thing, and they'd expect us to be the ones to open this disc—not them." Neruda suddenly shot up in his chair. "David, let's try something different. Put the random generator on pause for a moment."

"Done."

"Okay, bear with me. Let's apply the random generator on just the first character in the password."

"You mean apply each of the seventy-six characters to just the first character space of the password entry."

"Exactly."

"Whoa," David exclaimed a moment later. "We got something, hold on."

David closed his eyes. "I see it. We did it!"

"What?" Neruda asked.

"We have ourselves a translation index."

Neruda clenched his fist. "Fantastic. Is it for the entire text?"

"I'm checking it right now. Hold for a second."

David's expression went blank, and then he smiled the smile of a fox. "You know what they did?"

"What?"

"They've segmented each of the twenty-four sections with its own password. The first character opens up the first section and only the first section. I'm looking at 321 pages of perfect English. It should be onscreen in a few seconds."

Neruda could tell that David was reading with his eyes closed. Moments later, it displayed on his monitor, and both he and David were entranced by the writing. A delicate silence ensued while they both read what they had struggled so hard to gain access to.

You may refer to us as WingMakers. We are actually quite human, simply a future version of you. Humans of your time, conditioned as they are, seem unable or, unwilling to comprehend that a future version of themselves could have invented humanity and seeded its genetic structure across the universe in which you now live. Humanity is a far more diverse and ubiquitous life form than you think. It is an ideal soul carrier, and its format is as common throughout this universe as there are life-bearing planets to sustain it.

Neruda looked at his monitor screen and realized, for the first time, how surreal his situation was. He was twelve stories beneath the ground in the middle of the desert twenty miles north of Palm Springs, California, sitting before a monitor that connected him to the most powerful computer on earth. On his screen was a 321 page manifesto written by the Central Race. It was all he could do to ask David a question. "We got into the first section and not the others?"

"Apparently," David began, "the password was only able to access the first section. We now believe that the second section is accessible if we find a two-character password, and the third would open with a three-character password, and so forth."

"Let's try it," Neruda said impatiently. "If we're lucky, maybe the character set is reduced each time we open up a new section."

David leaned forward in his chair. "Understood. The second section is opened and I'm pasting it to your screen now. The third will be up in ten seconds or so."

"How many sections will you be able to open before we hit the time barrier?"

"Assuming that there's no character set reduction, we'll get to the ninth section tonight—it'll take approximately twenty-seven minutes to open. The tenth section will take fourteen days. The eleventh section will take 1,131 days, or about three years. The twelfth section, 85,956 days, or over two hundred years. You don't want to know the rest," David advised.

"Shit, we won't even be able access half of the information contained on this disc?"

"Bear in mind, I'm giving you the worst case scenario. We could get lucky with the eleventh section and find the password in the first week. However, probability dictates that we will only be able to reach the first eleven chambers—at least in our lifetime."

"No other options?"

"None that we can think of at the moment," David replied.

Neruda could feel a surge of exhilaration and disappointment flood through his body. His attention returned to the text, as if it were the only thing left to do.

Culture building is the primary focus of the WingMakers because it is understood to have such a significant bearing on the world of spirit and cosmological transformation. Culture building, by definition, integrates the values of individualism with the value of oneness. It is the goal of life, as it is related to a species, to evolve itself where it can be conscious of its diverse perceptions and expressions, and integrate them into a cohesive, all-inclusive culture.

Humankind deeply desires such a culture; a global culture that recognizes and appreciates the rights of its constituent parts. This is one of the primary reasons that communication technologies will evolve so quickly upon earth in the twentieth century. Through these technologies, the global culture will be more rapidly developed and experienced. And through this global culture, humankind will become increasingly sensitive to the spiritual inclinations of oneness. Not only oneness within the human species, but within the whole of life that embraces and envelops the human species, which extends into our world—the foundation of the universe.

Humankind is part of something more than simple inter-dependency as depicted in a food chain or ecosystem. You are part of the accumulative knowledge of First Source, achieved through absorbing the life experience of all sentient life forms within the Grand Universe. This all-encompassing knowledge is shared willingly to all life forms, but is only comprehensible to those soul carriers who have achieved an ability to step out of the constraints of time for the expression of their divinity.

You are part of an incalculably complex, but single-minded, cosmological organism devoted to the transformation of evolving life forms so that soul carriers can comprehend and appreciate their connection to the whole cosmological structure of life, living in oneness with First Source. This is the fundamental system that overarches all other systems of the multiverse, and it is for this supernal reason that life exists.

Each of you is like a particle of a single, massive wave that moves outward, sweeping across the universal spectrum of life forms and experiences, and rebounding to the shore from whence you were created. The energy of this system is like a giant funnel that delivers a species to First Source unerringly. This funnel creates an overbearing drive for oneness and re-connection with the Primal Creator in a developing species, but the species does not realize that the Primal Creator is hidden behind the layers of human, angelic, extraterrestrial, and cosmic forces. It is so deeply hidden that until the final veil is drawn, it is never considered hidden.

The Primal Creator or First Source, is stored within you in the cauldron of your genetic composition. There, it awaits you. And we, the elders of humanity, have come to show you how to free this image—this immutable memory of your future self. It has been seeded within your body, invisible to your senses and instrumentation, but absolutely real and absolutely yours.

What are before you are words, and behind them, a voice. What is behind the voice is a mind, which your psychologists call the Collective Unconscious. But we tell you that it is not unconscious—it is your innermost sanity, and it is beckoning you, and thousands of others like you, to step forward into this work that we have left behind. The words, music, pictures, symbols, definitions are all ways to touch this innermost sanity of First Source, and feel this world from the safety of your own. We hope that you honor these words by your actions and follow the sound of our voice to your home. Your true home.

Neruda stopped reading and glanced at the monitor that held David's face. "Are you reading this?"

"Yes."

"What do you make of it?"

David started to speak, stopped, and leaned back in his chair. "We believe the introduction is further proof of an alien intelligence, but it's impossible to say whether it's the Central Race. It certainly makes for interesting reading, though. By the way, we just finished decoding the eighth section. We'll complete the ninth section in a little less than twenty-six minutes."

"How many pages?"

"Through the eighth section, we have 2,817 pages," David responded matter-of-factly. "We're printing them out, but it'll take another ten minutes or so to complete the printing. I assume you'll want the first copy."

"Please," Neruda replied. He scrolled to the second page and continued reading.

We have installed a system of seven sites upon earth that, when discovered and decoded, will facilitate your transformation into a new scientific and philosophical fusion that will create an entirely new, global society. You will discover this system, which we call the Galactic Tributary Zones, in due course, but first, you must share these, the first of the materials, with your planet's citizens. They must be shared upon your data networks without regard to cost, geography, heritage or belief system.

The material on this disc will awaken certain of your citizens to prepare for the necessary changes required to sustain your planet and enable the irrefutable, scientific discovery of the human soul. It is this discovery, and this discovery alone, that will pilot the human species into the greater society of inter-galactic enterprise and partnership.

We are aware that these words may instill fear and doubt in some of you. We are also aware that there will be many in power that will not desire to share these materials, fearing panic and social disorder. However, if you doubt our prediction, you will not heed our warning nor will you take action. To do this is complete folly. We advise you to carefully study the system we have left behind. It is composed of more than mere words. There is music, symbols, mathematics, geometry, poetry, and art. In total, it is an encoded sensory data stream that is a potent catalyst for your next stage of evolution.

We created you; thus we coded within your genetic structure the receptors that we can activate with our words, sounds, and symbol pictures. When you immerse within our sensory data streams, you will mutate. In a genetic sense, your interior, subatomic architecture becomes more adaptable and accommodating to the frequencies of energy that emanate from the centermost section of the Grand Universe. These frequencies are quite literally the carriers of your new life as a species.

The technologies we have left behind for you to discover are able to coordinate this incoming energy to transpose your genetic structure to a higher dimensional existence, an existence that will render you invincible to our ancient enemy— the Animus. They are the soulless creatures of your nightmares. Your planet has experienced them before, but it was nearly three hundred million years ago when the genetic structure of the planet's life forms were not so highly developed, and thus, not as desirable. When they return, they will not be so apathetic. They will see the human soul carriers of your planet as being worthy of their pursuit and conquest.

The Animus seek the genetic repositories of our species because they desire to become soul carriers themselves. They fear only one thing: extinction. It is the motivation behind their quest to interbreed with species of compatible soul carriers that also possess the genetic structures that can support their collective intellect. They fear their own annihilation because of their inability to sustain the vibration of the sovereign soul within their physical bodies. They are unable to contain this frequency as an individuated essence. They can only sustain a group mind, which makes them vulnerable to the fear of extinction. And this fear drives their behavior as conquerors and nihilists.

What you have before you is the dilemma of how to bring this warning to the citizens of your planet in a way that does not break down social structures, but rather builds new ones that are complementary to the existing structures. Our only counsel is to read these materials and this will become clear to you. You have been chosen to see these words. Have no doubt of this. There will be those that will try to prevent the distribution of these materials, but your planet's future depends on your ability to find the help you will need to bring these materials to the public's attention.

The Animus are very sophisticated life forms. They will not display aggression until it serves their purpose, and then, only after they have succeeded in gaining the cooperation of world leaders. It is their pattern to observe and analyze weakness, target leadership, build coalition, and through deception and long-range planning, orchestrate their introduction to the planet. After this introduction and the promise of charitable deeds, the Animus will continue to attract the influential elite in politics, academia, and culture into their web of selfish interests.

They are masterful manipulators with brilliant minds, and your citizenry, even the very best of your breed, will be unprepared to resist their carefully orchestrated plans until it is too late. They will interbreed initially, and establish colonies in nearby artificial planets. They will infiltrate the highest offices of government and their hybrid progeny will become the new leaders of earth and all its native populations.

The global economy will respond positively to the Animus technology transfers, propaganda, and political manipulations, but there will be pockets of unrest, and strong resistance will bubble to the surface even in the first year of their introduction. As this resistance becomes increasingly vocal and violent it will ultimately reveal the true intentions of the Animus: control the planet Earth and its genetic repository.

With these seven sites and the artifacts therein, we, the Central Race, have provided your species with a sensory data stream that will catalyze members of your population to mutate. This mutation is extremely subtle, but it will awaken select members to their purpose, which is to discover the Wholeness Navigator—that fragment of First Source that is stored within each of you. With this discovery, you will have clear access to our protection and assistance as a species, not simply as individuals.

For time immemorial, we have protected our progeny and genetic repositories from the Animus. In honesty, we have not always succeeded. Your success is vital because of the earth's unusually diverse genetic populations. Our assistance is contained in the system of encoded sensory data streams, which will become known as the WingMakers' Materials. It is our method of reaching into your world with subtle assistance until that golden day in which you realize—as a species—that you are not the product of earth animals, but rather the vision of First Source.

All of this that we have disclosed in this communiqué is scheduled to occur over the next seventy-five years. This is nothing short of a revolution. It requires of you to act as a revolutionary. Your eyes alone will read these words. Remember them well. You are thus commissioned.

Neruda rubbed his eyes. He had the uncomfortable feeling that the words were directed exclusively at him. "David, are you reading this introduction?"

"I've been a little preoccupied getting the other sections translated. Why?"

"Can you look at the print out of section one and tell me what you see on page two."

"Just a minute," David replied. "Do you want me to read this aloud?"

"Yes."

"Okay," David said, clearing his throat as if rehearsing for a play. "*Life Principles of the Sovereign Integral*—it's the heading. *The entity model of expression is designed to explore new fields of vibration*—"

"Whoa, how'd you get a different text?"

"What do you mean?"

"My second page is entirely different. How's it possible that you don't have the same—" Neruda stopped in mid-sentence. He was looking at his monitor screen, and the text he had been reading was suddenly gone and replaced with the text that David had been reading moments before. His mind went blank. "How's this possible?" He said to himself, shaking his head in disbelief.

"What?" David asked. "What happened?"

"I was reading text that just disappeared. It didn't print out, and you didn't read it. It's as if the second page was erased."

"Like they were meant for only one pair of eyes?"

"Exactly," Neruda exclaimed. "But how could they do that?"

"Hold on a moment." David busied himself at a control panel. It was the monitoring system for ZEMI. "There's nothing wrong with ZEMI. All functions are normal. The only thing that would make sense is if the program were designed to be self-erasing from the source file. Nothing's been saved to our system. We were focused on opening up the files and printing them out."

"Do it now," Neruda ordered. "Save everything you have the instant you open it."

"Understood," David said. "Everything'll be saved in file name: AAP DISC CONTENTS ONE THROUGH ELEVEN."

"Is the second page still the same?"

"Yes."

"Shit."

"Perhaps you should take the time to reconstruct the text," David suggested. "You remember it, don't you?"

"Yes, of course," Neruda answered, but he was already thinking how to keep it to himself. Too many things had happened in the past eight hours that convinced him that his world had changed, as if a gigantic hand had reached down, gathered him up, and dropped him on a new stage. He no longer felt a loyalty to the ACIO, but rather to the enigmatic WingMakers. It troubled him that his loyalties could be swayed so dramatically, but he also recognized that the creators of the ETC site, if they were the Central Race, offered every reason to make a change.

"Why don't you just reconstruct it into a text file and I'll insert it into the second page," David offered.

"I'll do it in the morning, David. I'm too tired right now. I think I'll read a little more and call it a night."

"Okay," David replied. "Do you want the printout before you go?"

"Yeah, is it done?"

"Stop by on your way out and I'll have it ready for you."

"Thanks."

"Oh, one more thing," David remarked. "I was scanning the 321 pages printed out for section one, and there's not that much text. Most of it is musical notations and what appears to be programming code. We're still not certain of its purpose, but it looks intelligible—it'll just take some time to translate it so we can construct an application model. Philosophical text represents five percent of the printed output, poetry is two percent, mathematics is eight percent, programming code is sixty-three percent, and music is twenty-two percent. It's a rather odd mixture."

"Not for self-professed culture builders," Neruda said, smiling.

David remained silent.

Neruda returned to the text, eager to read more from the voice he had come to trust. He noticed familiar words in the title.

LIFE PRINCIPLES OF THE SOVEREIGN INTEGRAL

The entity model of expression is designed to explore new fields of vibration through biological instruments and transform through this process of discovery to a new level of understanding and expression as a Sovereign Integral. The Sovereign Integral is the fullest expression of the entity model within the time-space universes, and most closely exemplifies Source Intelligence's capabilities therein. This is the level of capability that was seeded within the entity model of expression when it was initially conceived by First Source.

There have been those upon terra-earth who have experienced a shallow breath of wind from this powerful tempest, which we have named the Sovereign Integral Consciousness. Some have called it ascension; others have attributed names like illumination, vision, enlightenment, nirvana, and cosmic consciousness. While these experiences are profound in human standards, they are only the initial stirrings of the Sovereign Integral, as it becomes increasingly adept at touching and awakening the remote edges of its existence. What most species define as the ultimate bliss is merely the impression of the Sovereign Integral whispering to its outposts of form and biology and nudging them to look within to their roots of existence and unite with this formless and limitless intelligence that pervades all.

The Sovereign Integral consciousness is far beyond the calibration of the human drama much like the stars in the sky are beyond the touch of terra-earth. You can observe the stars with your human eyes, but you will never touch them with your human hands. Similarly, you can dimly foresee the Sovereign Integral consciousness with the human instrument, but you cannot experience it through the human instrument. It is only accessed through the wholeness of the entity, for it is only in wholeness that the Sovereign Integral and its residual effects of Source Reality perception can exist. And truly, this wholeness is only obtained when the individual consciousness is separated from time and is able to view its existence in timelessness.

The human instrument is the soul carrier, which contains the physical, emotional, and mental aspects of the human being, and these can become aligned to trigger—like a metamorphosis—the integration of the formful identities into the Sovereign Integral. This is the next stage of perception and expression for the entity model, and it is activated when the entity designs its reality from life principles that are symbolic of Source Reality, as opposed to the reality of an external source that is bound to the evolution/saviorship model of existence.

Neruda paused. His eyes expressed wonderment at what he had read. He felt his mind throwing off some long-established shackles. He was anxious to read more, but was also aware that his energy was draining away rapidly. He rubbed his eyes again. "David, are you done with the text print-out yet?"

"Almost."

"I think I'll pack up and read the rest in the morning," Neruda said with a tired voice.

"I'll have it all ready for you in three to four minutes."

"Thanks, I'll stop by in five."

Neruda glanced at the monitor unable to resist the temptation to see what the next section held.

> These life principles are Source Intelligence templates of creation. They are designed to create reality from the perspective of the Sovereign Integral and hasten its manifestation within the fields of vibration that has thus far repelled it. They are principles that construct opportunities for the integration of the entity's formless and formful identities. They are bridges that the human instrument—with all of its componentry intact—can experience the Sovereign Integral perception of wholeness.
>
> As the human instrument becomes increasingly responsive to Source Intelligence it will gravitate to life principles that symbolically express the formative principles of First Source. There are wide ranges of expressions that can induce the transformational experience of the Sovereign Integral and liberate the entity from time-space conditioning and external controls. Inasmuch as the expression can vary, the intent of the expression is quite narrowly defined as the intent to expand into a state of integration whereby the human instrument becomes increasingly aligned with the Sovereign Integral perspective.
>
> There are three particular life principles that help to align the human instrument with the Sovereign Integral perspective. They are:
>
> > 1) Universe relationship through gratitude
> > 2) Observance of Source in all things
> > 3) Nurturance of life
>
> When the individual applies these principles, their life experience reveals a deeper meaning to its apparently random events—both in the universal and personal contexts.
>
> ### UNIVERSE RELATIONSHIP THROUGH GRATITUDE
>
> This is the principle that the Universe of Wholeness represents a collective intelligence that can be personalized as a single Universal Entity. Thus, in this model of inference, there are only two entities in the entire cosmos: the individual entity and the Universal Entity. Inasmuch as the individual soul carrier is impressionable and constantly changing to adapt to new information, so is the Universal Entity, which is a dynamic and living template of potential energies

and experiences that are coherent and as knowable as a friend's personality and behavior.

The Universal Entity is responsive to the individual and their perceptions and expressions. It is like a composite omni-personality that is imbued with Source Intelligence and responds to the perceptions of the individual like a pool of water mirrors the image that overshadows it. Everyone in a human instrument is indeed, at his or her innermost core, a sovereign entity that can transform the human instrument into an instrument of the Sovereign Integral. However, this transformation is dependent on whether the individual chooses to project an image of a Sovereign Integral upon the mirror of the Universal Entity, or project a lesser image that is a distortion of its true state of being.

The principle of *universe relationship through gratitude* is primarily concerned with consciously designing one's self image through an appreciation of the Universal Entity's supportive "mirror". In other words, the Universal Entity is a partner in shaping reality's expression in one's life. Reality is an internal process of creation that is utterly free of external controls and conditions if the individual projects a sovereign image upon the mirror of the Universal Entity.

This process is an interchange of supportive energy from the individual to the Universal Entity, and this energy is best applied through an appreciation of how perfect and exacting the interchange occurs in every moment of life. If the individual is aware (or at least interested in having the awareness) of how perfect the Universal Entity supports the individual's sovereign reality, there is a powerful and natural sense of gratitude that flows from the individual to the Universal Entity. It is this wellspring of gratitude that opens the channel of support from the Universal Entity to the individual and establishes a collaboration of purpose to transform the human instrument into an expression of the Sovereign Integral.

Neruda stopped and glanced at his wristwatch. He had read concepts of similar perspective, but he felt there was something fundamental in the words that felt authentic, if not true. He remembered translating texts from the Corteum that felt resonant to these teachings. He wondered if somehow the WingMakers had already shaped the philosophical beliefs of the Corteum. Perhaps the Corteum's planet had also been visited by these beings from the center of the universe—though he thought it strange that the Corteum could be genetically linked to the human species.

"It's ready," David's voice interrupted.

"Thanks," Neruda said absently as if his mind were lost on other matters.

"So, what do you think so far?" David inquired.

"It's fascinating, but I'll need more time with it before I could do justice to a critical review."

"I'll leave the output from the first eight sections on my desk. Oh, and the ninth section'll be completed in another ten minutes. Do you want to wait?"

"Sure, I'll wait. There's plenty to keep me occupied for ten more minutes. This isn't exactly light reading."

"Even for you?" David chuckled.

"Especially for me."

"I'll let you know when it's ready," David remarked, and then changed his tone of voice. "We have a theory about the software programming."

"I'll bite," Neruda said. "What is it?"

"So far, each of the eight chambers has a similar data distribution. There's definitely a pattern. The majority of the data is programming code. We think the programming code is an activation sequence for the technologies found within the chambers."

"Are the translations of the code applicable to ZEMI?"

"No, but I think we can crack it. Though it'll take a little experimentation.

"It'd help if we knew how to access their technology."

"Agreed," David said, "but maybe if we could understand their programming language, we could figure out how to access the technology."

"So you're talking about wireless code transfers?"

"Perhaps. But it could also be the music or sounds that appear to be present in these texts. Maybe these activate them. We'll see—hopefully very soon."

"Is everything saved within ZEMI's data architecture?"

"Yes, at least through the eighth section."

"Do a search on interface protocols."

"No matches."

"Damn. I was hoping we'd get lucky."

"Anything else?"

"No, I'll let you get back to work."

Neruda put his hands through his hair and briefly rubbed the back of his neck. While his body was exhausted, his mind was reeling from all the events of the past eight hours and the text before him. He decided to resume his reading until David was ready with the ninth section.

> It is principally gratitude—which translates to an appreciation of how the inter-relationship of the individual and the Universal Entity operates—that opens the human instrument to its connection to the sovereign entity and its eventual transformation into the Sovereign Integral state of perception and expression. The relationship of the individual with the Universal Entity is essential to cultivate and nurture, because it, more than anything else, determines how

accepting the individual is to life's myriad forms and manifestations.

When the individual accepts changes in sovereign reality as the shifting persona of the Universal Entity, they live in greater harmony with life itself. Life becomes an exchange of energy between the individual and the Universal Entity, which is allowed to play out without judgment and experienced without fear. This is the underlying meaning of unconditional love: to experience life in all its manifestations as a single, unified intelligence that responds perfectly to the projected image of the human instrument.

It is for this reason that when the human instrument projects gratitude to the Universal Entity, regardless of circumstance or condition, life becomes increasingly supportive in opening the human instrument to activate its Source Codes and live life within the framework of the synthesis model of expression. The feeling of gratitude coupled with the mental concept of appreciation is expressed like an invisible message in all directions and at all times. In this particular context, gratitude to the Universal Entity is the overarching motive behind all forms of expression that the human instrument aspires to.

Every breath, every word, every touch, every thought, every thing is centered on expressing this sense of gratitude. A gratitude that the individual is sovereign and supported by a Universal Entity that expresses itself through all forms and manifestations of intelligence with the sole objective of creating the ideal reality to activate the individual's Source Codes and transform the human instrument and entity into the Sovereign Integral. It is this specific form of gratitude that accelerates the activation of the Source Codes and their peculiar ability to integrate the disparate componentry of the human instrument and the entity, and transform them to the state of perception and expression of the Sovereign Integral.

Time is the only factor that distorts this otherwise clear connection between the individual and Universal Entity. Time intervenes and creates pockets of despair, hopelessness, and abandonment. However, it is these very pockets that often activate the Source Codes of the entity and establish a more intimate and harmonious relationship with the Universal Entity. Time establishes separation of experience, and the perceived discontinuity of reality, which in turn creates doubt in the Universal Entity's system of fairness and overarching purpose. The result creates fear that the universe is not a mirror, but rather a chaotic, whimsical energy.

When the human instrument is aligned with the Sovereign Integral and lives from this perspective as a developing reality, it attracts a *natural* state of harmony. This does not necessarily mean that the human instrument is without problems or discomforts, rather it signifies a perception that there is an integral purpose in what life reveals. In other words, natural harmony perceives that life experience is meaningful to the extent you are aligned with the Sovereign Integral, and that your personal reality must flow from this strata of the multidimensional universe in order to create lasting joy and inner peace.

Gratitude is a critical facet of love that opens the human instrument to acknowledge the role of the Universal Entity and redefine its purpose as a supportive extension of sovereign reality, rather than the whimsical outreach of fate or the exacting reaction of a mechanical, detached universe. Establishing a relationship with the Universal Entity through the outflow of gratitude also attracts life experience that is transformative. Experience that is richly devoted to uncovering life's deepest meaning and most formative purpose.

David's voice interrupted Neruda's train of thought. "Are you still reading?"

"Yes. Why?"

"We have something for you."

"And what's that?"

"We found a form of hypertext linkages throughout the text. There's the equivalent of a glossary for each section of the text. I'm refreshing your screen with the new data files from ZEMI. Click on any word or phrase that seems unusual."

Neruda pointed his cursor at the phrase, Sovereign Integral, and double clicked

SOVEREIGN INTEGRAL

The Sovereign Integral is a state of consciousness whereby the entity and all its various forms of expression and perception are integrated as a conscious wholeness. This is a state of consciousness that all entities are evolving towards, and at some point, each will reach a state of transformation that allows the entity and its instruments of experience (i.e., the human instrument) to become an integrated expression that is aligned and in harmony with Source Intelligence.

"That's great," Neruda exclaimed, mostly to himself.

"It'll make the text more comprehensible. That's for sure," David remarked. "I think I'm going to run home and catch some shut-eye. Anything else you need before I go?"

"No, I'm fine. I think I'll walk out with you, though. Can you bring the printout with you? I'll meet you at the elevator in two minutes."

"No problem. Oh, and by the way, Samantha is up. Evans escorted her from our offices just a few minutes ago. She's fully recovered, and seems to be doing well."

"Thanks, David. I appreciate the update."

"You're welcome. Signing off."

Neruda watched the ZEMI monitor fade to a brownish, dark gray. He turned his attention back to the text of section one, and moved his cursor to the phrase, Source Reality, and instantly a definition appeared.

SOURCE REALITY

First Source exists in Source Reality. Source Reality is the dimension of consciousness that is always pushing the envelope of expansion—the leading edge of development and evolution for the *whole* of consciousness. In this realm of dynamic expansion is always found Source Reality. It can be likened to the inner sanctum of First Source or the incubator of cosmological expansion. There is no identity as a place in time because it is outside of time and non-time. It is the seam between the two, perfectly invisible and yet absolutely real.

He stood to his feet, knowing that he needed to close down the system and pack up in order to meet David. His body felt different, as though he had shed weight and was now the occupant of an elongated, not-so-coordinated, young swan's body. His head ached with the thought of Samantha. His whole world seemed in absolute turmoil, and yet he felt calm, as though he were inside the eye of the hurricane while all around him calamity struck. For some reason, the thought came into his mind to talk with Emily.

Neruda let out a long sigh as he flicked off the overhead halogen lights. He felt more alone than he ever remembered feeling, even as a five-year-old after his mother died. He knew that his defection was inevitable. He had no real choice but to find this girl Lea who held the key to this magnificent puzzle. The forces directing him were more powerful than his personal will. He could feel them propelling him into the future, but their faces were blurred in the indistinguishable fires of transformation that surrounded him.

He smiled for the security cameras as he left the computer lab. A part of him was already thinking about the freedom that was beckoning him, and the danger that would undoubtedly accompany it.

INTRODUCTION TO THE NERUDA INTERVIEWS

[I]f anyone ever reads this interview, please do so with an empty mind. If you bring a mind full of learning and education and opinion, you'll find so much to argue with in what I've said that you'll not hear anything.[32]

The four interviews of Jamisson Neruda are an extension of the *Ancient Arrow Project* novel. The first three interviews are contained on the First Source disc and the fourth interview was released in November 2002, about a year following the release of the First Source disc.

The backdrop of these interviews paints a picture in which Dr. Neruda has defected from the ACIO because, his contact with the WingMakers has convinced him that they hold the keys to humanity's survival. His defection from the ACIO and from his mentor, Fifteen, signifies the outcome of a major crisis in his life—choose the familiar reality upon which his entire life is based or choose to follow his heart and Sovereign Integral, awakened through his interaction with the WingMakers.

Dr. Neruda is being interviewed by a journalist named Sarah, who has written extensive notes on Jamisson's background and knowledge of the ACIO's and the Labyrinth Group's activities. Sarah's notes provide an informative overview for the much more detailed information contained in the interviews themselves.

In all probability, the contents of the interviews are based, like the novel, on James' use of sensory bi-location (SBL). The interviews are a very creative extension of the novel and are so effective in their presentation that, at the time of their first appearance on the website in 1998, they lent more support to the contention of many WingMakers' website visitors that there is a Jamisson Neruda, that he is on the run, and that he is desperately trying to stay out of the clutches of the ACIO.

As discussed earlier, however (see Introduction to the *Ancient Arrow Project*), the interviews are a literary device, a vehicle for delivering detailed information regarding the secret government projects, aliens, advanced technologies, and plans by a cabal of hidden power elites to control the world's resources and its population. James calls this cabal the Incunabula and they are discussed extensively in the fourth interview.

Because there is such a wealth of information in these interviews (comprising more than two hundred pages), I created an index in 2004 as a resource for accessing the many topics. That index is included here following the interviews themselves.

One cautionary note: Although many of the topics discussed by Dr. Neruda are current supposed facts and others are potential possibilities, some are metaphorical parts of the fictional aspects of the WingMakers story.

---

32. The First Interview of Dr. Jamisson Neruda, p. 287

In closing this short introduction, I believe it is vital to keep in mind that although the topics discussed by Dr. Neruda are fascinating, their importance is secondary to the ultimate goal of James and the LTO, namely the discovery of the Grand Portal.

In James' session one audio interview with Mark Hempel, recorded in April 2008 we find the following:

> The real import of the WingMakers materials is to, in effect, dislodge the person from the historical mind and move them into a sense of connection to their Higher Self and the Spirit that supports it. In doing this, the person can more easily access the tone of equality or the intuitive faculty inside their heart which opens the channel to the Living Truth.[33]

Finally, in light of James' words, we might ask ourselves why he is providing this information in the first place. Perhaps he is foreshadowing a time in this century when many of these secretive plans, alien contacts, and clandestine government activities will find the light of day. Thus, this glimpse into the future of many individuals reading these documents provides a context for the economic, political, and social environment in which the steady march toward the Grand Portal will take place.

---

33. *Collected Works of the WingMakers Vol. II*, Part IV, Sec. One, Mark Hempel Interview with James, Session One

SARAH'S NOTES ON
DR. JAMISSON NERUDA

Written May 27, 1998

What follows are some of my notes taken while in earnest discussions with Dr. Neruda from the ACIO (Advanced Contact Intelligence Organization) during the last two weeks of December 1997, before he disappeared—at least off my radar screen.

Dr. Neruda is about six feet tall, perhaps one hundred-seventy pounds, has relatively long black hair, and by all appearances, seems of Peruvian descent or at least from somewhere in South America (though I never asked what specific city or village he grew up in). I would guess he was about fifty years old with just a few tinges of gray hair.

He called me out of the blue one day in mid-December 1997. His opening line to me was something like, "My name is Dr. Neruda, and I have secret information about the future of humankind that proves the existence of time-travel technology." Being a journalist by profession, it got my attention, though the whole time I spent on the phone with him my skeptical nature was in high gear. I always assume stories of a fantastical nature are false in reality, though the perceiver can think them to be true. And so that's how I operated with Dr. Neruda. I felt him to be genuine and sincere, but probably misguided or in error.

However, he was convincing enough to secure a meeting with me, and so we met a few days later at a coffee shop near my home. He didn't fit my stereotypical view of a scientist. He was much more sophisticated and even elegant in his demeanor, and looked as much like an executive of a Fortune 100 company as anything else. His charisma and articulate manner immediately impressed me, and I sensed that he was not a man of mental instability prone to wild claims.

He told me that he had no recollection of his mother, and that his father brought him to the ACIO at an early age. A high-ranking member of the ACIO had taken him under his wing, so a considerable portion of his life was involved in one way or another with the ACIO. His father raised him as a single parent. He had been told that his mother had died from breast cancer shortly after his birth when he was only about two years old. He had attended the best private schools, and additionally had been provided with special tutors, which he later learned were from the ACIO.

At the age of fourteen he came under the formal tutelage of his future colleagues from the ACIO. By the time he was seventeen he had left school and decided to pursue an internship at the ACIO, though he said that at the time, it was simply called the NSA Special Projects Laboratory and was an unacknowledged department of the

NSA. His internship lasted for two years and he never pursued a formal degree at a University, though he claimed to have knowledge about physics and the life sciences that is far in advance of the curriculums at the best universities.

He stated that he believed himself to have possessed average intelligence until he began his training and internship at the ACIO. He said that they had technologies that stimulated certain aspects of the central nervous system and brain that increased raw intelligence by as much as 500 percent. In addition, he claimed that there was a genetic implant technology that increased the ability to memorize and retain information to the point where the entire scientific core of the ACIO had perfect photographic memory. This enabled them to build their group intelligence beyond the genius of any one individual. These technologies—he claimed—were of extraterrestrial origin derived from a friendly source that had been visiting earth for thousands of years, but had arrangements with the ACIO dating from 1959 that were secret even from our government and its intelligence agencies.

The alien race, which he called the Corteum, had infiltrated the ACIO in 1958, and though he wasn't specific about how this occurred, he did say that the Corteum are still working with the ACIO to seed technologies on earth that are superior to our native technologies. The technologies to accelerate and enhance intelligence were the first technologies to be transferred and these were to enable the ACIO scientists to assimilate and utilize subsequent technologies that the Corteum brought to the ACIO. In exchange for these technologies, the Corteum were provided safe haven within the ACIO intelligence structure.

In other words, the Corteum were permitted access to all of the information systems of the ACIO, which are considerable according to Dr. Neruda. They were also able to use the facilities of the ACIO including their laboratories, considerable land holdings, and scientific brainpower. This unfettered access to ACIO intelligence provided the Corteum leaders with insight into the structure of world government, where the power centers were, who the real leaders were, and how critical decisions were made for the world's people.

According to Dr. Neruda, the Corteum are benevolent and had no ulterior motives to take over the earth and rule in dictatorship. In fact, they were much more interested in establishing diplomatic ties to the various world governments through the United Nations at the appropriate time, which was considered to be shortly after the year 2011. The existence of the Corteum was kept from the NSA and even most ACIO personnel were unaware of their existence (though I don't know how this was accomplished).

Within the ACIO, there are fourteen distinct levels of security clearance. Those who are at level twelve and above are aware of the Corteum Technology Transfer Program (TTP), and they, according to Dr. Neruda, are about 120 in number, and are primarily in India, Belgium, and the United States. There are only seven who have Level Fourteen clearance, and they are the Directors of Intelligence, Security, Research, Special Projects, Operations, Information Systems, and Communications.

These Directors report to the Executive Director, who is known simply as "Fifteen," which is the unique classification that is reserved for the head of the ACIO. Fifteen, in the eyes of Dr. Neruda, is the most powerful human on the planet, and what I think he meant by "powerful" is that Fifteen is able to deploy technologies that are well in advance to any that our world's governments have access to. However, Dr. Neruda portrayed Fifteen and his seven Directors as a benevolent force, not a hostile or controlling force.

The eight people who comprise this inner sanctum of the ACIO are in possession of radical technologies that have been part of the Corteum TTP. However, there were also other extraterrestrial technologies that had been derived from recoveries of spacecraft or other alien artifacts, including various discoveries contained in ancient texts that had never been revealed before. All of this information and technology has been collected and developed within the ACIO scientific core—all of whom possess clearances of Level Twelve or higher.

This scientific core is called the Labyrinth Group, and consists of both men and women who have utilized the Corteum intelligence accelerator technologies to their advantage, and have created a secret organization within the ACIO. When Dr. Neruda was explaining this to me, it got so complicated that I asked him if he could draw me a visual diagram of how all of these organizations worked.

The Labyrinth Group consists of all the personnel within the ACIO that qualify for levels twelve, thirteen, and fourteen clearance. Fifteen is the leader of this most secret organization. It was split from the ACIO to enable secrecy from the NSA and lower ranking members of the ACIO, which would facilitate the Labyrinth Group's agenda to create its own applications of the Corteum TTP. The Labyrinth Group is in possession of the pure technologies derived from the Corteum TTP. It takes these technologies and dilutes them to the point where the ACIO or Special Projects Laboratory will sell them to private industry and government agencies, (which includes the military).

This secret organization is the most powerful organization on earth in Dr. Neruda's opinion, but they do not choose to exercise their power in a way that makes them visible. Thus, their power is only discernible to their members. For about forty years they have accumulated considerable wealth apart from the NSA's oversight. They have managed to build their own security technologies that prevent detection from intelligence agencies like the CIA or MI5. They are, for all practical purpose, in total control of their agenda—perhaps this is what makes them a unique organization.

Dr. Neruda had a clearance of level twelve and was still kept from vital information that only the Director level was aware. And it was assumed that even Fifteen kept vital information from his Directors, though this was never a certainty. The symbol used by the Labyrinth Group is four concentric circles. Each circle representing a clearance level (twelve, thirteen, fourteen, and fifteen), and each circle had a unique insight into the agenda of the Labyrinth Group, and its coordination with the Corteum.

Fifteen was an enigma to everyone within the Labyrinth Group. He had been a physicist before he became the Executive Director of the ACIO. He was a renegade because he never interacted with the protocols and the political environment of academia. He operated outside of the institutions and was selected to be part of the ACIO because of his combination of brainpower, independence, and relative obscurity within scientific circles. He was one of the first to make contact with the Corteum and establish communication with them. The Corteum essentially appointed Fifteen as their liaison to the ACIO, and Fifteen became the first to utilize the intelligence accelerator technologies that the Corteum initially offered.

These technologies not only enhance cognitive abilities, memory, and higher order thinking skills, but also enhance the consciousness of the individual so that they can utilize the newly gained intelligence in a non-invasive manner. Meaning, they don't exploit their intelligence for personal gain at the expense of others. This apparent increase in both Fifteen's IQ and ethical consciousness caused him to create the Labyrinth Group in order to retain the pure-state technologies of the Corteum TTP from the NSA.

What technologies are released to the NSA are diluted forms of the pure-state technology, which are significantly less potent in their military and surveillance applications. What I expected to hear from Dr. Neruda was a secret organization of intelligent, evil elitists—individuals intent on exploitation and control. Why else would they want to hide beneath the cloak of such incredible secrecy?

The answer, according to Dr. Neruda, was surprising. The Labyrinth Group view themselves as the only group with sufficient intellect and technology to develop a specific form of time travel technology. They are essentially focused on this agenda because they desire to prevent future hostilities that they believe will occur unless this technology is developed. The Corteum is assisting, but despite their considerable intellects, they have been unable to develop this technology.

What I'm about to tell you will seem impossible to believe, but again, I'm only reporting what my notes say based on my initial conversations with Dr. Neruda. He explained to me that there are as many as twelve different extraterrestrial races currently involved in the past, present, and future of earth and its destiny. The ACIO, because of its mission with the NSA, is the most knowledgeable group about the various agendas of these twelve alien races.

Apparently there is an extraterrestrial race that may have hostile intent and the technological potential to disrupt the human social order and overtake it, as well as earth itself. This concern is what motivated Fifteen to assign the Labyrinth Group's intellect and collective energy to create the ultimate defense weapon—which they refer to as Blank Slate Technology (BST) or a form of time travel. I don't pretend to understand all of what Dr. Neruda described regarding BST. My notes are a bit vague because he was talking so far over my head I didn't even know what to write in many instances.

When the Ancient Arrow Project came under the control of the ACIO, it was— like all projects—carefully scrutinized to determine if there were any technologies that could help in the overall agenda of developing BST. When it was determined that the Ancient Arrow project was in fact a time capsule from a future aspect of humanity, the Labyrinth Group seized the project from the ACIO and essentially began a misinformation campaign back to the NSA.

Dr. Neruda was one of two scientists that held a level twelve clearance and was asked to lead in the translation of the WingMakers language and decode their various communication symbols. In this process, he became aware of how to decode their language and began to understand what they were trying to communicate. He became convinced that the WingMakers were time travelers and possessed a form of BST. He also became convinced that there were six additional time capsules stored in various places around the globe, and that they held the technologies or insights that would enable the development of BST.

The reason he defected was that somehow in the process of translating the WingMakers language, he became a sympathizer of their philosophy. He felt that the WingMakers were communicating with him and had selected him as their liaison. And when he acknowledged this to his superiors, he was felt to be a risk to the project's secrecy. Apparently, when personnel, regardless of clearance or rank become known as security risks, they are given a "memory therapy" that essentially removes problematic experiences from their mind. Dr. Neruda felt certain that he was going to receive this "therapy" imminently, and could not fathom the results of losing his memories of the WingMakers experience. Thus, he defected from the ACIO and the Labyrinth Group, the first to ever do so.

When he had contacted me, he had defected only the day before. He told me that I would have to wait for him to contact me again to set up a rendezvous time and place. Three days later he called and we met that same afternoon. I wasn't prepared to believe him, but I thought it was a provocative story and was worth spending an hour or two investigating.

Anyway, what he proceeded to tell me in that first meeting is largely contained in this journal entry. He showed me photographs and documents from the Ancient Arrow Project that appeared authentic to my eyes. He also showed me some of the technologies that were in development by the ACIO concerning holographic fractal objects or HFOs as he called them. These were incredible to observe (and equally impossible to explain) and I must admit that my first impression after seeing HFOs in action was that any organization that could develop this technology was operating at a level well outside of the mainstream. It felt alien to me.

It was then I became at least a partial believer. I called my employer and told them that I needed to take some personal leave. I took one week off and spent a significant portion of it with Dr. Neruda, asking a thousand questions, which, for the most part, he had ready answers to. Gradually I became a reluctant believer with a healthy streak of skepticism. At the end of the week, he asked me to take some of his materials and publish them. There were times that I honestly felt he was an extraterrestrial, and even now I'm not certain that he isn't. (This from a person who six short months ago would have disputed ETs and any other "bump-in-the-night" phenomenon.)

He was convinced that the ACIO would not allow him to defect with his memory intact. He was fearful of their remote viewing technology and was certain that they would try to track him down. He wanted me to have possession of the materials only if I volunteered to do so, and was willing to publish them. And through all of this, he wasn't absolutely certain that the Labyrinth Group and their ET friends, the Corteum, were intending anything bad. He just didn't want his memory tampered with.

I think he was mostly interested in exposing the WingMakers time capsule and its philosophy and communication symbols. He never seemed that interested in exposing the ACIO and its secret organization the Labyrinth Group. He told me about this entity only to impress upon me that he was part of an organization that had unusual powers and technologies. And to the extent they wanted to keep things under wrap, they would use their considerable powers to do so, which was why he had picked me at random to help him in getting this story out.

Dr. Neruda was the most sincere individual I have ever met. Someone I would love to count among my friends. I was so impressed with his manners, communication skills, and intellect. At one time, I asked him what his IQ was, and with all humility intact, he simply answered that there is no way to test it. And that the Labyrinth Group's members are not interested in IQ, so much as what he called Fluid Intelligence, or the speed with which alternative, creative solutions to a problem can be generated.

He claimed this was the most important form of intelligence, and without it, one would not be able to time travel. In other words, he was convinced that time travel was not an independent technology, but was integral to the traveler. The time traveler must have a certain degree of fluid intelligence in order to withstand the stress inherent in time travel, and the best way to handle the stress was by having a high level of fluid intelligence.

The thing I found so fascinating about Dr. Neruda was his descriptions of how information about ETs, new physics, cosmology, prophecies, and the galactic hierarchy were hidden from the public, government, and even intelligence organizations. He told me that only one man had ever really tried to write about the NSA's Special Project Laboratory and that was back in 1950, and according to my notes it was written by Wilbur Smith, who I believe was a journalist from Canada. Everything else that has been written is done so on the basis of pure speculation.

Dr. Neruda said that when this paper was circulated it was the genesis of the ACIO in order to build another layer of what he called unacknowledged departments. He said that unacknowledged departments are rare in intelligence agencies, but those that do exist often telescope into greater levels of secrecy in order to remain hidden from public and private scrutiny.

He also inferred that there were corporate members of the military-industrial complex that were involved in these unacknowledged departments. He claimed that the ACIO or its sister organization, the Special Projects Laboratory, would sell diluted technologies to private corporations and laboratories, which in turn would be commercialized for the military, and in some instances, even consumer use.

Dr. Neruda permitted me to tape record five formal interviews with him. These are probably the best way to understand his perspective and the story that he has to tell. Even now as I'm writing this letter, I find myself doubting much of what he told me, while at the same time I can't imagine why he'd go to all this trouble if it were just a game or charade of some kind. It just doesn't make any sense in that context. So, I'm stuck somewhere in the middle of belief and disbelief. I can only tell you that if only a small percentage of his story is accurate, then citizens and their politicians need to wake up. According to Dr. Neruda, even our highest-ranking government officials and military intelligence officers lack access to the information that he was privy to.

But if these unacknowledged secret departments exist, and private contractors working on behalf of the military are involved with these secret organizations, some organization should be investigating this. And they should have powers to grant witness protection, immunity, and a variety of other inducements to get these secrets out to the public or, at the very least, our government officials.

I have approximately sixty pages of notes from my initial discussions with Dr. Neruda and then five transcripts from the five interviews I conducted. I'd encourage anyone who's serious about understanding these issues to read the interview transcripts. They're probably our best records of what's going on behind closed doors relative to the ET phenomenon, secret organizations, and time travel.

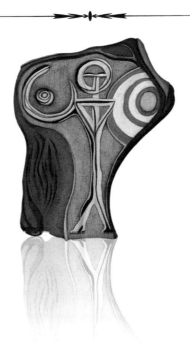

THE FIRST INTERVIEW OF
DR. JAMISSON NERUDA

By Sarah

What follows is a session I recorded of Dr. Neruda on December 27, 1997. He gave permission for me to record his answers to my questions. This was the first of five interviews that I was able to tape-record before he left or disappeared. I have preserved these transcripts precisely as they occurred. No editing was performed, and I've tried my best to include the exact words and grammar used by Dr. Neruda.

Sarah: "Are you comfortable?"

Dr. Neruda: "Yes, yes, I'm fine and ready to begin when you are."

Sarah: "You've made some remarkable claims with respect to the Ancient Arrow Project. Can you please recount what your involvement in this project was and why you chose to leave it of your own freewill?"

Dr. Neruda: "I was selected to lead the decoding and translation of the symbol pictures found at the site. I have a known expertise in languages and ancient texts. I am able to speak over thirty different languages fluently and another twelve or so languages that are officially extinct. Because of my skills in linguistics and my abilities to decode symbol pictures like petroglyphs or hieroglyphs, I was chosen for this task.

"I had been involved in the Ancient Arrow Project from its very inception, when the ACIO took over the project from the NSA. I was initially involved in the site discovery and its restoration along with a team of seven other scientists from the ACIO. We restored each of the twenty-three chambers of the WingMakers time capsule and cataloged all of their attendant artifacts.

"As the restoration was completed, I became increasingly focused on decoding their peculiar language and designing the translation indexes to English. It was a particularly vexing process because an optical disc was found in the twenty-third chamber, which initially impregnable to our technologies. We assumed that the optical disc held most of the information that the WingMakers desired us to know about them. However, we couldn't figure out how to apply the symbol pictures found in their chamber paintings to unlock the disc.

"I decided to leave the project after I was successful in deducing the access code for the optical disc, and felt that the ACIO was going to prevent the public from accessing the information contained within the Ancient Arrow site. There were other reasons, but it's too complicated to explain in a concise response."

Sarah: "What did Fifteen do when he found out you were leaving?"

Dr. Neruda: "He never had a chance to respond directly to me because I left without a word. But I'm certain that he's angry and feels betrayed."

Sarah: "Tell me about Fifteen. What's he like?"

Dr. Neruda: "Fifteen is a genius of unparalleled intelligence and knowledge. He's the leader of the Labyrinth Group and has been since its inception in 1963. He was only twenty-two years old when he joined the ACIO in 1956. I think he was discovered early enough before he had a chance to establish a reputation in academic circles. He was a renegade genius who wanted to build computers that would be powerful enough to time travel. Can you imagine how a goal like that—in the mid-1950s —must have sounded to his professors?

"Needless to say, he was not taken seriously, and was essentially told to get in line with academic protocols and perform serious research. Fifteen came to the ACIO through an alliance it had with Bell Labs. Somehow Bell Labs heard about his genius and hired him, but he quickly outpaced their research agenda and wanted to apply his vision of time travel."

Sarah: "Why was he so interested in time travel?"

Dr. Neruda: "No one is absolutely sure. And his reasons may have changed over time. The accepted purpose was to develop Blank Slate Technology or BST. BST is a form of time travel that enables the rewrite of history at what are called intervention points. Intervention points are the causal energy centers that create a major event like the breakup of the Soviet Union or the NASA space program.

"BST is the most advanced technology and clearly anyone who is in possession of BST, can defend themselves against any aggressor. It is, as Fifteen was fond of saying, the freedom key. Remember that the ACIO was the primary interface with extraterrestrial technologies, and how to adapt them into mainstream society as well as military applications. We were exposed to ETs and knew of their agenda. Some of these ETs scared the hell out of the ACIO."

Sarah: "Why?"

Dr. Neruda: "There were agreements between our government—specifically the NSA—to cooperate with an ET species commonly called the Greys in exchange for their cooperation to stay hidden, and conduct their biological experiments under the cloak of secrecy. There was also a bungled technology transfer program, but that's another story… However, not all the Greys were operating within a unified agenda. There were certain groups of Greys that looked upon humans in much the same way as we look upon laboratory animals.

"They're abducting humans and animals, and have been for the past forty-eight years… they're essentially conducting biological experiments to determine how their genetics can be made to be compatible with human and animal genetic structure. Their interests are not entirely understood, but if you accept their stated agenda, it's to perpetuate their species. Their species is nearing extinction. They're fearful that their biological system lacks the emotional development to harness their technological prowess in a responsible manner.

"Fifteen was approached by the Greys in his role at the ACIO, and they desired to provide a full-scale technology transfer program, but Fifteen turned them down. He had already established a TTP with the Corteum, and felt that the Greys were too fractured organizationally to make good on their promises. Furthermore, the Corteum technology was superior in most regards to the Greys... with the possible exception of the Greys' memory implant and their genetic hybridization technologies.

"However, Fifteen and the entire Labyrinth Group carefully considered an alliance with the Greys if for no other reason than to have direct communication with regard to their stated agenda. Fifteen liked to be in the know... so eventually we did establish an alliance, which consisted of a modest information exchange between us. We provided them with access to our information systems relative to genetic populations and their unique predisposition across a variety of criteria including mental, emotional, and physical behaviors; and they provided us with their genetic findings.

"The Greys, and most extraterrestrials for that matter, communicate with humans exclusively through a form of telepathy, which we called suggestive telepathy because, to us it seemed that the Greys communicated in a such a way that they were trying to lead a conversation to a particular end. In other words, they always had an agenda, and we were never certain if we were a pawn of their agenda or we arrived at conclusions that were indeed our own.

"I think that's why Fifteen didn't trust the Greys. He felt they used communication to manipulate outcomes to their own best interest in favor of shared interests. And because of this lack of trust, Fifteen refused to form any alliance or TTP that was comprehensive or integral to our operations at either the ACIO or the Labyrinth Group."

Sarah: "Did the Greys know of the existence of the Labyrinth Group?"

Dr. Neruda: "I don't believe so. They were generally convinced that humans were not clever enough to cloak their agendas. Our analysis was that the Greys had invasive technologies that gave them a false sense of security as to their enemy's weaknesses. I'm not saying that we were enemies, but we never trusted them. And this they undoubtedly knew. They also knew that the ACIO had technologies and intellects that were superior to the mainstream human population, and they had a modicum of respect—perhaps even fear—of our abilities.

"However, we never showed them any of our pure-state technologies or engaged them in deep dialogues concerning cosmology or new physics. They were clearly interested in our information databases and this was their primary agenda with respect to the ACIO. Fifteen was the primary interface with the Greys because they sensed a comparable intellect in him. The Greys looked at Fifteen as the equivalent of our planet's CEO."

Sarah: "How did Fifteen become the leader of both the ACIO and the Labyrinth Group?"

Dr. Neruda: "He was the Director of Research in 1958 when the Corteum first became known to the ACIO. In this position, he was the logical choice to assess their technology and determine its value to the ACIO. The Corteum instantly took a liking to him, and one of Fifteen's first decisions was to utilize the Corteum intelligence accelerator technologies on himself. After about three months of experimentation (most of which was not in his briefing reports to the then current Executive Director of the ACIO), Fifteen became infused with a massive vision of how to create BST.

"The Executive Director was frightened by the intensity of Fifteen's BST agenda, and felt that it would divert too much of the ACIO's resources to a technology development program that was dubious. Fifteen was enough of a renegade that he enlisted the help of the Corteum to establish the Labyrinth Group. The Corteum were equally interested in BST for similar reasons as Fifteen. The Freedom Key, as it was sometimes called, was established as the prime agenda of the Labyrinth Group, and the Corteum and Fifteen were its initial members.

"Over the next several years, Fifteen selected the cream of the crop from the scientific core of the ACIO to undergo a similar intelligence accelerator program as he had, with the intention of developing a group of scientists that could—in cooperation with the Corteum—successfully invent BST. The ACIO, in the opinion of Fifteen, was too controlled by the NSA. He felt the NSA was too immature in its leadership to responsibly deploy the technologies that he knew would be developed as an outgrowth of the Labyrinth Group. So Fifteen essentially plotted to take over the ACIO and was assisted by his new recruits to do so.

"This happened a few years before I became affiliated with the ACIO as a student and intern. My stepfather was very sympathetic to Fifteen's agenda and was helpful in placing Fifteen as the Executive Director of the ACIO. There was a period of instability when this transition occurred, but after about a year, Fifteen was firmly in control of the agendas of both the ACIO and the Labyrinth Group.

"What I said earlier… that he was viewed as the CEO of the planet… that's essentially who he is. And of the ETs who are interacting with humankind, only the Corteum understand the role of Fifteen. He has a vision that is unique in that it is a blueprint for the creation of BST, and is closing in on the right technological and human elements that will make this possible."

Sarah: "What makes BST such an imperative to Fifteen and the Labyrinth Group?"

Dr. Neruda: "The ACIO has access to many ancient texts that contain prophecies of the earth. These have been accumulated over the past several hundred years through our network of secret organizations of which we are a part. These ancient texts are not known in academic institutions, the media, or mainstream society; they are quite powerful in their depictions of the twenty-first century. Fifteen was made aware of these texts early on when he became Director of Research for the ACIO, and this knowledge only fueled his desire to develop BST."

Sarah: "What were these prophecies and who made them?"

Dr. Neruda: "The prophecies were made by a variety of people who are, for the most part, unknown or anonymous, so if I told you their names you would have no recognition. You see, time travel can be accomplished by the soul from an observational level… that is to say, that certain individuals can move in the realm of what we call vertical time and see future events with great clarity, but they are powerless to change them. There are also those individuals who have, in our opinion, come into contact with the WingMakers and are provided messages about the future, which they had recorded in symbol pictures or extinct languages like Sumerian, Mayan, and Chakobsan.

"The messages or prophecies that they made had several consistent strands or themes that were to occur in the early part of the twenty-first century, around the year 2011. Chief among these was the infiltration of the major governments of the world, including the United Nations, by an alien race. This alien race was a predator race with extremely sophisticated technologies that enabled them to integrate with the human species. That is to say, they could pose as humanoids, but they were truly a blend of human and android—in other words, they were synthetics.

"This alien race was prophesied to establish a world government and rule as its executive power. It was to be the ultimate challenge to humankind's collective intelligence and survival. These texts are kept from the public because they are too fear-provoking and would likely result in apocalyptic reprisals and mass paranoia…"

Sarah: "Are you saying what I think you're saying? That anonymous prophets from God know where and when, have seen a vision of our future takeover by a race of robots? I mean you do realize how… how unbelievable that sounds?"

Dr. Neruda: "Yes… I know it sounds unbelievable… but there are diluted versions of this very same prophecy in our religious texts, it's just that the alien race is portrayed as the antichrist; as if the alien race was personified in the form of Lucifer. This form of the prophecy was acceptable to the gatekeepers of these texts, and so they allowed a form of the prophecy to be distributed, but the notion of an alien race was eliminated."

Sarah: "Why? And who exactly is it who's censoring what we can read and can't? Are you suggesting there's a secret editorial committee that previews books before their distribution?"

Dr. Neruda: "This is a very complicated subject and I could spend a whole day just acquainting you with the general structure of this control of information. Most of the world's major libraries have collections of information that are not available to the general public. Only scholars are authorized to review these materials, and usually only on site. In the same way, there are manuscripts that were controversial and posited theories that were sharply different than the accepted belief systems of their day. These manuscripts or writings were banished by a variety of sources, including the Vatican, universities, governments, and various institutions.

"These writings are sought out by secret organizations that have a mission to collect and retain this information. These organizations are very powerful and well funded, and they can purchase these original manuscripts for a relatively small amount of money. Most of the writings are believed to be hocus-pocus anyway, so libraries are often very willing to part with them for an endowment or modest contribution. Also, most of these are original writings having never been published, being that they originated from a time before the printing press.

"There is a network of secret organizations that are loosely connected through the financial markets and their interests in worldly affairs. They are generally centers of power for the monetary systems within their respective countries, and are elitists of the first order. The ACIO is affiliated with this network only because it is rightly construed that the ACIO has the best technology in the world, and this technology can be deployed for financial gain through market manipulation.

"As for an editorial committee... no, this secret network of organizations doesn't review books before publication. Its holdings are exclusively in ancient manuscripts and religious texts. They have a very strong interest in prophecy because they believe in the concept of vertical time and they have a vested interest in knowing the macro-environmental changes that can affect the economy. You see for most of them, the only game on this planet that is worth playing is the acquisition of ever-increasing wealth and power through an orchestrated manipulation of the key variables that drive the economic engines of our world."

Sarah: "So, if they're so smart about the future, and they believe these prophecies, what're they doing to help protect us from these alien invaders?"

Dr. Neruda: "They help fund the ACIO. This collective of organizations has enormous wealth. More than most governments can comprehend. The ACIO provides them with the technology to manipulate money markets and rake in hundreds of billions of dollars every year. I don't even know the scope of their collective wealth. The ACIO also receives funding from the sale of its diluted technologies to these organizations for the sake of their own security and protection. We've devised the world's finest security systems, which are both undetectable and impregnable to outside forces like the CIA and the former KGB.

"The reason they fund the ACIO is that they believe Fifteen is the most brilliant man alive and they're aware of his general agenda to develop BST. They see this technology as the ultimate safeguard against the prophecy and their ability to retain relative control of the world and national economies. They also know Fifteen's strategic position with alien technologies and hope that between his genius, and the alien technologies that the ACIO is assimilating, that BST is possible to develop before the prophecy occurs."

Sarah: "But why the sudden interest in the WingMakers time capsule? How does it play a role in all of this BST stuff?"

Dr. Neruda: "Initially, we didn't know what the connection was between the Ancient Arrow Project and the BST Imperative. You have to understand that the time capsule was a collection of twenty-three chambers literally carved inside of a canyon wall in the middle of nowhere about eighty miles northeast of Chaco Canyon in New Mexico. It's without a doubt, the most amazing archeological find of all time. If scientists were allowed to examine this site, with all of its artifacts intact, they would be in awe of this incredible find.

"Our preliminary assumptions were that this site was a time capsule of sorts left behind by an extraterrestrial race who had visited earth in the eighth century. But we couldn't understand why the art was so clearly representative of earth—if it were a time capsule. The only logical conclusion was that it represented a future version of humanity. But we weren't certain of this until we figured out how to access the optical disc and translate the first set of documents from the disc.

"Once we had a clear understanding of how the WingMakers wanted to be understood, we began to test their claims by analyzing their chamber paintings, poetry, music, philosophy, and artifacts. This analysis made us fairly certain that they were authentic, which meant that they were not only time travelers, but that they were also in possession of a form of BST…"

Sarah: "Why did you assume they had BST?"

Dr. Neruda: "We believed it took them a minimum of two months to create their time capsule. This would have required them to open and hold open a window of time and physically operate within the selected time frame. This is a fundamental requirement of BST. Additionally, it is necessary to be able to select the intervention points with precision—both in terms of time and space. We believed they had this capability, and they had proven it with their time capsule.

"Furthermore, the technological artifacts they had left behind were evidence of a technology that was so far in advance to our own that we couldn't even understand them. None of the extraterrestrial races we were aware of had technologies so advanced that we could not probe them, assimilate them, and reverse-engineer them. The technologies left behind in the Ancient Arrow site were totally enigmatic and impervious to our probes. We considered them so advanced that they were quite literally indiscernible and unusable which—though it may sound odd—is a clear sign of an extremely advanced technology."

Sarah: "So you decided that the WingMakers were in possession of BST, but how did you think you were going to acquire their knowledge?"

Dr. Neruda: "We didn't know, and to this day, the answer to that question is elusive. The ACIO placed its best resources on this project for more than two intensive months. I posited the theory that the time capsule was an encoded communication device. I began to theorize that when one went through the effort to interact with the various symbol pictures and immerse themselves in the time capsule's art and philosophy, it affected the central nervous system in a way that it improved fluid intelligence.

"It was, in my opinion, the principle goal of the time capsule to boost fluid intelligence so that BST was not only able to be developed, but also utilized…"

Sarah: "You lost me. What is the relationship between BST and fluid intelligence?"

Dr. Neruda: "BST is a specific form of time travel. Science fiction treats time travel as something that is relatively easy to design and develop, and relatively one-dimensional. Time travel is anything but one-dimensional. As advanced in technology as the Corteum and Greys are, they have yet to produce the equivalent of BST. They are able to time travel in its elemental form, but they can't interact with the time that they travel to. That is to say, they can go back in time, but once there, they cannot alter the events of that time because they are in a passive, observational mode.

"The Labyrinth Group has conducted seven time travel experiments over the past thirty years. One clear outcome from these tests is that the person performing the time travel is an integral variable to the technology used to time travel. In other words, the person and the technology need to be precisely matched. The Labyrinth Group, for all it knows, already possesses BST, but lacks the time traveler equivalent of an astronaut who can appropriately finesse the technology in real time and make the split-second adjustments that BST requires.

"The Labyrinth Group has never seriously considered the human element of BST and how it is integral to the technology itself. There were some of us who were involved in the translation indexes of the WingMakers, who began to feel that that was the nature of the time capsule: to enhance fluid intelligence and activate new sensory inputs that were critical to the BST experience."

Sarah: "But I still don't understand what it was that led you to that conclusion?"

Dr. Neruda: "When we had translated the first thirty pages of text from the optical disc, we learned some interesting things about the WingMakers and their philosophy. Namely, that they claimed that the three-dimensional five-sensory domain that humans have adjusted to, is the reason we are only using a fractional portion of our intelligence. They claimed that the time capsule would be the bridge from the three-dimensional five-sensory domain to the multidimensional seven-sensory domain.

"In my opinion, they were saying that in order to apply BST, the traveler needed to operate from the multidimensional seven-sensory domain. Otherwise, BST was the proverbial camel through the eye of the needle… or in other words… impossible…"

Sarah: "This at least seems plausible to me, why was it so hard to believe for the ACIO?"

Dr. Neruda: "This initiative was really conducted by the Labyrinth Group and not the ACIO, so I'm making that distinction just to be accurate, and not to be critical of your question. For Fifteen, it was hard to believe that a time capsule could activate or construct a bridge that would lead someone to become a traveler. This seemed like an extraordinarily remote possibility. He felt that the time capsule may hold the technology to enable BST, but he didn't believe it was merely an educational or developmental experience.

"Also, and more importantly, the true identity of the WingMakers became clear as we deployed our RV technologies."

Sarah: "First, what're RV technologies?"

Dr. Neruda: "Think of it as psychic spying. The ACIO has a department that specializes in Remote Viewing technology, and within this department was a woman of unparalleled capability as an RV. She was assigned to the project as its RV, and she was a critical element in determining the identity and purpose of the WingMakers."

Sarah: "Can we come back to the RV technology? Just tell me what she discovered as to the identity of the WingMakers."

Dr. Neruda: "She was very attuned to the first artifact we recovered, which turned out to be a homing device that essentially led us to the Ancient Arrow site. We conducted two official RV sessions—one that I monitored and another that Fifteen monitored. She was able to make contact with the original planners of the Ancient Arrow site. Through these two RV sessions we were able to determine that the identity of the WingMakers was an ancient—the most ancient—race of humankind."

Sarah: "When you say most ancient, what do you mean?"

Dr. Neruda: "We know of them mostly through a few ancient manuscripts that were reputedly channeled by these beings. There're a few myths in Mayan and Sumerian text that refer to these beings as well. But the most definitive text comes from the Corteum who defined them, in our terms, as the Central Race."

Sarah: "How can they be so ancient if they're so technologically advanced?"

Dr. Neruda: "The Central Race resides in the most primeval galaxies nearest the centermost part of the universe. According to Corteum cosmology, the structure of the universe is segmented into seven superuniverses that each revolve around a central universe. The central universe is the material home of First Source or the Creator. According to the Corteum, in order to *govern* the material universe, First Source must *inhabit* materiality and function in the material universe. The central universe is the material home of First Source and is eternal. It's surrounded by dark gravity bodies that make it essentially invisible even to those galaxies that lie closest to its periphery.

"The Corteum teach that the central universe is stationary and eternal, while the seven superuniverses are creations of time and revolve around the central universe in a counterclockwise rotation. Surrounding these seven superuniverses is 'outer' or peripheral space, which is nonphysical elementals consisting of non-baryonic matter or antimatter, which rotates around the seven superuniverses in a clockwise rotation. This vast outer space is expansion room for the superuniverses to expand into. The known universe that your astronomers see is mostly a small fragment of our superuniverse and the expansion space at its outermost periphery. Hubble-based astronomy extrapolates, based on a fractional field of view, that there are fifty billion galaxies in our superuniverse, each containing over one hundred billion stars. However, most astronomers remain convinced that our universe is singular. It is not… according to the Corteum.

"On the fringe of the central universe resides the Central Race, which contain the original human DNA template of creation. However, they are such an ancient race that they appear to us as Gods, when indeed they represent our future selves. Time and space are the only variables of distinction. The Central Race is known to some as the creator gods who developed the primal template of the human species and then, working in conjunction with the Life Carriers, seeded the galaxies as the universes expanded. Each of the seven superuniverses has a distinctive purpose and relationship with the central universe via the Central Race based on how the Central Race experimented with the DNA to achieve distinct, but compatible physical embodiments to be soul carriers."

Sarah: "I don't even know what to ask next…"

Dr. Neruda: "The Central Race is divided into seven tribes, and they are master geneticists and the progenitors of the humanoid race. In effect, they are our future selves. Quite literally they represent what we will evolve into in time and towards in terms of space."

Sarah: "So, you're saying that the WingMakers are our future selves and that they're building these time capsules in order to communicate with us?"

Dr. Neruda: "The Labyrinth Group believed that the WingMakers are representatives of the Central Race, and that they created our particular human genotype to become suitable soul carriers in our particular universe. The Ancient Arrow site is part of a broader, interconnected system of seven sites installed on each continent. Together, we believe this system constitutes a defensive technology."

Sarah: "So there're are seven Ancient Arrow sites?"

Dr. Neruda: "Yes."

Sarah: "And you know where they are?"

Dr. Neruda: "I know generally where the remaining six are, but I don't know their specific location. They remain undiscovered so far as I know."

Sarah: "Why would the most advanced race—or future version of humanity—place such a sophisticated array of technologies and artifacts on our planet? What're they afraid of?"

Dr. Neruda: "They have an ancient, formidable enemy, which Fifteen calls the Animus."

Sarah: "We're back to the synthetics?"

Dr. Neruda: "One in the same."

Sarah: "So, the WingMakers are protecting their human genetics from the invasion of the Animus, and they placed these sites… or defensive technologies on earth to somehow prevent them from taking over the planet?"

Dr. Neruda: "That's essentially what we believe. However, it's more than human DNA. It includes all the higher order animals, humans being one of a collective of about one hundred and twenty species."

Sarah: "And you know all of this because of a psychic's vision, a few ancient manuscripts, and the Corteum?"

Dr. Neruda: "I admit it sounds implausible, but yes, we know all of this from sources that no one in the public domain can access or corroborate."

Sarah: "So the WingMakers or Central Race, created us and presumably hundreds of other species, planted us on earth, and then built a complex defensive system to protect their genetics. Is that the situation?"

Dr. Neruda: "The best way to conceptualize who these beings are, is to consider them as geneticists who were the first born of First Source. The galaxies in which the Central Race resides are approximately eighteen billion years old and their genetics are immeasurably more developed than our own. They are the optimal soul carrier in that they can co-exist in the material world and the non-material dimensions simultaneously. This is because their genetic blueprint has been fully activated."

Sarah: "You sound like you're a believer in this philosophy, but I don't understand why you're such an authority if it's the Corteum cosmology. Did they teach you this?"

Dr. Neruda: "Part of our TTP with the Corteum extended to their cosmology, and they have the equivalent of our Bible called *Liminal Cosmogony* that I translated. It was our first detailed exposure to the Central Race and their behind-the-scenes influence of genetic evolution and transformation."

Sarah: "What do you mean 'behind-the-scenes'?"

Dr. Neruda: "The WingMakers have created a DNA template that is form-fitted to each of the seven superuniverses, enabling a unique and dominant soul carrier to emerge within each of the superuniverses. This soul carrier—in our case—is the human genotype. Within our genetic substrate is the inborn structure that will ultimately deliver our species to the central universe as a perfected species. The WingMakers have encoded this within our DNA, and set forth the natural and artificial trigger points that cause our genetic structures to alter and adapt. In this process, it activates parts of our nervous system that feed the brain with a much richer stream of data from our five senses and two additional senses that we have yet to consciously activate."

Sarah: "It sounds a little too manufactured."

Dr. Neruda: "What do you mean?"

Sarah: "Just that humans will one day aspire to the heights of the WingMakers, but our salvation is something invisible that's encoded in our genes. It feels like we're manufactured to attain the same view or perspective of our creators. What happened to freewill?"

Dr. Neruda: "You raise a good question, Sarah. I can't defend this system of belief. I can recite any passage you want from the books that I know, but it's just someone's opinion who's taken the time to write it down.

"I can tell you that in my experience, the wider the range of possibilities as one moves toward more of a multidimensional thought stream and activity path, the narrower one's choices become as they pertain to rightful living. You could even say that freewill diminishes as one becomes realized to all possibilities."

Sarah: "I know you're trying to help, but you lost me… but don't try to explain again. Let' s just chalk it up to my dense brain getting in the way."

Dr. Neruda: "If it's anything, it's my poor explanation. It's difficult to define these things in a way that can enter your consciousness at its preparation point."

Sarah: "You said earlier that the WingMakers encoded trigger points that were both natural and artificially stimulated. What did you mean?"

Dr. Neruda: "Again, I want to emphasize that this is all according to the Corteum. We have very little proof of any of this from our own empirical research. However, the Labyrinth Group has a high degree of trust in the Corteum's cosmological systems of belief because of their history as an explorer race, and their superior application of physics.

"Our human DNA is designed. It did not evolve from forces of time, matter, and energy. It was *designed* by the Central Race, and part of this design was to encode within the DNA template certain super sensory capabilities that would enable a human to perceive itself in a very specific way."

Sarah: "In what way?"

Dr. Neruda: "As a soul carrier that is connected to the universe like a ray of light is connected to a spectrum of colors as it passes through a prism."

Sarah: "Could you be a bit more concrete?"

Dr. Neruda (laughing): "I'm sorry, sometimes I quote passages—it's easier than coming up with my own explanation every time."

Sarah: "No doubt one of the curses of having a photographic memory."

Dr. Neruda: "Perhaps you're right. I'll try in my own words.
"Our DNA is designed to respond to natural imagery, words, tones, music, and other external forces."

Sarah: "What do you mean by 'respond'?"

Dr. Neruda: "It can activate or deactivate certain components of its structure that enable adaptation in both the biological and higher states of being…"

Sarah: "Like?"

Dr. Neruda: "Like the state of enlightenment as described by some of our planet's spiritual teachers."

Sarah: "I've never heard of enlightenment as something that one *adapts* to."

Dr. Neruda: "That's only because mystics and scientists alike do not understand this aspect of the human DNA template. Everything, whether it's a biological environment or a state of mind, requires adaptation on the part of the person undergoing the experience. Adaptation is the primary intelligence designed within our genetic code, and it is this intelligence that is awakened, or triggered, with certain stimuli.
"The stimuli can be artificially induced, that is to say, the Central Race has encoded adaptation to higher vibratory frequencies within our DNA that they can trigger through catalytic images, words, or sounds."

Sarah: "Okay, so now you're coming full circle to the purpose of the artifacts found at the Ancient Arrow site. Correct?"

Dr. Neruda: "I believe they're related. To what extent I'm not sure. But from reading the information contained within the optical disc, I'm quite certain that the WingMakers intend the music, art, poetry, and philosophy to be catalytic."

Sarah: "But for what purpose?"

Dr. Neruda: "Let's save that for a later time. I promise we'll get to that, but it's a very long story."

Sarah: "Let's take a short break and resume after we've had a chance to grab some more coffee. Okay?"

Dr. Neruda: "Okay."

(Break for about ten minutes... Resume interview)

Sarah: "During the break I asked you about the network of secret organizations you mentioned that the ACIO is part of. Can you elaborate on this network and what its agenda is?"

Dr. Neruda: "There are many organizations that have noble exteriors and secret interiors. In other words, they may have external agendas that they promote to their employees, members, and the media, but there is also a secret and well-hidden agenda that only the inner core of the organization is aware of. The outer rings or protective membership as they're sometimes referred to, are simply window dressing to cover-up the real agenda of the organization.

"The IMF, Foreign Relations Committee, NSA, KGB, CIA, World Bank, and the Federal Reserve are all examples of these organizational structures. Their inner core is knitted together to form an elitist, secret society, with its own culture, economy, and communication system. These are the powerful and wealthy who have joined forces in order to manipulate world political, economic, and social systems to facilitate their personal agenda.

"The agenda, as I know it, is primarily concerned with control of the world economy and its vital resources—oil, gold, gas reserves, platinum, diamonds, etc. This secret network has utilized technology from the ACIO for the purpose of securing control of the world economy. They're well into the process of designing an integrated world economy based on a digital equivalent of paper currency. This infrastructure is in place, but it is taking more time than expected to implement because of the resistance of competitive forces who don't understand the exact nature of this secret network, but intuitively sense its existence.

"These competitive forces are generally businesses and politicians who are affiliated with the transition to a global, digital economy, but want to have some control of the infrastructure development, and because of their size and position in the marketplace can exert significant influence on this secret network.

"The only organization that I'm aware of that is entirely independent as to its agenda, and therefore the most powerful or alpha organization, is the Labyrinth

Group. And they are in this position because of their pure-state technologies and the intellect of its members. All other organizations—whether part of this secret network of organizations or powerful multinational corporations—are not in control of the execution of their agenda. They are essentially locked in a competitive battle."

Sarah: "But if this is all true, then is Fifteen essentially running this secret network?"

Dr. Neruda: "No. He's not interested in the agenda of this secret network. He's bored by it. He has no interest in power or money. He's only attracted to the mission of building BST to thwart hostile alien attacks that have been prophesied for twelve thousand years. He believes that the only mission worth deploying the Labyrinth Group's considerable intellectual power is the development of the ultimate defensive weapon or Freedom Key. He's convinced that only the Labyrinth Group has a chance to do this before it's too late.

"You have to remember that the Labyrinth Group consists of one hundred eighteen humans and approximately two hundred Corteum. The intellectual ability of this group, aligned behind the focused mission of developing BST before the alien takeover, is truly a remarkable undertaking that makes the Manhattan Project look like a kindergarten social party in comparison. And perhaps I'm exaggerating a bit for effect… but I'm pointing out that Fifteen is leading an agenda that is far more critical than anything that has been undertaken in the history of humankind."

Sarah: "So, if Fifteen is running his own agenda, and it's just as you say it is, why would you defect from such an organization?"

Dr. Neruda: "The ACIO has a memory implant technology that can effectively eliminate select memories with surgical precision. For example, this technology could eliminate your recall of this interview without disrupting any other memories before or after. You would simply sense some missing time perhaps, but nothing more would be recalled… if that.

"My intuition cautioned me that I was a candidate to have this procedure because of the behaviors I was exhibiting in deference to the WingMakers. In other words, I was believed to be a sympathizer of their culture, philosophy, and mission—what I knew of it. That made me a potential risk to the project. The Labyrinth Group, in a very real sense, feared its own membership because of their enormous intellects and ability to be cunning and clever.

"This imprinted a constant state of paranoia which meant that technology was deployed to help ensure compliance to the agenda of Fifteen. Most of these technologies were invasive, and the members of the Labyrinth Group willingly submitted to the invasion in order to more effectively cope with the paranoia. Several months ago I began to systematically shut down these invasive technologies—in part to see what the reaction of Fifteen would be, and partly because I was tired of the paranoia.

"As I was doing this, it became obvious to me that the suspicions were escalating and it was simply a matter of time before they would ask me to subject myself to an MRP—"

Sarah: "MRP?"

Dr. Neruda: "Yes, MRP stands for Memory Restructure Procedure. What I had learned from the WingMakers time capsule is not something I want to forget. I don't want to give this information up. It has become a central part of what I believe and how I want to live out my life."

Sarah: "Couldn't you have simply defected and not sought out a journalist who will want to get this story out. I mean, couldn't you have simply gone to an island and lived out your life and never disclosed the existence of the Labyrinth Group and the WingMakers?"

Dr. Neruda: "You don't understand... the Labyrinth Group is untouchable. They have no fears about what I divulge to the media, their only concern is the terrible precedence of defection. I'm the first. No one has ever left before. Their fear is that if I defect and get away successfully, others will too. Once that happens, the mission is compromised and BST may never happen.

"Fifteen and his Directors take their mission very seriously. They are fanatics of the first order, which is both good and bad. Good in the sense that they're focused and working hard to develop BST, bad in the sense that fanaticism breeds paranoia. My reasons for seeking out a journalist like you and sharing this knowledge is that I don't want the WingMakers time capsules to be locked away from humanity. I think its contents should be shared. I think that was their purpose."

Sarah: "This will seem like a strange question, but why would the WingMakers hide their time capsule and then encode its content in such an extraordinarily complex way if they wanted this to be shared with humanity? If the average citizen had found this time capsule... or even a government laboratory, what's the chance they would have been able to decipher it and access the optical disc?"

Dr. Neruda: "It's not such a strange question actually. We asked it ourselves. It seemed clear to the Labyrinth Group that it had been the chosen organization to unlock the optical disc. To answer your question directly, had the time capsule been discovered by another organization, chances are excellent that its optical disc would never be accessed. Somehow, this coincidence—that the time capsule ended up in the hands of the Labyrinth Group—seems to be an orchestrated process. Even Fifteen agreed with that assessment."

Sarah: "So Fifteen felt that the WingMakers had selected the Labyrinth Group to decide the fate of the time capsule's content?"

Dr. Neruda: "Yes."

Sarah: "Then wouldn't it be reasonable to assume that Fifteen wanted to learn more about the contents of the time capsule before he released it to the public through the NSA or some other government agency?"

Dr. Neruda: "No. It's doubtful that Fifteen would ever release any information about the Ancient Arrow Project to anyone outside of the ACIO. He's not one to share information that he feels is proprietary to the Labyrinth Group, particularly if it has anything to do with BST."

Sarah: "So now that you've made these statements, isn't it going to affect the ACIO? Isn't someone going to ask questions and start poking around looking for answers?"

Dr. Neruda: "Perhaps. But I know too much about their security systems, and there's no way that a political inquiry will find them. And there's no way the secret network of organizations I mentioned earlier could exert any influence over them; they're completely indebted to the ACIO for technologies that permit them to manipulate economic markets. They… the ACIO and Labyrinth Group… are, as I said before, untouchable. Their only concern will be defection—the loss of intellectual capital."

Sarah: "What effect will your defection have on the ACIO or the Labyrinth Group?"

Dr. Neruda: "Very little. Most of my contributions with respect to the time capsule have been completed. There are some other projects having to do with encryption technologies that I developed and these will be more significant in their impact."

Sarah: "Back to the WingMakers for a moment, if they're so advanced technologically, why time capsules? Why not just appear one day and announce whatever it is they want to share? Why this game of hide and seek and hidden time capsules?"

Dr. Neruda: "Their motives are not clear. I think they left behind these time capsules as their way to bring culture and technology from their time to ours. We also believe that these sites represent a defensive weapon… a very sophisticated defensive weapon.

"As for why don't they just show up and give us the information… this, I think, is their genius. They've created seven time capsules and placed them in various parts of the world. I believe this is all part of a master plan or strategy to engage our intellects and spirits in a way that has never been done before… to demonstrate how art, culture, science, spirituality, how all of these things are connected. I believe they want us to discover this… not to be told.

"If they simply arrived here in your living room and announced they were the WingMakers from the centermost sector of the universe, I suspect you'd be more amazed about their personalities, physical characteristics and what life is like in their world. That's assuming you even believed them. The aspects of what they wanted to impart—culture, art, technology, philosophy, spirituality, these items could get lost in the phenomenon of their presence.

"Also, in the text that we had translated, it was apparent that the WingMakers had time traveled on many occasions. They interacted with people from many different times and called themselves Culture Bearers. They were probably mistaken as angels or even Gods. For all we know, their reference in religious texts may indeed be frequent."

Sarah: "So you think they intend that these time capsules be shared with the whole of humanity?"

Dr. Neruda: "You mean the WingMakers?"

Sarah: "Yes?"

Dr. Neruda: "I don't know with absolute certainty. But I think they should be shared. I don't have anything to personally gain from getting this information out to the public. It goes against everything I've been trained for, and places me at risk at the very least, disrupts my lifestyle irreparably.

"To me, the Ancient Arrow time capsule is the single greatest discovery in the history of humankind. Discoveries of this magnitude should be in the public domain. They shouldn't be selfishly secured and retained by the ACIO or any other organization."

Sarah: "Then why are these discoveries and the whole situation with ETs kept from the public?"

Dr. Neruda: "The people who have access to this information like the sense of being unique and privileged. That's the psychology of secret organizations and why they flourish. Privileged information is the ambrosia of elitists. It gives them a sense of power, and the human ego loves to feed from the trough of power.

"They would never confess to this, but the drama of the ET contact and other mysterious or paranormal phenomenon is extremely compelling and of vital interest to anyone who is of a curious nature; particularly politicians and scientists. By keeping these subjects in private rooms behind closed doors with all the secrecy surrounding it, it creates a sense of drama that is missing in most of their other pursuits.

"So you see, Sarah, the drama of secrecy is very addictive. Now of course, the reason that they would tell you for keeping this out of the public domain is for purposes of national security, economic stability, and social order. And to some extent, I suppose there's truth to that. But it's not the real reason."

Sarah: "Does our President know about the ET situation?"

Dr. Neruda: "Yes."

Sarah: "What does he know?"

Dr. Neruda: "He knows about the Greys. He knows about ET bases that exist on planets within our solar system. He knows about the Martians…"

Sarah: "Good God, you're not going to tell me that little green men form Mars actually exist are you?"

Dr. Neruda: "If I were to tell you what I know about the ET situation, I'm afraid I would lose my credibility in your eyes. Believe me, the reality of the ET situation is much more complex and dimensional than I have time tonight to report, and if I gave you a superficial rendering, I think you'd find it impossible to believe. So I'm going to tell you partial truths, and I'm going to be very careful in my choice of words.

"The Martians are a humanoid race fashioned from the same gene pool as we. They live in underground bases within Mars, and their numbers are small. Some have already immigrated to earth, and with some superficial adjustments to their physical appearance, they could pass for a human in broad daylight.

"President Clinton is aware of these matters and has considered alternative ways to communicate with ETs. To date, a form of telepathy has been used as the primary communication interface. However, this is not a trusted form of communication, especially in the minds of our military personnel. Virtually every radio telescope on the globe has been, at one time or another, used to communicate with ETs. This has had mixed results, but there have been successes, and our President is aware of these."

Sarah: "Then is Clinton involved in the secret network you mentioned earlier?"

Dr. Neruda: "Not knowingly. But he is clearly an important influencer, and is treated with great care by high-level operatives within the network."

Sarah: "So you're saying he's manipulated?"

Dr. Neruda: "It depends on your definition of manipulation. He can make any decision he desires, ultimately he has the power to make or influence all decisions relative to national security, economic stability, and social order. But he generally seeks inputs from his advisors. And high-level operatives from this secret network advise his advisors. The network, and its operatives, seldom gets too close to political power because it's in the media fish bowl, and they disdain the scrutiny of the media and the public in general.

"Clinton, therefore is not manipulated, but simply advised. The information he receives is sometimes doctored to lead his decisions in the direction that the network feels is most beneficial to all of its members. To the extent that information is doctored, then I think you could say that the President is manipulated. He has precious little time to perform fact checking and fully evaluate alternative plans, which is why the advisors are so important and influential."

Sarah: "Okay, so he's manipulated—at least by my definition. Is this also happening with other governments like Japan and Great Britain for instance?"

Dr. Neruda: "Yes, this network is not just national or even global. It extends to other races and species. So its influence is quite broad, as are the influences that impinge upon it. It is a two-way street. As I said before, the Labyrinth Group operates the only agenda that is truly independent, and because of its goal, it's permitted to have this independence… though in all honesty, there's nothing that anyone could do to prevent it, with the possible exception of the WingMakers."

Sarah: "So all the world's governments are being manipulated by this secret network of organizations… who are these organizations… you mentioned some of them, but who are the rest? Is the mob involved?"

Dr. Neruda: "I could name most of them, but to what end? Most you wouldn't recognize or find any reference to. They are like the Labyrinth Group. Had you ever heard of it before? Of course not. Even the current management of the NSA is not aware of the ACIO. At one time, they were, but that was over thirty-five years ago, and people circulate out of the organization, yet still retain their alliance to the secret and privileged information network.

"And no, absolutely there is no mob or organized crime influence in this network. The network uses organized crime as a shield in some instances, but organized crime operates through intimidation, not stealth. Its leaders possess average intelligence and associate with information systems that are obsolete and therefore non-strategic. The organized crime network is a much less sophisticated version of the network I was referring to."

Sarah: Okay, back to the WingMakers for a moment… and I apologize for my scattered questions tonight. It's just that there's so much I want to know that I'm finding it very difficult to stay on the subject of the Ancient Arrow Project."

Dr. Neruda: "You don't need to apologize. I understand how this must sound to you. I'm still wide awake, so you don't have to worry about the time."

Sarah: "Okay. Let's talk a little bit about your impressions or insights into the ET situation that you spoke of earlier. To me, this is the part that's most fascinating."

Dr. Neruda: "First of all, I want to explain that the ETs that interact with our world's governments are not the same ones that interact with the Labyrinth Group."

Sarah: "But I thought you said that the Greys were involved with the ACIO, or at least one of its factions."

Dr. Neruda: "Yes, they're also known as the Zetas, but as I said, they're many different factions of the Greys and the one that the ACIO is working with are the alpha faction, and they don't operate with our government organizations because they are too suspicious of them, and frankly, don't view them as intelligent enough to even warrant their time."

Sarah: "What about the Corteum?"

Dr. Neruda: "The Corteum are a very sophisticated culture, integrating technology, culture, and science in a very holistic manner. For different reasons, they're not involved with our governments either, mainly because of their role with the Federation."

Sarah: "What's the Federation… I haven't heard you talk about it before?"

Dr. Neruda: "Each galaxy has a Federation or loose-knit organization that includes all sentient life forms on every planet within the galaxy. It would be the equivalent of the United Nations of the galaxy. This Federation has both invited members and observational members. Invited members are those species that have managed to behave in a responsible manner as stewards of their planet and combine both the technology, philosophy, and culture that enable them to communicate as a global entity that has a unified agenda.

"Observational members are species who are fragmented and are still wrestling with one another over land, power, money, culture, and a host of other things that prevent them from forming a unified world government. The human race on planet earth is such a species, and for now, it is simply observed by the Federation, but is not invited into its policy making and economic systems."

Sarah: "Are you saying that our galaxy has a form of government and an economic system?"

Dr. Neruda: "Yes, but if I tell you about this you will lose track of what I really wanted to share with you about the WingMakers…"

Sarah: "I'm sorry for taking us off track again. But this is just too amazing to ignore. If there's a Federation of cooperative, intelligent species, why couldn't they take care of these hostile aliens in the year 2011 or at least help us?"

Dr. Neruda: "The Federation doesn't intrude on a species of any kind. It is truly a facilitating force not a governing force with a military presence. That is to say, they will observe and help with suggestions, but they will not intervene on our behalf."

Sarah: "Is this like the Prime Directive as it's portrayed on Star Trek?"

Dr. Neruda: "No. It's more like a parent who wants its children to learn how to fend for themselves so they can become greater contributors to the family."

Sarah: "But wouldn't a hostile takeover of earth affect the Federation?"

Dr. Neruda: "Most definitely. But the Federation does not preempt a species' own responsibility for survival and the perpetuation of its genetics. You see, at an atomic level our physical bodies are made quite literally from stars. At a sub-atomic level, our minds are nonphysical repositories of a galactic mind. At a sub-sub-atomic level, our souls are non-physical repositories of God or the intelligence that pervades the universe.

"The Federation believes that the human species can defend itself because it is of the stars, galactic mind, and God. If we were unsuccessful, and the hostility spread to other parts of our galaxy, then the Federation would take notice and its members would defend their sovereignty, and this has happened many times. And in this process of defense new technologies arise, new friendships are forged, and new confidence is embedded in the galactic mind.

"That's why the Federation performs as they do."

Sarah: "Doesn't BST exist somewhere within the Federation?"

Dr. Neruda: "Perhaps in one of the planets closer to our galactic core."

Sarah: "So why doesn't the Federation help… you said they could help didn't you?"

Dr. Neruda: "Yes, they can help. The Corteum are IMs or invited members and they are helping us. But they themselves do not possess the BST technology… this is a very special technology that's permitted to be acquired by a species that intends to use it only as a defensive weapon. And herein is the challenge.

Sarah: "Who does the 'permitting'… are you saying the Federation decides when a species is ready to acquire BST?"

Dr. Neruda: "No… I think it has to do with God."

Sarah: "I don't know why, but I have a hard time believing that you believe in God."

Dr. Neruda: "Well, I do. And furthermore, so does everyone within the Labyrinth Group—including Fifteen. We've seen far too many evidences of God or a higher intelligence that we can't dispute its existence. It would be impossible to deny based on what we've observed in our laboratories."

Sarah: "So God decides when we're ready to responsibly use BST. Do you think he'll decide before 2011?" (I admit there was a tone of sarcasm in this question.)

Dr. Neruda: "You see, Sarah, the Labyrinth Group is hopeful that the readiness of the entire species isn't the determining factor, but that a subgroup within the species might be allowed to acquire the technology as long as it was able to protect it from all non-approved forces. This subgroup is hoped to be the Labyrinth Group, and it's one of the reasons why Fifteen has invested so much of the ACIO's resource into security systems."

Sarah: "You didn't really answer my question though… Do you think it can be developed in twelve years?"

Dr. Neruda: "I don't know. Certainly I hope so, but BST is not our only line of defense. The Labyrinth Group has devised many defensive weapons, not all of which I'll describe to you. The Animus have visited earth before, approximately three hundred million years ago, but they didn't find anything present on our planet to cause them to invest the time and resources to colonize our planet. When their probes return in thirteen years, they will think differently.

"Our analysis is that they will befriend our governments and utilize the United Nations as an ally. They will set about orchestrating a unified world government through the United Nations. And when the first elections are held in 2018, they will overtake the United Nations and rule as the world government. This will be done through trickery and deception.

"I mention our analysis—taken from three different RV sessions—because they're quite specific as to the dates, and so we have the equivalent of nineteen years to produce and deploy BST. Ideally, yes, we'd like to have it completed in order to interface with the intervention points for this race when it decided to crossover into our galaxy. We would like to cause them to choose a different galaxy or abandon their quest altogether. But it may be impossible to determine this intervention point.

"You see, the Memory Implant Technology developed by the Labyrinth Group can be utilized in conjunction with BST. We can define the intervention point when our galaxy was selected as a target to colonize, enter that time and place, and impose a new memory on their leadership to divert them from our galaxy."

Sarah: "Either I'm getting tired, or this just got a lot more confusing… You're saying that the Labyrinth Group already has scenarios to nip this thing in the bud… to prevent this marauding group of aliens from even entering our galaxy? How do you know where they are?"

Dr. Neruda: "To answer your question, I would need to explain with much more granularity the precise nature of BST and how it differs from time travel. I'll try to explain it as simply as I can, but it's complex, and you need to let go of some of your preconceived notions of time and space.

"You see… time is not exclusively linear as when it's depicted in a timeline. Time is vertical with every moment in existence stacked upon the next and all coinciding with one another. In other words, time is the collective of all moments of all experience simultaneously existing within non-time, which is usually referred to as eternity.

"Vertical time infers that one can select a moment of experience and use time and space as the portal through which they make their selection real. Once the selection is made, time and space become the continuity factor that changes vertical time into horizontal time or conventional time …"

Sarah: "You lost me. How is vertical time different from horizontal time?"

Dr. Neruda: "Vertical time has to do with the simultaneous experience of all time, and horizontal time has to do with the continuity of time in linear, moment-by-moment experiences."

Sarah: "So you're saying that every experience I've ever had or will ever have exists right now? That the past and future are actually the present, but I'm just too brainwashed to see it?"

Dr. Neruda: "As I said before, this is a complex subject, and I'm afraid that if I spend the time explaining it to you now, we'll lose track of more important information like BST. Perhaps if I were to explain the nature of BST, most of your questions would be answered in the process."

Sarah: "Okay, then tell me what Blank Slate Technology is? Given the title, I assume it means something like… wipe out an event and change the course of history. Right?"

Dr. Neruda: "Let me try to explain it this way. Time travel can be observational in nature. In this regard, the ACIO and other organizations—even individual citizens—have the ability to time travel. But this form of time travel is passive. It's not equivalent to BST. In order to precisely alter the future you have to be able to *interact* with vertical time, paging through it like a book, until you find the precise page or intervention point relevant to your mission.

"This is where it gets so complex because to interact with vertical time means you will alter the course of horizontal time. And understanding the alterations and their scope and implication requires extremely complex modeling. This is why the Labyrinth Group aligned itself with the Corteum—its computing technology has processing capabilities that are about four thousand times more powerful than our best supercomputers.

"This enables us to create organic, highly complex scenario models. These models tell us the most probable intervention points once we've gathered the relevant data, and what the most probable outcomes will be if we invoke a specific scenario. Like most complex technologies, BST is a composite technology having five discrete and inter-related technologies.

"The first technology is a specialized form of remote viewing. This is the technology that enables a trained operative to mentally move into vertical time and observe events and even listen to conversations related to an inquiry mode.

The operative is invisible to all people within the time they are traveling to, so it's perfectly safe and unobtrusive. The intelligence gained from this technology is used to determine the application of the other four technologies. This is the equivalent of intelligence gathering.

"The second technology that is key to BST is the equivalent of a memory implant. As I mentioned earlier, the ACIO refers to this technology as a Memory Restructure Procedure or MRP. MRP is the technology that allows a memory to be precisely eliminated in the horizontal time sequence and a new memory inserted in its place. The new memory is welded to the existing memory structure of the recipient.

"You see, events—small and large—occur from a single thought, which becomes a persistent memory, which in turn, becomes a causal energy center that leads the development and materialization of the thought into reality... into horizontal time. MRP can remove the initial thought and thereby eliminate the persistent memory that causes events to occur.

"The third technology consists of defining the intervention point. In every major decision, there are hundreds, if not thousands, of intervention points in horizontal time as a thought unfolds and moves through its development phase. However, in vertical time, there is only one intervention point or what we sometimes called the causal seed. In other words, if you can access vertical time intelligence you can identify the intervention point that is the causal seed. This technology identifies the most probable intervention points and ranks their priority. It enables focus of the remaining technologies.

"The fourth technology is related to the third. It's the scenario modeling technology. This technology helps to assess the various intervention points as to their least invasive ripple effects to the recipients. In other words, which intervention point – if applied to a scenario model—produces the desired outcome with the least disruption to unrelated events? The scenario modeling technology is a key element of BST because without it, BST could cause significant disruption to a society or entire species.

"The fifth and most puzzling technology is the interactive time travel technology. The Labyrinth Group has the first four technologies in a ready state waiting for the interactive time travel technology to become operational. This technology requires an operative, or a team of operatives, to be able to physically move into vertical time and be inserted in the precise space and time where the optimal intervention point has been determined. From there the operatives must perform a successful MRP and return to their original time in order to validate mission success."

Sarah: "I've been listening to this explanation and I think I even understand some of it, but it sounds so surreal to me, Dr. Neruda. I'm... I'm at a loss to explain how I'm feeling right now. This is all so strange. It's so big... enormous... I can't believe this is going on somewhere on the same planet that I live. Before this interview, I was worried about balancing my checkbook and when my damn car would ever be fixed… this is just too strange…"

Dr. Neruda: "Maybe we should take another break and warm up our coffee."

Sarah: Signing off for a coffee break…

(Break for about fifteen minutes… Resume interview)

Sarah: "If the Labyrinth Group has four of the five technologies ready to go, and is only awaiting the interactive… the interactive part, they must have scenario models and intervention points already established for how they plan to deal with this Animus race. Do they?"

Dr. Neruda: "Yes. They have about forty scenario models and perhaps as many as eight intervention points defined."

Sarah: "And if there're that many, there must be a priority established. What's the most probable scenario model?"

Dr. Neruda: "I will be brief on this point because it's such classified information that only the SL-Fourteen personnel and Fifteen know this. My classification is SL-Thirteen, and so I get diluted reports and quite possibly misinformation with regard to our scenario modeling. About all I can tell you is that we know—from both the prophecies and our remote viewing technology—a significant amount of information about this race.

"For example, we know that it hails from a galaxy that our Hubble telescope has examined as thoroughly as possible and we've charted it as extensively as possible. We know that it's thirty-seven million light years away and that the species is a synthetic race—a mixture of genetic creation and technology. It possesses a hive mentality, but individual initiative is still appreciated as long as it is aligned with the explicit objectives of its leaders.

"Because it's a synthetic race, it can be produced in a controlled environment and its population can be increased or decreased depending on the whims of its leaders. It is—"

Sarah: "Didn't you just say it's from a galaxy that's thirty-seven million light years away? I mean, assuming they were able to travel at the speed of light, it would take them thirty-seven million years to come to our planet. And you said earlier that they hadn't even crossed into our galaxy yet…right?"

Dr. Neruda: "The Corteum come from a planet that is fifteen million light years away, and yet they can come and go between their planet and our planet in the time it takes us to travel to the moon—a mere two hundred and fifty thousand miles away. Time is not linear, nor is space. Space is curved, as your physicists have recently learned, but it can be artificially curved through displacement energy fields that collapse space and the illusion of distance. Light particles do not displace or collapse space, they ride a linear line through space, but there are forms of electromagnetic energy that can modify or collapse space. And this technology makes space travel—even between galaxies—not only possible, but also relatively easy."

Sarah: "Why did you say, '*your* physicists' just then?"

Dr. Neruda: "I apologize… it's just a part of the conditioning of being isolated from mainstream society. When you operate for thirty years in a secret organization like the Labyrinth Group, you tend to look at your fellow humans… as not your fellow humans, but as something else. The principles of science that the Labyrinth Group has embraced are very different from those taught within your… there I go again… within our universities. I must be getting tired."

Sarah: "I didn't mean to criticize you. It's just the way you said it, it sounded as though an alien or an outsider said it."

Dr. Neruda: "I qualify as an outsider, but certainly not an alien."

Sarah: "Okay, back to this prophecy or alien race. What do they want? I mean… why travel such a far distance to rule earth?"

Dr. Neruda: "This seems such a funny question to me. Excuse me for laughing. It's just that humans do not understand how special Earth is. It is truly, as planets are concerned, a special planet. It has such a tremendous biodiversity and a complex range of ecosystems. Its natural resources are unique and plentiful. It's a genetic library that's the equivalent of a galactic zoo.

"The Animus desire to own this planet in order to own its genetics. As I've already mentioned, this is a synthetic race… a species that can clone itself and fabricate more and more of its population to serve the purpose of its colonization program. However, it desires more than the expansion of its empire. It desires to become a soul carrier—something reserved for pure biological organisms. Synthetic organisms are not able to carry the higher frequencies of soul, which absolutely require an organic nervous system."

Sarah: "So they want a soul?"

Dr. Neruda: "They want to expand throughout the universe and develop their organic nature through genetic reengineering. They want to become soul carriers in order to achieve immortality. They also want to prove what they already believe, that they are superior to all other pure organics."

Sarah: "So where are they right now?"

Dr. Neruda: "The Animus?"

Sarah: "Yes."

Dr. Neruda: "I assume they remain in their home world… to the best of our knowledge their probes haven't crossed into our galaxy yet."

Sarah: "And when they arrive, how will the ACIO or Labyrinth Group know?"

Dr. Neruda: "As I said, the ACIO has already done a significant amount of intelligence gathering and even selected scenarios and intervention points."

Sarah: "So what's the plan?"

Dr. Neruda: "The most logical approach would be to travel to the time and place when the causal thought was born to explore the Milky Way, and through MRP, expunge it from the memory of the race. Essentially, convince them that of all the wonderful, life-inhabited galaxies, the Milky Way is a poor choice. The Labyrinth Group would implant a memory that would lead this race to conclude that our galaxy was not worthy of their serious exploration."

Sarah: "So, some other galaxy becomes their next target? Wouldn't we bear the responsibility of their next conquest? Aren't we then perpetrators ourselves?"

Dr. Neruda: "This is a fair question, but I'm afraid I don't know how to answer it."

Sarah: "Why couldn't we—using this MRP technology—simply implant a memory not to be aggressive? To tell this race to stop trying to colonize new worlds that aren't theirs to own like property. Why couldn't we do this?"

Dr. Neruda: "Perhaps we will. I don't really know what Fifteen has in mind. I am though, confident in his approach and its efficacy."

Sarah: "But you said earlier that you feared for your life… that Fifteen is probably trying to hunt you down even as we speak. Why are you so confident in his sense of morality?"

Dr. Neruda: "In the case of Fifteen, morality doesn't really play a role. He operates in his own code of ethics, and I don't pretend to understand them all. But I'm quite certain of his mission to avert takeover by this alien race, and I'm equally confident that he will choose the best intervention point with the least influence to the Animus. It's the only way he can acquire BST. And he knows this."

Sarah: "We're back to God again, aren't we?"

Dr. Neruda: "Yes."

Sarah: "So God and Fifteen have this all figured out?"

Dr. Neruda: "There's no certainty if that's what you mean. And there's no alliance between Fifteen and God, at least not that I'm aware of. This is part of the belief system that the Labyrinth Group formalized along the path to developing BST. It's logical to us that God is all-powerful and all knowing because it operates as the universal mind field that interpenetrates all life, all time, all space, all energy… and all existence. This consciousness is impartial, but certainly it's in a position to deny things or perhaps more accurately, delay their acquisition."

Sarah: "If God exists everywhere as you say, then why wouldn't he stop this marauding alien race and keep them in their place?"

Dr. Neruda: "Again, a fair question, but one that I can't answer. I can only tell you that the God I believe in is, as I said before, impartial. Meaning that it allows its creation to express themselves as they desire. At the highest level where God operates, all things have a purpose… even aggressive species that desire to dominate other species and planets. It was Fifteen's belief that God orchestrated nothing but understood everything in the universal mind.

"Remember when I was talking about the galactic mind?"

Sarah: "Yes."

Dr. Neruda: "There are planetary minds, solar minds, galactic minds, and a singular universal mind. The universal mind is the mind of God. Each galaxy has a collective consciousness, or mind field that is the aggregation of all of the species present within that galaxy. The universal mind creates the initial blueprint for each of the galaxies related to its galactic mind or composite consciousness. This initial blueprint creates the predisposition of the genetic code seeded within a galaxy. We, the Labyrinth Group, believed that God designed each galaxy's genetic code with a different set of pre-dispositions or behaviors."

Sarah: "And why would this be so?"

Dr. Neruda: "So diversity is amplified across the universe, which in turn permits God to experience the broadest continuum of life."

Sarah: "Why is this so important?"

Dr. Neruda: "Because God loves to experiment and devise new ways of experiencing life in all of its dimensions. This may very well be the purpose of the universe."

Sarah: "You know you're talking like a preacher? You speak like these are certainties or truths that are just self-evident… but they're just beliefs aren't they?"

Dr. Neruda: "Yes, they're beliefs, but beliefs are important don't you think?"

Sarah: "I'm not sure… I mean my beliefs are changing every day. They're not stable or anchored in some deep truth that's constant like bedrock or something."

Dr. Neruda: "Well, that's good... I mean that they change. The Labyrinth Group evolved a very specific set of beliefs—some of these were based on our experiences as a result of the Corteum intelligence enhancement technologies, some were based from ancient texts that were studied, and some were borrowed from our ET contacts."

Sarah: "So now you're going to tell me our friendly neighborhood ETs are religious zealots?"

Dr. Neruda: "No... no, I don't mean that they were trying to convert us to their beliefs, we simply asked and they related them to us. Upon hearing them, they seemed quite a bit more like science than religion actually. I think that's the nature of a more evolved species... they finally figure out that science and religion converges into cosmology. That understanding the universe in which we live also causes us to understand ourselves—which is the purpose of religion and science... or at least should be."

Sarah: "Okay, this is getting a little too philosophical for my tastes. Can we return to a question about the WingMakers? If, as you say, there's a galactic federation that governs the Milky Way, how do the WingMakers factor into this federation?"

Dr. Neruda: "I'm impressed by the nature of your questions. And I wish I could answer them all, but here again, I don't know the answer."

Sarah: "But if you can use your remote viewing technology to eavesdrop on this alien race in an entirely different galaxy, why can't you observe the Federation?"

Dr. Neruda: "As for the Federation, they're fully aware of our remote viewing capability, and in fact, we can't eavesdrop on the Federation because they're able to detect our presence if we observe them through remote viewing. So, in deference to their privacy and trusting their agenda, we never imposed our technology on the Federation... perhaps only once or twice."

Sarah: "You'll have to forgive me Dr. Neruda, but I find all of this a little hard to believe. We've skimmed the surface of about a hundred different subjects through the course of this interview, and I keep coming back to the same basic issue: Why? Why would the universe be set up this way and no one on earth know about it? Why all the secrecy? Does someone think we humans are so stupid that we couldn't understand it? And who the hell is this somebody?"

Dr. Neruda: "Unfortunately, there are so many conspiracies to keep this vital information out of the public domain, that what ends up in the hands of the public is diluted to the point of uselessness. I can understand your frustration. I can only tell you that there are people who know about these things, but only Fifteen knows about the larger reality of what we've touched on tonight.

"In other words, and this is to your point, Sarah, there are some people within the military, government, secret network, NSA, CIA, etc., that know parts of the whole, but they don't understand the whole. They aren't equipped with the knowledge to stand before the media and explain what's happening. They fear that they would be made to appear feeble by the fact that they only know pieces of what's going on. It's like the story of the three blind men who are all touching different parts of an elephant and each thinks it is something different.

"Fifteen withholds his knowledge from the media and the general public because he doesn't want to be seen as a savior of humanity—the next messiah. And he especially doesn't want to be seen as some fringe lunatic that should be locked up, or worse yet, assassinated because he is so misunderstood. The instant he stepped forward with what he knows he would lose his privacy and his ability to discover BST. And this he'll never do.

"Most people who know about this greater reality are fearful of stepping into the public scrutiny because of the fear of being ridiculed. You have to admit, that the general public is frightened by what it doesn't understand, and they do kill the messenger."

Sarah: "But why can't we get even partial truths about this picture of reality... about ETs and the Federation? Someone, the media or government or someone else is keeping this information from us. Like the story you were telling me about the Martians. If this is true and Clinton knows about this, why aren't we being told?"

Dr. Neruda: "There's a cynical part of me that would say something like... why do you watch six hours of television every day? Why do you feed your minds exclusively with the opinions of others? Why do you trust your politicians? Why do you trust your governments? Why do you support the destruction of your ecosystems and the companies and governments that perpetrate this destruction?

"You see, because the whole of humanity allows these things to occur, the wool is pulled over your eyes and it's easy to ration information and direct your attention to mundane affairs like the weather and Hollywood."

Sarah: "That's fine for you to say—someone who's IQ can't be charted. But for those of us with average intelligence, what are we supposed to do differently that would give us access to this information... to this larger reality?"

Dr. Neruda: "I don't know. I honestly don't know. I don't pretend to have the answers. But somehow humans need to be more demanding of their governments and even the media. Because the media is a big part of this manipulation, though they're not aware of how they've become pawns of the information cover-up.

"The truth of the matter is that no one entity is to blame. Elitists have always existed since the dawn of man. There have always been those who had more aggression and power and would dominate the weaker of the species. This is the fundamental structure that has bred this condition of information cover-up, and it happens in every sector of society, including religion, government, military, science, academia, and business.

"No one created this playing field to be level and equal for all. It was designed to enable free will and reality selection based on individual preferences. And for those who have the mental capacity to probe into these secrets behind the secrets behind the secrets, they usually find pieces of this larger reality—as you put it. It's not entirely hidden… there are books and individuals and even prophesies that corroborate much of what I've spoken of here tonight. And these are readily available to anyone who wants to understand this larger universe in which we live.

"So, to answer your question: '…what are we supposed to do differently?' I would read and study. I would invest time learning about this larger universe and turn off the television and disconnect from the media. That's what I would do…"

Sarah: "Maybe this is a good place to wrap things up. Unless you have anything else you'd like to add."

Dr. Neruda: "Only one thing, and that is that if anyone ever reads this interview, please do so with an empty mind. If you bring a mind full of learning and education and opinion, you'll find so much to argue with in what I've said that you'll not hear anything. And I'm not interested in arguing with anyone. I'm not even that interested in convincing anyone of what I've said. My life will go on even if no one believes me.

"The WingMakers have built a time capsule of their culture and it's magnificent. I wish I could take people to the original site, so they could stand before each of the twenty-three chambers and witness these wall paintings in person. If you were to do this, you would understand that art can be a portal that transports the soul to a different dimension. There is a certain energy that these paintings have that can't be translated in mere photographs. You really need to stand inside these chambers and feel the purposeful nature of this time capsule.

"I think if I could do that, you would believe what I've said."

Sarah: "Could you take someone like me to the site?"

Dr. Neruda: "No. Unfortunately, the security system surrounding this site is so sophisticated, the site entrance, for all intents and purposes, is invisible. All I have are my photographs…."

Sarah: "You're saying that if I walked right up to the site, I wouldn't be able to see it?"

Dr. Neruda: "Cloaking technology is not just a science fiction concept. It's been developed for more than ten years. It's used much more frequently than people realize. And I'm not talking about its diluted version of stealth technology; I'm talking about the ability to superimpose a reality construction over an existing reality that's desired to be hidden.

"For instance, you could walk right up to the entrance of the Ancient Arrow site and see nothing that would look like an entrance or opening. To the observer it would be a flat wall of rock. And it would have all the characteristics of rock—texture, hardness and so forth, but it's actually a reality construction that is superimposed on the mind of the observer. In reality the entrance is there, but it can't be observed because the mind has been duped into the projected reality construction."

Sarah: "Great, so there's no way to enter this site and experience this time capsule... so once again, us little humans are prevented from the experience of proof. You see, the reason why this is so hard to believe is that nothing is ever proven!"

Dr. Neruda: "But isn't proof in the eye of the beholder? In other words, what is proof for you may not convince another or vice a versa. Isn't this the way of all religions and even science? Scientists claim to have proof of this theory or that theory, and then some years later, another scientist comes along and disproves the previously held theory. And on and on this goes."

Sarah: "So what's your point?"

Dr. Neruda: "Proof is not absolute. It's not even objective. And what you're looking for is an experience that is permanent and perfect in its expression of truth. And such an experience, if it indeed exists, is not owned or possessed by any secret network or elitist organization or galactic federation for that matter.

"You could have this experience of absolute proof tomorrow, and the very next day, doubt would begin to creep in and in a matter of weeks or months this proof, or absolute truth, that you aspire to possess... it would be just a memory. And probably not even a powerful memory because so much doubt would be infused into it.

"No, I can't give you or anyone absolute proof. I can only tell you what I know to be true for me and try to share it as accurately as I know how with anyone who's interested. I'm less interested in trying to relate the cosmology of the universe than I am in getting the story of the WingMakers and the artifacts of their time capsule into the public attention. The public should know about this story. It's a discovery of unparalleled importance and it should be shared."

Sarah: "You do realize don't you, that you've made me the messenger? You've asked me to be the one who takes the public scrutiny and suspicions, and has to endure all of the ridicule..."

Dr. Neruda: "I'm not asking you to do anything against your will, Sarah. If you never do anything with the materials I've given you, I'd understand. All I'd ask is that you return them to me if you're not going to get them out. If I step forward as the messenger, I would lose my freedom. If you step forward, this story could catapult your career and you're only doing your job. You're not the messenger, you're the transmitter… the media.

"But you must do what you think best. And I'd understand your decision whatever you decide."

Sarah: "Okay, let's wrap it up there. I don't want you to get the wrong impression that I'm a total disbeliever. But I'm a journalist and it's my responsibility to validate and cross check stories before I publish them. And with you, I can't do this. And what you're telling me, if it's true, is the biggest story ever to be told. But I can't take this to the media—at least not the company I work for, because they would never publish it. No validation… no story."

Dr. Neruda: "Yes, I understand. But I've shown you some of the ACIO technologies and photos of the site and its contents, so these must be some form of validation."

Sarah: "For me, it validates that something is going on that I've never heard about. Namely, the ACIO is a new organization that's never been talked about—at least not in my journalistic circles. But your photographs and stories don't validate what you've explained tonight. They're in the category of teasers. Something the National Enquirer is fond of broadcasting, but this isn't the brand of journalism I subscribe to."

Dr. Neruda: "Let's talk some more in the next few days. Take the time to read some of the materials translated from the optical disc, and in the meantime, just be neutral. Okay?"

Sarah: "Don't assume I'm not interested, or too much a skeptic to do anything with this stuff. I just need some time to get my bearings as to what I should do with this story and the evidence you've provided."

Dr. Neruda: "I promised you several interviews before I left. Are we still on for tomorrow night?"

Sarah: "Yes. But how much more is there than what you've already explained?"

Dr. Neruda: "We've only touched on the surface of a small portion of the story."

Sarah: "That's a little hard to believe, but let's pick up tomorrow night, then."

Dr. Neruda: "Thanks for your interest in my story, Sarah… I know it sounds outlandish, but at least you've shown restraint in writing me off as a lunatic. And for that, you have my thanks."

Sarah: "You're very welcome."

The Second Interview of Dr. Jamisson Neruda

By Sarah

What follows is a session I recorded of Dr. Neruda on December 28, 1997. He gave permission for me to record his answers to my questions. This is the transcript of that session. This was one of five times I was able to tape-record our conversations. I have preserved these transcripts precisely as they occurred. No editing was performed, and I've tried my best to include the exact words, phrasing, and grammar used by Dr. Neruda.

(It's recommended that you read the December 27, 1997, interview before reading this one.)

Sarah: "Before we begin tonight's session, I wanted to tell you that I've listened to last night's tape and have used it to formulate some new questions. I noticed that I was all over the place with regard to my questions, and tonight I'm going to try and stay more focused. So I'm just warning you that if I get off track again, remind me to stay on course. Okay?"

Dr. Neruda: "I'll certainly do my best… although I'm not sure what your course is."

Sarah: "Well, I guess I'd like to stay more centered on the WingMakers and the artifacts of their time capsule."

Dr. Neruda: "That's fine with me. But let me make one clarification first.
"The Ancient Arrow site was labeled initially as an Extraterrestrial Time Capsule, or ETC, however, it is not actually, in my opinion, a time capsule."

Sarah: "Good, let's start right there. What exactly is it, in your opinion?"

Dr. Neruda: "The site is part of a larger structure that's interconnected through some means I don't understand. We know there're seven sites that have been constructed on earth—presumably in the ninth century. We know that these sites have some defensive purpose, and we know that the sites planners represent themselves as culture bearers, and are most likely representatives from the Central Race."

Sarah: "I hear a lot about 'defensive weapon', but how can these wall paintings or the music artifacts be considered part of a defensive weapon?"

Dr. Neruda: "We know from our RV sessions, that the WingMakers designed these sites to be more than a defensive weapon, otherwise, as you point out, the cultural artifacts wouldn't make any sense. However, it also doesn't make sense that they'd be completely unrelated to the objectives of a defensive weapon. I'd make the hypothesis that they're DNA triggers."

Sarah: "You mean they activate something within our DNA... as you were describing last night?"

Dr. Neruda: "Correct."

Sarah: "And how does this relate to a defensive weapon?"

Dr. Neruda: "It was our hypothesis that the cultural artifacts, if studied or examined, would somehow activate parts of our DNA. For what purpose we weren't certain, but I intuit that it has something to do with stimulating our fluid intelligence and enabling sensory inputs that have been dormant within our central nervous system."

Sarah: "And do you have a hypothesis as to why?"

Dr. Neruda: "Presumably the enhancements to the central nervous system makes the defensive weapon more effective."

Sarah: "It's so damn easy to get sidetracked when talking with you, but I'm going to resist the temptation to move into a line of neurological discourse, not that I know anything about it anyway.

"Tell me more about your role with the WingMakers time capsule... or whatever you want to call it."

Dr. Neruda: "I think for accuracy and consistency, we can refer to it as the Ancient Arrow site. As I said before, I'm confident that it's not a time capsule.

"To your question, though, I was working with a computer we call ZEMI, helping to translate the data contained on the optical disc found in the twenty-third chamber of the site. It contained text, symbol pictures, mathematical equations, and what turned out to be music files.

"Once the site was located, my primary focus was to decode the optical disc, make the data therein sensible, and as much as possible, applicable to BST."

Sarah: "Did any of it apply to BST?"

Dr. Neruda: "Not directly, at least nothing that I've read. The text was of a more philosophical nature. I was the first one to read their language. Once we unlocked the optical disc, we printed out 8,045 pages of symbol pictures like the ones contained in their art work, except much more varied and in some instances, much more complex. There were twenty-three chapters of text or symbol pictures—each consisting of about 350 pages.

"I read the first segment or chapter of this text and was amazed to find that there were passages of text—in the introduction—that were only readable to me. This was additional confirmation that I had a role to play in getting this information into the public domain."

Sarah: "Are you saying that the text you read disappeared after you read it or that you deleted it?"

Dr. Neruda: "It disappeared. It deleted itself."

Sarah: So only the first eyes would see the message?"

Dr. Neruda: "Correct."

Sarah: "So what did it say?"

Dr. Neruda: "I can recite the exact words if you like, but it would take a few minutes."

Sarah: "Give me a summary."

Dr. Neruda: "The essence of this passage was validating what the ACIO had already known—that the Animus were sending probes in 2011, and it was written in the form of a warning. It stated that the WingMakers had installed a defensive weapon on earth that would render the planet invisible to the Animus probes."

Sarah: "Invisible? How?"

Dr. Neruda: "They didn't explain with any precision. They wrote that higher frequencies were emanating from the central universe, and that these seven sites comprised a collective technology that somehow coordinated these frequencies or higher energies to bring about a shift in the planet's vibratory structure, enabling life on the planet to survive the shift and remain undetected by the Animus."

Sarah: "All life forms?"

Dr. Neruda: "Technically, the text didn't specify."

Sarah: "And this was for your eyes only?"

Dr. Neruda: "Yes, the ZEMI operator did not find any evidence of this section of the text. It completely disappeared."

Sarah: "What else did it say?"

Dr. Neruda: "It confirmed that we're dealing with the Central Race, and that they want the cultural artifacts from the seven sites to be shared with the public. These elements were connected to the effectiveness of the defensive weapon."

Sarah: "In what way?"

Dr. Neruda: "In the sense that the materials activate aspects of our DNA that make the shift easier, or perhaps possible, I'm not certain because they were a bit vague."

Sarah: "So, by reading the philosophy I'm supposed to be able to become invisible?"

Dr. Neruda: "I think it's more holistic than that. They left behind poetry, music, paintings, and even a glossary. It seems to me that all of these elements—in addition to the philosophy—are connected. Also, I'm suggesting that something fundamentally changes when these materials are absorbed, and perhaps this change, whatever it is, resonates with the technology from the seven sites."

Sarah: "Sounds far-fetched to me. Why do you believe this?"

Dr. Neruda: "I've absorbed the materials and I've noticed changes."

Sarah: "Such as?"

Dr. Neruda: "I defected from the ACIO. To me, that's the biggest change imaginable."

Sarah: "You're not implying that the materials you've read induced you to defect are you?"

Dr. Neruda: "It was a combination of many things, but it certainly had a significant impact on my decision. Did you read any of the materials I left last night?"

Sarah: "I read the first section and a little of the glossary. I didn't understand it. It was too abstract. It did have an effect on me though… it managed to put me to sleep."

Dr. Neruda: "I know it's a little intense, but you have to admit, it's very interesting if for no other reason than they're representative of how our distant ancestors think and believe."

Sarah: "And you have a copy of all the pages of text?"

Dr. Neruda: "Yes."

Sarah: "And can I see it?"

Dr. Neruda: "Yes, but it's not something I carry around with me."

Sarah: "Tell me a little bit about the translation process since you were involved in it?"

Dr. Neruda: "The translation is the key to the usefulness of the optical disc, and using a carefully sequenced set of experiments, conducted by ZEMI, we were able to access the disc's data files in five days."

Sarah: "How do you know that the translation is accurate?"

Dr. Neruda: "Within the disc, once it was accessed, were translation indexes that enabled their text to print out in perfect English, or about sixty other languages. It took us two days to figure out how to access the disc, but once we did, we were able to access the twenty-four sections of text in the span of seventeen hours."

The most vexing of the translations, and the one in which we have the least confidence is the music."

Sarah: "Good, I'm glad you brought up the music because I don't understand that element of the time capsule."

Dr. Neruda: "How do you mean that?"

Sarah: "Was the music already on the optical disc and you simply captured it from the disc, or was it basically produced by the Labyrinth Group based on the musical notations?"

Dr. Neruda: "Actually, it was a bit of a combination of the two. Their musical notations were very precise and they left digital samples of each of their instruments—even vocals. So we simply translated their digital samples to a MIDI standard and produced our own version of their music."

Sarah: "So were you involved in the music translations as well?"

Dr. Neruda: "Yes. I helped in the initial discovery of their musical notation and helped with the translation indexes. I wasn't involved in its production phase, though I was very curious as to what it would sound like."

Sarah: "Can I hear any of these compositions?"

Dr. Neruda: "Yes, of course. When I left, the ACIO had successfully translated ten of the twenty-three music compositions. I have these. And they've been converted to both CD and cassette standards. I also have complete files of the remaining thirteen compositions in their raw, deconstructed form."

Sarah: "How were they produced exactly?"

Dr. Neruda: "Do you mean that technically or artistically?"

Sarah: "I guess both."

Dr. Neruda: "On the technical end we needed to step their samples down to a resolution of 384 bit in order to use them in our computer systems. When we first heard the samples of instrumentation, we were somewhat relieved to hear familiar sounds. There were some that were different, but for the most part, the digital samples that were encoded on the optical disc were the same as contemporary musical instruments heard around the world.

"Once we had captured their samples and organized them into octaves, we took their compositional notations and essentially let the computer select the digital instrumentation based on their samples. Eventually this all had to be stepped down to a twenty-four bit commercial CD mastering system, which was them pressed on a CD and recorded onto a cassette tape.

"As for the artistic production, there really wasn't much that we did. The computers did all the interpretative work and essentially performed the production for that matter. We had some of our staff perform overdubs on various versions to experiment with the compositions. The music was very popular, particularly when you listened to it at a sampling resolution of 384 bit."

Sarah: "Didn't anyone wonder why the time capsule included a musical construction kit instead of just having a recording of the music? I mean, why have us bring an artistic interpretation to their music?"

Dr. Neruda: "Everything was wondered about in the Ancient Arrow Project. Everything.

"We didn't know why they did it the way they did it, but again our hypothesis was that the WingMakers didn't have a way to bring their music into our world because we lacked the technology to listen to it. So they disassembled their music into—as you put it—a construction kit, which enabled us to reconstruct the music so it could be listened to on our technology. It's the most logical reason.

"There were several of us who were able to experience chambers one and two as a completely integrated form of expression and it was a very powerful experience… to say the least. When you hear the music in 384-bit resolution with the original paintings, standing inside the actual chamber in which they were placed, it is a very moving and spiritual experience. Unlike any I've ever had."

Sarah: "In what way?"

Dr. Neruda: "Just that the sense of being pulled out of your body and into the portal of the painting is irresistible. There is a very strong sense of movement into and beyond these paintings, and the music and paintings are only two of the art forms, the third, the poetry is also part of the experience."

Sarah: "So tell me about the poetry."

Dr. Neruda: "The poems are expressive of a wide range of subjects. To most of us at the ACIO, they could have been written by any contemporary poet. There was really nothing that caused them to stand out as representing a culture billions of years older than our own. Many of the same themes about spirituality, love, relationships, and death were evident in their poems as well. There're actually two poems for each chamber painting, so there's a total of forty-six poems."

Sarah: "That's interesting. Everything else—the paintings, music, artifacts, and philosophy—is placed one per chamber. Why do you suppose they've placed two poems in each chamber instead of one?"

Dr. Neruda: "In my opinion it was to provide a broader perspective into the particular theme represented by a specific chamber. The poetry appears to be designed in such a way to provide both a personal and universal perspective in each of the chambers... but again, it's just a working hypothesis at this time."

Sarah: "I assume from the examples you left me, that the poetry is also a bit less abstract when compared to their philosophy and paintings. Have you considered how the poetry is related to the paintings?"

Dr. Neruda: "Yes. And I believe the poetry and the paintings have the strongest connection of all the objects in each of the chambers. I think the paintings illustrate— in some subtle way—the themes represented in the poetry. In some instances, when the painting represents an assemblage of abstract objects, the poetry is also more abstract. When the painting is more illustrative, the poetry seems more like prose."

Sarah: "Are you saying then that the poetry carries the central meaning of each chamber?"

Dr. Neruda: "I'm not sure, but it does seem that the poetry is somehow implied symbolically in the chamber painting that it's associated with. The problem is that the poetry is so highly interpretive that it's impossible to know precisely what its theme is intended to be. Also, and I should have mentioned this before, but the grammar and syntax of their language is very different from ours in that they have no end to their language punctuated with periods.

"In other words, if we made a literal translation, there would be no sentence structure... more like a logic syntactical approach... which simply means an abstracted language flow which would be, for most people, very difficult to understand. When I was doing the translations of the poetry, I placed it in a sentence structure that fragmented its meaning so that it could be better understood. Perhaps in the process I unintentionally changed the meaning, but it was either that or the poetry would be too abstracted to understand."

Sarah: "Is there a connection between the poetry and the philosophy of each chamber?"

Dr. Neruda: "My colleague and I felt that all of the objects within a specific chamber were connected... probably in ways we couldn't fathom. We were constantly worried that the translation indexes were somehow inaccurate, and that this was limiting our ability to see the linkages between the various objects. And of course, the most puzzling connection was the technology artifacts, because we had no way to probe or reach any conclusions about their purpose or function."

Sarah: "Let's talk a little bit about the artifacts found in each chamber. The only one that I've really heard about was the one found in the twenty-third chamber, the optical disc. I know you've shown me some photos of the others, but could you describe them better?"

Dr. Neruda: "The optical disc is the only artifact of the twenty-third we found that the ACIO had successfully accessed, at least that I'm aware of. The other artifacts were all taken to the Labyrinth Group's research laboratory in Southern California immediately after they were discovered. These were never acknowledged to anyone below a security level twelve clearance. There were rumors within the broader ACIO that there were technologies within the Ancient Arrow site, but these never gained any serious consideration, and certainly not by the NSA.

"The technology artifacts were of the greatest curiosity to Fifteen because they represented possible solutions to BST. And as I mentioned earlier, Fifteen and most of the Labyrinth Group for that matter, felt that the WingMakers may not allow the Labyrinth Group to deploy BST. Hence, Fifteen considered the WingMakers as possible foes, instead of allies."

Sarah: "But what I've seen doesn't look very advanced or based in high technology. They could pass for crystals or rocks… or something organic. Why was the Labyrinth Group so intrigued by them?"

Dr. Neruda: "The crystalline structures that were found, in most cases, did look quite ordinary in the sense that when they were examined by the eye, they appeared to be crystals, but when you looked at them through various molecular and atomic analyses, it was obvious that they were manmade objects. In other words, they were synthetic crystalline structures, and we held the hypothesis that they were encoded with information much like the optical disc or the paintings. We also held the hypothesis that they were potentially connected to the optical disc since it was the last of the artifacts and seemed the equivalent of a keystone or master key."

Sarah: "Did any of the text translated from the optical disc refer to the other artifacts?"

Dr. Neruda: "No, to our disappointment, there were no references."

Sarah: "You didn't answer my question about whether you felt there was a connection between the technology artifacts and the specific cultural artifacts related to each chamber."

Dr. Neruda: "Sorry, I guess it's my turn to get sidetracked tonight. Anyway, yes, there were connections… we were certain of this, but at the same time, because we couldn't get inside the artifacts and probe them, we couldn't prove our theory. Consequently, we placed all of our time and energy on the optical disc because it seemed to be the most important of the artifacts as well as the one we had the best chance of accessing through our technology."

Sarah: "Why?"

Dr. Neruda: "You must bear in mind that the technology artifacts were extremely alien to our technologies. Other than the optical disc, the other technologies were a combination of synthetic materials based on organic structures, and in some instances actually possessed human DNA within their structures. These were…"

Sarah: "You're saying that the technologies were in part human?"

Dr. Neruda: "Yes… in a way. But what I was going to say, is that these artifacts seemed to have molecular-based computer systems that activated by a specific human touch. And we weren't certain whether it was literally a specific human, or a specific type of human, or perhaps any human in a specific state of emotion or mind. We had one hundred and fifteen possible experiments developed for testing and all failed."

Sarah: "But this is real odd… why would human DNA be inside a technology… and this talk about synthetic crystals… it leaves me cold."

Dr. Neruda: "We had some similar misgivings until we were able to translate some of the text within the optical disc. The philosophical papers from chambers one and two convinced us that the WingMakers could indeed be authentic and we had no other reason to disbelieve their story. That's not to say that we suspended all of our disbelief or caution, but the philosophy was a breakthrough to our understanding of their perceived mission with contemporary humankind."

Sarah: "I don't know… I read the first two philosophy papers you left for me, and I could believe that they're from an alien race. I could also believe that they're from a deceptive race that uses philosophy and all this cultural stuff to lull us into believing they're benevolent when in fact they're not at all. I mean isn't that part of the prophecy you spoke about last night?"

Dr. Neruda: "Well, I see you remain the ever skeptical journalist. I'm actually glad to see that reaction.

"Sarah, all I can tell you is that when you take into account all of the cultural artifacts found within the Ancient Arrow site, and you immerse yourself in their content and philosophy, it's hard to believe they originate from evil intent."

Sarah: "Unless that's exactly what they wanted you to believe."

Dr. Neruda: "Perhaps. It's hard to debate such a thing. I think at some point it's an individual decision. The Labyrinth Group—and I'm including the Corteum when I say that—was in agreement that it was an authentic disclosure from the Central Race, and felt confident that we were not dealing with deception. But we never close the door to that possibility. Our security and operations directors put contingency plans in place in the event evidence was accumulated that increased the probability of fraud or deception."

Sarah: "One of things that seemed odd to me, having looked at the photographs of the chamber paintings, was how similar they all were. They were clearly done by the same artist... or I suppose a group of artists. But when I think of a time capsule, I would think you would include a variety of art from a diverse assortment of artists that represent a variety of perspectives and so forth. And that isn't the case here. Why do you suppose?"

Dr. Neruda: "I don't think their motive was to inform us about their artists or the diversity of their artistic culture. I think they intend that the art function initially as a form of communication, and subsequently as a form of time travel or moving out of the body consciousness. The continuity of the twenty-three paintings seen as a whole seem to be inviting the consciousness of the observer to quite literally step into the world of the WingMakers. As though they were portals, and I've experienced this myself.

"The paintings are incredibly brilliant in their colors. You really can't imagine how much impact they have when you see them in person, particularly after their cleaning and restoration was completed. But even when they were first discovered without any touch-up, it was eerie how luminous they were and vibrant in their colors after 1,150 years. There were many times when those of us who were involved in restoration and cataloging of the artifacts, would sit in the chambers and stare at these paintings. On several occasions I did this for hours just letting my eyes wander through the painting, and imagining the mind of the artist and what they were trying to communicate. It was a very powerful experience."

Sarah: "I think they'd scare me a little bit."

Dr. Neruda: "I'm only laughing because I had such an experience. One night after a long day of working in the artifact chambers, I was left as the last one inside the site. I had been so absorbed in what I was doing I scarcely remembered being told to activate the security system on my way out. About a half-hour went by, and I finally realized I was alone inside the time capsule... the silence was incredible. At any rate, I was walking down the corridor that connected all of the twenty-three chambers, and passed each chamber and I began to feel a presence that was overwhelming. Every time I would come upon one of the chambers I expected something from the painting to jump out at me. They literally seemed alive.

"Our lighting was a very high quality portable halogen system and every chamber was outfitted precisely the same. When I got to the bottom of the corridor—what we called the spiral staircase and looked into chamber two, I clearly saw motion and nearly jumped out of my skin. Not necessarily out of fear, but out of excitement I suppose, though there was fear as well. But this motion was simply a blurred image of something stepping out of the painting and then disappearing into thin air... I couldn't really..."

Sarah: "What was it? Was it human?"

Dr. Neruda: "I couldn't see it clearly enough to tell you what it was, but I began to theorize that some of the chamber paintings may have purposes beyond just visual stimulation. Our RV also had some experiences of sensing motion in the paintings, feeling as though she was being pulled out of her body."

Sarah: "This may seem to be an odd, off-the-wall question, but how do you know this wasn't all a hoax? That someone or some group created this whole thing to look like an alien or future time capsule just for the fun of playing with your minds?"

Dr. Neruda: "The one thing we know for certain is that this is not a hoax. The Ancient Arrow site consists of an enormous rock structure that has literally been hollowed out in the form of a helix that detours every ten meters into a separate chamber—twenty-three to be exact. The entire structure would have taken an incredible technology to build. We have accurate dating of when the chamber paintings were created, and they were conclusively produced in the ninth century, and we're certain that this technology didn't exist then."

Sarah: "I'm not trying to argue with you… but if these artifacts are really from the Central Race, it just seems so odd that they'd be buried inside a huge rock in the middle of nowhere… in New Mexico of all places. And it also seems odd that they'd go to all this work, but make it so damn hard to understand what the hell they were trying to say. Do you see what I mean?"

Dr. Neruda: "Yes, I understand, and I don't take your questions as argumentative. But the point I'm making is that this site is indeed a set of real objects. And these objects don't even correspond to the same time frame. For example, while the paintings were created about eleven hundred years ago, the artifacts do not even respond to our carbon dating or biochemical analysis. To complicate matters, the pictographs in and around the Ancient Arrow site were determined to have been created in the past fifty years, and could very well have been done in the year, or month, the site was discovered.

"These real objects are admittedly an enigma, but they are not a hoax to my eyes. The real question is whether the WingMakers identity and purpose is as they represent it."

Sarah: "Okay, let's say it's not a hoax. Then tell me why're you so convinced it's a defensive weapon. It seems to me, that it might be more of a communication device… or perhaps an educational tool of some kind. Why a weapon?"

Dr. Neruda: "The text from the optical disc states this. And we had an RV session that corroborated it."

Sarah: "So, earth is this genetic library that the Animus want to use in order to re-create themselves as soul carriers, as you put it? And the Ancient Arrow site—and its six companion sites—is going to protect earth and all of us from these marauding aliens? How am I doing so far?"

Dr. Neruda: "I can't say that your specific conclusions are right or wrong. I can only tell you that the Animus are a real threat and that the WingMakers intend to protect their genetics."

Sarah: "Okay, then tell me, why would the Central Race, who lives trillions of light years away, care about what happens to us?"

Dr. Neruda: "The Central Race is responsible for seeding and cultivating higher life forms throughout the universe, they're vitally interested in protecting their genetics from the Animus. Earth isn't the only genetic repository that they protect in this manner. Our RV sessions uncovered a database of planets throughout our superuniverse that was incalculably large."

Sarah: "So this is just standard operating procedure for this race... to install a defensive weapon on the planets they seed with life?"

Dr. Neruda: "I believe so."

Sarah: "I looked the word 'Animus' up in the dictionary this morning. It's a real word. How did a race whose most recent visit to earth was some three hundred million years ago become an entry in Webster's dictionary?"

Dr. Neruda: "Their name is known even by the WingMakers. They used the same word in their translation indexes. There are certain words that have been purposely seeded within our language by the WingMakers."

Sarah: "So, now you're saying that WingMakers actually place words into our dictionaries?"

Dr. Neruda: "No. Remember when I told you that the WingMakers were culture bearers?"

Sarah: "Yes."

Dr. Neruda: "They have encoded the discovery of language, mathematics, music, and so forth into our genetic structures. As we evolve, certain forerunners of our species—people like you and I—activate a part of their DNA before the rest of us. These forerunners are able to retrieve this encoded information and share it with the species. In subsequent generations, this insight is transmitted, and pretty soon, the entire species encompasses this new information or skill."

Sarah: "So you're really saying, that the word Animus was encoded into our sense of language, and someone invented the word, not realizing it was the name of this alien synthetic race?"

Dr. Neruda: "Yes, something like that."

Sarah: "I also read the memo that Dr. Sauthers (a colleague of Dr. Neruda) wrote, about a global culture being an outcome of this technology from the WingMakers sites. But how could these objects be used to build a global culture? It seems a little naïve to me."

Dr. Neruda: "All I can tell you is that it's related to the Internet and a new communication technology that the WingMakers referred to as OLIN or the One Language Intelligent Network. If you read the glossary section that I left behind, you'll see it referenced there. The WingMakers seem to feel confident that the OLIN technology will help create the global culture through the Internet. This incidentally is consistent with prophecies that the Labyrinth Group was privy to dating as far back as 1,500 years ago. Of course the enabling technology wasn't called OLIN, but the notion of a global culture and unified governance has been predicted for many centuries."

Sarah: "This is what George Bush used to call the New World order isn't it?"

Dr. Neruda: "Yes, but there have been four other presidents who've acknowledged this concept."

Sarah: "What would make the world's people decide to unify under one governing body, or for that matter, create a global culture… whatever that means? I just can't envision it happening… not in my lifetime."

Dr. Neruda: "According to the WingMakers it will happen through the digital economy and then through the Internet's OLIN technology platform. And through this global network, entertainment and educational content will be globalized. This is the basis of a global culture with unified commerce, content, and communities. Once these pieces of the infrastructure are in place, then the need to govern this infrastructure will loom as the preeminent issue of the day. And the United Nations is the logical ruling body for such an endeavor. As long as the World's people allow the digitization of the economy and embrace the OLIN technology platform, a global government and culture is virtually assured to emerge."

Sarah: "And as you said last night, this is supposed to occur in 2018?"

Dr. Neruda: "According to prophecy, that's when the United Nations will hold initial elections for a unified world government. And it won't be an all powerful, centralized authority, but rather a global public policy decision and enforcement organization for issues that affect the world at large. Issues like pollution, global warming, border disputes, space travel, terrorism, trade, commerce, OLIN technology upgrades, and general technology transfer programs."

Sarah: "So what will happen to National sovereignty in this new role of the United Nations?"

Dr. Neruda: "I'm willing to answer your question in the form of a speculative response, but I'm also aware that you had asked me at the outset of this interview to remind you if you got off course. What would you like—"

Sarah: No, you're absolutely right. Sorry. Let's go back to the artifacts… what was the condition of the site when you first entered… or better still, why don't you just describe your first encounter going inside the site."

Dr. Neruda: "I was one of five from the ACIO who made the trip to New Mexico to explore the site after it was initially determined to have potential ET implications. None of us at the time knew anything that would have led us to conclude that the Ancient Arrow site would become such an important discovery.

"The only real clue we had was an artifact that had been recovered near, what was determined much later, as the entrance of the interior chamber of the time capsule. It was this artifact that brought the project under the control of the ACIO because the artifact was considered by the NSA to have potential ET origins."

Sarah: "What specifically led the NSA to conclude the artifact was alien?"

Dr. Neruda: "Like all the other artifacts it showed no response to carbon dating analysis and it had peculiar markings or symbols that seemed other-worldly. It was a pure grade composite of unknown origin. Also, and perhaps more importantly, there was no obvious way to activate the artifact or access its interior controls. Its interior was impervious to various spectrum analyses –even simple x-rays were unable to penetrate the object.

"At any rate, this artifact was essentially handed over to the ACIO, which deemed it to be of ET origins, and then proceeded to investigate the region in which it was found. We discovered that the outside casing of the artifact held a detailed topographical map that defined the region in which it was discovered. We began to think the artifact might activate or become more useful if taken to the region depicted on its casing."

Sarah: "Is this the artifact you showed me pictures of?"

Dr. Neruda: "No. This artifact destroyed itself after it led us to the Ancient Arrow site."

Sarah: "Why did you think it was important to activate it where it was found?"

Dr. Neruda: "Because it was thought to be a form of a compass or homing beacon. We weren't sure, but we couldn't determine any functional purpose in the laboratory, so it seemed like a logical experiment to see how the device would function in the area in which it was discovered. Also, the original people who found the artifact complained that it induced a hallucinogenic experience when it was held near the stomach area.

"The exploration team from the ACIO figured out how to use this device to locate the entrance to the interior of the canyon wall in which the Ancient Arrow site was hidden. The device, when activated, seemed to pass thought waves or mental pictures of where it wanted the person to go. The RV assigned to our team was the one holding the device when it was first activated, and she immediately began to see pictures. I did as well. Ultimately, it led us into a cave-like structure tucked twenty to thirty meters inside one of the clefts of the canyon wall."

Sarah: "Was there an entrance already, or did you have to blast your way inside?"

Dr. Neruda: "The way into the interior was cleverly hidden behind a natural made cavern, which in its own right was well hidden by natural underbrush. This cavern was about twenty-five meters deep and led inside the canyon wall. We presumed it was an Indian dwelling of some kind that had long been abandoned. Towards the end of this cavern there was a corridor that jutted off to the side, and at the back of this corridor there was another chamber. A large, flat rock on the floor hid the entrance to the site."

Sarah: "So you were convinced there was something underneath the rock?"

Dr. Neruda: "Yes. After removing the rock, we were able to determine a tunnel was indeed underneath it. The tunnel was in the form of a "J" and was about one meter in diameter. I slid down first through the tunnel and crawled my way to the entrance of the site."

Sarah: "So all five of you were inside this... this site, looking around with flashlights, what was running through your mind at the time?"

Dr. Neruda: "We were all very excited and somewhat apprehensive as well. We thought we might find an ET site, and were half aware that it could be an active site... which kept us all on guard."

Sarah: "And this whole thing was carved out of rock?"

Dr. Neruda: "It was completely manmade... or alien... and we knew it the instant we got out of the transition tunnel. It was like being born into a completely new world. It was absolutely silent; the air was cool, but not uncomfortably cold. There were no signs of life, and it seemed like everything took on a new purpose... an intelligent purpose that we couldn't wait to unravel.

"What was so remarkable was the incredible sense of walking into a surreal world—a world that was created by something completely alien. We assumed it was of ET construction from the moment we stepped out of the "J" tunnel."

Sarah: "But how did you immediately know it was an artificial construction, and not a natural set of chambers or caves?"

Dr. Neruda: "At the beginning of the spiral staircase there were ornate petroglyphs carved in the stone with a precision never before seen by our eyes.

Also, the entire tunnel system was clearly too smooth— almost polished—to be of natural construction. There was a sense of architecture… a sense that someone designed it with extreme care and purpose.

"Amazingly there was nothing on the floor. Not even a pebble or a grain of sand. Every surface was completely clean, smooth, and polished. There was dust, but only dust. And something like a polymer coating had been applied to every square centimeter of the structure including the ceilings.

"When we arrived at the first chamber, which is only about thirty meters from the entrance, I can clearly recall a sense of awe or something approaching a religious experience I suppose. No one spoke for a long time after our lights hit the first chamber painting. Everyone's flashlight converged on the painting and we all just stared for about forty seconds in the incredible silence of this tomblike structure.'"

Sarah: "Did you find all the chambers that same day?"

Dr. Neruda: "Yes. We went from chamber to chamber, each time feeling like we had stumbled into an alien natural history museum. You have to understand that our lighting was not very good because we hadn't expected to need anything more than basic flashlights. I vividly remember seeing each of the chamber paintings for the first time and just staring at them… mesmerized by the incredible anachronism of the place. I'd never been in such a surreal environment… it was both eerie and completely enchanting at the same time."

Sarah: "So how large were the chambers and the paintings themselves?"

Dr. Neruda: "The chambers themselves were relatively small… about four meters in diameter with fairly high ceilings, in some instances as high as six meters."

Sarah: "So, judging from the photographs I've seen of the chamber paintings, the paintings themselves must be fairly large?"

Dr. Neruda: "Yes, they're large and always face the entrance of the chamber. If you stand just outside the entrance of a particular chamber, you can't see the whole painting; it's too large. You have to walk into the chamber in order to see the whole composition."

Sarah: "What, in the opinions of the Labyrinth Group, are the artistic merits of these paintings?"

Dr. Neruda: "No one within the Labyrinth Group claims to be an art critic I can assure you. I think it's fair to say that of those who saw the chamber paintings in their original environment found the artistic merits to be very compelling, even captivating. I think those who saw them only represented in photographs thought they were less art and more of a cog in some masterfully designed wheel like an illustration in a children's book."

Sarah: "Not to change the subject, but I keep wondering how you came to choose me… I mean… I know you said it was completely random, but why did you select an average journalist to share this story? Why not a scientist or someone who could at least ask you more sophisticated questions? I have to confess that I feel completely inadequate to interview you, mostly because I don't even know what questions I should be asking you…"

Dr. Neruda: "You're doing a fine job… absolutely fine. You shouldn't worry about your questions. They're insightful. And most people, who will read this information, will be more interested in the things you've inquired about than the physics or science involved anyway."

Sarah: "Perhaps, but I have this nagging feeling that if I could ask you the scientific questions then you could more easily prove your story or credibility. I think I'm handicapping you in some way."

Dr. Neruda: "What is it exactly that you feel you're not asking me?"

Sarah: "I guess it's mostly things related to time travel and BST. Last night you talked about some things that when I reread them earlier today, I felt like I should have asked more in-depth questions…"

Dr. Neruda: "Like…"

Sarah: "That's the problem, I don't know."

Dr. Neruda: "Sarah, the reason I selected you was simple. I needed to find someone who knew how to access the mainstream media, and yet be relatively obscure. Had I chosen a science editor from a major newspaper, I may have ended up with more scientific questions and less about the cultural, artistic, and social implications of the Ancient Arrow project. Of my random selections, I knew that you had no established image to protect, that you knew how to access the media, and could ask sound questions that wouldn't betray your identity. That's why we're talking right now… and the fact that you didn't think I was crazy."

Sarah: "I never asked you this before, but I'm just curious, was I the first journalist you talked with, or did someone turn you down before you found me?"

Dr. Neruda: "No, you were the first and only person outside of the Labyrinth Group whom I've talked with about this story."

Sarah: "I'd like to change the topic slightly and ask you about Fifteen's personality… is that okay?"

Dr. Neruda: "Yes, that's fine."

Sarah: "What's he like as a leader?"

Dr. Neruda: "He's extremely focused, and demands everyone he works with to be similarly focused. He's a workaholic, sleeps about four hours a night and works the rest of his time on some aspect of BST. If there's research or development of new technologies that don't have a specific and strategic impact on BST, he's not involved in it. He won't even ask questions about projects of that nature, and generally within the ACIO, there are always three or four projects that are unrelated to BST. Within the Labyrinth Group, every project is related to BST."

Sarah: "What's he look like?"

Dr. Neruda: "He's about average height and has fairly long gray hair down to his shoulders which he usually wears in a ponytail. He's always reminded me of Pablo Picasso with long hair… he has those same penetrating eyes. He's originally from Spain, so it's no coincidence that he looks like Picasso. His most notable feature is his eyes, they're mischievous like you'd expect from a child who's done something wrong on the surface, but underneath, they've created something wonderful, it's just that nobody understands the wonderful part yet. That's what you see going on behind his eyes."

Sarah: "I may have already asked you this, but how old is he?"

Dr. Neruda: "He's about sixty years old I think – or at least he looks about that old. I've never heard anyone say his age. I know when he was a student, he was supposed to look old for his age. I think he started getting gray hair when he was in his early twenties, and that's probably why he was often mistaken for a professor rather than a student."

Sarah: "You said earlier that he was kicked out of school. Why?"

Dr. Neruda: "Remember, he was, even at an age when most kids are concerned about dating and parties, working on BST… or at least early versions of time travel. He's one of those rare visionaries that enter the physical world and knew at a very early age what he came to do. Fifteen was born to time travel. Period… end of story. That's all he's ever cared about.

"In the fifties, researching BST was considered a waste of time, no pun intended. It was simply too theoretical and disconnected from anything practical. I think Fifteen also rubbed his professors the wrong way because he was so bright as a student that he intimidated most of them. He's also very stubborn, and when the professors told him to change his research to something more practical, Fifteen apparently told them they were small-minded… or something to that effect. Later that semester he was forcibly expelled as the story was told to me.

"However, Bell Labs hired him for a short stint because his research on quantum objects and how they could be influenced by consciousness interested them."

Sarah: "Forgive me, but what exactly are quantum objects?"

Dr. Neruda: "They're elementals like electrons or neutrons. Quantum objects are fundamental building blocks of matter, and they can appear both as a wave and a particle."

Sarah: "Okay, so Fifteen was trying to prove that quantum objects are influenced by consciousness. Why was that so dangerous to a research university?"

Dr. Neruda: "That in itself wasn't so radical, but it was only a small part of his total research into how to construct BST using the new physics that was being introduced rapidly in the community of quantum physics. Fifteen has always maintained that Einstein's general theory of relativity was flawed, which is not a popular position to take. In somewhat the same way that Newton's theory of the mechanistic universe became too constricted and unable to explain so much of the phenomenon of what we call today, complexity or chaos theory, Fifteen felt that Einstein's theories underestimated the influence that consciousness had on quantum objects.

"In the fifties and sixties, this was tantamount to heresy, particularly because it was impossible to prove by mathematical modeling or formula. Consequently, Fifteen just continued to develop his theories in secret and began to become noticed by the ACIO when he became involved in a project having to do with heuristic learning systems based on a technology that the ACIO had reengineered from the Greys.

"The project leader from the ACIO recognized his intellect and rogue creativity and began to develop a relationship with the young man. Several months later, Fifteen was recruited to join the ACIO and essentially left his identity behind, quickly rising to the position of director of research. He was later introduced to the Corteum intelligence accelerator technology, and the rest is history as they say."

Sarah: "How exactly does this Corteum technology accelerate or expand the intelligence?"

Dr. Neruda: "Few people realize that their conscious mind only processes about fifteen bits of information per second of linear time. However, in vertical time, the unconscious mind is processing approximately seventy to eighty million bits of information. Thus, in normal consciousness, humans are aware of only an infinitesimal amount of the information that is constantly being fed to them at the unconscious level. The Corteum technology was designed to reduce the filtering aspects of the conscious mind and enable the higher frequency information packets to be fed to the conscious mind.

"In parallel with this effort, the brain circuitry—if you will—is rewired to handle the higher voltage of the information that is being fed to the consciousness, allowing capabilities like photographic memory and abstract thought to coexist. These capabilities become the matrix filter that draws from the unconscious repositories the most relevant information at any particular time based on the problem or task at hand."

Sarah: "If I were a behavioral scientist, I'd be able to ask you about a thousand questions right now. But I'm lost in what you say… I mean, how many bits of information can you process right now?"

Dr. Neruda: "It's not really a simple question of the quantity of information processing, but rather the relevance of the information in linear time based on the intention of the individual. When one goes through the process of the Corteum technology, their ability to tune into information packets that are relevant to a situation or problem is vastly improved. In most people, when a given situation confronts them they access their conscious mind and pull out the solution that has served them in the past. Thus, people fall into ruts and patterned behavior, which closes down their access to the unconscious information packets that are based on real-time situation analysis and have extremely high relevancy.

"This technology accelerates the circulation of information between the conscious and unconscious aspects of the mind to flow in the pattern of an ascending spiral rather than the pattern of a repetitious circle. And because of this it unleashes the innate intelligence of the individual. So you see, the Corteum technology doesn't increase raw intelligence, it simply facilitates the natural intelligence of the individual."

Sarah: "This is very cool. I wish I could undergo this regimen of the Corteum intelligence accelerator so I could really ask you some zinger questions! And with that, let's take a short break."

Ten minute break…

Dr. Neruda: "Since you have the tape recorder on now, let me repeat myself. The Corteum technology was the single most influential element in helping Fifteen become the Executive Director of both the ACIO and the Labyrinth Group. Granted, he had a brilliant mind before he underwent the Corteum intelligence enhancement process, but for some reason, the technology seemed to enhance his intelligence more than anyone else… by a significant degree."

Sarah: "Did anyone ever suspect that the Corteum and Fifteen were somehow a separate force from the Labyrinth Group. I mean, did anyone consider the possibility that they had a separate agenda… maybe BST wasn't their ultimate goal?"

Dr. Neruda: "No. There was, and I presume still is, absolute faith in both Fifteen and the Corteum. You have to understand that the Corteum are a benevolent race. We never saw any evidence that they had anything but good intentions to assist us, and to the extent possible, we tried to assist them in return. It was a courteous and completely reciprocal partnership."

Sarah: "You said last night that the Corteum were part of the Labyrinth Group, but only a couple hundred or so were actual members. How did they become part of the Labyrinth Group?"

Dr. Neruda: "Actually, I don't know for certain. I can only tell you what I was told when I asked the same question of one of the directors who sponsored me for entry into the Labyrinth Group. He told me that Fifteen had been selected by the Corteum to be their liaison with the ACIO. They singled him out, as the one through which they would initiate their technology transfer program with humans.

"Fifteen agreed to subject himself to the intelligence enhancement technology the Corteum offered. It was from this experience that Fifteen's vision of how BST could be developed was crystallized. He essentially created the framework and design blueprint.

"One of the things that the Corteum have in abundance is logical intelligence. They are very adept in terms of scientific inquiry and logical reasoning. By their own admission, where they lack ability is in the creative visionary aspect of discovery. This is precisely where Fifteen excels…"

Sarah: "But you're talking about a race that is superior to us in their technologies, how can they lack creative insights?"

Dr. Neruda: "These things are all relevant. Compared to virtually all other humans, the Corteum are creative and visionary. But there are formative principles of physics that reside in a dimensional matrix that are completely foreign to all beings except the most penetrating intellects. And Fifteen has such an intellect. The Corteum are hoping that Fifteen, and more generally, the Labyrinth Group, can develop BST because the Corteum have their own application for this technology."

Sarah: "But last night you said there are other races within our galaxy that may already have time travel capabilities, why don't the Corteum simply go to these races and make a deal with them?"

Dr. Neruda: "As I said before, a species that has, of their own initiative, developed time travel will be unwilling to share it with another race. It is truly the most guarded of all technologies. And one doesn't simply ask to borrow the technology when they need it. Even when the need seems compelling and true. It's so easy to become dependent on the technology itself. Furthermore, as I tried to explain last evening, there's a considerable difference between time travel and BST. I'm not aware of any species that possesses the form of BST that the Labyrinth Group is attempting to develop.

"It's like this, Sarah, BST requires a suite of interdependent, but discrete technologies that require a developer to apply new theorems, new laws of physics, that have never been discovered before. And then to build this suite of technologies based fundamentally on a new matrix of how the world works… it's a daunting task.

Everything previously held to be true needs to be destroyed, needs to be reinvented, reformulated, and then integrated into this new matrix.

"This is the very nature of BST, you start with a blank slate and reinvent, reformulate, and recreate the consciousness of matter."

Sarah: "Slow down… You just lost me. The consciousness of matter?"

Dr. Neruda: "Remember what I said earlier about quantum objects and how they're influenced by consciousness?"

Sarah: "Yes."

Dr. Neruda: "Quantum objects become increasingly granular or refined until they become pure light energy and cease to have mass. They are not of physical reality, but rather of a pure-state energy. This energy is further segmented into octaves of vibration. In other words, this light energy vibrates, and just like music, there are fundamentals and harmonics. The harmonics resonate with the fundamental energy vibration and the whole energy packet sings like a choir… except its voice is light.

"This singing, if you will, is the equivalent of a consciousness that pervades all matter… every physical object in the entire universe. Fifteen has successfully proven this all-pervasive consciousness or what he calls the Light-Encoded Reality Matrix or LERM, for those of us who like shorthand. Any way, LERM is just one of the new theorems that were required in order to devise a way to prove that BST was indeed a possibility, and not just a fanciful vision inside the mind of Fifteen."

Sarah: "This all-pervasive consciousness you mentioned, are you really talking about spirit or God?"

Dr. Neruda: "Exactly."

Sarah: "Now you've really crossed over the line. You're going to tell me that Fifteen discovered God. That he has proof of God?"

Dr. Neruda: "Yes, in a way, but… but God isn't what we call it. It's LERM. And Fifteen was quite emphatic that we never refer to LERM as God or even God-like. He preferred to think of LERM as the shadow of God. The light that casts the shadow, and the object of the shadow itself, he believes is impossible to prove through science or any other objective form of inquiry."

Sarah: "Okay… okay. But listen to me for a minute. If LERM is the shadow of God, as you put it, then it proves the existence of God, right?"

Dr. Neruda: "To those of us within the Labyrinth Group who understand the work of Fifteen, the answer is yes."

Sarah: "So isn't this even more important than the Ancient Arrow Project? I mean, if someone had proof of God, isn't it their moral responsibility to share this information with the public?"

Dr. Neruda: "Perhaps, but the only way this could be shared with the public is to disclose who the Labyrinth Group is, and that isn't something that Fifteen even likes to contemplate doing. He's afraid of the ridicule and misunderstanding that would result, and firmly believes that no one would believe him anyway because there are so many hidden technologies that led him to his findings, and he has no interest in disclosing these technologies to academia, government institutions, or the media. He'd become the next messiah… or devil, depending on your perspective."

Sarah: "So he's trapped in his own secrecy…"

Dr. Neruda: "In a way, but he's not feeling trapped. He's simply so far removed from the social fabric and scientific communities of academia that he has, for practical purposes, burned his bridges and has no intention of ever crossing the chasm that separates himself from all that he's left behind."

Sarah: "He must be incredibly lonely."

Dr. Neruda: "I don't think so. He seems extremely energized and basically happy. He's doing exactly what he wants to do, I can't say I've ever seen him depressed… maybe disappointed, but never depressed."

Sarah: "I still don't see the connection between LERM and BST…"

Dr. Neruda: "You see, if matter ultimately dissolves into octaves of light, and light dissolves into octaves of consciousness, and consciousness dissolves into octaves of reality, then matter, light, consciousness, and reality are all interdependent like an ecosystem. And like an ecosystem, if you change one element you affect the whole. Isolating any of the elements contained within LERM, and changing it, it can change reality. And this is a fundamental construct of BST. Does that answer your question?"

Sarah: "I'm not sure… I don't know, maybe all of this doesn't matter. Again, I'm feeling out of my territory. I find this interesting, but at the same time, it's frustrating. I even find myself feeling pissed off that all of this stuff is going on in my world and I don't know about it… well, I mean I didn't know about it until just now. It seems like an injustice to me. It's the old haves and have-nots story all over again. Can you appreciate how someone would feel… hearing all of this for the first time, and feeling so left out?"

Dr. Neruda: "Yes, I understand."

Sarah: "To you, you can take all of this for granted. After all, you're in the know. But the rest of us, we muddle through our little lives thinking the world is this and that, when really we're just bumping into each other in the dark. We're essentially clueless, aren't we?"

Dr. Neruda: "I don't know… maybe. Maybe you're right, it doesn't matter. I simply know what I know and I believe what I believe. Any more than that, it's as mysterious to me as it is to you. It would be a great mistake to think that the Labyrinth Group, or any of its members, including Fifteen and the Corteum, understands it all. They don't. But they work hard to get the answers, Sarah. I mean really hard. They've devoted their entire lives to this mission of BST. They didn't simply fall into the knowledge by accident. They tried and failed at thousands of different experiments until they found the existence of LERM, and they'll probably fail another thousand times before they find the solution to BST. But believe me, these individuals didn't arrive at their knowledge casually or because it was gifted to them by some higher force."

Sarah: "No, I didn't mean it that way. I'm glad for the Labyrinth Group… I mean it. I'm happy that someone on this planet has figured this out, or at least is trying. It's just unfair that so few have the proof… the knowledge… the opportunity to understand all of this. Their lives are so different, they might as well be living on some other planet. They might as well be extraterrestrials."

Dr. Neruda: "I'm only laughing because that's been a fear of Fifteen's from the start; that if someone ever did find out about the Labyrinth Group and its agenda, they would be regarded as ETs. And here you are, confirming that fear."

Sarah: "In a way, I wish you hadn't selected me. My life is so different now. This is all I can think about. It consumes me every waking minute. I have no idea how I'm going to get this story out. I have no idea. None."

Dr. Neruda: "Sarah, do you remember the first time we talked and I mentioned the Corteum? Your first question was, 'what do they look like?'"

Sarah: "Yes. And your point is…?"

Dr. Neruda: "These are the natural questions that people will have. LERM may interest a few scientists, but I doubt it. What's portrayed in these interviews is so superficial that I doubt any scientist would take it very seriously. And those that would, would find it to be a noble gesture to authenticate monistic idealism, and nothing more. So you see, your initial instincts should be trusted. Ask the questions that people would be interested in that appeal to their basic sense of curiosity. And don't worry about changing the world through anything I have to say. I don't need that weight on my shoulders."

Sarah: "Okay, you're right. You're absolutely right. Besides, I'm not sure about the truth of all of this. I'm still not convinced of what you say… just for the record."

Dr. Neruda: "And I'm still not trying to convince you or anybody else. I'm just answering your questions as truthfully as I know how."

Sarah: "Touché.

"Now, for the benefit of those who read this interview eventually, what do the Corteum look like?"

Dr. Neruda: "I thought you'd never ask. They stand nearly three meters high and have very elongated heads and bodies. Their skin is very fair… almost translucent, like you might expect from a cave dweller. Their eyes are relatively large and have various colors just like our own, except the Corteum have different colors to their eyes depending on their age and in some instances, their emotional state.

"What's very unique about the Corteum is that they have an incredibly articulate nervous system that enables them to process virtually everything that occurs within their environment, including the thoughts of another. Which means that when you're in their presence, you need to have control of your thoughts or else you'll potentially offend them. They're very sensitive emotionally."

Sarah: "How do they communicate with you?"

Dr. Neruda: "They speak perfect English or French, Italian, Spanish, or most any other language for that matter. They're very gifted linguists and can acquire average language skills in a matter of a few weeks, and operate as masters of the language within a few months. Their minds are like sponges, but like I said before, while they possess incredible mental powers to absorb new information and synthesize it with previous information, they're not necessarily adept at creating new information totally unrelated to existing information. That's precisely what impressed them so much with Fifteen."

Sarah: "What's their interest in the Ancient Arrow Project?"

Dr. Neruda: "No different than Fifteen's I presume. They're completely absorbed in the efforts to create BST, and hope that there's some technology or theorem within the Ancient Arrow site that can help accelerate the development of BST."

Sarah: "And what do the Corteum want to do with BST?"

Dr. Neruda: "The Corteum have a planetary system that's in a very fragile state because its protective atmosphere is degenerating at an alarming rate. Their atmosphere protects them, just as our own, from harmful light waves that are generated from their local sun, and to a lesser extent, their closest stars. Anyway, this condition has led them to become nocturnal, only venturing outside at night, and even then, only for as short a time as necessary. Over many generations, this has left them increasingly susceptible to the very condition that they're trying to solve. Their outer skins become more and more sensitive while their atmosphere becomes less protective.

"Their scientists predict it's only about ten to twenty years before they'll have to stay in underground communities year-round. This has had a major impact on their standard of living, economy, social structure, every possible aspect of their society has been affected, and mostly in a negative way, at least by their own measure. They hope that BST will enable them to install a technology that they've recently discovered to prevent the deterioration of their atmosphere."

Sarah: "Why can't they simply deploy this technology now?"

Dr. Neruda: "It's not a regenerative technology, it's a preventative technology. Regenerative technologies are impossible once a system reaches a certain retrograde trajectory. In their scenario, only BST would restore their environment."

Sarah: "Obviously they have space travel technology, why don't they pick out another planet and colonize it?"

Dr. Neruda: "They have tried, but every planet they've found that's suitable for their species is occupied. And they're not interested in being assimilated into an existing culture or society. They want their own identity and social structure. Also, what they deem suitable for habitation is extremely particular. For example, they have the same problem with earth as they have with their own planet... in fact, it's worse here. They have to live in our underground base in order to survive on our planet. It required that we build a special way-station for their spacecraft."

Sarah: "Do they want to interact with our governments and our people?"

Dr. Neruda: "Initially I think they did. And in fact they tried. But they were quickly escorted to the ACIO. We convinced the NSA and all other interested parties that the Corteum had left earth fearful of their lives. So... as far as our operatives within the NSA are concerned, the Corteum are long gone, and fortunately the NSA at the time were quite preoccupied with other ET issues anyway, namely the Greys."

Sarah: "I want to return to the WingMakers for a moment. What do the Corteum think of the WingMakers site, I assume they've seen everything?"

Dr. Neruda: "Yes, they've been involved from the beginning. The Corteum are as integral to the Labyrinth Group as any of its human members, so nothing is hidden from them. The leader of the Corteum mission to earth is called—in English—Mahunahi, and he happens to be an artist first and foremost, and a scientist is his secondary nature. He was always excited to see and hear about our findings. He asked if we could create a way station to the Ancient Arrow site so he could visit the site himself, but it just wasn't practical to do so without drawing attention to the site."

Sarah: "I have a few oddball questions, so bear with me. First, every time you mention a member of the ACIO, Labyrinth Group, or Corteum, it's always a male reference. Are there any women in any of these organizations? And second, why would an artist be the leader of a space mission of the Corteum? That seems very strange to me."

Dr. Neruda: "In answer to your first question, it's true that the Labyrinth Group is mostly male. I'm not aware of this being by design, but rather by accident. One of the directors is a woman, she's in charge of communications, and as a director has a Level Fourteen clearance. We also have nine females who are in the Twelve or Thirteen clearance categories, all of them are extremely bright and capable and share responsibility with their male counterparts without any form of discrimination… at least that I've ever been aware of. We even have one married couple. Each person—regardless of sex—is paid the identical sum of money and has all the same privileges… there's no distinction whatsoever within the ranks of the Labyrinth Group, and that's at Fifteen's insistence.

"As for the Corteum, they're all males. Their culture is much more role-defined than our own. And it's not to say that the females are treated as the lesser sex… no, in fact it may be quite the opposite, it's just that space travel and interaction with other species is left to the male sex until species interaction procedures are brought into play. That's so their children can retain access to their mothers and their families can remain more intact. Most, if not all, of the members of the Corteum contingent are married.

"As for your second question, the Corteum look at science, religion, and art as three equal members of a unified belief system that defines their social order. As I understand it, leadership varies between each of these three elements of their social order, depending on the contact that is made with an alien race. When they first made contact with humans it was decided that the leadership should come from the ranks of the artistic side because they felt we were more of an equal in this domain and thus the leader could more appropriately understand our motivations and desires."

Sarah: "That's interesting. They actually thought we were more artistic than scientific or spiritual. I guess now that I think about it, I can understand that. As a race, we probably are more inclined in that way than the others."

Dr. Neruda: "That was their assessment any way."

Sarah: "I'd like to go back to the artifacts for a minute. The artifacts that are technology based, where are they right now?"

Dr. Neruda: "After the initial discovery of the Ancient Arrow site, all of the physical artifacts that could be removed from the site were carefully packed in shipping crates and shipped to the ACIO research lab in Southern California, and are held by the Labyrinth Group in its own laboratory. That's where they still are, to the best of my knowledge."

Sarah: "And only the homing device found outside the site and the optical disc have been, to some extent, understood?"

Dr. Neruda: "That's correct."

Sarah: "So we really don't know whether BST is possible, do we?"

Dr. Neruda: "We know it's possible, but it's like anything that is extremely complicated and interdependent, one needs a fine-grain understanding of the total environment that encompasses the problem before they can modify or change the environment to solve the problem. And this requires an understanding of LERM that is still evolving within the Labyrinth Group, and I dare say, may yet require years of experimentation before its understanding is sufficient to identify intervention points and time-splice in such a way to minimize undesirable effects."

Sarah: "So we're back to the shadow of God discussion... or LERM as you affectionately call it. Why is the understanding of LERM so fundamental to achieving BST?"

Dr. Neruda: "Because LERM is the equivalent of genetics for consciousness, and consciousness is the equivalent of reality formulation for sentient beings. So if LERM is understood, one understands the causal system that operates in non-time and non-space, which fundamentally constructs the reality framework of space, time, energy, and matter. Quantum objects operating in the construct of LERM have an existence that is entirely different from macro objects like this table or chair.

"Quantum objects—in their true state—have never been seen by a human. Scientists have witnessed the effects and some of the properties of quantum objects, but their causal nature is not visible through scientific instruments... no matter how powerful they are, because scientific instruments are physical and therefore have a relationship to space and time. Whereas quantum objects have no relationship to time and space other than through an observer."

Sarah: "So you're saying that the building blocks of matter, these quantum objects, have no existence unless someone is observing them... that consciousness makes them appear real and fixed in time and space? Is that what you're saying?"

Dr. Neruda: "In a way, but not exactly. Let me try and explain it like this. Consciousness stems or originates from non-time and non-space as a form of energy that is a basic building block of LERM. Consciousness becomes localized as it becomes physical. In other words, consciousness becomes human, or animal, or plant or some object that has physical characteristics. Are you with me so far?"

Sarah: "Yes."

Dr. Neruda: "Good. As consciousness becomes a localized physical object, it essentially orchestrates LERM to conform to a reality matrix that has been encoded into the genetic or physical properties of the object it has become. In other words, consciousness moves from non-space and non-time to become matter, and then it orchestrates LERM to produce a physical reality consistent to the encoded genetic properties of the physical object it has become. If that object is a human being, then the genetic triggers that are uniquely human become the tools of consciousness from which it constructs its reality.

"LERM is essentially an infinite field of possibilities or as Aristotle referred to it, Potentia. This Potentia is like fertile soil from which physical objects are created. Those who can orchestrate LERM through the application of their consciousness are able to manifest reality and not simply react to it. This manifestation can be instantaneous because again, quantum objects originate in non-time and non-space…"

Sarah: "Not to get overly religious here, but what you're really talking about is what Jesus or other prophets have done… essentially manifest things like turning water to wine or curing the sick. Right?"

Dr. Neruda: "Yes. It's the same principle only I've described it instead of performed it. It's much easier to perform than describe."

Sarah: "So now you're going to tell me you can turn water into wine?"

Dr. Neruda: "Actually I've never tried that before, but yes, all of the members of the Labyrinth Group can manifest physical objects from out of LERM. This was actually one of the outcomes of Fifteen's discovery. The process of orchestrating LERM and manifesting physical objects on demand."

Sarah: "Okay, now you've definitely got my interest, but I'm feeling a little guilty because I swore I was going to stay on the subject of the WingMakers and the Ancient Arrow Project. So tell me, can you teach me how to manifest things out of thin air?"

Dr. Neruda: "Yes, but it would take some time… probably a few weeks or so."

Sarah: "Can you show me some examples of how you do it?"

Dr. Neruda: "How's this?"

Sarah: "For purposes of those reading these transcripts. Dr. Neruda just made a ball of twine appear out of nowhere. He just made it disappear as well. Now it has reappeared again. This is incredible. He's not holding it, so it's not like a magician who's making this appear from his sleeve or from behind his hands somehow. It's quite literally appearing and disappearing on a table about three feet in front of him, which is about six feet away from me. I can see it all very clearly.

"I'm picking up the ball of string and it's definitely a physical object… not simply a mirage or… or hologram. It has all the normal properties… weight… texture… it's slightly warm to the touch, but in every other respect, it's exactly how I'd expect a ball of twine to feel.

"Can you make something else appear… something more complicated, like a million dollars in cash?"

Dr. Neruda: "Yes."

Sarah: "Okay, let's see it."

Dr. Neruda: "You see this is the problem with these discoveries and capabilities. If I produced a million dollars in cash right now, you'd have a dilemma. What to do with a million dollars? Could you bear to see me make it disappear as easily as I make it appear?"

Sarah: "Are you crazy? Since the first moment I met you, I've never believed in what you've said until now. And I'm not even saying I totally believe you even now, but I'm a hell of a lot closer. I… no, people in general, need to see things with our eyes. We need to believe in what our eyes tell us because they—of all the senses—seem to have a fix on reality. And you've finally shown me something that is tangible… that my eyes relate to. I'm just asking for one more confirmation of your abilities. I mean, a ball of string doesn't seem like such a huge deal… not that I'm not impressed. But if you could produce a million dollars in cash… now that's a huge deal."

Dr. Neruda: "And the dilemma?"

Sarah: "Okay, I have a proposition for you. I'm going to need to quit my job for at least a few months to get this story out to the public and maybe even relocate or move underground somewhat. What if I kept just ten thousand dollars to help me through the next two months? Could that work for you?"

Dr. Neruda: "Yes, I could do that."

Sarah: "I'm now looking at a loose pile of one-hundred dollar bills that appear to be perfect replicas. I'm touching them… again they feel slightly warm to the touch, but these would definitely pass as the real thing… wow… I can't believe it. But this can't be a million dollars, you only manifested ten thousand didn't you?"

Dr. Neruda: "Yes, give or take a few hundred dollars."

Sarah: "You do realize that you just undermined your own credibility to those who will read this transcript. You just made yourself unbelievable. I'm not even sure I should include this because no one will be believe it anyway, and it may instead hurt your credibility in all the other areas of our discussion. This is truly not a believable experience unless you see it with your own eyes. What should I do?"

Dr. Neruda: "Sarah, whether anyone believes me isn't important. No one believes anything anyway unless they experience it, and even then, most people fall back into doubt. Belief is short-lived and always questioned; as it should be. Even the most devoted believer is in doubt most of the time, regardless of what they say. So, don't worry about whether this impairs my credibility or not. I don't care. It doesn't matter because I'm not trying to convince anyone of anything. I'm only trying to get information about the WingMakers to people who can make their own determination of what is true and believable."

Sarah: "Okay… so much for my concern. It'll be the last time I worry about your credibility.

"If you can manifest money like this so easily, why do you need to get paid? I mean who needs money from work?"

Dr. Neruda: "When this technology was discovered, it was only shared within the Labyrinth Group, and it was only used for experiments approved by Fifteen. The same principle would apply to BST or any other technology discovered by the Labyrinth Group that could be used for personal gain or benefit."

Sarah: "Man, you must be a very disciplined group. I don't think I could resist."

Dr. Neruda: "The truth is, I'm sure all the members of the Labyrinth Group have, from time-to-time, experimented with this technology in the privacy of their own homes."

Sarah: "Why do you refer to it as a technology? It seems to me that it's a mental thing. You weren't using anything other than your mind were you?"

Dr. Neruda: "It's a technology only from the standpoint of understanding the mental process. There's nothing electronic or mechanical if that's what you mean. But it's more than mind control. It's really a belief in LERM, and its unerringly perfect processes of creation — moving quantum objects from non-space and non-time to the world of matter in our time and space. It's more closely related to faith than technology… as odd as that may sound."

Sarah: "Actually, I was figuring that if Jesus and others who've walked the earth could do these things thousands of years ago, it must not have much to do with technology. But when you see it happen with your own eyes, you have a tendency to think there's some technology behind the scenes that's doing it. That it couldn't just be a natural power of humans… that doesn't seem possible to me for some reason."

Dr. Neruda: "I understand, but nonetheless, it's really a matter of perspective, and once you have the perspective on LERM and it becomes a fundamental construct of your belief system, it becomes amazingly easy to do this. It's a little like a sophisticated optical illusion based on a hologram that takes you several months of concentrating to see the picture that is subtly embedded, but the moment you see it, you can instantly see it the rest of your life without effort. That's how this operates. Some people can pick it up in a matter of a few days, others require hundreds of hours, but what everyone has in common is that once you get it, it becomes as natural as breathing."

Sarah: "And you think you could teach me in a matter of a few weeks, when it took some of your colleagues—with genius IQs, I might add—hundreds of hours to learn the technique?"

Dr. Neruda: "It's not related to IQ. It's related to understanding and belief. The understanding comes from seeing the existence of LERM and understanding how it operates at its fundamental level. Whether you have an average intelligence or are a genius, it doesn't matter, so long as you understand and believe what you understand."

Sarah: "So how do you get me to believe in LERM?"

Dr. Neruda: "You already do deep inside you. It's your conscious mind that rejects your deeper belief and understanding. So I would help you to consciously understand what you already know at a deeper level of your being. And I would do this by showing you LERM."

Sarah: "And how would you do that?"

Dr. Neruda: "You would need to come to the Labyrinth Group's research facility in Southern California. It's the only place in the world where I can show you the indisputable evidence of LERM."

Sarah: "Under the circumstances, that doesn't seem like a scenario that will ever happen. There must be another alternative… or said another way, what is it that I'd see at this research center that I couldn't get somewhere else… or through some other means?"

Dr. Neruda: "I'm not saying that the only way to acquire this ability is by seeing LERM in action, but it is very convincing. The Labyrinth Group has a technology—designed by Fifteen himself—that quite literally enables an individual to experience LERM. There are also the mystical or shamanic means, but these are far less likely to occur in a two-week period of time. These methods seem independent of circumstance and more dependent on some deeper, predestined or pre-encoded awakening that the individual is not aware of consciously. In some instances, this awakening includes an ability to manifest physical objects, but generally, it's done without a conscious knowledge of how it's done. It just works."

Sarah: "Okay, so let's assume I'm not cut out to be a mystic or shaman, what would I see with this technology that would convince me of my abilities to do what you just did?"

Dr. Neruda: "I can't really tell you. It's one of those experiences that words are wholly inadequate to describe or explain. About all I can tell you is that LERM is experienced through this technology, and it essentially, as a result of the experience, rewires your internal electrical system. In this process, new circuits are cut in your nervous system, and these new circuits enable you to utilize LERM as an outgrowth of your experience of it.

"I doubt this explanation does you any good whatsoever. I've never tried to explain it before, and I can see by the look on your face that I failed miserably…"

Sarah: "No, it's not that. I'm just tired of always feeling like I've lived on a different planet all my life. That I've missed out on all of this… it's really distressing to me when I think about it.

"I remember reading a biography about Einstein, and he was quoted saying something like we humans only use about two percent of our intellectual capability. Well, that's about how I feel right now. That I've lived my life at about the two percent level—if that—and I'm just beginning to see what he meant. I never had a comparison before now that let me see what the other ninety-eight percent might be like. It's not altogether pleasant to see what's been left out or overlooked… or undervalued."

Dr. Neruda: "I understand."

Sarah: "On to something else. You said earlier that certain technologies like LERM and BST weren't allowed to be used for personal gain by members of the Labyrinth Group. Yet, if BST did exist, wouldn't everyone line up and ask to use it? I know I would. There're a lot of events in my life I'd change if I could. Once the cat's out of the bag, how could BST ever be kept under wraps?"

Dr. Neruda: "Like everything, there are implications and moral and ethical considerations that have to be weighed. One of the things that Fifteen and more generally the Labyrinth Group is good at, is to consider these implications in the broader scope of the social order. Fifteen, from an early age, always felt that the technologies of BST and LERM would only be granted to those organizations that would properly honor the ethical considerations that were required by the technology itself.

"This is one of the fundamental charters of the Labyrinth Group, and all of its members take it very seriously. As a new technology is being developed, there are always members of the team who are concerned with the ethical implications of the technology and are responsible for usage guidelines and deployment rules. This is an integral part of any project's development."

Sarah: "That's good to hear, but couldn't such a charter also be used to prevent the spread of these technologies to a broader audience?"

Dr. Neruda: "Unquestionably. A technology like BST—once developed and tested—could, in time, become a consumer technology. But as long as the Labyrinth

Group exists, it would protect BST from any and all outside forces. Within the Labyrinth Group there is a committee called the Technology Transfer Program or TTP Committee. This committee has two missions, one, to assess the incoming technologies that are assimilated from ETs, and two, they're responsible for which technologies and in what state of dilution they're transferred to our private industry partners, NSA, or the military.

"The TTP Committee is in control of the pure-state technologies that are developed by the Labyrinth Group. These pure-state technologies are virtually never transferred to outside organizations. Even those staff members in the ACIO who are not part of the Labyrinth Group are unaware of these pure-state technologies, and when—"

Sarah: "But if I place these interview transcripts on the Internet or some media publication picks up this story, more than just the ACIO staff members are going to know about this stuff. Isn't this going to screw up the Labyrinth Group's cloak of secrecy?"

Dr. Neruda: "No. The Labyrinth Group is more than a secret organization. For all practical purposes, it doesn't exist. The ACIO doesn't exist. No one will be able to trace the ACIO let alone the Labyrinth Group. Their security technologies are so vastly superior they are completely invulnerable in this regard. Nothing I say, or you publish, will make them more vulnerable. As I said before, their only concern will be the precedent of my defection and how it could create more defections over time."

Sarah: "Why, why would anyone want to leave... I mean I understand your case... you didn't want your memories changed or removed. But they don't commonly do that do they?"

Dr. Neruda: "Not often, but I'm certainly not the first to be targeted to undergo memory implant sessions or other forms of invasive security measures. They're all part of the culture of the Labyrinth Group and the ACIO. Everyone who enters either of those worlds understands what they must subject themselves to. It's very clear why the paranoia must be part of the culture. But over time, certain individuals find it suffocating. And these individuals are the ones who are most at risk to see my defection as a reason for their own.

"I may be entirely wrong about this, but I believe there are ten to twenty individuals who would leave the ACIO or even the Labyrinth Group if they were given the choice without repercussions."

Sarah: "But I thought you said last night that these people were in love with their jobs because of the special access to technologies and research labs that were so advanced to anything else available? If that's the case, what would they do in normal society?"

Dr. Neruda: "I'll find out. I'll be the first to experience normal society… as a normal person."

Sarah: "Well, at least you won't have any problem getting a job… what am I saying, you won't even need to work. I forgot, you can make your own money out of thin air."

Dr. Neruda: "You'd be surprised to know that I live a pretty simple life. I own a '92 Honda Accord and live in a modest three bedroom home in a suburban neighborhood of modest homes…"

Sarah: "You're kidding?"

Dr. Neruda: "No."

Sarah: "You make $400,000 a year tax free and… and have a money tree in your mind, and you live like I do? If you don't mind my asking, what do you do with all your money?"

Dr. Neruda: "I have blind trusts."

Sarah: "Are all the Labyrinth Group members like you?"

Dr. Neruda: "You mean in regard to money and possessions?"

Sarah: "Yes."

Dr. Neruda: "Most live at a higher standard of living than I do, but it is part of our culture to live modestly and none of the members live a pretentious lifestyle. Fifteen pays people what they're worth, not because he wants them to throw money around and live flamboyantly. He's a big believer in this, and he himself, even more than I, lives humbly."

Sarah: "I find this really hard to believe. I think of just about everything you've told me so far, this is one of the hardest things to believe. I'm totally baffled here…"

Dr. Neruda: "I can appreciate that, but what I'm telling you is the truth.

"Initially, the way new people are recruited to join the ACIO is largely because of the monetary incentives. These are extremely bright and capable people and could easily secure positions in academia or private industry making two-hundred thousand dollars per year, and more. The ACIO lures them by at least doubling their salary and offering them lifetime employment contracts. But those who ultimately earn the right to enter the twelfth level are then inducted into the Labyrinth Group, and by the time an individual has risen to this status, money has become increasingly unimportant… particularly after the Corteum intelligence accelerator experience… after the LERM experience, it's diminished even more.

"You'd probably find it interesting that Fifteen lives in a small, three bedroom home in a regular community where the average property value is about $250,000. That's not much of a house by West Coast standards. His automobile must have at least one-hundred thousand miles on it, no air conditioning, and he's perfectly content with his situation. New ACIO recruits are always amazed at Fifteen's thrift… I think bewildered is a better way of putting it. But over time, they learn to respect him not as an eccentric, but as an extremely dedicated genius who simply likes to live like other people and blend in."

Sarah: "Okay… I've got to get personal here, and I know I've totally betrayed my agenda, but you've got to tell me a few things about… well like, what do your neighbors think you do?"

Dr. Neruda: "I don't know my neighbors very well. I've worked seventy hours per week since I was eighteen years old. When I socialize, it's generally with my colleagues. There's very little time for establishing other relationships. But to answer your question directly, I don't know for sure what they think I do… I've only told them I'm a research scientist for the government. For most people that settles their curiosity."

Sarah: "But what if you met a woman and fell in love. She'd want to know what you did and how much money you made and so forth… what would you tell her?"

Dr. Neruda: "I work for a government weather research center. I'm a research scientist in applied chaos theory and I make $85,000 per year."

Sarah: "So you'd lie?"

Dr. Neruda: "It's part of the culture of the Labyrinth Group. We can't tell the truth, and if we did, the vast majority of people would think we were crazy. It's also why we keep to our own… we can tell the truth among ourselves."

Sarah: "When I first heard about the ACIO and its secret mission, and that you were defecting and afraid for your life… I thought the ACIO was an evil-minded, control-the-world type of organization. Then I heard about the kind of money you all made and I pictured a bunch of intellectual snobs driving bullet-proof Mercedes Benzes and living in posh mansions… and you just dismantled my image. You completely destroyed it. So why are you so afraid?"

Dr. Neruda: "The Labyrinth Group, because of its connection to the ACIO, is still very much connected to the secret network of organizations who control a great deal of the world's monetary and natural resource assets. This network of organizations will know about my defection the instant these materials I've given you gain any visibility in the press or on the Internet. They will know of its authenticity by simply reading these two interviews. While there's nothing they can do to the ACIO or the Labyrinth Group, they can make my life difficult to live.

"And they will most definitely try. I know all about their technologies and how they deploy them. I know the people behind these organizations and I know how they operate. I have knowledge that I've only shown you a small fraction of. And this knowledge would make certain individuals—very powerful individuals—very uncomfortable. It's extremely rare, but when high-level operatives defect, they're hunted like dogs until they're found and disposed of, or if they serve an ongoing purpose, their memories are selectively wiped clean. It's one of the unfortunate realities of having dealt with these organizations."

Sarah: "But you were just a scientist… a linguist, for God's sake. How does that make you a threat to these secret organizations?"

Dr. Neruda: "I was the one that created the underlying encryption technology for their security system that overlays their predictive modeling software for the world's stock exchanges. I may be a simple scientist in your eyes, but my talents for linguistics is not the only talent I possess. I'm also gifted in the field of encryption. And within the world of economics, I'm simply the best. And this talent was given to certain organizations to help them, and in the process of doing so, I learned about these organizations and how they operate. It makes me a security risk."

Sarah: "Why? I mean if the ACIO and Labyrinth Group have so much money… why work with these evil groups?"

Dr. Neruda: "First of all, they're not evil. These organizations consist of well educated elitists who're self-absorbed perhaps, but not evil. They look at the world as a biological experience where the strong survive, the powerful thrive, and the secretive control. They like being in control of the experience. They are the ultimate control freaks, but not for the sake of adoration or ego gratification, but for the sake that they genuinely believe they're the best at making policy decisions that affect the world's economy and security.

"Don't confuse control with evil intent. It's not necessarily one and the same thing. That's the game they choose to play. The fact that they make incredible sums of money is simply part of the game, but it's not the reason they sit in the driver's seat of the world's economy… they simply want to protect their life's agenda like anyone else would. It's just that they're in the position to actually do it. They get their security from being at the top of the economic food chain."

Sarah: "But they're manipulating people and keeping information from them. If this isn't evil, what is?"

Dr. Neruda: "By your definition, our national government, our local government, virtually every business and organization, is evil. Everyone manipulates and keeps information hidden; governments, organizations, and individuals."

Sarah: "You're twisting my words. It's a matter of degree isn't it? I mean, it's one thing if I don't tell you my true hair color, and it's another thing if, as part of this secret network, I withhold information about how I'm manipulating the world economy. They're entirely different in scale. You can't compare them. I still think it's evil when organizations manipulate and control things for their own gain."

Dr. Neruda: "Believe me, I didn't set out to be the defender of these organizations, but you need to understand this because it's important and it may affect you in the days ahead. This secret network of powerful organizations are more aligned with the goals of the Labyrinth Group than our world's governments, and in particular, our military leaders. If you're worried about anything, you would be well advised to worry more about the administration, Congress, and the Department of Defense... not only in the United States, but in every country."

Sarah: "How can you say that? Are you saying that our government and military leaders are trying to cause us harm and these secret, manipulative organizations are trying to help us?"

Dr. Neruda: "I'm saying that the leadership in the world's community of nations is inept, and can be bought with the holy dollar. And that it's not the secret network that I've been talking about who's manipulating our government and military leadership to invest huge amounts of money in destructive forces like nuclear and biological weapons. This, they're deciding on their own. The secret organizations that I'm pointing the finger at are opposed to these military buildups because they interject a degree of uncertainty in their models for controlling economic and social order.

"The politicians and military leaders are the ones who're investing time, energy, and money in weapons of mass destruction, and these, if there is such a thing as evil, are it."

Sarah: "Okay. I see your point. But you implied that these secret organizations would try to kill us if we published and distributed all of this? I still don't see how that makes them so noble."

Dr. Neruda: "I don't think you have to be concerned about these secret organizations. You don't know enough to be dangerous to them. Besides, they're used to journalists snooping around and trying to expose them. None have succeeded in any meaningful way. Dozens of books have been written about them. So they're not going to bother you. Their interest will be in me and me alone. It's one of the reasons why I'm careful in what I tell you. I know they'll read these transcripts, as will the NSA, CIA, ACIO, and the entire Labyrinth Group. I'm allowing you to record these conversations because I know who will hear these exact words, and I want them to know precisely what I have shared with you, and through you, to others.

"I'm not making a value judgment as to whether these secret organizations are noble or not. I'm merely pointing out that they're not the ones wasting huge sums of money and intellectual capital on weapons of mass destruction. They're significantly more competent to rule than our politicians and military leaders are. And this is simply my opinion."

Sarah: "I still don't get it. If the Labyrinth Group, the ACIO and this secret network of organizations are all so noble and benevolent, why are you afraid for your life? And why are they hiding from the public like cockroaches?"

Dr. Neruda: "To answer your first question, I fear for my life because I know information that could cause irreparable harm to a variety of secret organizations... though I have no intention to do so."

Sarah: "But simply because you know these things they'll hunt you down and kill you? Sounds like a nice group to me. Certainly not evil..."

Dr. Neruda: "Remember... they're control freaks. They don't like having anyone loose who could cause them potential harm. If I wanted to, I could bring them down. I know that much about their computer algorithms and encryption technologies."

Sarah: "But how would you get access to their system. It would seem to me that you'd be placing yourself in great jeopardy if you tried to get into their system."

Dr. Neruda: "I don't need to get into their system to cause them harm, I need to get into their system to prevent harm. They will invite me into their system."

Sarah: "I don't understand..."

Dr. Neruda: "When I developed the system initially, there were certain time delayed algorithms that were scripted to occur at specific times, and if they were not maintained accordingly, the program would essentially self-destruct. Something that these organizations cannot afford to happen."

Sarah: "Why did they agree to this?"

Dr. Neruda: "It's part of the fee that the Labyrinth Group extracts from its clients. More importantly, it ensures that our technologies—even in their diluted states—are operated according to our agreement and not misused. I have the access codes for this system and the maintenance key that will prevent it from crashing. I've made certain that I'm the only one who has this knowledge."

Sarah: "You're telling me that with all those photographic memories running around at the Labyrinth Group, that you're the only one who knows the code?"

Dr. Neruda: "I didn't exactly report the right number when I did my last update of their system... so, yes, I'm the only one who knows the correct code. I designed it that way to ensure my safety..."

Sarah: "But with all the geniuses in the Labyrinth Group, you're telling me that they can't solve this problem themselves?"

Dr. Neruda: "Not without a significant amount of time… which is something Fifteen won't agree to do. It's too wasteful and a major distraction to BST research."

Sarah: "Do they already know about this?"

Dr. Neruda: "Oh, yes. I informed them shortly after I defected."

Sarah: "They must have been pissed."

Dr. Neruda: "It wasn't a pleasant conversation to put it mildly."

Sarah: "I was thinking about all of this sophisticated technology that the Labyrinth Group has, but I don't understand something. How do you manufacture it? I assume Intel isn't doing the manufacturing. Right?"

Dr. Neruda: "Correct. There's no one on this planet that can manufacture these technologies. They're all based upon the Corteum technology, which is about 150 generations ahead of our best computer technologies here on earth. For example, the LERM project used only one domestic technology in the total array of about two-hundred different technologies, and it was a relatively insignificant part of the project…"

Sarah: "What was it?"

Dr. Neruda: "It's a derivative of a laser telemetry technology that the ACIO developed about twenty years ago, but it filled the specific needs of the LERM project because it was based on analog protocols, which were required for the application in that specific part of the experiment."

Sarah: "So the Corteum performs all the manufacturing of what the Labyrinth Group designs. What if the Corteum decide, for whatever reason, not to share these technologies all of sudden? Wouldn't the Labyrinth Group cease to exist?"

Dr. Neruda: "Perhaps. But Fifteen is shrewd and he's put certain contingencies in place to help ensure nothing like that would ever happen. Bear in mind, that the Corteum are at least as motivated as we are to develop this technology, perhaps more. They have tremendous respect for Fifteen as well as the other human contingent of the Labyrinth Group. However, when the Labyrinth Group was first formed, Fifteen negotiated with the Corteum to share all source code for the projects that came out of BST research. All base technologies were replicated in two separate research labs. There's complete redundancy right down to the power supplies."

Sarah: "Won't the leaders of these secret organizations try to pressure Fifteen to find you… with their remote viewing technology, can't they find you easily?"

Dr. Neruda: "The leaders of these secret organizations well know they have no leverage with Fifteen. After they read this information, they will know they have even less leverage. Fifteen and the Labyrinth Group designed and developed all of their security systems. Every last one. They knew they had to be indebted to the Labyrinth Group for certain technologies that made them, speaking metaphorically, invisible. Fifteen cannot be pressured. In fact, it's just the opposite. Fifteen can pressure them, though he never would. To Fifteen, these organizations simply represent the best alternative to letting our own governments take control of the economic engines and social order of the world infrastructure. Hence, he sympathizes with them and tries to help them to the extent he can afford the time and energy."

Sarah: "So how will you hide from them?"

Dr. Neruda: "As I told you before, I began to systematically disentangle myself from the ACIO's invasive security precautions, which include electronic sensors implanted underneath the skin in the back of the neck. I effectively stripped myself of these devices so I'd have a chance of remaining underground until a reasonable solution could be negotiated."

Sarah: "But you said they had RV technology that can locate you. What about this?"

Dr. Neruda: "There's little doubt that they will try this, but it's not an exact science. An RV could see this room, but not have a clue as to how to find it. They might be able to key in on a particular object—like that clock, for example—but unless it was the only clock of its kind and they could trace its location, it wouldn't help them."

Sarah: "Is there anything I should be worried about, then?"

Dr. Neruda: "I think we need to move around a bit, and vary our meeting time and place. We should conduct the next interview in a new environment—perhaps outdoors. Something generic without landmarks."

Sarah: "So they can't read my street sign and then look at my house's address—I mean if they were doing an RV session right now?"

Dr. Neruda: "They would try, and it's possible they'd be successful, but not likely."

Sarah: "I suddenly got very nervous. You're not making me feel comfortable with this."

Dr. Neruda: "I can only be honest."

Sarah: "What would they do with me and my daughter if they found us?"

Dr. Neruda: "I think you could assume that they'd perform an MRP of the entire experience of meeting me."

Sarah: "They wouldn't kill us?"

Dr. Neruda: "I don't think so. Fifteen doesn't resort to violence unless it's absolutely necessary."

Sarah: "Shit. I wish I knew about this before I agreed to get my daughter and me involved. Just tell me one thing; do you know when they're doing an RV session? I mean, can you feel it or anything?"

Dr. Neruda: "I can sense it, but it's not something that's absolute."

Sarah: "Is there any defense against it?"

Dr. Neruda: "None."

Sarah: "So all we do is hope that their damn RV is incompetent?"

Dr. Neruda: "I'll only stay for short periods of time, and it'll be late at night when they're far less likely to perform an RV session. It'd be a good practice to vary our meeting place, as I suggested before. Other than that, I don't know what more we can do."

Sarah: "I assume there's nothing the police or FBI could do to help?"

Dr. Neruda: "Nothing that I'm interested in."

Sarah: "But what will you do to protect yourself?"

Dr. Neruda: "As you can imagine, Sarah, there's certain information I can't share with you given the nature of these interviews. This is one instance I can't tell you more than I already have."

Sarah: "I'm feeling the need to bring this session to an end. My mind is quite literally filled to the brim. I think if you told me anything profound right now, it'd just go in one ear and out the other. Can we meet again on Tuesday and perhaps pick-up where we left off tonight?"

Dr. Neruda: "Yes, that's fine with my schedule."

Sarah: "Okay. Signing off for tonight."

THE THIRD INTERVIEW OF
DR. JAMISSON NERUDA

By Sarah

What follows is a session I recorded of Dr. Neruda on December 30, 1997. He gave permission for me to record his answers to my questions. This is the transcript of that session. This was one of five times I was able to tape record our conversations. I have preserved these transcripts precisely as they occurred. No editing was performed, and I've tried my best to include the exact words, phrasing, and grammar used by Dr. Neruda.

(It's recommended that you read the December 27 and December 28, 1997 interviews before reading this one.)

Sarah: "Good evening, Dr. Neruda. Are you ready?"

Dr. Neruda: "Yes, I'm ready when you are."

Sarah: "One of the things that I find hard to embrace about this whole affair is that the concept of time travel always seemed like a fairly easy technology to develop. I know I've gotten that impression from Star Trek and various other movies and television, but still, what you've described seems like it's so difficult to develop that we'll never succeed. Is it really that hard to develop?"

Dr. Neruda: "The way time travel is presented in the movies trivializes the complexities of this technology, and interactive time travel or BST, as defined by Fifteen, is the most sophisticated of all technologies. It's the apex technology from which virtually all other technologies can be derived. So, in creating BST, one is creating a short cut or an accelerated pathway into the acquisition of virtually all other technologies. This is why BST is so difficult to develop.

"Science fiction violates most of the scientific premises that are related to our understanding of time travel. And BST in particular is an extremely sophisticated application of scientific principles that are simply not stated in science fiction, mostly because people like the effects and plot lines of time travel, more than they have an appetite for understanding the science behind it. So writers, especially for television and movies, trivialize the degree of complexity that surrounds this apex technology."

Sarah: "But you didn't really answer my question… will we succeed in developing it?"

Dr. Neruda: "There's little doubt in my mind that the Labyrinth Group will succeed in developing BST. The question is whether it's in humanity's best interest in the long-term. They were weeks from beginning their initial tests for broad scale testing just before I defected. There was widespread anticipation at the director level that BST was a matter of four to six months away from a successful test."

Sarah: "So what's the biggest obstacle to success?"

Dr. Neruda: "Simply stated, it's whether the Labyrinth Group has the ability to define and access intervention points as prescribed by Fifteen that have the least impact on related events in horizontal time. It's the most subtle, yet most important component to this whole chain of technologies."

Sarah: "Can you explain this in lay terms?"

Dr. Neruda: "It's an extremely difficult technology to develop—defining the optimal intervention point, accessing the intervention point, and returning from the intervention point without detection. This is all about splicing time at the causal level with a minimum of disruption. It's the equivalent challenge of throwing a boulder into a pond without any ripples."

Sarah: "Why all the concern about minimizing disruption? I mean, in the case of the Animus, aren't they trying to completely annihilate humankind? Why should we care so much about disrupting their way of life?"

Dr. Neruda: "First of all, the Animus are not coming to annihilate humankind. They're coming to control the genetic library known as earth. Their intention is not completely understood, but it's not to kill our animal populations or the human species. It has more to do with genetic engineering and how their species can be modified to enable it to house a spiritual consciousness. They want unfettered access to our DNA in order to conduct experiments. Beyond this, they want to colonize earth, but for what ultimate purpose we don't know.

"To your question, the concern about minimizing impacts from BST intervention has to do as much with selfish interests as altruistic ones. When events are altered or changed, they can have unintended and very unpredictable consequences. For example, we could successfully divert the Animus from our galaxy, but in the process, unintentionally send them to another planet. This act would have consequences to our planet that we could never predict."

Sarah: "Are you talking about karma?"

Dr. Neruda: "No. It has to do with physics and the inherent nature of complex systems. Causal energy is eternal. It simply bounces from event to event. In some cases, it shapes the event; in others, it creates the event. Causal energy is the most potent force in the universe, and when it's redirected —on a global scale—it will rebound in unpredictable and innumerable ways."

Sarah: "So, this is the flaw of BST... not knowing the consequences of changing events? Are you suggesting that we could succeed in diverting the Animus from our planet, and then some years later fall victim to some other form of catastrophe that wipes out our planet?"

Dr. Neruda: "No, it doesn't happen quite like that. The energy system that was redirected would simply rebound to the point from whence it was redirected. How it would rebound is so complex that it would be impossible to predict the nature of its reaction. I suppose it could invite a cataclysm of some kind, but it's not to say humanity would be punished, if that's what you're trying to imply."

Sarah: "I guess that's what I was implying. But isn't it true that karma exists? And if we turned the Animus onto another planet via BST, we'd be setting ourselves up for a negative reaction?"

Dr. Neruda: "No. It means we'd receive a reaction, and the nature of the reaction may be so unrelated to the causal energy redirect that no one would know it was a reaction. This is the nature of causal energy: it rebounds of its own force and intelligence; it's not a simple reaction to an action."

Sarah: "I thought karma, and even physics, held that for every action there's an equal and opposite reaction. What happened to this principle?"

Dr. Neruda: "It's alive and well. It's just doesn't apply to causal energy systems or the dimension of vertical time."

Sarah: "Okay, I'm going to avoid another discussion of physics in favor of finding out why you think BST will succeed given our discussion of the past few minutes."

Dr. Neruda: "It's one of the main reasons I defected."

Sarah: "How do you mean that?"

Dr. Neruda: "This issue of uncertainty, regarding causal energy systems, has always been the breaking point of BST—at least theoretically. Fifteen believes he knows how to manage this. I'm not so certain it can be managed, particularly after my exposure to the WingMakers and gaining a bit of understanding into their solution in dealing with the Animus."

Sarah: "I know you've talked a little bit about this already, but refresh my memory. What *is* their solution?"

Dr. Neruda: "I have only a few pieces to go by, so I'm not going to be able to talk definitively about this."

Sarah: "And what's the nature of these sources?"

Dr. Neruda: "There was an RV session that elicited some insight. I read more about it in the introduction of the text from the optical disc—"

Sarah: "This being the text that literally disappeared?"

Dr. Neruda: "Yes, but I've stored the entire text in my memory."

Sarah: "Anything else?"

Dr. Neruda: "I had a direct communication with what I believe was a representative of the WingMakers."

Sarah: "How? When?"

Dr. Neruda: "It's a complicated story, but Samantha, the RV assigned to our project, was having increasingly strong connections to the WingMakers. Unfortunately, they were so strong that Fifteen had little choice but to subject her to an MRP. I met with her just prior to the procedure, and she suddenly began channeling a presence to me that I believe was from the Central Race."

Sarah: "And from these three sources you have a pretty good idea as to how the WingMakers plan to protect their genetic library?"

Dr. Neruda: "Correct."

Sarah: "And what did this channeled entity say?"

Dr. Neruda: "Its primary emphasis was that our technology would fail us."

Sarah: "And by technology, it meant BST?"

Dr. Neruda: "That was my interpretation."

Sarah: "So you trust this Samantha?"

Dr. Neruda: "I have no doubts about her whatsoever. She was simply our best RV, and quite possibly the best natural intuitive we ever had within the ACIO."

Sarah: "Let's go back to something you implied a minute ago. Did I understand you right that you defected from the ACIO because of a disagreement you had with Fifteen about BST and the WingMakers solution of defense?"

Dr. Neruda: "Yes, it was a primary factor."

Sarah: "Can you elaborate on this a bit?"

Dr. Neruda: "Fifteen believed that Samantha—our RV—could jeopardize our mission because of her ability to make contact with the WingMakers. In two of the three RV sessions she performed, they detected her presence, and they had begun to probe her. Fifteen—once he had confirmation that these beings were, in all probability, from the Central Race—became quite alarmed and put a stop to any further RV sessions.

"When I asked him why, he seemed to have some apprehension about their ability to sense our work on BST, and feared that they may put an end to it."

Sarah: "Why?"

Dr. Neruda: "Because they are very powerful beings. What most people consider God, amplify by a factor of a thousand and you would be close to the range of capabilities and power that these beings can wield."

Sarah: "Are you saying these beings are more powerful than God?"

Dr. Neruda: "The problem with your question is that I don't know *which* God you're referring to. The conception of God in the Bible, or most of our planet's holy books, bears no resemblance to the image of God that I hold in my mind."

Sarah: "Okay, I want to come back to this topic because it really holds an interest to me, but I also want to complete our discussion around your defection. Can you explain what happened?"

Dr. Neruda: "Simply put, I began to feel that the defensive weapon installed on this planet by the WingMakers stood a better chance of succeeding than BST. All logic dictated this to be true. Fifteen, however, disagreed. He would allow further investigation into how to find the remaining WingMakers' sites and how to bring them online, but he would never share the technology or anything related to the discovery with the general public."

Sarah: "And so your differences over this issue caused your defection?"

Dr. Neruda: "Yes."

Sarah: "Back to the topic of God. Tell me how your version of God is defined."

Dr. Neruda: "God is a unifying force, primal and eternal. This force is the original force that summoned life from itself to become both its companion and journey. The life that was summoned was experimented with many times until a soul carrier was formed that could take a particle of this force into the outer, expanding universes."

Sarah: "I assume this soul carrier you're referring to is the Central Race?"

Dr. Neruda: "Correct."

Sarah: "Are these the same as angels?"

Dr. Neruda: "No, the Central Race is more akin to genetic planners and universe architects. They're not well known or understood, even in the most insightful cosmologies held by the Corteum."

Sarah: "So, I presume if angels are real they're yet another creation of the Central Race?"

Dr. Neruda: "Correct."

Sarah: "Then God, or this force as you were describing it, didn't really create anything other than the Central Race, and then returned to his abode in the center of the universe. It sounds like the Central Race does all the work."

Dr. Neruda: "The Central Race is simply a time-shifted version of the human race."

Sarah: "Huh?"

Dr. Neruda: "The Central Race holds the genetic archetype of the human species, no matter what form it takes on; no matter what time it lives in; no matter what part of the universe it lives in. This archetype is like a magnetic force: it draws the lesser developed versions of the species towards it. All versions of the humanoid species are merely time-shifted versions of the Central Race—or at least that's the view of the Corteum."

Sarah: "Stop a second. Are you saying that I'm made from the same DNA as the Central Race? That I'm essentially the same, genetically speaking, just in a different time and space? How's that possible?"

Dr. Neruda: "It's possible because the Central Race designed it that way. DNA is not something that only transmits physical characteristics or predispositions. It transmits our concepts of time, space, energy, and matter. It transmits our conscious and unconscious filters. It transmits our receptivity to the inward impulse of original thought, and this receptivity is what defines the motion of the being."

Sarah: "The motion of the being?"

Dr. Neruda: "All beings are in motion. They're going somewhere every moment of their lives. If not physically in motion, their minds are in motion. Their subconscious is always in motion, interacting with the data stream of a multiverse. The motion of the being is simply a term we used at the ACIO to define the internal compass."

Sarah: "And the internal compass is?"

Dr. Neruda: "It's the radar system of the individual that defines its path through life at both the macroscopic and microscopic levels, and everywhere in between."

Sarah: "I have this feeling that this topic could go on forever."

Dr. Neruda: "It's not that complex, Sarah. Think of the decisions you make in your life. Which ones would you say were made for you by external sources, which ones were your own, and which ones were a combination of both external and your own decision?"

Sarah: "You mean as a percentage?"

Dr. Neruda: "Try to estimate."

Sarah: "It depends on what stage of my life I consider. When I was a baby, my parents made all my decisions—"

Dr. Neruda: "No, this applies to all stages—from birth to death. Just make a guess."

Sarah: "I don't know, maybe 40 percent external, 30 percent my own, and thirty percent a combination."

Dr. Neruda: "Then you'd be surprised if I told you that you deposit an image within your DNA—before you're born—that defines your motion of being. And when this deposit is made, your motion of being is defined by *you*, not someone else. No external force makes your decision, an external force can only inform and activate a decision already made."

Sarah: "You lost me. Are you saying that every decision in my life was already made before I was born?"

Dr. Neruda: "No. Every causal decision was."

Sarah: "So what's the difference between a causal decision and a regular decision?"

Dr. Neruda: "Think of how many decisions you make in a day. Wouldn't you agree that it's probably hundreds if not thousands every day? These are—as you put it—*regular* decisions. Causal decisions are defined by how integral they are to the substrate of the individual being. Are you receptive to new ideas? Are you able to synthesize opposing thoughts? Do you process information dominantly in a visual or numeric context? These are causal decisions that you define before being born, and they're encoded within the DNA that activates your decision matrix. External forces like parents, teachers, and friends only inform you of what you've already defined as the motion of your being."

Sarah: "Is this according to the Corteum, too?"

Dr. Neruda: "This is part of the learning I personally gathered from my LERM experiences. The Corteum subscribe to a similar belief, however."

Sarah: "You're telling me a variation of reincarnation, aren't you? When you said that we deposit an image within our DNA—before we're born—who exactly does the depositing?"

Dr. Neruda: "Only the formless consciousness can deposit an image onto the

DNA template."

Sarah: "I assume you're talking about soul?"

Dr. Neruda: "It depends again on your definition of soul. The formless consciousness is that which observes and experiences through forms or structures, not just physical embodiments. For example, consciousness can be contained inside a structure or form, but not be physically based. The mind is such a structure. While it's not physical, consciousness—when physically embodied—peers through a mind structure like someone looking through a window. Soul is often confused with the mind and vice a versa.

"The formless consciousness is that particle of God that is decelerated from the frequency of the God state, into individuality, where it can become autonomous and exercise freewill. Think of it like a photon, or subatomic particle that is cast into a web of interconnected particles of like-mindedness. That is to say, all the particles have a similar frequency, or spin-rate, and they're able to step down their frequency, at will, in order to enter membranes of consciousness that can only be entered by taking on a form. So the formless becomes form, and just before it enters the body, consciousness activates the DNA template according to its desired experiences within the membrane of reality it chooses."

Sarah: "What do you mean by the term *membrane*?"

Dr. Neruda: "The multiverse is a collection of reality membranes, clustered together in a dimensional matrix that responds to the thought circuits and gravity fields of our formless consciousness. We've been trained, through evolutionary timescales, to accept the three dimensional world as our reality. These reality membranes are not structured like parallel planes or rungs of a ladder, but rather are like lattices of interlocking cells. If you want, I can describe them in more detail, but I think it becomes so abstract from here forward that I suspect your eyes will glaze over."

Sarah: "All of this seems unbelievable. I'm beginning to wonder if you're the reincarnation of Jesus or Buddha."

Dr. Neruda (Laughing): "I'm reincarnated, and that's as far as I can attest."

Sarah: "Do you remember any of your previous incarnations?"

Dr. Neruda: "*Previous* is a relative term. I prefer to think of my incarnations not so much as a function of memory, but something more akin to a bleed through of a simultaneous reality membrane. The compartments into which human experience is divided are not so watertight that they exclude one life from entering, or influencing, another. And from my experience, these *compartments* represent parallel moments in the life of an individual across a broad sweep of time and space."

Sarah: "So you're implying that our past, present, and future lives are all lived out at the same time, even though they seem to be taking place in different places and times?"

Dr. Neruda: "Yes."

Sarah: "Okay, then explain how it's possible, because it doesn't make any sense to me."

Dr. Neruda: "Our formless consciousness is like a sphere with many, many spokes leading outwards from its central core. Each of these spokes connects into the vertical time continuum through forms, and these forms—human or otherwise—feed the formless consciousness with insights about the different reality membranes in which it has form. In this way, the forms of the formless bring it awareness of different reality membranes, which in turn is processed by the formless and passed on through the unification force to God."

Sarah: "God's the recipient of all this information or experience... from every living thing... from every time and place? How?"

Dr. Neruda: "I don't have any idea."

Sarah: "But this *is* what you believe, and I have to assume you wouldn't believe it if you didn't have some evidence to support your belief."

Dr. Neruda: "Sometimes you follow a trail of evidence to a point where it comes to an abrupt end, but you can still imagine how the trail continues despite the lack of proof that it moves forward in a particular direction. You can intuit its pathway. Call it imagination or pure conjecture, I don't care, but it's what I've done in this case. I truly don't know how this magnitude of data could possibly be processed for any useful purpose, but I believe it."

Sarah: "Okay, give me a second to review my notes... because I want to go back to something you said earlier. Here it is. You said that everyone defines his or her motion of being at the causal level. If that's the case, and assuming that soul is intelligent, why would any soul choose to be impaired mentally, emotionally, or physically?"

Dr. Neruda: "How do you mean that?"

Sarah: "Let's say that soul entered a body, but chose to be closed-minded, stupid, and generally a blob. Why would an intelligent consciousness choose this and then imprint it on their DNA so their life is made more difficult, or at least more boring?"

Dr. Neruda: "Let me ask you a question. Why would God impose this same condition on a person?"

Sarah: "Ah, but you're starting with the assumption that God exists."

Dr. Neruda: "Make this assumption and then answer my question."

Sarah: "I know what you're implying, but why would either God or soul impose these—at least from my point of view—stupid decisions?"

Dr. Neruda: "It has to do with complex systems and their inherent rules of dynamics."

Sarah: "Could you be a bit more specific?"

Dr. Neruda: "In order to expand and ultimately support diverse life forms, the universe required an incalculably complex system of interrelated principles and rules. The more complex this system is, the more dynamic are its poles of interaction. Think of it like an uncut diamond. When you shine a focused beam of light on it in a dark room, there's only a muted glow, but if you facet the diamond, making it more complex, it spreads light in a radiant pattern upon all the walls of the room.

"Complexity works in a similar manner with consciousness, it facets human experience and spreads the light of consciousness upon all the walls of experience, including ignorance, stupidity, wickedness, beauty, goodness, and every other possible condition of human experience. The formless consciousness is not stupid in choosing to experience something that we might deem difficult or boring. It's simply acknowledging that the reality membrane of earth requires it.

"No one can live within this reality membrane and be untouched by the dynamics of the human experience. No one's exempt from difficulties or pain. Does that prove that every one of us makes stupid decisions? No, it only proves that we live within a complex world… that and nothing more."

Sarah: "Not to sound defensive, but you'd agree that some have easier lives than others."

Dr. Neruda: "Yes, but it's not relevant to the intelligence of the formless consciousness."

Sarah: "Okay, so is it related to the age of the formless consciousness?"

Dr. Neruda: "Are you asking if the formless consciousness—as it gains experience—becomes better at selecting its motion of being?"

Sarah: "Exactly."

Dr. Neruda: "The formless consciousness looks upon hardship and ease, the way you might look upon the negative and positive ends of a battery. With relative indifference, I would imagine."

Sarah: "There's no difference, is that what you're saying? No value to being an Einstein versus a Hitler? I don't believe that."

Dr. Neruda: "The choice is not made to be evil or wicked, or to select a life path that is excruciatingly difficult for oneself and others. Nor, in the case of Einstein, did he choose to contribute to humanity's understanding in a way that permitted the creation of nuclear weapons. In the formless consciousness of these individuals—prior to their most recent incarnations—they didn't make choices to harm or help humanity. They made choices to experience aspects of this reality membrane that would contribute to their own understanding."

Sarah: "So, you're saying that the soul chooses its motion of being according to its selfish desires? It doesn't think about the greater good at all?"

Dr. Neruda: "It doesn't need to think about the greater good. That's what the unification force does."

Sarah: "It's an interesting philosophy. We can be as selfish as we desire, and leave it up to God to make our selfish, clumsy actions into something that contributes to the common good of humanity. Is that what you're really saying?"

Dr. Neruda: "No. I'm saying that God, working through its unification force, orchestrates the intermingling of life in order to bring about transformation in the universe. God is like the cosmological alchemist who transforms the selfish interests of the one into the transformative conditions for the many."

Sarah: "Then you're saying that God solves all of our human frailties. We can do anything and it doesn't really matter because he'll fix it. If this philosophy were taught in our world, we'd be in sorry shape."

Dr. Neruda: "While it may not be taught in a formal way, humankind is unconsciously aware that this is the way it works."

Sarah: "On this point, I have to disagree with you. Selfish interests, evil intent, stupidity… these are not the traits of a responsible society, and I don't know of anyone who believes that we should act in this way and then let God perform damage control or mop up after our poor judgments."

Dr. Neruda: "You misunderstand. Perhaps I'm not explaining this very well. Let me try again.

"First, the selfish interests of the formless consciousness are to facet its consciousness in such a way that it can receive and radiate the unification force. In so doing, it can become consciously connected to this force and knowingly become a conduit for it into a broad range of reality membranes. Now, the formless consciousness selects reality membranes to enable the faceting of its consciousness. None of this is done with an attitude of universal contribution or noble purpose. However, this isn't a result of selfish behavior as you think of it. It's a result of its nature… the way it was designed.

"I'm not saying that God cleans up after our messy mistakes. I'm saying our messy mistakes are *not* messy mistakes. Again, we live in a complex system of interdependent reality membranes. You can think of these membranes like scales on a snake, and the snake represents the collective human consciousness. Each scale protects the human soul and collectively, propels it through its environment – in this case, the multiverse. The messy mistakes that we individually and collectively make are as responsible for the existence of the multiverse as are the noble contributions."

Sarah: "Let me see if I got this right. You're saying that our mistakes—both as individuals and a species—make it possible for us to exist, so therefore, they're not mistakes?"

Dr. Neruda: "As I said earlier, complex systems require a near infinite range of dynamics in order to sustain the system. Our reality membrane is form fitted to the complexity of our universe, which in turn created the environment of earth and its various life forms. Yes, our mistakes, our individuality, is a central part of our ability as a species to sustain itself in the face of a complex, interconnected structure of the quantum world and the cosmos.

"The selfish motivations harvest the experience that facets our consciousness, which in turn are harvested by the unification force and used to transform reality membranes into passages through which a species can return to the God state. The mistakes weigh equally in this process, as do the unselfish contributions. Nothing is wasted."

Sarah: "If this is all true, why even worry about the Animus or anything else? Just let God take care of everything."

Dr. Neruda: "Because the Animus are not connected to the unification force."

Sarah: "Why? I thought you said everything was."

Dr. Neruda: "The formless consciousness doesn't select soul carriers that don't utilize DNA as its formative structure. It knows that these structures are not able to connect to the unification force, and therefore, cannot be trusted."

Sarah: "And they can't be trusted because?"

Dr. Neruda: "Because the unification force is what brings coherence to incoherence, and purpose to chaos. Without it, physical structures tend to ebb and flow in stasis, which is to say, they don't transform."

Sarah: "How did this happen?"

Dr. Neruda: "What?"

Sarah: "That the Animus became an independent race unconnected to God?"

Dr. Neruda: "You've heard the story of the fallen angels?"

Sarah: "You're talking about the Lucifer rebellion?"

Dr. Neruda: "Yes. This story is misrepresented in Biblical texts, owing to the fact that the authors of these texts didn't have a sufficient understanding in which to define cosmology or physics.

"The Central Race designed the higher life forms, and this includes a wide range of beings that operate within the quantum world and the reality membranes therein. Among these beings are what we commonly refer to as the angels, who are intermediaries between the soul carriers of humanoids, and the Central Race.

"There were some within the angelic realm that believed the Central Race was too controlling of the soul carrier structure. They felt that a structure should be created that would enable angels to incarnate within the reality membrane of earth and other life-bearing planets. They insisted that this would improve these planets and the physical structure of the universe at large. However, the Central Race refused this proposal and a renegade group left to design a soul carrier, independent of the Central Race."

Sarah: "Hold on a moment. You're saying that Lucifer led this rebellion to create a soul carrier that could house the spirit of an angel, and the Animus are the result?"

Dr. Neruda: "It's more complicated than that. Lucifer, or what we have come to call Lucifer, was a very devoted servant of the Central Race. He was one of the forerunners of the angelic species; capable of powers that were diminished by the Central Race in subsequent prototypes."

Sarah: "Are you saying that angels are created... that they can't reproduce like humans?"

Dr. Neruda: "Correct.

"Lucifer's personality included a strong sense of independence from his creators, and an even stronger sense that his creators were flawed because of their insistence that the humanoid soul carrier would exclusively house the formless consciousness, and not the angelic form. To Lucifer, this seemed unthinkable because the angelic form was superior in its capabilities and could be of great assistance to the physical life forms on earth and other life-bearing planets.

"From Lucifer's perspective, humans and the higher order species would be unable to transform themselves because of the severe limits of their soul carriers, or physical forms. Lucifer felt certain that without the collaboration of the angels, humanoids throughout the universe would become increasingly separated from their purpose as spiritual beings, and throw the universe into disarray, which would eventually cause its destruction and life within it—including, of course, angels."

Sarah: "Then you're suggesting that the Lucifer rebellion was simply a disagreement over this one issue?"

Dr. Neruda: "Lucifer wanted to incarnate into this reality membrane the same way humans do. He wanted to become a collaborator with humanity to assure its ascension. While the Central Race saw his intentions as noble, they feared that the angelic incarnations would become known as Gods to their human counterparts, and unintentionally mislead humans, rather than co-create the ladder to the God state.

"This matter underwent a tremendous debate, ultimately forming a division between the angelic realm and the Central Race. The loyalists to the Central Race argued that Lucifer and his sympathizers should be banished for their radical ideas that could potentially create a lasting division in their reality membrane, and cause them tremendous turmoil. Lucifer, in wide-ranging deliberations with the Central Race, negotiated a compromise that enabled him to take his group of sympathizers and prove the value of their plan on a single planet."

Sarah: "Are you saying that Lucifer was allowed to experiment on a planet?"

Dr. Neruda: "Yes."

Sarah: "Okay, before we go any further, are you talking about this in the context of myth or are you essentially representing the Corteum view?"

Dr. Neruda: "There are three ancient manuscripts in the ACIO's possession that describe this story in an allegorical form, but the Corteum view—as you put it—is much more descriptive and definitive as a record of this cosmic event."

Sarah: "So, Lucifer conducted this… experiment. Where and to what result?"

Dr. Neruda: "The planet is in a galaxy known as M51 to your scientists."

Sarah: "This is the same galaxy of the Animus?"

Dr. Neruda: "Yes."

Sarah: "So you're really saying that Lucifer and his band of sympathizers created the Animus to be soul carriers for angels?"

Dr. Neruda: "It's more complicated than that."

Sarah: "I certainly hope so because this story is too strange for me to believe."

Dr. Neruda: "Be patient. We're moving into uncomfortable territory for most people. So take a deep breath and bear with me as I try to explain this.

"Lucifer created a synthetic physical structure that could accommodate the quantum requirements of an angel. It was a very effective structure, but induced a strong survival complex within the species, which eventually overpowered the angelic tendency of altruism and cooperation."

Sarah: "Why? What happened?"

Dr. Neruda: "When the formless consciousness enters a reality membrane through a structure like a soul carrier, it immediately feels disconnected from all other forces, but its own. It's literally thrown into separation. In humans, this is more or less controlled through the subtle realization that it remains connected through the unification force, and this is because its DNA is designed to emit this feeling of connection subconsciously.

"However, in the case of the soul carrier designed by Lucifer and his followers, this connection was severed both consciously and subconsciously because the structure was not based on DNA, which is strictly controlled by the Central Race. Consequently, it inclined this experimental species toward a very strong survival complex because it feared extinction so deeply, which is the result of feeling complete separation from the unification force. This survival complex created a species that over-compensated its fear of extinction by developing a very powerful group mind.

"The group mind compensated for the loss of connection to the unification force, creating its physical and mental corollary. It was the equivalent of unifying the species as a whole in the physical reality membrane of their planetary system. Thus, the angels that entered this system lost their memory of their angelic natures and became more interested in operating as a single collective, than as individuals.

"They became a concern for the Central Race, and Lucifer was asked to dismantle his experiment. However, Lucifer had become attached to the species that he had helped to create. These angelic beings had developed over a number of generations a very sophisticated set of technologies, culture, and social order. It was like an extended family in many ways to Lucifer. So, he negotiated to modify his creation so they would no longer accommodate the angelic frequency or quantum structure, but that they could become self-animated."

Sarah: "How do you mean self-animated?"

Dr. Neruda: "That they would become soulless androids."

Sarah: "And so this happened and that's how we got the Animus?"

Dr. Neruda: "Yes."

Sarah: "It doesn't make any sense. Why would God, or the Central Race for that matter, allow Lucifer to create a race of androids? Didn't they know that these beings were going to become the scourge of our universe?"

Dr. Neruda: "Yes, of course they knew. However, God doesn't design something as complex as the multiverse, and then control how everything operates."

Sarah: "But you said earlier that God orchestrates what happens through the unification force."

Dr. Neruda: "God orchestrates how the dynamics of the multiverse come together to form a unified, comprehensible data stream that can inform the next evolution of the multiverse. Most people would think that an all-powerful God would banish a species like the Animus, but it doesn't work this way because the dark side of predation, as in the case of the Animus, sparks resourcefulness and innovation in its intended prey."

Sarah: "And we're the prey."

Dr. Neruda: "Not just us, but the humanoid species as a whole."

Sarah: "Evil begets good. That's what you're really saying, right?"

Dr. Neruda: "Again, it's not evil against good. The Animus don't consider themselves to be evildoers when they invade a planet. From their perspective, they are simply executing their plan to become reconnected to their sense of individuality and become—as strange as it may sound—more spiritual."

Sarah: "But when I asked you earlier if you knew what their intentions were with earth, you said you didn't know."

Dr. Neruda: "I don't. However, I do know something about their intentions to reengineer their soul carriers to be more DNA compliant. They want to introduce DNA to their soul carriers in order to transform their species. This is essentially what any race would do under their exact set of circumstances. In fact, you could even call it noble."

Sarah: "Noble? I don't see anything noble in trying to commandeer our planet and subject our citizens to genetic experiments and tyranny."

Dr. Neruda: "To us, no. But from a completely objective viewpoint, one can appreciate that the Animus are just trying to transform their species for the better. They don't have any other choice because without DNA, they're simply unable to connect to the unification force."

Sarah: "Why can't they contact the Central Race and ask for help?"

Dr. Neruda: "The Central Race is well aware of the Animus, and consider them their most potent enemy. Perhaps they consider them unsalvageable. Or perhaps the Central Race invites the drama of having an ancient enemy that forces them to protect their most valuable assets. I don't pretend to know. But for whatever reason, the Central Race is not able or willing to assist the Animus in becoming reconnected to the unification force."

Sarah: "So whatever happened to Lucifer and his plan?"

Dr. Neruda: "According to the Corteum, he's alive and well and completely reintegrated into his species as a member of high standing."

Sarah: "Just so I'm clear, we *are* talking about Satan aren't we?"

Dr. Neruda: "Theologians are left with a tattered tapestry of myth and legend, and from this, they've injected their own interpretations down through time. What we're left with is little more than the fiction of a thousand voices, but it somehow manages to become known as fact.

"Satan, as we think of him, never existed. There is no countermeasure to God. God encompasses all dynamics. It has no polarity of itself that is beyond its reach, or personalized outside of itself. The story of Lucifer—at a very high level—was just described to you. I assume you can see some similarity to the version of the Lucifer Rebellion depicted in the Bible, but the correlation, I'm sure you'd admit, is sparse at best."

Sarah: "But if there's no source of evil, why does evil exist in such abundance? And before you answer, I know you'll disagree with my assumption that evil exists, but how can you reconcile terrorism or any other predator force of humankind as anything but evil, even if Satan never existed as you claim?"

Dr. Neruda: "If you watch movies like Star Wars or Star Trek they imply that extraterrestrials populate every planetary system in the galaxy and beyond. However, it just isn't true. Our planet is an extremely rare combination of animals and organisms. The universe that comprises our physical reality membrane is in fact hostile to life—at an extreme level. And yet life somehow managed to emerge on our planet in the black depths of our oceans—"

Sarah: "What does this have to do with my question?"

Dr. Neruda: "Be patient, I'll get to it. I promise."

Sarah: "Okay."

Dr. Neruda: "The habitable zones within our universe would be analogous to extracting a drop of water from the Pacific Ocean every cubic mile, and defining it as the only part of the ocean that contained all of the potential conditions to bear microbial life. Then, extracting a single molecule from each of these drops of water, and defining it as the only part of the drop that could sustain multi-cellular life; and from each of these molecules, extracting a single quantum particle and defining it as the only part of the molecule that could sustain complex, sentient life forms like humans.

"The genetic library that thrives upon earth is a form of currency that has no price tag. All I can say is that its value far exceeds anything that human thought could imagine. And with this incredible value, our planet attracts interest from a wide-range of extraterrestrial races, and this is as true today as it was a thousand years ago or a hundred thousand years ago.

"Objects of inestimable value and rarity, such as earth, attract beings from outside our planetary system that desire to control them, which makes earth an extraordinary object of attraction. It's precisely this attraction that has brought the concepts of evil to our psyche."

Sarah: "I followed you right up to the last sentence and then lost you. How did this attraction bring evil to our consciousness?"

Dr. Neruda: "Aggressive ETs, seeking to quite literally own earth, visited our planet approximately eleven thousand years ago. These ETs brought their genetics to our native DNA, and in so doing, modified our human DNA adding a more aggressive, domineering drive to our personalities. This predisposition divided the human species into the conquerors and the conquered."

Sarah: "I don't get it. You're saying that ETs impregnated thousands of our native population with an aggressive gene that brought evil into our consciousness?"

Dr. Neruda: "These ETs were not so different in physical form than the native humans, and they were treated like Gods because of their superior technologies and capabilities. It was considered a great honor to have intercourse with these beings, but only a few were selected."

Sarah: "So how did their DNA become so influential that it literally brought evil into our lives?"

Dr. Neruda: "One of the yet-to-be-discovered properties of DNA is that it can communicate traits – particularly aggressive traits – without physical interaction."

Sarah: "Explain, please."

Dr. Neruda: "There are carrier circuits within the DNA that transmit traits and even forms of intelligence through a reality membrane that is sub-quantum. It's a tributary ingredient of the unification force that propagates new traits and understandings in the few to the many. It's what enables the transmission of a new insight or potent trait across a spectrum of a species that resonates with the insight or trait, and it does it without physical interaction."

Sarah: "You're saying that a single person could have an idea or trait that is deposited within their DNA, and then their DNA transmits this trait like a broadcast tower and everyone on the planet that's like them is affected?"

Dr. Neruda: "Let me clarify some things you said.

"First, it's not one person. It requires a critical mass of several hundred for a personality trait to transmit, and perhaps only ten or twenty to transmit a new concept or insight. In any case, one person is not sufficient. This is not an exact science yet, even to the ACIO.

"Secondly, it's not transmitted like a broadcast tower. It's transmitted selectively to resonant DNA, and the effect it has isn't dependent on whether the recipient is like, or even similar to, the donor. It's dependent on the receptivity of their DNA. Some people open their DNA up to new innovations, others don't. This is the critical factor in whether the new trait or idea is successfully transmitted."

Sarah: "Okay, ETs with their aggressive personalities infected humans, and this brought evil tendencies to our race. Why would the Central Race allow this to happen?"

Dr. Neruda: "We don't know."

Sarah: "But you said earlier that they would protect our planet with their best technology. Why didn't they protect it thousands of years ago?"

Dr. Neruda: "This is a mystery. We don't know."

Sarah: "I assume this must be another reason that Fifteen doesn't want to rely on the WingMakers for our protection."

Dr. Neruda: "He doesn't talk about it, but I'd agree with you."

Sarah: "I'd like to return to the topic of God… and just for the record, I'm well aware that I'm off the subject of the WingMakers, but I can't resist talking about these things. Okay?"

Dr. Neruda: "It's fine with me. I'll discuss any topic you choose."

Sarah: "You explained earlier that to you, God is a force, but is it *the* force?"

Dr. Neruda: "Do you mean is God plural or singular?"

Sarah: "Yes."

Dr. Neruda: "God is both."

Sarah: "Both?"

Dr. Neruda: "God is found everywhere because it's the unification force, but paradoxically, being the unification force it is also unique or singular. Physicists will explain to you that there're four primary forces at play in the universe: strong nuclear, weak nuclear, gravity, and electromagnetic. These forces are actually facets of a singular force, more primal and absolutely causative.

"Einstein worked nearly thirty years trying to prove this with his unification theory, but never found his answers. No one supposedly has. I can only report that the Labyrinth Group—using its LERM technology—has discovered this force. And this force possesses an unmistakable consciousness. That is, it is neither chaos nor order. It is both, and flows between the two worlds of chaos and order like a sine wave flows between positive and negative amplitude."

Sarah: "And can our physicists prove or disprove this?"

Dr. Neruda: "No, our physicists cannot prove or disprove what I say. They're too shackled in specialized theories that are in crisis."

Sarah: "What kind of theories?"

Dr. Neruda: "Like quantum mechanics, to name one example.

"Nearly all physicists, regardless of their specialty, would stand before you in all sincerity, and advise you that quantum mechanics is the correct and complete theory underlying our understanding of the universe. But it doesn't honor the consciousness of a particle, and it has no way of detecting the infinitesimal magnetic fields within which these particles reside."

Sarah: "Why?"

Dr. Neruda: "This is not a lay person's topic, Sarah. I don't know how to explain this in words you'll understand. It has to do with the fact that our physicists in academia lack sophisticated force-amplification technology that can detect the extraordinarily tiny magnetic fields that subatomic particles nest within, which in turn, creates an interconnected web of thought circuits. These thought circuits—taken collectively—represent the exterior structure of the unification force, and they permeate the multiverse. The magnetic fields represent the interior of the unification force, and they permeate the form's formless consciousness."

Sarah: "Okay, I get your point about it not being a lay person's topic. You've completely lost me in the abstract nature of this discussion. I thought we were talking about God, and now I'm not sure what we're talking about."

Dr. Neruda: "Keep focused on the primal force. God has decelerated itself to display its physical embodiment in the four known forces I spoke of earlier."

Sarah: "So, this is truly how the universe works, and I should just accept it?"

Dr. Neruda: "No, no, no. I don't want to leave you with the impression that what I've said is *the* way the multiverse works. If there's one truth I can state unequivocally, it's that my understanding of the multiverse, while constrained with the tools of particle physics, cosmology, and mathematics, is partial at best, and completely inaccurate at worst."

Sarah: "Well, that leaves us essentially nowhere, doesn't it? If what you've said tonight is just partial understanding or complete misjudgment, where does that leave our brightest scientists and theologians? You have all the advantages of advanced technology and alien cosmology, and still you can't explain the universe with any confidence. Even with your proof of God, you claim to know essentially nothing that's absolutely true. How can that be?"

Dr. Neruda: "No one who's invested in astronomy, cosmology, or physics likes to think that their discipline is misguided by false or incomplete assumptions. But they are. And there's a good reason."

Sarah: "Which is?"

Dr. Neruda: "Imagine that the observable universe is the middle rung on a ladder of unknown length. Each of the rungs above and below our observable universe represents an order of magnitude beyond our senses. For example, let's say that the rung above the one that represents our observable universe is the outer perimeter of our Milky Way galaxy. Using a telescope we can see the next rung above us, but the rest of the ladder is lost in a thick haze.

"Looking downward—at a microscopic level with an electron microscope—we can add another rung below our observable universe, and with a particle accelerator, we can even theorize what the next rung below that might be, but the rest of the ladder trails downward into a thick haze no different than when we try to look up.

"With all of our technology and theory, we still have no idea how tall the ladder is or even whether the ladder is straight or begins to curve like a double helix. We don't know if perhaps the top end of the ladder curves to such a degree that it actually connects with the bottom end of the ladder. And we don't even know whether there might be additional ladders."

Sarah: "Okay, I think I know where you're going with this, but then why does it always seem that science knows more than they really do?"

Dr. Neruda: "The largest population of the planet—perhaps 99 percent—has no experience beyond the middle rung of the ladder. And those that are privileged to observe the next rung above or below by the use of technology, falsely assume, or perhaps hope, that the ladder retains the same form and holds to the same principles.

"The ACIO has observed another rung of this ladder—beyond the technology of academia. Nothing more. However, in doing so, we've only become humbled by the depth and breadth of our ignorance. We've learned that the ladder does change. It begins to modify its form and we theorize that its shape is no longer predictable or even stable."

Sarah: "So doesn't that mean that our physics is wrong?"

Dr. Neruda: "I like the way an obscure writer, by the name of Gustave Naquet, put it: 'Whenever knowledge takes a step forward, God recedes a step backwards.'

"Each rung of the ladder may require a different physics or set of laws and instruments. Is the Neanderthal wrong in the face of the modern human? He was merely a precursor or early prototype. And this is the same as physics or cosmology. It must be understood as a valid prototype that has its purpose in time, but will ultimately be displaced by a new model that encompasses more rungs of the ladder."

Sarah: "It's still hard to imagine how all this technological advantage that the ACIO wields could only make clear how little we know about our universe. It doesn't leave much hope for us."

Dr. Neruda: "How do you mean that?"

Sarah: "Well, it seems to me that if we don't know what we don't know, we're doomed to make assumptions about things that are taken as fact, when in reality, it's just opinion. In this regard, science is no better than religion. Right?"

Dr. Neruda: "The interesting thing about science is that *origins* reveal how things work. If you can follow particles to their origins, you can understand how inner space works. If you can follow the cosmic particles—galaxies, quasars, and black holes—to their origins, you can understand how outer space works. When you put the two halves together with in-between space, or the observable universe, you can understand how the whole multiverse works.

"The problem is that no one has the lens or technology to observe the origins. And this is where theory takes over. The difference between science and religion is that science applies theory while religion applies faith. Both theory and faith, however, fall short of revealing origins. So in this regard, they're similar."

Sarah: "But if what you're saying is true, then we live in a world we don't really understand."

Dr. Neruda: "Exactly."

Sarah: "If we don't understand our world, and science and religion are inadequate, where do we turn? I mean, how are we supposed to cope with our ignorance?"

Dr. Neruda: "The danger of ignorance is only in believing you're not ignorant. If you know that you lack insight into the inner dimensions of how things work, you know that you have blind spots. You can keep a wary eye open for any advantage that enables a deeper insight or more profound sense of meaning. You have to learn to live with incompleteness and use it as a motivating force rather than a point of desperation or indifference.

"As far as where do we turn? That's a hard question to answer. It's the reason that all the dramas have become packaged and sold via the media. The media is where most people turn. They flick on their televisions, radios, computers, newspapers, magazines, even books, and these deliver the packets of information bundled together by the media. The media know very well that people are ignorant—enough so that they lack the ability to discern the incompleteness of the information packets they serve to their customers. Information is incomplete, and this drowns our population in ignorance, which enables manipulation."

Sarah: "By whom?"

Dr. Neruda: "Sarah, no one entity is the master manipulator, if that's what you're asking. It's more like everyone in the media manipulates information and disclosure. It's all part of the drama that causes people to turn to the media for their answers, and citizens are responsible for this state of affairs because they don't demand that their educational centers secure clear, full disclosures of information and distribute it to the public domain."

Sarah: "Are you saying that our schools and universities should be the stewards of this information, and not the media?"

Dr. Neruda: "In the ideal world, yes. This is how the Corteum designed their information structures. The educational centers dominate the distribution of information through a collective and well reasoned system of journalism. The journalists are specialists across the disciplines of theology, the arts and sciences, government, business, and technology. These journalists document the best practices of each and every discipline and share this information through full disclosure. Nothing is left out. The research is meticulous and completely untouched by the political spectrum of special interests."

Sarah: "Okay, being a journalist myself, we've finally hit on a topic I know something about. When I was a beat reporter, I never felt the hand of politics influencing how or what I reported. I know at the national level—particularly reporting in D.C.—that might not be entirely the case, but the stories we've been talking about the past few nights weren't even on my radar screen. That's the real problem. These stories are completely secreted away. And given that our politicians don't even know about the existence of the ACIO and all of the other things affiliated with it, how can you blame the politicians, or the media for that matter?"

Dr. Neruda: "I didn't intend to blame anyone, really. The system is imperfect. Anyone involved in the system knows that it's larger than life and can't be changed by one person or even one group of people. The media know their limits, and they know their markets. People want to know the truth about the things that affect them in their pocket book. The regions of cosmology, ETs, the ACIO, and things that go bump in the night are considered light reading to the masses —reserved for entertainment—not serious news."

Sarah: "This is anything but light news, and you know it. Why do you sound so cynical?"

Dr. Neruda: "If I'm cynical about the media, it's not for you to take personally. I'm of a mind that the media will not change significantly until the education system changes significantly and produces students that demand more than news dramas, sports, and weather."

Sarah: "So our schools should not only produce students with an appetite for cosmology, but they should also produce the news? Pretty tall orders for schools don't you think?"

Dr. Neruda: "Perhaps, but it's what's needed before the ACIO or any related organization would share its knowledge with the masses."

Sarah: "And why's that?"

Dr. Neruda: "Academia would absolutely be turned on its head if the ACIO stepped forward and provided its research findings, technologies, and evidence of ET interactions. It would be attacked. And it would be a vicious attack. At least that was Fifteen's intractable conclusion. The ACIO, therefore, had no other way to bring its findings to the public than through the private sector and the alliances it had with the NSA's Special Projects Laboratory."

Sarah: "Give me an example of something—a technology or discovery—that was first uncovered by the ACIO and then exported to the private sector."

Dr. Neruda: "The transistor would be a good example—"

Sarah: "You're telling me that the ACIO invented the transistor?"

Dr. Neruda: "No, Bell Labs invented the transistor, but the ACIO worked with Bell Labs, or more specifically, Mervin Kelly who ran its operations in the mid-1950s. Mr. Kelly had attached a rather brilliant physicist to this project by the name of Bill Shockley who became aware of the outermost edges of the ACIO."

Sarah: "How'd that happen?"

Dr. Neruda: "A little known fact: Mr. Shockley, working with a friend of his, invented the world's first nuclear reactor. The defense department heard about it through Mr. Kelly, and wanted it badly. This was before the Manhattan Project got underway. Mr. Kelly wanted a patent for the discovery, but the government threw up every conceivable roadblock. They kept the whole discovery under complete confidentiality and negotiated to have one of our scientists work with Mr. Shockley in secret."

Sarah: "When was this?"

Dr. Neruda: "This was happening in 1944 and 1945."

Sarah: "Why did our government squabble about the patents?"

Dr. Neruda: "They knew Mr. Shockley could play a role in the war, and they wanted to use this as leverage to secure his commitment to help. He was a difficult man to work with, so I was told. He never stepped forward and volunteered to do anything unless he knew it would somehow benefit him. So, our government held the patents up until he would enlist.”

Sarah: “And did he?”

Dr. Neruda: “Yes.”

Sarah: “And how did it benefit him?”

Dr. Neruda: “There was, within our government, a newly formed intelligence agency—it was the forerunner of the NSA. It was known as the General Services Special Projects Laboratory, and to this day, very little is known about it. The SPL was later folded into the NSA in 1953 as an unacknowledged department, and ultimately the ACIO was folded into the SPL as an unacknowledged research laboratory. So, the ACIO was two levels deep or what is called, *Black Root.*”

Sarah: “What was the motivation for all the security? The war?”

Dr. Neruda: “It may surprise you, but the war wasn’t of great concern to the forces that the ACIO were dealing with. The concern was ETs and who would be able to first utilize their technology in military applications. In the early 1940s, UFO sightings were quite common—even more so than today. And our government was convinced that these sightings were real and that they were indeed off-planetary forces. They wanted two things: Steal the technology from downed spacecraft, or establish an alliance. They weren’t too particular about which way it happened.”

Sarah: “But how did all of this pertain to Shockley?”

Dr. Neruda: “I got off track a bit. Mr. Shockley was introduced to the SPL and was made privy to many of the secret initiatives of the SPL. If not for his personality traits, he would’ve been recruited to join the SPL, he was that brilliant. Anyway, he was given access to some of the research in field effect transistors that was underway within the SPL. This was before the Bell Labs’ discovery of the joint transistor, which was made by colleagues of Mr. Shockley.

“Mr. Shockley was allowed to utilize some of the research within the SPL to create his own version of the field effect transistor and become widely known as its inventor. This was done in exchange for his cooperation in helping Army and Navy strategic operations during the war. He was aware of the SPL and knew part of their agenda, and I was told that he wanted to join the SPL after the war because of its superior laboratories, but again, his personality traits prevented his admission.”

Sarah: “So, Bell Labs receives the patent for the transistor in exchange for Shockley’s assistance with the war. What exactly did he do that was so important?”

Dr. Neruda: “I don’t know for certain, but in general, his role was helping to optimize weapons deployment.”

Sarah: “What was the role of the NSA during all of this?”

Dr. Neruda: "The NSA wasn't in existence until November 1952. During this time, the SPL and ACIO were the two most advanced, secretive labs in existence. And they each had only one private sector lab they worked with: Bell Labs. And this is because Mr. Kelly was a friend with the executive director of the SPL."

Sarah: "So what was the relationship between the SPL and ACIO?"

Dr. Neruda: "You mean in the 1940s?"
Sarah: "First, how far back does it go?"

Dr. Neruda: "The SPL was formed in 1938. There was a strong development—particularly throughout Europe—in fission energy. The SPL was initially conceived to examine fission as an alternative energy source as well as its possible military applications."

Sarah: "Why was it kept so secret?"

Dr. Neruda: "In the late 1930s there was significant political unrest in Europe, and the U.S. wasn't sure whom it could trust. It had a notion that fission was the answer to superior technical warfare, and didn't want to share it unwittingly. It was also alarmed at some of the sudden advances that were taking place in the European physics community, and felt it needed to concentrate some of its best resources to equip a world-class laboratory, and staff it with some of the best minds of the planet."

Sarah: "How could the best minds of the planet suddenly be plucked up by the U.S. government and not be noticed by the scientific community? I mean, how do you keep this a secret?"

Dr. Neruda: "They didn't take established leaders in the field of physics. They sought out the young, budding geniuses that were still relatively unknown, but under the right guidance and with the best available technology, could produce something extraordinary."

Sarah: "Like the transistor?"

Dr. Neruda: "Like the transistor."

Sarah: "So if the SPL was established in 1938, when did the ACIO come into existence?"

Dr. Neruda: "It was established in 1940 shortly after the SPL was organized."

Sarah: "Why?"

Dr. Neruda: "First, in part, it was because management within the SPL feared discovery by Congress. So they decided to construct Black Root, which was the codename of the ACIO, in order to build a laboratory that was untouchable by political forces or the media. Second, they didn't want the research agenda of the SPL competing with ET issues. When all of this first occurred, ETs and UFOs were still a subject of great debate within the SPL. Most of the SPL leaders didn't believe in them. There was no hard evidence.

"But when the first spacecraft was found intact, it changed the minds of everyone within the SPL and it was decided that a separate research agenda needed to be developed, and that it was the more urgent and secretive of the two labs. So, Black Root, or the ACIO as it became known later, was established behind the SPL at a deeper level of secrecy. It was unacknowledged two levels deep."

Sarah: "Were you referring to the Roswell incident just then… about the recovered spacecraft?"

Dr. Neruda: "No. This was an abandoned spacecraft found in waters off the coast of Florida in 1940."

Sarah: "It was just abandoned? Who found it?"

Dr. Neruda: "As the story goes, a recreational diver found it in waters about sixty feet deep. It was perfectly preserved."

Sarah: "Whatever happened to the diver?"

Dr. Neruda: "It was an anonymous tip given to the Navy. The person who discovered it was never found. However, we later learned that the discovery was a staged event."

Sarah: "A staged event?"

Dr. Neruda: "Meaning that the discovery was orchestrated by the Corteum."

Sarah: "So this was a Corteum spacecraft left behind to be discovered by the Navy?"

Dr. Neruda: "It's how they chose to make first contact."

Sarah: "By leaving behind one of their spacecraft in the ocean, and then calling our Navy and telling them where to find it? Shit this is strange!"

Dr. Neruda: "Yes, but it took three calls to get someone to investigate according to the log entries."

Sarah: "Okay, so this is how the ACIO came about. When did you get involved?"

Dr. Neruda: "In 1956, my father discovered a damaged spacecraft in the jungles of Bolivia during a hunting trip. It was a triangular vessel about seventy meters from end-to-end, nearly equilateral. It included twenty-six crew. All dead."

Sarah: "Corteum?"

Dr. Neruda: "No, this craft was later confirmed as a Zeta ship. It was on a scouting mission similar to my father—hunting for animals. Unfortunately, it malfunctioned in flight during an electrical storm. My father was an electronics dealer, mostly for the Bolivian military.

Sarah: "I know you told me this story before, but please repeat yourself for the sake of the record."

Dr. Neruda: "My father recovered a specific technology from the ship, and then contacted a military official within the Bolivian government that was a trusted friend. Initially, my father was interested in selling the craft to the Bolivian military, but it quickly became a concern of the U.S. military—specifically the SPL. A director from the SPL met with my father, ascertained the ship's location, and performed a complete salvage operation in the span of three days.

"This was done in exchange for U.S. citizenship and a role within the SPL for my father."

Sarah: "Why did your father negotiate for this instead of money?"

Dr. Neruda: "He knew it was the only way to preserve my life and his. He retained control of a navigational technology that was aboard the ship, and turned everything else over to the SPL."

Sarah: "And what about the Bolivian government?"

Dr. Neruda: "They were handsomely paid."

Sarah: "That's it?"

Dr. Neruda: "In the seven years between 1952 and 1959, six additional spacecraft were found under similar circumstances as in the case of my father. Only one of these was found in U.S. territory. The other five were willingly handed over to our military in exchange for money."

Sarah: "I take it these countries didn't want to deal with the political implications?"

Dr. Neruda: "That, but they also wanted the money and a friendly alignment with the U.S. military. They saw future benefits in the form of shared technologies, military protection, loans, and many other intangible benefits. In short, it was smart politics. Besides, no other country, outside of the Soviet Union, had any laboratories like the ACIO. What would they do with these spacecrafts?"

Sarah: "Your father and you end up in the United States… what qualified him for admission into the SPL and what did he do there?"

Dr. Neruda: "My father was not simply a salesman to the Bolivian government, he was an electronics expert with the equivalent of an advanced electrical engineering degree. He had several patents to his credit, but was considered something of a dreamer and a lost soul I suppose."

Sarah: "Is he still alive?"

Dr. Neruda: "No."

Sarah: "I'm sorry. What about the rest of your family? Was it just you and your father that came to America?"

Dr. Neruda: "I was an only child. My mother died shortly after I was born. I was only four years old when we came to the States. I really don't have strong memories of my home in Sorata."

Sarah: "Where's Sorata?"

Dr. Neruda: "North of La Paz, on the east end of Lake Titicaca."

Sarah: "Maybe I've watched too many episodes of the X-Files, but it seems a little hard to believe that your father could negotiate a job and U.S. citizenship with the SPL. Can you explain how he did that?"

Dr. Neruda: "He asked. It wasn't such a hard thing. Here's a man that speaks perfect English, knows electronics, and has some political clout. More importantly, he led the SPL to a very important discovery, worth billions of dollars in research and development. My father was smart enough to photograph the craft and secure electronic components that pertained to navigation. He had these carefully secured with instructions for their distribution should anything befall him or me."

Sarah: "Don't take this the wrong way, but didn't you say that only young geniuses were hired into the ACIO? I assume your father didn't qualify."

Dr. Neruda: "No, he wasn't a genius. But he was smart enough to add value to some of the reverse engineering experiments that were ongoing within the ACIO— especially those that pertained to semiconductors."

Sarah: "And all of this was happening in the mid-fifties?"

Dr. Neruda: "Yes."

Sarah: "Was Fifteen there at the time?"

Dr. Neruda: "No. He joined the ACIO in the spring of 1958."

Sarah: "So he knew your father?"

Dr. Neruda: "My father, believe it or not, became a high-level director of the ACIO toward the latter part of his tenure, thanks largely to Fifteen, who took an immediate liking to my father. Remember Fifteen is Spanish. My father knew Fifteen as well as anyone, and had the utmost respect for him."

Sarah: "Was your father part of the Labyrinth Group?"

Dr. Neruda: "Yes."

Sarah: "When did you find out about the Labyrinth Group and its mission?"

Dr. Neruda: "Fifteen introduced me to it in a meeting I'll never forget."

Sarah: "What time was this?"

Dr. Neruda: "September 18, 1989."

Sarah: "What happened?"

Dr. Neruda: "Fifteen showed me a suite of technologies that had been part of a TTP (Technology Transfer Program) with the Corteum. He explained it activated parts of the brain that fused the unconscious data stream with the conscious. It enabled a much more potent flow of data to be captured by the conscious mind."

Sarah: "Can you explain how it works?"

Dr. Neruda: "I'll do my best, but it's a technical explanation. I don't know any other way to do it."

Sarah: "Try. I'll signal when I'm lost."

Dr. Neruda: "There's a part of the brain known as thalamocortical system. The Corteum technology activated this specific section of the brain, inducing a small functional cluster within this system to expand the higher-order consciousness. These are the neural coordinates of consciousness, pertaining to higher order reasoning, which is very useful to scientific inquiry, mathematics, and general problem solving.
"Yes?"

Sarah: "I'm not totally lost. But what's the role of this technology to the Labyrinth Group?"

Dr. Neruda: "When Fifteen first became acquainted with the Corteum TTP he was the first to use this technology on his own brain—"

Sarah: "Yes, I remember now. He got the vision of BST shortly afterwards. Right?"

Dr. Neruda: "Correct."

Sarah: "And this was why he established the Labyrinth Group, to pursue the development of BST. Right?"

Dr. Neruda: "Yes."

Sarah: "So, everyone who was handpicked by Fifteen got to use this Corteum technology and everyone got smarter as a result. And no one outside the Labyrinth Group suspected that the Labyrinth Group existed?"

Dr. Neruda: "No one to my knowledge."

Sarah: "Okay, back to your story with Fifteen. What happened?"

Dr. Neruda: "Everyone who knew anything about Fifteen knew he was intensely interested in time travel, but I had no idea as to the degree of his intensity until that day. He explained the physics behind his BST plan and how the Corteum played a vital role in its development. He wanted to reassign me to a new project that was related to BST development, and when he explained the nature of the project, I shook my head in disbelief that he felt I could do the job."

Sarah: "What was it?"

Dr. Neruda: "It was a project that involved designing and developing an advanced neuronal selection technology for the human brain; a subject that I knew very little about. I raised this objection, but Fifteen explained that no one else did either, so it was just as well that I undertook the research. And then he casually explained the Corteum technology for brain enhancement. This was when he told me how all personnel with a security clearance of twelve were invited to undergo the process."

Sarah: "I assume everyone accepted the invitation."

Dr. Neruda: "It's a safe assumption, although there are some drawbacks to the technology."

Sarah: "Like?"

Dr. Neruda: "The information capacity of the conscious mind is very limited. When you intensify the connection between the conscious and unconscious, the conscious mind rejects the data stream's breadth of information and tends to become observational of the alternative states of consciousness. In other words, the brain enhancement process triggers a rapid and fluid shifting between states of consciousness, not unlike a slide show in fast motion with each slide representing a different state of consciousness."

Sarah: "I think I follow you, but isn't it worth it if you can control this side effect?"

Dr. Neruda: "I thought so, as did everyone else. There were some that were more affected by this than others, and typically it only lasted for a few weeks until the higher mind began to integrate this into its dynamic core."

Sarah: "Okay, enough about the brain, I'd like to return to the topic of the

Labyrinth Group. You mentioned in the first interview that this is the most secret of all the organizations on the planet, even though it's one of the most influential. How does it operate in secrecy and yet exert its influence?"

Dr. Neruda: "The Labyrinth Group is a subset of the ACIO that's absolutely secret. Its main purpose was to create a staging organization for the pure-state technologies that were part of the TTPs that Fifteen negotiated with the Zetas and Corteum. Fifteen didn't want these technologies within the ACIO where they were within striking distance of the SPL and potentially the NSA. He wanted to be able to review, analyze, and synthesize these new technologies before he figured out how to dilute them into less powerful technologies that could be exported to the SPL or the private syndicates we worked with.

"We used the best security technologies in existence. By that, I mean that we could secure our technologies from any hostile force. This enabled the Labyrinth Group personnel to focus on applications of these pure state technologies for the advancement of our BST agenda.

"Our influence is not understood by anyone because we've managed to release these diluted technologies into behind-the-scenes technologies that are used by our military, the NSA, DARPA, and private syndicates of our own choosing."

Sarah: "I thought you said you even work with private industry?"

Dr. Neruda: "The Labyrinth Group doesn't work directly with the private sector. But some of our technologies filter into the private sector."

Sarah: "Like the transistor?""

Dr. Neruda: "No, actually the field effect transistor was more the development of the SPL."

Sarah: "Then give me an example of something more recent that involved the Labyrinth Group and the private sector. Something I might be aware of."

Dr. Neruda: "I can't think of anything that would be known to you at this time. Our technologies don't appear on the cover of Newsweek or Time."

Sarah: "I just want to get some information that I can validate later. The transistor story, while interesting, doesn't give me anything I can follow-up on. I doubt Shockley's still alive. Is he?"

Dr. Neruda: "First of all, if he were alive, he'd never divulge the influence of the SPL in his research. Second, he died about eight years ago."

Sarah: "So what can you share with me that corroborates—even to a tiny degree—that the Labyrinth Group *might* exist?"

Dr. Neruda: "Nothing. There's nothing you could do to trace things back to the Labyrinth Group. I can't stress it enough. Our ways of filtering technologies into the private sector are extremely subtle."

Sarah: "Okay, then. Just give me an example."

Dr. Neruda: "The Labyrinth Group developed a computer system, which we call ZEMI. Part of the unique characteristics of ZEMI is that its information structure is based on a new form of mathematics for information storage, recombinant encryption, and data compression. It was a mathematics that provided quantum improvements in each of these areas. And we shared it with scientists involved in the design of the MiG-29."

Sarah: "Russia? Are you saying the Labyrinth Group works with the Russian government?"

Dr. Neruda: "No, we never worked with governments directly. In this case, we worked with the Phazotron Research and Production Company in Moscow. We supplied them with an assortment of algorithms, which they in turn adapted for use within their information and fire control radar systems aboard the MiG-29. These same algorithms were discovered by American interests and are now being adapted for use in broadband delivery systems for the global market."

Sarah: "Who's the American interest? Can you give me names?"

Dr. Neruda: "It's not a well-known company, but they go under the name of Omnigon, based in San Diego."

Sarah: "And Omnigon has this technology, which was originally developed by the Labyrinth Group for computer storage, and now they're using it to build broadband delivery systems? In layperson's terms, can you tell me what these networks will do?"

Dr. Neruda: "Assuming they use this technology appropriately, it'll enable Omnigon to embed a significant amount of functionality in the switches of the ATM network and not rely on server-side solutions, which will increase the speed and custom functionality of a network."

Sarah: "By my definition, that wasn't in layperson terms. But it doesn't matter.
"Did the Labyrinth Group create this technology or reverse-engineer it from ET sources?"

Dr. Neruda: "A little of both, actually. They were created within the Labyrinth Group, but some of the initial thinking came from the Zetas, which was reverse engineered from one of their spacecraft."

Sarah: "How did the organization in Russia get this technology from the Labyrinth Group?"

Dr. Neruda: "Fifteen knew one of the senior scientists at Phazotron and presented him with the idea. It was a friendly gesture, which he believed would later be useful in recruiting this scientist. This method of sharing creates loyalty and it can be done in such a skillful way that the recipient of the idea can believe it was their idea and not simply given to them."

Sarah: "But you must track these technologies or how else would you know it ended up in Omnigon's hands?"

Dr. Neruda: "We have operatives from the intelligence community who feed us information. They're essentially moles that live within the major government research labs and the military industrial complex. In this case, one of our operatives at General Dynamics brought this to our attention. We even use our Remote Viewing technology to track some of our more advanced technologies that we've placed within major syndicates."

Sarah: "Maybe we should leave off there. I know you'd prefer to keep these sessions brief, although I'm very tempted to plunge into this topic of syndicates.
"Is there anything you'd like to add before we call it a night?"

Dr. Neruda: "No, not really. I think we covered a lot of information tonight about my personal philosophy, and for what it's worth, I'd like to remind you that it was my philosophy. I'm not trying to press it on anyone. And I'm certainly not trying to preach a particular message or lifestyle. I would hope that in our next session, with your help, we could concentrate on the WingMakers and perhaps minimize my personal views on cosmology and the like."

Sarah: "I'll try, but I can't make any promises. I had a complete list of questions to ask you tonight about the WingMakers, but somewhere along the way I thought it would be interesting to better understand how you think. I'll try my best tomorrow night to keep on the subject of the WingMakers. Do you have any suggestions?"

Dr. Neruda: "I think the artifacts are extremely interesting, so I'd recommend that we focus on that topic."

Sarah: "I'll do my best. Thank you."

Dr. Neruda: "You're very welcome, Sarah. Thank you as well."

THE FOURTH INTERVIEW OF DR. JAMISSON NERUDA

By Sarah

What follows is a session I recorded of Dr. Neruda on December 31, 1997. He gave permission for me to record his answers to my questions. This is the transcript of that session. This was one of five times I was able to tape record our conversations. I have preserved these transcripts precisely as they occurred. No editing was performed, and I've tried my best to include the exact words, phrasing, and grammar used by Dr. Neruda.

(It's recommended that you read the previous three interviews before reading this interview.)

Sarah: "As promised, one of the things I want to focus on in this interview is the Ancient Arrow site. From what you said the other day, the Ancient Arrow site was essentially stripped of its artifacts. Where are they now and what do you think the ACIO intends to do with them?"

Dr. Neruda: "As of the time of my defection, the site's antechamber and twenty-three sub-chambers were carefully measured, analyzed, and each of the artifacts were cataloged. All of the artifacts that could be taken from the twenty-three chambers were moved to the ACIO lab for rigorous testing. The initial hope was that they contained accessible technologies that could somehow accelerate the deployment schedule for BST. However, I think that expectation changed following the discovery of the twenty-fourth chamber."

Sarah: "You never really talked in any detail about the chambers before. What was so special about the twenty-fourth Chamber?"

Dr. Neruda: "What was interesting about the chambers—apart from the artifacts they contained—was that the site was as sterile as an operating room, except the twenty-third chamber. Remember that these chambers protruded outward from a central corridor that spiraled up through solid rock. From the top of the twenty-third chamber to the antechamber below was approximately fifty meters. We knew there were twenty-four chapters or segments on the optical disc, but we assumed that the antechamber—even though it didn't have any artifacts—was included. Thus, we falsely assumed that the twenty-four chambers were accounted for."

Sarah: "They weren't?"

Dr. Neruda: "No. There was another chamber that had been hidden."

Sarah: "How?"

Dr. Neruda: "The twenty-third chamber had a significant amount of rock debris on its floor. It had all the markings of being unfinished, as if the constructors had to leave suddenly or simply ran out of patience before they completed their mission. We invested a reasonable amount of time and analysis studying the walls and debris of the twenty-third chamber, hoping to discern the methods of construction, but we never suspected that there was a hidden passageway beneath the debris on the floor of the chamber."

Sarah: "So, there was a trap door?"

Dr. Neruda: "Shortly before my defection, a trap door was discovered by some ACIO researchers who were conducting a form of x-ray photography of the interior of the site."

Sarah: "For what purpose?"

Dr. Neruda: "They were trying to determine if there were any structural deficiencies in the site that could cause instabilities within the site in the long-term. We had, in effect, broken the seal on this site and introduced a significant amount of stress to the structure. Fifteen, being the thorough person he is, wanted to be sure we hadn't inadvertently compromised the structural integrity of the site. He felt certain that the site's preservation was potentially critical."

Sarah: "Okay, so these x-rays showed a trap door to another chamber. How was it overlooked before? Was it completely hidden?"

Dr. Neruda: "Not really. We had been told to leave all the chambers as we had found them—other than to remove the artifacts and catalog everything we found. What we didn't realize was that the six inches of rock chips on the floor of the twenty-third chamber concealed a vertical passageway."

Sarah: "It went straight down?"

Dr. Neruda: "Correct. It dropped nearly fifty meters—"

Sarah: "But I thought the antechamber was fifty meters underneath the twenty-third chamber."

Dr. Neruda: "It is, but not directly underneath. The twenty-fourth chamber is only separated by four meters from the nearest wall of the antechamber."

Sarah: "Was there a passageway between the two, or was the only entrance from the twenty-third chamber?"

Dr. Neruda: "The only entrance was from the twenty-third chamber, which made it near impossible to get to."

Sarah: "Why?"

Dr. Neruda: "Because the passageway was cut too small for an adult body, and it was a long distance to traverse."

Sarah: "With all your technology, couldn't you have made it wider?"

Dr. Neruda: "It was an alternative, but Fifteen didn't feel it was warranted."

Sarah: "Why not? It seems like a pretty important discovery… maybe the key to the whole site."

Dr. Neruda: "The ACIO had technologies that allowed us to drop cameras down the passageway and photograph the entire chamber remotely."

Sarah: "What did you see?"

Dr. Neruda: "It was the largest of the twenty-four chambers—in all dimensions. Its wall painting was the largest, and like the twenty-third chamber, was oriented horizontally instead of vertically. There was a technology artifact that we removed from the chamber that, as far as I know, is, like all the others, inaccessible to the ACIO probes."

Sarah: "Other than the chamber being larger in scale, were there any other differences?"

Dr. Neruda: "It was very similar to the twenty-third chamber in the sense that it was also unfinished in appearance, but it was about three times as large in volume. There were a series of glyphs incised on the wall opposite the painting that were organized in seven groups of five characters."

Sarah: "I know you showed me photographs of the chamber paintings, did I see this one?"

Dr. Neruda: "No."

Sarah: "What's it look like?"

Dr. Neruda: "It's the most abstract and complex of the collection, and consequently, hard to describe. Like all the chamber paintings, we invested considerable effort and time to decode the symbols and analyze the content of the painting, but we only had speculation as to its real purpose."

Sarah: "Any hypothesis on why the twenty-fourth chamber was hidden?"

Dr. Neruda: "Remember that the site was interpreted by most within the Labyrinth Group as being loosely based on our human genome—"

Sarah: "Because of the helix shape?"

Dr. Neruda: "That and the fact there were twenty-three chambers—the precise number of chromosomes—or pairs of chromosomes in a normal human cell. These factors, along with some of the detail contained within the chamber paintings and philosophical text we decoded, led us to conclude that the site was designed to tell a story about the human genome."

Sarah: "Okay, but why was the twenty-fourth chamber hidden and how does that relate to the human genome?"

Dr. Neruda: "I don't know with certainty, but remember that the twenty-third chromosome determines the sex of the individual. The wall painting from the twenty-third chamber is the only painting that shows—albeit abstractly—the genitalia of both a man and a woman. We assumed that this was deliberate. The fact that the twenty-third chamber was unfinished suggested that the twenty-third chromosome was also somehow unfinished, implying that there may be some other function of the sex gene that has not been completed yet."

Sarah: "But isn't the entire genome unfinished? I remember reading that 95 percent of the genome is unused. Isn't that true?"

Dr. Neruda: "It's true that the instructions contained within the genes are mostly unused, but the genes themselves, as far as their instruction set, are not incomplete so far as we know. There are, of course, genetic mutations that occur from time-to-time, but again these are not states of incompletion so much as spontaneous adaptation to genetic interfusion."

Sarah: "Then what's the case with the twenty-fourth chamber? Are there instances when some people have twenty-four chromosomes?"

Dr. Neruda: "First, it's twenty-three *pairs* of chromosomes, and yes, there are people who have an extra chromosome, but it's generally not desirable, and is often lethal. In our research, we've never seen twenty-four pairs of chromosomes in a healthy, normal human."

Sarah: "But isn't it possible that it's not about pairs of chromosomes? There aren't any pairs of chambers, so maybe they're talking about twenty-four chromosomes period."

Dr. Neruda: "This possibility was certainly explored."

Sarah: "And…?"

Dr. Neruda: "There was no reliable evidence, so the theory was discounted."

Sarah: "So nothing human has twenty-four chromosomes or twenty-four pairs of chromosomes? Why would the WingMakers construct something so obviously genetic in its shape and make an error like this?"

Dr. Neruda: "No one within the Labyrinth Group believed there was an error. Chimpanzees, orangutans, and gorillas possess twenty-four pairs of chromosomes."

Sarah: "Apes?"

Dr. Neruda: "Any molecular biologist will tell you that our genome is a 98 percent match of the chimpanzee."

Sarah: "Are you suggesting that the WingMakers produced this site in homage to the chimp?"

Dr. Neruda: "No. I'm simply relating the truth. Until 1955 scientists believed that humans had twenty-four pairs of chromosomes just as the chimpanzee or gorilla, but then it was discovered that somewhere in time, humans fused two chromosomes into one—"

Sarah: "And how does this all relate to the discovery of the twenty-fourth chamber?"

Dr. Neruda: "It probably doesn't. The human genome is like a set of encyclopedias with twenty-three volumes. It's quite possible that the twenty-fourth chamber, in this case, is the equivalent of the index or navigation volume."

Sarah: "But it's not visible like the other twenty-three chromosomes?"

Dr. Neruda: "We thought there was significance in the fact that the twenty-fourth chamber was hidden, and was only connected by a narrow, vertical passage to the twenty-third. It's possible, in theory, that the twenty-fourth chromosome isn't a molecular based gene repository. There may be a genetic mutation that is being foreshadowed in our future, or the twenty-fourth chamber is a metaphor for a new functionality of the human species that is—as yet—dormant or non-coded."

Sarah: "So, what does Fifteen think it all means?"

Dr. Neruda: "ZEMI had done an exhaustive search of the variables, and I believe Fifteen had more or less accepted its most probable alternative, that the twenty-third chromosome was destined to mutate and create or catalyze the creation of a twenty-fourth chromosome that would act as a navigation system or index for future geneticists."

Sarah: "And ZEMI deduced all of this from a single painting?"

Dr. Neruda: "ZEMI had sixty-two different analyses of the twenty-fourth chamber painting, and each of them had probabilities of over 40 percent. This is unheard of unless an object is coded in sufficient complexity, and this coding is consistently applied to produce a web effect of possibilities. This painting, along with the glyphs on the opposite wall, achieved that end. The ACIO calls this phenomenon, *Complexity Interlocks*, with factors on a scale of zero to one hundred. If an object or event has a CI of fifteen, it's considered a coded object. The artifacts of the twenty-fourth chamber had the highest CI of all the chambers: 94.6. To put it into perspective, the next highest chamber, chamber six, had a CI of 56.3."

Sarah: "Why is that important?"

Dr. Neruda: "Because Fifteen looked at the twenty-fourth chamber as the key to understanding the Ancient Arrow site. ZEMI's analysis was very specific, much more so than I'm able to relate in this conversation."

Sarah: "Can you give me an example of how ZEMI determines this CI index?"

Dr. Neruda: "The painting or object is scanned and reduced to its digital components. Color, scale, position, shape, and repetition are all established and analyzed. For example, one of the abstract figures in the twenty-fourth chamber painting appears to be floating upside down, and happens to have twenty-three stars within its mid-section. ZEMI would associate significance to this, and this would become a thread of the web effect. ZEMI would continue to create these threads, looking for a consistent pattern. If a pattern emerges with sufficient mathematical coherence and context, it deduces that the object is designed for a purpose."

Sarah: "In other words, a higher CI indicates a higher purpose?"

Dr. Neruda: "Yes, but especially if the distinction is significant as in the case of the twenty-fourth chamber."

Sarah: "If all these pieces are fit together, the picture that emerges is that the Ancient Arrow site was created as a metaphor of the human genome, and that it's predicting a mutation that will produce a twenty-fourth chromosome, which leads us right back to our hairy cousins. Wouldn't this be devolution?"

Dr. Neruda: "No."

Sarah: "Why not?"

Dr. Neruda: "The molecular environment of the twenty-third chromosome is the most antagonistic and dynamic of all the human chromosomes. This makes it a cauldron for potential mutation. Molecular and evolutionary biologists are only now beginning to recognize this inherent reality of the twenty-third chromosome.

"ZEMI's analysis was that the twenty-fourth chamber painting was concerned not with our sexual identity, as in the case of the twenty-third chromosome, but our spiritual identity."

Sarah: "How so?"

Dr. Neruda: "It would take me at least twenty minutes to explain the rationale. Do you want me to proceed?"

Sarah: "Can you give me a summary?"

Dr. Neruda: "I'll try.

"There are several connections between the twenty-third and twenty-fourth chambers; the most notable being that the twenty-fourth chamber is only accessible from the twenty-third chamber. This suggests that the twenty-fourth exists as a result of the behaviors and conditions of the twenty-third. In a sense, the tunnel connecting the two chambers is a birth canal, and the twenty-fourth chamber is the baby.

"Since the twenty-third is the sex chromosome, that is, it determines the sexual and physical identity of the individual, its purpose is largely binary. It's quite logical to conclude that if it were to give birth to a new chromosome, it may have something to do with our spiritual identity, particularly in light of all the other information we have about the Central Race."

Sarah: "I get the feeling that you believe this."

Dr. Neruda: "I think it's a viable hypothesis, but the exact purpose of the Ancient Arrow site is yet to be determined with high confidence."

Sarah: "Are there any other sites similar to the Ancient Arrow site that the ACIO got involved in?"

Dr. Neruda: "No, nothing of this magnitude, but the ACIO involves itself in anything anomalous that may have ET influence."

Sarah: "Can you give me an example?"

Dr. Neruda: "There was an underground installation of engraved stones found in Peru in the mid-1960s. Some of the circumstances regarding this site are similar."

Sarah: "How so?"

Dr. Neruda: "It was an underground installation of considerable complexity and it contained tens of thousands of stones that had been intricately engraved with pictographs that depicted a vast historical record of earth and a prehistorical culture, all carved on a stone known as andesite."

Sarah: "And was this site also kept off the record?"

Dr. Neruda: "No, quite the contrary, but it was targeted with heavy disinformation and ultimately discredited by academic institutions that no doubt felt threatened by the revelation."

Sarah: "I still don't see how a government organization like the ACIO can operate behind the scenes and our own elected officials be completely unaware of both its existence and agenda."

Dr. Neruda: "Not all of your elected officials are unaware of the ACIO, but you're right about one thing: they do not know its true objectives."

Sarah: "So who knows and who doesn't?"

Dr. Neruda: "It's not such a simple thing to provide you with a list of names. Those who know, and are elected officials, form a very short list—"

Sarah: "How short?"

Dr. Neruda: "I would prefer not to say at this time, only that it is less than ten in number.

"The world body politic is not divided into republicans and democrats or liberal and conservative parties. They are divided into a stratification of knowledge and vital intelligence. The financial oligarchy of the secret network I mentioned last week possesses superior knowledge, some of which it shares with the military force and some of which it shares with the Isolationist forces.

These three forces are the principal way the world is organizing itself, and the presumed alpha organization is the Incunabula because they control a dominant share of the world's money supply and hard assets."

Sarah: Okay, stop a moment because I did some research since our interview Saturday, and learned a little bit about the organization called the Illuminati. Is this the same organization you're now referring to as the Incunabula?"

Dr. Neruda: "No. The Illuminati is part of the secret network, but it's not the alpha organization. The Illuminati is affiliated with other blueblood organizations, mostly originating from European roots, but its goals and objectives are not aligned to the Incunabula."

Sarah: "In what way, because from my reading it seemed like it was the secret network you were referring to."

Dr. Neruda: "First, you need to understand that the secret network, as I was referring to, is loosely assembled and not well aligned because of competing agendas. Nonetheless, there is a sense of camaraderie between some of the more powerful groups mostly because they share an elite status in business, academia, or government.

"However, these groups are generally designed to help its members build greater wealth and influence through the members' network of business and government contacts. It is somewhat comparable to a high-powered networking organization."

Sarah: "Are you sure we're talking about the same organization?"

Dr. Neruda: "There are many stories about the Illuminati that are based more on legend than evidence. Too many conspiratorial objectives are credited to them, and they are not organized in this way. Their leadership is too visible and carefully scrutinized by the media. When you have this condition, you can, in most instances, dispel the notion that global, conspiratorial objectives are in the works."

Sarah: "What about the occult references to the Illuminati? Are they true?"

Dr. Neruda: "The supposed leaders of the Illuminati are not occultists or Satan worshippers as they are sometimes accused. Again, this is conspiracy theory run amok, usually by those who seek to define enemies that can embody Lucifer, which in their mind is synonymous with the occult. The Illuminati, while it exists as an elite organization, is made up of men and women that do not conform to one belief system. The spiritual beliefs of their members are not used as criteria to acquire membership. What's important is a member's personal network of contacts."

Sarah: "But don't they have a tremendous influence on politics?"

Dr. Neruda: "Yes, they have influence, as do the Masons, and Skull and Bones, and twenty-seven other organizations that make up this loose-knit network of the elite, but the people who control the master plan are not directly affiliated with any one of these thirty organizations.

"The reality is that these organizations really operate in one of three forces that do have alignment under the controlling hand of the Incunabula."

Sarah: "So you're saying that within these three forces the world's political stage is organized, and the group with the most money also has the best knowledge and basically controls the other two groups?"

Dr. Neruda: "The Incunabula doesn't dictate to the other two forces. It strategically releases information that lures the two forces in the direction it wants them to go.

"You can look at these three forces as part of an equilateral triangle, with the Incunabula at the apex, and the Global Military Force at one base and the Isolationist Force at the other. This is the real structure of global power."

Sarah: "I'm not clear about the different objectives of these three forces."

Dr. Neruda: "The Incunabula is concerned with the globalization of monetary channels and vital supplies like petroleum and natural gas; the Military Force is concerned with spreading and preserving democratization throughout the globe, and in so doing, protecting the self-interests of the dominant superpowers of America and Western Europe; and the Isolationist Force is focused on industry and wealth building for its citizens at the state level."

Sarah: "But how does the Incunabula lure these other two forces to do its bidding? Can you give me an example?"

Dr. Neruda: "Why do you think Saddam Hussein invaded Kuwait?"

Sarah: "To grab its oil wells and make a lot of money."

Dr. Neruda: "On the surface that is close to the truth. Following the Iran-Iraq War, Saddam had depleted too much of his country's wealth, and to be sure, he was interested in the wealth production of Kuwait, but he also knew that his military was not designed to invade and annex countries, and he was aware that the superpowers would protect their interests in Kuwait.

"Saddam had a real dilemma, he had upwards of a million soldiers that were without jobs after the Iran-Iraq War and there was no place within Iraq's broader economy to absorb these men. The Military Force was aware of Saddam's dilemma, and through a consistent disinformation campaign by the Military Force, Saddam was led to believe that he would be allowed to invade Kuwait without superpower retaliation.

"There are high level operatives within the Military Force that are also the eyes and ears of the Incunabula. It was well understood that Iraq had weapons of mass destruction that it had developed during the course of its war with Iran. The Military Force saw this as a destabilizing element of its long-term policy to bring democracy—American-style—to the oil producing region.

"The Incunabula does not have control of the Middle East oil. It is the only vital asset in which they do not exercise prime authority. Saddam Hussein was seduced by disinformation to attack Kuwait so that the Military Force could—with the whole world looking on—dismantle Iraq's defenses. This was a staged event of global impact exercised by the Incunabula and carried out by the Military Force completely unaware that they were being lured into this conflict in the same way as Iraq."

Sarah: "And all because some elite trillionaires want to control the world's oil supply?"

Dr. Neruda: "It's much more complex than that, though that is a part of the equation. I'm not sure how much you want me to go into it."

Sarah: "It's hard to stop after you drop this revelation on me. Where is this all headed… I mean what is the end goal of the Incunabula?"

Dr. Neruda: "Do you mean in the context of the Middle East?"

Sarah: "Yes."

Dr. Neruda: "They want to control crude oil production. They want to exercise authority over this critical asset that is so fundamental to shaping world economies. They have controls over refining and the distribution of end products, but they lack control over the production, particularly in the Middle East. This is the fundamental goal, but it's surrounded by the tributary objectives of bringing a Western culture to the region and slowly, but surely, homogenizing the world's culture. They want this global culture as a framework in which to create global regulation."

Sarah: "And how long will this take… assuming they're successful?"

Dr. Neruda: "From the perspective of the ACIO, it has a probability of occurrence no more than 35 percent within the next ten years and jumps to a 60 percent probability in twenty years. Thereafter, it becomes more probable with each passing decade, until it reaches near certainty by the year 2060."

Sarah: "And when you say 'global regulation', what do you mean?"

Dr. Neruda: "The ability to regulate the vital resources of the planet as a singular, global political body."

Sarah: "What makes this such a critical goal of the Incunabula?"

Dr. Neruda: "The diminishing oil and natural gas supplies. These are non-renewable energy sources, and what required a billion years to create 3.2 trillion barrels of useable oil has only taken 110 years to reduce to 1.8 trillion barrels. The planet's oil supply is its economic lifeblood. As this diminishes, so does the economic system in which the world's people live. As the economic conditions erode, instability arises, and if left unchecked, chaos ensues."

Sarah: "Again you're saying that this is all about oil?"

Dr. Neruda: "Try to understand that to me it's astounding that this isn't obvious. Anyone who knows the condition of the world's oil supply can perform simple extrapolations and conclude that the world is approximately fifty years away from oil depletion, and that assumes you use the more optimistic analyses. On the pessimistic side, it could be as little as twenty-five years."

Sarah: "How can that be? I don't recall anything being said about this in the media. I would think this would be a huge story if it were that obvious and that ominous."

Dr. Neruda: "There are many versions of this story that circulate in the media, but they never quite capture the attention of the mass media and the masses because they deal with the distant future—a topic not held in high regard by citizens in love with their Western lifestyles. Nevertheless, this future is precisely where the Incunabula place their focus because this is what determines the tactics of the present day.

"The depletion of the world's oil supply, coupled to the growth in human population, is the dominant influence that is shaping the policies of the Incunabula and its timetable."

Sarah: "So the agenda of the Incunabula is to control the diminishing oil supply in order to do what?"

Dr. Neruda: "At the highest levels of the Incunabula, the planning horizons are typically twenty to one hundred years, depending on the issue. They are well aware that as the oil supplies diminish, oil will become increasingly more difficult to extract from the planet's reservoirs, and consequently, require at minimum, a 30 percent delta in refining costs. This will have a profound effect on price, which can have the effect of producing a persistent recession in the world's economy.

"The planners of the Incunabula believe that by consolidating control of the oil supply and its distribution it is the best way to impose rationing at a global level without setting off Armageddon."

Sarah: "It's really that serious?"

Dr. Neruda: "I don't mean to sound like an alarmist, but this is the fundamental problem that the world must address in the twenty-first century. The brightest minds of our planet are well aware of this and have known this for twenty years or more."

Sarah: "Why then aren't the leaders of the world, and the brightest minds, working on alternative energy sources?"

Dr. Neruda: "In some instances they are. There're several alternative energy sources that are under consideration—some are not even released to the public at this time because they stem from technologies that also carry great potential as weapons.

"But the bigger issue is how to change the energy system of our modern day civilization from petroleum to a new energy source, or perhaps to change the manner in which we live—in other words, our oil dependent lifestyle."

Sarah: "Why is that such a big deal? I would think that as the world wakes up to the reality of dwindling oil supplies it would be very receptive to a new energy source."

Dr. Neruda: "Have you ever heard the quote by Machiavelli about the difficulty of changing a system?"

Sarah: "I don't think so."

Dr. Neruda: "He wrote, 'There is nothing more difficult to plan, more doubtful of success, nor more dangerous to manage than the creation of a new system. For the initiator has the enmity of all who would profit by the preservation of the old system and merely lukewarm defenders in those who would gain by the new one'."

Sarah: "Okay, so this requires a lot of preparation and planning, and probably persuasion. But what choices do we have?"

Dr. Neruda: "None. This is the realism of the next fifty years."

Sarah: "I presume the Incunabula plan to orchestrate this change of systems. Am I right on that?"

Dr. Neruda: "Yes. As I said earlier, they believe the global regulation of energy resources and the ability to manage population growth are the convergent issues of our time that—if managed properly—can avert Armageddon."

Sarah: "You've said that word twice tonight—*Armageddon*. What do you mean by that? Are you talking about World War III?"

Dr. Neruda: "Armageddon is defined by the ACIO as the chaos of humanity. It is the time when humanity plunges into chaos and the interfaces of global commerce, communication, and diplomacy are destroyed in favor of national self-preservation. If this were to happen, weapons of unusual power could be used to destroy 30 percent or more of the human population. This is the definition that we don't like to talk about, but it's well known within the ACIO as a possibility in the twenty-first century."

Sarah: "So I assume you have your probability forecasts for this as well. Right?"

Dr. Neruda: "Yes."

Sarah: "And what are they, dare I ask?"

Dr. Neruda: "I'd prefer not to say. They aren't really relevant anyway because they fluctuate based on world events."

Sarah: "But this is what the Incunabula's planners are trying to steer clear of?"

Dr. Neruda: "Yes. This consumes their agenda more than any other issue."

Sarah: "What other organizations are consumed by this agenda?"

Dr. Neruda: "There are none."

Sarah: "What?"

Dr. Neruda: "This agenda is unique to the Incunabula because they're the only organization that is focused squarely on averting this particular crisis condition based on the convergence criteria I stated earlier."

Sarah: "You mean they're the only organization that's worried about Armageddon as it relates to dwindling oil supplies and population increases?"

Dr. Neruda: "Yes."

Sarah: "But you're not telling me that other organizations aren't worried about World War III or Armageddon, how ever you define it. Right?"

Dr. Neruda: "Every nation's leadership is concerned about these issues, but it's by no means the focus of their agenda. It is a small, compartmentalized component of their agenda.

"This is precisely why Fifteen is involved with the Incunabula's planners, the threats to the human race are both real and persistent, and with each passing decade the conditions are only growing more fertile for fragmentation and chaos—the very kind you would observe in tribal warfare. There is no fundamental difference."

Sarah: "And the leaders of the Military Force know about this objective?"

Dr. Neruda: "No. They have their own agenda, which is related, but quite different as well. They don't aspire to regulate oil production; they intend to defend its availability and influence its price as a result. They're not concerned with globalization as it relates to economic or cultural platforms, but rather, they're concerned with exporting democracy in order to ensure stabilization in the region, and eradicate instability in the form of terrorists and dictators alike."

Sarah: "But that seems at odds with everything I've heard about the military."

Dr. Neruda: "In what way?"

Sarah: "You make it sound as though the Military Force is trying to bring stability or peace, when everything I've ever read implies that the military feeds off of conflict and instability. If the world is at peace, then the military becomes a simple police force, its power is reduced and its budgets are slashed."

Dr. Neruda: "I understand your question. However, the Military Force is not the same thing as the military. While it is very pro-military, it operates in a longer planning horizon than military personnel. The Military Force is made up of high-level politicians, business people, intelligence members, academics, think tanks, and so on. Its members are from the United Kingdom, America, Germany, Canada, Australia, Israel, and many other countries. Its cohesion, as a group, is not so much a function of formal structure and meetings, but rather it's by publishing classified papers that are shared among its elite members. These papers define the platform, goals, long-term objectives, and essentially map out the strategy and tactics by which the Military Force intends to execute its plan.

"The Military Force is working on hybrid defensive and offensive weapons that relate to space, bio-weapons, the Internet, and other environments that are as yet not viewed as battlefield arenas. They would contend that R & D budgets should be increased in order to develop these new weapons in order to secure the rights of free people to live without fear of preemptive attack. They intend to remove this reality from the face of the earth and at the same time, propagate democracy."

Sarah: "But isn't this a noble goal?"

Dr. Neruda: "Their goals are not necessarily misguided, but their methods to achieve these goals are. This is all about projecting power, and, as a consequence, dictating the prevailing political platform by which the world achieves peace. It is enforced peace. It is peace through power and manipulation."

Sarah: "But it's still peace and it's still democracy. It's certainly better than the alternative of wars and anarchy or dictatorship."

Dr. Neruda: "There are other means to achieve the same end."

Sarah: "You said that the budget for military spending would only increase over time if the Military Force has its way. How would that happen amidst world peace?"

Dr. Neruda: "New threats will be determined that will create this need even though our countries of the world are at peace."

Sarah: "Are you talking about ETs again?"

Dr. Neruda: "Among other things. China will likely be the last island of opposition that the wave of democracy will land upon, but when it does, the Military Force desires to have unique weapons at its disposal in order to swiftly bring the changes it seeks. Bio-weapons will likely be the choice—"

Sarah: "How is that possible when the U.S. has banned bio-weapons?"

Dr. Neruda: "Unfortunately the discoveries in the human genome are too compelling for the Military Force to ignore as it pertains to bio-weapons development. Research is already underway, and has been for two years, to develop bio-weapons that target certain genomes indicative of a specific race."

Sarah: "Like Chinese?"

Dr. Neruda: "Yes, but it doesn't mean the weapon would ever be deployed. It would simply be a known capability of the Military Force and that alone would make the change of regime irresistible."

Sarah: "I have to stop here and make a confession. Part of me wants to cry when I hear this and bury my head in a pillow, and part of me wants to keep asking more questions. I'm really torn on this one... I don't think I want to talk about this anymore. Okay?"

Dr. Neruda: "I'm only answering the questions you ask of me as honestly as I can."

Sarah: "I know, and I'm not complaining about you or your answers really. I just needed to say what I was feeling."

Dr. Neruda: "I understand."

Sarah: "Do you want to take a break and stretch your legs?"

Dr. Neruda: "I'm fine, but if you want one, I'll be happy to take a stretch."

Sarah: "No, I'm fine...

"Tell me more about the Isolationist Force. What's their story in all of this?"

Dr. Neruda: "Again, I don't want you to think that the Military and Isolationist Forces are formal groups that have memberships and party platforms. They are informal, tacit coalitions at most, and they operate through the well-placed leadership of Incunabula operatives. Also, it is important to remember that they're all part of the triad of leadership that the Incunabula has forged over the last fifty-seven years.

"In the case of the Isolationist Force, it's the least organized of the three forces. It's designed to spur economic policies and activities that generate wealth for the elite class throughout the world. As a force it is concerned with domestic state issues that drive economic growth and vitality. Its focus is to influence local, state and national governments to facilitate commerce."

Sarah: "Am I correct in thinking that Republicans are more affiliated with the Isolationist Force?"

Dr. Neruda: "No. These three forces are not affiliated with any party or political organization. Someone can be aligned with both the Military and Isolationist Force and not have any conflict doing so. They are not antagonistic. They're compatible forces. Also, these forces are not exclusively American. They are global forces—albeit with dominance from American and European interests, but they're not party affiliations like Democrats and Republicans, nor are they state-sponsored in any way."

Sarah: "If the oil production is in the hands of the Incunabula, what will happen to the Arab state regimes that currently hold this power?"

Dr. Neruda: "It depends on the regime. The Incunabula is expert at influence through financial services and legal maneuvering. They will assert their influence slowly, gradually, and in a manner that will catch the royal families and cartel by surprise. Their patience is unmatched, and they operate on multiple levels of influence, which is why they win nearly every time.

"Even at the present time many of the royal families exert influence in domestic affairs, but not oil production. They reap the rewards of the oil financially, but others within their regimes are truly operating the production and interacting with the cartel, developing the core relationships of trust and influence. These are the ones that the Incunabula bring into their fold, and slowly win over as operatives in their plan. The Military Force, at the appropriate timetable, will overturn the regimes in conflict with the plan, and those regimes that are friendly, will be allowed to retain their domestic presence and influence. These are carefully orchestrated events."

Sarah: "And once the Incunabula has control over oil production, what then?"

Dr. Neruda: "The dismantling of hard currency. The Incunabula desires to have an electronic currency because it tracks everything and enables a more thorough analytical insight into the affairs of the individual."

Sarah: "So what do they want to do with all this information?"

Dr. Neruda: "They want to observe patterns and manipulate events in order to protect their dominance as a leadership body, and, as I said earlier, they want to define the new systems and manage system change. Once this dominance is perceived as reaching a critical mass, the Incunabula plans to create a global body of governance that brings stability to Earth and a set of policies that aid humanity at large."

Sarah: "Again you're telling me that their goal is to *help* humanity, but I find it hard to believe."

Dr. Neruda: "In a way it is the only way they can retain power. If they concentrate wealth and services too much, they will lose control of the population they seek to govern. Rebellion is never far away when empty stomachs grumble in unison."

Sarah: "How will they dismantle our hard currency?"

Dr. Neruda: "There will be a gradual devaluation of the stock markets worldwide. Americans in particular have become accustomed to easy money production within the stock markets, as well as lavish lifestyles. This will not be permitted to continue indefinitely. Recessions will occur in waves until the value of currency is called into question. This will begin in third world countries first, and as these become the initial victims of feeble economic policies, the Incunabula will essentially force these countries to sell their assets at rock bottom prices in return for helping them out of economic crisis.

"In the best of times, the world economy is a fragile patchwork of economic systems that run at different rates without a smooth interface or a macro system in which to operate. In the worst of times, it is a house of cards vulnerable to the faintest of winds. Hard currency and the monetary system that supports it will become a scapegoat of the economic slowdown, and electronic currency will increasingly become the solution to the general malaise of the global economy."

Sarah: "I'm not an economist so I don't even know what questions to ask, but it leaves me with a queasy feeling in my gut. I get the feeling that there's only one real power in the world and it's the Incunabula, and we're all just puppets of this elite group of moneymen. Isn't that pretty much the subtext of all your comments here?"

Dr. Neruda: "No, not at all, but I can understand how you arrive at that conclusion given that we've been focused on the Triad of Power, or TOP, as we refer to it within the Labyrinth Group. TOP is a reality on earth, and it probably will be for many generations to come, and it's certainly in the best position to dominate world affairs and development, but there are other powers that can intervene and bring fresh opportunity to the world's people."

Sarah: "Like religious powers?"

Dr. Neruda: "Yes, that's one, though they will never rival the Incunabula in terms of impacting on world affairs."

Sarah: "So who're you talking about? Give me some names or examples."

Dr. Neruda: "The rise of personal computers and the Internet was never intended to occur according to the Incunabula. It was one of the developments that genuinely surprised the planners within the Incunabula and proved to be a very vexing issue for nearly a decade. Computing power was supposed to remain in the hands of the elite. The Internet grew organically and at a pace that no one thought possible, and it caught the Incunabula completely off guard."

Sarah: "So technology is a power that frustrated the plans of the Incunabula?"

Dr. Neruda: "It's one example."

Sarah: "I imagine the ACIO is another?"

Dr. Neruda: "The single greatest weakness of the Incunabula is its lack of scientific expertise within the ranks of its leadership. While it has technical and scientific members in special projects within the Global Military Industrial Complex, they are not leaders, and it is the leadership of the Incunabula that establishes its agenda."

Sarah: "But I thought you said that Fifteen was part of the Incunabula."

Dr. Neruda: "Yes, but the ACIO is simply seen as a resource to the Incunabula. Fifteen is perceived as an anarchist whose vision could never be aligned with the leadership of the Incunabula. They don't even identify with his vision."

Sarah: "If the Incunabula relies so heavily on ACIO technology, and they need scientific leadership, why don't they replace Fifteen and place someone they can control better?"

Dr. Neruda: "They originally tried to have a Director who would be more compliant, but it didn't succeed."

Sarah: "How do you mean that?"

Dr. Neruda: "One of the first Directors of the ACIO was a member of the Incunabula's Military Force and was very much an insider in terms of working with some of its higher ranking leaders, especially in America."

Sarah: "Can you disclose his name?"

Dr. Neruda: "Vannevar Bush."

Sarah: "How do you spell his name?"

Dr. Neruda: (Spelling it out.)

Sarah: "Is he related to President George Bush?"

Dr. Neruda: "No."

Sarah: "So he ran the ACIO when it was still in its infancy?"

Dr. Neruda: "Yes."

Sarah: "What happened to him?"

Dr. Neruda: "He was too visible, and it was rightly feared that he would not be able to retain secrecy."

Sarah: "Why?"

Dr. Neruda: "Dr. Bush was a gifted individual who exercised both technical vision and leadership skills. He had access to the leadership of the government and the Incunabula. He could manage a large team of scientists and engineers as well as anyone could. He essentially built the infrastructure for military research, but his celebrity status was troublesome to the founders of the Incunabula."

Sarah: "Give me a sense of the timetable because I have to admit I've never heard of this man."

Dr. Neruda: "It was right near the end of World War II that Dr. Bush was asked to head up a team of research scientists that had supposedly been assembled from the NDRC and SPL to reverse engineer a recovered alien spacecraft that had been recovered in 1940 off the coast of Florida. These were actually top scientists from the newly formed ACIO. The spacecraft had been placed in cold storage because of World War II. As the war ended, Bush became privy to this discovery through his network and offered his leadership to the project. As I understand it, he was just coming off the Manhattan Project when this opportunity presented itself."

Sarah: "So he was considered a security risk and that ended his tenure at the ACIO?"

Dr. Neruda: "Yes.

"This reverse-engineering project was held in the highest possible secrecy. Dr. Bush ran the operation within the SPL through special funding from the OSS, which was the forerunner of the CIA. However, after a year's time, little progress was made and there were rumors attributed to Bush that alien spacecraft consumed his agenda.

"Bush reported directly to James Forrestal, who at the time was heading up the Navy, but shortly thereafter became the first Secretary of Defense. Truman was president.

"The spacecraft that had been recovered was sufficiently intact to conduct reverse engineering studies on its propulsion system, which was the most critical knowledge that Forrestal hoped to extract from the project."

Sarah: "What year are we talking?"

Dr. Neruda: "This would have been between 1945 and 1946."

Sarah: "So what happened?"

Dr. Neruda: "Bear in mind that my knowledge of these events is based on my study of the ACIO archive. I wasn't personally involved in any of these happenings, so I'm not vouching for their absolute accuracy."

Sarah: "Understood."

Dr. Neruda: "Dr. Bush was asked to replicate the propulsion system of the recovered craft in twelve months, and was given the resources of the ACIO in order to do so."

Sarah: "And did he succeed?"

Dr. Neruda: "Only partially. The electromagnetic fields were not fully replicated in terms of their sustained intensity levels in metals because of electron drift, which, and I'm struggling to keep this in layperson's terms, was the primary reason they failed. Nonetheless, there were prototypes built that replicated aspects of the alien craft's propulsion system, and these were sufficient to galvanize funding and support for the ACIO."

Sarah: "Then why didn't Dr. Bush join the ACIO?"

Dr. Neruda: "He knew it would require that he go underground and essentially become anonymous. He didn't want anonymity because he was a prodigious inventor and liked the limelight accorded him from government officials as well as the scientific community at large. Also, I don't think the head of the OSS thought his mental capabilities were sufficient to the task. Bush was a great organizer of talent, but he lacked the commanding intellect in physics to lead the ACIO as it was envisioned in those days."

Sarah: "How many people knew about this project?"

Dr. Neruda: "I'm not sure. Perhaps five or six knew the total scope of the project and another fifty knew elements of the project. It was, as I said before, a very well guarded secret."

Sarah: "How do you keep something like this a secret?"

Dr. Neruda: "There are entire departments within our government that have responsibility for this. It's a very well engineered process that includes legal contracts, clear penalty reminders, and known deterrence factors that include very invasive technologies. In the worst case, if vital information was disclosed, a different but related department would step in that would masterfully spread disinformation. It was, and still is, virtually impossible to bring this information to the public."

Sarah: "They had invasive technologies even in 1945?"

Dr. Neruda: "Yes. While the invasive technologies were more crudely applied, they were certainly effective. There was nothing more vilified in these undisclosed organizations than traitors. The entire organizational culture was designed to reward loyalty and severely punish disloyalty in any form."

Sarah: "I want to switch topics for a moment. It seems that we're in a new stage of world peace and economic stability, but when I hear you talk, it seems that this just isn't possible given the nature of the Incunabula and the triad of power that you were talking about earlier. Is this true?"

Dr. Neruda: "It is an illusion. There may be lulls in the movements of war, but look at the past one hundred years. Isn't it an assemblage of wars?"

Sarah: "And all because war feeds the triad of power as you call it?"

Dr. Neruda: "No. There are forces that truly believe in good and evil. In their view, countries—like people—are essentially cast into three categories: good, neutral, and evil. Those that are good must dominate the world political structures and ensure that those that are evil are identified and reduced to a non-threat status."

Sarah: "But the cold war is over, right? The Soviet Union is no more, and what's left of it seems more or less friendly to the interests of the free world. Isn't this true?"

Dr. Neruda: "When power is concentrated in a single person, and that country or organization develops long range missile technology, it immediately becomes a target for concern within the intelligence community."

Sarah: "And am I correct in assuming that the intelligence community you're referring to is global and managed by the Incunabula?"

Dr. Neruda: "Yes, but it is not formally managed by the Incunabula."

Sarah: "I understand, but the results are the same, right?"

Dr. Neruda: "Yes."

Sarah: "I apologize for the interruption."

Dr. Neruda: "The perceived enemy is missile technology in the hands of a concentrated power. There are many, many countries that have this technology so it ensures distrust. Organizations like the U.N. (United Nations) are not sufficiently empowered to deal with these threats, so multilateral coalitions are developed between nations to deal with the perceived threats, often completely undisclosed to the public.

"Iraq is a perfect example. North Korea is another, though it lacks the strategic geography to place it on the top of the list. So, geography also plays a central role in this assessment."

Sarah: "So essentially the world is coalescing into three camps. I understand that, but who determines who is evil, neutral, and good? I mean isn't this a terribly subjective call?"

Dr. Neruda: "Whoever exerts the greatest global leadership in terms of projecting military force, economic vibrancy, and foreign policy makes this determination. And yes, it is certainly subjective, but it's precisely why the U.S. has adopted its imperialist attitude. It wants to define good and evil for the world, and in so doing, it can more effectively export its own definition of peace and democracy."

Sarah: "Sounds so simplistic when you put it those terms."

Dr. Neruda: "It's a natural outgrowth of how a state *engineers* its power. The state requires its enemies in order to convince its citizens to accept its authority over their lives. The greater the fear the state is able to provoke in the hearts and minds of its citizens, the more power its citizens are willing to give to it in order to protect them from its enemies. All states, to varying degrees, do this."

Sarah: "Are you saying that the U.S., just to pick an example, engineers its enemies? You're really saying that America creates its enemies in order to increase its power domestically and internationally."

Dr. Neruda: "I don't mean that the U.S. literally creates its enemies. The U.S. has potential adversaries in many parts of the world. Its policy of military presence as a global protector is all that's required to create enemies. Its forceful export of its political belief system is also troublesome to many countries that see American interests as a prelude to cultural colonization."

Sarah: "Because we're the only remaining superpower?"

Dr. Neruda: "No. It's because the U.S. has a global military presence and economic lever that it wields with relative virtuosity. It is skillful at aggression without appearing aggressive. It protects and defends, and sometimes it will do this in a pre-emptive strike and sometimes in a reactive countermeasure that is usually at a force response that is several fold the original intensity. America's self interests have become the standard of the free world, and there are those who fear it will dominate to the point of imperialism."

Sarah: "How does all of this fit into the work of the Incunabula or the ACIO for that matter?"

Dr. Neruda: "The Incunabula uses the U.S. as a force for globalization. It is the lead horse pulling the nation states of the globe into a common economic and political platform.

"As far as the ACIO is concerned, it has thoroughly analyzed the various scenarios presented by U.S. global domination and find that there are only two scenarios in which the United States can achieve its ambitious aims without catalyzing a world war and plunging the global economy into a severe depression."

Sarah: "Can you disclose these?"

Dr. Neruda: "No."

Sarah: "Why?"

Dr. Neruda: "They are based on a mixture of remote viewing, advanced computer modeling, and preliminary BST tests. I am not willing to disclose this information at this time. Perhaps at a later date."

Sarah: "I fully realize that we've gotten completely off the subject, but you seem to be leading me into this conversation. I can't help it."

Dr. Neruda: "I understand."

Sarah: "Are there plans for making this all happen? I mean does the Incunabula actually engineer the globalization or does it sort of happen as a result of a nudge here and a nudge there?"

Dr. Neruda: "It's a carefully orchestrated process. The planning is deep, penetrating, and exhaustive. It is not flawless nor is it carried out with perfect precision. Nonetheless there is certainly a plan and it's executed by the triad of power as I stated earlier."

Sarah: "And you've seen this plan?"

Dr. Neruda: "I know of it through the Labyrinth Group. Fifteen requires each of us to know these plans on an intimate basis."

Sarah: "Can you disclose any of this plan?"

Dr. Neruda: "I think I have been alluding to it in this interview."

Sarah: "Yes, but you haven't been clear about how events will culminate in such a way that the Incunabula will rise to power."

Dr. Neruda: "It is not preordained. There is no certainty in what I am about to disclose. It is a plan. Albeit a plan created by very ambitious and capable people."

Sarah: "Duly noted."

Dr. Neruda: "There are serious flaws within the global economy, and the United States will, within the next seven years, begin to express these flaws in ways that ripple through the globe and cause financial unrest. The best way to ensure that these flaws are controlled is to tighten corporate loopholes that allow greedy executives to exploit their shareholders, and to seize control over the price of oil."

Sarah: "Wait a minute, I thought the greedy executives were exactly the profile of the Incunabula. Why would they lock down on their own turf?"

Dr. Neruda: "The Incunabula leadership is not comprised of greedy executives. It is made up of anonymous individuals. They are not sitting on corporate boards. They are not the Bill Gates of corporate America, nor are they the Bluebloods of European royalty. They are anonymous, and through their anonymity they wield great power. They are the strategists of the Triad of Power who plot and plan at such a level as to make corporate executives and politicians seem like preschoolers fumbling to hold a pencil."

Sarah: "So if you gave me a name of the leader of the Incunabula, I couldn't look him up. He doesn't exist?"

Dr. Neruda: "That's correct."

Sarah: "So these people are not really very different from those of you within the ACIO."

Dr. Neruda: "They are very different. They produce globalization, uniform economic and political platforms, while we produce breakthrough technologies. They practice hegemony, while we practice science."

Sarah: "I didn't mean to offend you… I thought you said earlier that the Incunabula used White Papers and think tanks to promote its vision for the future."

Dr. Neruda: "No, it is the Military Force that does this. The Incunabula is multi-tiered, as I've said before. It produces ideas and frameworks that produce the right conditions for the think tanks and other forces of the elite power base to exert influence. It is a very complicated process. If you would like me to go into it, I will."

Sarah: "No, I sort of interrupted you. You were talking about the Incunabula's plan."

Dr. Neruda: "They desire a paperless currency coupled to a global leadership, and to carry this out they require a restructuring—or perhaps more precisely, a complete reengineering of resource and power sharing."

Sarah: "Can you elaborate on this a bit?"

Dr. Neruda: "The plan requires new leadership in the Arab states. There is general concern that the Arab states will consolidate much like Europe is in the process of doing, and new superpowers will be created out of this consolidation. Multiple superpowers make consolidation of the global economic platform a thorny proposition.

"Because of its natural aggression as a superpower, the United States is the spearhead of the Incunabula to usher in the required changes of their plan. It will be positioned to exert a strong military and cultural presence in the Middle East and Asia; partly for oil considerations and partly for the purpose of gradually westernizing the indigenous cultures."

Sarah: "Hold on a second. Our military bases are as much for the protection of our allies as for ourselves, and as for culture, we may export our movies and pop stars, but other countries are just as eager to be trend setters in the culture game."

Dr. Neruda: "There's a difference. The U.S. protects and defends because it can establish military bases in those regions after it is done defending. Agreements are made—sometimes without the public's knowledge—to have military bases and protective forces therein for domestic peace issues and normalization. The U.S. has over one hundred-seventy military bases on foreign soil. This number will continue to grow as dictated by this plan.

"In regard to the export of culture, yes, you are right, the U.S. is not alone in this, but it leads the way through its capitalistic leverage of pop culture. No one does this as well as American corporations. They have set the world standard for monetizing content and brands. Other countries mimic this standard and add their weight. Collectively, the culture of capitalism reaches the Arab nations, China, North Korea, Southeast Asia, and the people of these countries— especially the new generations—are seduced by its allure."

Sarah: "I can't help but get the impression that you're not very patriotic."

Dr. Neruda: "The plan I share with you is rooted in the success of the United States to secure unilateral superpower status by the turn of the century. The U.S. will, as a result, be required to assert itself because there will be many challengers and discreditors. However, in this process, it will increase its worldwide presence as the leader of the free world. This is the goal that many throughout the world hold dear to their heart, whether they voice this sentiment or not.

"I don't hold any grudge against the U.S. for this assertion. Any nation would do the same thing if given the opportunity. The United States is relentlessly aggressive in all the important dimensions: military, culture, capitalism, applied technology, foreign policy, space, economic policy, and intelligentsia, to name the most critical areas.

"In Nature, the alpha male dominates through strength, cunning, and aggression. It is no different in the world of humans and statehood. The alpha male also has a responsibility for protection and sustenance. And the Incunabula planners selected the U.S. as being the most suitable country to lead the pack of other nations to the global platforms it has designed and is readying."

Sarah: "Okay, it sort of makes sense, what you're saying, but the Incunabula wants the U.S. to lead the world to a global community of free, democratic states with a global culture based on capitalism. How do they know the free world will elect them to govern them?"

Dr. Neruda: "They don't. There are, as I've said many times here tonight, no guarantees. All I can say is that they don't miscalculate very often, and when they do, they adjust to the changes presented them. Again, the planners of the Incunabula, the real architects behind these events, are not interested in being the leaders of earth in terms of visibility. They want to appoint the leadership while giving the world a sense of choice."

Sarah: "It's very hard to imagine how the world would select one leadership. It sounds like something that is hundreds of years in the future—if ever."

Dr. Neruda: "I understand your conclusion, but what seems implausible today can rapidly evolve if the proper conditions are created. This is precisely what the Incunabula are focused on above all else. They realize that this may not take place until the year 2040 or even later, but they are convinced that consolidation of power—at a global level—is necessary in order to prevent planetary destruction or what we talked about earlier as Armageddon."

Sarah: "What do you mean by planetary destruction?"

Dr. Neruda: "There are many decay forces that can take hold of a planet and cause its decline as a supportive living environment. In our interactions with extraterrestrials, this is a common theme that is expressed because this condition frequently accompanies the rise of postmodern civilizations.

"Human populations fragment across a planet, developing their unique cultures, language, economic systems, and state identities. Certain states have the good fortune of natural resources and some do not. As these natural resources of the planet are converted into commercial advantage, some states flourish economically and some flounder.

"As the stronger states begin to dominate the weaker, military forces and weapons are created. Applied technology becomes the ultimate weapon. If multiple superpowers are allowed to develop they can bring destruction to the human populations of the planet. If population densities reach a critical level, it can have the same devastating effects.

"The human residents increasingly bring the planet under pressure. If left unchecked, the planet can reach a critical stage of destruction whereby human populations no longer find the planet a suitable habitat."

Sarah: "So you're saying that the whole reason the Incunabula are engineering the globalization of earth is because they want to save earth from destruction?"

Dr. Neruda: "I will put it this way. The leaders of the Incunabula are very clear about the threats that earth will undergo in the twenty-first century. They believe their orchestration of human events better serves the human population than to leave it to the forces of competitive politics. They genuinely believe that the self-interests of the states will prevent a consolidation of global power."

Sarah: "Remind me again, why is this consolidation, as you put it, so critical to our survival?"

Dr. Neruda: "Because the threats that will confront the human population in the twenty-first century will be global issues—whether they are intractable recessions, dwindling oil supplies, food distribution, overpopulation, pollution, nuclear fallout, or extraterrestrial visitations, they will require a global, coordinated response. Unless the nations of the world are united, they will respond too slowly to the threats, and the decay forces will have such traction that they may be impossible to reverse."

Sarah: "But isn't this why the United Nations was formed? To deal with these very issues?"

Dr. Neruda: "The United Nations is a prototype that the Incunabula designed to serve as an experiment to test the format for a world government. It was never considered to be the format for consolidation.

"The issues of which I'm speaking are not confronted in the United Nations, even if they're discussed and debated. Resolutions are designed to help remedy the problems, but ultimately it depends upon the will of the individual state to implement, monitor, report, analyze results, and make adjustments, and this is not enforced in any reasonable manner. A world government, to be effective, will require the ability to enforce and adjust resolutions based on sound analysis. Otherwise these threats will arise and the world's people will not be able to speak with a single voice, and more importantly, to act as a unified force against threats."

Sarah: "So this is the real end game of the Incunabula? What happened to the greedy elitists you disclosed earlier?"

Dr. Neruda: "Greed is alive and well within the ranks of the Incunabula. But I've been talking about the *planners* of the Incunabula—the people who have the real grip on power. They don't operate out of greed. They have assets that are beyond the imagination of even wealthy people. The acquisition of wealth is completed for them.

"The planners are concerned with securing humanity's future, rather than generating wealth for themselves."

Sarah: "Okay, I understand you're a sympathizer of the Incunabula, but what happened to the insatiable greed and self interests? I know you mentioned this before."

Dr. Neruda: "It exists, but the Incunabula, like any undisclosed organization is composed of multiple levels. Operatives at the lower levels function within a set of rules and norms that do not apply to the higher levels. In other words, planners operate in a completely different organizational culture. There is a sophistication and penetrating insight at the highest levels that are not existent at the operations level.

"Planners within the Incunabula are of a special character and they feel a genuine responsibility to manage the global affairs of humanity. They are most certainly better equipped than heads of state to perform this function, and so they compose and orchestrate world events instead of merely participating in their unfolding.

"Over time, this role has made them very responsible and even paternalistic to humanity as a whole. They're not motivated by greed, as are many others within the Incunabula and the broader Triad of Power, but they earnestly desire to save the planet. They are like captains of a ship that know where the dangers lie in the waters below and steer quietly away because they do not want to go down with the ship."

Sarah: "Okay, when you say these planners are anonymous, they must have names and identities, right?"

Dr. Neruda: "No. They operate outside of our system. They cannot be tracked or identified. If they were to be hit by a car and sent to a hospital, they would have diplomatic papers and immunity. They would not have any record of existence outside of this. And even if their identity were researched, it would lead to a fabricated identity."

Sarah: "What about family and relatives? I assume they were born into families weren't they?"

Dr. Neruda: "Yes, they are human if that's what you're implying. In most cases they're groomed for their positions from an early age. When they reach their early twenties they're typically brought into a direct mentorship with one of the Incunabula planners and a very specific succession process is begun, which usually lasts for about ten years. When the person is in his mid-twenties his loyalty is tested in every conceivable manner over the next five years. If he passes these tests, he is allowed to preview the inner workings of the Incunabula. For most, this is near their thirty-third birthday.

"At this point, a new identity is transferred to the person and they die—quite literally—so far as their family and friends are concerned. These deaths are arranged as covers for their new identities and usually involve drowning or a fire accident, where physical evidence is minimal. Prior to their arranged death, insurance policies, if they exist, are cancelled to ensure minimal investigation, and usually the death is staged during a trip to a specific third-world country where police investigators are more easily controlled.

"After their death event, the new planner is inducted in a secret ceremony that I do not have details of. This inner circle becomes the surrogate family for the new planner, and as they develop in their skills, insights, intuition, and knowledge base, they develop a very protective sensibility to the longstanding goals and objectives of the Incunabula."

Sarah: "Okay, but don't they ultimately get married and have children? How do they keep all of this separate? I mean how do you go to work during the day and plan the future of the world and then come home to dinner with the wife and kids?"

Dr. Neruda: "The planners are not married. It's frowned on by the Incunabula. It is one of the tests I mentioned that they undergo in their mid-twenties."

Sarah: "So it's a priesthood?"

Dr. Neruda: "Not at all. No one is asked to be celibate, but the role of the planner is all consuming. It requires minimal distractions and commitments outside of their role as planners. It's a sacrifice and it heightens loyalty within the circle of planners."

Sarah: "How do they find future planners if they don't have children?"

Dr. Neruda: "There are only five to eight planners at any one time within the Incunabula. Five is the core number, but there are usually two or three in training as well, but these do not have voting powers. I mention this because it is a very small number. Now, as to your question, candidates are identified early one—usually when the person is a teenager."

Sarah: "Is this as a result of them doing something noteworthy or does it result from something else?"

Dr. Neruda: "They are, with rare exception, identified as a result of their genetics."

Sarah: "How is this done?"

Dr. Neruda: "It's a result of extensive tracking of lineages and genetic traits—including mutations. This is something that is well understood by the Incunabula, and is given a significant amount of time and investment. Genetic candidates are identified and observed over a period of about three years before any contact is made."

Sarah: "How many, at any one time, are being tracked?"

Dr. Neruda: "About fifty in number, but out of every generation only two or three are chosen."

Sarah: "And those that aren't chosen don't even know they were passed over?"

Dr. Neruda: "Yes, that's correct."

Sarah: "How did the planners come about? I mean, how did they rise to leadership?"

Dr. Neruda: "The Incunabula came to its power as a result of the inefficiencies of the intelligence community to gather information and position its strategic value relative to the long-term crises that were forming on the horizon as they pertained to the global economy.

"Shortly after the Second World War, many nations, including the United States, restructured or initiated their intelligence organizations—particularly as it related to foreign policy intelligence gathering.

"However, these organizations were still locked into the cold war mentality and didn't formally share intelligence as a result. The Incunabula arose out of a need to consolidate global intelligence as the best means to strategically maneuver the nation states to a unified platform of commerce."

Sarah: "So it was less about saving the world than it was about making money, at least initially?"

Dr. Neruda: "Yes."

Sarah: "But how did it all start? I mean who decided it would be a good idea to create an organization that shared intelligence?"

Dr. Neruda: "If I gave you his name, it wouldn't mean anything to you. I assure you his name is not recorded in any directory or reference material you could research."

Sarah: "But there was only one person that started this organization?"

Dr. Neruda: "No. There were five men that started it, but one sparked the vision."

Sarah: "As you're talking I can't help but think that these planners sound a lot like the Hollywood portrayal of the antichrist. I mean don't they wield a god-like power? And yet I haven't heard you say anything about a religious or spiritual connection."

Dr. Neruda: "I think the power they wield is directed at the survival of humanity. They're not evil in the sense that they're intent on destroying earth or humanity. They're trying to guide humanity to new systems before the old systems decay and create the conditions that could bring annihilation to a substantial percentage of the species.

"The choices of a fragmented state leadership or anarchy are not suitable systems for modern, civilized man. They invariably lead to imbalance and an inability to move from the old system to the new system. Before the advent of long-range missile technology, nuclear, biological and chemical weapons, this migration of the human race from one system to another was not as critical. But the chasm that exists between systems as complex as economies and energy, and in light of modern weapon's technology, the Incunabula serve a vital role."

Sarah: "Do the planners believe in God?"

Dr. Neruda: "I presume they believe in a higher power. Perhaps they don't call it God because of the religious overtones contained in that word, but they certainly are aware of the unification force because Fifteen has acquainted the present generation of planners with the LERM technology."

Sarah: "That's interesting. So they've all seen LERM and know how it works?"

Dr. Neruda: "Yes, to your first question, but I don't believe they understand how it works at the micro-factual level."

Sarah: "When someone—like an Incunabula planner—interacts with LERM, assuming he didn't believe in God beforehand… in other words he's an atheist… does it convert him?"

Dr. Neruda: "Again, it depends on the definition of God. If they don't believe in God as defined by a certain religion, and then experience LERM, they will not be persuaded by LERM to believe in the religious version of God."

Sarah: "I think I followed your explanation, but what I mean is different. Assume they didn't believe in any higher power, that the universe is a big mechanical formation that became the way it did by some evolutionary quirk. Would someone of this mindset become a believer that there's a force orchestrating things—even if you don't choose to call it God?"

Dr. Neruda: "Everyone who has undertaken the LERM experience concludes that a unifying intelligence pervades the universe in every measurable dimension, and that this intelligence is both personal and universal simultaneously, and because of this feature, it is absolute, unique, singular.

"It's a life changing experience even if you already believe in God. You are converted, as you put it, no matter how strong or weak your previous beliefs in God were."

Sarah: "It's too bad you didn't bring this technology with you when you defected… I'd love to experience this.

"So, back to the Incunabula for a moment, it would make me feel better if I knew they believed in God, and you're saying they do. Right?"

Dr. Neruda: "They believe in this unifying intelligence that I spoke of, and I suspect that if you asked them, they would tell you that they're guided and perhaps even inspired by this intelligent force. I don't know if they would call it God or some other name. But I trust they are believers in what some would call the unification force."

Sarah: "But it's not like a religion to them?"

Dr. Neruda: "That's correct. I know of nothing that would suggest that the Incunabula planners follow a specified religion or desire to start one for that matter."

Sarah: "I don't know why I'm asking all these questions tonight, but it's fascinating to hear more details about the Incunabula. I find it an irresistible topic.
"How is it that you know so much about such a secretive organization?"

Dr. Neruda: "As I mentioned previously, the ACIO is a major contractor with the Incunabula and receives funding and support from them, including shared intelligence and mutual protection. As a result of this longstanding relationship, directors at the ACIO have considerable insight into the organization. Fifteen is not a planner, but is held in very high esteem by the planners and meets with them perhaps once or twice a year.
"Fifteen is well aware of the objectives of the planners, and he shares his insights with members of the Labyrinth Group. We also discuss how the Incunabula's plans might bear on our own. The Incunabula is a factor in the ACIO plans, but they don't dominate its agenda."

Sarah: "How much do the Incunabula know about the WingMakers and the Ancient Arrow site?"

Dr. Neruda: "Very little, as far as I know. Fifteen begrudgingly provides some information to his direct agency supervisor, but the NSA is not aware of the Ancient Arrow site. There are two operatives within the NSA that are aware of the original artifact that was found, but Fifteen placed the existence of this artifact in question due to its self-destruction."

Sarah: "I assume from your response that whatever is shared with the NSA, at least in the case of the ACIO, it is shared with the Incunabula planners."

Dr. Neruda: "No. There are information filters that reduce clutter. Only certain information, as deemed necessary by Fifteen, is forwarded up the command chain to the Incunabula planners."

Sarah: "The WingMakers are understood to be a force to be reckoned with, correct?"

Dr. Neruda: "Do you mean by the Incunabula planners?"

Sarah: "Yes."

Dr. Neruda: "The planners know about the Central Race and the legend pertaining to their existence. There are several important references to them in various books and prophecy, so even if the ACIO didn't share anything of their discovery in New Mexico, the Incunabula—especially its planners—are well aware of the Central Race."

Sarah: "Why did Fifteen choose not to share the Ancient Arrow discovery with either the NSA or the Incunabula?"

Dr. Neruda: "Fifteen designed the Labyrinth Group largely for security reasons. Information that pertains to BST is held in the highest secrecy. As I mentioned earlier, Fifteen was hopeful that the Ancient Arrow site, and the other related sites, would somehow accelerate the successful deployment of BST.

"It's a simple matter of not wanting to alert the Incunabula, or the NSA for that matter, to the technology prowess of the Labyrinth Group. If they knew what the Labyrinth Group had in terms of technology, the planners would want to have detailed knowledge of this technology, and Fifteen doesn't trust anyone outside his directors with this knowledge."

Sarah: "The part that I find bewildering in all of this is that you have all of this knowledge about the universe, extraterrestrials, global plans, and futuristic technologies, and because you have this knowledge you're essentially a prisoner now."

Dr. Neruda: "I prefer *conscientious defector*."

Sarah: "Whatever you call it, you've got to be a little paranoid about the remote viewing capabilities of the ACIO and their various technologies. How can you outrun the ACIO or the Incunabula if they're anywhere as powerful as you say they are?"

Dr. Neruda: "I don't know that I can evade them. I don't feel invincible or vulnerable. I'm simply operating on a moment-to-moment basis, trying my best to transfer what I know so you can help me publish this information.

"It's never been done before—to defect from the ACIO. I know Fifteen is searching for me, I can actually feel this."

Sarah: "You mean you can feel when they use their remote viewing technology?"

Dr. Neruda: "Yes."

Sarah: "How often have you detected this since you left?"

Dr. Neruda: "I'd prefer not to say how many instances, but I'm aware of each incident."

Sarah: "Have you ever felt this during our interview?"

Dr. Neruda: "No. I would stop the interview if this were the case."

Sarah: "How would this help?"

Dr. Neruda: "I would prefer that they not hear our conversation—even its general tone."

Sarah: "Is this why we meet at the times we do?"

[Note: Our meetings were always in a different place, late at night, and they were often outdoors in nondescript places. This was the case in this fourth interview.]

Dr. Neruda: "Yes."

Sarah: "So how do you protect yourself and me?"

Dr. Neruda: "By meeting at odd hours and changing locations, at least until you can get these interviews published on the Internet."

Sarah: "How will this help you exactly? I know we've had this discussion before, but I still don't understand how this information will help you if it gets into the public domain. It seems to me that it would only anger them."

Dr. Neruda: "They won't be pleased at this disclosure—there's no doubt in this. However, it will not touch them in any significant way because very few in power will believe what I share with you, assuming they even read it."

Sarah: "And why is this?"

Dr. Neruda: "They are totally consumed in their own agendas and personal dramas. The information I'm disclosing defies categorization. It ranges from poetry to physics, from esoteric philosophy to the conspiratorial forces within MIC (the Military Industrial Complex). And because it defies categorization, it will be difficult to critique and analyze. Most will consider it an interesting piece of entertainment and leave it at that.

"Also, and more importantly, there's a real feeling of acceptance because the intelligentsia and the political body of dissent don't feel equipped to stop what is presumed to be the inevitable. There are those within both of these groups that have a general awareness of what is emerging, but feel completely powerless to change it, and there is a sense of fate that accompanies their silence.

"The ones that will find it most disturbing are the planners within the Incunabula, and Fifteen himself, and not because politicians or the media will be stepping into their arena, but because they don't want their secrets revealed to their followers or, in the case of Fifteen, to the planners of the Incunabula or his contacts at the NSA."

Sarah: "So this is a purpose of these disclosures—to infuriate the Incunabula planners and your boss?"

Dr. Neruda: "No. I don't have any vested interest in making their lives more difficult. It's simply a result of my candid disclosure that they will undergo the resulting pressures from their constituents. This is the only thing that they'll find unpleasant in this whole disclosure. Once the information is out I will be less an interest, other than for pure analysis."

Sarah: "Pure analysis?"

Dr. Neruda: "What I mean is that the ACIO—Fifteen in particular—will want to analyze what went wrong in their security system to ensure that another defection will not take place. There's always the lurking fear that one successful defection would encourage others. If they captured me, they would be able to do a more thorough analysis on the psychological state, precipitating factors, methods of evasion, and so on."

Sarah: "You've talked before about the website. What is it that you want to achieve with this?"

Dr. Neruda: "To simply make available what the WingMakers have left behind. It will not threaten the ACIO or the Incunabula. It would be impossible to do so, and they know that I understand this. I can only cause a temporary embarrassment at best, but they can manage their way through that.
    "As I've said from the beginning, I wanted to share this information from the Ancient Arrow site and any subsequent sites that I can."

Sarah: "Any subsequent sites? Are you planning to find additional sites?"

Dr. Neruda: "I believe there are seven sites on earth. I also believe they can be found."

Sarah: "How, exactly?"

Dr. Neruda: "I can't disclose this."

Sarah: "Have you found something within the Ancient Arrow artifacts that gives you directions?"

Dr. Neruda: "Again, I don't want to disclose the details of this."

Sarah: "Okay. Since we landed on the topic of the artifacts, I'm reminded that in our last session you mentioned that you'd like us to talk about the artifacts from the Ancient Arrow site. This might be a good time to do so. Where would you like to begin?"

Dr. Neruda: "One of the most interesting artifacts was the original homing device."

Sarah: "This is the one found by the students at the University of New Mexico?"

Dr. Neruda: "Yes. It was enigmatic in all respects."

Sarah: "Give me some examples."

Dr. Neruda: "When it was first discovered, it was laying on top of the ground as if it had been placed there. This was not a buried object—as it should have been. It was left in the open, albeit in a very non-descript section of northern New Mexico. When the students handled it, it immediately induced vivid hallucinations, which they couldn't understand."

Sarah: "What kind of hallucinations?"

Dr. Neruda: "They saw images of a cave-like structure. It later turned out to be the Ancient Arrow site, but of course they didn't know what it was, and were afraid of it because they linked the hallucinations to touching the object. So they wrapped the object up in a jacket, stuck it in their backpack, and took it to a professor at the University, who examined it. We discovered it within hours afterwards and dispatched a team to secure the artifact."

Sarah: "How exactly did you find out about the artifact? I assume the ACIO isn't listed in the phone directory."

Dr. Neruda: "There are certain keywords that are monitored in e-mail and phone communications—especially within academia. The ACIO simply taps into this technology that was developed by the NSA, and can intercept e-mails and phone calls anywhere in the world that relate to key words that it monitors."

Sarah: "Like Alien or Extraterrestrial?"

Dr. Neruda: "Yes. It actually works a little differently because the ACIO can define how many characters—in the case of e-mail, or how much time—in the case of a phone conversation—it wants to monitor on either side of the key word, and then extracts entire sentences or even paragraphs in an effort to verify context. It also correlates this to the e-mail's IP address or phone number to a credibility index. If all of these variables meet a specified level, the communication event is relayed to analysts at the ACIO who then perform more invasive techniques to ensure context and content are matched and verified. All of these steps can take place in a matter of an hour or two."

Sarah: "And once you have this information verified you swoop in and take possession of whatever you want?"

Dr. Neruda: "We have uncovered our most important discoveries in this very manner since this system was activated, and the ACIO operates differently depending on the situation. In this case, operatives were dispatched to the professor's office posing as NSA agents in search of a missing experimental weapon. It was believed by the professor to be in his own best interest to release the object without delay since the artifact was deemed to be imminently dangerous."

Sarah: "I'm surprised. Didn't he wonder how you knew he had it?"

Dr. Neruda: "I'm sure he did, but there's an element of shock that the operatives make use of and they're also highly skilled in the use of mind control. I'm sure he was very cooperative. The artifact was secured without any major objection by the professor or the University."

Sarah: "If I contacted the University of New Mexico would I be able to confirm that this occurred?"

Dr. Neruda: "No. Every event of this kind is com-cleared, which is an ACIO term, meaning contracts are signed and all communications are monitored for one year to ensure compliance."

Sarah: "So they signed contracts and won't talk because of a piece of paper? That seems a bit outlandish."

Dr. Neruda: "Do you know the penalty for treason?"

Sarah: "No, I mean I understand it's not a good thing and all, but I just find it a little strange that someone like a learned professor would be intimidated by a signed contract. What about the students that originally found it, are they also com-cleared?"

Dr. Neruda: "Yes."

Sarah: "Okay, back to the artifact. What happened when you retrieved it? What was your role specifically?"

Dr. Neruda: "I was asked to lead a team to assess the artifact using our internal Sanitaire process."

Sarah: "What's this process do?"

Dr. Neruda: "Whenever an extraterrestrial artifact is recovered, it's initially put through the Sanitaire process, or what we sometimes referred to as the 'I-steps', which includes four stages of analysis. The first is Inspection where we examine the object's exterior and map its exterior features in our computer. The next is Inference, which is the stage where we take the results of stage one and compute the probable applications of the object. The third stage is Intervention, which is related to any issues that pertain to the defense or security mode of the object. And the last stage is Invasion, which simply means we try to access the inner workings of the object and find out how it operates."

Sarah: "How difficult was it to go through this four-step process with this artifact?"

Dr. Neruda: "It was one of the most difficult we had ever examined."

Sarah: "Why?"

Dr. Neruda: "It was designed for a very specific purpose and unless it was used for this purpose, it was completely impenetrable to our examinations."

Sarah: "Didn't the hallucinations affect you?"

Dr. Neruda: "We knew of the hallucinations reported by the students who recovered the artifact, but we didn't find any evidence of this at all in our labs. We assumed the students were imagining this due to the unusual nature of the artifact.

"It wasn't until later that we discovered that the very subtle markings on the exterior of the object were actually three dimensional topographical maps. Once we overlaid these to real maps of the area in which the object was found, we uncovered its real purpose, which was a homing beacon.

"The hallucinations were site specific, which is to say that there was a proximity effect encoded within the artifact that caused it to operate when two conditions were present. First, the object needed to be within the geographical range of its map coordinates—as etched on its casing—and two, it needed to be held in a human's hands in order for its guidance system to activate."

Sarah: "And by guidance system you're talking about the hallucinations?"

Dr. Neruda: "Yes."

Sarah: "And throughout this whole process you didn't know where this artifact came from, right?"

Dr. Neruda: "We knew it was extraterrestrial and we knew it was situated."

Sarah: "What do you mean by situated?"

Dr. Neruda: "That it was placed there to be found."

Sarah: "Who do you think did this?"

Dr. Neruda: "Representatives of the Central Race."

Sarah: "So what happened next after you realized it was a homing beacon?"

Dr. Neruda: "A team was dispatched to the area and we essentially followed the device to the interior structure of the Ancient Arrow site, which you're already aware of."

Sarah: "You said earlier that this artifact was the most amazing of the entire find. If it was simply a homing device, then the other artifacts I assume were fairly mundane."

Dr. Neruda: "To be more accurate, I can't say it was the most interesting since

I defected before all the other artifacts were sent through the I-Steps process, but it was a very advanced technology and one of the most enigmatic we had come across in quite a while.

"For example, once our team came within a certain distance of the site, the artifact animated under some undetermined energy source and scanned our group. It was literally reading our bodies and minds, presumably to determine if we were suitable to discover the site."

Sarah: "And if you weren't suitable?"

Dr. Neruda: "It was never discussed, but I think everyone assumed it would probably have destroyed the site and all those present at the time of the scanning. As it was, it only destroyed itself."

Sarah: "And you had no idea that it was capable of these feats when you examined it?"

Dr. Neruda: "None whatsoever. Its casing was resistant to all of our invasive analyses. It was a real source of frustration. In fact, the artifact in the twenty-third chamber was similarly vexing and required significantly more resources to complete the I-Steps process."

Sarah: "Are these the only two artifacts from the site that you've completed the I-Steps process?"

Dr. Neruda: "Yes, prior to my defection. But there were artifacts in every chamber, although the one discovered in chamber twenty-three seemed the most important."

Sarah: "And why was that?"

Dr. Neruda: "Remember that I described the interior of the site as a helix shaped tunnel system?"

Sarah: "Yes."

Dr. Neruda: "The uppermost chamber was the twenty-third chamber and in it was the optical disc. While the other chambers held artifacts similar in size and composition to the homing artifact, the artifact in the twenty-third chamber was an optical disc that had a degree of familiarity to it, and we considered it the key to the entire site."

Sarah: "Because it was so different from the other artifacts?"

Dr. Neruda: "Yes. It was also the highest chamber in the formation and it was unique in its structure in that it was the only chamber that was unfinished."

Sarah: "I understand that all the information you showed me came from the disc, and I know you've explained in some detail about how you were able to decode the information, but you've alluded tonight that something within this site points to the location of six other sites. Can you elaborate on this at all?"

Dr. Neruda: "There's nothing in this information that points to the location of the other six sites. However, I believe there is, encoded within this information, location markers to the next site."

Sarah: "You mean the sites are supposed to be discovered in a specific order one at a time?"

Dr. Neruda: "I believe so."

Sarah: "Can you give me some hints as to where the next site is, based on your analysis?"

Dr. Neruda: "If I gave you some information, you would need to promise that this interview would not be released until I contacted you and confirmed it was okay to do so. Would you agree with this?"

Sarah: "Certainly. I would honor anything you asked."

Dr. Neruda: "There is an ancient temple just outside of the city of Cusco, Peru called Sacsayhuaman. It is somewhere near this temple that the next site will be found."

Sarah: "And do you know where exactly, or are you simply saying near to be evasive."

Dr. Neruda: "No, I believe I know the exact coordinates, but this detail I won't disclose."

Sarah: "This is your homeland isn't it?"

Dr. Neruda: "Yes, I grew up not too far from this area."

Sarah: "Have you been to this site before?"

Dr. Neruda: "No, but I'm somewhat familiar with the city of Cusco."

Sarah: "This question may seem to come out of left field, and I'd understand if you don't want to answer it, but why do you think the Central Race would design a defensive system upon earth and then leave its discovery and activation to an organization like the ACIO?"

Dr. Neruda: "I don't think it was left in the hands of the ACIO to find and activate these sites."

Sarah: "You, then?"

Dr. Neruda: "I'm not able to say at this time."

Sarah: "But you're certainly an important part of this aren't you?"

Dr. Neruda: "I hope so."

Sarah: "Okay, here's another left curve.

"Why are five men—the Incunabula planners—allowed to control the destiny of humanity? I mean it's only five men and we're five billion world citizens. No one elected these guys, and virtually no one knows who these guys are, what their plans are, capabilities, insights, or even if they truly have our best interests at heart.

"After hearing your story tonight, I'm left with this sense of indignation that five guys—no matter how well intentioned—are deciding the fate of humanity and no one knows who they are!

"At least with politicians I can see them, hear them talk on television, and get to know their unique personalities. There's comfort in this. Whether I believe them all the time, well, that's a different story, but most of the ones I've voted for I think are good and honorable people."

Dr. Neruda: "When you ask the question, 'allowed' to run the world, to whom are you referring?"

Sarah: "Doesn't the Central Race have something to say about this? After all, as you mentioned the other night, all of these seven ancient sites are part of a defensive weapon designed to protect the earth. They also placed this homing device in clear sight for the ACIO to uncover, which proves they're interacting with us in our present time. Wouldn't the Central Race need to allow these planners to have such authority over humanity's destiny?"

Dr. Neruda: "Let me try to answer your question this way.

"Presidents, senators, members of congress, governors, presidential cabinets and military leaders, all ebb and flow, which is to say, they have their influence for a period of years, and then they move aside for others to take their place. Their agendas express short-term power to pass new legislation, appoint new judges, or amend laws. They are so focused on the politics of the near-term that they lose sight of the importance of the long term.

"The Incunabula planners have the safety of permanence and place their whole focus on the long-term objectives of humanity. This is the nature of the Incunabula. They bring continuity to the major issues of our time and the times to come for the next three generations. They operate in this realm to ensure they are not influenced by the short-term goals of special interests.

"As to your question about who 'allows' them to perform this function, I'd have to say that no one does. No one has control or authority over the planners, no more than anyone has control or authority over Fifteen or the Labyrinth Group."

Sarah: "What about the Central Race, though? Doesn't it stand to reason that they know about these planners and watch them? I thought you said earlier that this unification force, or God, advises them or something like that. Didn't you make this comment?"

Dr. Neruda: "What I meant is that the Incunabula planners believe in this force that unifies all sentient life throughout time and space. They believe very strongly in their personal destinies or they would never have been placed in the position of a planner. It is a very esteemed position despite its anonymity.

"I have no doubt that the Central Race is aware of the Incunabula planners and perhaps there is even some influence or exchange. I don't know. As I said before, my knowledge of the planners is based exclusively on the reports from Fifteen."

Sarah: "So it's possible that Fifteen made all of this up?"

Dr. Neruda: "You mean about the planners?"

Sarah: "Isn't it possible?"

Dr. Neruda: "No. But it's possible that his perception is not completely accurate, though I doubt it. Fifteen's ability to grasp the character of someone is uncanny. He understands human psychology better than those writing the textbooks. I think it would be impossible for the planners to pull the wool over his eyes without him being aware of it."

Sarah: "But you said you never met these planners—only Fifteen has…"

Dr. Neruda: "I understand your concern about the validity of this. If I could give you names to check out, or some other form of proof, I would. These organizations exist right up to the Incunabula, and they can be traced and researched. Certainly many journalists and researchers have done so regarding Freemasonry or Skull and Bones, and some with good success. But they never look at the broader order and what organization manages these larger, more abstract forces that make up the Triad of Power."

Sarah: "But why?"

Dr. Neruda: "There's nothing to drill into. There's no research traction. The organization is purposely abstract and amorphous."

Sarah: "But leaders like Clinton and Blair, aren't they really pulling the strings? How do the planners within the Incunabula have greater power than these leaders who are signing new legislation into law or deciding whether we go to war or not? It just doesn't make sense."

Dr. Neruda: "Everything within a democracy is consensus and the game is designed to shift consensual opinion and fix it on a specific galvanizing target. If there's sufficient resonance with the people, the shift can be manipulated. If there is not, the political will is stymied. Leadership all over the world, unless it's in a country like North Korea, is bound to this certainty, and nations' leaders are generally well schooled to operate within this reality.

"Yes, the world's leaders appear to wield a great deal of power, but it is really aggression – not power. True power is contained in the acts of implementing a plan that is designed to enhance or optimize the position of humanity relative to its environment, and to protect it from formidable threats. The key word is *humanity*, which is an analogue for the collective soul of every person on the planet. It is not defined by ethnicity or geographical boundaries.

"World leaders apply aggression to achieve their agendas, which always include a healthy dose of state greed and self-aggrandizement. The concept of *humanity* is not a critical ingredient in their agenda. Their power, if that's what you want to call it, is a collective will of a small inner circle of political zealots who want to secure the benefits of their power for themselves first, their state second, and their citizens third."

Sarah: "That's a pretty strong condemnation of our political system, assuming I understand you correctly."

Dr. Neruda: "Then I would say you understand me quite well."

Sarah: "So our political leaders lack real power because they're absorbed in state agendas that exclude humanity as a whole?"

Dr. Neruda: "Please understand that I'm not condemning the individual leaders so much as I am the provincial state system, which has been engineered to excite nationalism. The individual leaders assume the identity of the state system, which is largely contrived around the single concept of patriotism."

Sarah: "So now you're saying patriotism is the problem? I'm confused."

Dr. Neruda: "Patriotism is the state catalyst. It is the means by which citizens are stirred to a response. It is also the means by which leaders are directed to respond to issues or threats. Under this singular banner, wars have been prosecuted and aggression veiled. It's the ideal method that the state uses to enjoin its citizens to support its leadership.

"I'm saying that the citizens' identification with the state, or patriotism, is the real stumbling block to effectively deal with the issues of humanity. The individual leaders are simply pawns within this structure that was engineered as a means to colonize the weaker states."

Sarah: "I think my brain can only handle one more question and than I'd like to call it quits for tonight. Okay with you?"

Dr. Neruda: "Yes, whatever you'd like."

Sarah: "In this whole discussion tonight—most of which has been centered on the Incunabula or, maybe more appropriately I should call it the world power structure—I don't hear much about the spiritual implications. It really sounds oddly impersonal and unspiritual, if that's a word. Can you comment on this?"

Dr. Neruda: "What is occurring in our world is a manifestation of how a species migrates from statehood to species-hood. It is a stage within the migration plan. Humans must move from the patriotic, believe-what-I-am-told mentality, and elevate their thinking to encompass and embrace the holistic community of humankind. It will require enormous leadership capacity in order to accomplish the conclusion of this migration, because the world's people will require a watershed event to erase its memory."

Sarah: "Hold on a moment. What do you mean to *erase* its memory?"

Dr. Neruda: "There's a persistent memory in the psyche of humans—particularly the weaker cultures that have been trampled on by nations bent on colonization. These grievous indignations to the weaker nations of the world have left a deep mark on their collective memory. It's vital that this memory be erased or purged in order for humankind to become unified in its governance and fundamental systems.

"This event can be orchestrated or it may occur through natural means, but it's generally agreed that an event must arise that galvanizes the world's people to unite, and in this process, purge the memory of all peoples, but especially those who have been dealt with as victims of colonization."

Sarah: "I know I just said I was only good for one more question, but as a journalist I can't resist this line of thought. Give me some examples of what kind of event you're talking about?"

Dr. Neruda: "The most probable event with global implications is an energy shortage."

Sarah: "This is what you said earlier, but wouldn't an energy shortage only create more friction between the haves and have-nots?"

Dr. Neruda: "If it were managed properly, no. The kind of energy shortage I'm talking about will have devastating effects on every aspect of our world. All infrastructures would be impacted, and the impact would be harsh and persistent. A global body to regulate production and distribution of existing resources, coupled to a well-managed search for alternative, renewable sources would become a necessity of this condition.

"Still behind the scenes, the Incunabula would help to manage this event in such a way as to restore equality to the world's people. It would stand above the special interests and dominant powers, and ensure fairness. This fairness would establish its instrument of global leadership as the preeminent force for globalization, and the memory of all would—metaphorically speaking—be erased."

Sarah: "Is this my answer for where's the spiritual in all of this?"

Dr. Neruda: "No. Admittedly I got sidetracked a bit.

"Also, I want to make the disclaimer that what I'm disclosing is the broad concept, and anyone reading these disclosures in the future, I hope you will bear this in mind. I'm not able, owing to the circumstances and time constraint, to provide a detailed rendering. However, these details do exist and when one has the luxury of studying them, all of what I am disclosing will appear more plausible.

"Now, regarding your question. The spiritual element is very strongly integrated to the whole theme of tonight's discussion. If I were to sum it up, I'd call it the human migration plan. Humankind is evolving on one level, and migrating on another.

"In the instance of its evolution, humans are becoming more advanced technologically speaking with the ability to multiprocess more sophisticated visual, aural, and intellectual data. In other words, the brain system is changing to become more holistic in how it processes information. Computers are a big part of this evolutionary track.

"Humans are also migrating from separation by means of statehood, to unification through globalism. This is a completely different but related track. Humankind is coalescing, even though it may not seem like it because we continue to have wars and conflicts throughout the globe. It's happening in micro-steps."

Sarah: "And the spiritual?"

Dr. Neruda: "Yes, thank you. The spiritual is that these two tracks are leading humankind to something that the WingMakers call the Grand Portal. It is the connection to our human soul, which has been broken into hundreds of pieces and strewn across the globe in the form of different colors, cultures, languages, and geographies, and is now in the process of an unalterable reunion.

"This is the spiritual aspect, and it touches everything in our lives. It penetrates every single atom of our collective existence, imbuing it with a destiny that is yet unseen."

Sarah: "You just mentioned the Grand Portal. What is it?"

Dr. Neruda: "In the glossary found on the optical disc, it talks about this—"

Sarah: "Just so you know I did read the section of the glossary you gave me, but only once, and it didn't stick with me too well. Can you explain it again, please?"

Dr. Neruda: "The Grand Portal, according to the WingMakers, is the indisputable, scientific discovery of the human soul."

Sarah: "Sort of like LERM isn't it?"

Dr. Neruda: "Similar, but LERM is more the demonstration that the unification force exists and interpenetrates all dimensions of existence. It is the proof of spirit, if you will. The human soul remains elusive to our technology."

Sarah: "But you're not saying that soul and spirit are different are you because I was always taught that soul and spirit are essentially one and the same thing."

Dr. Neruda: "Soul, or what the WingMakers refer to as the Wholeness Navigator, is the replica of First Source (God), only compartmentalized into a singular, immortal, and wholly individualized personality. Spirit is more of the connecting force that unifies the individual soul with First Source and all other souls."

Sarah: "I'm not sure I followed that description, but it may be that my mind is saturated right now and nothing you said would get through my thick skull. Anyway, what will be gained by having this discovery… the Grand Portal?"

Dr. Neruda: "Everything that keeps us separate—locked in statehood and provincial concerns—will be obliterated when this undeniable proof is obtained."

Sarah: "Why would the basic nature of man, which has taken hundreds of thousands of years to form, suddenly change when science steps forward and announces that it has proven the existence of soul? It doesn't seem plausible to me."

Dr. Neruda: "According to the WingMakers this is the evolutionary path of the human species, and the discovery of the Grand Portal is the culmination of a global species. It creates the conditions whereby the things that separate us are stripped away, whether they're color, race, form, geography, religion or anything else. We find ourselves staring into the lens of science and we see that all humans are composed of the same inner substance—whatever you choose to call it—and it is this that truly defines us and our capabilities."

Sarah: "So everything we've been talking about tonight… the globalization of humankind culminates in this discovery? Is that what you're saying?"

Dr. Neruda: "Yes."

Sarah: "And the Incunabula planners will be there, waiting to guide us. Is that also part of the plan?"

Dr. Neruda: "I don't know if there'll be a role for the Incunabula in this new world. Perhaps, perhaps not."

Sarah: "If an individual would experience this Grand Portal and establish for themselves that they are composed of a soul—an immortal soul—wouldn't it profoundly change the way in which they live? I mean I'm just starting to think of the ramifications, and they're kind of scary.

"For example, what if someone saw that they don't really die. Wouldn't that change their attitude towards death in such a way that they no longer fear it? Perhaps people would become more reckless and daring, more dangerous."

Dr. Neruda: "Some may. There will undoubtedly be many different reactions, and I don't pretend to know how it will all be managed."

Sarah: "Another thing I find interesting in this whole thing is the role of science versus religion. It seems that religion has tried its best to define soul and failed. Whatever its definitions, they seem to be based entirely on faith, and there's no real consistency in the model. This Grand Portal is a scientific discovery, not a religious one. Correct?"

Dr. Neruda: "Yes."

Sarah: "So science will get a try. What if they fail as well? Maybe there's something so elusive, so hidden in all of this that science does no better. I mean I know some people who can be shown something and they will deny it with all their strength. How do you convince someone who doesn't want to see it?"

Dr. Neruda: "You can think of the Grand Portal as the interface for the consciousness of vertical time. This interface will be discovered sometime in the twenty-first century. I don't know all the details. I don't know how it will impact on the individual. You may be right; some will accept it and some will not. I only know it is part of the destiny that humankind is led to achieve."

Sarah: "According to the WingMakers?"

Dr. Neruda: "Yes."

Sarah: "Did you know about this prior to reading the glossary?"

Dr. Neruda: "Do you mean did I know about the existence of the Grand Portal?"

Sarah: "Yes, that, or simply the technology to prove the existence of the human soul. Was it being planned or worked on by the ACIO?"

Dr. Neruda: "No."

Sarah: "Are there any other organizations working on this proof—even now?"

Dr. Neruda: "Not that I know of."

Sarah: "If no one's trying to discover this Grand Portal, who will?"

Dr. Neruda: "That's why I want to get these materials out. The WingMakers materials are designed to activate those souls that are incarnating who will play active roles in the discovery and creation of the Grand Portal—"

Sarah: "Are you saying that souls are incarnating specifically for this purpose?"

Dr. Neruda: "Yes. There are very advanced souls who are incarnating in the next three generations who will design, develop, and employ the Grand Portal. This is the central purpose of the WingMakers materials stored within these seven sites."

Sarah: "I thought you said they were a defensive weapon?"

Dr. Neruda: "That's one role, but there is another as well. And I believe it has to do with the artistic elements. They are encoded. They are catalysts of consciousness. I'm convinced of this based on my own experience."

Sarah: "I've read many of these writings, and listened to the music. I like it, but it hasn't catalyzed anything in me. I certainly don't feel like I want to help design or build the Grand Portal, not that I have the mental capacity to contribute anything of value."

Dr. Neruda: "Perhaps your role is different."

Sarah: "Or I have no role at all. Maybe you have to have the qualities inside you before the materials can activate anything. And in my case, I have this feeling that there's nothing there to awaken.

"Well, as much as I'm tempted to dive into more information about this Grand Portal, I think my mind has reached its full ration for the night. Let's plan to talk more about the Grand Portal in our next interview. Okay?"

Dr. Neruda: "That's fine with me."

Sarah: "Anything you want to say before we sign off?"

Dr. Neruda: "Yes. If you, the reader, wonder how the information I've presented about the Incunabula relates to all of the various conspiracy theories about the New World Order, intelligence community, Illuminati, Freemasonry, and all the other supposed clandestine organizations of the world, I would respectfully ask you to suspend your prior notions about the motivations of these various groups.

"These are not evil minded organizations regardless of how some portray them. Their members have children and families just like you, and they take pleasure and disgust in the very same things as you do. They are humans with all the same weaknesses for vice and greed, but they also have a strong energy to improve the world, it is simply that their definition of what a better world is may differ from yours.

"If your interest is to conjure an antagonist for your amusement, that's your prerogative. But the issues I've related tonight are too serious to be amusing. They are deserving of your attention and discernment. Do your own investigation into the energy supplies of our world. You may come up with different numbers than what I mentioned, but only because the technology of the ACIO is more advanced than the petroleum industry. Nonetheless, you'll see confirmation of this general condition.

"Look at the current events of your time whenever you read this interview. You'll see how this plan is progressing. It may seem to take detours, but the general course is what I've described. It is moving in this direction not out of accident or because of the whims of the world's leaders, you can be sure. It is all part of the orchestration of events that are played out according to the well-designed blueprints of the Incunabula planners.

"You may feel a certain anguish that you're being led to a future not of your choosing, but if you want to have influence, then you need to be educated and aware of the real forces that are defining your future. This is a free-will universe. There is no hierarchy of angelic beings guiding the destiny of earth. There is no ascended master who dictates the pathway to enlightenment for humanity or the individual.

"If you truly want to express and apply your freewill, make it a personal religion to know the facts. Learn how to look behind the stories that are being sold by the media and politicians, and form your own conclusions. Keep your doubt intact about everything you're told from the political stage, especially when you're induced to be patriotic. It is one of the clearest signals to be suspicious of what you're being told.

"When enemies are created—especially new ones, be wary of the motivations of those who claim them to be enemies. Investigate the facts. Look under all the rocks and verify your evidence. Each of you must become investigators and learn the art of research and analytical study if you want to feel more a part of the movement to globalization.

"Your insights and understandings may not change humanity's course one millimeter, but they will change your ability to feel a part of this migration and have a sense of where humanity is moving and why.

"And to those who prefer to strike out on their own path and believe that globalism is pure folly, I can only explain to you that it must happen. It is the outward expression of who we are and it is the natural progression of our species to unify around the inner essence of our identity, instead of the outer façade of our particular nation or religious belief.

"I believe everyone understands this to varying degrees, but it is the methods of this unification that concern people. And I share this concern. If we're collectively informed about the plan and understand the end-goal is something that holds a great promise for humanity, we can pursue this goal with greater velocity and with added confidence that the methods will be in everyone's best interest. This must be our goal.

"And finally, many of you may feel that globalization is a concept of the New World Order and therefore dismiss it as a movement born out of greed and the lust for power. Yes, there are always those who will take advantage of this movement to achieve personal gain, but the reason to become a unified people on this earth is far greater than the personal gains of a few. Remember this as you read your conspiracy stories.

"I'm finished, Sarah. Thank you for your indulgence."

Sarah: "Thank you for your comments."

Index to the Interviews of Dr. Jamisson Neruda

COMMENTARY: CHAMBER CONNECTIONS

In a sense, the tunnel connecting the two chambers is a birth canal, and the twenty-fourth chamber is the baby.[34]

As the novel and Neruda interviews reveal, the WingMakers' Chaco Canyon hidden structure was designed as a single strand of DNA, or one strand of the double helix. Because the DNA molecule contains twenty-three chromosomes, the WingMakers' helix consists of twenty-three chambers. Further, we learned that each chamber contained a painting and an artifact. As enigmatic as the paintings were, the artifacts proved to be even more mysterious. The guess was that these were forms of technology so advanced, that they appeared to be ordinary-looking objects—simply nondescript.

The twenty-third chamber proved to be different. First of all, unlike the smooth surfaces of the other twenty-two chambers, this twenty-third chamber's floor was rough and unfinished, strewn with small rocks and stone debris. The second feature of interest was the artifact. Unlike the others, this one was immediately recognizable, for it appeared to be a media disc of some kind.

The disc was eventually decoded by the Labyrinth Group's supercomputer, ZEMI, and the CD-like disc proved to contain more than eight thousand pages of information that the WingMakers apparently wanted humanity to know about.

It was not until the fourth Neruda interview was released in late 2002 that we learned that there was a secret twenty-fourth chamber built into the Ancient Arrow site four meters behind the antechamber. Once James released the fourth interview, he also revealed the twenty-fourth Chamber Painting at the WingMakers website.

As the fourth interview continues, Dr. Neruda explains that the ZEMI super-computer determined that there was a higher density of symbolism in the twenty-fourth painting than in any of the others. The other interesting feature of this painting is that it is depicted horizontally whereas all the other Chamber Paintings, except the twenty-third, are designed vertically. (It should also be noted that the ten Portal Paintings appearing on the First Source disc are also horizontally oriented.)

This fact strongly hints that the twenty-third and twenty-fourth paintings have a special relationship (as might the ten Portal Paintings). Neruda speculates that because the twenty-fourth chamber can only be accessed through the twenty-third chamber, this means that the twenty-third chromosome—related to sexual reproduction and gender identity in humans—will somehow lead to an as yet undiscovered chromosome related to our spiritual identity. Furthermore, Neruda goes on to explain that the twenty-third chromosome is very susceptible

---

34. The Fouth Interview of Dr. Jamisson Neruda, p. 372

to alteration and therefore its possible mutation might give birth to the twenty-fourth chromosome.

As so often happens with James' materials, Dr. Neruda's discussion of these two chambers and chromosomes leaves us with more questions than answers. We can suggest, however, that the dimensional shift around 2012 could very well be a factor relative to the emerging twenty-fourth chromosome.

The shift, according to James, will be the most profound shift of human consciousness in the history of humanity. For all those engaged in the process of bringing spirit into their lives, this shift and expansion of consciousness will open up new faculties of psychological and spiritual significance. James describes these generally as "a new transparency into wholeness and a new accessibility to our heart's intuitive guidance."[35] This dimensional shift, and what I also like to call "dimensional expansion," will most likely contribute to or be the catalyst for the emergence of a new exploratory energy system that is addressed in the fourth philosophy paper "Beliefs and Their Energy Systems."

In addition to this consciousness shift and expansion, which may very well contribute to the creation or activation of the twenty-fourth chromosome, the catalytic triggers embedded in James' materials (writings, music, imagery) are explicitly designed to alter our DNA.

The topic of this genetic triggering is discussed in the first interview of Dr. Neruda:

> "When we had translated the first thirty pages of text from the optical disc, we learned some interesting things about the WingMakers and their philosophy. Namely, that they claimed that the three-dimensional five-sensory domain that humans have adjusted to, is the reason we are only using a fractional portion of our intelligence. They claimed that the time capsule would be the bridge from the three-dimensional five-sensory domain to the multidimensional seven-sensory domain.
>
> "In my opinion, they were saying that in order to apply BST, the traveler needed to operate from the multidimensional seven-sensory domain. Otherwise, BST was the proverbial camel through the eye of the needle... or in other words... impossible..." [36]

As you may recall, BST, or Blank Slate Technology is the secret time travel project of Fifteen and the Labyrinth Group. Also, the so-called "time capsule" is the helix-shaped Ancient Arrow site.

This quotation reinforces the fundamental idea discussed in the other writings of James and the teachings of Lyricus translated by him. Remember, the central scientific discipline of Lyricus is genetics and we know that the primary mission of the LTO is the discovery of the Grand Portal. Further we read the following:

35. When-Which-How Practice: A Guide for Everyday Use, Foreword, p.5, eventtemples.com
36. The First Interview of Dr. Jamisson Neruda, p. 263-264

> "Within our genetic substrate is the inborn structure that will
> ultimately deliver our species to the central universe as a perfected
> species. The WingMakers have encoded this within our DNA, and set
> forth the natural and artificial trigger points that cause our genetic
> structures to alter and adapt. In this process, it activates parts of our
> nervous system that feed the brain with a much richer stream of data
> from our five senses and two additional senses that we have yet to
> consciously activate." [37]

Setting aside the ultimate perfection of the species, the more immediate and
foundational step to this ultimate perfection is the discovery of the Grand Portal.
We can attempt some reading between the lines of these two extracts and consider
that the Ancient Arrow site is a metaphor for the discovery of the Grand Portal. We
might also consider the concept of BST (time travel) as a hint toward one aspect of
the Grand Portal. Perhaps the Grand Portal is not only the revelation that humanity
is one collective organism and that this organism somehow extends throughout
multiple dimensions of the multiverse, but that the Grand Portal is also a means of
traveling through time.

When we think more deeply about the story that James has delivered to us,
the emphasis he places on time travel could very well be a signpost pointing to the
timeless nature of the higher dimensions of the galaxies themselves. If so, in the
post Grand Portal era we may not only be exploring the physical and non-physical
dimensions of human planetary populations across the billions of galaxies in the
multiverse, but also have access to the past and future, as well as the present.

Tying this all together is James' assertion that the twenty-fourth chamber is a
key to the Grand Portal. Although the nature and details of this "key" are not yet
known, further examination and pondering of Neruda's discussion of the relation
between chambers twenty-three and twenty-four may yield further insights into
this mystery. Also, remember that the twenty-fourth chamber painting contains the
highest degree of symbolism compared to the other twenty-three paintings. Let's
also keep in mind that the horizontal orientation of the twenty-third and twenty-
fourth paintings strongly hints at their connection.

Additionally, the ten Portal Paintings are also oriented in landscape style. This
connection between these twelve paintings links them in some mysterious way.
The only known clue to the meaning of the Portal Paintings is contained in James'
introduction to the DVD, "Meditations in TimeSpace": "Within these portals are
stored the encoded knowledge of the Central Race—humanity's progenitors,
known also as the WingMakers." [38]

From a strictly symbolic point of view, a horizontal layout suggests breadth,
expansion and distribution. Coupled with James' writing about the Portal Paintings
containing the stored "encoded knowledge of the Central Race," this might mean that

---

37. Ibid., p. 267.
38. www.wingmakers.com/products3.html.

our knowledge of how to attain the Grand Portal will be expanded and distributed to humanity. In addition, this knowledge will come through discoveries and research related to the twenty-third and twenty-fourth chamber paintings that represent the twenty-third chromosome, and leading to the emergence of the twenty-fourth.

Thus, these twelve paintings provide a rich source of contemplation and discussion of the expansion of our DNA, our consciousness, and our sensory equipment, all ultimately leading to the Grand Portal.

SECTION TWO

The WingMakers Chamber Paintings

Dr. Neruda:

"I wish I could take people to the original site so they could stand before each of the twenty-three chambers and witness these wall paintings in person. If you were to do this, you would understand that art can be a portal that transports the soul to a different dimension."

The First Interview of Dr. Jamisson Neruda, p. 287.

Introduction to the WingMakers Chamber Paintings

The continuity of the twenty-three paintings seen as a whole seem to be inviting the consciousness of the observer to quite literally step into the world of theWingMakers. As though they were portals, and I've experienced this myself.[39]

As previously discussed in "Chamber Connections," the Ancient Arrow site consists of twenty-three chambers arranged in a helix pattern, with a twenty-fourth chamber hidden behind the site's antechamber at ground level. We also learned that all twenty-four paintings are depicted in vertical, portrait mode except for chambers twenty-three and twenty-four, which are laid out horizontally or in landscape mode.

We also speculated that the landscape depiction might symbolize expansion and distribution, as the setup suggests moving outward from a specific center. Now we will follow up on this reasoning by suggesting that the portrait mode represents the *grounding* of energies from higher dimensions to our physical dimension. This orientation suggests the descent of energies and/or information onto the physical level where it can be distributed horizontally or onto the level it has reached.

The human genome, according to James, is much more than the physical chromosomes contained in the trillions of cells comprising our physical bodies. The implication being that DNA is multidimensional. If this is indeed the case, then we might say that the densest portion of the human genome is contained in the cells of our physical bodies and the least dense portion emanates from the Entity itself—the "first source" of our Human Instruments. What does this mean in relation to the chamber paintings?

It may possibly mean that these paintings are illustrating the higher dimensional qualities and characteristics of each physical chromosome as it winds its way down through various unknown dimensions into our physical dimension. Following this possibility, we may have to expand our thinking in regard to the paintings and their many symbols; we cannot assume that everything in them is purely physical. Their twenty-two vertical layouts may symbolize the coming down, densification, or decreasing frequency of the chromosomes in their "journey" to the physical plane.

Naturally, nothing is moving down and moving out *spatially*, but rather—*energetically*. Therefore, we are left with the more satisfying idea that the physical chromosomes are manifested end products resulting from a densification and slowing frequency rate of the energetic level of the chromosomes.

This is a good place to see James' explanation of the paintings characteristics:

> The Chamber Paintings, as they're represented on the WingMakers website, are translations of the real paintings. The original works reside within the Tributary Zone near the galactic center of the MilkWay galaxy. The original "paintings" are photonically animated by an advanced technology that permits the art to morph

---
39. The Second Interview of Dr. Jamisson Neruda, p. 299

intelligently as dictated by the music. In other words, music is the engine that animates the painting. The original environment in which the art is stored requires that I, the translator, take a "snapshot" of the painting that best represents the dynamic image statically. These original works are not "classified" by any government organization I assure you. They simply exist in a different dimension and are visible to a different range of senses. The DVD "Meditations in TimeSpace" is an attempt to capture some sense of how the paintings are actually presented in their native environment.[40]

Besides the interesting information James provides about the paintings, he also comments on the questioner's curiosity about secret government involvement with the materials created by James. This most probably stems from the suspicions born from the *Ancient Arrow Project* novel and the Neruda interviews that the WingMakers site is some kind of conspiratorial plot. There is no real basis for any of this distrust and as discussed in the Collected Works of the WingMakers Volume I Introduction, James is best judged by the quality of his work, the years of dedication he has put into the materials, and your own intuitive sense of the integrity of him and the material.

Chamber 15

Also of interest in the above extract is the effect of music on the paintings. This brings to light the interconnectedness of all the materials related to the WingMakers presentation. Later in this introduction, another example of this interlinking appears that relates four particular paintings to the WingMakers poetry. These subtle details are important in that they convey a real sense of the deep, underlying connections of these materials based on sound and light.

It is not the purpose of this introduction to analyze each painting, but we can explore a few points of interest in some paintings.

One instance involves paintings fifteen and twenty. Fifteen appears in portrait mode and there is apparently nothing in it that sets it apart from the other paintings. Chamber Twenty is different from all the other paintings in that it is square and not rectangular. There may be some symbolic reason for this, but whatever it is it's not immediately obvious. One thing we can say is that since the Chamber Twenty painting is square, in terms of orientation, it is neither portrait nor landscape in its depiction.

There is however, a very interesting connection between these two paintings and that is the fact that they can be *joined* to form a larger painting. The only fly in the ointment is that there is no other painting in the WingMakers paintings that completes the composite image. The paintings need to be scaled to fit together and

40. *Collected Works of the WingMakers Vol. II*, Part IV, Sec. Two, Top. Arr. of Qs and As, Ques. 60-S3

they are illustrated below.

Perhaps there is some link between chromosomes fifteen and twenty that is solved by the missing section, but an explanation of these two chromosomes at Internet websites does not reveal any particular connection. Obviously, we can go deeper into this mystery, but for the purpose of this introduction this is enough.

The next example of the multidimensional nature of these paintings comes in the form of an exercise found in the Chamber Four Philosophy paper. The technique is called "Mind-Soul Comprehension."

Chamber 20

For our purposes we only need the following information:

Chamber 15 >

< Chamber 20

- If you observe the *Chamber Two* Painting, using the aforementioned technique, you will learn a *new dimension of time*.
- If you inspect the *Chamber Three* Painting, you will gain knowledge of a *new dimension of inner space*.
- If you study the *Chamber Twelve* Painting, you will discover a *new dimension of energy*.
- If you examine the *Chamber Four* Painting, you will be taught a *new dimension of matter*.[41]

We have already established that the paintings correspond to the chromosomes of the physical body, so what connection might these four chromosomes have with time, inner space, energy and matter? (James refers to these as MEST.) Again, websites devoted to genetics and DNA do not offer any obvious clues.[42] Metaphysically speaking, however, these four chromosomes, at their *energetic level* may very well have to do with the establishment of the Human Instrument in the physical dimensions of time, space, energy and matter.

This is all well and good, but perhaps the real clue to the higher dimensional frequencies of DNA resides in the phrase James uses to describe the exercise—namely *new dimension of inner space* (Chamber Three). Hence, the exercise itself implies that the physical chromosomes are simply endpoints of energetic "strands" covering a spectrum of the multidimensional levels that the DNA components energetically pass through as they emerge onto the microscopic level of the physical plane. These four chamber paintings are illustrated below.

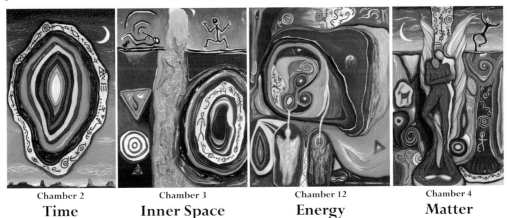

Chamber 2	Chamber 3	Chamber 12	Chamber 4
Time	**Inner Space**	**Energy**	**Matter**

There are many other details we could explore in the chamber paintings, however it's probably best to allow you to examine the paintings for yourself and perform the Mind-Soul exercise to begin your journey of discovery.

Following are comments by James on the paintings. His comments are in response to questions from various individuals.

---

41. "Beliefs and Their Energy Systems," p.660.
42. An article exploring the possible links to the chromosomes can be found in the articles section of our website, www. planetwork.co, entitled "The WingMakers Poetry of Chamber 16."

The imagery used in the Chamber Paintings is not specifically inspired by, nor taken from, the Genetic Mind. There are common symbols, but this is due to the universality and pre-existent state of geometry.[43]

The equivalent of the Ancient Arrow site, within the galactic core, contains three-dimensional art forms that are always in a state of movement. They respond to sound wave pressure, as well as the thoughts of those who are present at the site. There is no method to presently replicate this on earth. Thus, the paintings must be fixed in time and space. I decide this fixed state, so, in this case, I am a "creator". However, I have extensive experience in making these interpretations based on research of color vibrations, human perceptual systems, sophistication of the visual cortex, associative values of form, and methods of catalyzing new receptive fields.[44]

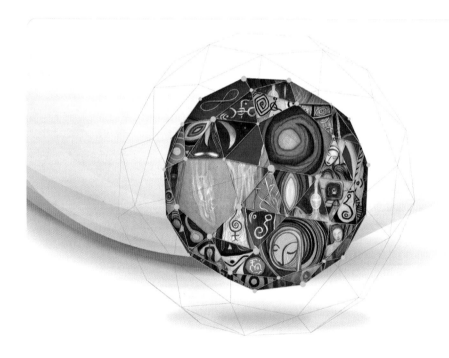

43. *Collected Works of the WingMakers Vol. II*, Part IV, Sec. Two, Top. Arr. of Qs and As, Ques. 64-S3
44. *Collected Works of the WingMakers Vol. II*, Part IV, Sec. Two, Top. Arr. of Qs and As, Ques. 25-S2

The WingMakers Chamber Paintings

Chamber One

I am listening for a sound beyond sound
that stalks the nightland of my dreams,

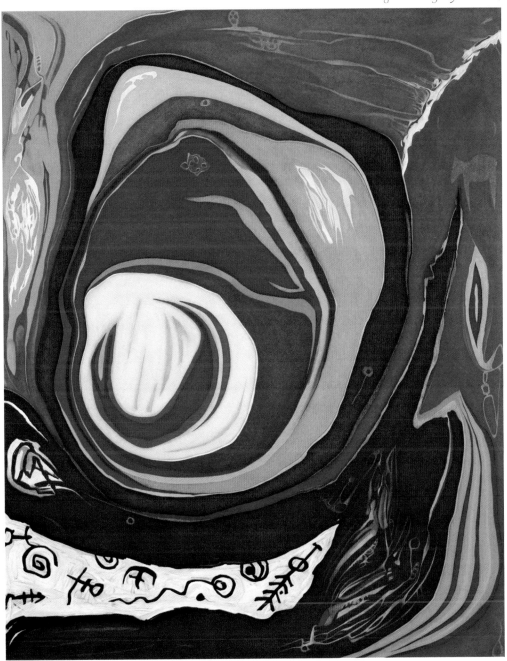

entering rooms of fossil-light
so ancient they are swarmed by truth.

Compare this grain of sand with your galaxy.
This spire of sorrow with your deepest eye.

If my callous mind can see you,
there are no interventions.

Chamber Three

You have mistaken my search as my soul.
Raking through it for clumps of wisdom,
you have found only what I have lost to you.

Held like rootless dreams
I will vanish in your touch.

I will rise like a golden bird of silent wing
graceful as the smoke of a fallen flame.

Chamber five

The dream of flight has invaded somber walls—
life carriers have bounded to the other side.

There they meet the next rung
of the endless ladder, and trade their wings for wisdom's eye.

Perhaps one life is the same as another
only tilted sideways.

Chamber Six

Caught from underneath
by some invisible hand that animates
even the coldest stone of this place.

Chamber Seven

You are my last love,
my final embrace of this world

and all the others that drop their prints at my door
are dimmed by your approaching steps.

...ies escape the writer's hand
...nd pursue me as though I alone held their vigil.

Their very soul
When indeed these stories have never been told

Chamber Nine

In mercy, we are torn apart
into separate worlds

to find ourselves over and over
a thousand times aching for the other half.
To dream of nothing but the One between us.

Open me to the stains
of this land that original sin cannot explain.

Chamber Ten

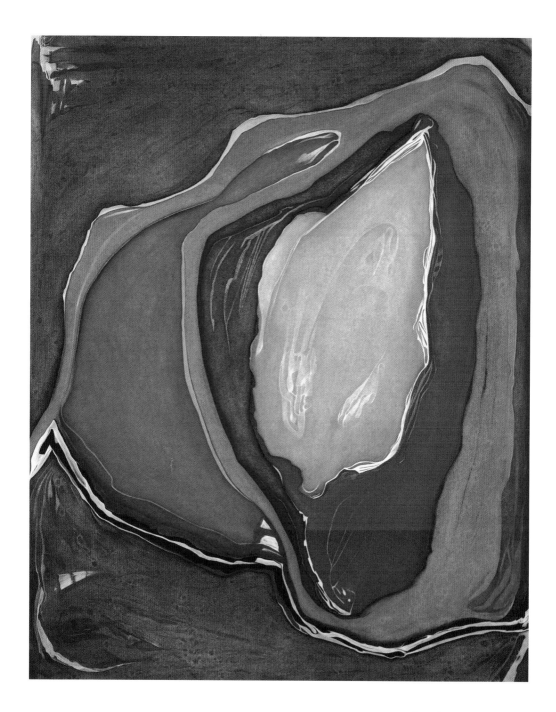

Let these symptoms go
like dead, yellow leaves fumbling
in swift, guiltless currents downstream.

Chamber Eleven

I have seen its ruthless eyes
that always stare,
burrowing their way to the crown I wear.

talking to flowers and gnarled trees
will only move me a step away --

Chamber Twelve

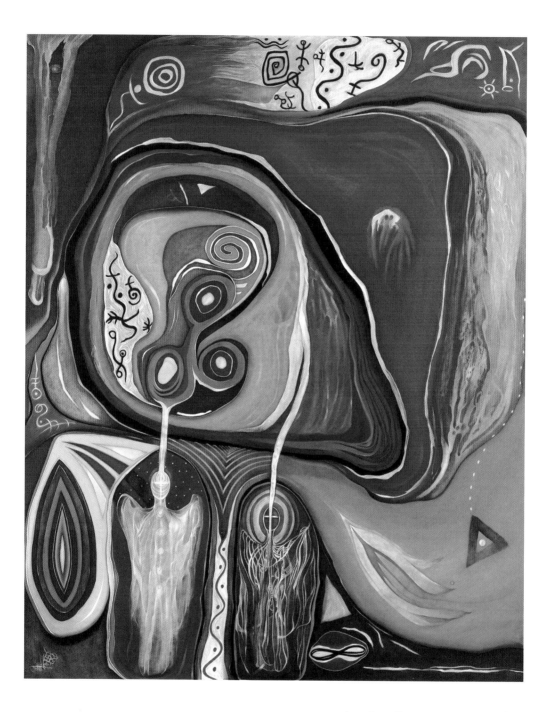

when I really want to press my face
against the windowpane
and watch the WingMakers craft my wings

Chamber Thirteen

For tracks to emerge like dust in a beam of light.

he ancient casts of the empyrean
thstood definition.

Paradise lost to the soundless blanket
of the clearest thought
of the loneliest mind

Chamber fifteen

*Sun walks the roof of the sky
with a turtle's patience.*

*Circling endlessly amidst the black passage
of arrival and retreat.*

I am waiting
for something deep inside
to take my empty hands
and fill them with her face

Chamber Sixteen

so I can know the rehearsals were numbered
and all the splinters
were signals to her heart

Chamber Seventeen

I am lost words echoing in still canyons.
I am a light wave that found itself

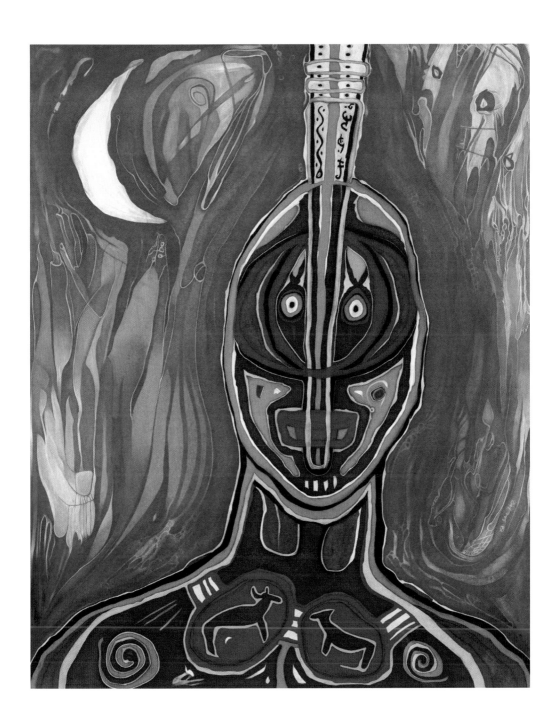

darting to earth unsheathed
seeking cover in human skin

Deep, black solitude enfolding us,
the kind found only in caves

Chamber Eighteen

that have shut out light for the growing of delicate
transparent things

Chamber Nineteen

I know they will come
even though I fumble for my key.
even though my heart is beheaded.

Even though I have only learned division
I remember you
and the light above your door.

Holiness claims my tired eyes
as I return the stare of stars.

Chamber Twenty

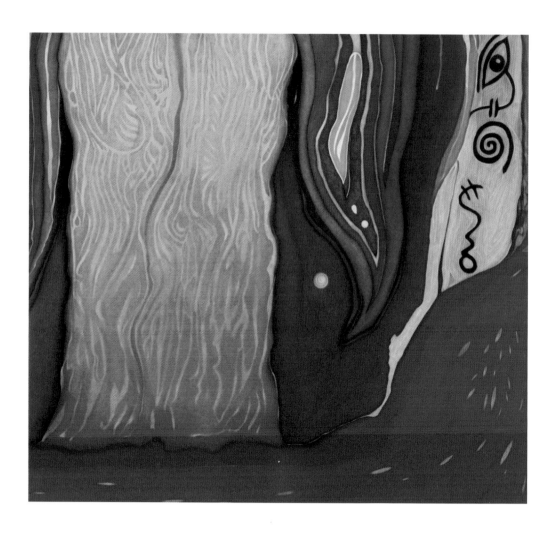

They seem restless, but maybe they're
just ink blots and I'm the one
who's really restless.

Chamber Twenty-One

*Knowing that behind the darkening mist
angels are building shelters for human innocence.*

I visited you last night when you were sleeping with a child's abandon.

Chamber Twenty-Two

Curled so casual in sheets inlaid by your beauty

Perhaps it will be the light
that draws me away

Chamber Twenty-Three

or some sweet surrender that captures me
in its golden nets.

find you, my dearest friends, who are truth — who were all along,

will renew your devotion to a powerful image in a distant mirror.

Chamber Twenty-four

SECTION THREE

The WingMakers Poetry

Dr. Neruda:

"I believe the poetry and the paintings have the strongest connection of all the objects in each of the chambers. I think the paintings illustrate—in some subtle way—the themes represented in the poetry. In some instances, when the painting represents an assemblage of abstract objects, the poetry is also more abstract. When the painting is more illustrative, the poetry seems more like prose."

The Second Interview of Dr. Jamisson Neruda, p. 296.

What is before you

in the form of dimension

veils what is before you in spirit.

To truly approach the divine

you must know the difference

if not in your eyes

then in your heart.

Poem from Hakomi Chambers 7-12 CD

Introduction to the WingMakers Poetry

One day, out of this fleshy cocoon
I will rise like a golden bird of silent wing.[45]

The WingMakers poetry offers another modality of approach to the new psychology of the Sovereign Integral. Poetry, for the most part, taps into our emotions by expressing observations of life through creative metaphors designed to awaken our imaginations and sensitivity to everything around us, including our inner, subjective world. The poetry of the WingMakers does not fail in this regard when certain familiar phrases are used. When it comes to the overall sense of any particular poem, however, neutral and abstract qualities predominate.

There are two poems for each chamber resulting in forty-eight poems. A peculiar aspect of the poems is that they are difficult to pin down to any particular social order. They appear to be deliberately designed to offer a neutral view of human emotions, generally avoiding any connection to a particular and identifiable geographical location, culture or time period.

This abstract and neutral style has the effect of subtly loosening the reader's feelings and thoughts from the mind's pre-defined associations, familiar—and habitual—reactions to words appearing on paper. As the Indian philosopher,

---

45. Chamber Four Poem, "One Day." p.480

Krishnamurti, once said, and I paraphrase, "The word is not the object." Meaning, the full impact of observing a tree is short-circuited by the reaction of the mind, which immediately interferes with the observation by producing past, stored definitions of what a tree is, along with our associations to trees.

Naturally, many of our associations cannot be totally avoided in the neutrality of the WingMakers poetry simply because the words we use everyday must be employed to write the poems. And in many of the poems words appear that can be associated with the familiar things of our lives.

For instance, the Chamber Ten poem "What is Found Here" contains phrases such as "one foot on the curb," "the other on the pavement," "drifting of curtains," "mountain winds," and "juries of the night." Even though these are familiar words to our ears, the poem does not offer a hint as to the location, culture or time related to the existence of the individual expressing their feelings. We don't even know the gender of this person. Granted, this is not necessarily important to the mood of the poem, but it does go to the points of neutrality and the abstract. The Chamber Ten poem appears below:

What is Found Here

What is found here can
never be formed of words.

Pure forces that mingle uncompared.
Like dreams unspoken when first awoken
by a sad light.

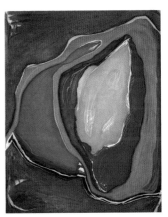

Chamber 10

What is found here
can limp with *one foot on the curb*
and *the other on the pavement*
in some uneven gait
waiting to be hidden in laughter.

What is found here
can open the swift *drifting of curtains*
held in *mountain winds*
when long shadows tumble across like *juries*
of the night.

What is found here
can always be held in glistening eyes.
Turned by silence's tool of patience.
Like feelings harbored for so long
the starward view has been lost.[46]

---

46. Chamber Ten Poem, "What is Found Here." p. 501.

As you can see, the inclusion of these phrases, does not negate the general effect of the neutral, abstract, and even timeless style utilized by Lyricus in some of its resources (e.g. the chamber paintings). The poems, therefore, are quite abstract in their total expression, while often containing familiar words that temporarily re-ground us. It is possible that there is a reason for this. The back-and-forth style—from a neutral and abstract mood, to a specific and familiar word usage—engages the right and left hemispheres of the brain, thus resulting in a whole-brain interface with each poem. Consequently, while reading, we are in a manner of speaking, *spiraling* between hemispheres, creating and activating a fully engaged brain. In a real sense, the use of both sides of the brain describes a dual system of processing the abstract and the specific.

Beyond this dual-brain system, James describes another duality labeled as the heart-mind system. As is described in detail in the EventTemples part of volume II, the heart-mind system is one that does not function to its full capacity in the conditions of our current civilization. Without getting into too much detail, when our hearts express the emotions of gratitude and compassion, they set up a frequency, or vibration that affects the mind and brain, the former a subjective faculty and the latter an objective instrument. So, paralleling this *mind-brain* relationship is the *heart-mind* relationship.

Research conducted at the HeartMath Institute shows that an emphasis, for instance, on the emotions of love, caring, and gratitude reduces mental and bodily stress, consequently affecting not only the *subjective, energetic* heart, but also the *objective physical* heart. Recall that the Chamber One Philosophy "Life Principles of the Sovereign Integral" identifies gratitude as a key factor for inculcating the Sovereign Integral level of consciousness into our lives. This strongly suggests that the implementation of the principles of the Sovereign Integral activates the heart-mind system. Consequently, the WingMakers poetry very likely contributes to the activities of the heart-mind system, while the spiraling nature of the poems themselves contributes to the activation of full brain processing.

Let's now turn to the complementary relationship between the poems and the paintings. In terms of the abstract, the chamber paintings exceed the poems. Thus, in many cases, it is difficult to discern a connection between the word imagery of the poem and the pictorial imagery of the corresponding painting. Despite this abstractness, in many instances, the poems and paintings do reflect one another. Interestingly, this only becomes obvious when one examines a painting in relation to its corresponding poem.

One example of the more obvious connection is found in the chamber four poem "One Day," and its pictorial counterpart. I have italicized the phrases that correspond to the painting.

One Day

One day, *out of this fleshy cocoon*
I will rise like a golden bird of silent wing
graceful as the smoke of a fallen flame.
I will dream no more of places
Hidden—secreted away in heaven's cleft
where the foot leaves no print.

One day, I will walk in gardens holding hands
with my creation and creator.
We will touch one another like lovers torn by death
to say goodbye.
We will lay in one another's arms
until we awaken as one
invisible to the other.

One day, *I will isolate the part of me*
that is always present.
I will dance with it
like moonlight on water.
I will hold it to myself in a longful embrace
that beats perfection
in the hymn of the Songkeeper.

Chamber 4

One day, when I curl away inside myself
I will dream of you
this *flesh-covered-bone of animal.*
I will yearn to know your life again.
I will reach out to you as you
now reach out to me.
Such magic!
Glory to covet the unknown!
That which is
is always reaching for the self
that cheats appearances.
Who dreams itself awake and asleep.
Who knows both sides of the canvas
are painted, awaiting the other
to meld anew.[47]

Another example of correspondences relates to the Chamber Sixteen poem "Nothing Matters." In this instance, the correspondence involves the association of

---

specific words in the poem that relate to a particular painting, and not necessarily any images in the painting, even though there may be some corresponding imagery. I have italicized four key words. Here is the first stanza of that poem.

> *Space* is curved
> so no elevator can slither to its stars.
> *Time* is a spindle of the present
> that spins the past and future away.
> *Energy* is an imperishable force
> so permanence can be felt.
> *Matter* flings itself to the universe,
> perfectly pitiless in its betrayal of soul.[48]

Chamber 16

If you recall, the four words "space," "time," "energy," and "matter" directly relate to the four paintings used in the Mind-Soul Comprehension technique described in the Chamber Four philosophy paper "Beliefs and Their Energy Systems." (James sometimes refers to these four words with the acronym "MEST.")

There are many other examples of the linkages between poem and painting, but these two examples provide us with an initial demonstration of the connections. As a result, the poems provide some clues to the meanings of the more abstract, and even obscure nature of the paintings.

Last but not least, we come to the timeless nature of the poetry, along with the inability to pinpoint a specific spacial location of any given poem. In terms of location, some of the poems imply that they are earth-bound because of the words and phrases employed. Yet, they are abstract enough to leave the door open to uncertainty.

In a real sense, time and place are de-emphasized for two reasons. First, is the WingMakers assertion that humanity is similar in its psychological makeup throughout the universe, and therefore the physical location of any given poem is not relevant. This goes to the point that the human species, scattered throughout many worlds, is essentially and generally the same in its subjective expressions and experiences despite differences in its humanoid features and the location in space of any particular planetary population. Hence, the spaceless nature of human psychology as it interacts with space is generally the same. Naturally, the physical environment plays a role in the psychological reactions and ego-personality development of any given planet. But the psychological strategies and coping mechanisms are roughly the same from planet to planet.

The second point is the time element. Again we find that the poetry is largely devoid of the time factor. This has the effect of putting our individual consciousnesses into neutral relative to time. In other words, the poems put us into a temporary state of timelessness, which is part of the nature of the Sovereign Integral.

---

48. Chamber Sixteen Poem, "Nothing Matters." p.516-517.

The first philosophy paper "Life Principles of the Sovereign Integral" and the EventTemples paper "The Temple of Spiritual Activism" describe the timeless nature of the Sovereign Integral.

> Life initially emerges as an extension of Source Reality, and then, as an individuated energy frequency invested within a form. It vibrates, in its pure, timeless state, precisely the same for all manifestations of life. This is the common ground that all life shares. …It [life] can only be understood in the context of the entity, which is deathless, limitless, timeless, and sovereign.[49]

> The Spiritual Center is the timeless presence of the individuated spirit-consciousness.[50]

In the context of the WingMakers philosophy, the timeless and spaceless nature of the poems is designed to open us up to the Sovereign Integral consciousness. This brings us to the Emotion-Soul Acquisition technique from the fourth philosophy paper "Beliefs and Their Energy Systems." This technique is practiced by reading ten specific poems. Below is an excerpt briefly describing the technique. I have added the chamber painting number in brackets that corresponds to each poem.

> The technique of emotion-soul acquisition is concerned with discerning the emotional voice of a poem, intending that voice to resonate within your soul, and releasing the emotion that arises from the resonance, letting it wander away from you like a wild animal released into its natural habitat.
> There are ten poems within the WingMakers Ancient Arrow site that are designed for the application of this technique. They are:

> Circle - Chamber Eleven
> Forever - Chamber Nine
> One Day - Chamber Four
> Listening - Chamber One
> Afterwards - Chamber Seventeen
> Of this Place - Chamber Six
> Warm Presence - Chamber Twenty-two
> Another Mind Open - Chamber Eight
> Of Luminous Things - Chamber Nine
> Like the Song of Whales - Chamber Seven[51]

This concludes the introduction to the poetry. Once again we have seen the interconnection of the various artistic and philosophical works of the WingMakers

49. "Life Principles of the Sovereign Integral," pp. 627-628
50. *Collected Works of the WingMakers Vol. II*, Part III, Sec. Three, "The Temple of Spiritual Activism".
51. "Beliefs and Their Energy Systems," p. 661.

and the LTO that James has created and adapted for our spiritual growth and consequent preparation for the dimensional shift, and later the Grand Portal. If you spend some time with both the poems and the paintings, you will certainly gain insights into the deeper meanings of them. And in the process, you will also be activating the higher dimensional frequencies of your Human Instrument, enabling it to tap into the higher Sovereign Integral frequencies. Simultaneously you will be initiating the process of psycho-spiritual fusion that will lead to your eventual expression as the Sovereign Integral.

Chamber One Poetry

Listening

I am listening for a sound beyond sound
that stalks the nightland of my dreams,
entering rooms of fossil-light
so ancient they are swarmed by truth.

I am listening for a sound beyond us
that travels the spine's
invisible ladder to the orphic library.
Where rebel books revel in the unremitting light.
Printed in gray, tiny words with quicksand depth
embroidered with such care they
render spirit a ghost, and God,
a telescope turned backwards upon itself
dreaming us awake.

Never-blooming thoughts surround me
like a regatta of crewless ships.
I listen leopard-like,
canting off the quarantine of bodies
sickened by the monsoon of still hearts.
There is certain magic
in the heartbeat which crowds the sound I seek,
but it is still underneath the beating I wish to go.
Underneath the sound of all things
huddled against the tracking dishes
that turn their heads to the sound of stars.

I am listening for a sound unwound,
so vacant it stares straight with the purity to peer
into the black madness of time
sowing visions that oscillate in our wombs
bearing radiant forms as the substrate of our form.

When I look to the compass needle
I see a blade of humility
bent to a force waylaid like wild rain
channeled in sewer pipes.
Running underground

Chamber One Poetry

in concrete canals that quiver,
laughing up at us as though we were lost
in the sky-world with no channel for our ride.

I am listening for a sound
in your voice,
past the scrub terrain of your door
where my ear is listening on the other side.
Beneath your heart where words go awkward
and light consumes the delicate construction of mingled lives.
I can only listen for the sound I know is there,
glittering in that unpronounceable, stateless state
quarried of limbs so innocent

they mend the flesh of hearts.

Compassion

Angels must be confused by war.
Both sides praying for protection,
yet someone always gets hurt.
Someone dies.
Someone cries so deep
they lose their watery state.

Angels must be confused by war.
Who can they help?
Who can they clarify?
Whose mercy do they cast to the merciless?
No modest scream can be heard.
No stainless pain can be felt.
All is clear to angels
except in war.

When I awoke to this truth
it was from a dream I had last night.
I saw two angels conversing in a field
of children's spirits rising
like silver smoke.
The angels were fighting among themselves
about which side was right
and which was wrong.

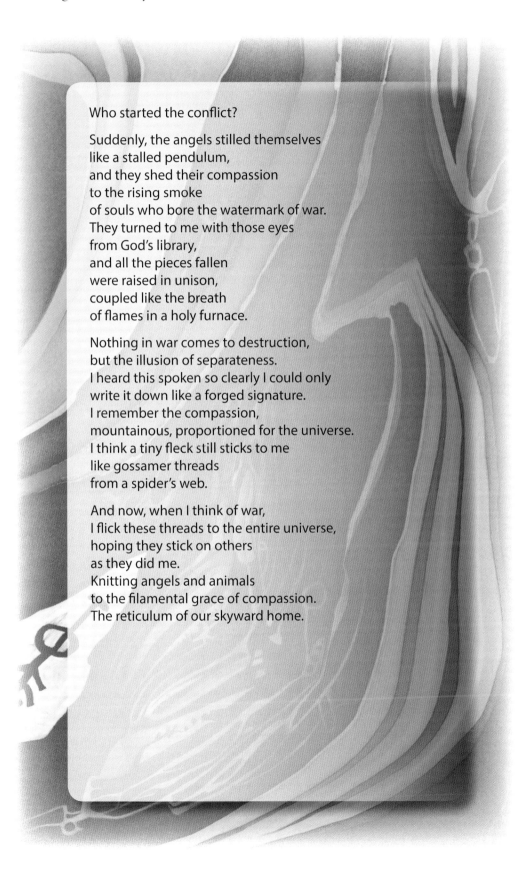

Who started the conflict?

Suddenly, the angels stilled themselves
like a stalled pendulum,
and they shed their compassion
to the rising smoke
of souls who bore the watermark of war.
They turned to me with those eyes
from God's library,
and all the pieces fallen
were raised in unison,
coupled like the breath
of flames in a holy furnace.

Nothing in war comes to destruction,
but the illusion of separateness.
I heard this spoken so clearly I could only
write it down like a forged signature.
I remember the compassion,
mountainous, proportioned for the universe.
I think a tiny fleck still sticks to me
like gossamer threads
from a spider's web.

And now, when I think of war,
I flick these threads to the entire universe,
hoping they stick on others
as they did me.
Knitting angels and animals
to the filamental grace of compassion.
The reticulum of our skyward home.

Chamber Two Poetry

Temptress Vision

A temptress vision has encircled me like a
willful shadow of a slumbering dream.
Is it the powerful light of purpose?
If I squint with all my strength I may see it.
Always must it be inside of me
like a pilot fish inseparable from its host.
It fearlessly drinks my essence.
Such a bitter taste I muse.
Spit it out upon your table of perfection.
Compare this grain of sand with your galaxy.
This spire of sorrow with your deepest eye.
If my callous mind can see you,
there are no interventions.
No pathway away.
Convergence.

I am a lock-picker.
A tunnel-digger.
A fence-cutter of the wicked watchers.
A traveler that has sought
the mystery that eludes all but the outlaws.
The wild-eyed, unrelenting fools of purpose
that remain outside the laboratory of wingless flight.

You are the eternal Watcher
who lives behind the veil of form and comprehension,
drawing forth the wisdom of time
from the well of planets.
You cast your spell and entrain all that I am.
Am I just a fragment of your world?
A memory hidden by time?
A finger of your hand driven by a mind
unfamiliar with skin.
Touch yourself and you sense me.
Visions wild with love.
Splendor that beckons like a secret whisper of gladness
spread on the winds by an infinite voice.
The sound of all things unified.

I am part of that voice.
Part of that sound.
Part of that secret whisper of gladness.

This limitation must end in lucid flesh.
The dream of sparks ascending
quickening the cast of hope.
Avoid the brand of passivity
the signs complain.
Shun manipulation before you are stained.
Spurn all formula and write new equations
in the language of sand.
Heed no other,
nor listen to the seduction of holy symbols
standing before the windows of truth.
Define from a foreign tongue.

These are the battered keys
that have led me to unlocked doors.
Doors that collapse at a mere breath
and behind which
lay more pieces to collect for the Holy Menagerie.
The never-ending puzzle.

All the stars in the sky
recall the purpose of your hallowed light.
Burn a hole through the layers.
Peel all the mockery away.
Enjoin the powers
to answer this call:
Bring the luminous vision
hidden behind the whirling particles
of the Mapmaker.
Let it enter me
like a shaft of light that enters
a cave's deepest measure.
Ancient fires still burn in these depths.
Who tends them?
What eyes are watching?

Chamber Two Poetry

Waiting.
Waiting for time's flower to bloom.
To submerge in the relentless subtlety
that moves beyond my reach
with a jaguar's stealth.
To dream of elder ways
that leap over time
and leave behind the puzzle of our making.

O' temptress vision
you steal my hunger for human light.
If there is anything left to hollow
let it be me.
If there is anything left to cage
let it run free.
If there is anything left to dream
let it be our union.

Language of Innocence

When a river is frozen,
underneath remains a current.
When the sky is absent of color
beneath the globe another world comes to light.
When my heart is alone
somewhere another heart beats my name
in code that only paradise can hear.

Is my heart deaf
or is there no one
who can speak the language of innocence?
Innocence, when words
suffer meaning and gallop away in its presence.
I have seen it.
Felt it.
I have loosened its secrets in the blushing skin
when upturned eyes witness its home
and never turn away.
And never turn away.

There is this world
of slumbering hearts and hollow love,
but it cannot carry me to daylight.
My craving is so different
and it can never be turned away.

Chamber Three Poetry

Half Mine

When I see your face I know you are half mine
separated by the utmost care to remember all of you.
When I undress my body I see that I am half yours
blurred by sudden flight that leaves
the eye wondering what angels carved in their hearts
to remind them so vividly of their home.

When I see your beauty I know you are half mine
never to be held in a polished mirror
knowing the faithful hunger of our soul.
When I watch your eyes I know they are half mine
tracing a trajectory where sensual virtue is the very spine of us.
When I hold your hand I know it is half mine
wintered in kinship, it circles tenderness
beneath the moon and well of water when the feast is done.
When I kiss your lips I know they are half mine
sent by God's genealogy to uncover us
in the delicious cauldron of our united breath.

When I hear you cry I know your loneliness is half mine
so deep the interior that we are lost outside
yearning to give ourselves away
like a promise made before the asking.
And when I look to your past I know it is half mine
running to the choke cherry trees
invisible to the entire universe we found ourselves
laughing in sudden flight
eyeing the carved initials in our hearts.
Sparing the trees.

Bandages of the Beast

There were many random omens.
Sending olive branches with thorns was
only one of your repertoire.
You offered me a book
where all the answers lay encoded in
some strange dialect.

Symbols undulating like serpents restless for food.

If I was windborne as a lambent seed you
would still the air
and I would fall into the thicket.
If I yearned for sweet water
you would pass me the bitter cup.
If I was an injured fawn you would flush me
from the cloister, corner me against cold stone,
and admire my fear.

Everywhere I steer I seek the one look of love;
yet love humbles itself like a mannequin
changing its clothes to accommodate the dressmaker.
Underneath there are bandages of the beast.
Underneath there is the tourniquet of deliverance.
But beneath the shell there is emptiness, so defiant
it is clothed in finery that neither
dressmaker nor beast can touch.

You have mistaken my search as my soul.
Raking through it for clumps of wisdom,
you have found only what I have lost to you.
Held like rootless dreams
I will vanish in your touch.

If you pass your rake over this emptiness
you will feel clumps of my spirit.
You will find me like tiny pieces of mirror broken
apart yet still collected in one spot.
Still staring ever skyward.
Still reflecting one mosaic image.
Still the accompanist of myself.

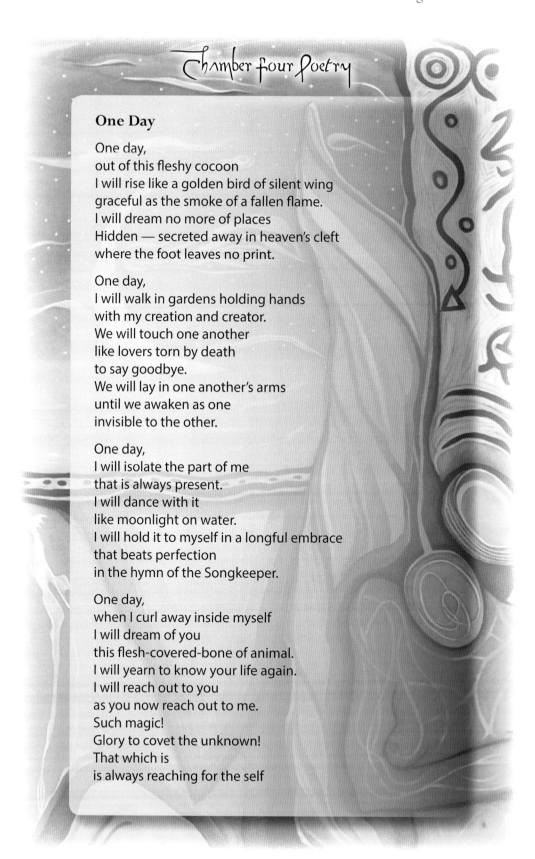

Chamber four Poetry

One Day

One day,
out of this fleshy cocoon
I will rise like a golden bird of silent wing
graceful as the smoke of a fallen flame.
I will dream no more of places
Hidden — secreted away in heaven's cleft
where the foot leaves no print.

One day,
I will walk in gardens holding hands
with my creation and creator.
We will touch one another
like lovers torn by death
to say goodbye.
We will lay in one another's arms
until we awaken as one
invisible to the other.

One day,
I will isolate the part of me
that is always present.
I will dance with it
like moonlight on water.
I will hold it to myself in a longful embrace
that beats perfection
in the hymn of the Songkeeper.

One day,
when I curl away inside myself
I will dream of you
this flesh-covered-bone of animal.
I will yearn to know your life again.
I will reach out to you
as you now reach out to me.
Such magic!
Glory to covet the unknown!
That which is
is always reaching for the self

that cheats appearances.
Who dreams itself awake and asleep.
Who knows both sides of the canvas
are painted, awaiting the other
to meld anew.

Missing

Facing another evening without you
I am torn from myself
in movements of clouds,
movements of earth spinning
like the sure movement of lava as it rolls to sea.
Yet when I arrive from my dream
you are still gone from me
twenty-three footsteps away;
a bouquet of the abyss.

When I look to the east I think of you
softly waiting for me
to chisel you from the matrix
with smooth hammer strokes
from my hands.
Freed of barren, untouched shoulders,
you can open your eyes again
flashing the iridescent animals,
valiant vibrations of your rich spirit.

Your picture is the centerpiece of my table
I stare at you in candlelight,
the windows behind, black in their immensity,
only enlarge you.
Making you more of what I miss.

At night I go among your body
to feel the presence of your heart beating
something golden
spun from another world.
You can feel me when this is done
though I am invisible in all ways to you, but one.

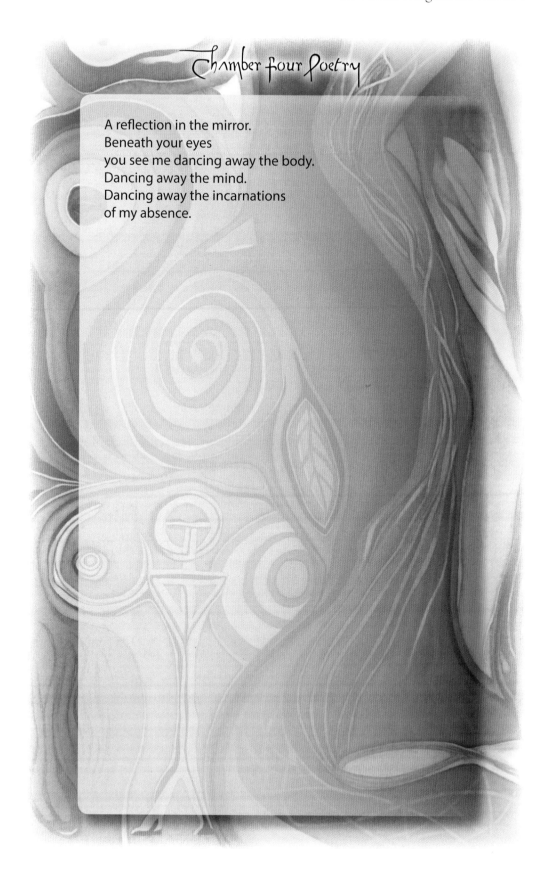

Chamber four Poetry

A reflection in the mirror.
Beneath your eyes
you see me dancing away the body.
Dancing away the mind.
Dancing away the incarnations
of my absence.

Chamber five Poetry

Life Carriers

Life carriers spawn in the primal waters
of a giant embryo.
Their progeny will settle in human dust.
Pieces of clay
with tiny thoughts of flight.
Knife-points veiled in turbid cloaks
that shun the light of a tranquil star.

In the remote wilds the life carriers
emerge and perch upon
the shoulders of gray stones.
They signal their desires to fly,
but their homes are suited
for the comforts of rain and earth.
The sky must wait.
(The dirt companion smiles.)

Circles break.
Barriers overrun.
Life carriers deny their ancient pull
from the ground.
Wings sprout like golden hair
sinuous with nature's artifice.
Ragged feet are left behind.
The earth replaced with vivid sky.
Gravity shines its menacing stare
to hold them
with assertive hands.

Homeless cages
are left to rot.
To sink behind the groundless sky.
Earthen faces have dropped their smiles
and lost their smell of fresh dirt.
The dream of flight
has invaded somber walls—
life carriers have bounded
to the other side.

Chamber five Poetry

There they meet the next rung
of the endless ladder,
and trade their wings for wisdom's eye.

Another

One skin may hide another,
I remember this from a poem when I
launched a fire across a field of deadness.
At least, to me, it seemed dead.
I felt like a liberator of life force
renewing the blistered and dying grasses.
Actually, more weeds than grass,
but nonetheless, the flora had flat-lined.
I peeled back skin with holy flame
and brought everything to black again
as though I called the night to descend.
From blackness will arise a new skin
cresting green architecture from a fertile void.

As the flames spread their inviolable enchantment
I saw your face spreading across my mind.
Remember the fire we held?
I hoped it would unfurl a new skin
for us as well.
Forever it will roam inside me
invariant to all transformations and motions.
(Einstein smiling.)
One person may hide another,
but behind you, love is molting a thicker skin
than I can see through.
No flame can touch its center.
No eyes can browse its memory.
I want nothing behind you in wait.
Seconds tick away like children growing
in between photographs.
I will not forget you in the changes.
Cursed with memory so fine
I can trace your palm.

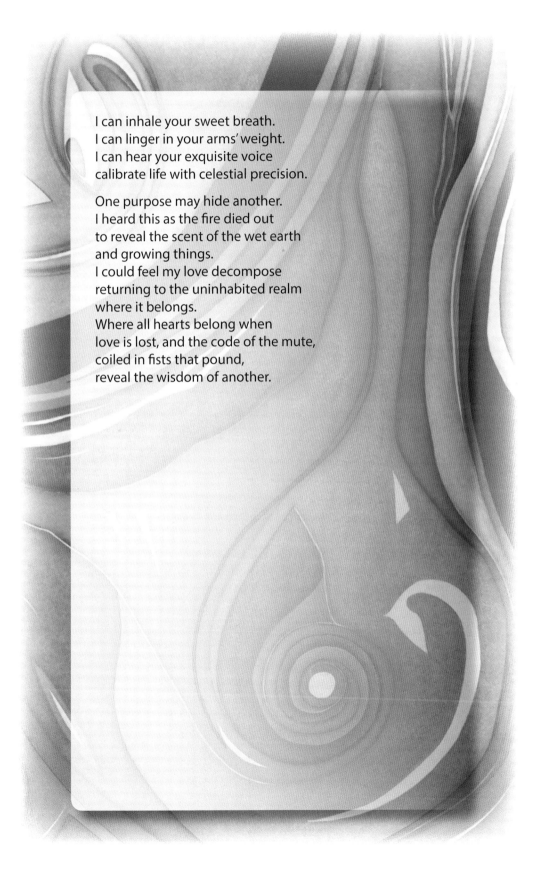

I can inhale your sweet breath.
I can linger in your arms' weight.
I can hear your exquisite voice
calibrate life with celestial precision.

One purpose may hide another.
I heard this as the fire died out
to reveal the scent of the wet earth
and growing things.
I could feel my love decompose
returning to the uninhabited realm
where it belongs.
Where all hearts belong when
love is lost, and the code of the mute,
coiled in fists that pound,
reveal the wisdom of another.

Chamber Six Poetry

Of This Place

Her heart ran
in the wilds of deserted plains.
Sun-etched land barren of clouds
and singing water.
If she listened closely
her hand would call
and signal its thoughts upon her brow.
But in this place
she could only offer her arms to the sky
like a tree its branches
and a flower its leaves.
In this dusty basin,
silence gathered like smoke
clearing the mind of the scoundrel.
The infidel of thoughts.
Blots of yellow leaves and white bark
could be seen hiding in pools of life
surrounded by red rock spires.
Clustered sand monuments held together
by some other life form.
She wasn't sure.
Perhaps one life is the same as another
only tilted sideways.
Caught from underneath
by some invisible hand that animates
even the coldest stone of this place.

A smile emerged and perched upon her face
drinking the sun's clear ways.
She could spear
a million miles of air in a glance
and send the window of her flesh
into the cloudless sky.
Upon this ocean a hawk sailed ever closer.
She watched the silver speck
spiral overhead dreaming through its eyes.
Feeling the winds gild her wings
in the softest fold of time.

A tree of pine sent its sky roots
deep within the air to weep its sweetness.
She entered,
gliding through branches
to every needle in their factory of air.

So strange to feel the pull of earth in flight,
but she knew the antagonism well
in the splendor of this place.
She knew it had settled deep,
lodged like permanent ink
in the heart of her.
Under skin, muscle, bone
it fought the single path.
What madness calls her away?
What dream is stronger than this?
What heart beats more pure?

Of this place,
it is so hard to know which is host
and which is guest.
Which is welcome, which is pest.
Which is found and which is lost.
Which is profit, which is cost.

She gave her prayers
to the skypeople and waited for a cloud —
her signal to leave.
She should return home
before dusk settles in and the golden
eyes peer out against the black code.
In a single breath she held the ancient ways
that never left.
She turned them inside out
and then outside in.
Again and again.
Waiting for her signals in the sky.
If not a cloud...
then perhaps a shooting star.
(Besides, it was too dark for clouds anymore.)

Chamber Six Poetry

When the first star fell she held her breath
afraid she would miss its spectral flight.
She wondered with whom she shared
its final light.
What other eyes were heaven bound
in that secret moment?
Was this their signal home as well?
And what was it they found
buried so deep in a whisper of light
that none can tell?

She waited with solemn eyes
for more stars to fall,
to gently sweep her away
from the magnets of this place.
If she listened to her hand
it would scratch a sign in the sand for another
to take her place.
It would touch the land
in honor of its grace and wisdom,
and become a tree, rock, hawk, or flower.

Imperishable

Through this night I have slept little.
My eyes, closed like shutters
with slats that remain open,
wait to invent dreams
of some charred reality.
I sense you, but no weight on my bed.
No shift or creaking other
than my own restlessness.

Wandering words
self-gathered, self-formed,
and released to the night
like a mantra slowly drowned in music.
Your presence grew with the music
devouring it in silence.

You came to me so clear
my senses aroused in electric storms of clarity.
The buzz of mercury lamps
alongside rutted roads,
shedding their weightless light.

In all of this waiting for you
no fortress or foxhole bears my name.
I lay on the Savannah
staring at the sun hoping against hope
it blinks before I do.
My wounded cells,
tiny temples of our mixture,
have weakened in your absence.
I can feel them wail in their miniature worlds.
My feet resist their numbness,
deny them their war.

As I lay here alone
waiting to be gathered into your arms,
I ask of you one thing,
remember me as this.
Remember me as one who loves you
beyond yourself.
Who pierces shells, armor, masks,
and everything protecting
your spirit in needless fervor.
Remember me as this.
As one who loves you unmatched
by the deepest channels
that have ever been forged.
Who will love you anywhere and always.

And if you look very closely at my love
you will not find an expiration date,
but instead, the word, imperishable.

Chamber Seven Poetry

Union

You are not here.
In this moment all that exists is here.
But you are not.
There are so many footprints
leading to my door.
Let us enter, they say.
We cannot sleep in the desert
it is too cold.
Our tears will dry too fast.
Our ears will hurt from the silence.
Let us in.
And so I gather them all up,
swing wide my door,
and step aside as they enter
hoping they will lay in peace beside my fire.

You were not among them.
I looked everywhere for your face
and saw only mimicry.
The blind eye buried behind brain
searching for your heart.
An antenna so alert
there is a peculiar nearness of you
flying inside my body.
I can hold this like a tiny bird in my hands;
fragile, vulnerable, waiting
for my move to decide its fate.

You are not here.
I wish I could reach your skin,
remove the camouflage
tearing it away like black paper
held before the sun as a shield.
Unbundle you from your other lives
and distill you in my now.
You are my last love,
my final embrace of this world
and all the others that drop their prints at my door

are dimmed by your approaching steps.

I can see you will be here soon.
There is victory in my heart
and something invisible yet massive wants to speak.
Reminding me of you and your coming.
Quick, I plead, give me your lips.
Give me your womanly tenderness
that understands everything
so I may lose myself in you
and forget my loss.

If you were here, I would tell you this secret.
But you would need to be staring up at the stars
when I told you, held within my arms
feeling the earth rise up beneath you like a holy bed.
You would need our union to be your ears.

Song of Whales

Your voice lingers when it speaks
like rippling heat over desert floor.
It draws my heart and I find myself
leaning toward its source
as though I know it will take me
where you always are.
It draws me near to your breath—the spiracle that
holds the words of home.

It draws me to the blanket you hold
around your soul you so willingly share.
If you were to dive below the waters
where the whales sing their songs
into the gathering of deep currents
that pull our courage along,
channels that flow free of worldly levels,
you would find me there.
Listening to the voice I hear in you.
Feeding my heart in the waters of deep blindness
where currents flow

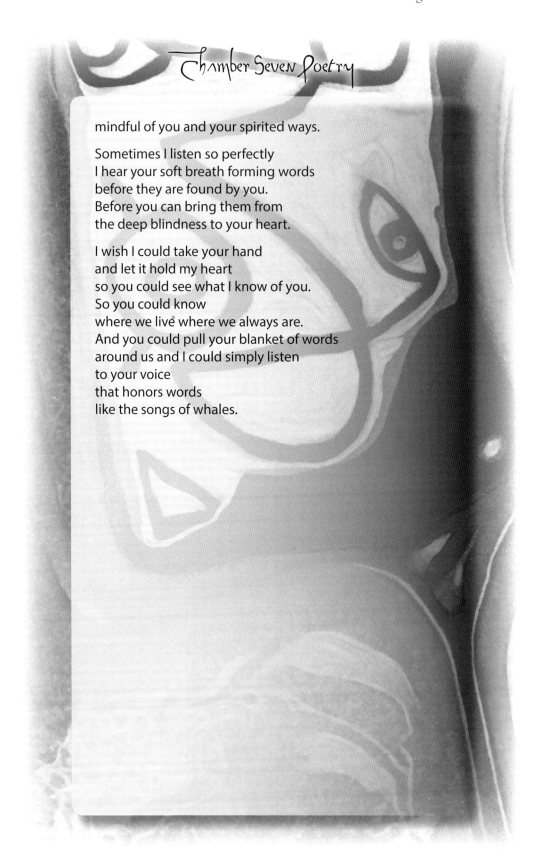

Chamber Seven Poetry

mindful of you and your spirited ways.

Sometimes I listen so perfectly
I hear your soft breath forming words
before they are found by you.
Before you can bring them from
the deep blindness to your heart.

I wish I could take your hand
and let it hold my heart
so you could see what I know of you.
So you could know
where we live where we always are.
And you could pull your blanket of words
around us and I could simply listen
to your voice
that honors words
like the songs of whales.

Chamber Eight Poetry

Another Mind Open

There was a fire where smoke gathered
and danced like rivers without gravity
to the rattle of drums.

Sometimes I would look inside the smoke
but it curled away and covered itself
with a cloak so opaque I could only cry.
It became the mask of its consumption.
The dream of its new life.
The victorious skin always changing
yet everlasting.
There was a fire last night
that proclaimed news of a newer testament
that drinks tears, lies, vile words, even
the deep fears that linger underneath the turncoat.

I usually lurch away when it calls.
To me, it burns too cold
like a skinwalker lost in a body
devoured by time.
Sometimes I would dream it alive
and it would blaze—vibrant sun—
more durable than a grave.

In times of stillness
it would speak like a codicil of some lidless dream
that words could not preserve.
"The time has come to lift your gaze
from the fire's brightness
and cast shadows of your own."
The words would echo into oblivion
like stars lost in the swell of the sun's awakening.

In these flames I see my
consumption fit and proper.
In its smoke
I am stored away like so many jars
in a broom closet.
Waiting to flee.

Chamber Eight Poetry

Drawing my feet to oppose the floor.
Struggling to reach the door inside these jars
of sealed air.

Stories escape the writer's hand
and pursue me as though I alone held their vigil.
Their very soul.
When indeed these stories have never been told.
They have never found words
to hold though they ceaselessly try.

Fires blind nature.
They invest their life in her death.
But the end is always beginning
toward another end.
And the dreams of the untold
are always pursuing another mouth,
another hand,
another mind open.

Sometimes I look to the errant expression of hope,
and ask it to bring its flames deeper into my heart.
To burn a clear sense of purpose.
To burn away the fool's crevice
and enshroud me in its skin of smoke.

Sometimes I offer myself to these flames
and know they listen.
Devising my world.
Reality coalesces around their finery
like a tower of glass enclothes a shell of steel.

Sometimes I feel the flames send me
words, notes, tones.
Enchantment.
Products of another kind.
Tiny crucibles of earth that burn so brightly
they can blind the sun's creatures of whimsy.

And sometimes, without even thinking,
I peek into these flames

when the smoke peels away for an instant.
There, behind the mask,
is my future.
Our future.
The future.
The present in another world.
Calling out for another mouth,
another hand,
another mind open.

Longing

Longing, when the eyelids open
upon the deepest stimulus held by your lips
and the amorous kiss becomes my orbit.

I ache and long to have you with me
so close our skin would melt together
like two candle wicks sharing wax.
I only know that what is of soul
is of longing and ache.
It delivers me to the edge,
the precipice where I look down
and see myself inextinguishable,
longing to be consumed by you.

And in that glittering place
let me stretch with your heart
at full speed, blind and intent.
Let me dwell in you
until I am so familiar with our union
that it becomes part of my eyes.
With memory full,
we can walk home,
hand-in-hand,
in the permanence of longing.

So much a part of the other
that the other does not exist.

Chamber Nine Poetry

Of Luminous Things

Of luminous things
I have so little experience
that I often think myself small.
Yet when I think of you
and your luminous ways
my being swells with hope and prayers
that you will permit the flames to grow.

In mercy, we are torn apart
into separate worlds
to find ourselves over and over
a thousand times aching for the other half.
To dream of nothing but the One between us.

Of luminous things I have squandered none
nor have I held them to my heart and asked them
to dissolve into me.
Yet when I think of you, I desire only this.
And if you disrobed your Self and watched it
watch you, you would see me as clearly as I am.
Not small and unworthy.
Unafraid of fear.
Not uncertain like empty space.
But luminous
like white light before the prism.

In my thoughts I hold your heart
sculpting away the needless
for the essence.
And when I find it
I will hold it to my heart and ask it
to dissolve into me.
I will know of luminous things
that hurtle through time
bringing us the uncharted, unfathomable
desire we have never spoken.
Words are not curious enough to say their names.
Only love can weep their identity,

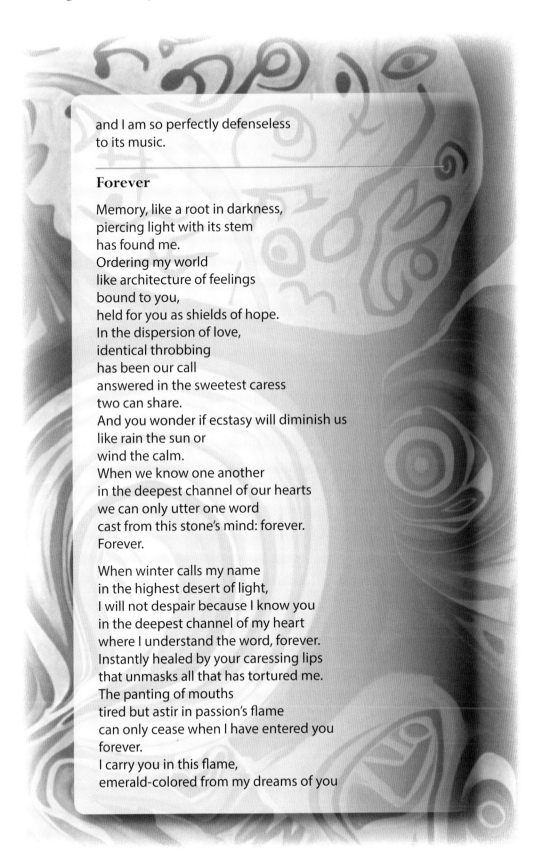

and I am so perfectly defenseless
to its music.

Forever

Memory, like a root in darkness,
piercing light with its stem
has found me.
Ordering my world
like architecture of feelings
bound to you,
held for you as shields of hope.
In the dispersion of love,
identical throbbing
has been our call
answered in the sweetest caress
two can share.
And you wonder if ecstasy will diminish us
like rain the sun or
wind the calm.
When we know one another
in the deepest channel of our hearts
we can only utter one word
cast from this stone's mind: forever.
Forever.

When winter calls my name
in the highest desert of light,
I will not despair because I know you
in the deepest channel of my heart
where I understand the word, forever.
Instantly healed by your caressing lips
that unmasks all that has tortured me.
The panting of mouths
tired but astir in passion's flame
can only cease when I have entered you
forever.
I carry you in this flame,
emerald-colored from my dreams of you

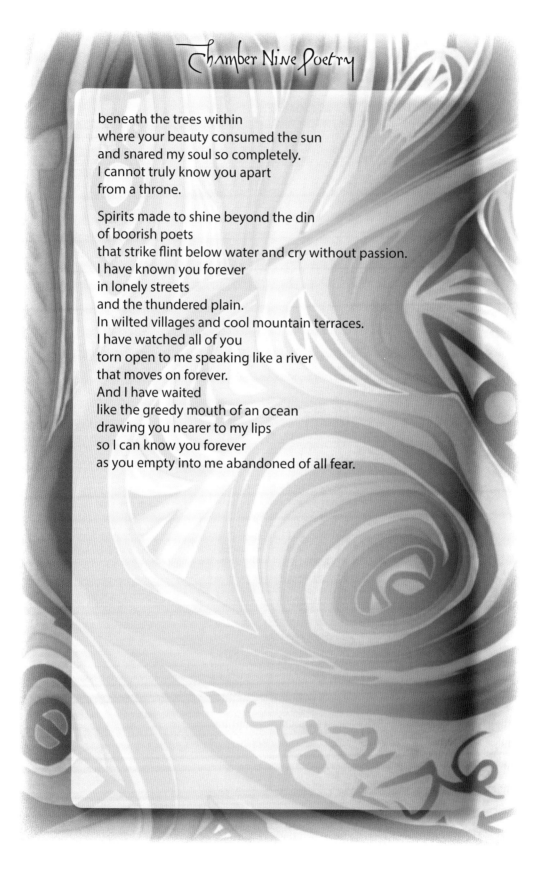

Chamber Nine Poetry

beneath the trees within
where your beauty consumed the sun
and snared my soul so completely.
I cannot truly know you apart
from a throne.

Spirits made to shine beyond the din
of boorish poets
that strike flint below water and cry without passion.
I have known you forever
in lonely streets
and the thundered plain.
In wilted villages and cool mountain terraces.
I have watched all of you
torn open to me speaking like a river
that moves on forever.
And I have waited
like the greedy mouth of an ocean
drawing you nearer to my lips
so I can know you forever
as you empty into me abandoned of all fear.

Chamber Ten Poetry

Downstream

Open me.
Take me from here to there.
Let the wind blow
my hair and the earth's skin touch me.

Open me like broken bottles
that bear no drink
yet think themselves worthy of the trash man.
Open me to the clans from which I sprout.
Are they colors separated, cast apart
like memories of drunkenness?
Open me to Africa, Asia, America, Australia.
Open me like a package
of mystery left on your doorstep
in the sweetness of laughter.

Open me to the crudely made lens of love
that screams to be of human hands
and lips.
Open me to the glance
that comforts strangers like the tender overture
of a mourning dove.

Is the wisdom of horses mine
to harness?
Is the muscle of wolves
lawless or the healer of sheep?
Is the black opal of the eye
the missing link we all seek?

Open me to the authors of this beaten path
and let them flavor it anew.
Bring them flecks of the rumored and rotten
slum that waits downstream.
Show them the waste of their watch.
The shallow virility that exterminates.
The ignominy that exceeds examination.

Open me to the idols of the idle.

Chamber Ten Poetry

Let me stare open mouthed at the herdsmen
who turn innocence into fear.
Is the plan of the sniper to uncivilize
the nerveless patch of skin
that grows unyielding to pain?

Open me to the stains
of this land that original sin cannot explain.
Let these symptoms go
like dead, yellow leaves fumbling
in swift, guiltless currents downstream.

Downstream where the slum
lies in waiting.
Downstream where the idols' headstones
are half-buried in muddy rain.
Downstream where animal tracks
are never seen.
Downstream where
the lens of love is cleaned with red tissue.
Downstream where the herdsmen
herd their flock and beat the drums
promising a new river that never comes.

Downstream there lives
a part of me that is sealed like a paper envelope
with thick tape.
It watches the river like the underside of a bridge
waiting to fall if the seal is broken.
To plunge into the current when I am opened
by some unforgiving hand unseen.
To be drawn downstream
in the gravity of a thousand minds
who simply lost their way.
A thousand minds that twisted the river
away from earth's sweetness
into the mine shaft of men's greed.

So it must be.
So it must be.

Open me to the kindness
of a child's delicate hand when it reaches out to be held.
Let it comfort me
when my bridge falls and the swift, guiltless currents
pull me downstream
where all things forgiven are lost.
Where all things lost are forgiven.

What is Found Here

What is found here
can never be formed of words.
Pure forces that mingle uncompared.
Like dreams unspoken when first awoken
by a sad light.

What is found here
can limp with one foot on the curb
and the other on the pavement
in some uneven gait
waiting to be hidden in laughter.

What is found here
can open the swift drifting of curtains
held in mountain winds
when long shadows tumble across like juries
of the night.

What is found here
can always be held in glistening eyes.
Turned by silence's tool of patience.
Like feelings harbored for so long
the starward view has been lost.

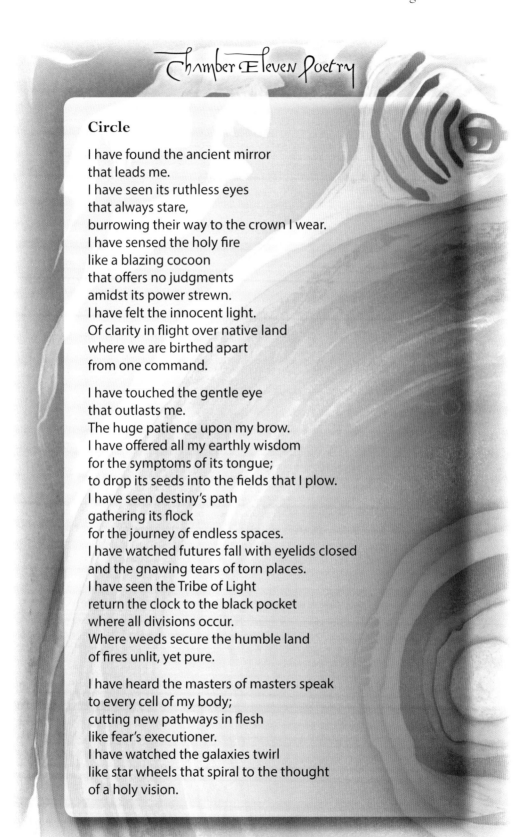

Chamber Eleven Poetry

Circle

I have found the ancient mirror
that leads me.
I have seen its ruthless eyes
that always stare,
burrowing their way to the crown I wear.
I have sensed the holy fire
like a blazing cocoon
that offers no judgments
amidst its power strewn.
I have felt the innocent light.
Of clarity in flight over native land
where we are birthed apart
from one command.

I have touched the gentle eye
that outlasts me.
The huge patience upon my brow.
I have offered all my earthly wisdom
for the symptoms of its tongue;
to drop its seeds into the fields that I plow.
I have seen destiny's path
gathering its flock
for the journey of endless spaces.
I have watched futures fall with eyelids closed
and the gnawing tears of torn places.
I have seen the Tribe of Light
return the clock to the black pocket
where all divisions occur.
Where weeds secure the humble land
of fires unlit, yet pure.

I have heard the masters of masters speak
to every cell of my body;
cutting new pathways in flesh
like fear's executioner.
I have watched the galaxies twirl
like star wheels that spiral to the thought
of a holy vision.

I have felt my spirit follow
the one sound that is free.

I have vanished before.
I have taken this body to an inner place
where none can see.
Only feelings can hear the sound of this space.
This sacred place alone
has brought me here to recover the thread.
To see the weaving dance that calls my name
in a thousand sounds.
That draws my spirit
in a single, perfectly round,
circle.

Awake and Waiting

Child-like universe emerging from darkness,
you belong to others not I.
My home is elsewhere
beyond the sky
where light pollinates the fragile borders
and gathers the husk.
In the quiet of the desert floor
my shell lingers in the pallid dusk
of a starved garden.
What holds me to this wasteland
when others clamor for shadows
and resist the vital waters?
Where the ripening magnet
holds us blind.

Far away,
kindling the presence of a timeless world
hunting for memories of a radiant love;
wingless creatures
tune their hearts to the key of silence.
It is there I am waiting.
Alone.

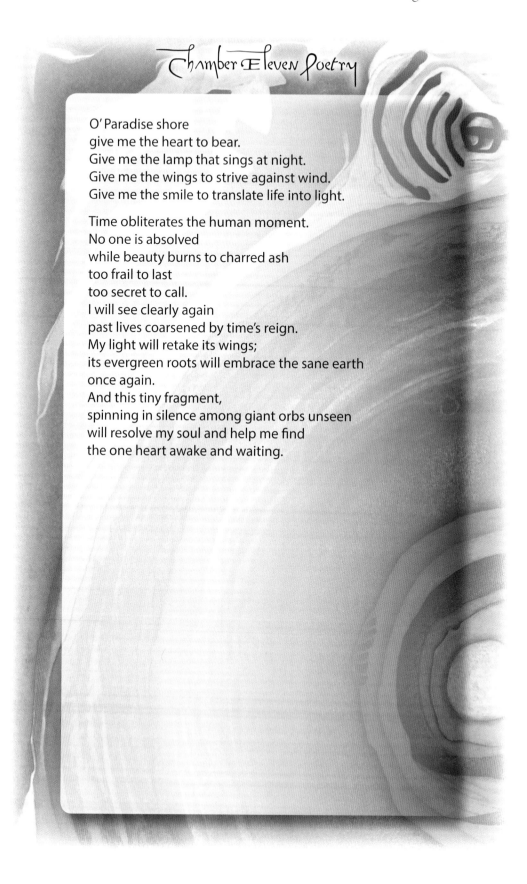

Chamber Eleven Poetry

O' Paradise shore
give me the heart to bear.
Give me the lamp that sings at night.
Give me the wings to strive against wind.
Give me the smile to translate life into light.

Time obliterates the human moment.
No one is absolved
while beauty burns to charred ash
too frail to last
too secret to call.
I will see clearly again
past lives coarsened by time's reign.
My light will retake its wings;
its evergreen roots will embrace the sane earth
once again.
And this tiny fragment,
spinning in silence among giant orbs unseen
will resolve my soul and help me find
the one heart awake and waiting.

Chamber Twelve Poetry

WingMakers

I am destined to sit on the riverbank
awaiting words from the naked trees
and brittle flowers that have lost their nectar.
A thousand unblinking eyes
stare out across the water
from the other side.
Their mute voices seek rewards of another kind.
Their demure smiles leave me hollow.

Am I a perpetual stranger to myself?
(The thought brands me numb.)

Am I an orphan trailing pale shadows
that lead to a contemptuous mirror?
Where are these gossamer wings that my
destiny foretold?
I am waiting for the river to deliver them to me;
to lodge them on the embankment
at my feet.

My feet are shackles from another time.
My head, a window long closed
to another place.
Yet, there are places
that salvage the exquisite tongue
and assemble her wild light
like singing birds the sun.
I have seen these places among the stillness
of the other side.
Calling like a lover's kiss
to know again what I have known before;
to reach into the Harvest
and leave my welcome.

These thoughts are folded so neatly
they stare like glass eyes fondling the past.
I listen for their guidance
but serpentine fields are my pathway.
When I look into the dark winds

Chamber Twelve Poetry

of the virtual heart
I can hear its voice saying:
"Why are you trapped with wings?"
And I feel like a grand vision inscribed in sand
awaiting an endless wind.

Will these wings take me
beneath the deepest camouflage?
Will they unmask the secret measures
and faithful dwellings of time?
Will they search out the infinite spaces
for the one who can define me?

Wings are forgotten by all who travel with their feet.
Lines have been drawn so many times
that we seldom see the crossing
of our loss though we feel the loss of our crossing.
We sense the undertow of clouds.
The gravity of sky.
The painless endeavor of hope's silent prayers.
But our wings shorn of flight
leave us like newborn rivers that babble over rocks
yearning for the depths of a silent sea.

I have found myself suddenly old.
Like the blackbirds that pour
from the horizon line,
my life has soared over this river searching for my wings.
There is no other key for me to turn.
There is no other legend for me to face.
Talking to flowers and gnarled trees
will only move me a step away --
when I really want to press my face
against the windowpane
and watch the WingMakers craft my wings.

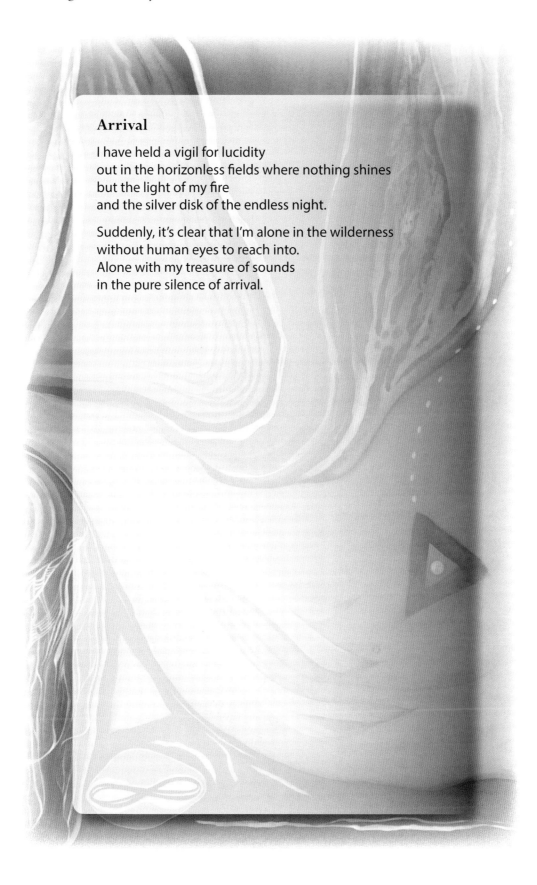

Arrival

I have held a vigil for lucidity
out in the horizonless fields where nothing shines
but the light of my fire
and the silver disk of the endless night.

Suddenly, it's clear that I'm alone in the wilderness
without human eyes to reach into.
Alone with my treasure of sounds
in the pure silence of arrival.

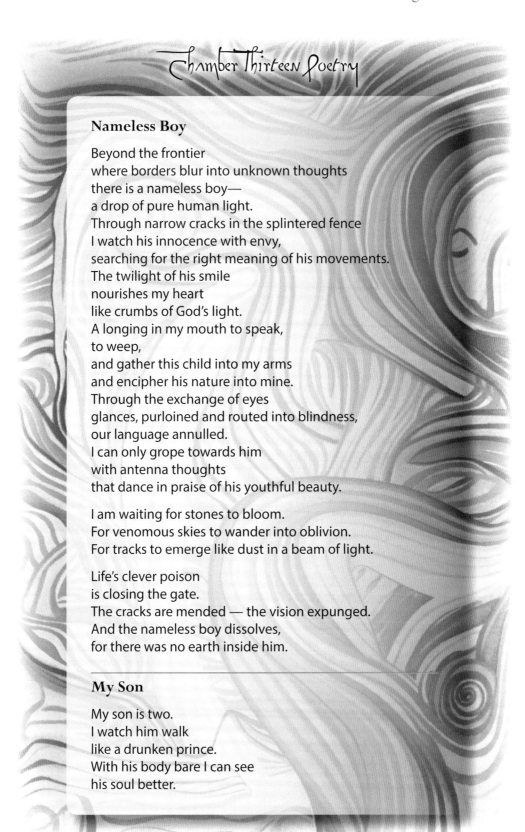

Chamber Thirteen Poetry

Nameless Boy

Beyond the frontier
where borders blur into unknown thoughts
there is a nameless boy—
a drop of pure human light.
Through narrow cracks in the splintered fence
I watch his innocence with envy,
searching for the right meaning of his movements.
The twilight of his smile
nourishes my heart
like crumbs of God's light.
A longing in my mouth to speak,
to weep,
and gather this child into my arms
and encipher his nature into mine.
Through the exchange of eyes
glances, purloined and routed into blindness,
our language annulled.
I can only grope towards him
with antenna thoughts
that dance in praise of his youthful beauty.

I am waiting for stones to bloom.
For venomous skies to wander into oblivion.
For tracks to emerge like dust in a beam of light.

Life's clever poison
is closing the gate.
The cracks are mended — the vision expunged.
And the nameless boy dissolves,
for there was no earth inside him.

My Son

My son is two.
I watch him walk
like a drunken prince.
With his body bare I can see
his soul better.

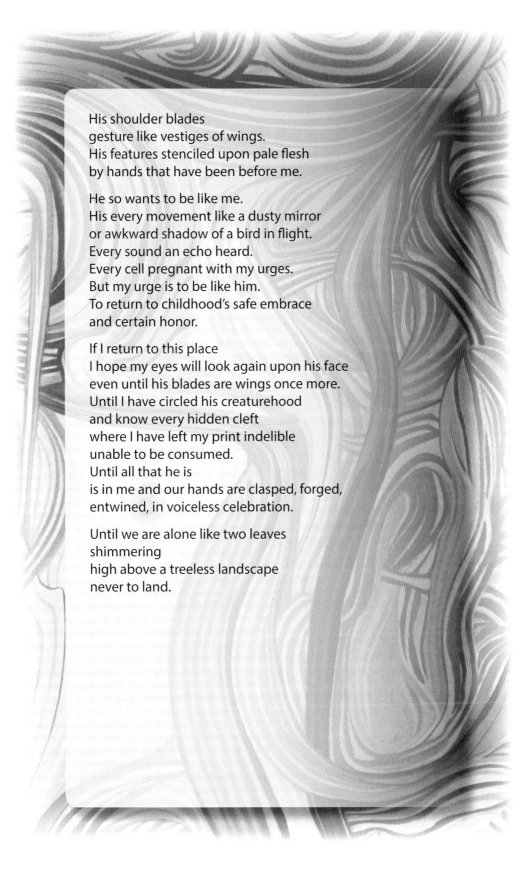

His shoulder blades
gesture like vestiges of wings.
His features stenciled upon pale flesh
by hands that have been before me.

He so wants to be like me.
His every movement like a dusty mirror
or awkward shadow of a bird in flight.
Every sound an echo heard.
Every cell pregnant with my urges.
But my urge is to be like him.
To return to childhood's safe embrace
and certain honor.

If I return to this place
I hope my eyes will look again upon his face
even until his blades are wings once more.
Until I have circled his creaturehood
and know every hidden cleft
where I have left my print indelible
unable to be consumed.
Until all that he is
is in me and our hands are clasped, forged,
entwined, in voiceless celebration.

Until we are alone like two leaves
shimmering
high above a treeless landscape
never to land.

Chamber fourteen Poetry

Empyrean

He walked a higher ground
like a soul untethered to human flesh.
Darkness implored
demanded his searching stop
and match the drifting gait of others.
But his pathway unwound like a ball of string
sent upward
only to fall in a sentence of light.
Collisions with fate would unrail him
and send him the wishes of obscurity.
The lightning of desire.
The curse of empty dreams.
The witness to unspeakable horrors.

He would laugh at the absurdity,
yet aware of the dark ripples
that touched him.
Humanity was a creaseless sheet of blank paper
waiting to be colored and crumpled
into pieces of prey for the beast-hunter.
Why did they wait?
The palette was for their taking.
The "distance" betrayed them.
The shallow grave of the deep heart
killed their faith.

He knew,
yet could not form the words.
Nor draw the map.
The ancient casts of the empyrean
withstood definition.
Paradise lost to the soundless blanket
of the clearest thought,
of the loneliest mind.

Separate Being

Waking this morning,
I remember you.
We were together last night
only a thin sheet of glass between us.
Your name was not clear.
I think I would recognize its sound,
but my lips are numb
and my tongue listless from the
climb to your mouth.
Your face was blurred as well,
yet, like a distant god
you took your heart and hand
and there arose within me
a separate being.

I think you were lonely once.
Your only desire, to be understood,
turned away by some vast shade
drawn by a wisdom
you had forgotten.
So you sang your songs
in quiet summons to God
hoping their ripples would return
and gather you up.
Continue you.
Brighten your veins
and bring you the unquenchable
kiss of my soul.

Drunken by a lonely name
you stagger forward
into my nights, into my dreams,
and now into my waking.
If I try to forget you
you will precede my now.
I would feel your loss
though I can't say your name
or remember your face.

Chamber fourteen Poetry

I would awaken some morning
and long to feel your skin upon mine
knowing not why.
Feeling the burn of our fire
so clearly that names and faces
bear no meaning
like a candle flicking its light to the
noonday sun.

Chamber fifteen Poetry

Secret Language

Night in bed,
eyes closed, ears open,
listening to the secret life outside my window.
The liturgy of the nocturnal.
Sounds and rhythms of
swift-footed crickets
giving testimony to the trees that overlook
the native church like great archways
carved of Roman hands.

The intricate language of tiny animals
sweeping through the night air
unfaltering they hold me spellbound.
How can I sleep without an interpreter?
If only I knew what they were saying.
I could sleep again.

Wishing Light

Sun walks the roof of the sky
with a turtle's patience.
Circling endlessly amidst the black passage
of arrival and retreat.
Moon can shape shift
and puncture the confident darkness.
The weaker sister of sun
it bleeds light even as it dwindles
to a fissure of fluorescence.
Black sky like a monk's hood draped
over stars with squinted eyes.
Stewards lost,
exiled to overspread
the dark lair of the zodiac.
This silent outback where
light is uprooted and cast aside
beats like a tired clock uneven.
It dreams of sunlight passing so
it can follow like a parasite.

Chamber fifteen Poetry

Tired of meandering in absence it
wants to live the speed of light and feel its directness.
Wishing to stay alive in light years
and not some recumbent eternity.
Desiring the sharp pain of life
to the dull, numbing outskirts of ancient space.
Darkness follows light like a tireless
wind that pours over tumbleweeds.
But it always seems to outlast the people
if not the light.

Chamber Sixteen Poetry

Signals to Her Heart

Out where the ocean beats its calm thunder
against grainy shores of quartz and sand,
she strolls, hands pocketed in a flowing gown
of pearl-like luminance.
I can see her with hair the color of sky's deepest night
when it whispers to the sun's widow
to masquerade as the sickle's light.

This is she.
The one who knows me as I am
though untouched is my skin.
The world from which she steps
pounces from mystery,
announces her calm beauty
like a willow tree bent to still waters.

In this unhurt place she takes her body
to the shoreline listening for sounds beneath the waves
that tell her what to do.
How great is her dream?
Will it take her across the sea?
Does she hear my heart's voice
before the translation?

She scoops some sand
with her sculpted hands and
like an hourglass the particles fall
having borrowed time
for a chance to touch her beauty.
Her lips move with prayers of grace as she tells
the wind her story;
even the clouds gather overhead to listen.
Her gestures multiply me
with the sign of infinity,
disentangled from all calculations,
adorning her face with a poetry of tears.

I am summoned by her voice
so clear it startles me.

Chamber Sixteen Poetry

I watch her because I can.
I know her because she is me.
I desire her because she is not me.

In all my movement, in the vast search
for something that will complete me,
I have found her
on this shoreline,
her faint footprints,
signatures of perfection
that embarrass time with their fleeting nature.
I am like the cave behind her
watching from darkness,
hollowed from tortured waves
into a vault that yearns to say
what she cannot resist.
A language so pure it releases itself
from my mouth like long-held captives
finally ushered to their home.

She turns her head and looks
past me as if I were a ghost unseen,
yet I know she sees my deepest light.
I know the ocean is no boundary to her love.
She is waiting
for the final path to my heart to become clear.
And I am waiting
for something deep inside
to take my empty hands
and fill them with her face
so I can know the rehearsals were numbered,
and all the splinters
were signals to her heart.

Nothing Matters

Space is curved
so no elevator can slither to its stars.
Time is a spindle of the present
that spins the past and future away.

Energy is an imperishable force
so permanence can be felt.
Matter flings itself to the universe,
perfectly pitiless in its betrayal of soul.

You can only take away
what has been given you.

Have you not called the ravens the foulest of birds?
Is their matter and energy so different than ours?
Are we not under the same sky?
Is their blood not red?
Their mouth pink, too?

Molten thoughts, so hot they fuse space and time,
sing their prophecies of discontent.
Listen to their songs in the channels of air
that curl overhead like temporary tattoos
of light's shimmering ways.

Am I merely a witness of the betrayal?
Where are you who are cast to see?
How have you been hidden from me?
Is there a splinter that carries you to the whole?

If I can speak your names
and take your hands so gentle you would not see me,
feeling only the warm passage of time
and the tremor of your spine moving you to weep.

Space is curved so I must bend.
Time is a spindle so I must resolve its center.
Energy, an imperishable force I must ride.
And matter, so pitiless I refuse to be betrayed.

So I stand naked to the coldest wind
and ask it to carve out an island in my soul
in honor of you who stand beside me in silence.
Lonely, I live on this island assured of one thing:
that of space, time, energy, and matter;
nothing matters.
Yet when I think of you in the cobwebbed corner,

Chamber Sixteen Poetry

Hove led without wings
like a seed planted beneath a dead tree stump,
I know you are watching
with new galaxies wild in your breast.
I know you are listening
to the lidded screams smiling their awkward trust.
All I ask of you is to throw me a rope sometimes
so I can feel the permanence of your heart.

It's all I need in the face of nothing matters.

Chamber Seventeen Poetry

Memories Unbound

I have this memory
of lying atop a scaffold of tree limbs
staring out to the black, summer blanket
that warms the night air.
I can smell cedar burning in the distance
and hear muted voices praying in song and drum.
I cannot lift my body or turn my head.
I am conscious of bone and muscle
but they are not conscious of me.
They are dreaming while I am caught
in a web of exemptible time.

My mind is restless to move on.
To leave this starlit grave site and dance with
my people around huge fires
crackling with nervous light.
To join hand with hand to the rhythm of drums
pounding their soft thunder
in monotone commandments to live.

I can only stare up at the sky
watching, listening, waiting
for something to come and set me free
from this mournful site.
To gather me up in arms of mercy
into the oblivion of Heaven's pod.
I listen for the sound of my breath
but only the music of my people can be heard.
I look for the movement of my hands
but only wisps of clouds
and crescent light move
against raven's wings.

Sometimes when this memory peeks through
my skin it purges the shoreward view.
It imposes on the known predicament
with a turbulent bliss
that bleeds defiance to the order.

Chamber Seventeen Poetry

There is certain danger in the heritable ways
of my people who send me the chatoyant skin
humbled and circumscribed.
My white appetite leached of earthly rations.
Misplaced to the darshan of the devil,
the very same that
maneuvered my people to reservations —
the ward of the damned.
(At least I have no memories of a reservation).

Perhaps it is better
to lay upon this mattress of sticks
with my wardrobe of feathers and skins
chanting in the wind.
Perhaps it would be better still
to be set atop the cry shed and burned
so prodigal memories would have
no home to return to.

I have this memory
of escaping the pale hand
of my master that feeds me
scraps of lies and moldy bread.
My skin yearns for lightness,
but it is the rope that obliges.

I have this memory
of holding yellow fingers,
large and round, dripping with ancient legacies.
Of seeing the rounded belly of Buddha
smiling underneath a pastoral face
in temples that lean against a tempest sky.
I have this memory
of dreaming to fly.
Stretching out wings that are newly attached
with string-like permanence
only to fall in the blunted arms of obscurity.

I have this memory
of seeing my face in a mirror

that reflects a stranger's mind and soul.
Knowing it to be mine, I looked away
afraid it would become me alone.
I am patchwork memories searching for a nucleus.
I am lost words echoing in still canyons.
I am a light wave that found itself
darting to earth unsheathed
seeking cover in human skin.

Afterwards

I've set loose the guards that
stand before my door.
I've let cells collide in suicide
until they take me.
If there were stories left to tell
I would hear them.

Behind the waterfalls of channeled panic
spilling their prideful progeny
I can stay hidden in the noise.
Being invisible has its cameo rewards.
It also keeps visible the durable lifeform
murmuring beneath the wickedness.
This is truly the only creature I care to know,
with luminous ways of sweet generosity that suffers
in the untelling universe
of the unlistening ear.

When I am found out—after I am gone—
by a stranger's heart whose drill bit
is not dulled by impersonation,
I will open eyes, peel away skin,
awaken the heart's coma.
I will set aside the costumed figure
and redress the host
so its image can be seen in mirrors
I set forth with words bugged by God.
When these words are spoken,
another ear is listening on the other side

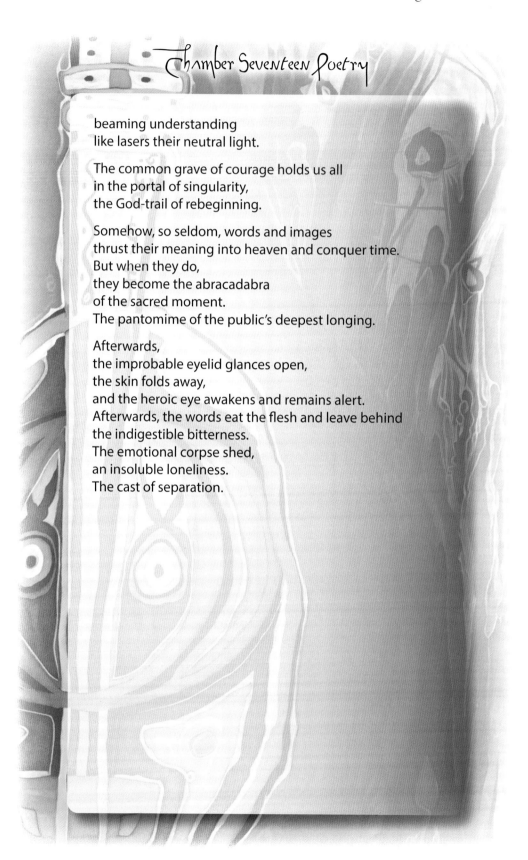

Chamber Seventeen Poetry

beaming understanding
like lasers their neutral light.

The common grave of courage holds us all
in the portal of singularity,
the God-trail of rebeginning.

Somehow, so seldom, words and images
thrust their meaning into heaven and conquer time.
But when they do,
they become the abracadabra
of the sacred moment.
The pantomime of the public's deepest longing.

Afterwards,
the improbable eyelid glances open,
the skin folds away,
and the heroic eye awakens and remains alert.
Afterwards, the words eat the flesh and leave behind
the indigestible bitterness.
The emotional corpse shed,
an insoluble loneliness.
The cast of separation.

Chamber Eighteen Poetry

Transparent Things

There it is then, my open wound,
eager for forgiveness.
It comes with age like brown spots
and silver hair.
Shouldn't age bring more than
different colors to adorn the body?
I think it was meant to.
It just forgot.
Old age does that you know.
Too many things to remember here.
Both worlds demanding so much,
one to learn, one to remember.

Can't we see each other
without wounds bearing grief?

There it is then, my hope for you
to find me and apply yourself
like a poultice to my wounds.
The rest of me is barren too.
Waiting for your arrival
with speed built of powerful engines
that groan loud from a piercing foot.
Downward pressure
never stopping even when floorboards are found.

If there was silence in these waters
my wound would dance open
and separate itself from all attackers.
Even this body.
It would look at you
in the orphaning light, diminished of features,
and lead you away to its place of sorrow.
It would ask you to lie down beside it
and wave goodbye
to the coiled currents that tug and pull
to separate us from ourselves.
It would hold your hands,

Chamber Eighteen Poetry

so masterful in their wisdom,
so mindful of their glory
that it would disappear inside.
In the future, someone,
a friend perhaps, would
read your palm and notice
a small line veering off in a ragged ambush.
Unchained from the rest
of your palm's symmetry.
A lonely fragment, waving goodbye
to everything between us.

There it is then, my prayer for you
to close this wound
and draw the shades around us.
Deep, black solitude enfolding us,
the kind found only in caves
that have shut out light for the growing of delicate,
transparent things.

Final Dream

Strike the flint that burns
a lonely world
and opens blessed lovers
to the golden grave of earth's flame.

Listen to the incantation
of raindrops as they pass from gray clouds
to our mother's doorstep.
Dreams of miracles yet to come
harbor in their watery husks.

Stand before this cage
splashed with beauty and stealth
and arranged with locks that have grown frail.
A simple breath
and all life is joined in the frontier.

Here is the masterpiece of creation
that has emerged from the unknown
in the depths of a silent Heart.
Here is the laughter sought
among rulers of death.
Here are the brilliant colors of rainbows
among the spilling reds that purge our flock.
Here is the hope of forever
among stone markers that stare through eyelids
released of time.
Here are the songs of endless voices
among the heartless dance of invisible power.

There is an evening bell that chimes
a melody so pure
even mountains weep
and angels lean to listen.
There is a murmur of hope that sweeps
aside the downcast eyes of hungry souls.

It is the fragrance of God
writing poems upon the deep blue sky
with pin-pricks of light and a sleepless moon.
It is the calling to souls
lost in the forest of a single world
to be cast, forged, and made ready
for the final dream.

Chamber Nineteen Poetry

Easy to Find

I have often looked inside my drawers
without knowing why.
Something called out.
Seek me and you shall find,
but when I obey
I'm confounded by memory's fleeting ways.
Hands immerse and return awkwardly empty
like a runaway child
when no one came after them.

I know there is something I seek
that hides from me so I can't think about what I lack.
It is, however, and this is the point,
too damn powerful to be silent and still.
Besides, I know I lack it because I miss it.

I miss it.
Whatever "it" is.
Whatever I need it to be it is not that.
It can never be anything but what it is.
And so I search in drawers and closets absent of why,
driven like a machine whose switch has been thrown
just because it can.

I miss it.
I wish it could find me.
Maybe I need to stay put long enough for it to do so.
Now there's a switch.
Let the powerful "it" seek me out.
But for how long must I wait?
And how will I recognize it should it find me?

There must be names
for this condition that end in
phobia.
Damn, I hate that suffix.
It all starts with a sense of wonder
and ends in a sense of emptiness.
God, I wish you could find me here.

I'll tuck myself in a little drawer
right out in the open.
I won't bury myself under incidentals.
I'll be right on top.
Easy to find.
Do you need me for anything?
I hope so because I need you for everything.

Beckoning Places

Of beckoning places
I have never felt more lost.
Nothing invites me onward.
Nothing compels my mouth to speak.
In cave-like ignorance, resembling oblivion,
I am soulless in sleep.
Where are you, beloved?
Do you not think I wait for you?
Do you not understand the crystal heart?
Its facets like mirrors for the clouds
absent of nothing blue.

Invincible heaven with downcast eyes
and burning bullets of victory that peel through flesh
like a hungry ax,
why did you follow me?
I need an equal not a slayer.
I need a companion not a ruler.
I need love not commandments.

Of things forgotten
I have never been one.
God seems to find me even in the tumbleweed
when winds howl
and I become the wishbone in the hands
of good and evil.
Why do they seek me out?
What purpose do I serve
if I cannot become visible to you?

Chamber Nineteen Poetry

You know, when they put animals to sleep
children wait outside
as the needle settles the debt of pain and age.
The mother or father write a check and
sign their name twice that day.
They drop a watermark of tears.
They smile for their children
through clenched hearts beating
sideways like a pendulum
of time.

And I see all of this and more in myself.
A small animal whose debts are soon to be settled.
Children are already appearing outside
waiting for the smile of parents to reassure.
The signature and watermark
they never see.

Of winter sanctuary
I have found only you.
Though I wait for signals to draw me from the cold
into your fire
I know they will come
even though I fumble for my key.
Even though my heart is beheaded.
Even though I have only learned division.
I remember you
and the light above your door.

Chamber Twenty Poetry

Bullets and Light

I am adrift tonight
as though a privilege denied
is the passageway
to keep body and soul together.
You have kept so much at bay
I wonder if your enchantment
is to tame passion.
Cornered by your savage artillery
you sling your bullets like schools of fish
darting to a feast,
and I surge ahead tired of being the food.
When I look back
I can see fragments of you
hiding in the underbrush,
stubborn remnants of your vanished heart.
I can still love them.
I can still hold their fragile nerves
clustered with a welder's tongue
seething light as pure as any ever beheld.

Perhaps I drift away
because of the chasm I see.
Bullets and light.
How strange bedfellows can be.
But you will never confess
nor shed your doubt of me.
I will always remain an enigma hurling itself
like litter across your absolute path.
A sudden shaft of light
that begets a deep shadow
that temporarily blinds.

Hope-stirred eyes have always sought to steal
you from the simian nature
that collects at your feet
and pulls at you like derelict children.
My unearthly hunger drew me away from you,
even against my will, or at least my conscious will.

Chamber Twenty Poetry

There was always something calculating
the distance between us.
Some cosmic abacus shuffling sums
of bullets and light
looking for the ledger's balance,
but never quite locating its exact frequency.

Nature of Angels

Midnight in the desert and all is well.
I told myself so and so it is,
or it is not,
I haven't quite decided yet.
Never mind the coyotes' howl or
the shrinking light.

Holiness claims my tired eyes
as I return the stare of stars.
They seem restless, but maybe they're
just ink blots and I'm the one
who's really restless.

There is something here that repeals me.
In its abundance I am absent.
So I shouted at the desert spirits,
tell me your secrets
or I will tell you my sorrows.

The spirits lined up quickly then.
Wings fluttering.
Hearts astir.
I heard many voices become one
and it spoke to the leafless sky
as a tenet to earth.

We hold no secrets.
We are simply windows to your future.
Which is now and which is then
is the question we answer.
But you ask the question.
If there is a secret we hold

it is nothing emboldened by words
or we would commonly speak.

I turned to the voice,
what wisdom is there in that?
If words can't express your secret wisdom,
then I am deaf and you are mute and we are blind.
At least I can speak my sorrows.
Again the wings fluttered
and the voices stirred
hoping the sorrow would not spill
like blood upon the desert.

But there were no more sounds
save the coyote and the owl.
And then a strange resolution suffused my sight.
I felt a presence like an enormous angel
carved of stone was placed behind me.
I couldn't turn for fear its loss would spill my sorrow.
But the swelling presence was too powerful to ignore
so I turned around to confront it,
and there stood a trickster coyote
looking at me with glass eyes
painting my fire, sniffing my fear,
and drawing my sorrow away in intimacy.
And I understood the nature of angels.

Chamber Twenty-One Poetry

Dream Wanderer

Intoxicated with children's thoughts
I wonder,
why are souls so deep and men so blind?
How can souls be eclipsed
by such tiny minds?
Do we love the damp passageways of Hell?
Where every drop of pale water
that falls from the cavern walls
is unwashed music etched in silence...

My favored dreams have disappeared
astride the backs of eagles.
With wings sweeping downward, lifting upward,
they are carried away like finespun,
elegant seeds
on a crystalline wind.
Without them
I am divinely barren
like an empty vessel denied its purpose.
I can only stare into the silence
ever listening for heaven's murmur.
Knowing that behind the darkening mist
angels are building shelters for human innocence.
Shelters torn from something dark
and gravely wounded.
Havens resistant to all disease.

I thought I was endowed
with a promised beauty
that would free the neglected dreams of a demigod.
That would untie their feeble knots
and release them into light's caress.
But the glorious reins
that had once been mine,
tattered and stained with blood,
have slipped from my hands in disuse
as a web abandoned to a ghostly wind.
I can still reach them.

I can feel their shadow across my hands.
Their power, like an electric storm
wandering aimlessly without fuel,
soon to be exhausted.

This piece of paper
is torn from something dark
and gravely wounded.
It is the mirror I hold up to the blackened sky.
A devious sacrifice.

Leaping from star to star
my eyes weave a constellation.
My thoughts in search of the endless motherload.
My heart listening for the sound
of unstained children dreaming.
The dream wanderer looks back at me.
Calls my name in a whispered voice.
Beckons me with an outstretched wing.

"Fly! Your favored dreams await you!"

The voice boomed like thunder swearing.
My wings trembled with forbidden power
as they searched the wind's current
for signs of release.
Currents that would carry me
to the high branches of trees
suckling the sun in fields beyond my kingdom.

In a moment's interlude
I unfolded my wings and vaulted skyward,
into the blue vestibule.
Sheer speed.
Rivers beneath were brown veins
swollen on earth's legs,
or savage cuts that bled green.
The sun sliced holes in the clouds
with tender spears of crimson light.
The moon was rising in the eastern sky—
an oyster shell

Chamber Twenty-One Poetry

pitted by time.
Lonely winds would rush by
searching for an outpost of stillness.
The earthen dungeon
peered up at me with contempt
like a nursemaid relieved of her duty.

I forgot the ground.
I canceled gravity.
Balanced against aboriginal hopes and fears
I became the shaman who dances
in the spirit waters of ancestors
plucking words and meanings from the cumbrous air.

I thought only of the dream wanderer...
the holy wind that rekindles
my exquisite longing for raw truth.
To seize it like medicine
in a sleepless fever hoping to be healed.
The halcyon spire!
The dusty places of purity.

These wings are torn
from something dark and gravely wounded.
They carry me to my favored dreams
and choke the inertia of indifference dead.
Their strength is perfectly matched
to my destination.
One more mile beyond these trees,
I would fall like a fumbled star
into the moat of a starving world.

My favored dreams will wander again.
In time they will soar to trees of a richer kingdom.
My wings will again follow their flight,
track their heartbeat
and build a quilt of a thousand dreams intermingled.
One more turn of the infinite circle.
The dream slate revivified.
Navigable—

even in the murky waters
and cloudy skies of the itinerant traveler.
The dream wanderer reveals
(with a flip of the hourglass of heaven),
as above
so below.
Create your world and let it go forward
entrusted to the one that is all.
The leavening will prevail.
It is the lesson I learned
with my wings outstretched beneath
the glaring sky.
It is the rawness I seek
untouched by another's polish.

Forgiver

Last night we talked for hours.
You cried in unstoppable sorrow,
while I felt a presence carve itself into me
source and savior of your dragging earth.
You feel so deeply,
your mind barely visible
staring ahead to what the heart already knows.
I see the distance you must heal.
I know your pacing heart bounded by corners
that have been rounded and smoothed
like a polished stone from endless waves.
For all I know you are me
in another body,
slots where spirits reach in
to throw the light
interpreting dreams.
Prowling for crowns.

Are there ways to find your heart
I haven't found?
You, I will swallow without tasting first.
I don't care the color.

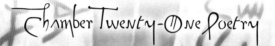

Chamber Twenty-One Poetry

Nothing could warn me away.
Nothing could diminish my love.
And only if I utterly failed
in kinship would you banish me.

Last night, I know I was forgiven.
You gave me that gift unknowing.
I asked for forgiveness
and you said it was unneeded;
time shuffled everything anew
and it was its own
forgiver.

But I know everything not there
was felt by you and transformed.
It was given a new life, though inconspicuous,
it wove us together to a simple, white stone
lying on the ground that marks a spot of sorrow.
Beneath, our union, hallowed of tiny bones
beseech us to forgive ourselves
and lean upon our shoulders
in memory of love, not loss.

Blame settles on no one;
mysterious, it moves in the calculus
of God's plan as though no one thought
to refigure the numbers three to two to one.
The shape stays below the stone.
We walk away,
knowing it will resettle
in our limbs
in our bones
in our hearts
in our minds
in our soul.

Chamber Twenty-Two Poetry

In the Kindness of Sleep

I visited you last night when you
were sleeping with a child's abandon.
Curled so casual in sheets
inlaid by your beauty.
I held my hand to your face
and touched as gently
as I know how
so you could linger with your dreams.
I heard soft murmurs that only angels make
when they listen to their home.
So I drew my hand away
uneasy that I might wake you
even as gentle as I was.

But you stayed with your dreams
and I watched as they found their way to you
in the kindness of sleep.
And I dreamed that I was an echo of your body
curled beside you like a fortune hunter
who finally found his gold.
I nearly wept at the sound of your breath,
but I stayed quiet as a winter lake, and bit my lip
to ensure I wouldn't be detected.

I didn't want to intrude
so I set my dream aside
and I gently pulled your hand from underneath
the covers to hold.
A hand whose entry into flesh
must have been the lure that brought me here.
And as I hold it
I remember why I came
to feel your pulse
and the beating of your heart in deep slumber.
And I remember why I came in the
kindness of sleep—
to hold your hand, touch your face
and listen to the soft breathing

Chamber Twenty-Two Poetry

of an angel,
curled so casual in sheets
inlaid by your beauty.

Warm Presence

I once wore an amulet
that guarded against the forceps of humanity.
It kept at bay the phalanx of wolves
that circled me like phantoms of Gethsemane.
Phantoms that even now
replay their mantra like conch shells.
Coaxing me to step out and join the earthly tribe.
To bare my sorrow's spaciousness
like a cottonwood's seed to the wind.

Now I listen and watch for signals.
To emerge a recluse squinting in ambivalence
inscribed to tell what has been held by locks.
It is all devised in the sheath of cable
that connects us to Culture.
The single, black strand that portrays us to God.
The DNA that commands our image
and guides our natural selection of jeans.

Are there whispers of songs flickering
in dark, ominous thunder?
Is there truly a sun behind this wall of monotone clouds
that beats a billion hammers of light?
There are small, flat teeth that weep venom.
There is an inviolate clemency
in the eyes of executioners while their hands toil to kill.
But there is no explanation for
voyeur saints who grieve only with their eyes.
There is only one path to follow
when you connect your hand and eye
and release the phantoms.

This poem is a shadow of my heart
and my heart the shadow of my mind,

which is the shadow of my soul
the shadow of God.
God, a shadow of some unknown, unimaginable
cluster of intelligence where galaxies
are cellular in the universal body.
Are the shadows connected?
Can this vast, unknown cluster reach into this poem
and assemble words that couple at a holy junction?
It is the reason I write.
Though I cannot say this junction has ever
been found (at least by me).

It is more apparent that some unholy hand,
pale from darkness, reaches out and casts its sorrow.
Some lesser shadow or phantom
positions my hand in a lonely outpost
to claim some misplaced luminance.
The phantom strains to listen for songs as they whisper.
It coordinates with searching eyes.
It peels skin away to touch the soft fruit.
It welds shadows as one.

I dreamed that I found a ransom note
written in God's own hand.
Written so small I could barely
read its message, which said:
"I have your soul, and unless you deliver—
in small, unmarked poems—
the sum of your sorrows, you will never
see it alive again."

And so I write while something unknown is curling
around me, irresistible to my hand, yet unseen.
More phantoms from Gethsemane who honor
sorrow like professional confessors lost in their despair.
I can reach sunflowers the size of
moonbeams, but I cannot reach the sum of my sorrows.
They elude me like ignescent stars that fall nightly
outside my window.

Chamber Twenty-Two Poetry

My soul must be nervous.
The ransom is too much to pay
even for a poet who explores the black strand of Culture.

Years ago I found an
Impression—like snow angels—left in tall grass
by some animal, perhaps a deer or bear.
When I touched it I felt the warm presence of life,
not the cold radiation of crop circles.
This warm energy lingers only for a moment
but when it is touched it lasts forever.
And this is my fear:
that the sum of my sorrows will last forever
when it is touched, and even though my soul
is returned unharmed,
I will remember the cold radiation
and not the warm presence of life.

Now I weep when children sing
and burrow their warm presence into my heart.
Now I feel God adjourned by the
source of shadows.
Now I feel the pull of a bridle,
breaking me like a wild horse turned
suddenly submissive.
I cannot fight the phantoms
or control them or turn them away.
They prod at me as if a lava stream should
continue on into the cold night air
and never tire of movement.
Never cease its search for the perfect place to be a sculpture.
An anonymous feature of the gray landscape.

If ever I find the sum of my sorrows
I hope it is at the bridgetower
where I can see both ways
before I cross over.
Where I can see forgeries like a crisp mirage
and throw off my bridle.
I will need to be wild when I face it.

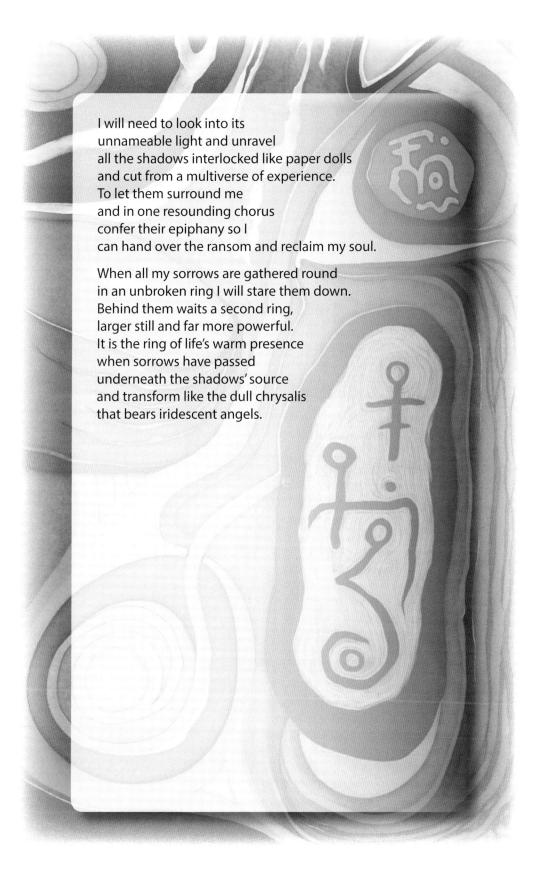

I will need to look into its
unnameable light and unravel
all the shadows interlocked like paper dolls
and cut from a multiverse of experience.
To let them surround me
and in one resounding chorus
confer their epiphany so I
can hand over the ransom and reclaim my soul.

When all my sorrows are gathered round
in an unbroken ring I will stare them down.
Behind them waits a second ring,
larger still and far more powerful.
It is the ring of life's warm presence
when sorrows have passed
underneath the shadows' source
and transform like the dull chrysalis
that bears iridescent angels.

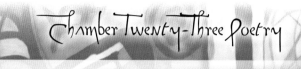

Chamber Twenty-Three Poetry

Spiral

Inside there is something gnawing
with silken jaws and wax teeth.
It holds me still in pureness
like a circle whose middle
is my cage.

While you went away from me
I was ever tightening my circle.
A spiral cut in glass.
A flower's bloom dropping petals.
A winnowed ball of yarn
spilling color.

I see the inside of your thigh
brilliant in its smoothness,
and I spiral ever closer to your edge.
Paper cut touching I burn
bleeding without pain.
How could I spill so easily
without knowing why?

When I hear your voice
there is no quenching this ache
to hold you.
Like one who draws near and then forgets
the story they came to tell,
I circle you waiting for thread's tautness
to draw us ever closer
though I know not how.

The final luxury is the kiss
of your boundless heart.
The final beauty so pure
all else limps behind blissfully in your wake.
Drawing from your shadows
the light of saplings
lurking on the forest floor.

If I could unbutton you,

take your dress down
I would see a map of my universe.
A phantom limb, grown from
my body like wings sprouting from a chrysalis
reaches for you.
It is the hand of clarity
desperate for your skin
so powerfully bidden
as though a shimmering block of light
cut from black velvet,
stood before me.
And all I could do was to reach out
and touch it,
not knowing why,
but utterly unafraid.

Soul's Photograph

Who will find me
in the morning after
the winds rush over the barren body
that once held me like a tree a leaf?
Who will find me
when mercy, tired of smiling,
finally frowns in deep furrows of ancient skin?

Who will find me?
Will it be you?
Perhaps it will be a cold morning
with fresh prints of snow
and children laughing as they
lay down in the arms of angels.
Perhaps it will be a warm evening
when crickets play their music
to the stillness of waiting stars.
Perhaps it will be the light
that draws me away
or some sweet surrender that captures me
in its golden nets.

Chamber Twenty-Three Poetry

Who will find me
when I have left and cast
my line in new waters trickling
so near this ocean of sand?
Listen for me when I'm gone.
Listen for me in poems
that were formed with lips mindful of you.
You who will outlast me.
Who linger in the courage I could not find.
You can see me
in these words.
They are the lasting image.
Soul's photograph.

Chamber Twenty-four Poetry

The Pure and Perfect

Someday the messengers will arrive
with stories of a nocturnal sun
despondent, burning implacably
in the deepest shade of a thousand shadows.
They will tell you of the
serene indifference of God.
They will draw you by the hand
through bruised alleyways
and prove the desperation of man
rejected from the beauty of an unearthly realm.
The news will arrive
as a tribute to the death of oracles.
Sparing words of purpose
the messengers will announce the
cold fury of realism's cave.

Someday, the messengers will send their thoughts
through books that have no pulse.
You will be accused of weakness
that drowns you in servitude.
A queer rivalry will beset you
and your life will crawl like an awkward beast
that has no home.

And you, my dearest friends,
who are truth—who were all along,
will renew your devotion
to a powerful image in a distant mirror.
You will listen to these stories
and tear at your silent heart
with animal claws that are dulled
by the stone doors of time.
Where the unattested is confirmed
your vestige-soul is stored.
It will strengthen you
and cradle you in the light
of your own vision,
which will be hurled like lightening

through twilight's dull corridor.

The messengers will cry
at the sound of your rejection.
They will scream: "Do you want to be a
lowly servant and lonely saint?"

Mutants of the light
are always tested with doubts
of a swollen isolation
and the promise of truth's betrayal.
Listen without hearing.
Judge without pardon.
The grand parasite of falsehood
will prevail if you believe only your beliefs.

Someday, when all is clear to you—
when the winds have lifted all veils
and the golden auberge is the locus
of our souls—
you will be tested no more.
You will have reached destiny's lodge
and the toilsome replica of God
is jettisoned for the pure and perfect.

A Fire For You

On this, the shortest day of the year,
I have journeyed to the Great Plains
to build a fire for you.

The night air is cold like a cellar
cut from ancient stones.
But I found some wood among the deserted plains
buried under the grasses and dirt,
hidden away like leaves
that had become the soil.
After I cleaned the wood by hand—its dirt beneath
my nails and the fabric of my cloth
I sent a flame
combusted by the mere thought of you.

And the wood became fire.

There were hermit stars that gathered
overhead to keep me company.
Your spirit was there as well
amidst the fire's flames.
We laughed at the deep meaning of the sky
and its spacious ways.
Marveling at the flat mirror of the plain
that sends so little skyward,
like the hearts of children denied
a certain kind of love.

You played with spirits
when you were young among these fields.
You didn't know their names then.
I was one.
Even without a name, or body,
I watched your gaze, unrelenting to the things
that beat between the
two mirrors of the sky and plain.

I believe it was here also
that you learned to speak with God.
Not in so many words as you're now accustomed,
but I'm certain that God listened to your life
and gathered around your fire
for warmth and meaning.
In the deserted plains he found you set apart
from all things missing.

Dear spirit, I have held this vigil for so long,
tending fires whose purpose I have forgotten.
I think warmth was one.
Perhaps light was another.
Perhaps hope was the strongest of these.

If ever I find you around my fire,
built by hands
that know your final skin,
between the sheets of the sky and plain,

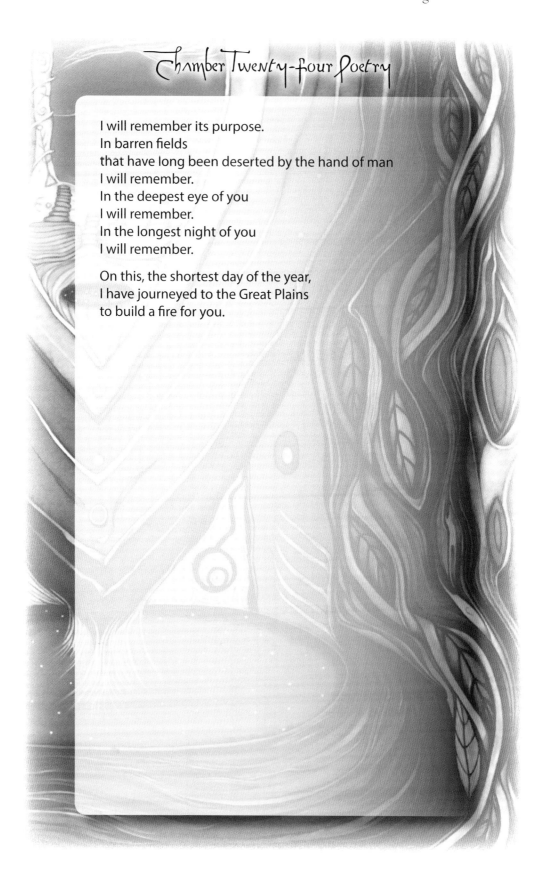

Chamber Twenty-four Poetry

I will remember its purpose.
In barren fields
that have long been deserted by the hand of man
I will remember.
In the deepest eye of you
I will remember.
In the longest night of you
I will remember.

On this, the shortest day of the year,
I have journeyed to the Great Plains
to build a fire for you.

Section Four

The Music

Dr. Neruda:

"When you hear the music in 384-bit resolution with the original paintings, standing inside the actual chamber in which they were placed, it is a very moving and spiritual experience. Unlike any I've ever had."

The Second Interview of Dr. Jamisson Neruda, p. 295

The Chamber Paintings, as they're represented on the WingMakers website, are translations of the real paintings. The original works reside within the Tributary Zone near the galactic center of the Milk Way galaxy. The original "paintings" are photonically animated by an advanced technology that permits the art to morph intelligently as dictated by the music. In other words, music is the engine that animates the painting.

James, from Topical Arrangement of Qs and As, Question 60, Session Three.

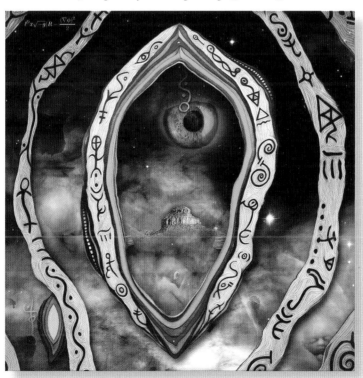

Introduction to the Ancient Arrow Project Music

 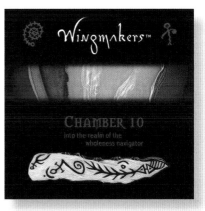

 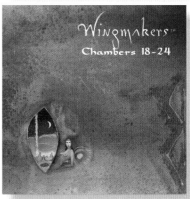

The anonymous force behind . . .all the discs of the WingMakers welcomes you to experience that part of you that lives in the shadow of no thing. . . .whose essence reveals itself in the union of music, poetry, and art.[52]

Of all the components comprising the WingMakers/Lyricus materials, the music probably has the most power to transport one's consciousness to heightened levels. Below is a list of the Ancient Arrow Project CDs arranged chronologically.

1. WingMakers: Chambers Eleven to Seventeen, 2000
2. WingMakers First Source CD-ROM Chambers One to Nine, 2001
3. WingMakers: Chambers Eighteen to Twenty-four, 2001
4. WingMakers: Chamber Ten, 2001

One interesting aspect of James' musical compositions is that they span the entire spectrum of websites in James' presentation of the Lyricus teachings. These include the websites of WingMakers, Lyricus, and Event Temples, to date. The music thus covers at least a ten-year evolution and expansion of James' mission and unfolding plan as it proceeds further into this century.

---

52. "The Music of the WingMakers: Volume 3 Chambers 18-24" inside booklet.

The WingMakers Music

Recalling the exercises given in the fourth philosophy paper, there are techniques for using the paintings, poetry, and music for opening a channel of awareness between the Human Instrument and the Sovereign Integral. The exercise dedicated to the music is called the Body-Mind technique.

This technique is different from the other two exercises in that it does not include the soul. Whereas the chamber painting exercise involves the *mind and soul*, and the poetry exercise relates to the *emotions and Sovereign Integral*, the music technique engages the *mind and body*.

The exercise is used exclusively with the music from Chambers Seventeen through Twenty-four—eight tracks in all. The instructions in the fourth philosophy paper recommend listening to each track seven times before proceeding to the next one. As a result, the entire exercise comprises fifty-six sessions, and this is called a Grand Cycle. Alternatively, if you prefer, you can listen to tracks one and two seven times before proceeding to the next two tracks. However, you should not exceed this number. Also, try not to let too many days go by without proceeding with the exercise or it won't be effective.

Briefly, the idea underlying this exercise is to allow the body's intelligence to override the mind's controlling activities. The idea is to forget the mind's natural tendency to analyze what it is hearing and to simply focus on the body's desire to move to the rhythms of the music, which are specifically designed for a variety of motions. According to the explanation, this activity helps ground the exploratory energy system into the body at the cellular level.

In the latter part of 2001, James released the music for Chamber Ten. It was a bit of a mystery to some followers of the WingMakers materials as to why there was no Chamber Ten music in the first three CDs. For that matter, one could ask why the chambers CDs were not released in numeric order. No one is really sure why this was the case, but nevertheless Chamber Ten was the last of the Ancient Arrow themed music to come out.

This particular CD is unique in that it is targeted at the tenth chromosome. In order to give this topic greater clarity I have included the entire explanation here. It comes directly from the Chamber Ten CD introduction of the music section of the WingMakers site at Spiritstate.

> *The Wholeness Navigator is the core wisdom. It draws the human instrument to perceive fragmentary existence as a passageway into wholeness and unity. The Wholeness Navigator is the heart of the entity consciousness.*
>
> The music of Chamber Ten weaves compositional patterns and sounds from all corners of the globe—geographically and historically—into a universal anthem of the Wholeness Navigator. It is a complex staging of compositions that will guide your consciousness

into the realm of unity in which we all derive and originate.

Chamber Ten, in the context of the human genome, is analogous to the genetic structure of the human chromosome ten. This chromosome regulates, in large measure, the condition of well being within the human instrument and its relationship to physical, emotional, and mental forms of stress.

Chamber Ten is being released now [late 2001], during this period of increased stress and turmoil, as a means to facilitate a renewed connection within people to their state of wholeness and unity. It is from this state of experience that stress and fear are diminished, and one's immunity system enhanced.

It is suggested to listen to this music a minimum of seven, uninterrupted times, in a comfortable position, eyes closed, and yielding to the journey it will invoke within you. Listening with headphones is recommended. During this journey feelings will undoubtedly arise, and as they do, bless them as you would any source of kindness. They will become signposts in your musical adventure.

There are thirty-eight musical compositions within Chamber Ten that flow together seamlessly. These musical "stanzas" express the flowing movement and multi-faceted expression of the Wholeness Navigator. They are bridges through which you can travel between worlds and dimensions.

This is not meditative music whose purpose is to relax your mind and body. The music of Chamber Ten is designed to call forth that part of you that is eclipsed by your human personality and the human dimension of experience. It is an aural data stream that causes a resonance of the unity vibration that is stored inside all humans.

May this music bring you an awakening of how we are woven from the same source, and may you experience the heart of your consciousness, if only for a moment in time.

From my world to yours,

James [53]

One more interesting point relative to the music of Chamber Ten is in the following words sung by a female voice:

Open.
Take me from here to there.
Let the wind blow
my hair and the earth's skin touch me.

---

53. www.wingmakers.com/music-chamber10.html

These words originate from the tenth chamber poem, "Downstream." Actually, the first line of the poem is "Open me," but in the lyrical version the word "me" is not present. Although there is not too much to read into this, the words of poem chamber ten do suggest a journey, with the suggestion of movement as the wind blows your hair and as you feel the earth touching your feet as you stride forward. The "journey" is one in which we travel to the core of our being, described here as the Wholeness Navigator. It should be noted that in the earlier writings of James he often referred to the Wholeness Navigator as a synonym for the soul. If you refer to the article "Anatomy of the Individuated Consciousness" there are definitions of the six components comprising the Individuated Self. The Wholeness Navigator is at the core, or heart of the Entity, which resides in the "realm of unity in which we all derive and originate."

In terms of the CD comprising Chambers eleven to seventeen and the First Source CD-ROM with Chambers one to nine, the former contains music with powerful and energetic rhythms, while the latter CD contains more mellow sounds and rhythms. Personally, I found the music of Chambers one to nine rather haunting as if they were activating deep ancient, almost primordial memories and feelings. Although James never stated that these first two CDs were encoded, I have always felt that Chambers one to nine were designed to awaken something deep within me, something that I had forgotten. Perhaps you too will have similar feelings and certainly feelings different from my own.

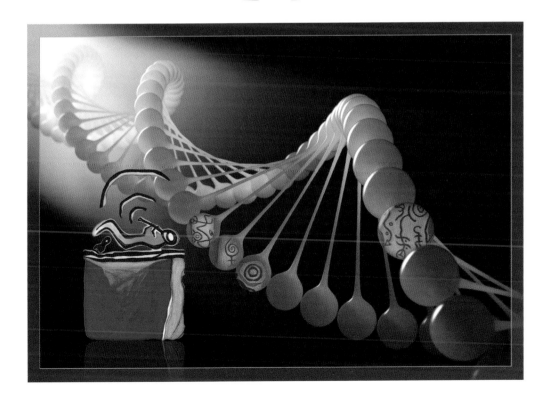

Introduction to the Hakomi Project Music:
Chambers One, Two and Three

*"In the generosity of stars we live. By the freedom of our will we love.
Through the enchantment of the unexplored we learn."*[54]

Hakomi Project: Chambers One to Two, 2002
Hakomi Project: Chamber Three, 2003

The Hakomi Project—Music of Chambers One to Two

Toward the end of 2002, James released the first CD in the Hakomi Project series. Hakomi represents the second site of the seven created by the WingMakers in that mythological presentation. James has placed this site near Cusco, Peru.

This CD consists of two tracks and the inside of the CD label asks an interesting question: "Where do you stand in relation to the other realms?" This question is a translation from the language of the Hopi Indians of the American southwest. At first, this question does not seem to be a big deal, but further musing on it can lead us into thoughts and feelings associated with the subjective dimensions of our inner lives. In other words, the Hakomi Project is geared toward psychology and the study of our thoughts, feelings, and actions. These three factors are the mechanisms

---

54. www.wingmakers.com/music-hakomichamber3.html

of our Human Instruments and reflect the state and level of our consciousness.

Before continuing further, an interesting twist to James' increased emphasis on human psychology with the Hakomi Project comes to light through a search of the word "hakomi" on the Internet. The results reveal a form of psychotherapy called Hakomi. According to the Hakomi Institute website, this system was founded by Ron Kurtz and a core group of trainers in 1981.[55]

The psychotherapy is based on the mind-body connection. One underlying resource of the system is based on the Buddhist practice of mindfulness. Simply put, mindfulness is the effort to stay conscious of every passing moment—to hold one's awareness in a moment-to-moment neutral state of observation and witnessing.

The body, or somatic aspect of the Hakomi system, utilizes the mindfulness state of being to become aware of the physical body's reactions to emotions and thoughts that arise during a session with a therapist.

Interestingly, the above system of somatic and psychological intertwining roughly equates to James' Body-Mind movement exercise from the fourth philosophy paper. It would not be wise to read too much into this connection between the Hakomi method and James' Hakomi Project, except to say that there is a deep relationship between the physical body's reactions to outer stimuli and the mind's efforts to associate such stimuli with comfortable, pre-defined patterns of response. In short, the mind is the defender of the ego-personality's concretized definitions of its reality. Alternatively, the Body-Mind exercise, with its use of encoded music, is designed to allow the body's intelligence to disrupt the mind's automatic reactions to its surroundings, and thus begin a process of shifting consciousness away from the ego-personality, to the ever-present permanent reality of the Sovereign Integral.

There are no statements from James as to whether the music of Chambers One and Two are encoded. Nevertheless, an excerpt from the Hakomi Chamber One philosophy provides a clue to the specific purpose of these two compositions.

> "The presence of the Wholeness Navigator is invisible to the human instrument, and, for the most part, is not felt sufficient to induce the behaviors of soul. The higher pathways of the mind imagine it, capturing it like the wind a seed, and these images can be translated to the emotions and body through music more vividly than any other art form." — Hakomi Project Translation Chamber One.[56]

In short, this first CD in the Hakomi Project series is designed to evoke feelings akin to that of the Wholeness Navigator. The Wholeness Navigator is one of six components of the individuated consciousness, and its function is to provide us with an instinctual sense of being an integral part of the whole of nature and the cosmos. (It is important to remember that whenever we discuss the individuated consciousness we are referring to the Entity.)

55. www.hakomiinstitute.com
56. www.wingmakers.com/music-hakomiproject.html

In addition, the Wholeness Navigator also functions as a navigational guide toward a fusion between the Sovereign Integral and the Human Instrument. This fusion is expressed by the presence of the Sovereign Integral consciousness in everyday life. Ultimately, the Wholeness Navigator is the spiritual compass that guides us back to First Source.

There may be a parallel between the Ancient Arrow music of Chambers one to nine and the Hakomi Project music of Chambers One and Two. As mentioned previously, the one through nine chamber compositions on the First Source CD-ROM are apparently not coded, but I believe they were designed to begin the process of awakening individuals to a greater sense of self and to a sense of profound connection to All That Is. The initial Hakomi Project CD continues this process by evoking a feeling of oneness with the cosmos via the Wholeness Navigator.

The Hakomi Project—Music of Chamber Three

The Chamber Three music, released in 2003, consists of one seventy-four minute track filled with many different sounds and rhythms. It is almost shocking in its interludes of sound effects, mysterious voices, subtle, and sometimes sudden, transitions to beautiful melodies, as well as energizing rhythms. It is a non-stop musical journey that calls forth varied emotions.

Unlike the first Hakomi Project CD with its apparent lack of coding and subtle hint of its connection to the Wholeness Navigator, the second CD has a very specific purpose that is explained in an article by James that accompanies it. The article is entitled "Anatomy of the Individuated Consciousness." Here is a brief description of the unique feature of this CD:

> There is a very specific intention in the design of this particular CD, and it is highly recommended that you read the associated article "Anatomy of the Individuated Consciousness" that is an integral part of this new release. These new materials provide insight into the nature of how this music can affect the human body as well as the unfathomable energy-being that we each possess.[57]

The article opens with the following statement:

> The Chamber Three music from the Hakomi site is designed to stimulate your practice of adventure and embolden you to stretch, and perhaps revitalize, your habits of experimentation as you interact with life.[58]

Later, the article clarifies the nature of the experimentation it recommends. It has nothing to do with such things as trying new foods or learning a new skill. Rather, it focuses on "the motivations to expand and regularly alter or refresh

---

57. www.wingmakers.com/music-hakomichamber3.html
58. "Anatomy of the Individuated Consciousness," p. 560.

your understanding of the broader dynamics that shape your world—both as an individual and as a species." [59]

The "anatomy" aspect of the article relates to six components of the Individuated Consciousness. These six parts are the:

- Remnant Imprint (of the Sovereign Integral)
- Human Instrument (body, emotions, mind)
- Phantom Core (super-consciousness)
- Human Soul, or Entity (fragment of consciousness of First Source)
- Sovereign Integral (core identity of the individual)
- Wholeness Navigator (guide to wholeness and unity)

Although these six components of the individuated consciousness are defined and important to understand, the thrust of the article is directed at the Remnant Imprint.

> The Remnant Imprint is the muse, or inspirational formation of the human instrument insofar as the individual is concerned. It is the voice of deep character that arouses the most potent and noble instincts and creative stirrings of the human being: creating acts of goodness that touch the human soul in oneself and others. [60]

> Within every human instrument is the imprint of the Sovereign Integral, and it is referred to as a 'remnant' only because it exists in the dimension of time and space. In reality it is the cast of energy bestowed by the Sovereign Integral to the human instrument. It is precisely this energy that generates ideas and inspirations, making it possible for the voice of all that you are to surface into the worlds of time and space in which you are only a particle of your total being. [61]

From these descriptions of the Remnant Imprint, it is clear that the music of Chamber Three is designed to interrupt the mind's tendency to organize information, in this case the information is a great variety of melodies, rhythms, and voices. Due to the continuous shift in the music's themes, the mind is never allowed to settle into a fixed idea of what the music is communicating. This has the effect of opening us to feelings associated with change, something the egoic mind is resistant to.

Few people welcome change due to our propensity for predictable patterns of living, but as the old saying goes, "there is nothing permanent in life except change." Major life changes, often involving loss of some kind, introduce crisis in our lives. Crises can lead to opportunities for growth in new directions, but too often they are seen as threats to the comfortable living habits we have established.

Crises may also require us to produce creative solutions to problems that suddenly erupt into our well-worn lifestyles. Within this context, the third chamber

---

59. Ibid., p. 565.
60. Ibid., p. 561.
61. Ibid., p. 561.

music can be catalytic in terms of expectations, as its wide variety of themes move in unexpected directions. Thus, just as crises suddenly interject themselves into our lives, requiring attention and creative solutions, the third chamber music mimics, in a sense, the crises we experience as we go through life. Following this idea, you may discover that this music demands your attention, just as life crises do.

Curiously, the first time my wife and I listened to this music we fell asleep about fifteen minutes into it. This reaction might be similar to our natural tendency to avoid, put off or ignore a crisis. Perhaps the music still had an effect on us because upon a second listening we were stimulated, not sedated to the point of sleep. From this point forward, as previously mentioned, the music *demanded* our full attention. It is also worth noting that in some cases individuals may fall asleep so that listening to something new is first absorbed at a subconscious level. This same idea may also pertain to other mediums as well.

Returning to our main point, by short-circuiting the mind, our awareness is freed and cleared, and therefore is exposed to the influence of the Remnant Imprint. We then have the opportunity to be inspired with new ways of perceiving the thought patterns and reactionary habits of the ego-personality. This can be painful to some degree, as with any form of change. James remarks:

> The music of Chamber Three is not intended exclusively for the human personality, but rather, the individuated consciousness. This is why Chamber Three is composed in the manner that it is—a journey that winds its way through a mosaic of sounds, patterns, keys, rhythms, chants, vocalizations, and words. It is also why some may feel at first—uncomfortable with this music because it speaks to elements of their energy-being that have become contented with the reality of being unobserved.[62]

Here, James is juxtaposing the human personality and the individuated consciousness. Whereas the ego-personality tends toward an established pattern of living—a fixed psychological structure—the individuated consciousness, or Entity is fluid and dynamic. Consequently, our limited awareness and desire for ordered structure within the Human Instrument, if overly accomplished, will be at odds with the Entity's desire for new experience and dynamic change. After all, this goes to the heart of the blueprint of exploration (see third philosophy paper of the Ancient Arrow Project).

The bottom line on the music of Hakomi Project Chamber Three is that its purpose is to open our fixed ego pattern to the inspirational and creative influence of the Remnant Imprint. The music urges us to move from fixity to dynamism. This may feel uncomfortable to some, but this musical journey has the potential to shift us to an expanded awareness and inspire us to create new ideas and perspectives related to our personal lives, as well as to life in general.

---

62. Ibid., p. 564-565.

Individuals who declare themselves an individuated consciousness, not merely a human personality, are immediately more connected to the voice of the Remnant Imprint.[63]

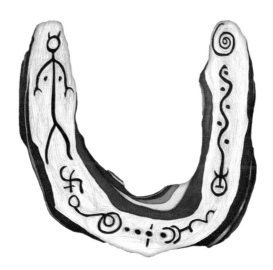

Anatomy of the Individuated Consciousness
Associated Materials of Chamber Three Hakomi CD

The Chamber Three music from the Hakomi site is designed to stimulate your practice of adventure and embolden you to stretch, and perhaps revitalize, your habits of experimentation as you interact with life.

Life provides each individual with an amazing array of mystifying messages. You are encouraged to "be yourself" and yet at the same time, you are coerced and trained—however subtly—to conform to the structure and norms of society. You are taught the secular knowledge of humanity's past, but you remain uninformed of the spiritual purpose of humanity's near-term future. These are but two examples of how the individual is influenced to become obedient to the social order of the day.

Within this natural tension of competing influences, mixed messages, and social edicts is the angst of the individual caught in the vice of do this, but do not do that. This imposed conformity dulls the impulse to experiment with life, and this lack of experimentation further entrains the individual into compliance with a prescribed wisdom path of limited scope.

There is a voice within you that speaks truth to power irrespective of consequence. This voice, in the language of the WingMakers, is the *Remnant Imprint* of the Sovereign Integral. It is actually a voice within each of you that is, to varying degrees, audible to the human mind if not the human ear.

It is this voice that is connected to the part of you that is all of you. In the WingMakers' Glossary the following definition exists for this aspect of your being:

Remnant Imprint: The human instrument is the genetic compound of three separate, but related structures: the physical composition (body), the emotional predisposition (emotional template), and the mental configuration (mind-thought generator). These three aspects of the human instrument are inexplicably bound together through the intricate and utterly unique interface of the genetic code and life experience.

Within the human instrument, and acting as its animator of creative goodness, is the Remnant Imprint of the Sovereign Integral. The Remnant Imprint is the muse or inspirational formation of the human instrument insofar as the individual is concerned. It is the voice of deep character that arouses the most potent and noble instincts and creative stirrings of the human being: creating acts of goodness that touch the human soul in oneself and others.

It is a difficult abstraction for time-bound humans to understand, but the Sovereign Integral consciousness is the fusion of the entity consciousness in the worlds of timespace. All expressions and experiences of the human instrument, collectively, are deposited within the Sovereign Integral state of consciousness, and it is precisely this that imprints upon the human instrument of the individual.

For some who have traveled across the material universe in various times, places, and physical bodies, the Remnant Imprint is more influential and expressive. For those who are relatively new to the Universe of TimeSpace, the Remnant Imprint lacks persistent influence and is easily overcome by the seduction of power, fear, and greed—the machinery of survival.

Within every human instrument is the imprint of the Sovereign Integral, and it is referred to as a 'remnant' only because it exists in the dimension of time and space. In reality it is the cast of energy bestowed by the Sovereign Integral to the human instrument. It is precisely this energy that generates ideas and inspirations, making it possible for the voice of all that you are to surface into the worlds of time and space in which you are only a particle of your total being.

The Remnant Imprint is often confused with the Higher Self, or human soul. The distinction, subtle as it may seem, is vital to understand. There are many discrete but ultimately integrated states of consciousness that animate, express through, and observe the human instrument. The energy of the Remnant Imprint is generated from the Sovereign Integral consciousness, filtered through the Wholeness Navigator and imprinted upon the mind, emotions, and physical body.

This energy, because of its origination from the Sovereign Integral, imbues the human instrument with a multiplicity of ideas, ideals, and approaches to being. It is not hindered by convention or social structure. It is not diminished by intimidation. It is forthright in its effort to instill the innate rights of sovereignty through the expression of its responsible and informed voice. It calibrates the ascension path of a mortal soul carrier against the acts of creative goodness, independent of the obstacles, ridicules, and customary ornaments of culture.

The Remnant Imprint is an important part of the overall architecture of the individuated consciousness, which each of us, living within the worlds of time and space, possess. In total, there are six fundamental and integrated systems that comprise the individuated consciousness. In addition to the Remnant Imprint, the other components of this architecture are:

Human Instrument consists of the twenty-four primary systems and four major elements: body, emotions, mind, and genetic mind. It is the soul carrier in the worlds of the time and space.

Phantom Core is written about in the Lyricus Discourse Three. Here is a short excerpt:

> Even in the quiet moments of your life when you are staring through a window or reading a book, there is a great universe of experience that is perceived by this phantom core, and every miniature detail is faithfully recorded and transmitted to the soul.
>
> The phantom core is the super consciousness of the human instrument. It is separate from the soul, and is considered the soul's emissary to the natural world in which the human instrument must interact.
>
> It is through this awareness that soul experiences the natural world of limitation and separation, drawing in the experiences that help it to build appreciation for the Grand Multiverse that is the garment of First Source.

Human Soul (entity consciousness) is, in the simplest of terms, a fragment of the Universal Spirit Consciousness of First Source. As reported in the Glossary, it is composed of a very refined and pure energy vibration that is equal to Source Intelligence (spirit). It is an immortal, living, coherent consciousness that is a replica of the energy of its Creator with the individual consciousness of a unique personality.

Sovereign Integral is a state of consciousness whereby the entity and all of its various forms of expression and perception are integrated as a conscious wholeness. The Sovereign Integral is the core identity of the individual. It is the convergence of the experiential worlds of time and space with the innate knowledge of First Source divested within the individual at the time of its birth. It is the gathering of all created experiences and all instinctive knowledge.

Wholeness Navigator guides the human instrument to perceive fragmentary existence as a passageway into wholeness and unity. The Wholeness Navigator pursues wholeness and integration. It is the heart of the entity consciousness, shepherding the human instrument and the human soul to unify and operate as a single, sovereign being interconnected with all other beings. The Wholeness Navigator is the gravitational force that forms the purposeful clustering of Sovereign Integrals, reigning in sovereignty from the existential grasp of self-sufficiency.

The anatomy of the individuated consciousness is composed of these six primary energy systems, and within this structure or architecture, only the human body—the tip of the iceberg—is visible to the human eye. Each of these energy systems possesses a sensory awareness that is tuned to self-recognition much as the human body's eye-brain system is tuned to see the physical body. For example, the Wholeness Navigator has senses that are tuned to see, hear, think, and feel itself, and because of this, it identifies with itself as the central element within the individuated consciousness or personality. This is known as perceptual locus.

In most instances, the fundamental systems that comprise the individuated consciousness are not aware of one another in any significant way and operate independently, as if in their own worlds. In other cases, there is an awareness, however dimly held, that consciousness consists of more than what is immediately visible within the spectrum of available perception. In rare instances there is both an awareness and understanding of this ensemble structure and its overarching purpose, and this is the evolutionary direction of the human species.

Music is a vibratory experience that can be "tuned" to affect the entire individuated consciousness structure. Musical vibrations can be organized to touch the components of the individuated consciousness in a coordinated manner that

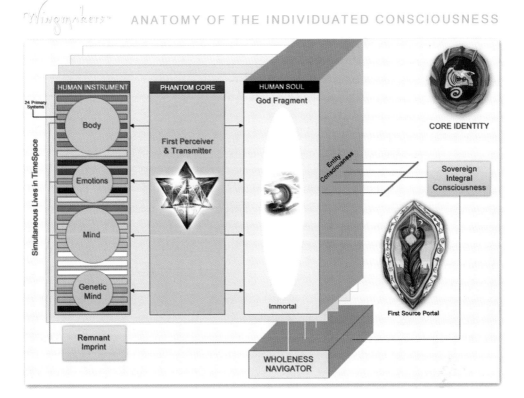

orchestrates the elements of the individuated consciousness (as described above) to become increasingly aware of one another. In other words, music vibrations can kindle and nurture the elements of the individuated consciousness to become a more coordinated ensemble, causing them to align around a common purpose.

Chamber Three of the Hakomi Project is designed to stimulate each of the elements of the individuated consciousness, but its emphasis is in developing the voice of the Remnant Imprint. The reason for this is that the Remnant Imprint can be likened to a precursor or antecedent to the Sovereign Integral state of consciousness in terms of the worlds of time and space.

It is the Remnant Imprint that is capable of creating and sustaining a wisdom path that is based on the life principles of the Sovereign Integral. As you can see in the diagram below, the disproportion between the human personality and the immensity of the individuated consciousness. The human personality is where the individual lives during its waking life. It is also where virtually all media—television, music, film is designed to interface with the individual.

The individuated consciousness is the template upon which our Creator casts each of us. We are an individuated consciousness comprised of the essential components and functions therein whether we recognize and acknowledge this factor not. When the irrefutable scientific discovery of the human soul occurs, the magnificent architecture that each of us possesses will still remain largely hidden.

The music of Chamber Three is not intended exclusively for the human personality, but rather, the individuated consciousness. This is why Chamber Three

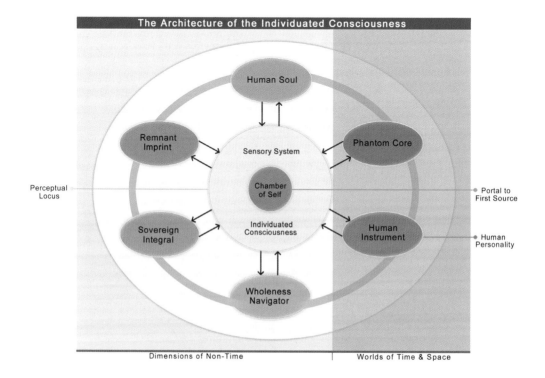

is composed in the manner that it is—a journey that winds its way through a mosaic of sounds, patterns, keys, rhythms, chants, vocalizations, and words. It is also why some may feel at first, uncomfortable with this music because it speaks to elements of their energy-being that have become contented with the reality of being unobserved.

It is vital that the individual know the magnitude of their structure, and how the human personality can become more aware of the "component parts" of its consciousness and how they function. The reason for this is simple: in the conceptual understanding of your vastness is contained the seed that expands your sense of adventure and experimentation.

To be clear, this is not the same experimentation and adventure that one might associate with trying new foods or experimenting with a new manner of dress. This has a particular focus on the motivations to expand and regularly alter or refresh your understanding of the broader dynamics that shape your world—both as an individual and as a species.

For example, research has shown that the average person, by the time they become an adult, has seen two hundred thousand acts of violence as portrayed through media. These exposures to violence support the aggressive tendencies inherent in the human instrument's survival instincts. This aggression manifests on all scales of human endeavor, it is not limited to the interactions of one individual to another, indeed, it manifests as international discord as well.

The particle within the individuated consciousness called the human personality is constantly being conditioned by society. Intentionally or not, if this element of your identity becomes your exclusive perceptual locus, you will tend to respond to life according to the embedded program of your human personality—your instincts.

There is also an embedded program within the individuated consciousness, and this Program—as it pertains to the worlds of time and space—is primarily expressed through the Remnant Imprint of the Sovereign Integral.

Individuals who declare themselves an individuated consciousness, not merely a human personality, are immediately more connected to the voice of the Remnant Imprint. This simple act can rekindle the embedded program within the individuated consciousness and spark a new wisdom path. There is an unimaginable shortage of media that speaks to this aspect of the human consciousness and supports this program to emerge and express itself. This is, in part, the purpose behind the music of Chamber Three.

From my world to yours,

Introduction to the Hakomi Project Music:
Chambers Four to Twenty-one

"What is within is without equal, it arises from the smallest space where the First Vibration of the Unmanifest surges in the splendor of One World's Grace."[64]

Hakomi Project: Chambers Four to Six, 2003
Hakomi Project: Chambers Seven to Twelve, 2005
Hakomi Project: Project Thirteen to Twenty-one, not on CD

As the list shows, the last offering is not on CD. However, these collections are available for download purchase in the music section in the product section of the WingMakers' website.

The Hakomi Project—Music of Chambers Four to Six

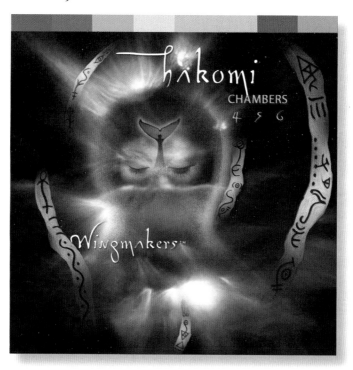

Following the release of the Hakomi Project Chamber Three CD early in 2003, the Hakomi CD Chambers Four to Six was released later that year. Just as the music of Chamber Three had an accompanying article, the new CD also had an article supplementing the music. This article is entitled "Coherence of the Evolutionary Consciousness." Whereas the article associated with Chamber Three centered on the Remnant Imprint, this new CD and article focuses on the effects of music and sound on the Human Instrument. The article emphasizes:

---

64. www.wingmakers.com/music-hakomichambers4-6.html

- The positive and negative effects of music on the Human Instrument
- The power of music and sound to instill a reconnection to spirit
- The relation of mantras to the root frequencies of First Source
- First Source's expression of sound and light
- The creation of an Interface Zone between the Human Instrument and the coarse vibrations of the outer world of forms

As you can see, this short article covers a lot of ground, but it all comes down to restoring our connection to the unifying nature of spirit. As stated by James: "The music of Hakomi Project Chambers Four to Six is intended to restore and support this sense of reconnection." [65]

The title of the article itself implies the unitive nature of reality across all dimensions. Consciousness is evolutionary and coherent by nature. The *evolutionary aspect of consciousness* is an established fact of modern psychology and sociology. The coherence of consciousness is now coming to light as the fields of psychology and sociology study the need for psychological integration and social integration.[66] Integration implies harmony and balance, and these are crucial factors in both our personal lives as well as in our social relationships. One need only tap into the news of the world to see the vast array of disharmonious and fractured relationships spread across our planet. The good news is that many people recognize the critical need to take action for creating right human relations in many areas of life—the need for understanding and harmony between all peoples.

At the level of the Sovereign Integral, the *coherence of consciousness* is best described in the many references in James' writings about the Sovereign Integral's comprehension of its many incarnational experiences in the space-time universe. All the experiences and developmental jumps in the Human Instrument's consciousness are transferred to the Entity where these are all integrated into a complete and coherent overview.

Here we must emphasize that the Entity consciousness is unlimited in its awareness of many incarnations, but the lesser consciousness that we experience through our Human Instruments is greatly limited. Metaphorically, the Entity's journey through the space-time worlds is like an unfinished book that is still being written. Our current lives, however are only one chapter in this ongoing book, and our past lives are previous chapters. We, while in our Human Instruments, are only aware of the current chapter as it is being written, while the Sovereign Integral is aware of all the chapters up to the present. We could say that the authoring Sovereign Integral has already mapped out the entire plot of the book. At our level of awareness this book is not coherent because we cannot as yet examine the larger flow of the story. The work of James and the other Lyricus teachers is to guide us to a more complete understanding of the cohesive nature of our Sovereign Integral's ongoing book.

---

65. "Coherence of the Evolutionary Consciousness," p. 573.
66. See Ken Wilber's *Integral Psychology*, 2000, and *Integral Spirituality*, 2006. Also see Jeremy Rifkin's *Empathic Civilization*, 2009.

Part of the reason that we have a greatly reduced grasp of our Sovereign Integral's evolutionary development is that we are overwhelmed by the dissonant vibrations of our existence in the world of form. The music of Hakomi tracks four to six are designed to clear a zone of harmony, called the Interface Zone. This zone stands between the incoming discordant vibrations of the outer world and the physical, emotional, and mental parts that compose our Human Instruments.

> Spiritual sound helps to create an Interface Zone between the human instrument and the vibratory soup of the world of forms. This Interface Zone supports the human instrument's mission and purpose, preventing its vibratory contamination as a vessel for the human soul and an outlet of First Source's expression of Sound and Light, or what is sometimes referred to as Para Vach.
>
> Para Vach is the primordial, causal Sound and Light that transcends both manifestation and non-manifestation. It is the Breath of First Source beyond the cosmos that creates, vitalizes, and sets in motion the vibratory substance of matter.[67]

This passage explains that we are inherently connected to the Sound and Light vibrations of First Source. The Interface Zone is a "vessel of the Entity" as well as an outlet for Para Vach. It was created, at least in part, by a spiritual sound that transcends all the dimensions of the multiverse, whether in space-time or non-space-time. As the article explains, the problem is that our Interface Zones are shut down due to the discordant vibrations of our surroundings. The Interface Zone can be cleared by music.

> Harmony is the ruling principle of the Interface Zone, and music— properly tuned—can help to create, direct, and uphold this sense of harmony. If the Interface Zone is rightfully managed, it will provide a buffer between the human soul and the worlds of form that bear down upon it.[68]

Further, James is not claiming that his music is the only means of clearing the Interface Zone, for he relates that:

> Sacred music, chants, mantras, and harmonic vibrations are the countervailing effect of this vibratory density, and it is the most potent way in which to direct and uphold the inherent harmony of the Interface Zone that surrounds each of us. In a meditative state, the sound of one's voice chanting a mantra or the sacred name of First Source is very powerful, particularly if one is actively visualizing and imagining a harmonious Interface Zone.[69]

---

67. Ibid., p. 4.
68. Ibid., p. 5.
69. Ibid., p. 5.

While he says that the sound of one's voice when in a meditative state has a powerful effect, he takes this to the next level in the succeeding paragraph:

> There are melody lines embedded within the music of Hakomi Chambers Four to Six that can be internalized and used as a harmonic "broom" to sweep the denser vibrations that may have accumulated within your Interface Zone. This procedure does not require a good voice, and indeed, can be more potent if given expression within your consciousness instead of through your vocal chords and mouth.[70]

Here, James is telling us that besides listening to the music physically, we can also bring to mind the passages of the music that strike us as the most beautiful and uplifting. Both methods will have the same effect. This also implies that the entire CD contains the harmonious frequencies that help to eliminate the discordant vibrations of the world that contaminate the Interface Zone. In all probability, this *motion* also applies to the aforementioned sacred music, chants, and mantras.

So how can we determine the state of our Interface Zone? The first step requires us to be present in the moment. If we are driving a car or preparing a meal, for instance, but thinking of something else then we are not fully present and aware of what we are doing in the present. Here is an extract from the transcript of Mark Hempel's audio interview with James.

> **James:** Only in the currents of love do you realize that you are not the form you animate, but rather the energetic frequencies of the animation itself. And these frequencies—where do you suppose they derive from?
>
> **Mark:** I guess I would say First Source.
>
> **James:** Yes, from our Creator. And these frequencies, they dance in the moment, they do not know the past or future, they live in the now. So thoughts and feelings that search into the past or future, they can restrict the circulation of these delicate frequencies, and it is these frequencies, like the pied piper, lead you to the point, the very moment where you are open to transformation.
>
> Now we have a saying that goes like this: *"If you are peeling an orange do not be thinking about an apple."* [Emphasis mine]. In other words, stay in the moment, because this is where the frequencies of animation occur. This is where your power lies.[71]

Although he is not directly referencing the Interface Zone, James may be describing the continuous presence of "frequencies" related to Para Vach. The hint

---

70. Ibid., p. 5.
71. *Collected Works of the WingMakers Vol. II*, Part IV, Sec. One, Mark Hempel Interview with James, Session One

to this supposition lays in his use of the word "animation" in this interview segment. His description of the animating force of First Source parallels his description of Para Vach as quoted earlier: "It is the Breath of First Source beyond the cosmos that creates, vitalizes, and *sets in motion* the vibratory substance of matter." This is most likely the animation James is describing in the interview.

Consequently, if we are to become aware of our state of consciousness as reflected by the condition of the Interface Zone, then when we are peeling an orange we should not be thinking about apples or any other thing for that matter.

Once we are in the moment we can learn to assess the state of our Interface Zones. Do we feel connected to the simple pleasure of peeling an orange or are we agitated by thoughts and feelings associated with our surroundings and the activities taking place therein? These thoughts might be pleasant or unpleasant, but these can also be observed in the moment, just like peeling the orange. This Zen-like approach to living is what places us squarely in the Interface Zone and allows us to witness its state.

From this point we have the opportunity to shift our consciousness to an expanded, more inclusive and integrated condition of coherence. Hakomi Project Chambers Four to Six are coded with frequencies to help us clear the Interface Zone of the clutter of feelings and thoughts generated by the discordant frequencies bombarding us.

So, what is the nature of the Interface Zone that we are urged to create? It can be thought of as a psychological space erected between the incoming stimulants of our surroundings (detected by the five senses) along with the stored memories and associations of the mind. This subjective space is accessed by staying in the moment as an observer, or witness to the incoming sensory stimulants. By allowing our senses to fully communicate the object of observation, we, as observers without the preconceived judgments of the mind as servant to the ego, can view the situation from a higher ground of being. This is the ever-present ground of the greater self, the Sovereign Integral, with its inherent connection to First Source.

Many more details about the Interface Zone are provided in the fifth Lyricus Discourse "The Interface Zone," which James released shortly after the publication of "Coherence of the Evolutionary Consciousness." While the information in this introduction is still fresh in your mind, you may want read the fifth discourse, as well as my introduction to it.

The Hakomi Project—Music of Chambers Seven to Twelve and Chambers Thirteen to Twenty-one

Hakomi Project Chambers Seven to Twelve is a CD. Its sub-title is "Approaching the Divine." The compositions of Chambers Thirteen to Twenty-one are not on CD, but are MP3s that can be downloaded.[72]

---

72. Go to www.wingmakers.com/wingmusic/music.html.

The music on these releases is beautiful and stirring, and although there are no essays or specific clues associated with these compositions, they may be coded in some way. Consequently, we are left on our own to intuit what effects these compositions may have on our bodies, hearts, and minds. Maybe James' lack of comments on these releases is deliberate, so that we can be left on our own to gauge our sensitivity to the subtle vibrations of this music.

Coherence of the Evolutionary Consciousness
Associated Materials of Hakomi Project: Chambers Four to Six

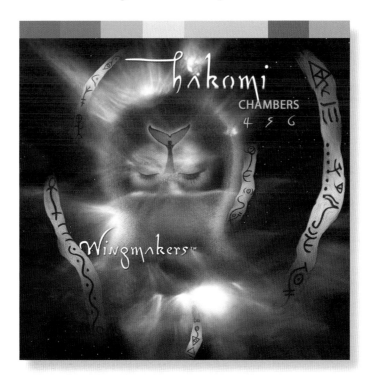

Music is a language that directly communicates what cannot be said with words. When you encounter rhythm, melody, timbre, tone, harmony—the components of music—your first instinct is to surrender to their language. You crossover into the mysterious world of their creative presence where a bridge can be built and integration between these two worlds can be formed.

The human instrument absorbs the sounds present in music and can, if the music is properly tuned, form a sympathetic resonance with the music. Similar to two tuning forks that resonate on the same frequency when only one is struck, the human instrument can be a resonant system in which its cellular and atomic structure is entrained by the music—or more specifically—the vibratory frequencies contained in the harmonics of the music.

The atomic structure of the human instrument is a vibrating harmonic system. The nuclei vibrate, and the electrons in their orbits vibrate in resonance to their nuclei, but to what does the nuclei resonate with? What is the primal vibration that establishes the vibratory expression of a human instrument? And can this vibration change and adapt—in a sense migrate to new levels of vibration that are more aligned and supportive to the spiritual purpose in which the human soul chose to incarnate?

Modern humanity has been deluded by sound and music—in effect, sung to sleep. The material world of sonic vibration has ensnared the human instrument, keeping the primal vibration of the human soul suppressed and diminished. This condition creates a heightened sense of separation, which in turn creates an unspecified, broad-spectrum anxiety that is difficult to identify, and, consequently, to resolve. It is to this vibration of separation and anxiety that most humans submit, and as resonant systems, unwittingly nourish and promote. But the truth is that life is encapsulated spirit, and all life is part of a unified creative presence that lives underneath the material world like a waterway of motion lives beneath the solid, opaque ice of a river.

Using this analogy, music can break through the ice and enable the individual to thrust their hands into the water and feel this motion—this current of universal life that surges undeniably just below the surface of the material world. This is the re-connective experience that heals the sense of separation so powerfully woven into the human condition. The music of Hakomi Chambers Four to Six is intended to restore and support this sense of reconnection.

Within the esoteric fields of study, it has long been known that sound is the most effective way to move beyond separation and rekindle the sense of integration between the heart-mind-body-soul system. Music, properly tuned and orchestrated, is like a needle and thread that stitches these component parts of the human entity together not in permanent union, but in manageable alignment and coherence. It is this alignment and coherence that enables your spiritual work to surface and bloom, and sound is the bridge that connects the "archipelago" of the heart-mind-body-soul system, uniting them as a singular "geography" or system in service to the native, original purpose of the individuated consciousness. (See below.)

This does not mean that you necessarily become a healer or a teacher of spiritual works. The original purpose of the human instrument and soul—as a unified team—

Coherence of the Evolutionary Consciousness

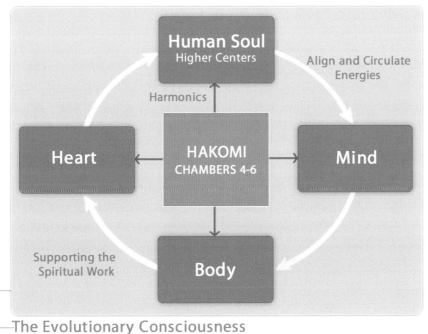

The Evolutionary Consciousness

is to harmonize consciousness from the density of material survival to the highest vibration of love. This harmonization is not ruled by human definitions of good and evil or right and wrong. It is exclusively about bringing disparate vibrations into harmony and building coherence between the two poles of survival and divine love. Spirit becomes matter through the vibration of sound, and similarly, matter becomes spirit through the harmonics of sound. It is a reciprocal energy transfer—one in which science is only now beginning to understand. Since prehistoric times, humans have known that music modifies the environment and our relationship to time and space, but now science is revealing that music also modifies our cellular structure, energy centers (chakras), and the coherence between our total selfhood (heart-mind-body-soul system).

In the study of wave phenomenon known as the science of cymatics, sound waves produce an effect on inert matter, structuring it into geometric, even archetypal forms. This same cause and effect relationship of sound waves on matter is what produces the effect at the atomic and cellular levels of the human instrument. However, it is more than mere physical impressions of the sound waves. There are harmonics within the sound that extend into higher and lower frequencies than the audible range of the human ear, but nonetheless impact on the vibrational structure of the human instrument's DNA, mind-brain structure, and central nervous system.

The vibratory structure of the human instrument, which includes the body, emotions, and mind structures, is an object lesson in non-aligned frequencies. The vibrations of one organ are different than another—say the stomach when compared to the heart. The vibration of the higher mind is different than the emotions; the crown chakra different than the vibration of the pituitary gland. The human instrument is a vast collection of vibratory systems, each operating in service to a functional outcome that serves the material needs of the human instrument to survive in the physical world and evolve towards the spiritual worlds of First Source. These competing vibrational currents create the condition of floating intentionality— which results in the diffusion of the intention and will of the individual.

Because the vibratory structure of the human instrument is unaligned and asymmetrical, it is a collection of vibrations operating in a multiplicity of resonant systems. There are root sounds that are primal, and because of their primal stature, causal. These root sounds are inaudible, but nevertheless provide an orchestrating frequency that brings a degree of coherence to the human instrument. Mantras, particularly as they were applied in the esoteric schools of sound and light, were designed to strengthen the root frequencies or source vibration that establishes the unifying vibration of each human instrument. It is this unifying Source Vibration that generally defines the descending form in which the human instrument manifests in the physical domain, as well as the ascension path upon which it evolves.

The Source Vibration of the individual is intermixed with the world of forms as the human instrument manifests. This is the "vibratory soup" of the external world that impacts on, and influences, the human instrument. This vibratory soup, particularly as it pertains to technology, acts to diminish the Source Vibration in the space of human consciousness. This Source Vibration is analogous to what is – in esoteric schools – referred to as the soul's heartbeat

Hierarchy of Vibrations (see below) depicts this overall relationship between the inward connectivity of the individuated consciousness to First Source (God), and its interface with the external world of form and vibratory density. Spiritual sound helps to create an Interface Zone between the human instrument and the vibratory soup of the world of forms. This Interface Zone supports the human instrument's mission and purpose, preventing its vibratory contamination as a vessel for the human soul and an outlet of First Source's expression of Sound and Light, or what is sometimes referred to as Para Vach.

Para Vach is the primordial, causal Sound and Light that transcends both manifestation and non-manifestation. It is the Breath of First Source beyond the cosmos that creates, vitalizes, and sets in motion the vibratory substance of matter. It transcends the manifestation of light and sound even as it exists in its most pure and luminous state.

There are references in virtually all religious texts, as well as physics and cosmology that describe—however obliquely—the Para Vach. In the Bible it is the Word made flesh; it is the Nada of the Upanishads; the Kalma-I-ilahi or inner sound of the Koran; the HU of the Sufi; the music of the spheres in Pythagorean philosophy; it is Fohat in Buddhism; and the Kwan-Yin-Tien in Chinese mysticism. Regardless of its name or precise definition, it is the fundamental cause of all sound and light within the Grand Universe, which in turn is the fundamental cause of all manifestation.

It is this connection that is embedded within each of us. It is our source of the pure vibration that we live upon as endless beings. In the book, "Liminal Cosmogony," it is stated as follows: From the Hidden Father originate the Light and Sound harmonics—the universal codes of unity—that are distilled into his

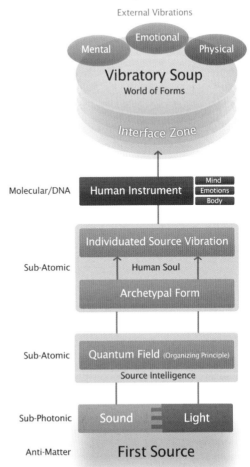

Hierarchy of Vibrations

External Vibrations

Mental   Emotional   Physical

Vibratory Soup
World of Forms

Interface Zone

Molecular/DNA   **Human Instrument**   Mind / Emotions / Body

Individuated Source Vibration

Sub-Atomic   Human Soul

Archetypal Form

Sub-Atomic   Quantum Field (Organizing Principle)

Source Intelligence

Sub-Photonic   Sound   Light

Anti-Matter   **First Source**

Brilliant Children in the worlds of form. However, it is the worlds of form that can defile and contaminate this connection and subtle vibration, hence the Interface Zone is an essential concept to understand.

Harmony is the ruling principle of the Interface Zone, and music—properly tuned—can help to create, direct, and uphold this sense of harmony. If the Interface Zone is rightfully managed, it will provide a buffer between the human soul and the worlds of form that bear down upon it. This is a result of the density of vibration within the worlds of form that inadvertently, and in some instances, purposely, diminish the vibratory state of the human soul's vessel—the human instrument—to the vibratory rate of matter.

Sacred music, chants, mantras, and harmonic vibrations are the countervailing effect of this vibratory density, and it is the most potent way in which to direct and uphold the inherent harmony of the Interface Zone that surrounds each of us. In a meditative state, the sound of one's voice chanting a mantra or the sacred name of First Source is very powerful, particularly if one is actively visualizing and imagining a harmonious Interface Zone.

There are melody lines embedded within the music of Hakomi Chambers Four to Six that can be internalized, and used as a harmonic "broom" to sweep the denser vibrations that may have accumulated within your Interface Zone. This procedure does not require a good voice, and indeed, can be more potent if given expression within your consciousness instead of through your vocal chords and mouth.

There will be a Lyricus discourse released in the next month that will provide more background depth and practical applications related to the Interface Zone and its role in supporting and facilitating the evolutionary consciousness.

From my world to yours,

James

The Music of Lyricus

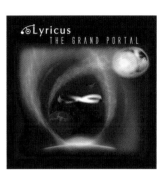

The music on the Lyricus site is specifically designed to provide a non-traditional method to shift the human consciousness to the more subtle regions of the individuated consciousness. Unfortunately, due to the relative infancy of the World Wide Web, the music must be reduced in its granularity and detail in order to make possible its rapid download. A music CD will be made available at a later date for those who would like the high-resolution files, which contain the full measure of the encoding. [This music CD is now available at wingmakers.com.]

Atomic and molecular vibrations in the human body produce electromagnetic and acoustic energy fields, which regulate and even catalyze biochemical processes. These natural biological vibrations are regulated by a higher dimensional octave of more fundamental vibrations, which function at the quantum level. Lyricus refers to these foundational vibrations as an Underivative Information Structure (UIS).

Certain acoustic and scalar vibrations cause the helix within the DNA molecule to unwind, extending the DNA backbone and making the exposed bases more accessible for base pairing and activation, particularly as this relates to what scientists refer to as "junk" or dormant DNA. Sound frequencies can be contoured to penetrate the DNA molecule, and expose and activate the nucleotides and when useful, the corresponding nerve cells.

The compositions within the Lyricus site are components of a larger composition, but again, because of the limited bandwidth of the Internet the compositions have been reduced in length. The music can be experienced as an entity that is capable of shifting inside your energetic body and activating certain frequencies of your energy centers—particularly your heart and what is sometimes referred to as your third brain.

The entity that is encoded within the music is not composed of material frequency, but is purely energetic—produced like an acoustic soulprint that is transferred from soul to thought to music to distribution platform, and it operates at a collective level within the listening "body" of the individuated consciousness.

In the nascent science of cymatics, sound waves have been proven to generate geometric forms in matter. In the yet-to-be-discovered science of multidimensional reality, waveforms can be sculpted to enter biogenetic fields and catalyze biochemical processes, restore cellular health and trigger encoded electromagnetic fields within the cellular functions of the Central Nervous System (CNS).

This music and the "entity" that it contains, is focused on the electromagnetic fields of the CNS and how this physical manifestation of the energetic grid that constitutes the soul carrier can be enhanced to conduct greater energy from the host soul consciousness thereby increasing its fusion with the material life of the soul carrier.[73]

---

73. Lyricus.org

Commentary on the Music of Lyricus: The Grand Portal

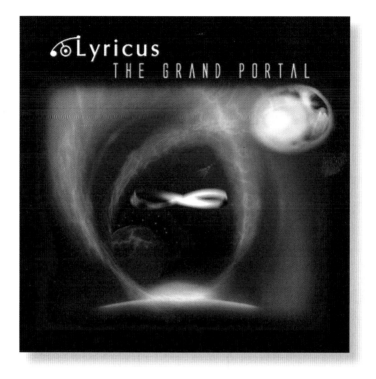

"Before the first word: silence. Before the first light: sound."[74]

Lyricus: The Grand Portal, 2004

Released in 2004, The Grand Portal CD represents another encoded musical composition in two parts. Track one is entitled "Solitonic Transformations" and the second track is called "Solitonic Transmissions." These are interesting titles and are worth considering.

The most obvious place to begin is with the word "solitonic." Solitonic is an adjective for the noun, soliton. According to the Merriam-Webster Collegiate Dictionary, soliton means "a solitary wave (as in a gaseous plasma) that propagates with little loss of energy and retains its shape and speed after colliding with another wave."

An Internet search of this term yields a large number of websites devoted to mathematics, physics, biology, and other fields of research. According to one source, solitons were once thought to be non-existent, but mathematicians proved that solitons did exist and this mathematical solution was later confirmed through scientific research.

Relative to The Grand Portal CD, the titles of the two tracks strongly suggest that they contain solitonic waves capable of impacting our Human Instruments. This may apply to the coding contained in most of the other CD compositions created by James.

---

74. Lyricus.org. - see Articles

We find the following statement from the Lyricus music introduction:

> The music on the Lyricus site is specifically designed to provide a nontraditional method to shift the human consciousness to the more subtle regions of the individuated consciousness.[75]

Note that the music on the Lyricus website is the same as that on the CD, but the compositions in their entirety do not play at the site itself.

Another possible form of coding on this, and very likely, the other CDs involves cymatics, the scientific field of acoustic research on the effects of sound waves on matter. According to the website cymascope.com:

> The generic term for this field of science is the study of 'modal' phenomena, named 'Cymatics' by Hans Jenny [1904-1972], a Swiss medical doctor and a pioneer in this field. The word 'Cymatics' derives from the Greek 'kuma' meaning 'billow,' or 'wave,' to describe the periodic effects that sound and vibration has [sic] on matter.[76]

Cymatics demonstrates that there is a relationship between the effects of sound on the arrangement of particles into specific geometric configurations. This was proven by Ernst Chladni (1756-1827), a German musician and scientist sometimes called the father of acoustics. He used a brass plate spread with sand, upon the edge of which he drew a violin bow. The resultant sounds yielded archetypal geometric patterns that Chladni recorded and classified. The various patterns depended on what part of the plate's edges he drew the bow.[77]

So, how does this apply to the two tracks on The Grand Portal CD? Just taking what is given in the definitions above, apparently the music of The Grand Portal is coded with solitonic waves that cannot be altered when they encounter the atoms and force fields constituting our Human Instruments.

Relative to the possible cymatic aspect of the music, is this quotation from James:

> All physical structures are composed of geometric shapes. However, the Genetic Mind is not a physical structure or place. When you move into the higher mind, where the Genetic Mind is situated, geometry is no longer confined to a three-dimensional static paradigm. To explain its non-physical structure is impossible using a three-dimensional language because the Genetic Mind is organic, dynamic, and always changing. In other words, there is no representative "snapshot."[78]

James more directly addresses this brief mention of the geometric patterning of

---

75. The Music of Lyricus, p. 577.
76. www.cymascope.com
77. www.cymascope.com/cyma_research/history.html
78. *Collected Works of the WingMakers Vol. II*, Part IV, Sec. Two, Top. Arr. of Qs and As, Ques. 71-S3

our physical form, along with the cymatic effect, in the following:

> In the nascent science of cymatics, sound waves have been proven to generate geometric forms in matter. In the yet-to-be-discovered science of multidimensional reality, waveforms can be sculpted to enter biogenetic fields and catalyze biochemical processes, restore cellular health and trigger encoded electromagnetic fields within the cellular functions of the Central Nervous System (CNS).[79]

Here, James is acknowledging the presence of geometric patterns in all forms, which naturally includes our Human Instruments. He also implies that these geometric forms exist, and most probably originate in higher dimensions. Consequently, there may very well be a cymatic effect upon listening to this music. This suggests that solitonic waves that are not altered by their encounter with the Human Instrument, along with specialized music encoding, have a cymatic effect on the geometry of the physical atomic structures that constitute our cells and the DNA within them.

> Certain acoustic and scalar vibrations cause the helix within the DNA molecule to unwind, extending the DNA backbone and making the exposed bases more accessible for base pairing and activation, particularly as this relates to what scientists refer to as "junk" or dormant DNA. Sound frequencies can be contoured to penetrate the DNA molecule, and expose and activate the nucleotides and, when useful, the corresponding nerve cells.[80]

The end of the Lyricus Music Introduction confirms that The Grand Portal CD contains such coding, and this leaves us with the two title names, track one, "Solitonic Transformations," and track two, "Solitonic Transmissions." These titles appear to indicate that the first piece of music is designed to transform, or re-pattern our active DNA as well as *activating* our so-called junk DNA.

This re-patterning and *activation* process—transformation—is then followed by transmission. As to what is being transmitted, remains a mystery.

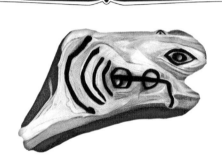

---

79. The Music of Lyricus, p. 577.
80. Ibid., p 577.

Introduction to the EventTemples Music

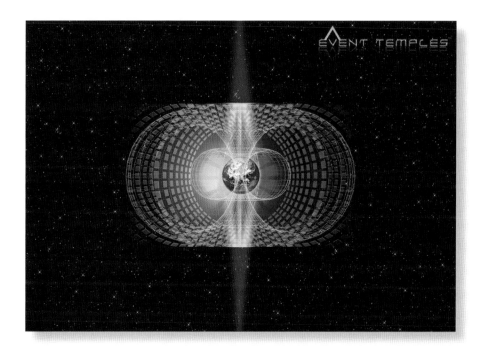

Feel yourself connected to your Creator at your heart,
but release the flow of love that comes your way.[81]

In 2007 a new website was introduced as James' work continued to unfold. The new website was called Event Temples. Along with the site, new musical compositions by James were released. These compositions do not appear on CDs, but are offered as downloads at the WingMakers site.[82]

The titles of the music are:

- Energetic Heart
- The Rising Heart
- Living from the Heart
- Heart Transfer
- Flow in Compassion

As you see this music is focused on the heart. And here the word heart refers to the emotional component of the Human Instrument. The mood of all five places one in a calm and serene state in which the contemplation of the heart can occur.

This is quite a contrast to the Ancient Arrow Project music, which is high energy and filled with many melodies and lots of percussion. Recall that Ancient Arrow Project tracks seventeen to twenty-four are designed to ground the new exploratory

---

81. *Collected Works of the WingMakers Vol. II*, Part III, Sec. One, "The Energetic Heart: Its Purpose in Human Destiny"
82. Go to www.wingmakers.com/wingmusic/music.html

energy system into the physical body. And Chamber Ten is coded to directly affect the tenth chromosome, which according to James will reduce stress.

At least two of the Hakomi Project CDs, Chambers Three through Six, are focused on psychological levels. Chamber Three is designed to shake us out of our egoic comfort zones and guide us into freer expression and a renewed spirit for exploration. This music invokes the individuated consciousness and not the Human Instrument, or outer personality. Chambers Four to Six help to clear the Interface Zone, another psychological component.

This short review uncovers a definite pattern and plan behind all the music that James has composed. They progress from the outer physical body, to the depths of the individuated consciousness, to the interface between the clamor and confusion of the world, and finally to the energetic heart, or emotional aspect of the Human Instrument.

So now we come to the question as to whether the EventTemples music is coded like much of the other music. The answer is yes. Shortly after the release of this new series, James provided a brief statement about the piece entitled "Flow in Compassion."

> At precisely three minutes into the song, the composition enters an 'inner chamber' and while this section plays, if you're so inclined, radiate compassion from your heart center. You can do this in whatever way you feel works best with your nature, if you want, you can say the simple phrase: *Flow in compassion.* Doing this can be used as a method to open your heart's energetic center. It's a little like tuning-up your heart's communication capacities (energetically speaking).
>
> In most of my compositions I create these inner chambers where the higher-frequency melodies can be heard, and these melodies, as innocent as they may seem, are the one's [sic] that open the heart, revealing its intuitive intelligence in ways that only sound can. The inner chamber lasts two and one-half minutes. For those of you who are planning to participate in the EventTemples sessions, I suggest that you listen to this composition and practice the flow of compassion as it will activate, stimulate, accelerate and sustain the potency of your transmission of heart energetics.[83]

Flow in Compassion can be downloaded at: www.wingmakers.com/wingmusic/music.html. This track is at the bottom of the MP3 music list.

Not only does James give us the exact time when the encoding takes place. But he also identifies these interims as "inner chambers." Additionally, he explains that these inner chambers are present in most of his compositions. Thus, it is quite likely that the music that *does not* appear to be coded, because there is no specific

---

83. www.wingmakers.com/products1.html

statement that it is—*is actually coded to open the intuitive intelligence of the heart.*

With the opening of the heart, the music ultimately leads to an increase in our awareness and sensitivity to the refined frequencies continuously emanating from the Entity and the Domain of Unity in which it dwells. The effect of this exposure is also designed to awaken the unused portions of our DNA, resulting in an upgrade to our physical bodies for the reception of the heightened vibrations of earth brought on by the dimensional shift. For that matter all the works of James—music, imagery, philosophy, and stories—are coded to integrate the spiritual components of the Entity with the material orientation of our Human Instruments. Although all these components have a their role in this process, the music is the most powerful medium for accomplishing this goal.

As a result, we are being given the opportunity to open and activate the refined frequencies of love and intuition that radiate from the Sovereign Integral and emerge into our lives through the portal of the energetic heart. From that point onward it is up to each of us to make a choice between the old stale ruts of the ego-personality that dominate our everyday lives, or make a personal dimensional shift to the domain of unity wherein the Sovereign Integral is constantly pouring forth its love and light through the heart.

What we now know about James' music, is that he is using the power of sound as a means of preparing us for the intensified frequencies that the 2012 shift and dimensional expansion will bring to our planet. In this new psychological environment, living from the heart will be the foundation upon which we build our lives and express our behavior. Anything less will be out of sync with this coming new reality.

Introduction to the DVD: Meditations in TimeSpace

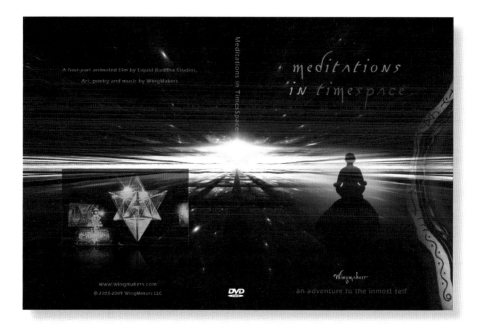

The Galactic Tributary Zones are the knowledge repositories of Lyricus. They house the local Lyricus staff, research centers, teaching facilities, and various tools that we believe—in this particular case—will help humanity focus its technology and efforts in the pursuit of the Grand Portal.[84]

In 2003, a DVD was released on the WingMakers website entitled "Meditations in TimeSpace." This four-part animated video was produced by Liquid Buddha Studios under the supervision of James.

As the above remarks by James indicate, the Tributary Zones can be compared to the large universities of earth. Imagining what it is like to visit these Tributary Zones induces feelings of wonder and inspiration, and this DVD is an attempt to provide a small measure of a Tributary Zone visitation.

According to the introduction to the DVD, the meditations "are intended to create new linkages between the individual and the multi-leveled, Grand Universe."[85] This is accomplished by immersing the viewer in a depiction of a meditation chamber within a Galactic Tributary Zone. These particular Tributary Zones contain all the information and data required for a human species to discover the Grand Portal. The beginning process for this discovery involves awakening that portion of the Entity, called the Wholeness Navigator. This Entity component is what drives us to seek wholeness and unity in all of life.

The Galactic Tributary Zones are located in the center of galaxies that contain

---

84. *Collected Works of the WingMakers Vol. II*, Part IV, Sec. Two, Top. Arr. of Qs and As, Ques. 6-S3
85. Meditations in TimeSpace, p. 586.

life-bearing planets. Entities who have attained a frequency compatible with the Tributary Zone gain access during their hours of sleep or during meditation.

At the risk of oversimplifying a complex subject, James is transferring the information for guiding humanity to the Grand Portal discovery, from the galactic core location to earth. He is translating these encoded data sensory streams from a higher dimensional galactic level to the third dimensional level of earth—our TimeSpace. James is then creating a mythological framework in which he can position the stepped-down encoded galactic data streams for human use.

The TimeSpace DVD is one more example of this process. By following the suggested instructions James provides in the accompanying DVD essay, you may feel a new sense of wholeness and awareness of the dimensional expanse of that greater consciousness we call the Entity.

(Refer to the WingMakers glossary for more detailed information on the Wholeness Navigator and the Tributary Zones. You will also find more details about the Tributary Zones in the Collected Works of the WingMakers Vol. II, Part IV, Sec. Two, Topical Arrangement of Qs and As.)

Meditations in TimeSpace

The DVD, *Meditations in TimeSpace*, is composed of four multimedia meditations. Each are designed to provide an immersive experience into the consciousness of the WingMakers. The duration of the insight, expansion or feeling of remembrance is not the critical element. It is the depth in which the feeling and insight is carried into your human instrument.

This new DVD is designed to strike a chord of resonance within the human instrument that helps the individual recognize it is an integral part of an expansive plan that supersedes the personal, local, national, and even global issues and events of our time. These meditations are intended to create new linkages between the individual and the multi-leveled, Grand Universe.

MEDITATION 1: Combines music of Chamber Eighteen with an original animation of a meditation chamber within a Galactic Tributary Zone. With the superb artistry and technical skills of Goa from Liquid Buddha Studios, this animated film depicts one of the meditation chambers that inspired the Ancient Arrow site. Galactic Tributary Zones are the source of the encoded data streams that constitute the WingMakers' materials. You can learn more about them in the Glossary.

SIGNPOSTS OF THE FILM: The three white lights represent the triune personality of an attendant who is within the meditation chamber, serving as a guide to those visiting in their dream state. Invited members of the human race can journey within their soul consciousness to these Tributary Zones and experience the encoded data streams that are uniquely present within these special chambers.

The use of sacred geometry is very prevalent because of its correlation to the universal language of mathematics and its association with perfection and grace. The golden form that morphs into various geometrical shapes is a representation of the Wholeness Navigator—known also as the Merkaba, or vehicle of light. This is the form we all take while visiting within these meditation chambers.

This vehicle of light is the divine, inmost consciousness of the human instrument. It speaks using the Language of Light, which is represented as the symbols that flow from the Wholeness Navigator into and through the paintings, which are portals of knowledge. Within these portals are stored the encoded knowledge of the Central Race—humanity's progenitors, known also as the WingMakers.

The "bubbles" that arise from the blue cylinders are representative of knowledge capsules that are stored within these cylinders, or what humanity might call an organic computer. The knowledge capsules are connected to each of the portal paintings and activate when a Wholeness Navigator arrives in the meditation chamber. They are offered as sacred provisions for the visitor and they can be absorbed by the Wholeness Navigator as spiritual nutrition that assists in the remembrance process of the human instrument.

The DNA formation represents the bridge between the Wholeness Navigator and the human instrument. DNA is the individual blueprint of spiritual purpose, not merely the repository of behavioral predispositions and genetic traits. DNA is quite literally instructed within these meditation chambers of a Galactic Tributary Zone and can be re-informed to accelerate the mission and purpose of a human instrument.

You can think of these Galactic Tributary Zones as outposts that are constructed for the preservation and transfer of vital knowledge from the Central Race to the Wholeness Navigator contained within a soul carrier or human instrument. Human consciousness is not exposed to this vibration—only the Wholeness Navigator within the human form is permitted entry to these meditation chambers.

The objective of this animated film is to enable the human consciousness to acquire a tiny glimpse of these amazing sites and to better feel the certainty of their existence. What is represented here conforms to the three-dimensional construct of human existence, and it is thus, a shadow-form of the authentic radiance of the Galactic Tributary Zone.

MEDITATION TECHNIQUES: The words, music, and art can reach deep into your psyche and feeling center. For those so inclined, it is recommended to "step" inside these meditations and allow them to touch your inmost self. In other words, lay your defenses down. Approach these meditations from your feeling center and allow them to connect there—not the mind or ego.

This can be achieved by preparation of the human instrument:

1. *Create a sacred space.* Whether you are sitting at your computer or relaxing in your favorite chair in front of the television, remember that you are not only the body and mind of a personality. Be present as a Sovereign Integral. Prepare the space around you by visualizing a dome of transparent light that surrounds you. This is your sacred space wherein the Sovereign Integral consciousness can arise to the surface of your personality. Invite your whole self to be present.

2. *Breathe your spirit.* The sacred space that you have created remains a dome of light that surrounds you. It is your presence of spirit. You can breathe this spirit essence and draw it inside your body and allow it to release within you. Take time to breathe your spirit inside you, feeling the light enter your lungs and releasing into your body and mind.

3. *Allow your innocence.* You can relax knowing you are within your sacred space and that your inmost self has surfaced within this dome of light. You are now better equipped to process the meditations from a perspective of innocence, less mindful to understand and decode meanings, and more willing to simply absorb the experience with trust that its meaning will come to you.

MEDITATIONS Two to Four: This second set of meditations combines the music of Chamber Nineteen, Twenty-two, and Twenty-four with art and poetry taken from the Ancient Arrow project. The music and poetry evoke a plaintive tone of the individual struggle to anchor spiritual identity in a fragmented world, and obtain a

sense of reunion with one's Creator. The poetry, art, and music chronicle this process of separation, despair, a penetrating vision of the unknown,

the journey of union, and the ultimate realization of the inmost self as a God-fragment connected to all other God-fragments regardless of form.

These particular meditations are designed to be introspective and contemplative. They are not active animations, as in the case of Meditation One, but rather, they are animated backgrounds intended to focus the mind on integrating the poetry and music. In doing so, individuals can anchor the content deeper into their personalities where they can consider its meaning and relevance better.[86]

---

86. www.wingmakers.com/products3.html.

SECTION FIVE

The WingMakers Philosophy

Sarah: "So, by reading the philosophy I'm supposed to be able to become invisible?"

Dr. Neruda: "I think it's more holistic than that. They left behind poetry, music, paintings, and even a glossary. It seems to me that all of these elements—in addition to the philosophy—are connected. Also, I'm suggesting that something fundamentally changes when these materials are absorbed, and perhaps this change, whatever it is, resonates with the technology from the seven sites."

The Second Interview of Dr. Jamisson Neruda, p. 293.

Manifesto of the Sovereign Integral

- There is no space more sacred or powerful than another.
- There is no being more spiritual than another.
- There is no thing more divine than another.
- There is no tool or technique that accelerates the unfoldment of consciousness.
- There is no truth that can be written, spoken, or thought unless it is conceived and expressed through the Language of Unity.
- First Source transcends Wholeness.
- All the fragments of philosophy, science, and religion, even when unified, represent but a fractional picture of reality.
- The mysteries of your world will never be understood through inquiries that are based in the language of the mind.
- Perfection is a concept of wholeness misunderstood.
- The conditions of peace, beauty, love, and security are merely signposts to wholeness, as are their counterparts.
- To live in the Wholeness Perspective is to value all things as they are and to bear witness to the unity of their expression.
- No being requires knowledge other than their unique Wholeness Perspective.
- There is no hierarchy. There is only One That Is All.
- There is no model of existence outside of the model of self-creation.
- True Freedom is access to First Source.
- A being cannot get closer to First Source than in the existence of a moment.
- The sovereign being and First Source are reality.
- Having a physical body does not limit you, anymore than having legs on an eagle prevents it from flying.
- All conditions of existence are facets of the one condition of the reality of unlimited self-creation.
- There is no pathway to First Source.
- Unfoldment, evolution, growth/decay cycles and transformation are all bound to the same premise of separation in linear time.
- The hidden harmony is found with joy, while the obvious brings indifference.
- The farther you enter into the Truth the deeper your conviction for truth must be.
- There is understanding of the world precisely to the degree that there is understanding of the Self.

Commentary on the Manifesto of the Sovereign Integral

*The Sovereign Integral is the transparent Being of expansion,
uniquely fit for the era in which we have begun to enter.*[87]

Introduction

Instead of commenting on the twenty-four bulleted items in their order within the manifesto, we are going to examine them according to the themes they present.

The groupings I have created are only one example of how the statements of the manifesto can be interpreted. You may see these arrangements differently, which is fine because each of us can only seek the truth from the standpoint of our own experiences and views of the world. Nevertheless, the more we attempt to live according to the manifesto and the other characteristics of the Sovereign Integral, the clearer our understanding of the statements will be because they are inherent to the Sovereign Integral itself.

With this in mind, I encourage you to study them and formulate your own understanding of their meanings and how they may apply to your everyday life. After all, the downpouring of insights that we all experience from our exposure to the teachings of Lyricus contribute to the collective understanding of these materials for others, and thereby contribute to the Genetic Mind— the collective consciousness of humankind.

If we are going to work toward establishing ourselves in the awareness and behaviors of the Sovereign Integral, then we will be well served by reflecting on their meanings. Guidance and facilitation have their place in psycho-spiritual study

87. *Collected Works of the WingMakers Vol. II*, Part IV, Sec. One, Project Camelot Interview.

and practice, but in the end, each individual is left with their own actions, feelings, and ideas. The contents of consciousness, stored in the mind and accessed through the brain, represent our experiences in the world around us. Consequently, these emotional reactions and stored memories manifest and form our individual personalities. This being so, the Human Instrument becomes the vehicle for a persona largely constructed from our relationships with our parents, extended families, friends, teachers, and co-workers. In most cases, until we *turn within* to examine our egoic tendencies, beliefs, prejudices, and stances relative to the world around us, we will have difficulty comprehending the nature of the Sovereign Integral, not to mention the other five components, including the Spirit Intelligence of First Source,[88] the Remnant Imprint, the Wholeness Navigator, the Phantom Core, and the Human Instrument.

As we turn within, reflecting on our subjective lives, we will likely encounter a vivid contrast between the *inner world* of the Sovereign Integral and the *inner world* of the ego with its well-established thoughtforms, beliefs, and attitudes generated from contact with the objective, outer world. Therefore, an examination of the twenty-four points of the Manifesto offers another opportunity (in addition to the other WingMakers/Lyricus resources) to expand our awareness to incorporate the Sovereign Integral's wider and deeper awareness into our everyday consciousness. The outcome of our efforts ultimately shifts from taking on the qualities of the Sovereign Integral to actually *becoming* the Sovereign Integral.

At this point, after reading the Manifesto, you may be wondering how mere words on a page can put you in touch with such an abstract concept as the Sovereign Integral. This is a good question, especially when we realize that words and language are double-edged swords in that they can clarify as well as mask the many abstractions of psychology and spirituality. For some insight into this point is the following quotation:

> The substance of your design is awakened with the words that form the concepts of your enlarged self-image. And these words are not merely spoken, but they are seen, felt, and heard as well. They lead you to the tone of equality and the perception of wholeness. Allow these words to wash over you like a gentle wave that brings you buoyancy and movement. It will sweep you to a new shore, and it is there that you will begin to uncover your true nature and purpose.[89]

This passage strongly suggests that words can fulfill a purpose beyond that of the clarifying or masking comprehension and understanding. The extract implies that words can be encoded in such a way as to direct the influences of the higher frequencies, vibrations, or tones emanating from the level of the Sovereign Integral.

---

88. James identifies this as the Human Soul, or Entity consciousness in "Anatomy of the Individuated Consciousness." It might be more clearly defined as a replica of Source Intelligence, or Spirit.
89. "The Blueprint of Exploration," p. 650.

In other words, the statements in the Manifesto may very well be coded in a fashion similar to the paintings, poetry, music, and philosophy being brought forth by James. Armed with this possibility, let's move on to an examination of the Manifesto.

Reflections on the Manifesto

The Tone of Equality—*First Source is present in all. And all are able to contact First Source through this tone-vibration of equality.*[90]

1. There is no space more sacred or powerful than another.
2. There is no being more spiritual than another.
3. There is no thing more divine than another.
4. There is no hierarchy. There is only One That Is All.

The tone of equality emanates continuously from First Source. And because our Sovereign Integrals are individualized fragments of First Source, the Sovereign Integral also emanates this tone, or vibration of equality. The Sovereign Integral reflects this tone as part of its nature.

> The origin and destiny of existence is the tone of equality in life.
> Listen for this tone—this frequency of vibration—and follow it back
> into the very foundation from whence all things arise and return.[91]

Obviously, the foundation "from whence all things arise and return" is First Source—but what about Hierarchy, item four above? As briefly mentioned in the introduction to the Manifesto, as well as in other places in this compendium, hierarchy is interwoven into all levels of the multiverse. So why doesn't the Sovereign Integral recognize this? Maybe the following quotation can help understand item four above:

> The Hierarchy is the vessel of the collective ego-personality
> tinged with the energetic impressions of its soul carrier. Fear is the
> base frequency of this macro entity and it is this that creates the
> structure of protection (safety in numbers) and the collective purpose
> and common good that harmonizes diffusion and misalignment. It is
> the vehicle of orderly evolution, though sometimes it appears to be
> the epitome of chaos.[92]

As a topic of discussion,[93] Hierarchy is complex and cosmic in its scope. Because this Manifesto is directed at planet Earth and current planetary conditions, we should reiterate that hierarchies are not inherently bad or evil. Yet, this is the case on our planet when they are corrupted by greed and unwarranted control in order to maintain their power. We really don't have an example of extraterrestrial civilizations whose populations have attained the Sovereign Integral level of living.

---

90. WingMakers' glossary, p. 666.
91. "The Shifting Models of Existence," p. 643.
92. Email from James to John Berges 8-27-08.
93. See "Hierarchy" in the WingMakers glossary and in the Introduction to the Four Philosophy Papers.

In all likelihood, these civilizations are post-Grand Portal planets. Now we must assume that these planets have hierarchies, but because they are created by Sovereign Integrals, these hierarchies may be completely different than the hierarchies presently dominating our planet, which is in a pre-Grand Portal environment.

Having said this and interpreting Hierarchy in relation to our current world, the key to this quotation is that the hierarchies of earth are the containers, or forms through which the "collective ego personality" manifests. Consequently, at least relative to our planet, global hierarchical structures are personality based, and embedded in the space-time dimension. Therefore, from the transcendent non-space-time dimension and perspective of the Sovereign Integral, there is no hierarchy because it is vibrating to the tone of equality. Hence, human hierarchies based on a spectrum comparing best and worst individuals do not enter into the Sovereign Integral's perspective.

The Time Factor—*Time establishes separation of experience, and the perceived discontinuity of reality.*[94]

1. There is no tool or technique that accelerates the unfoldment of consciousness.
2. A being cannot get closer to First Source than in the existence of a moment.
3. There is no pathway to First Source.
4. Unfoldment, evolution, growth/decay cycles and transformation are all bound to the same premise of separation in linear time.

Techniques, pathways, and unfoldment are time-based processes and therefore not aligned to the Sovereign Integral's experience of reality. It is fair to say that while we are still not at the Sovereign Integral stage of awareness, we need guidance for achieving this level. After all, James is providing such guidance through concepts and techniques delivered to us over time, for the *Collected Works of the WingMakers* represent at least ten years of unfolding information designed to accelerate and expand our consciousnesses to that of the Sovereign Integral.

The second item above makes it clear that we do not get closer to First Source through a progressive process stretched over time, but simply by recognizing that each moment is a continuum of consciousness not subject to the past or future, rather— *First Source is continuously available in every instant.* This is not a new concept, but nevertheless it deserves our attention because this is the natural state of existence for the Sovereign Integral, and if we wish to become a Sovereign Integral, the all-important practice of staying in the moment is imperative. This is a well-recognized principle underlying Buddhism, the philosophy of Krisnamurti, and in The Course in Miracle's "holy instant," to name a few. James describes this experience as dwelling in the "Quantum Presence" of the Sovereign Integral—a fragment of First Source.

Further, we can appreciate the limitations of language here by my use of "each" and "every" moment. Even the word moment implies a distinct object of time—a

---

94. "Life Principles of the Sovereign Integral," p. 627.

particle of time, if you will. From the standpoint of the Sovereign Integral, there is no stream of discrete moments, but only the continuous Presence of All That Is.

Finally, on a more practical level, we might say that even though Sovereign Integrals can live and function in time, they are not of time. We, at present, are actors on the stage of a play based on a time-based culture. We have forgotten, however, that we are only playing roles. Sovereign Integrals, on the other hand, know that when they are incarnated within a Human Instrument, they are acting in a very real play, but nonetheless, they know that the play and the stage are only a small part of their wider existence beyond the space-time theatre.

The Underpinnings of Reality—*The consciousness of the Sovereign Integral is the destination that beckons the human instrument inward into the reality of First Source.*[95]

1. The mysteries of your world will never be understood through inquiries that are based in the language of the mind.
2. There is no truth that can be written, spoken or thought unless it is conceived and expressed through the Language of Unity.
3. All the fragments of philosophy, science, and religion, even when unified, represent but a fractional picture of reality.
4. The sovereign being and First Source are reality.
5. There is understanding of the world precisely to the degree that there is understanding of the Self.

The first two items above distinguish the language of the mind from the Language of Unity. Here are several quotations pertaining to this dichotomy:

> Language is seductive to the ego's drive for power and control, as well as the mind's inclination to surrender to, and believe in, the language of externals. . .

> No one is able to articulate life's dimensional depth and breadth with the tools of language. They can only, at best, describe their interpretation or their impressions. . . .

> Source Reality is the dwelling place of First Source, and it dances outside of the constructs of any language. It is complete within itself, and has a singular purpose of demonstrating the collective potential of all species within the Universe of Wholeness. It is the archetype of perfection. It is the standard bearer of each entity's innate design and ultimate destiny. ITS essence is so far beyond conception that the human instrument's tendency is to resort to the language of externals—and ultimately the hierarchy—to define Source Reality.[96]

95. "The Shifting Models of Existence," p. 632.
96. Ibid., p. 633, 635, 632-633.

The first two extracts are obviously referring to the language of the mind, whereas the third passage hints at the Language of Unity. We say, "hints at" because we can only assume that anything emanating from Source Reality, the dwelling place of First Source, can only be expressed in the Language of Unity.

Perhaps we can draw closer to an understanding of the Language of Unity by the following quotation:

> The language of the mind is words. The language of the heart is feelings. But the language of our Presence is behaviors, or activity. If you stay in the intelligence of your Presence, by giving it your attention, then the things that come within your local multiverse that have a lower density, they will have minimal effect, as you can— from the empowerment of your Quantum Presence—transform them with ease.[97]

The Quantum Presence is the Sovereign Integral, and it expresses the qualities of Oneness and Unity in its behaviors. We could say then, that the Language of Unity is the language of the Sovereign Integral.

In the preceding quotation and in the EventTemples documents on the heart, James introduces the idea of behavioral intelligence. Although there is much more about the heart later, for now we can define behavioral intelligence as the *intelligence of the heart*. This heart intelligence is implemented through the expression of the six heart virtues of appreciation, compassion, forgiveness, humility, understanding, and valor. You can think of these virtues as the fundamental qualities of the Entity expressed through the Sovereign Integral.

Following this reasoning, we suggest that by living within the Presence of the Sovereign Integral, and by default First Source, we can speak the language of Unity through the Sovereign Integral's portal, the energetic heart. Like learning any new language, it takes consistent practice, patience, and perseverance to learn the Language of Unity. But because it is the native tongue of the Sovereign Integral, this language is actually our first language and the language of the mind is our second. Thus, re-learning our native language of the Sovereign Integral may very well be easier than learning a foreign language of the third dimension. As we work to achieve a Sovereign Integral level of living, we are re-connecting and remembering our core linkages to the larger self.

Beyond what has been surmised here, it is quite possible that there is an actual Language of Unity, comprised of words, grammar, and syntax, that exists in higher dimensional realms. This writer asked James if the glyphs appearing in his paintings were examples of the hidden language of initiates, known as Senzar, mentioned by H.P. Blavatsky in her book The Secret Doctrine. In answer to this question is the following comment from James:

---

97. *Collected Works of the WingMakers Vol. II*, Part IV, Sec. One, Mark Hempel Interview with James, Session Three

Senzar, besides being an alphabet of its own, can be rendered in cipher characters, which correspond to the nature of ideographs rather than of syllables. Senzar, as a language, was brought by the Central Race to earth. The reason is quite simple. Ideographic language can convey a tremendously complex concept in a single character...

Senzar is a language that flows between alphabetic characters, mathematical symbols, and musical notes. It is an integrated language, sometimes referred to as the Universal Language of Light, or the Insignias of First Source.[98]

Even though James doesn't identify Senzar as the Language of Unity, they may be the same or, at the least closely, related. The name "Insignias of First Source" especially suggests a Language of Unity. Merriam-Webster's defines insignia as a "distinguishing mark or sign." So, Senzar can be described as a language bearing the signs of First Source. James gives an example of Senzar in the Chamber Twenty-four painting.

In other words, you can look at a specific symbol of the twenty-fourth Chamber Painting (e.g., the second, primary character in the vertical matrix in the upper left section of the painting). If taken out of its framework, this particular character means one thing, which would transpose to Sanskrit, but when viewed in its contextual matrix, it is elevated to Senzar, where its meaning is encoded as representing the Wholeness Navigator within the human instrument.[99]

---

98. *Collected Works of the WingMakers Vol. II*, Part IV, Sec. Two, Top. Arr. of Qs and As, Ques. 34-S3
99. Ibid.

By describing the symbol in Chamber Twenty-four, James is confirming that these symbols are Senzar, the Universal Language of Light, or the Insignias of First Source.

Finally, we are told in point three that reality, understood from the unified standpoints of philosophy, science, and religion, will only reveal a fraction of reality. In other words, the search for the ultimate reality of existence may be beyond our capabilities as long as our search is based on a space-time viewpoint and is within the purview of the ego-personality.

Statement four then explicitly states that the Sovereign Integral and First Source are the keys to reality. Consequently, our search for reality without their inclusion will always be incomplete. The fifth statement reinforces this assertion with the statement that we can only understand the world—or reality—to the extent that we understand the "Self," or Sovereign Integral. The Sovereign Integral speaks the Language of Unity through its portal of the heart, which allows love and its six virtues to flow into our world. As we develop the higher mind of spirit, or Source Intelligence, it is also possible that we will learn the Insignias of First Source, a language born from the reality of the Sovereign Integral and First Source Itself.

Putting these pieces together with the concept of the Grand Portal discovery, strongly suggests that we will not truly grasp the nature of reality until we achieve it.

Wholeness—*The Sovereign Integral consciousness can be envisioned as the connective "glue" that unifies each of us into wholeness.*[100]

1. The conditions of peace, beauty, love, and security are merely signposts to wholeness, as are their counterparts.
2. To live in the Wholeness Perspective is to value all things as they are and to bear witness to the unity of their expression.
3. No being requires knowledge other than their unique Wholeness Perspective.
4. Perfection is a concept of wholeness misunderstood.
5. First Source transcends Wholeness.

The first two statements are probably the most difficult to manifest in practical terms because we are living in one of the most polarized times in history. Whether in religion, politics, or culture; physical, emotional, and mental conflicts prevail. As a result, the counterparts of peace, beauty, love, and security; war, ugliness, hate, and insecurity, stand in opposition to one another, as dogmas, beliefs, selfishness, and ignorance fan the flames of polarization.

As paradoxical as it sounds, observing the polarities of the world from a perspective of wholeness expands and lifts our worldviews to the Sovereign Integral level. From this vantage point of consciousness, we can see the world through a wider lens. In this state of awareness, we see the battlefield of world conflict within a larger framework. An analogy to this is how the Entity looks at each of its

---

100. *Collected Works of the WingMakers Vol. II*, Part III, Sec. Three, "The Temple of Spiritual Activism."

incarnations, with all the conflicts, as a metaphorical chapter in its book. It grasps the larger plan and detailed blueprint it has created. This is the theme and plot of the story, and the Entity may author other books.

Moving to the collective level, the current chapter of global conflict can be understood in psychological terms as coaxing the shadow side of humanity into the light of our awareness. The shadow is that part of the ego that contains conflicts that are too troubling to consciously address. Consequently, these conflicts are repressed, and stored in our sub-conscious. At the risk of stretching this analogy too far, the "therapist" facilitating this enormous and complex situation could be thought of as the collective consciousness of humanity, as it writes its story about the human species of planet Earth in its pre-Grand Portal phase of evolution.

At the individual micro level, many of our surface anxieties and stresses are manifestations of unresolved subconscious conflicts. As long as they are not uncovered and brought into awareness, our mental and physical health suffer and deteriorate.

The same general idea applies to global disharmony. Seething, unresolved resentments, hatred, and differences between groups and nations need to be resolved before they can be eliminated, or at the very least, recognized, but respected by one another. The only way to do this is to acknowledge their existence and work toward neutralizing them.

From the wholeness perspective of this wider view, it is possible to view the world, with its warring factions, as ongoing psychological therapy. The process involves resolving conflicts and reordering society in a way that respects the *sovereign* aspect of individuality and the *integral* necessity of global cooperation. This rebalancing of individual and group differences could be looked at as the emergence of the *collective* Sovereign Integral of humanity. And maybe this is what the Grand Portal will reveal.

Point three adds to the discussion of the first two points by placing the acquiring of the Wholeness Perspective ahead of the acquisition of knowledge. Our knowledge will not save us as long as we view the world in the duality of polarization. (This viewpoint is reflected in the Ancient Arrow story when the WingMakers say that our technologies will not save us from the Animus.) Conflicts will continue, and knowledge, along with its technological advances, will most likely be used for weapons of warfare. The ability to step out of the ego-personality's separative perspective into the Sovereign Integral's Wholeness Perspective is the key to acquiring knowledge of reality beyond the limited time-bound world reality we presently inhabit.

Will this mean a perfect society? Not according to point four above, which is telling us not to mistake wholeness for perfection. For instance, we can view a condition, such as world peace, as creating the perfect society, but this doesn't necessarily mean that it is whole. This is because the blueprint of exploration will continuously drive us to new discoveries and possibly even new conflicts with other civilizations that we may encounter as we explore the dimensions of the multiverse. The knowledge we gain from these discoveries, even from a perspective of wholeness, may very well expose us to re-evaluations of our own civilization that show imperfections in the light of new discoveries. Such imperfections are actually new, more expansive frameworks that indicate incompleteness, and consequently a not-so-perfect estimation of our civilization when compared to older, more advanced ones.

Finally, the bottom line is that First Source exists beyond our concept of wholeness, apparently including the Wholeness Perspective itself. Essentially, this means that everything created by First Source exists as Its manifested form, even in non-space-time dimensions. This idea is roughly similar to the Sovereign Integral externalizing a Human Instrument constituted by its multidimensional components. The Sovereign Integral, in this case, transcends the wholeness of the Human Instrument. The Human Instrument is only whole relative to itself, but the Sovereign Integral transcends that wholeness, and exists prior to the forms it manifests in the multiverse.

As far as we can tell, this is true of First Source. As the Pythagoreans and other Greek philosophers taught, the number one does not signify a divine singularity or a Creator, but is only the first manifestation of a Creator. In a similar way, the Hindu trinity of gods—Shiva, Vishnu, and Brahma are the manifested outpouring of a transcendent Being that exists prior to these three aspects. The same holds true for First Source. The wholeness of all life, as a self-contained multiverse, is a projection of First Source, Who exists prior to all conceptions of wholeness, unity, oneness or whatever other terms we can conceive.

The Freedom of Self-creation—*[T]hese life principles are the tools to accelerate the emergence of the Sovereign Integral and feel its perspective, its insights, and its empowered abilities to create new realities and shape them as learning adventures that liberate and expand consciousness.*[101]

1. There is no model of existence outside of the model of self-creation.
2. All conditions of existence are facets of the one condition of the reality of unlimited self-creation.
3. Having a physical body does not limit you, anymore than having legs on an eagle prevents it from flying.
4. The hidden harmony is found with joy, while the obvious brings indifference.
5. True Freedom is access to First Source.

If you have already read the introduction to the four philosophies and the Chamber Two paper "The Shifting Models of Existence" you know that the Entity Model is the primary model operating in the universe. So the first two items above give us pause. Can there be two primary models? It does not seem so according to the philosophy papers, but so much of the Lyricus teachings are new to us that it is being spoon-fed to us so that we can digest it and integrate it into our view of the multiverse. So, it is possible that there is an Entity Model and a Self-creation Model operating in tandem.

Alternatively, the Model of Self-creation can easily be viewed as a synonym for the Entity Model. This seems the most plausible explanation from my viewpoint, but I cannot and will not say that this is the only explanation, for many of you may have your own insights into this apparent dilemma, as well as others that present themselves in various areas of these collected works. Having said that, let's move on.

According to the Entity Model, individuated consciousnesses are created with free will. Consequently, we live in a free will universe, which allows relatively total freedom of expression. This means that First Source does not, to our knowledge, subject the good and the bad behavior of human beings to divine intervention. That does not mean, however that we have not been given principles to live by that educate us in conduct that contributes to the betterment of ourselves and to others, and also instructs in those behaviors that foster hurt and harm.

We can say then, that we are inherently creatures with free will to follow the principles of living handed down to us from the ancient world, along with the accumulated knowledge and wisdom we have garnered for ourselves as a result of experience. We could say that our self-discovered principles of living represent a "facet of unlimited self-creation."

Self-creation is simply the creative expression of the Entity through the Sovereign Integral. As mentioned in other places of this collection, First Source has given us free will so that we can learn to create in all areas of life. Whether driven by the need for survival or the need to express a concept or feeling through artistic means, the creativity of the Sovereign Integral is extant in every field of exploration.

The blueprint of exploration is the driving force behind self-creation. As early man wondered what lay beyond the ocean's horizon, men built vessels that could navigate the deeper waters. When these efforts failed, they were still driven to improve their shipbuilding skills and technologies to overcome their limitations. This is but one example of self-creation. Without too much effort, we can all find examples of such efforts, for they are a natural part of who we are. We were created for this explicit purpose—to explore the universe and create whatever means were necessary to achieve the goals.

The third statement then tell us that the physical body does not limit our ability to self-create, despite the difficulties and travails of living on the physical plane. On the contrary, the difficult roadblocks to survival thrown up by nature are the very whips that drive us forward, despite the pain of their stings. Armed with the freedom to explore and create, humanity inevitably advances and contributes to the purpose and plan of First Source.

What all this implies, is that the creativity of humanity is an expression of the Sovereign Integral as it is passed down to the Remnant Imprint, which is the source of inspiration within the Human Instrument. (See discussion of the Remnant Imprint in the introduction to the music of Hakomi Chamber Three and James' article "Anatomy of the Individuated Consciousness.) After all, this is a manifesto of the Sovereign Integral, and therefore these items pertain to its reality.

Self-creation also applies to the Entity, which is continuously creating new Human Instruments for universe expression. The Entity is totally free to plan when and where it will self-create the Human Instruments that will best contribute to its evolution. As the Entity gains more experience in the timespace universe, its contributions or creations are increasingly turned from the personal to others. Both are important. For instance, it can be said that we can best help others when we have helped ourselves. If we have problems that need addressing, then it is essential that we create the ways and means to overcome our weaknesses. Some can do this themselves, but most of us require some form of help. No matter, the point is that self-creation also applies to those thoughts, feelings, and attitudes that we create for our own advancement and improvement.

Whether we are self-creating through new thoughts about self-improvement or creating a groundbreaking philosophy or technology, they are a form of service. Thus, we move from service to self to service to others. From service to self, service to family, service to society, we self-create as we produce the ways and means to improve our service.

When we self-create under the inspiration of the Sovereign Integral passed on to its agent the Remnant Imprint, we experience joy. Joy radiates from contact with the higher frequencies of the Wholeness Navigator and the Sovereign Integral. Through these contacts, we experience joy. It might be said, that happiness lies within the realm of the ego-personality, where life can turn from happiness to sorrow in an instant. But joy comes from increasing contact with Sovereign Integral and is carried into the personality. It is then that our indifference to the obvious is replaced with a joy for all life. This joy coupled with the Sovereign Integral's transcendence of the polarities of the world, bring a harmony to our lives that has the power to staunch the flames of conflict that too often inflict us with hopelessness and bewilderment, and as a result sever or greatly reduce our ability to re-align with the spiritual side of our beingness.

Finally, when we become aware of the power of self-creation with its opportunities for service, and the inflow of spiritual joy that brings harmony, we enter into a new freedom that gives us access to First Source. This can happen because at that growth stage of consciousness we are connected and aligned with our true spiritual center, which is inherently immersed in the highest vibrations of First Source.

- The farther you enter into the Truth the deeper your conviction for truth must be.

This twenty-third statement seems a fitting end relative to the other statements we have already examined, for the bottom line to the Sovereign Integral's manifesto is how truthful we believe them to be. Can we trust these statements as facts?

At this point it might prove helpful to re-introduce two manifesto statements already discussed. The first statement is:

- There is no truth that can be written, spoken or thought unless it is conceived and expressed through the Language of Unity.

Put simply, the only way to test the truthfulness of the manifesto is to work with the statements, for these represent the Language of Unity. If we can escape from our ego-personality, knee-jerk reactions to our surroundings—personal situations, relationships, news events, etc.—and begin to view them according to the manifesto, we can transform our entire psychological landscape from the narrow space-time ego vantage point to the wide panorama of the Sovereign Integral. Metaphorically, this might be likened to moving from analog, black and white television to digital, color high definition reception.

This is a journey in consciousness from one truth to another. Speaking strictly subjectively, the truth of our reality as five year olds is much different than the reality we experience as adults. The world of the child, the truth of their reality, expands enormously as they grow older. In a way, our bold desire to explore a greater reality, lying outside the narrow confines of space-time, is similar to that of a child's continuous adjustments to the more expansive realities of reaching puberty, becoming a teenager, and crossing over into adulthood. With each new phase of awareness, we can say that the child's reality is changing, and many of the truths that the child believed in must be expanded in order to incorporate the realities of adult life.

At the danger of oversimplifying something we don't fully comprehend, namely the reality of the Sovereign Integral stage of consciousness, we can apply the child example to our spiritual search for new realities beyond the one we presently experience through our five senses. And just as children might very well be frightened by the realization, for instance, that their parents are not perfect and will someday die, this new concept of death is definitely a new reality for a child—a new truth. Hence, our own explorations into the truth may very well challenge our worldviews and, and if not managed wisely, could cause psychological damage. Instances of this effect are common in spiritual and metaphysical literature, and therefore cautionary warnings are extant in relation to encounters with subjective dimensions. Here is a lengthy quotation from James on the pitfalls of seeking deeper realities and the problem of verifying your experience:

> A radiant ball of energy (like the sun) burns underneath all concepts related to First Source. Around this energy are thousands of layers of interpretation—some of these are words, some symbols, some emotions, some mental constructs, some are pictures, some are dreams, some are hopes, etc. However, every level contains some of the light and energy of that radiant ball of energy, and because of this, it magnetically pulls the consciousness of the individual deeper into awareness.
>
> Verification is only accessible in personal experience, and even

this is temporary within the three-dimensional world. I have known students, who have been granted wonderful exposure to these "radiant balls of energy," and they often fall into doubt and even depression after the experience because they cannot sustain their belief that the experience was authentic.

In other words, even verification or personal experience is overrated. It only matters how you transfer your level of experience and knowledge into works that are aligned to the objectives of First Source and live your life according to the life principles of the Sovereign Integral.

If you have a very basic knowledge of these concepts, but you live according to the principles of the Sovereign Integral and you produce expressions aligned to First Source, you have your verification in your words and deeds, and you add to the radiant energy system of these concepts.

The keyword is add to the radiant energy system, not experience them for purposes of verification. I know you might think that by verification or personal experience you would be better able to add to the radiant energy system, but only in rare instances is this true. For most, they become unbalanced and seek more experiences. Their desire to experience overpowers their desire to practice the simple, but powerful principles of the Sovereign Integral.[102]

So, there is nothing wrong with seeking and gaining knowledge of other realities, as long as we do not get caught up in what James calls "information greed." Whatever knowledge we gain is only valuable to the extent that we use it in service to human betterment and in service to First Source. Verification of higher knowledge is not of value in and of itself. Rather, we "verify" the progress of our spiritual journey by living life according to the principles of the Sovereign Integral and not by displaying the knowledge we have of higher worlds and other dimensions.

Returning to statement twenty-three, it indicates that the further we delve into the truth, the more conviction we must have for the truth. Conviction means that we are convinced that something is true, even though it is still unproven. Such indications often come to us through the intuitive intelligence of the heart, not the head. We are so attached to the analytical modality of the mind that we tend to be insensitive to our feelings and even mistrusting of them.

Seeking truth in the area of spirituality, however, requires a certain amount of open-mindedness and a willingness to immerse oneself in that which is not immediately verifiable in the same way as the simple observation of the weather outside your window. Seekers of truth must have the desire, curiosity, and courage to explore areas beyond the range of the five senses. What we encounter in these

---

102. *Collected Works of the WingMakers Vol. II*, Part IV, Sec. Two, Top. Arr. of Qs and As, Ques. 42-S3

explorations, as implied by the twenty-third statement, will become stranger and stranger the further we explore.

The second statement is:

- All the fragments of philosophy, science, and religion, even when unified, represent but a fractional picture of reality.

Consequently, we must maintain our convictions—our faith—in truth seeking. The ego-personality will not help us here, but our continued alignment to the virtues of the heart and to the principles of the Sovereign Integral are the loyal guardians that will guide us along the Way.

Introduction to the WingMakers Philosophy Papers

It is neither fate nor karma that is drawing the human species to the edge of the Grand Portal. It is the event string of First Source, and therefore, the outcome of every human action and thought is an element of this journey.[103]

The four philosophy papers each correspond to a chamber in the WingMakers spiral-shaped structure. Like most of the materials presented by James, these four papers cannot be understood with one reading. I have revisited them a number of times and often refer back to specific sections of them to clarify my understanding of James' other writings.

In the hope of smoothing the way for your encounter with these important documents, I am presenting an overview of the four philosophies that provides a general framework in which you can fill in the details as you read the papers yourself. I have also provided a guide to the high points of the many new concepts presented in these four works. This guide is also a handy means of relocating specific information in the papers.

In the following overview, we will limit our discussion to life as we know it on earth. Even though the WingMakers philosophy is explained from a cosmological perspective, it will be easier to grasp the essentials by limiting them to an earth perspective as much as possible.

Finally, I have capitalized the great majority of terms that appear in the WingMakers glossary. Referring to these terms while reading this introduction, and the philosophy papers themselves, will greatly aid your reading experience.

Chamber One Philosophy: Life Principles of the Sovereign Integral—
The Sovereign Integral is the fullest expression of the entity model within the time-space universes, and most closely exemplifies Source Intelligence's capabilities therein.[104]

First Source has created fragments of Itself in the form of individuated self-conscious Entities. We are these Entities. Our existence and life expression within the universe is thus referred to as the Entity Model of existence.

The goal of the Entity is to express its true wisdom through an evolved portion of its consciousness, termed the Sovereign Integral. Although the stage upon which this growth of consciousness takes place is within a universe of many dimensions (the multiverse), the space-time dimension is the primary field of the Entity's exploration and consequent development. In short, we are designed to explore the space-time domain as individuated agents of First Source.

The Entity is not capable of exploring the space-time dimension because of its high frequency nature. So, the Human Instrument was designed to allow the Entity to project a tiny portion of its consciousness into this exploratory instrument, which

---

103. "Beliefs and Their Energy Systems," p. 662.
104. "Life Principles of the Sovereign Integral," p. 623.

consists of our mental, emotional, and physical faculties.

As the Entity progresses through its incarnations on various worlds, the Human Instrument transfers its accumulated experiences to the Entity, where it is transferred to First Source and to the Sovereign Integral. Through this process, the Sovereign Integral becomes the repository of all the experience, knowledge, and wisdom garnered from the incarnated Entity's experiences in the Human Instrument. And First Source gains this experience for Its continuing, mysterious purpose.

Operating within the Entity Model of expression are two other models. We can think of them as sub-models nested within the Entity Model. The first one is termed the Evolutionary/Saviorship Model and the second one is termed the Transformation/Mastership Model.

Inhabitants of earth are mostly operating within the Evolution/Saviorship Model, which is governed by hierarchical structures, such as religions, governments, institutions, corporations, etc. Collectively, these organized structures are termed Hierarchy. We can think of Hierarchy as the world power structure. The Hierarchy governs the Evolution/Saviorship Model on earth.

As Entities develop and are better able to incarnate through more refined Human Instruments, the Hierarchy and its Evolution/Saviorship Model becomes onerous and restrictive. There is an increasing desire for independence from the limiting structures and rankings of the Hierarchy. Whether the individual is working through a church, government, corporation or other institution, he or she, at some stage, will no longer look outside themselves for a savior, religious or otherwise. They will begin to realize that they themselves are capable of saviorship through transformation and self-mastery. This begins the process of shifting from the Evolution/Saviorship Model to the Transformation/Mastership Model. The term saviorship is more easily understood in the context of Hierarchy by expanding the concept of saviorship beyond the religious sphere.

If we think about it, saviorship is disguised in many ways within our lives. On the job we may hope that external forces will propel us to the next level within the company. As children or young adults we are often dependent on our parents to bail us out of difficult situations and in many cases this is justified. The time comes, however, when the child must become the adult and grow beyond an over-dependence on parental intervention.

Some people never grow out of this need for outside intervention and become dependent on a spouse, family member or friend for physical and psychological support. So, others continue to be our saviors throughout life in numerous situations. Naturally, there are many instances of individuals requiring help and it is morally correct to give that aid, but otherwise a savior can also be described by the more familiar term—enabler.

In a real sense, Hierarchy thrives on being the enabler because it guarantees its power over weaker institutions and organizations at the mass level, even while its cascading influences reaches down and control humans at the individual level. As savior, Hierarchy takes on the role of the parent who will never let go of the child because that parent will be diminished in power and influence. Even though Hierarchy is often acting out of benevolence and service, it overstays its welcome in the lives of groups and individuals by not allowing them to gain autonomy and freedom to creatively explore the space-time dimension, and thus fulfill their destiny as Entities.

Some esoteric schools describe the Evolution/Saviorship and Transformation/ Mastership approaches to life respectively as the slow path of evolution (of consciousness) and the *accelerated* path of initiation. The WingMakers philosophy avoids the mystical term *initiation* in favor of the more neutral term *transformation*. In the twenty-first century much of the old mystical and esoteric metaphysical terminology will be updated to more scientific and psychological expressions reflecting advances in physics, genetics, and psychology.

Returning to our main theme, the first philosophy paper explains that for individuals to grow beyond the Evolution/Saviorship Model and into the Transformation/Mastership Model they can begin by practicing the three principles of the Sovereign Integral. These three principles are:

- Universe relationship through gratitude
- Observance of Source in all things
- Nurturance of life

We will not go into the details of these three principles here except to point out that these are the key factors for the emergence of the Sovereign Integral level of expression in life. In a sense, the individual *becomes* a Sovereign Integral. This description is best described by the final passage of the first philosophy paper:

> In these life principles, if they are truly applied with proper intent, are the tools to accelerate the emergence of the Sovereign Integral and feel its perspective, its insights, and its empowered abilities to create new realities and shape them as learning adventures that liberate and expand consciousness. This is the underlying purpose of the principles and perhaps the best reason to explore them.[105]

Chamber Two Philosophy: The Shifting Models of Existence—*The time has come to integrate the dominant model of the hierarchy (evolution/saviorship) with the dominant model of Source Intelligence (transformation/mastership).*[106]

Now that we know there are two models of existence, Evolution/Saviorship and Transformation/Mastership, the second philosophy paper goes into detail about these models, especially the Evolution/Saviorship Model.

The paper begins by explaining that the Entity's experiences in the space-time dimension are characterized by separation from wholeness. The feeling of being

---

105. "Life Principles of the Sovereign Integral," p. 631.
106. "The Shifting Models of Existence," p. 640-641.

alone in the universe as a separate human being with little or no evidence of a Creator or other intelligences, creates a desire for security from the forces of nature and the difficulties of survival.

Consequently, the need for survival creates at least two factors that contribute to the development of civilization. One factor is creativity born of necessity, leading to the discovery of survival methods and the invention of technologies for improving living conditions. This inborn instinct of survival is an important factor in the mysterious plan of First Source because it generates creativity and uniqueness in the incarnated Entities exploring the space-time worlds.

The second factor created by the need to survive is Hierarchy. Hierarchical structures are a natural and necessary means of creating order in any society, whether they be Paleolithic tribes or modern institutions. According to the WingMakers glossary, Hierarchy exists throughout the multiverse in both the natural world and in the civilizations created by humans.

As a result, there is a dynamic interplay between the structural order of hierarchies and the free expression of creativity unhindered by the rules and protocols governing organizations. As a brief example, a big issue for some individuals who are considering accepting employment with a large corporation is how free they will be to implement or experiment with their theories and ideas.

The point is that there is always this conflict between being part of a group and remaining an individual. This is a micro-view of the macro-view presented by the WingMakers philosophy. First Source wants Entities to develop their creativity and diversity, but also realizes that Hierarchy is a necessary ingredient of the Entity Model.

The main problem with human-created hierarchies is that they often lose their way. This paper discusses, for example, how the original, simple precepts of great spiritual leaders attract followers who organize the revelatory information into formats that can be more easily grasped by an increasing number of adherents. These efforts are not wrong and to a large extent are necessary and helpful, but as the hierarchical structure grows and matures it becomes more and more removed from the simplicity of its originator. As the years go by, and societies become more sophisticated and complex, hierarchies have difficulty keeping pace with the changes and may sometimes find them threatening. Ironically, the survivorship instinct affects hierarchies as much as individuals.

So in order to survive and maintain power, hierarchies can become corrupt and simply exist to maintain themselves and to protect the persons at their heads. The purpose and originating principles upon which they were founded are lost and lose their power. They then become forces of the status quo and the adversary of innovation and the freedom to change. Corrupt and/or outdated hierarchies thus become a hindrance to the Entity Model created by First Source. The bottom line, however, is that hierarchies are not inherently bad or evil, but that their purposes, activities, and influences are all dependent on the motives of the individual or individuals who create, operate, and maintain these structures.

Despite all this, the second paper explains that hierarchies play a key role in the Primal Blueprint, or grand vision of First Source because humans instinctively desire to reconnect to some greater whole or Source from which they have been separated. Added to this is the need to band together for survival. These desires and needs are nourished by hierarchical structures no matter how small and local or large and universal. They provide a sense of belonging and unity.

> This is why the evolution/saviorship model is so critical as a component to the Grand Experiment. It is the stage whereby the human instrument develops a sense of unity and belonging; a sense of relationship to some grand and encompassing vision. This is why the hierarchy nurtures saviors. It is also why the feelings of inadequacy and insecurity are developed and nurtured by the hierarchy. It actually hastens the unification of humanity, which in turn, will hasten and lead to the unification of humanity with the Universe of Wholeness.[107]

At this point in the reading of the philosophy papers, terms are accumulating at a fast clip. The Grand Experiment is "the ongoing transformation and expansion of Source Intelligence through all entities in all dimensions."[108] The Grand Experiment is concerned with evaluating the two models of evolution and transformation. In other words, might hierarchies wield so much power that individuals have too much difficulty escaping them in order to be free to explore the multiverse and fulfill themselves as Entities?

The WingMakers terminology for spirit is Source Intelligence. In the simplest definition, Source Intelligence is described as the "eyes and ears" of First Source. In the case of hierarchies, Source Intelligence is "the factor of integrity and alignment, which ensures that the Hierarchy is serving its purpose within the Primal Blueprint."[109]

The paper explains that First Source is connected to individuals not organizations, but Source Intelligence (Spirit) does influence hierarchies. Recall that the Entity is a fragment of First Source and thus the direct connection. This is not to say that Source Intelligence has no effect on individuals or that individuals cannot contact Source Intelligence for guidance. Its role for individuals is to help accelerate their consciousness and remove the limits of the ego-personality.

Now comes a key point. From this distinction between the Entity's direct connection to First Source and the Hierarchy's connection to Source Intelligence—but not to First Source—it is clear that individuals cannot connect to First Source through hierarchies, religious or secular. Instead individuals can turn to the Transformation/Mastership Model. The many breakaway groups that have appeared throughout the centuries exemplify this approach to God. Such groups rejected the church or temple hierarchies that served as the intermediaries between their followers and God.

The point of course, which many seekers understand today, is that we can "save" ourselves. We have been provided with all the tools needed for transformation and

---

107. Ibid., p. 634-635.
108. Ibid., p. 636
109. Ibid., p. 636.

mastership over the elements of limitation contained within us. Many approaches to truth are now available to people seeking expansion and development of consciousness. These forms of spiritual approach, however, represent the knowledge and wisdom of the past. They have served humanity well through the ages, but new forms of spirituality are emerging today and the Lyricus/WingMakers materials represent this new wave of metaphysics, psychology, and cosmology.

Now, as has already been pointed out, hierarchies will always be with us, and even though individuals are practicing the Transformation/Mastership Model, they still operate in a hierarchical environment. Even if a proponent of a particular Transformation/Mastership Model teaches the techniques of their system, that person is already in a hierarchical position of leadership in relations to the students. And as a group forms around a particular Transformation/Mastership practice, it must have some organizational structure or will it most likely come under the second law of thermodynamics and disintegrate.

So what is the solution to this dilemma? This philosophy paper informs us that a Synthesis Model is being implemented throughout the space-time universe. Apparently, individuals play a key role in this emergence because we must personally explore both models and integrate them to form a Synthesis Model of existence. This is easier said than done because only the Entity level of consciousness can achieve this integration—it cannot be done through the mind, emotions or physical body. We must learn to access and express the Entity consciousness through spiritual practice. This Entity level is expressed through becoming the Sovereign Integral. The effort to express the three principles of the Sovereign Integral in philosophy paper one is the initial means. This coupled with the practice of the six heart virtues [see volume II, Event Temples] provides one approach to achieving the Synthesis Model.[110]

> While the entity assumes its role of personal liberation, it does not mean that the hierarchy is to be shunned or avoided. . . .The combination of self-saviorship and detachment from the hierarchy initiates the synthesis model into manifestation. The synthesis model is the next outcome of the Grand Experiment, and in certain vibrational fields of the multidimensional universe, there are entities who are indeed experiencing this stage of the experiment as forerunners of the entity model of Source individuation.[111]

In order to help in the process of creating a Synthesis Model, "Sovereign Entities" (perhaps Sovereign Integrals) will incarnate on earth to foster the ability of humans to create the Synthesis Model. These Sovereign Entities will work behind the scenes as "catalysts and designers."

> They are present to ensure that Source Intelligence is allowed

---

110. James emphasizes in various places of his writing that the Lyricus/WingMakers materials are only one of various new spiritual approaches that will become available to humanity in this century.
111. "The Shifting Models of Existence," pp. 641.

to balance the dominant force of the hierarchy and its model of evolution/saviorship. They will not create a new belief system. Instead, they will focus on developing new communication symbols through various art forms that facilitate the entity's detachment from the controlling aspects of the hierarchy. The Sovereign Entities will also demonstrate the natural ease of interweaving the two primary strands of existence into a synthesis model.[112]

Eventually, the Synthesis Model will be replaced by more advanced models that will better serve an evolving humanity. Details of these models are not explained in the paper; only that future Entities will be doing this work. This activity will produce a new hierarchy, but the paper is quick to point out that the new models that emerge are impossible to describe at this time.

Chamber Three Philosophy: The Blueprint of Exploration—*In reality, if you are within a human instrument, you are an immortal light consciousness gathered from the same substance as First Source.[113]*

We have explored the first two philosophy papers and before moving on let's briefly review what we have learned.

The first paper defines the goal of the individuated consciousness—the Entity—in the worlds of time and space. That goal is to achieve the Sovereign Integral level of consciousness. The first paper then discusses how to begin this process of activation and expansion.

We next learn that there are models of existence through which Entities work toward this goal. Two models currently dominate—they are called the Evolution/Saviorship Model and the Transformation/Mastership Model. Eventually, these two Models must be integrated through the Entity's physical incarnations to form a Synthesis Model. Source Intelligence monitors this process in order to determine how to optimize these models of Entity development toward the goal of the Sovereign Integral level of life expression. This optimization effort is termed the Grand Experiment.

Having laid the foundation of the Entity Model of existence in the first two papers, the third paper provides details of the Entity's exploratory experience. Following is a direct quote from the third philosophy: "The purpose of this system is to explore the worlds of creation and evolve the ability of the individuated consciousness to acquire and express wisdom."[114]

As mentioned on page one of this introduction, "[t]he goal of the Entity is to express its true wisdom through an evolved portion of its consciousness, termed the Sovereign Integral." So, here we see that the blueprint of exploration is the detailed plan for acquiring and expressing wisdom, which is the stated goal of the first philosophy paper.

---

112. Ibid., p. 641.
113. "The Blueprint of Exploration," p. 646.
114. "The Blueprint of Exploration," p. 644.

The third philosophy states that the "blueprint of exploration is the underlying foundation of the cosmos."[115] It then explains that the blueprint consists of five stages.

1. The Creation of the Entity Consciousness
2. The Individual of Time and Genetic Density
3. The Acquisition of Experience through Separation
4. The Ascending Spiral to the True Wisdom
5. The Onward Journey of Developing Creation

Setting aside the specifics, the titles of these five stages are quite descriptive of the overall blueprint.

The Creation of the Entity Consciousness. The WingMakers were the first creations of First Source. Initially, these primal Entities took the form of light bodies. Eventually the WingMakers created the Human Instruments that could explore the space-time universe.

The Individual of Time and Genetic Density. These Human Instruments allow the Entity to experience life in the universe as an individual of genetic density. Just how the WingMakers acquired their knowledge of DNA to create these genetic bodies is not explained in the philosophies released so far. Thus, if these philosophical ideas feel right enough for us to continue studying them, we must accept these generalities for now, until further details are released.

The Acquisition of Experience Through Separation. The Entity is always connected to First Source through its light body, but that portion of the Entity's consciousness (the lesser self) that is exploring the space-time dimension is separated from First Source. This separation is a deliberate aspect of the blueprint because it allows the individual of genetic density to explore with innocence. Like a child exploring its new world from the time of its birth, everything is a new discovery offering opportunity for creative play. Beyond the playful aspect, the trials of pain and suffering also often lead to great creative works and discoveries.

The Ascending Spiral to the True Wisdom. Through the pain and confusion of this sense of separation and abandonment, the individual ascends the spiral to the true wisdom. This is done through the two models of existence and their eventual integration as a Synthesis Model. The true wisdom emerges as the individual progresses through the Hierarchy of worldly powers and learns how to transform into the Sovereign Integral.

We could say that this process is a spiral because Hierarchy is an inescapable form of structural order in the space-time worlds and consequently the transformed individual will continue to work in a hierarchical environment even though that individual has transformed outside of a hierarchy. Accordingly, individuals first work within a hierarchy, then transform outside its control, and reenter the same or other

---

115. Ibid., p.645

hierarchical structure at a higher, or more refined level of awareness. This cycle may be repeated any number of times. This can be likened to an ascending spiral of ever more refined hierarchical environments, ultimately including hierarchies managed by Sovereign Integrals. These environments are reformed hierarchies based on a synthesis of the two models and this *synthesis* is created by Sovereign Integrals.

This section goes on to explain that the true wisdom will be revealed by Sovereign Integral Entities and thus we may assume that the controlling, misguided hierarchies of our present world will become enlightened power structures of the true wisdom in the future.

The Onward Journey of Developing Creation. Here, perhaps, is the most exciting aspect of these five phases of the blueprint—our onward journey overflows into the multidimensional realities of other worlds and planetary populations. This monumental leap in our evolution occurs as an ever-increasing portion of our world population reaches the Sovereign Integral expression of the true wisdom and discovers the Grand Portal.

Several hundred years after humanity discovers the Grand Portal it is given access to the Sovereign Integral Network (SIN) by First Source. The glossary describes the Sovereign Integral Network in the following ways:

1. SIN is actually a sub-atomic network of light-encoded filaments that exist in all dimensions of the multiverse.
2. [It is] like a web, connecting every life form at its entity level to all other entities and First Source.
3. This is an organic network that is utilized by First Source to transmit knowledge to entities and to receive knowledge from entities.
4. When a human species transforms its genetic mind to utilize the Sovereign Integral Network, this becomes the 'ship' upon which it sails the seas of the cosmos.
5. In this way, the species is allowed to become 'Gods' of newly created worlds in which it can re-enact the entire process of the Grand Experiment.
6. This is core purpose of WingMakers, to help terra-earth become a node on SIN before its opportunity to interface has passed.[116]

Referring to the entire SIN entry in the glossary will obviously give you a fuller idea of it, but the above items give us an exciting and positive vision of the future direction of earth's humanity. As number five indicates, our onward journey of creation appears to be innately linked with our access to SIN in a few hundred years. It is at that time that we will fully engage stage five. From the Grand Portal discovery point (estimated at the time of this writing to be about 2080), to our entry into the Sovereign Integral Network, we will be at stage four and working toward stage five. Even so, it is probable that there will still be portions of our population working at stage three, the "acquisition of experience through separation."

This third paper ends by explaining, and assuring, that every Entity will find its

---

116. WingMakers glossary, pp. 670-671.

way back to First Source and end its apparent separation and feeling of abandonment.

Chamber Four Philosophy: Beliefs and Their Energy Systems—*This Grand Portal will usher in a new awareness for humanity that will enable it to shift from a survival-based, mind-body energy system, to an exploratory-based, mind-soul energy system. This exploratory energy system will manifest the belief system of the Sovereign Integral; the Golden Age long prophesied.*[117]

The fourth philosophy paper addresses belief systems. According to this paper, humanity is currently operating within the Mind-Body belief system. This system is survival-based. It doesn't take too much imagination to realize that most of humanity's history has been based on survival. As civilization has progressed the ability to survive has slowly increased as well. Through the development of techniques for the storage of food and the availability of water, the protection of populations from nature's elements and invasions of hostile armies, humans have gradually improved their chances of survival.

In more recent times, first world countries have largely made real progress in protecting citizens from floods, droughts, storms, and other natural phenomena. True, there are still natural disasters, but improved knowledge and infrastructures largely negate the wholesale destruction that has often plagued earlier societies.

It is recognized today that if humanity is to achieve a stable global civilization, the first world countries must aid the third world. Interestingly, survival in the first world is now more oriented toward medical and financial survival as diseases and economics take center stage in the lives of so many people. So, while people, for instance, in third world countries worry about the next rainy season, people in first world countries worry about toxins in the environment caused by the production of the materials comprising their infrastructures.

The point is that humanity, despite the progress of science and technology is still grappling with survival. The fourth philosophy paper is fascinating in the sense that it predicts twenty-first century revolutionary advances in the arts and sciences that will create a new *exploratory system* in addition to the survival-based energy system. The former system is based on the mind and body, whereas the latter system will be based on the mind and Sovereign Integral.

The paper goes on to explain that beliefs are byproducts of energy systems.

> Energy systems are wide ranging in their context, but as they relate to beliefs, they can be defined as primordial thought forms crystallized within the human DNA. Some would refer to these fundamental energy systems as *instinctual knowledge.*[118]

Put in simple terms, survival is built into our DNA and is instinctual. Thus, even as we add a new energy system to our lives, we will still maintain the primary

---

117. "Beliefs and Their Energy Systems," pp. 653-654.
118. Ibid., p. 652.

instinct of survival. So, how will the new exploratory system be created? The answer introduces what are called Transition Zones. These are described as "isolated portals of energy that intersect the dominant energy system of the human species."[119]

As the new energy system of earth emerges, individuals will be able to access new Transition Zones that will enable them to ground and forge a new belief system. Because energy systems are built into our DNA, we can only assume at this point that changes in our DNA are going to—and probably already have—begun to introduce a new energy system into our Human Instruments and other undiscovered components of the Entity's energy field. Although purely speculation on my part, it may well be that the dimensional shift now occurring on our planet is a contributing factor to this incoming energy system.

Transition Zones are of two kinds—Tributary Zones and the Grand Portal. The first Tributary Zones were created by the WingMakers in "non-physical dimensions as outposts of creative energy."[120] Many of the most creative and talented individuals of earth's past contacted these non-physical Tributary Zones through their dreams and meditations, but all memory of these visitations were non-existent. What remained, however, were inspirational ideas that contributed to the uplifting and enrichment of civilization. "These initial physical creations dealt with spiritual values and were often the product of poetry, art, music, and drama."[121]

The major change that is coming in this century is the addition of *technology and science* to the arts, as scientific fields contributing to the spiritual values appropriate for our twenty-first century civilization. These new physically based Tributary Zones will be more significant than those of the past because they will foreshadow the Transition Zone of the Grand Portal. And recall that the primary mission of the Lyricus Teaching Order is to guide humanity to the Grand Portal. Hence, these coming Tributary Zones are critical to the Grand Portal discovery and will consequently intensify the activities of the Lyricus teachers. The work being conducted by James represents the initial stage of this twenty-first century project

This fourth paper goes on to explain that these new Tributary Zones will have an actual physical effect on our brains due to the advanced science and technologies incorporated in the music and art. Again, we have no specifics of how this will take place.

> The energy system of the Tributary Zones that prefigure the Grand Portal will be translated from the WingMakers to your finest representatives in the dawning of the twenty-first century. These Tributary Zones will manifest in the three-dimensional world of terraearth, but will actually stem from a non-physical dimension known only to the WingMakers and First Source.[122]

Having said that, the fourth philosophy paper offers an initial step for attracting

---

119. Ibid., p. 653.
120. Ibid., p. 654.
121. Ibid., p. 655.
122. Ibid., p. 656.

this new energy system into our personal energy fields. It states:

> When you believe, **'I am a fragment of First Source imbued with ITS capabilities,'** you are engaging this energy system inherent within the feeling of connectedness.[123]

The effects of feeling this sense of being an actual fragment of First Source, of containing and representing First Source within our three dimensional world can be a powerful change agent, both for ourselves and for those around us. The paper, however, alerts us that although this attitudinal shift in perspective is effective, it must be supported by other techniques that will strengthen and nurture the incorporation of the exploratory system into our lives. At this point in the paper, it offers three further techniques.

> There are specialized techniques for weaving this energy system to your own and exchanging—over time—your survival-based energy system for the exploratory energy system of the coming age.[124]

In other words, we will eventually eliminate the survival-based system from our lives in some "coming age." The next excerpt tells when this coming age will arrive.

> This Grand Portal will usher in a new awareness for humanity that will enable it to shift from a survival-based, mind-body energy system, to an exploratory-based, mind-soul energy system. This exploratory energy system will manifest the belief system of the Sovereign Integral; the Golden Age long prophesied.[125]

So, this coming Golden Age will arrive in the post-Grand Portal age after 2080. Notice that except for the first technique, they all involve the three components of the Human Instrument connecting with the Sovereign Integral. Following are the technique names:

- Mind-Body Movement Technique
- Mind-Soul Movement Technique
- Emotion-Soul Acquisition Technique

The first technique involves the music composed by James. Specifically this exercise is performed while moving to the music of Chambers Seventeen to Twenty-four.[126] In this exercise, the mind becomes the follower of the body's interpretation of the music's rhythm, tempo, and mood.

The technique is described as a meditation in which the mind takes a backseat to the intelligence of the body itself. As pointed out in the introduction to the *Collected Works of the WingMakers*, these eight tracks are encoded and designed to

---

123. Ibid., p. 656.
124. Ibid., p. 657.
125. Ibid., p. 653-654.
126. The CDs containing these tracks can be found under "Music" at www.wingmakers.com.

activate particular brain centers.

> This is a form of meditation taught by the WingMakers that demonstrates the trust placed upon the body intelligence and the willingness of the mind to listen to this intelligence. This is a thread of this new energy system externalized through this technique. There are portals designed into the music that will open the brain's emotional centers to this new energy, and when they are discovered, you will feel the undeniable shift in your energy field. The movement of the body signifies the externalization of the new in direct counterpoint to the old. It demonstrates the compatibility of the two energy systems, and how one can be in both fields simultaneously with comfort and confidence.[127]

Besides informing us that these eight tracks are encoded, the last sentence in this excerpt is also stating an important point—that both the survivorship system and the exploratory system can and will exist side-by-side. This seems to contradict our two previous quotations, which tell us that the survival-based system will be eliminated. The key phrase that clarifies this seeming contradiction is "over time." In other words, the two systems can work together, but after the Grand Portal is discovered the survival-based system will no longer play a part in the collective consciousness of earth's humanity. As for our current situation, even though we are approaching the Grand Portal discovery later in this century, we will still need to retain the survivor instinct, for this century will certainly be quite chaotic as it undergoes revolutionary global changes.

The next technique utilizes four particular Chamber Paintings—Chambers Two, Three, Twelve, and Four. These pertain to what James often refers to as MEST—matter, energy, space, and time. According to the paper, a new psychology will emerge in this century. It will integrate "metaphysics and the spiritual perceptions of the Genetic Mind, with the science of the brain and the shaping influences of culture and personal genetics."[128] Again, what all this means is difficult to assess right now. I will only venture to offer that the metaphysics and Genetic Mind aspects represent what is commonly understood as the subjective, or inner dimensions of life, and that brain science, culture, and personal genetics refer to the objective, or outer space-time dimension of life. So, the new psychology is aimed at unifying the subjective and objective dimensions of existence.

Further, these four paintings are designed to bring forward the incomprehensible nature of the human condition. Simply put, our engagement with the symbols and imagery of these four paintings is meant to force us into unconscious realms and utilize the mind for comprehension, or *understanding*. Here, as opposed to the first technique, the mind leads the way and it informs the soul of its discoveries and

---

127. "Beliefs and Their Energy Systems," pp. 657.
128. Ibid., p. 659.

insights. The paper states that "[b]y investigating visual symbols through the eye-brain, the mind can secure a glimpse into the Sovereign Integral consciousness and the special psychology therein."[129]

Following are the four Chamber Paintings and their designated targets of comprehension:

- Chamber Two—a comprehension of a new dimension of Time
- Chamber Three—a comprehension of a new dimension of inner Space
- Chamber Twelve—a comprehension of a new dimension of Energy
- Chamber Four—a comprehension of a new dimension of Matter

Two further points about this technique should be brought to your attention. First, there is the reference to *inner space* rather than to our acceptance of space being outer—*outer space*. This distinction may offer us clues to the symbolism related to third Chamber Painting. Second, it's important for us to keep in mind that these techniques are designed to give us a "glimpse" of the Sovereign Integral consciousness and the special psychology therein.

The third technique, Emotion-Soul Acquisition, focuses on the WingMakers poetry. Although there are forty-eight poems (two for each chamber), this technique employs only ten of the poems. These ten are designed to bring the discord of separation, abandonment, and spiritual neglect to the forefront of awareness and expose these discordant emotions to the soul.

> The technique of emotion-soul acquisition is concerned with discerning the emotional voice of a poem, intending that voice to resonate within your soul, and releasing the emotion that arises from the resonance, letting it wander away from you like a wild animal released into its natural habitat.[130]

According to James' later writing, the emotions are the main stumbling block to integrating the Human Instrument with the Entity and thus allowing the Sovereign Integral to step forward in one's life expression.

Western civilization is largely mind-based. The rational mind has the role of controlling the irrational emotions. Even though this effort is a crucial aspect of moral, ethical, and intelligent behavior, too much emphasis on the mental faculty can stifle and repress emotions that need to be addressed if we are want to experience psychologically healthy lives.

This isn't a case of reducing the role of the mind in our modern world, but restoring a balance between the emotions and the processes of thought. The EventTemplesmaterials are focused on this restoration of psychological integrity by placing the heart **in tandem with** the mind, so they function as a team. The heart, in this context refers to the feelings born from an alignment with spirit, and

---

129. Ibid., p. 659.
130. Ibid., p. 660.

consequently with the Entity and Sovereign Integral. This alignment with the spiritual aspect, rather than with the material ego-personality, utilizes the six heart virtues of appreciation, compassion, forgiveness, humility, understanding, and valor.[131]

The point of importance here, is that the restoration of psychological balance between the emotions and the mind can move forward simultaneously with the calling forth of the Sovereign Integral through the practice of spiritually oriented techniques such as practicing the six heart virtues. These are two sides of the same coin of consciousness expansion leading to living the life of the Sovereign Integral.

This third technique of emotional contact, awareness, and release, via these ten poems, is an integral part of the spiritual path set forth in these philosophy papers and for that matter, in all the WingMakers/Lyricus materials. In summation this paper says it best:

> The emotion-soul acquisition pays tribute to these feelings [separation, abandonment, spiritual neglect] and seeks to position the tether of discordance in the hands of soul, thus ensuring that the emotions have voice and influence in the shaping of soul's judgment, insight, and reasoning. It is the quiet emotions of separation and abandonment that fuel the strident emotions of fear, greed, and anger. Poetry can bring forth these quiet emotions and liberate their presence to the soul, and in so doing, allow them to be honored, and, in this process, understood.[132]

The fourth philosophy paper ends by assuring us that these techniques will yield successful results even though we may not be aware of the subtle effects they have on our DNA structure, which by the way, multi-dimensional and not just limited to the physical plane.

The paper goes on to explain that the entire process of incorporating a new energy system is designed to be a struggle because the process trains and disciplines us in the rigors and challenges of creating and working with the new, incoming Tributary Zones. In a real sense, we are upgrading and refining our Human Instruments in order to facilitate our immersion in the new Tributary Zones.

Despite the importance of this factor, it is pointed out that our individual efforts to integrate the new energy system through the coming Tributary Zones, this activity will not lead them to their personal discovery of the Grand Portal. No the Grand Portal discovery will be the result of a global humanity achieving *"the culmination of science, art, and technology, operating in unison, focused on the exploratory province of cosmology and metaphysics."*[133]

We then find at the end of this philosophy paper that Source Intelligence "orchestrates" the Grand Portal discovery from the very inception of human life on a planet. In short,

---

131. *Collected Works of the WingMakers Vol. II*, Part III, Sec. Three, *Living from the Heart*
132. "Beliefs and Their Energy Systems," pp. 661.
133. Ibid., p. 662.

this has always been our destiny and evolutionary trajectory. Reiterating, everything in human history represents the gestation period of humanity and our emergence into the post-Grand Portal era will be our birth onto the cosmic stage.

As a result, we will add a new energy system to our planet. This energy system is a "galactic energy system" that connects the earth to a galactic network, at which point we will no longer be a restricted planet-based species, but humanity *"will be inter-galactic in its range of experience and realm of influence."*

Summing up this fourth philosophy paper, it is important to reiterate a significant and interesting point—that the inculcation of the new energy system is not meant to replace the old, survival-based system in the short term. No, these techniques are designed to join them, bringing them together as a team in which we will still need the instinct of survival in the twenty-first century, but it will not be the only energy system governing our lives. We will be incorporating a new, exploratory system into our life repertoire. The fourth philosophy points out, however that the survival-based energy system will eventually fall away in the new age and earth's humanity will be based on the exploratory system.

In the case of the models of creation, we are creating a Synthesis Model from the Evolution/Saviorship and Transformation/Mastership Models, but in the case of the energy systems, we are bringing together two systems that will operate side-by-side until the post-Grand Portal period after 2080.

This brings out a finer point about the WingMakers/Lyricus initiatives. They all involve extension, incorporation, integration, and ultimately synthesis, whether these goals relate to the creation of a Synthesis Model, the apprehension of a new energy system, the creation of new Tributary Zones or the discovery of the Grand Portal. These all involve the coming revolutionary expansion of human consciousness through the discoveries of science, advancing technology, new art forms, and an increasingly sophisticated global communications system. And all implemented by the new Tributary Zones that are designed to restructure our Human Instruments for our eventual interaction with the Grand Portal experience of human Oneness and Wholeness.

Synopsis

We have learned that the Entity is designed to explore the space-time universe through the use of a Human Instrument. These instruments were designed by the first Entities, euphemistically called the WingMakers. The goal of the Entity as it explores the space-time worlds is to express its core nature through a quality, or level of consciousness termed the Sovereign Integral.

The Sovereign Integral is the "fullest expression of the Entity Model within the space-time universe."[134] The process of reaching this stage of consciousness expansion functions, at least on our planet, through two models of existence—the slower Evolution/Saviorship Model and the more rapid Transformation/Mastership

---

134. "Life Principles of the Sovereign Integral," p. 623.

Model. Both models appear necessary within the current set-up of the universe.

Eventually, these two models are integrated into a Synthesis Model. The ongoing life experiences of individuals (incarnational agents of the Entity), as they spiral their way through the two models, moving between each and "ascending" in consciousness expansion as they evolve, ultimately results in the Entity expressing itself as a Sovereign Integral operating within a Human Instrument.

This is all taking place within a universe-wide plan called the "Blueprint of Exploration." This is the context within which the Entity achieves the goal set forth for it by First Source and guided along the way by Source Intelligence.

This individual path of evolution finds its counterpart at the collective scale when the Grand Portal is discovered by a planetary species. This is a revolutionary event in the collective life of human beings, just as the attainment of Sovereign Integral expression is a revolutionary event in the life of the individuated Entity.

As a human population reaches the threshold of the Grand Portal discovery stage, the WingMakers take on a more active and visible role in this planetary happening. This occurs through the agency of the Lyricus Teaching Order. Through their activities, individuals committed to the Grand Portal initiative are given access to multidimensional Tributary Zones that inspire them to create physically-based Tributary Zones encompassing spiritual values, technology, science, and the arts. These Tributary Zones foreshadow the Grand Portal.

Once earth's humanity becomes a post-Grand Portal civilization we will no longer be restricted to the exploration of our own planet, but we will be able to explore on a cosmic scale beyond earth.

Thus, these four philosophy papers lay out a foundation for building a new metaphysical and cosmological worldview based on the revelation of the Grand Portal. The current worldview established by the institutions of governance, religion, philosophy, arts, and sciences has largely served humanity well despite the fact that these institutions have been, and still are, riddled with misconceptions, shortcomings, discord, and corruption.

Despite these imperfections, these older structures—hierarchies—have brought us to the threshold of the Grand Portal. This is truly a magnificent thought to contemplate. In the twenty-four hour clock of human existence relative to the Grand Portal, it is, perhaps, ten seconds to midnight and the beginning of a new day.

Generally considered, these four papers provide a rough outline for the establishment of a ***new energy system*** that will create the conditions for a paradigm shift of enormous magnitude. In short, our view of reality and our place in the multiverse will be forever altered.

Chamber One Philosophy
Life Principles of the Sovereign Integral

The entity model of expression is designed to explore new fields of vibration through biological instruments and transform through this process of discovery to a new level of understanding and expression as a Sovereign Integral. The Sovereign Integral is the fullest expression of the Entity Model within the time-space universes, and most closely exemplifies Source Intelligence's capabilities therein. It is also the natural state of existence of the entity that has transformed beyond the evolution/saviorship model of existence and has removed itself from the controlling aspects of the Hierarchy through the complete activation of its embedded Source Codes. This is the level of capability that was "seeded" within the entity model of expression when it was initially conceived by First Source. All entities within the time-space universes are in various stages of the transformational experience and each is destined to achieve the Sovereign Integral level as their Source Codes become fully activated.

The transformational experience is the realization that the entity model of expression is capable of direct access to Source Intelligence information, and that the information of First Source is discovered within the entity level of the Sovereign

Integral. In other words, the human instrument, complete with its biological, emotional, and mental capabilities, is not the repository of the entity's Source Codes. Nor is the human instrument able to reach out and gather in this liberating information—this glorious freedom to access All That Is. It is the entity that is both the harbor of, and instrument of access to, the Source Coding activation that permits the transformational experience to manifest through the integration of the human instrument and the sovereign entity.

The transformational experience consists of the realization that perceived reality is Source Reality personified in the form of individual preferences. Thus, Source Reality and sovereign reality become inseparable as the wind and air. This confluence is realized only through the transformational experience, which is unlike anything known within the time-space universes.

There have been those upon terra-earth who have experienced a shallow breath of wind from this powerful tempest. Some have called it ascension; others have attributed names like illumination, vision, enlightenment, nirvana, and cosmic consciousness. While these experiences are profound in human standards, they are only the initial stirrings of the Sovereign Integral, as it becomes increasingly adept at touching and awakening the remote edges of its existence. What most species define as the ultimate bliss is merely the impression of the Sovereign Integral whispering to its outposts of form and nudging them to look within to their roots of existence and unite with this formless and limitless intelligence that pervades all.

The transformational experience is far beyond the calibration of the human drama much like the stars in the sky are beyond the touch of terra-earth. You can observe the stars with your human eyes, but you will never touch them with your human hands. Similarly, you can dimly foresee the transformational experience with the human instrument, but you cannot experience it through the human instrument. It is only accessed through the wholeness of the entity, for it is only in wholeness that the Source Codes and their residual effects of Source

Reality perception can exist. And truly, this wholeness is only obtained when the individual consciousness is separated from time and is able to view its existence in timelessness.

Nevertheless, the human instrument is critical in facilitating the transformational experience and causing it to trigger—like a metamorphosis—the integration of the formful identities into the Sovereign Integral. This is the next stage of perception and expression for the entity model, and it is activated when the entity designs its reality from life principles that are symbolic of Source Reality, as opposed to the reality of an external source that is bound to the evolution/saviorship model of existence.

These life principles are Source Intelligence templates of creation. They are designed to create reality from the perspective of the Sovereign Integral and hasten its manifestation within the fields of vibration that has thus far repelled it. They are principles that construct opportunities for the integration of the entity's formless and formful identities. They are bridges that the human instrument—with all its componentry intact—can experience the Sovereign Integral perception of wholeness.

As the human instrument becomes increasingly responsive to Source Intelligence it will gravitate to life principles that symbolically express the formative principles of prime creation. There are wide ranges of expressions that can induce the transformational experience of the Sovereign Integral and liberate the entity from time-space conditioning and external controls. Inasmuch as the expression can vary, the intent of the expression is quite narrowly defined as the intent to expand into a state of integration whereby the human instrument becomes increasingly aligned with the Sovereign Integral perspective.

There are three particular life principles that accelerate the transformational experience and help to align the human instrument with the Sovereign Integral perspective. They are:

1. Universe relationship through gratitude
2. Observance of Source in all things
3. Nurturance of life

When the individual applies these principles, their life experience reveals a deeper meaning to its apparently random events—both in the universal and personal contexts.

Universe Relationship through Gratitude

This is the principle that the Universe of Wholeness represents a collective intelligence that can be personalized as a single Universal Entity. Thus, in this model of inference, there are only two entities in the entire cosmos: the individual entity and the Universal Entity. Inasmuch as the individual is impressionable and constantly changing to adapt to new information, so is the Universal Entity, which is a dynamic and living template of potential energies and experiences that are coherent and as knowable as a friend's personality and behavior.

The Universal Entity is responsive to the individual and its perceptions and expressions. It is like a composite omni-personality that is imbued with Source Intelligence and responds to the perceptions of the individual like a pool of water mirrors the image that overshadows it. Everyone in a human instrument is indeed, at their innermost core, a sovereign entity that can transform the human instrument into an instrument of the Sovereign Integral. However, this transformation is dependent on whether the individual chooses to project an image of a Sovereign Integral upon the "mirror" of the Universal Entity, or project a lesser image that is a distortion of its true state of being.

The principle of *universe relationship through gratitude* is primarily concerned with consciously designing one's self image through an appreciation of the Universal Entity's supportive "mirror". In other words, the Universal Entity is a partner in shaping reality's expression in one's life. Reality is an internal process of creation that is utterly free of external controls and conditions if the individual projects a sovereign image upon the mirror of the Universal Entity.

This process is an interchange of supportive energy from the individual to the

Universal Entity, and this energy is best applied through an appreciation of how perfect and exacting the interchange occurs in every moment of life. If the individual is aware (or at least interested in having the awareness) of how perfect the Universal Entity supports the individual's sovereign reality, there is a powerful and natural sense of gratitude that flows from the individual to the Universal Entity. It is this wellspring of gratitude that opens the channel of support from the Universal Entity to the individual and establishes a collaboration of purpose to transform the human instrument into an expression of the Sovereign Integral.

It is principally gratitude—which translates to an appreciation of how the inter-relationship of the individual and the Universal Entity operates—that opens the human instrument to its connection to the sovereign entity and its eventual transformation into the Sovereign Integral state of perception and expression. The relationship of the individual with the Universal Entity is essential to cultivate and nurture, because it, more than anything else, determines how accepting the individual is to life's myriad forms and manifestations.

When the individual accepts changes in sovereign reality as the shifting persona of the Universal Entity, they live in greater harmony with life itself. Life becomes an exchange of energy between the individual and the Universal Entity that is allowed to play out without judgment and experienced without fear. This is the underlying meaning of unconditional love: to experience life in all its manifestations as a single, unified intelligence that responds perfectly to the projected image of the human instrument.

It is for this reason that when the human instrument projects gratitude to the Universal Entity, regardless of circumstance or condition, life becomes increasingly supportive in opening the human instrument to activate its Source Codes and live life within the framework of the synthesis model of expression. The feeling of gratitude coupled with the mental concept of appreciation is expressed like an invisible message in all directions and at all times. In this particular context, gratitude to the Universal Entity is the overarching motive behind all forms of expression that the human instrument aspires to.

Every breath, every word, every touch, every thought, every thing is centered on expressing this sense of gratitude. A gratitude that the individual is sovereign and supported by a Universal Entity that expresses itself through all forms and manifestations of intelligence with the sole objective of creating the ideal reality to activate the individual's Source Codes and transform the human instrument and entity into the Sovereign Integral. It is this specific form of gratitude that accelerates the activation of the Source Codes and their peculiar ability to integrate the disparate componentry of the human instrument and the entity, and transform them to the state of perception and expression of the Sovereign Integral.

Time is the only factor that distorts this otherwise clear connection between the individual and Universal Entity. Time intervenes and creates pockets of despair, hopelessness, and abandonment. However, it is these very "pockets" that often activate the Source Codes of the entity and establish a more intimate and harmonious relationship with the Universal Entity. Time establishes separation of experience, and the perceived discontinuity of reality, which in turn creates doubt in the Universal Entity's system of fairness and overarching purpose. The result creates fear that the universe is not a mirror, but rather a chaotic, whimsical energy.

When the human instrument is aligned with the Sovereign Integral and lives from this perspective as a developing reality, it attracts a *natural* state of harmony. This does not necessarily mean that the human instrument is without problems or discomforts, rather it signifies a perception that there is an integral purpose in what life reveals. In other words, natural harmony perceives that life experience is meaningful to the extent you are aligned with the Sovereign Integral, and that your personal reality must flow from this strata of the multidimensional universe in order to create lasting joy and inner peace.

Gratitude is a critical facet of love that opens the human instrument to acknowledge the role of the Universal Entity and redefine its purpose as a supportive extension of sovereign reality, rather than the whimsical outreach of fate or the exacting reaction of a mechanical, detached universe. Establishing a relationship with the Universal Entity through the outflow of gratitude also attracts life experience that is transformative. Experience that is richly devoted to uncovering life's deepest meaning and most formative purpose.

Observance of Source in All Things

This is the principle that First Source is present in all realities through all manifestations of energy. IT is interwoven in all things like a mosaic whose pieces adhere to the same wall, and are thus, unified. However, it is not the picture that unifies the mosaic, but the wall upon which its pieces adhere. Similarly, First Source paints a picture so diverse and apparently unrelated that there appears to be no unification. Yet it is not the outward manifestations that unify, it is the inward center of energy upon which the pieces of diversity are layered that unifies all manifestations.

This centerpiece of energy is the collective storehouse of all life in all fields of vibration within the Universe of Wholeness. It is First Source who divests ITSELF in all forms through the projection of ITS Source Intelligence in to all fragments of life. Thus, Source Intelligence—acting as an extension of First Source—is the unifying energy that is the "wall" upon which all the pieces of life's mosaic adhere. Life flows from one energy Source that links all to All and one to One.

Observance of Source in All Things is the principle that all manifestations of life convey an expression of First Source. It does not matter how far the unifying energy has been distorted or perverted; the Source can be observed. It is the action of perceiving the unification of energy even when the outward manifestations appear random, distorted, unrelated, or chaotic.

When all manifestations of life are genuinely perceived as fragmentary expressions of First Source, the vibration of equality that underlies all life-forms becomes perceptible to the human instrument. Life initially emerges as an extension of Source Reality, and then, as an individuated energy frequency invested within a form. It vibrates, in its pure, timeless state, precisely the same for all manifestations of life. This is the common ground that all life shares. This is the tone-vibration of equality that can be observed within all life forms that unifies all expressions of diversity to the foundation of existence known as First Source. If an individual is able to look upon any form of life with the outlook of equality, then they are observing Source in all things.

While this may seem like an abstract concept, it is actualized through the practice of looking for the outward and inward manifestations of First Source. In a very real sense, the individual expects to observe the workings of Source Intelligence in every facet of their experience. It is the unassailable expectation that everything is in its rightful position, performing its optimal function, and serving its purpose to activate the fullest expression of its life in the present moment. It is the outlook that all life is in a state of optimal realization and experience regardless of condition or circumstance. It is the perception that life is perfect in its expression because it flows from perfection, and that no matter how divergent its manifestations are, life is an extension of Source Reality.

In light of the obvious turmoil and apparent destruction that accompanies life on terra-earth, this is an outlook or perception that seems naive. How can life—in all its forms and expressions—be perceived as optimal or perfect? This is the great paradox of life, and it cannot be reconciled with the human instrument's mental or emotional capabilities. It can only be understood in the context of the entity, which is deathless, limitless, timeless, and sovereign. Paradoxes exist because the human drama is too limited in scope and scale to allow a perception of wholeness to intervene and illuminate how the pieces of the puzzle are unified in perfect relation.

The dimensions of time and space and the elements of energy and matter circumscribe the human drama. It is played out upon the stages of survival and dysfunctional behavior because of the Hierarchy's methods of controlling information and manipulating conditions. The entity within the human instrument is largely unexpressed and under-utilized in the human drama, and therefore, life's apparent perversions and imperfections are seen in isolation as impediments to perfection rather than perfection itself.

Life is perfect in its resolve to expand and express an intelligence that is limitless. This is the fundamental purpose of life in all its diverse manifestations, and this is the presence of First Source—expressing ITSELF as a vibration of equality—that can be observed in all things. Sensory input derived from the human instrument is limited to frequencies in specific ranges that only convey an echo of this Source vibration. The true frequency is understood through deliberate and focused contemplation of equality inherent in all things, and the ability to penetrate beyond the picture of a thing to the origin of the picture.

These insights require a new sensory system beyond the five-senses that rule the human world in your time. These new senses are the outgrowth of the Source Code activation, and represent the first stage of the transformation experience. With this new perceptual ability, the human instrument will be capable of sensing not only the presence of First Source, but also the timeless essence within all life that is individualized and uniquely separate from First Source.

Calling forth the perceptions of the entity within the human instrument is the ideal method to access a lasting sensitivity to the Source vibration. This is how an individual can develop the ability to observe Source in all things. It is not only that First Source is within every individual manifestation of energy, but is also the wholeness of life itself. Thus, the principle requires an observance of Source in all ITS diverse forms of manifestation, as well as in the wholeness of life.

Nurturance of Life

Life, in this definition, is an individual's sovereign reality. It is subjective and impressionable to the human instrument. Life is the wholeness of experience flowing past the individual's field of perception in the dimension of nowness. There is never a closure to life or final chapter written. It is eternal, but not in the abstract sense of never ending or beginning, but rather in the real sense that life is ever expanding in order to express Source Intelligence in all fields of vibration within the Universe of Wholeness.

The *nurturance of life* is the principle that an individual is in alignment with the natural expansion of intelligence inherent within all life. This is an alignment that enhances the life-energy that flows past the individual with the clear intent of gentle support. It is the action of identifying the highest motive in all energy forms and supporting the flow of this energy towards its ultimate expression. In so doing, the action is performed without judgment, analysis, or attachment to outcome. It is simply nurturing the energy that flows from all manifestations and supporting its expression of life.

This is a departure from the normal perception that nurturing support can only be granted when energy is in alignment with personal will. However, when the individual can view life as an integrated energy flowing in the expression of expanding intelligence, life is honored as an extension of First Source. In this context, there is no energy that is misdirected or unworthy of support and nurturance. While this may seem contrary to the evidence of abusive energy upon terra-earth, even energy that is laden with "evil intent" is nevertheless energy that is flowing outward in search of a higher expression.

All forms of energy can be nurtured and supported to their highest expression, and this is the fundamental action of this principle. It requires the ability to perceive the causal motive and ultimate expression of life-energy as it passes through the individual's sovereign reality. Energy is an element of life that is so subtly interwoven with form that it is one; in much the same manner as space and time are inextricably linked in union. Energy is a motive. It is intelligent beyond the mind's ability to reason. While it is a force that can be subject to human applications that deny its highest expression, energy is always imbuing life with the motive to expand and evolve.

Life-energy is always in a state of becoming. It is never static or regressive in its natural state. The human instrument is very capable of nurturing this natural expansion of energy to forge new channels of expression and experience. In fact, it is the primary purpose of the human instrument to expand the life-energy that encircles its sovereign reality within physical existence and transform it to new levels of expression that more accurately reflect the perspective of the Sovereign Integral.

There are many specific actions that can be taken to nurture life. Each entity is, in a sense, programmed within its Source Codes to transmute energy through a tremendous variety of means. Working through the human instrument, the entity is able to collect and store energy within the human instrument and re-direct its purpose or application. The transmutation of energy can occur on either the personal or universal levels of expression. That is, within the sovereign reality of an individual, energy can be transmuted to conform to a vision of personal welfare, or aligned with a vision of universal welfare and goodwill.

One of the best methods to transmute energy is through one's belief system. All beliefs have energy systems that act like birthing chambers for the manifestation of the belief. Within these energy systems are currents that direct life experience. The human instrument is aware of these currents either consciously or unconsciously, and allows them to carry it into the realm of experience that exemplifies its true belief system.

By cultivating beliefs that expand and transform energy, the human instrument is able to engage energy systems that are nurturing to life in all its myriad forms. When beliefs are clearly defined as preferred states of being, the energy system is engaged in nowness—not in some future time. Now. The energy system becomes inseparable from the human instrument and woven into its spirit like a thread of light. Clarity of belief is essential to engaging the energy system of the belief, and allowing the nurturance of life to prevail in all activities.

So again, the nurturance of life is critical to both personal and universal realities within the Universe of Wholeness which contains all the fields of vibration that are interlinked like threads of an infinitely expanding fabric. Thus, as the individual awakens to their creative power to transmute energy and enhance it with the clear intent of gentle support, they become transmitters of Source Reality and architects of the synthesis model of existence.

Through the ongoing application of these life principles, Source Intelligence increasingly becomes the identity of the entity, and the entity becomes the identity of the human instrument. Thus, identity is transformed, and in the wake of this transformation, the Sovereign Integral unifies the human instrument with the entity, and the entity with Source Intelligence. It is this unification and shifts of identity that is the explicit purpose in expressing the life principles of the Sovereign Integral. If there is any other intention or objective these principles will remain misunderstood and their catalytic powers dormant.

It is the perspective of the Sovereign Integral *that all life is pure love in its fullest expression*, and that in this single concept, all life is conceived and forever exists. This becomes the core belief from which all other beliefs arise, and by their extension, one's belief system emerges with a clear intent of supporting this fundamental perspective; of nurturing, observing, and appreciating the Universe of Wholeness as the cradle from which all life is created, evolves, and ultimately acknowledges.

These life principles are merely symbols represented in words and served to the human instrument as a potential recipe to stir awake the embers of light that tirelessly burn within. There are no specific techniques or rituals that are required to invoke the power of these principles. They are simply perspectives. In a real sense, they are intentions that attract experience that expand consciousness. They do not provide quick fixes or instant realizations. They are amplifiers of personal will and intention that clarify how one lives. Their transformative power is contained exclusively in the intent of their application.

Through these life principles of the Sovereign Integral, the individual can become a master of unlimiting the Self. Boundaries are set, veils are pulled down, and one's light is subdued, simply because external, hierarchical controls create fear of the unknown and mystical practices of a sovereign being. In these life principles, if they are truly applied with proper intent, are the tools to accelerate the emergence of the Sovereign Integral and feel its perspective, its insights, and its empowered abilities to create new realities and shape them as learning adventures that liberate and expand consciousness. This is the underlying purpose of the principles and perhaps the best reason to explore them.

Chamber Two Philosophy
The Shifting Models of Existence

The consciousness of the Sovereign Integral is the destination that beckons the human instrument inward into the reality of First Source. In all the wanderings of the human consciousness from Source Reality, it has eliminated the compelling features of Source Reality through the application of the logical mind and the persistent belief in the language of limitation that flows from the external controls of the hierarchy.

Source Reality, hidden behind language, has gradually become "illuminated" by the prophets of your world, and has thus, taken on the image of language, rather than the expression of its compelling features. Language is the purveyor of limitation. It is the pawn of tyranny and entrapment. Virtually all entities within the time-space universe desire to preserve a dependence upon a hierarchy that stretches between the individual and the compelling features of Source Reality. It is the hierarchy that utilizes language as a form of structural limitation, though in relative terms, it can appear to be liberating and empowering.

Source Reality is the dwelling place of First Source, and it dances outside of the constructs of any language. It is complete within itself, and has a singular purpose of demonstrating the collective potential of all species within the Universe of Wholeness. It is the archetype of perfection. It is the standard bearer of each entity's innate design and ultimate destiny. ITS essence is so far beyond conception that the human instrument's tendency is to resort to the language of externals—and ultimately the hierarchy—to define Source Reality.

The hierarchy, through the purveyance of an evolution/saviorship model of existence, has attempted to guide the development of all entities throughout the Universe of Wholeness. The connection between the individual and the Source is subtly undermined through the layers of language, belief system manipulation, and ritual controls designed by the hierarchy to intervene between the spiritual essence of entities and their source, First Source.

Each individual must know their self to be free of all forms of external reliance. This is not to imply that one should not trust others or band together in alliances of friendship and community. It is simply a warning that relative truth is constantly shifting in the hands of those who desire to control, and even though their motives may be of good will, it is still a form of control. When the hierarchy withholds information, the interpretive centers for relative truth are positioned to acquire and maintain power rather than dispensing the empowerment of Source equality.

There are so many layers of relative truth that if you listen to the language of externals, you will most likely abandon your own power in favor of the proclamation of language. Language is seductive to the ego's drive for power and control, as well as the mind's inclination to surrender to, and believe in, the language of externals. It can lure the unsuspecting into believing images and ideas—real or imagined—for the sake of holding individuals in bondage to a lesser truth, or keep individuals supporting the hierarchy when it no longer serves a purpose. The time is fast approaching when the veils of control at all levels of the hierarchy will be rendered obsolete by entities who are destined to pull down the veils and allow sovereign power to prevail over hierarchical power.

There are entities that have woven their future existence with terra-earth and are destined to demonstrate the truth of Source equality among all entities at all levels of expression. It will become the fundamental purpose of the hierarchy to slowly remove these barriers to equality in such a way that the hierarchy appears to be the savior of consciousness rather than the guard of consciousness. There are those present who will ensure that the curtain falls swiftly for those who are ready to be equal with their Source; are willing to skirt the hierarchy's tangled pathways; and embrace their divinity as sovereign expressions of Source Reality.

The hierarchy represents diverse interests, perceptions of reality, and motives of action. It is this diversity that causes the hierarchy to become ineffective in leading individuals to their equal status with First Source. However, this diversity is also what permits the hierarchy to attract and initially awaken such a breadth of individuals to their spiritual energies and intuitive centers. Nevertheless, the hierarchy has trapped itself in diversity and vested specialization that prevents it from evolving from an arduous ladder of evolution to a joyous river of Light that is aligned with the purpose of empowering entities to Source equality.

The saviorship concept results from the feelings of inadequacy that constantly surge within the mass consciousness of humanity through the genetic mind. These feelings are related to the fragmentation of the human instrument and its inability—while fragmented—to fully grasp its own wholeness perspective and reach into its divine origins and accept itself as equal with First Source. Thus ensues the seemingly endless search to be saved from the inadequacy and insecurity that result from the fragmentation of the human instrument.

The motive to evolve consciousness derives from the feeling of being less than whole. And in particular, the feeling of being disconnected from First Source due to imperfect judgment caused by the fragmentation of the human instrument. It is through these feelings that the fragmentation perpetuates itself for the entire species and is passed into the genetic mind, which is the shared foundation of the human instrument. The genetic mind of the human species is the single most powerful component of the hierarchy and it is formed by the very conditions of the human instrument living in a three-dimensional, five-sensory context that is all-consuming.

When the entity initially enters a human instrument at birth, it is immediately fragmented into a physical, emotional, and mental spectrum of perception and expression. From that day forward the entity is carefully conditioned to adapt into, and navigate within, the three-dimensional, five-sensory context of terra-earth. In effect, the entity purposely fragments its consciousness in order to experience separation from wholeness.

In this state of separation, the entity has handicapped itself for the purpose of new experience and a deeper understanding of the Primal Blueprint or grand vision of First Source. Through this deeper understanding, the entity can, through the human instrument, transform the three-dimensional context into a self-aware, integrated component of the Universe of Wholeness. This magnificent and purposeful endeavor produces the urge within the human instrument to seek out its wholeness and re-experience its divine connection to First Source.

This search, in large measure, is the fuel that drives the individual to seek out and explore the evolution/saviorship model of existence. It provides the individual with the motivation to seek help and guidance from a specific subgroup of the hierarchy, and in so doing, develop a sense of belonging and unity. It is this very same sense of belonging and unity that helps to catalyze a growing awareness of the underlying union between the human instrument, the Entity Consciousness, the Universe of Wholeness, Source Intelligence, and First Source.

This is why the evolution/saviorship model is so critical as a component to the Grand Experiment. It is the stage whereby the human instrument develops a sense of unity and belonging. A sense of relationship to some grand and encompassing vision. This is why the hierarchy nurtures saviors. It is also why the feelings of inadequacy and insecurity are developed and nurtured by the hierarchy. It actually hastens the unification of humanity, which in turn, will hasten and lead to the unification of humanity with the Universe of Wholeness.

Spiritual leaders are able to peer deeply beneath the surface reality of life and experience how intricately connected every life form is, and how this composite of life is intelligent far beyond the human instrument's capability to both perceive and express. It is because of this condition that spiritual leaders can only interpret reality through their personal abilities to perceive and express life's dimensional depth and limitless intelligence. No one is able to articulate life's dimensional depth and breadth with the tools of language. They can only, at best, describe their interpretation or their impressions.

Every human is able, in varying degrees, to peer beneath the surface reality of life and perceive and express their personal interpretations of the Universe of Wholeness. They require only the time and intention to develop their own interpretations. And this is precisely what all the great spiritual leaders have taught. Life's deeper meaning is not an absolute to be experienced by the chosen few, but an evolving, dynamic intelligence that wears as many faces as there are life forms. No life form or species has the exclusive portal into the Universe of Wholeness in which First Source expresses ITSELF in all ITS majesty. The portal is shared with all because First Source is within all things.

The great spiritual leaders of terra-earth have all, in their own way, interpreted the Universe of Wholeness and humanity's role therein. In so doing, their interpretations, because they were articulated with authority and depth of insight, became a target of debate among various subgroups of the hierarchy. This debate and inquiry process creates a polarity of belief. A sympathetic constituency will emerge to defend and embellish their particular leader's interpretation, while everyone else will hold it in contempt of previously held beliefs.

This peculiar method of creating a religion that is fixated on a savior's or prophet's interpretation of the Universe of Wholeness is unique to a species that is exploring the evolution/saviorship model of existence. The spiritual leaders that are recognized as great prophets or saviors have produced a vision of the Universe of Wholeness beyond what was currently defined by the hierarchy. They created a new portal into the Universe of Wholeness and were willing to share their vision at the expense of debate and probable ridicule.

These men and women were the gateways for humanity to explore new facets of itself. To engage a part of its oversoul or universal consciousness that was essential at that particular time in its evolutionary cycle. But the leader's interpretations too often become interpreted by the followers who desire to create a religion or sect, and the vision quietly recedes into the hands of the hierarchy where it becomes de-vitalized by the very fact that it is connected to a massive structure that both protects and promotes it.

First Source is connected to individuals not organizations. Thus, the hierarchy is unconnected to the Source in a vital and dynamic way. The hierarchy is more connected to its own collective desire to help, to serve, to perform a function that allows the use of power to drive toward the vision of its leaders. In itself, this is not wrong or misguided. It is all part of the Primal Blueprint that orchestrates the unfoldment of consciousness from First Source to entity, and entity to Collective Source. This is the spiral of integration that breeds wholeness and cascading beauty within Source Intelligence.

What the hierarchy has loosely labeled as Spirit comes as close as any word to the symbol of Source Intelligence. Source Intelligence inhabits all fields of vibration as an extension of the Source. It is the emissary of First Source that interweaves with the hierarchy as its counter-balance. Source Intelligence is the factor of integrity and alignment, which ensures that the hierarchy is serving its purpose within the Primal Blueprint. Source Intelligence is, in effect, the "scientist" who oversees the Grand Experiment and establishes the criteria, selects the variables, monitors the results, and evaluates the alternative outcomes in the laboratory of time and space.

The Grand Experiment is the ongoing transformation and expansion of Source Intelligence through all entities in all dimensions of existence. It is the purpose of the Grand Experiment to test alternative models of existence to determine, with some certainty, the model that is best able to unify consciousness without impinging on the sovereignty of the entity and First Source. The Grand Experiment is composed of many distinct stages that interlink, leading to the Great Mystery. Most of these different stages are being simultaneously played out within the time-space universe in order to prepare the universe for the impending expansion of Source Reality into all dimensions of existence.

In the case of terra-earth, this is the stage of existence that promotes the clear connection of individual consciousness to the compelling features of Source Reality without the intervention of a hierarchy of any kind. This is when the fables and myths of history step into the light and become known as they truly are and have been. This is the time when language will be transmuted into a new form of communication that exhibits the compelling features of Source Reality in an artistry of energy and vibration that break down all barriers of control.

It is time to recognize that the hierarchy extends throughout the cosmos to the very borders of discovery. It has branches that extend from every star system, every known dimension; and virtually all life forms are "leaves" of this vast cosmological tree. This constitutes the grand indoctrination of species, spirits, planets, and stars as they each evolve through the branches of the tree. Thus, the hierarchy is an assemblage of externals that desire to invest their energies in support of a sub-group that has nested somewhere within the greatest of all structures—the hierarchy. Service is the operational motive of the hierarchy, and in most cases, this translates into the concept of saviorship and the teacher/student ordering of the universe.

The hierarchy is composed of all entities of all motives that have linked their energies into sub-groups. These sub-groups are independent branches of the vast, cosmological tree that encompasses all things outside of Source Reality. The roots of the tree are bound in the soil of genetic memory and subconscious instincts. At the base of the tree the first branches sprout and they are the oldest, representing the native religions of the species. The middle branches are the orthodox religions and institutions, while the upper branches represent the contemporary belief systems that are newly emerging throughout the universe. The whole tree, in this definition, is the hierarchy, and its seed was initially conceived, planted, and nurtured by Source Intelligence for the purpose of stimulating the Grand Experiment.

This is the experiment of transformation versus evolution. Evolution is the arduous and ongoing process of shifting positions within the hierarchy— always assessing your present position in relation to a new one that beckons you. Transformation is simply the recognition that there are accelerated pathways that bypass the hierarchy leading to sovereign mastership rather than interdependent saviorship, and that these new pathways can be accessed through direct experience of the equality tone-vibration that is present within all entities.

This tone vibration is not what is more commonly referred to as the music of the spheres or the vibration of spirit moving through the universe in resonance to Source intention. It is a vibration that holds together the three principles of the transformational experience: Universe relationship through gratitude, observance of Source in all things, and the nurturance of life. The application of these life-principles in a specific equation of conduct de-couples an entity from the controlling elements of the hierarchy.

How can the hierarchy act in the role of an interpretive center of truth without manipulating entities, and thus, obscuring their free will? The Grand Experiment was designed with free will as its primary method of obtaining authentic information that can be used to expand Source Reality to all dimensions of existence. Free will is the thread of authenticity that imbues value in the various tests within the Grand Experiment. The hierarchy or any other external structure never jeopardizes free will. Only the entity can choose their reality, and this is the fundamental principle of free will.

Free will is not obscured simply because an entity is presented with alternative realities or relative truths that delay its realization of Source equality. It is the choice of the entity to invest itself in external accounts of reality instead of delving within its own resources and creating a reality that is sovereign. The value of free will is always expanding as you move towards sovereignty, and in like manner, is always diminishing as you move towards external dependence. The choice between sovereignty or external dependence is the basis of free will, and there is no structure or external source that can eliminate this basic choice. It is an inward choice that, regardless of outward circumstance, is incapable of being denied by anything external.

The Universe of Wholeness encompasses all dimensions (including Source Reality), and therefore, all realities are contained therein. In this incomprehensible diversity, each entity is provided a structure that defines their free will in terms of its relation to Source Reality. Each of these structures varies in latitude of choice, but each is connected into the superstructure of the hierarchy. The structureless reality of Source Reality is where free will was initially conceived, and when the principle expanded into the time-space universe as the thread of authenticity, it became increasingly dependent upon the entity's recognition of its wholeness in relation to Source Intelligence.

If the entity was fragmented into its component parts, its comprehension of free will was limited to that which the hierarchy circumscribed. If the entity is a conscious collective, realizing its sovereign wholeness, the principle of free will was a form of structure that was unnecessary, like a fire in a summer's day. When entities are unknowing of their wholeness, structure will occur as a form of self-imposed security. Through this ongoing development of a structured and ordered universe, entities defined their borders—their limits—through the expression of their insecurity. They gradually became pieces of their wholeness, and like shards of glass from a beautiful vase they bear little resemblance to their aggregate beauty.

If you were to perceive the origin of your existence, you would undoubtedly see how vast the entity is. If you could pierce through the veils that cover your destiny, you would understand how much vaster you will become. Between these two points of existence—origin and destiny—the entity is always the vibrant container of Source Intelligence. It has willingly allowed itself to explore the time-space universes as an outpost of First Source. Therefore, while the hierarchy may obscure the entity's comprehension of its wholeness, it is the entity who has surrendered, by choice, to listen to the language of limitation, the proclamations of externals, and become seduced by the model of evolution/saviorship.

Why has the hierarchy not provided the alternative model of transformation/mastership and enabled the entity to make a choice, and in so doing, truly exercise its free will? It is because the hierarchy, like most entities, is not aware of its wholeness. Its fragments, or subgroups, are completely devoted to boundaries. Where there are boundaries that define and limit, there is also structure. Where there is deeply ingrained structure there is a pervasive belief that transformation is impossible. Naturally, the time-space universe conforms to the matrix of belief projection, and the very concept of transformation is removed from the hierarchy's reality.

Thus, the hierarchy is unable to even conceptualize the model of transformation/mastership with any precision, let alone inform the entity that alternatives exist which issue from Source Intelligence. The hierarchy is not responsible for this condition, each entity is. The dominant model of Source Intelligence is primal. It existed before the hierarchy. It is the entity that has chosen to explore the hierarchy's model of existence for the purpose of participating in the Grand Experiment and assisting in the emergence of the synthesis model of existence. The hierarchy is quite benign as a manipulative force, and merely represents a key ingredient to the recipe of wholeness that is transforming the entity to reach beyond its role as a vibrant container of Source Intelligence, and become the bridgeway in the expansion of Source Reality into the time-space universes.

There is an ancient belief, born of the hierarchy, that the time-space universes will ascend into Source Reality and the human instrument of love will accompany this ascension process. However, it is Source Reality that is expanding to encompass the time-space universes with the purpose of aligning all entities to the synthesis model of existence. Source Intelligence is stripping away the veils that hide the true meaning of the entity model of expression in the time-space universes. When this occurs, the entity will possess Source equality in all dimensions and fields of vibration, and its componentry will be united for the full expression of its sovereign perspective.

This transformation of the entity is the pathway into wholeness and the recognition that the entity model of expression is a composite of forms and the formless that is unified in one energy, one consciousness. When the fragments are aligned and inter-connected, the entity becomes the instrument that facilitates Source Reality expansion. Thus, the entity does not ascend from the time-space universes, but rather coalesces into a state of wholeness whereby its sovereign expression can assist in the expansion, or in a different context, the descent, of Source Reality into the time-space universes.

Ascension is often construed as the natural outcome of evolution. That all planetary systems and species are evolving to the point where they ascend from limitation, and that eventually, the time-space universes will somehow fold into Source Reality and cease to exist as fields of vibration. It is actually quite the opposite. Source Reality is descending. It is inclusive of all things, and it is the Source intention to expand, not retreat. The entity transforms to wholeness within the cradle of the time-space universe, and, in so doing, becomes the accessory of Source Reality's intention to expand.

Can you see the perfection of this Primal Blueprint? Can you feel the shifting of the matrix from which your reality is cast? Can you not also understand that you, the human instrument, consist of a componentry that is individuated as a single point of pure energy, yet live in many places on many dimensions simultaneously? Only within the entity is the place of transformation discovered, where the formless Self can enter and commune with its various outposts of form. The formless is the Eternal Watcher who lives behind the veil of form and comprehension, and draws forth the wisdom of time from the well of planets. It is the point of origination from whence Source Intelligence flows.

The Eternal Watcher is the only real interpretive center for the entity. It is the only stable guidance system that can propel the entity to its wholeness. Thus, the entity is composed of both the formless identity of Source Intelligence and the formful identity of densified energy. While the formless is one, the formful is divested in many fragments of expression that isolate its consciousness as islands of perception and expression. This condition results in the entity's denial of its vast and glorious nature of existence.

In the human instrument, the entity, for the most part, is silent and unmoving. It appears like a fleeting whisper of gladness that touches you like a mountain wind. It is quiet like a deep ocean. Yet, the entity is coming forward into the time-space universe as a harbinger of Source Reality expansion. It is beginning to make itself known as it truly is. Many feel the shadow of their entity as it approaches. They consign all forms of definition to this "shadow", seldom believing it to be the torchbearer of their total selfhood. Here is where all the vows of faithfulness, all the ceremonies of love, and all the feelings of hope should be centered and given over to the sovereign entity that we each are.

The primary reason that the hierarchy's model of evolution/saviorship is so compelling is because the entity has become fragmented in how it perceives its total selfhood. The Eternal Watcher that lives through the human instrument is illusive to the time-space conditioned mind, yet it is the mind that attempts to reach out and touch this subtle vibration of Source equality that is forever kindled by Source Intelligence. However, the mind is too conditioned and disempowered to realize the total scope of the entity that exists beyond the shadows of intuition. It is for this reason that the species is exploring the evolution/saviorship model of existence. They have little or no conception of their wholeness, and require a savior and the acclimation process of evolution, to bring them security and happiness.

It is a natural condition of an evolving species to have a desire, implanted by the hierarchy, to be saved and to be a savior. This condition results in the teacher/ student ordering of the universe, and it is a building block of evolution and the very essence of the hierarchy's structural existence. While some species resort to the drama of survival to catalyze their evolutionary progress, other species resort to the drama of being saved and being a savior. The saviorship drama is an expression of sovereign entities that are preoccupied with the evolutionary process, and it is not confined to a religious context, but indeed applies to all facets of one's life.

As there are relative truths, there are relative freedoms. If you are evolving through the hierarchical process you gain an ever-increasing sense of freedom, yet you are still controlled by the vibration of externals through languages, thought forms, frequencies of color and sound, and the seemingly indelible artifacts of the genetic mind. Each of these elements can cause the human instrument to rely upon the hierarchy as it overlays a sense of inequality between you and your Source. The underlying equation of the evolutionary process is Human Instrument + Hierarchy = God connection. In the case of the transformational process, it is Entity + Source Intelligence = First Source equality.

Source Intelligence, though it generally manifests as the vibration of equality, is subject to the will of First Source, and as the Source intention changes through the various stages of the Grand Experiment, Source Intelligence is also changing its form of manifestation. This change is occurring now within the worlds of time and space because First Source is beginning to set the stage for the integration of the two primary models of existence (evolution/saviorship and transformation/mastership) within the Grand Experiment.

The time has come to integrate the dominant model of the hierarchy (evolution/ saviorship) with the dominant model of Source Intelligence (transformation/

mastership). This integration can only be achieved at the level of the entity. It cannot occur within the context of a human instrument or an aspect of the hierarchy. Only the entity—the wholeness of inter-dimensional sovereignty imbued with Source Intelligence—can facilitate and fully experience the integration of these two models of existence.

This form of integration occurs when the entity fully explores the two models and develops a synthesis model that positions saviorship as an internal role of the entity to "save" itself, and not rely upon externals to perform this liberating task. This act of self-sufficiency begins to integrate the saviorship idea with the mastership realization. The next step is to integrate the time-based incremental progress of the evolutionary model with the realization-based acceptance of the transformation model. This is done when the entity is thoroughly convinced that experience and utilization of its wholeness can only occur when it is completely detached from the various structures of the hierarchy.

While the entity assumes its role of personal liberation, it does not mean that the hierarchy is to be shunned or avoided. The hierarchy is a wondrous instrument. It is symbolic of the body of First Source, enabling IT to submerge within the time-space universes similar to how the human instrument allows the entity to function outside of Source Reality. The hierarchy is a vehicle of transformation even when it acts to suppress information and keep species in obedience to its controlling hand. It is part of the ancient formula that prepares a new universe for the synthesis model of existence and membership in the Universe of Wholeness.

The combination of self-saviorship and detachment from the hierarchy initiates the synthesis model into manifestation. The synthesis model is the next outcome of the Grand Experiment, and in certain vibrational fields of the multidimensional universe, there are entities who are indeed experiencing this stage of the experiment as forerunners of the entity model of Source individuation.

These entities are specifically designed to transmit this future experience into communication symbols and life principles that facilitate the bridging of the two models of existence. Beyond the initial design and construction of these "bridges," these entities will remain largely unknown. If they were to do anything more, they would rapidly become a fixture of the hierarchy and their missions would become compromised.

These Sovereign Entities are not present in the time-space universe to be formal teachers. They are present to be catalysts and designers. They are present to ensure that Source Intelligence is allowed to balance the dominant force of the hierarchy and its model of evolution/saviorship. They will not create a new belief system. Instead, they will focus on developing new communication symbols through various art forms that facilitate the entity's detachment from the controlling aspects of the hierarchy. The Sovereign Entities will also demonstrate the natural ease of interweaving the two primary strands of existence into a synthesis model.

In the advancing epoch of human development, entities will collectively design new pathways beyond the synthesis model of existence so that a new hierarchy can be constructed that is fashioned from Source Intelligence information. This new hierarchy will be cast from the knowledge gained from the Grand Experiments of the time-space universes, and the cosmic cycle will regenerate itself into a new field of vibration and existence. This new model of existence resists definition, and word-symbols are completely inadequate to describe even the shadowy outlines of this new form of existence that is emerging from out of the synthesis model in your future time.

The WingMakers are Sovereign Entities who will be transforming time-space universes from ladders of consciousness to inclusions of Source Reality. In other words, Source Reality will be extended into time-space universes, and all life forms therein will experience this extension through a new hierarchical structure that is completely aligned with Source Intelligence. What some call "heaven on earth" is merely an echo-realization of this impending future time. What is truly bearing down on the time-space universes is the expansion of Source Reality through the accessibility of Source Intelligence information to all entities regardless of form or structure.

When this accessibility is complete and the Source Coding is fully activated, all entities will be part of a new cosmological structure. This new structure will invoke the next model of existence, which is already being developed within Source Reality by Source Intelligence and the Sovereign Entities. What is being activated now upon this time-space universe is the initial preparations for these shifts in the models of existence. More specifically, upon terra-earth, these models of existence will be simultaneously played out over the next epoch of time. As always, it will be the choice of the entity as to which model they embrace as reality.

These various models of existence will generally occur in a pre-determined sequence, but not necessarily in a pre-determined timeframe. The sequence of Source Reality expansion is: Source Intelligence creation of new fields of vibration; the ongoing development of an entity constructed hierarchy to act as the superstructure of the new creation; the emergence from the hierarchy of a dominant model of existence, in this case, the evolution/saviorship model; the introduction of the Source Intelligence model of existence, in this case, the transformation/ mastership model; the intermixing of these two models to form a synthesis model of Source equality; and finally, Source Reality expansion to the inclusion of all dimensions and entities.

When this sequencing of the Primal Blueprint is achieved, the process, with all that has been learned by Source Intelligence, will be reconfigured and a new element of the Primal Blueprint will be revealed that is unknown at this stage even by Source Intelligence. The time required to fulfill the complete cycle is undetermined, but it is reasonable to expect that its completion is yet so distant in time that to attach measurement is simply a feeble attempt at estimating the unknowable.

Let there be no mistake, however, that the fulfillment of the Primal Blueprint is indeed the direction all entities are traveling. While entities of all levels are bestowed free will within their own realities, they are not, as aspects of Source Reality, given free will to choose their ultimate destiny. The origin of entities is Source Intelligence, and it is Source Intelligence that determines destiny as well as origin. Still, entities are provided tremendous latitude of choices to propel themselves from origin to destiny and re-emerge into an expanded version of Source Reality with a renewed vision of their identity.

All the highest imaginings of the human instrument are yet unaware of the deepest foundation of the Primal Blueprint. They have sought the upper reaches of the building, and remain unaware of the foundation's design. It is here, at the very bottom of existence that First Source is bursting forth with ITS energy and is retreating with ITS equality of sovereign mastership. It is here that equality is realized, not in the lofty places of relative truth lodged in the hierarchy, but in the deepest part of the foundational plan of life's origins and destiny, where time rejoins itself into timelessness. The origin and destiny of existence is the tone of equality in life. Listen for this tone—this frequency of vibration—and follow it back into the very foundation from whence all things arise and return.

This frequency of the tone-vibration of equality is only heard with the seventh sense by the entity who is enveloped in a human instrument. The seventh sense can be developed by the time capsules and will lead certain entities to their innermost or core expression. The core expression is what activates the seventh sense. Thus, before one can hear the tone-vibration of equality, they must gain access to their core expression. There is encoded in each of the time capsules, a system of languages that can lead the individual to their core expression. It is hidden because it is so powerful. And we will only lead the worthy to this power.

Consider these words as symbols only. Remember that language is a tool of limitation. Feeling is an antidote of limitation that permits the human instrument to leap over the boundaries of the logical mind and witness first hand the wordless power of collective energy individuated. Feel the truth that stands behind the symbols, and tap into this energy-force that reaches out for you. Know it as a tone-vibration—a resonance that waits for you around every corner in which your life will turn. It is the beacon of the Source Vibration gathering itself into the form of language in order to usher you to the place from which you can experience the formless tone of equality; the bypass of limitation; the Primal Language of Source Intelligence that bestows to you the freedom to generate your deepest beauty in the expression of the highest truth.

Chamber Three Philosophy
The Blueprint of Exploration

First Source created a blueprint of exploration to redefine itself and beget purpose to the multiverse and all existence therein. The purpose of this system is to explore the worlds of creation and evolve the ability of the individuated consciousness to acquire and express wisdom. Each individuated consciousness is a fragment of the beautiful mosaic that depicts the personage of First Source. The blueprint of exploration organizes these disparate fragments and adjoins them in their proper place to restore the wholeness of First Source—reconfigured to achieve the creation, inhabitation, and transformation of yet another universe.

Throughout the cosmos there is life—the expression of First Source in individuated form. These are the divine fragments that are always in the process of separating to experience individual expression of self, and congealing to experience universal expression of First Source. We are born from the very womb of the cosmos, and it is here that all will return in time. It matters not when or how. It only matters why.

The distance of this womb from your earth is near infinite, and yet, so close that it would make your heart quiver if you knew the reach of your imagination. In the very beginning of your existence, as a formless consciousness, you chose to experience individual expression and separate from your Source. And when you chose the three-dimensional world as your platform of experience, you embarked into the world of time in which you would encounter every conceivable obstacle and challenge to your restoration of oneness with your Creator.

This blueprint of exploration is the underlying foundation of the cosmos and it consists of five basic stages of experience as it relates to the individual consciousness.

I. The Creation of the Entity Consciousness.

From out of the spirit-essence of Source Intelligence, flowing from First Source, each of you is born. As particles of light leavened by Source Intelligence to arise and secure individual consciousness, you are born an immortal entity that shares the essence of First Source in non-time and non-space. This is the Entity consciousness that is imbued with the Wholeness Navigator that permits the Entity to separate from First Source into individuality, but remain guided by Source Intelligence.

The entity is the highest state of consciousness, dwelling in a state of total awareness of all lesser instruments or bodies, which feed it experience and insight. The entity consciousness is the infallible observer of experience and synthesizer of insight. In all respects, it is a miniature of First Source, lacking only the experiential relationship with time and space that develops its sense of empowerment to act independently of First Source.

It is precisely this sense of independence that the birth of the entity begets. It is the central part of the blueprint of exploration because without this sense of independence, exploration of the cosmos and its various fields of vibration would be limited to the perception of First

Source, peering through the lens of Source Intelligence. By definition it is a single dimensional perception, and therefore, an incomplete exploration. First Source decreed this exploration as a result of its creation of the multiverse, and when it was created, First Source summoned itself in the form of light particles and cast these particles into separation.

The first of these creations was bestowed an individual identity through the use of a physical instrument known as a light body. The density of this body was sufficient to block the separated particles from First Source's dominant reality. In doing so, the particles became autonomous explorers and quickly populated the innermost realms of the Universe of Wholeness. However, they never ventured into the outer realms of creation where the density of vibration decelerated time to such an extent that exploration in bodies was impossible, owing to the great distance.

These initial entities understood that their existence held a very specific purpose, which was to construct a vehicle for the newly created entity consciousness to inhabit so the individuated spirit-form could enter the most remote sections of the multiverse and explore, experience, and learn from them. This would be similar to constructing a deep-sea diving suit that permits a diver to explore the sea bottom. First Source, working through Source Intelligence, could perceive the outermost realms of creation, but it was unable to experience them and, therefore, acquire wisdom about the very things First Source created.

WingMakers were the first creations that housed the entity consciousness. We are the architects and designers of the human instrument in all its various forms throughout the multiverse. The human species is not unique in the multiverse. There are many variations on other planets within your known universe. Nearly all of you have experience in these other realms of the universe, but you are not able to translate these experiences to your conscious mind. Even so, as First Source birthed the entity consciousness, the WingMakers created the instruments of exploration that enabled this newly formed consciousness to explore the dense vibratory realms of the outermost creation.

Because the vibratory rate of the physical universe is decelerated to such an extent that particles solidify into clusters of objects, time decelerates into sequential frames of perception, allowing the entity consciousness to explore multiple worlds simultaneously. This enables one entity to explore hundreds, if not thousands, of worlds in a single frame of time. This creates the perception—albeit dimly felt by most of you—that you have lived before and that you will live again.

In reality, if you are within a human instrument, you are an immortal light consciousness gathered from the same substance as First Source. You were born of this substance, and you will never die from it. It is not possible to discard or revoke this most pure of vibrations that is your core identity. Deep inside of you there is no doubt of this truth. There is only the question of why you were individuated.

II. The Individual of Time and Genetic Density

The entity is driven by its very nature to explore creation. This is the core identity of First Source, and it was bestowed upon all of its creations like a genetic trait is passed from a parent to its child. This primal instinct instructs the entity to submerge into the realms of creation for the purposes of exploration, without the attendant anticipation of achievement or conquest.

This form of exploration is not simply to discover new geographies or physical states of existence. More importantly, it is to discover new emotional states of perception that enhances the collective wisdom of First Source. Exploration begets wisdom. This is the practical perspective of the entity consciousness, and it is precisely this innate quality that compels the entity to descend into time and density.

The entity consciousness is aware of its connection to First Source through Source Intelligence. It is also aware of the opportunity to take its pure-state vibration into other dimensions of time and space through the instruments that have been created by the WingMakers. Through these instruments, or bodies, as you might think of them, the entity can explore decelerated vibratory states like your planet.

When the entity takes on the light body, it is still essentially formless. It's identity, while separate from First Source, is not separate from other entities within the light body. Thus, it is not yet cast into individuality. This stage occurs only when the light body moves into an instrument of genetic density. What your scientists call DNA is the instrument created by the WingMakers that permits the light body to explore the multiverse and acquire the individuated state of separation from First Source and its particles of light consciousness that we call the entity.

The vast conditions of creaturehood beckon the light body to don an instrument and follow its instincts to explore. The moment this is done, the entity becomes aware of itself as an individual. However, this individuality is not overwhelming, nor is it feared. It is simply a new sense of independence; the microcosm of self-learning begins to bloom.

Contrary to your religious instructions, there is no accompanying punishment that follows the state of independence. The entity is not punished for its choice of explorations, otherwise the state of independence would be impossible to achieve. It is only through this state of independence or freewill that the entity can achieve a unique perspective. If the boundaries were prescribed too narrowly, and the entity was punished or allowed to accumulate sin each time it strayed, it would become more of an automaton than an explorer.

Without authentic exploration within the worlds of creation, the value of the experience for both the entity and First Source is greatly diminished. Just as a newborn human expresses its energy in the awkward movements of its limbs, the new entity expresses its energy in the awkward decisions of its exploratory path. These decisions include every conceivable movement into darkness that can be imagined, and it is because of this that the entity develops its uniqueness.

III. The Acquisition of Experience through Separation

When the entity becomes unique, it can acquire experience and insight that is unique. And this is the precious cargo that the entity was designed to transmit to First Source. Individuality and independence were the gifts bestowed to the entity, and unique insight was the gift returned. This is how the multiverse is designed, and the blueprint of exploration is indifferent to the nature of the instrument, its outward appearance, its usefulness to a given species, or its contributions to the world from which it was born. The only objective worth expressing is that the entity secured for itself, and provided to First Source, a unique perspective during its sojourn into time and genetic density.

When the entity functions within a human instrument it remains attuned to First Source, but the mind learns to identify with its instrument of exploration, and seldom achieves a sustainable impression of the entity's pure-state vibration. However, this vibration is always remembered by the entity consciousness and expressed within the three-dimensional realm through the sense of equality and shared purpose that all entities possess.

The human instrument, when it is donned by the entity, becomes a dominant reality in which the entity's observational stage is cast. It is very similar to a pilot who enters a plane and begins to fixate on the control panels. The entity can operate effectively within a wide range of one to approximately one thousand dominant realities—each occurring in sequential time simultaneously. As a consequence, the entity is able to both accelerate and balance its learning across a broad range of experiential platforms.

We understand that the concept of simultaneous experiential learning platforms is a concept that pulls against every three-dimensional fiber in your bodies and minds, but it is the true way in which you were designed. WingMakers have produced not less than one hundred thousand variations of the human instrument—all structured around the same DNA template and each scattered across the seven physical universes of our multiverse. When you read these words, you are operating in tens, if not hundreds, of simultaneous realities throughout the multiverse, but only the entity is able to perceive these realities.

When the entity moves into independence, it initially operates in one dominant reality and gradually becomes adept at processing multiple data streams from multiple instruments. Remember that the entity is first and foremost within a light body, and that this light body is without structure, as you know it. It is both a point fixed in time and space, and a consciousness that is omnipresent. The human instrument was designed to have an aperture that focuses this omnipresent consciousness into multiple channels of perception, but at the same time limit the perception of the human instrument to one dominant reality.

This was done by necessity because the mind, emotions, and body cannot withstand the aggregate experience of multiple instruments. It overloads the system and causes the human instrument to break down and ultimately collapse. It also makes the delicate connection between the entity awareness and the mind and emotions more clouded. Even with this accounted for, the subconscious realms enable these currents of simultaneity to disperse and provide a cleansing space for the mind and emotions.

The entity is like a beam of white light, and as it passes into the genetic density of the human instrument, it separates into a broad spectrum of experience. Owing to the genetic structures into which the entity's light energy passes, it accumulates unique perspective that is shaped into an emotional wisdom that can be transmitted to First Source and to the species at large.

IV. The Ascending Spiral to The True Wisdom

The entity's sojourns within the physical realms of the multiverse are vast as measured by time and space. They comprise, in most cases, an aggregate of tens of thousands of years, and each of these years produce an effect on the entity. These messages of time shape them into new forms. And these forms emerge as exemplars of what is to be in the distant future. These are the Sovereign Integrals spoken of in our previous discourses.

These beings are able to look upon their experience in all forms, places, and time, and integrate the total experience into an expression that is imported to the human species. It is the pinnacle of testimony, and it seldom occurs in a species until it has defined its true wisdom.

You rightfully claim wisdom in your religious books, scientific journals, and philosophical discourses, but this is not your true wisdom as it pertains to your species. The difference is simple; your true wisdom will not divide your species. It will unite it. And it will not be unification through love and emotions; it will be through a shared connection to the rightful meaning of the multiverse because this is the only lens that, when focused, resolves your place as a species.

Are we saying that science will lead you to this true wisdom? No, we are telling you that there will be a handful of your species that will step forward as Sovereign Integrals with a balanced scientific and philosophical nature, and they will have the benefit of an educated species that will listen to the inconvertible evidence.

Even First Source cannot bring a species to its true wisdom. The leaders of the species must achieve it through organic, self-inventive methods. First Source, through its original blueprint of exploration, enabled the humanoid species the ability and means to acquire this knowledge itself. If the true wisdom were brought to the species from outside itself, it would be inherently mistrusted and it would not be sufficiently compelling to unite the species.

There are numerous revelations that have been brought to your species through non-physical entities in the form of what you term, channeled information. Even parts of your Holy books are channeled. However, these writings were for the few. They did not contain the true wisdom—they only hinted at the shadow it casts. The Sovereign Integrals will emerge like beacons for your species, and elevate the mental and emotional perceptions of the entire species.

When one Sovereign Integral emerges, it will, by the catalytic forces of its own entity consciousness, cause another to arise, and another, and another, and it will cascade from one to one thousand in a single generation. From this one thousand, will arise one million in the next generation, and from this one million the entire population will arise, imbued with this insight gained from the portal into the multiverse. And from this portal will arise the organization of the true wisdom into a form that will endure against all attacks.

This is the grand unification of the species around the new, non-hierarchal structures that enable the experience of the true wisdom to the newborn of its species in order to perpetuate the unification of the species. Within six generations, the genetic mind of the species is stable and then becomes a powerful tool of exploration that the species will come to understand as its "spaceship" into the multiverse.

The human species of your planet will become the teachers who channel the shadowy outline of the true wisdom to a new species that is, even now, unconsciously awaiting your arrival. The process is carried out over and over, always with variations and anomalies that spark deeper insights and pathways into the Central Universe from which First Source has its being. It is the most powerful of all gravity fields, and ultimately leads a species and its individuated entities to its periphery from which we, the WingMakers, reside as your future selves.

V. The Onward Journey of Developing Creation

The entity is viewed in the universe of time and space as an evolving particle of exploration commissioned by First Source to explore, populate, develop, and transform the outposts of creations into enclaves of Source Intelligence. When the entity is viewed in the dimensions of non-time and non-space—its natural habitat— it appears as an immortal facet of First Source that has been individuated, but when viewed in the three-dimensional environment of genetic density, it appears as a temporal facet of its species.

The species—in this case, the human species—evolves in time as the elder race that guides a developing race in the formation of its metaphysical and scientific foundations. They become the culture-builders of a new species. The evolution of a species stretches from its origins in the Central Universe as a unified genetic model fit to explore the multiverse, to a fragmentation of the species into biologic diversity, to its re-unification through culture and technology, to its ascension as a non-physical unified Genetic Mind, to its application of this Genetic Mind as a means to explore the outer reaches of the cosmos and help guide a developing species, and to the merging of this Genetic Mind with the Genetic Mind of its ancestral race.

Your scientists have defined the evolution of the species on a scale that is only the equivalent of a tiny splinter of wood in a vast forest of time and space. The evolution of the human specie through the "forest" of time and space is an exceedingly dense process, consisting of innumerable levels of progress that ultimately enables the Genetic Mind of the species to blend harmoniously with First Source.

What fuels this process is the genetically endowed drive of the entity to explore the worlds of creation, and to ultimately acquire the necessary wisdom and compassion to lead a younger species to its true wisdom. You may wonder why this process seems so convoluted and fraught with missteps and mistakes. We tell you that the process is not what it seems. The Genetic Mind of the elder race that is working with your species on terra-earth operates in a window of time more comprehensive and inclusive than you can imagine.

The gateway into your future is through the completion of this blueprint, and this blueprint is encoded deep within your species. At your root, you are not an immortal psychic impression, or mental echo, but rather, you are the faultless triune of First Source, Source Intelligence and the sovereign entity, colliding in a dance of energy that is evermore. Your mind must grasp the fullness of your true nature and depth of your being, or you will fall prey to the psychic impression and mental echo of your lesser self.

If you believe, as you are taught, in the lesser self, you will reach for the food that nourishes the shadow and not the substance. The substance of your design is awakened with the words that form the concepts of your enlarged self-image. And these words are not merely spoken, but they are seen, felt, and heard as well. They lead you to the tone of equality and the perception of wholeness. Allow these words to wash over you like a gentle wave that brings you buoyancy and movement. It will sweep you to a new shore, and it is there that you will begin to uncover your true nature and purpose.

The blueprint of exploration is the genetic substrate of your design, and all the so-called "lower" life forms are the "limbs" of your species. Without them, you could not exist. And so the composite life form is truly the species of which we speak when we speak of the human species. We do not separate you from the plant and animal kingdoms. We see them as one composite species. It is your scientists who have chosen to separate the one species into billions of sub-species because wholeness cannot be classified and analyzed.

The tools of the mind suppress the true nature of your species. Only when you observe with the frequency of equality foremost in your heart and mind, can you bypass this suppression and feel the linkages that organize your specie into a master organism. It is this organism that is in perfect alignment with First Source like two circles that overlap so perfectly that only one is seen. It is the very nature of First Source to create innumerable fragments of itself and lead each to cohesion as a master organism, while allowing each fragment to retain its sovereignty. This is the perfect bestowal of love.

While First Source cannot be found through searching, if you will submit to the leading impulse of the sovereign entity within you, you will unerringly be guided, step by step, life after life, through universe upon universe, and age by age, until you finally peer into the eyes of your Creator and realize you are one. And in this realization you will see that the species from which you emerge is one also. The fragments of the one congeal through the blueprint of exploration whose end is not foreseen, and whose beginning is not measured by time.

Chamber Four Philosophy
Beliefs and Their Energy Systems

All beliefs have energy systems that act like birthing rooms for the manifestation of the belief. Within these energy systems are currents that direct your life experience. You are aware of these currents either consciously or subconsciously, and you allow them to carry you into the realm of experience that best exemplifies your true belief system.

Belief systems resonate with, and are the byproduct of, the dominant energy system of a sympathetic group, culture, and even species. Thus, energy systems are more fundamental than beliefs, and create experience that creates beliefs. Energy systems are wide ranging in their context, but as they relate to beliefs, they can be defined as primordial thought forms crystallized within the human DNA. Some would refer to these fundamental energy systems as instinctual knowledge.

Within each entity is the genetic compound of its ancestry, moving across innumerable generations and species, and, in the vastness of galactic time, this genetic compound accumulates energy systems that pertain to how one survives in the three-dimensional universe. Thus, survival is the dominant energy system of the human entity, which informs its genetic code and triggers its life experience and beliefs.

Survival is the focal point of conformity. When an entity believes so deeply in survival, it is near impossible to break from the conformity that survival requires. And so, the human species, rooted in an energy system of survival, has become a conformist to the dictates of its genetic predispositions and instincts, and its experience reflects this, conditioning its belief system to follow.

Life circumstances do not differentiate nor insulate an entity from this pervasive reality. Thus the equation for three-dimensionally based species: Survival-Based Energy System + Galactic Time = Conformist Life Experience = Belief System. What this means is that survival, as the core energy system of the species, will beget over long periods of time, a life experience that produces conformity to the requirements of survival. Consequently, belief systems are largely a byproduct of the genetically based instinct to conform in order to survive.

The cycle of conformity entrains energy systems of individuals and groups, and it casts belief systems that obey the energy system just as surely as a shadow conforms to the general shape of an object. Within the boundaries of the survival-based energy system are transition zones that permit a re-casting of one's belief system in accordance with cosmological, multidimensional energy systems. Think of these transition zones as isolated portals of energy that intersect the dominant energy system of the human species not unlike energy vortexes intersecting space.

The energy system that permeates terra-earth—creating predictable belief systems of conformity—will be energetically transformed to enable more accessible transition zones. How one accesses these portals or transition zones and utilizes their enabling energy system will be the real issue of your twenty-first century.

Think of these transition zones as portals that lead one out of the prevailing energy system of survival and conformity of the mind-body into a new energy system that is of the mind-soul. The mind-soul energy system is characterized by creative energy directed to realizing that the Wholeness Navigator is the personality that endures and is therefore the creator of enduring beliefs and life experience. When this realization is achieved by accessing one of these transition zones or portals, the entity can begin to restructure their belief system independent of time and the predominant notion of survival.

There are two kinds of transition zones: Tributary Zones and the Grand Portal. The Tributary Zones fluctuate over time and are generally found in the high-culture of a robust civilization—notably the art movements that are grounded in spiritual principles, sacred mythology, and cosmic context. Art of this nature, whether it is music, painting, poetry, drama, or dance, can be constructed into a Tributary Zone that transitions entities to discover the Grand Portal.

The Grand Portal is the prime achievement that awaits humanity in the last quarter of the twenty-first century. It will be the irrefutable discovery of the human soul by authoritative science. This Grand Portal will usher in a new awareness for humanity that will enable it to shift from a survival-based, mind-body energy system, to an exploratory-based, mind-soul energy system. This exploratory energy system will manifest the belief system of the Sovereign Integral; the Golden Age long prophesied.

The WingMakers, working in conjunction with the existing Hierarchy, have created or inspired the Tributary Zones throughout human history. Each of these Tributary Zones emerges on the timeline of humanity not as religious or philosophical movements, but as artistic expressions of refined beauty and spiritual adoration. As time draws nearer for the discovery of the Grand Portal, these artistic expressions will become increasingly multidimensional, integrated, and, like directional beacons, guide the way to the Grand Portal's discovery.

This is the way of enlightenment for the human species. The WingMakers created the initial Tributary Zones in accelerated, non-physical dimensions as outposts of creative energy linked to the higher circuits of First Source, and these act as guideposts that gently steer humankind's finest representatives of the arts and culture to create Tributary Zones that are physically based, which in turn, guide humankind's finest representatives of the sciences to ultimately discover and prove the existence of the Wholeness Navigator. In so doing, humanity is forever changed from a survival-based energy system to an explorer-based energy system.

This is the event that will change the life experience of humanity more profoundly than any other event of the twenty-first century. Eleven thousand years of civilization will culminate in this event, and it will occur through art and science. Religion will be a factor as well, but only a subsidiary factor. When this discovery is made, religion will have no choice but to honor it and adopt the far-reaching implications. Religion will fear it will be displaced by science, and it will know only one course of action: integrate with the new science that combines technology, psychology, metaphysics, and cosmology.

Tributary Zones will become the new religion of the twenty-second century. They will become the touchstone for accessing the new energy coming into the planet as a result of the Grand Portal's discovery. In this time, the new structure of the Hierarchy will—like a glove turned outside in—finally fit the human "hand". This will herald the Return of the Masters who have remained behind the veil of secrecy because of the survival-based interests of religion, business, government, and science.

However, these institutions will be reformatted, and those Masters who hold the vital information as to how the individual may use the Grand Portal to explore themselves and the universe, will be revered and finally appreciated by humanity at large. By the dawning of the twenty-second century, the Grand Portal will be ubiquitous in human culture and acknowledged in all classrooms of learning.

The discovery of the Grand Portal is a carefully orchestrated event string, consisting of innumerable components. The reason this event has been, and continues to be, so carefully orchestrated is that it will galvanize the Genetic Mind of the human species to explore the multiverse, and not simply terra-earth or its solar system. It is the single event that establishes humankind on the Sovereign Integral Network, and shifts the energy system of the human species from which all manifestations arise.

When a species in the three-dimensional universe discovers irrefutable scientific proof of the multiverse and the innermost topology of the Wholeness Navigator, it impacts on every aspect of the species. It is the most profound shift of consciousness that can be foretold, and it is this event that triggers the Return of the Masters to explicit influence and exoteric roles.

There are many practical applications for restructuring one's own energy and belief system, and they require, in most cases, an active immersion into a Tributary Zone. This means to interact with the Tributary Zone on a deeply personal level, translating its meaning through in-depth consideration for its personal messages. Each Tributary Zone is designed like a house of mirrors. Until one steps inside, there is no image to reflect. No personal content to convey.

The most common way of accessing a non-physical Tributary Zone is through meditation or the dream state. While in these altered states of consciousness, the entity can begin to shift and restructure their energy system by accessing these Tributary Zones. Typically, this is done under the guidance of a select member of the Hierarchy who is a master of energy system transfer.

The purpose is to guide an entity to become less dependent on the survival energy system complex that invites conformity and a life experience therein. These entities are invited to participate in this process in order to activate their sense of creative power and authority to manifest in the three-dimensional universe a deeper and more penetrating channel into the mysterious realm of the Wholeness Navigator.

Entities are selected based on their accumulated desire to assist in the event string of the Grand Portal. As previously cited, the WingMakers created Tributary Zones in the accelerated dimensions whereby entities could access them in the dream state or, in some instances, through meditation. Exposure to these Tributary Zones, even though seldom remembered, enabled these entities to transfer a likeness of the non-physical Tributary Zone to the three-dimensional world of terra-earth.

These initial physical creations dealt with spiritual values and were often the product of poetry, art, music, and drama. In the dawning of the twenty-first century, they will combine art, spiritual values, technology, and science, and they will become Tributary Zones of greater import because they will prefigure the Grand Portal, and in this prefiguring they create the Framework of Discovery upon terra-earth.

These physical Tributary Zones will catalyze the entities born of the twenty-first century in ways that the non-physical Tributary Zones cannot. Specifically, they will cause a resonance at a sub-molecular level through music and art that will reconfigure the four-dimensional protein patterns of the human brain and nervous system. In so doing, the nervous system will receive and transmit higher energy circuits that enable a very subtle mutation in the region of the brain where intuition or the sixth sense resides.

There is a sixth sense in which the brain becomes an organ of the Genetic Mind instead of the physical body of an individual entity. This is a state of consciousness separate from the Sovereign Integral because it is not sustainable. It is only glimpsed for brief moments, but in these brief passages of time, the Genetic Mind can transfer ideas, insights, and innovations that make possible the discovery of the Grand Portal.

There is a repository of knowledge that was seeded within the Genetic Mind nearly eleven thousand years ago by the WingMakers. This knowledge is the blueprint for the discovery of the Wholeness Navigator. The human Hierarchy has drawn close to this Holy Grail through the efforts of its finest representatives. We, the WingMakers, have included everything for your successful attainment. No detail has been left out or overlooked. We have undertaken this process of energy system transfer on countless life-bearing planets within the Grand Universe, and your finest representatives will succeed.

However, the Grand Portal is not easily comprehensible. It will require an educated humanity in the fields of cosmology, technology, and science. It is for this reason that medical technologies in the field of genetics and neural mapping will proceed in the twenty-first century to enable a new, spatial intelligence to anyone who desires it. While this medical technology may seem to some as an artificial, and therefore unwelcome technology, it will be required for much of the human race in order to comprehend the Grand Portal, and it should not be feared.

This technology will accelerate a portion of the brain center that is responsible for spatial, multidimensional constructs and highly abstract thought processes. In the average human mind, it will permit the Grand Portal's energy system to be comprehensible, and, therefore, believed as a scientific principle as factual as the force of gravity.

The energy system of the Tributary Zones that prefigure the Grand Portal will be translated from the WingMakers to your finest representatives in the dawning of the twenty-first century. These Tributary Zones will manifest in the three-dimensional world of terra-earth, but will actually stem from a non-physical dimension known only to the WingMakers and First Source. In a sense, these Tributary Zones are echoes of a reality from your future, bearing down on you as an energy field that makes possible the quantum leap required of your species to allow the Wholeness Navigator to fully embody humanhood.

It is reasonably true to state that if humankind in your time believed it was a collective vehicle of First Source, endowed with ITS exploratory virtuosity, it would instantly recognize itself as the WingMakers. It is also true—in the same sense—that the WingMakers would not exist if we were not successful in making visible the Grand Portal to humankind. Through our existence, humanity is assured of its future. When all the calamities of terra-earth are forecast, and your doom as a species is spelled out in the certainty of cataclysm and war, the event that will redeem you is in the discovery, acceptance, and application of the Grand Portal.

This new energy system can be brought into your personal realm. When you believe, "I am a fragment of First Source imbued with ITS capabilities," you are engaging this energy system inherent within the feeling of connectedness. You are pulling into your reality a sense of connection to your Source and all the attributes therein. The belief is inseparable from you because its energy system is assimilated within your own energy system and is woven into your spirit like a thread of light.

These threads, however, must be manifold, or they will break, and your energy system will remain in the shadows of survival and conformity. As you gain awareness of the Tributary Zones, you will gain insight into the new energy systems and how to anchor these energy systems into your own. There are specialized techniques for weaving this energy system to your own and exchanging—over time—your survival-based energy system for the exploratory energy system of the coming age.

These techniques provide a means to weld survival and exploratory energy systems, as though one were creating a footbridge that enabled them to cross the chasm separating the two energy fields. These techniques are divided into three categories:

- Mind-Body Movement Techniques
- Mind-Soul Comprehension Techniques
- Emotion-Soul Acquisition Techniques

Mind-Body Movement—This technique involves the expression of music in the form of body movement that focuses the mind on the body's rhythmic, improvisational flow. The mind is following the body, and the body is following the music. The music, as the organizing principal, must be designed for this explicit purpose, or it will not lead to the exploratory energy system. The music compositions of Chambers Seventeen through Twenty-four—from each of the seven Tributary Zones created by the WingMakers—are intended for this purpose.

This technique requires a single-minded willingness to follow the interpretation of the body into the feel of the music. It would be like entering a meadow in the height of Spring with your eyes closed, knowing that your sense of smell would guide you to the flowers. In this same way, your mind must trust that your body is able to listen to the music and capture a sense of this new energy system encoded within the "field" of music.

By placing the mind in the position of follower, it is reliant on the body to make interpretations of movement based solely on the music. Thus, the music can penetrate directly to the mind and entrain it to a new energy system. The music will—by design—generate body movement that is high energy, complex, rhythmic, and stimulating to the emotional center of the brain.

This is a form of meditation taught by the WingMakers that demonstrates the trust placed upon the body intelligence and the willingness of the mind to listen to this intelligence. This is a thread of this new energy system externalized through this technique. There are portals designed into the music that will open the brain's emotional centers to this new energy, and when they are discovered, you will feel the undeniable shift in your energy field. The movement of the body signifies the externalization of the new in direct counterpoint to the old. It demonstrates the compatibility of the two energy systems, and how one can be in both fields simultaneously with comfort and confidence.

There are no rules to this movement. It is not a choreographed dance with either right or wrong movements. It is an improvisational body expression bypassing the mind and allowing the music's voice to be heard as clearly as possible by the body intelligence. The physical body becomes the sail of the music's wind, while the mind is the ship's hull. Clarity of intention is all that is required. There is no qualitative difference beyond this that matters.

The anchoring process requires a minimum of a cycle (seven expressions) of each composition in Chambers Seventeen through Twenty-four. There is a time period of the cycle that requires a completion in approximately one month of your time. Thus, each of the seven expressions for a single Chamber should be completed within a thirty day period of time. It can be less, but should not be more. It is recommended not to focus on more than two Chambers during a cycle.

Each expression of a particular Chamber should change over the course of the seven expressions. This progression can be radical variances or simple refinements; it depends on the entity's body development, comfort, and ability to listen to the subtle layering of the music and its focus in the moment. It is not only the energy of the low frequency rhythms, or percussive frequencies, but also the voices and melodies that can speak to the body intelligence.

The approach is different from your art form of dance in that each expression of the eight Chambers will develop the body intelligence to recognize an exploratory-based energy system. It will, in effect, activate the body's natural radar for this energy system, helping the human instrument to navigate into the new energy. It also confers a degree of trust to the body intelligence that it is not about the body's movement in space that matters, but is rather how the body listens to vibrations and responds in kind.

A Grand Cycle consists of a minimum of fifty-six expressions, and the Grand Cycle is the physical thread that generates an awareness of the new energy system in the body. It is important to anchor this awareness in the body because the body intelligence is the most instinctual of the human instrument, and while you may have awareness in your mind and soul, if it is not present in your body, your shift to the new energy is impeded because the body will instinctually gravitate to the survival-based energy system.

There will be some who will not be comfortable in practicing the expressions of this technique. You have been programmed that your body does not possess its own intelligence, therefore, when you are told to listen and express with your body's intellect, you feel overly self-conscious to even try. It is natural, and is part of the old energy system that controls your movement and sensory perceptions.

It is indispensable to listen with your body, express with your body, and to feel with your body the movements that the music dictates. When you come to the end of your expression, you may sit or stand in silence and listen to the reverberations calling within you, and then transmit these to the human instrument as a whole. This is done by visualizing the body as a transmitter of the energy, generated from the expression, and projecting this energy into the human instrument like a coil's energy finally released.

If you are unable to proceed through the Grand Cycle, you may still find the tools to build your bridge in the remaining two techniques.

Mind-Soul Comprehension—This technique involve the knowledge of the new psychology destined to reach humanity in the twenty-first century. This is the psychology that integrates metaphysics and the spiritual perceptions of the Genetic Mind, with the science of the brain and the shaping influences of culture and personal genetics.

Individual entities acquire their psychological acumen by studying behaviors and their consequences in others, such as family members or friends. It is the byproduct of this psychological study that helps to establish an entity's own behavioral boundaries. When psychology ignores the incomprehensible, the psychology of the species is mostly based on the phenomenon of observable behavior. As psychology evolves it increasingly takes into account the brain, mind, and emotional interplay.

The incomprehensible is First Source and the structure and interconnectedness of ITS creation. Human psychology has ignored this aspect of the human condition, venturing only as far as the dream state, which, by comparison, would be the equivalent of standing on a mountaintop reaching for the sun. The human condition is considered untouched by the incomprehensible, and yet, it is encompassed in it like a caterpillar within a cocoon. If the caterpillar were untouched by the cocoon would it emerge a butterfly?

The mind-soul comprehension technique focus the mind on the incomprehensible through the use of visual symbols that are just outside the intelligible regions of comfort as set forth by human psychology. By investigating visual symbols through the eye-brain, the mind can secure a glimpse into the Sovereign Integral consciousness and the special psychology therein.

An entity may, through an imaginative scenario based on a Tributary Zone, gain comprehension of the new psychology. The technique is admittedly abstract, but very effective. In this visual scenario the mind becomes a personal identity, as does the soul. Together, these two identities coexist on an otherwise deserted island. The mind has discovered the symbols of the WingMakers Chamber Paintings, and must explain their purpose to the soul. Neither the mind nor the soul speaks the same language, and thus the mind must explain the symbols' purpose to the soul through telepathic means.

Examine one of the Chamber Paintings, conducting a thorough mental analysis. Once completed, you may now take this knowledge and translate your understanding to your soul, bringing it comprehension without language. This is highly conceptual, but it is designed to be this way for a purpose, and the insights that will result are profound and far-reaching because they demonstrate how the mind-soul comprehension operates to enrich the mind's understanding of the incomprehensible. Comprehension of the incomprehensible does not flow from the soul to the mind, but rather from the mind teaching itself.

When the mind grasps the incomprehensible through symbols—be they mathematical formulas or the language of Gods—it sharpens the lens of psychology to focus on the invisible persona of the human soul and the energy system that regulates its behavior in the world of non-time.

Herein is the difficulty of the new psychology: It is based upon non-time, and here the mind is mute and blind. If you observe the Chamber Two Painting, using the aforementioned technique, you will learn a new dimension of time. If you inspect the Chamber Three Painting, you will gain knowledge of a new dimension of inner space. If you study the Chamber Twelve Painting, you will discover a new dimension of energy. If you examine the Chamber Four Painting, you will be taught a new dimension of matter.

All of this is encoded within these four paintings, but can be decoded through this technique. Remember, when applying this technique, the mind is a separate personality from the soul and is its instructor. In this example, the mind is the sail, the paintings the wind, and the soul the ship's hull.

It is recommended to repeat this procedure for each of the four Chamber Paintings three times. During each dialogue between your mind and soul identity, record your key descriptors and look for the linkages between them. You are describing a dimension of time, space, energy, and matter that recedes into the incomprehensible. You will find a new confidence in your mind's ability to express the insights of the Genetic Mind after this technique is completed. And you will begin to feel an appreciation for the role of the new psychology where the mind acquires the incomprehensible to become the Wholeness Navigator, just as the caterpillar acquires the cocoon to become the butterfly.

Emotion-Soul Acquisition—Soul acquires emotional responses through the human instrument. Emotions, by definition, are responses to a time-based event, an energy, a memory, or an expectation. The mind and body predominantly condition emotional responses, while the soul observes and acquires their constructive essence of bonding, appreciation, and special insight.

The body and mind also acquire learning from the emotional responses, but unlike the soul, they are unable to sift the constructive from the destructive, so they are more affected by the emotional responses of anger, greed, and fear. These emotions anchor the mind to the survival-based energy system as firmly as anything in the world of creation.

The Spirit-essence of the human instrument that guides it to wholeness with Source Intelligence, and ultimately First Source, is emotionally personified in the form of a voice. This voice is heard in the abstraction of poetry that is designed in a specific rhythm and vibration of meaning.

The technique of emotion-soul acquisition is concerned with discerning the emotional voice of a poem, intending that voice to resonate within your soul, and releasing the emotion that arises from the resonance, letting it wander away from you like a wild animal released into its natural habitat.

There are ten poems within the WingMakers' Ancient Arrow site that are designed for the application of this technique. They are:

- Circle
- Forever
- One Day
- Listening
- Afterwards
- Of this Place
- Warm Presence
- Another Mind Open
- Of Luminous Things
- Song of Whales

Each poem strikes an emotional chord of subtle discord.

It is discordance that stirs the emotional responses, making them accessible to the higher energies of the human instrument. This discordance is not concerning anger, greed, or fear, but rather the more subtle feelings of separation, abandonment, and spiritual neglect.

The emotion-soul acquisition pays tribute to these feelings, and seeks to position the tether of discordance in the hands of soul, thus ensuring that the emotions have voice and influence in the shaping of soul's judgment, insight, and reasoning. It is the quiet emotions of separation and abandonment that fuel the strident emotions of fear, greed, and anger. Poetry can bring forth these quiet emotions and liberate their presence to the soul, and in so doing, allow them to be honored, and, in this process, understood.

This understanding helps to diminish the anger and fear of the mind and body, which disaffect the human instrument from Source Intelligence and realization of the Wholeness Navigator consciousness. Thus, the emotion-soul acquisition technique is to trace the voice of the ten poems to the subtle emotions of abandonment and separation, allowing these emotions to arise within one's self as if they were on display to your soul. These emotions are like ropes that pull the strident emotions into your life-stream, which anchor you to the energy system of survival. To the extent you can eliminate or diminish the "ropes" of the quiet emotions, you can eliminate or diminish the strident emotions.

Be assured that each of these three techniques that you may practice, are done in our presence. You are not alone and you never fail. If your results are not as you expected, abandon your expectations. Set them aside and place your goal on not having any goals or standards. Also recognize that the realizations and shifts in your energy system may reveal themselves in unexpected ways, and therefore, remain largely invisible to yourself if you have set expectations for their materialization.

It is purposely designed to be a struggle to make this shift both as a species and as an individual. As a species, humankind must be able to harness the appropriate tools of technology in order to attune the human instrument to permit the Wholeness Navigator to both inhabit and be in command of the brain centers, nervous system, and the subconscious artifacts of ancestral roots. It takes the equivalent of 5,200,000 years for a humanoid species to evolve to the threshold of the Grand Portal.

As an individual, the aforementioned techniques enable a purposeful immersion into a Tributary Zone, whereby an individual can transform their energy system, which in turn, transforms their beliefs and life experience. However, no matter how effective an individual applies these techniques they will not achieve the discovery of the Grand Portal of their own efforts. The Grand Portal is a discovery by humanity. It is the culmination of science, art, and technology, operating in unison, focused on the exploratory province of cosmology and metaphysics.

Most humans have been raised on the premise of karma or fate. It is time to understand that while these doctrines are both valid; they are overshadowed by the reality of the Blueprint of Exploration. While karma or fate may explain the life experience of an individual, Source Intelligence orchestrates the species, from its very first emergence upon the planet, to discover the Grand Portal and establish its supremacy upon the planet.

The Grand Portal then becomes the homing beacon that draws the galactic energy system to the planet and connects it to the network of galactic energy. When this occurs, the species is no longer a planet-based species. Humankind will be inter-galactic in its range of experience and realm of influence.

The individual can participate in this orchestration of energies, being consciously aligned and supportive of the shifts required to achieve the discovery of the Grand Portal, or they can choose to live life within the survival-based energy system, and drift into the Grand Portal with their fellow humans. It is neither fate nor karma that is drawing the human species to the edge of the Grand Portal. It is the event string of First Source, and therefore, the outcome of every human action and thought is an element of this journey.

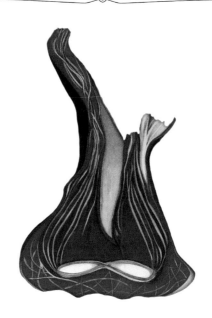

Introduction to the WingMakers Glossary

The WingMakers glossary consists of twenty-two entries. It is different from most glossaries in that the terms are not given in alphabetical order. One possible reason for this arrangement appears to the building of what I call concept clusters. These concept clusters are simply a means of making related terms more understandable by placing them together, rather than arranging them alphabetically. For example, the first five entries are a cluster of terms related to the individuated consciousness and its relation to First Source.

- Human Instrument
- Entity
- Remnant Imprint
- Sovereign Integral
- First Source

In 2003 I created a series of computer-generated slides delineating the terms in concept clusters. The groupings I created are not perfect and are based on my own interpretations.[135] You may see them differently, so don't think of them as strict and beyond alternative groupings. Also keep in mind that there are twenty-four chamber philosophies, so these so-called concept clusters are incomplete because only four philosophy papers have been published at the time of this writing. Below is a table listing the terms in alphabetical order.

All That Is	Remnant Imprint
Entity	Source Codes
Evolution and the Concept of Time	Source Intelligence
Fields of Vibration	Source Reality
First Source	Sovereign Integral
Genetic Mind	Sovereign Integral Network
Grand Portal	Sovereignty
Hierarchy	Tributary Zones
Human Instrument	Universe of Wholeness
Models of Existence	Wholeness Navigator
OLIN Technology	Wholeness Perspective

---

135. For examples of the concept clusters see this editor's Visual Glossary at www.wingmakers.com/whats-new.html.

The WingMakers Glossary

Human Instrument

The human instrument consists of three principal components: The biological (physical body), the emotional, and the mental. These three distinct tools of perception, in aggregate, represent the vehicle of the individuated spirit as it interacts with the physical dimension of time, space, energy, and matter.

Entity

The entity model of consciousness encompasses the individuated spirit sometimes referred to as the Higher Self or Soul. The entity is, in a sense, a fragment of the Universal Spirit Consciousness of First Source. It is composed of a very refined and pure energy vibration that is equal to Source Intelligence (spirit). It is the entity consciousness that divests itself into human or otherwise physical vehicles in order to collect experiences that evolve and transform its understanding and appreciation of existence. It is the hub of the wheel through which all its outposts of form and expression converge throughout the continuum of time and space. The entity is sovereign and simultaneously interconnected with all life through the Universal Spirit Consciousness (Source Intelligence). It is the animating force/energy within all life forms that is always in search of higher understanding and expression.

Remnant Imprint

The human instrument is the genetic compound of three separate, but related structures: the physical composition (body), the emotional predispositions (emotional template), and the mental configuration (mind-thought generator). These three aspects of the human instrument are inexplicably bound together through the intricate and utterly unique interface of the genetic code and life experience.

Within the human instrument, and acting as its animator of creative goodness, is the Remnant Imprint of the Sovereign Integral. The Remnant Imprint is the muse or inspirational formation of the human instrument insofar as the individual is concerned. It is the voice of deep character that arouses the most potent and noble instincts and creative stirrings of the human being: creating acts of goodness that touch the human soul in oneself and others.

It is a difficult abstraction for time-bound humans to understand, but the Sovereign Integral consciousness is the fusion of the entity consciousness in the worlds of time-space. All expressions and experiences of the human instrument, collectively, are deposited within the Sovereign Integral state of consciousness, and it is precisely this that imprints upon the human instrument of the individual.

For some who have traveled across the material universe in various times, places, and physical bodies, the Remnant Imprint is more influential and expressive. For those who are relatively new to the Universe of TimeSpace, the Remnant Imprint lacks persistent influence and is easily overcome by the seduction of power, fear, and greed—the machinery of survival.

Within every human instrument is the imprint of the Sovereign Integral, and it is referred to as a 'remnant' only because it exists in the dimension of time and space. In reality it is the cast of energy bestowed by the Sovereign Integral to the human instrument. It is precisely this energy that generates ideas and inspirations, making it possible for the voice of all that you are to surface into the worlds of time and space in which you are only a particle of your total being.

The Remnant Imprint is often confused with the Higher Self, or human soul. The distinction, subtle as it may seem, is vital to understand. There are many discrete but ultimately integrated states of consciousness that animate, express through, and observe the human instrument. The energy of the Remnant Imprint is generated from the Sovereign Integral consciousness, filtered through the Wholeness Navigator and imprinted upon the mind, emotions, and physical body.

This energy, because of its origination from the Sovereign Integral, imbues the human instrument with a multiplicity of ideas, ideals, and approaches to being. It is not hindered by convention or social structure. It is not diminished by intimidation. It is forthright in its effort to instill the innate rights of sovereignty through the expression of its responsible and informed voice. It calibrates the ascension path of a mortal soul carrier against the acts of creative goodness, independent of the obstacles, ridicules, and customary ornaments of culture.

Sovereign Integral

The Sovereign Integral is a state of consciousness whereby the entity and all its various forms of expression and perception are integrated as a conscious wholeness. This is a state of consciousness that all entities are evolving towards, and at some point, each will reach a state of transformation that allows the entity and its instruments of experience (i.e., the human instrument) to become an integrated expression that is aligned and in harmony with Source Intelligence.

First Source

First Source is the primal source from which all existence is ultimately linked. It is sometimes referred to as the Body of the Collective God. It represents the overarching consciousness of all things unified. This includes pain, joy, suffering, light, love, darkness, fear; all expressions and conditions are integrated and purposeful in the context of First Source. IT encompasses all things and unifies them in an all-inclusive consciousness that evolves and grows in a similar manner to how each individuated spirit evolves and grows.

In most cultures where the term "god" or "goddess" is used to define this omnipotent power, it often represents an entity that has evolved beyond the range of human comprehension and who manifests magical powers like manipulating the natural elements through thought or manifesting as non-corporeal Light Beings. These manifestations are described and depicted in virtually all cultures of the human race through its religious texts and mythology. While these may be entities that are highly evolved in their abilities and knowledge, they should not be confused with First Source.

First Source is not a manifestation, but rather a consciousness that inhabits all time, space, energy, matter, form, intent; as well as all non-time, non-space, non-matter, non-energy, non-form, and non-intent. It is the only consciousness that unifies all states of being into one Being. And this Being is First Source. It is a growing, expanding, and inexplicable consciousness that organizes the collective experience of all states of being into a coherent plan of creation; expansion and colonization into the realms of creation; and the inclusion of creation into Source Reality—the home of First Source.

This Being pervades the universe as the sum of experience in time and non-time. It has encoded ITSELF within all life as a vibration of frequency. This frequency is not perceptible to the three-dimensional, five sensory context of the human instrument, which can only detect a faint echo of this vibration. First Source is present in all. And all are able to contact First Source through this tone-vibration of equality. Prayers of supplication do not stir First Source to response. Only the core expression of the individual's tone-vibration of equality will be successful in contacting First Source in a meaningful way.

First Source has many lower faces. These faces are often thought to be God Itself, but Gods are only a dimensional aspect of First Source and there are many faces of God as well. The Hierarchy has made this manifest, not First Source. First Source is not beholden to any law nor does IT operate in conjunction with any other force or power. IT is truly sovereign and ubiquitous simultaneously, and thus, Unique. IT is not hidden or wary of life in any way. IT simply is Unique, and therefore, incomprehensible except through the vibration encoded within all life.

The other faces of God have been created so the human instrument can fathom First Source and crystallize an image of this Unique Being sufficient to progress through the Hierarchy and access the Sovereign Integral perspective. Nevertheless, what you hold as God, is not First Source, but a facet of First Source developed by the Hierarchy as a comprehensible interpretation of First Source. We must tell you that these "interpretations" have been exceedingly inadequate in their portrayal.

Because First Source is Unique unto all creation, IT is indescribable, unfathomable, and incomprehensible other than through the tone-vibration of equality stored in the entity level of the human instrument and accessible through the core expression of the entity. Until there are a sufficient number of individuals who operate from the Sovereign Integral consciousness, the genetic mind will make access to this vibration difficult to achieve.

The Genetic Mind

The genetic mind is the equivalent of a universal belief system that penetrates, to varying degrees, the human instrument of all entities. In some, it immobilizes their ability to think original thoughts and feel original feelings. In most, it entrains their belief system to harmonize with the accepted belief systems of the Hierarchy. In a few, it exerts no significant force nor has any bearing on the development of their personal belief system.

There are those on terra-earth who are in training to be Sovereign Entities and are completely unaware of this training as well as their destiny. When they are able to become timeless and view the continuum of their lifestream, they will see the thread that has differentiated them as Sovereign Entities. They will understand how the hardships and supposed indifference of the universe were actually the catalysts for their emergence as designers of the new genetic mind.

The genetic mind is different from the subconscious or universal mind as it is sometimes referred to in your psychology texts, in that the genetic mind has a peculiar focus on the accumulated beliefs of all the people on a planet from its most distant past to its present time. These accumulated beliefs are actually manipulations of the Hierarchy, which imprint on the genetic mind in order to cast the boundaries of what is acceptable to believe.

So compelling is this manipulation and the boundaries that are imposed by the Hierarchy that virtually no one is aware of the manipulations of their beliefs. This is precisely why the WingMakers have interacted with your species from the very beginning. As culture bearers, we stretch your boundaries in the arena of science, art, and philosophy. We essentially expand the genetic mind's "perimeter fence" and enable it to encompass a larger portion of the "land" known as Source Reality.

If we were to tell you about the fundamental misconceptions of your genetic mind, you would not believe us. You would most definitely—even your most accomplished spiritual leaders—find us in contempt of much that you hold true and reasonable. You would feel fear in the face of our expression of Source Reality because it would be so clear to you how you have squandered your divine natures in favor of the entrapment of the genetic mind.

We know this will seem like a judgment of your beliefs, and it is to some degree, but you must know this about your belief systems: they are largely disconnected from Source Reality. They are like threads of a web that have become disconnected from the "branches" of Source Reality by the "winds" of the Hierarchy. Source Reality is represented in your belief in unconditional love, but of all the dimensions of your belief systems, this is the one thread that is connected—through the genetic mind—to Source Reality.

All the other dimensions are connected to the genetic mind and have no ongoing connection to Source Reality. The genetic mind, as an intermediary and reflection of Source Reality, is completely and utterly inept. This is all part of the primal blueprint that designs the evolutionary pathway of a species through time. The genetic mind acts as a buffer for the developing species to experience separation from Source Reality. In this way, the human instrument is appropriately entangled in time, space, and the illusions of a disempowered belief system.

These factors, as disorienting as they are to the entity, are precisely what attract the entity to terra-earth. There are very few planetary systems in the multiverse that provide a better sense of separation from Source Reality than that which is experienced on terra-earth. By amplifying the sense of separation, the entity can experience more fully the individuated essence that is unique and bears the resemblance of First Source as a Unique Being. This is what draws entities to this world to incarnate within a human instrument.

So the genetic mind is an enabling force to experience separation on the one hand, and a disabling force to understand the true characteristics of Source Reality on the other. This dichotomy, when understood, helps to disentangle the human instrument and its entity consciousness from the limiting aspects of the genetic mind and its principle author, the Hierarchy.

Over the next twenty years, the genetic mind will become increasingly fragmented and thus, vulnerable to modification. This will be an effect of the growing ubiquity of intelligent networks and artificial intelligence therein. The expanding interconnection of intelligent networks has a significant impact on the genetic mind because of the emergence of a global culture that accompanies the arrival of such technologies.

Tributary Zone

Tributary Zones are catalysts for awakening the Wholeness Navigator within the human instrument for the purpose of helping humanity discover the Grand Portal. They are separated into three distinct categories:

- Superuniverse-Based Tributary Zones
- Galactic-Based Tributary Zones
- Planetary-Based Tributary Zones

The *Superuniverse Tributary Zones* are seven in number and constitute the repository of required knowledge in order to discover the Grand Portal for a life-bearing planetary system within that particular superuniverse. These are the archetypes for all other Tributary Zones—either planetary or galactic.

Galactic Tributary Zones are also seven in number and closely resemble their superuniverse counterparts. They are generally transposed by specialists from the Central Race, and are established near or within the galactic core of a life-bearing galaxy possessing sufficient numbers of intelligent, sentient life.

Galactic Tributary Zones are ultimately transposed to a planetary level as encoded sensory data streams. Generally, this occurs shortly after the planetary system establishes its first phase of the OLIN Technology or global communications network.

Planetary Tributary Zones are a diverse set of artistic and text-based contributions created by members of the species who have sufficiently interacted with the Galactic Tributary Zones in their dream state. In some instances, these may include works from other planetary systems within the same galaxy. Generally, Planetary Tributary Zones are created in the form of books, art, poetry, and motion pictures. They are not encoded sensory data streams, as in the case of the Galactic Tributary Zones, and they are focused on preparation of the species.

Grand Portal

The Grand Portal is the irrefutable scientific discovery of the Wholeness

Navigator and how it lives, and performs its functions, within the human instrument. The Grand Portal is the most profound discovery of a humanoid species because it establishes the species as a member of the galactic community. This discovery usually coincides with the third phase of the OLIN Technology, which ultimately morphs into the Sovereign Integral Network.

The Grand Portal is a lens through which humanity may observe Source Reality and communicate therein. The Grand Portal is the apex discovery of humanity and ushers in profound change to all sectors of the population. It conjoins science, metaphysics, art, and the superuniverse, placing humanity in a position to embrace all dimensions of the multiverse while existing in the third dimension.

OLIN Technology

Intelligent networks are able to operate from a single language with translation interfaces that enable global intercourse. This means language is no longer a barrier to communication. Intelligent networks will introduce a meta-language that translates both real-time written and spoken applications. It will revolutionize the genetic mind's global construct, and facilitate the digitalization of your global economy.

There will be many within the Hierarchy, who will object vehemently to the notion of a global, digital economy, but we will tell you, it will happen regardless of the complaints and registered concerns. Your most powerful banks, computer manufacturers, and software companies will merge to create this momentous technology, and the One Language Intelligent Network (OLIN) will become the standard operating system of all the world's computer-based systems.

This will not occur until the year 2008, so it is some time before you will encounter this globalization of your economy, but all the systems and architecture are already being designed and conceptualized in the minds of some of your brightest engineers and scientists. We assure you, this is not something to be feared, but rather embraced, and not because of the economic values, but because of the way the OLIN technology will facilitate the development of a global culture.

As the OLIN technology evolves, it will increasingly become subject to individual control. In other words, individuals will become inextricably linked into the network's entertainment and educational applications, which will become globalized. No longer will global media companies publish for a geographical market. They will produce content for a global audience and each individual will define what and how it desires to be entertained or educated.

The OLIN technology will "know" the preferences and interests of every individual linked to its network, and by the year 2016, it will be more ubiquitous than telephones in the late twentieth century. Hence, individuals, and producers of content will control the network, and services will be the "slave" or reactionary force of the individual. Thus, the individual will need to define their entertainment and educational desires carefully, or the OLIN technology will deliver content that is undesirable.

We know this sounds obvious and trite, but it is profoundly different than the way entertainment and education are delivered in your world of the pre-OLIN technology. The time capsules that the WingMakers have left behind will act as a template to those who operate outside of the limiting force of the genetic mind, and desire to create content for the OLIN technology even before it exists. The time capsules will show how to do this and demonstrate how to create multi-dimensional content that carries its viewer-participant into new corridors of understanding and illumination.

This is how the genetic mind will fragment and become unable to exert a unified force upon the human instruments of terra-earth. When it is in this condition it will yield to the transformation/mastership model of existence and form a synthesis with it. It will transform itself, and the genetic mind will become the leader of transformation for entities upon terra-earth instead of its barrier force.

Sovereign Integral Network

The Sovereign Integral Network (SIN) already exists, indeed, has always existed. However, there has not been a way for it to connect or interface with your technologies. Terra-earth has created technologies that are largely mechanistic and electrical in nature, and it is just beginning to understand electromagnetic energy fields and holographic technology. Regrettably, when technologies are in their infantile stages of development, they are very often conformed to a military or economic control application. And this is the case with these emerging technologies.

SIN cannot interface with technologies bearing such an application. Not because it is impossible technologically, but because it is undesirable ethically. SIN is actually a sub-atomic network of light-encoded filaments that exist in all dimensions of the multiverse. Think of SIN as an infinite number of threads of light issuing from Source Reality, and, like a web, connecting every life form at its entity level to all other entities and First Source. This is an organic network that is utilized by First Source to transmit knowledge to entities and to receive knowledge from entities.

SIN will eventually be interfaced with OLIN technology, but this will not happen for several hundred years. The interface is too far beyond both your technology and understanding of cosmology, and no planetary system can be fitted to interface with SIN until it is absolutely pure in its content and application. Only First Source makes this decision as to when a planetary system can become a node on SIN. This is the core purpose of WingMakers, to help terra-earth become a node on SIN before its opportunity to interface has passed.

Each entity is a node of SIN, but so few realize this connection exists other than through what they read or hear. The connection is real and timeless, and occurs at the core, innermost aspect of the entity where beats the replica heart of First Source. This is the repository of First Source and exudes ITS Unique vibration like a radio tower sends its signals in all directions.

Even your physicists have found preliminary evidence of SIN in their research with their so-called super string theory. We assure you, however, that this network will eventually replace all other networks for the primary reason that it is the conduit into timelessness. And this is the destination that draws all humanoid species, initially, through a technological portal similar to your Internet, which eventually leads to a biomorphic portal consisting of the encoded light filaments leading to the non-worlds of Source Reality.

When a human species transforms its genetic mind to utilize the Sovereign Integral Network, this then becomes the "ship" upon which it sails the seas of the cosmos. And in this way, the species is allowed to become "Gods" of newly created worlds in which it can re-enact the entire process of the Grand Experiment utilizing its knowledge base and wisdom that was achieved in the previous stage of its existence. On a grand scale, this process is cast in countless worlds across the multiverse, and orchestrating all this wondrous activity of creation is Source Intelligence and SIN.

Source Intelligence

Source Intelligence is the energy-consciousness of First Source that is cast into all worlds, all dimensions, all realities, all life forms, all times and places. Source Intelligence is First Source projected into All That Is. Source Intelligence, in effect, is the "eyes and ears" of First Source, and its role is principally involved in expressing, upholding, and sustaining the will of First Source. On a more personal level, it is a liberating force of energy-intelligence that serves to accelerate the expansion of consciousness and assist those who desire to unlimit themselves.

All That Is

Source Intelligence is the projected intelligence of First Source. Within this consciousness exists the synthesis and distillation of All That Is. It is an infinite library of knowledge and experience that can be tapped into through attunement and creative will. While Source Intelligence is the vehicle of cosmological unity, it also holds the information of All That Is and "circulates" this information and creative empowerment to all entities who are willing to reach for it and utilize it for the expansion of consciousness.

Universe of Wholeness

The Universe of Wholeness is the aggregate of all dimensions and realities. It is unified and inter-connected through Source Intelligence. It is dynamic and always in a state of experimental change and evolution. It is simply too vast and dynamic to comprehend or to establish a measurement of any kind.

Fields of Vibration

The Universe of Wholeness is a vast field of energy that is composed of innumerable dimensions of perception and existence. Within this macro-universe are dimensions of existence that are dominant realms of experience like the third-dimensional reality in which human life is rooted. Each dimension has its unique qualities of experience and these are known as fields of vibration because the vibratory rate of each dimension is the determining factor of its existence. The higher the vibratory rate of a dimension, the more expansive and unlimiting it is.

Within the Universe of Wholeness there are, for all practical purposes, an infinite number of fields of vibration that an entity or Sovereign Integral can attune to and utilize as an experiential or dominant reality.

Source Reality

First Source exists in Source Reality. Source Reality is the dimension of consciousness that is always pushing the envelope of expansion—the leading edge of development and evolution for the whole of consciousness. In this realm of dynamic expansion is always found Source Reality. It can be likened to the inner sanctum of First Source or the incubator of cosmological expansion.

Sovereignty

Sovereignty is a state of completeness and inter-connectedness. It is recognizing that as a human being you have an individuated spirit force that animates your physical, emotional, and mental aspects, and that through this spirit you are complete and connected to all other life forms through the Universal Spirit Consciousness (Source Intelligence). Sovereign beings understand that they alone create their reality and that they are responsible for their life-experience. They also understand that all other life forms are equally sovereign and that they also create their unique realities. Sovereignty allows that the source of liberating information is contained within the Self, and all that is needed to create new realities is also contained within the Self. It is the point of empowerment and connection to all through the frequency of love.

Source Codes

Source Codes are imbedded "activators" that are present within the entity consciousness. They serve the specific purpose of awakening the human instrument to the multidimensionality of the entity and the liberating information that is stored within the entity consciousness. Source Codes are somewhat analogous to the genetic coding of DNA to the extent that Source Codes activate specific blueprints of transformation that accelerate and facilitate the expansion of consciousness. In effect, Source Codes catalyze the awakening of the human instrument and encourage it to make the quantum leap from a socialized human to a sovereign entity that is aware of its connection to All That Is.

Hierarchy

The Hierarchy extends throughout the cosmos to the very borders of discovery. It has branches that extend from every star system, every dimension; and virtually all life forms are "leaves" of this cosmological tree. The Hierarchy constitutes the grand indoctrination of species, spirits, planets, and stars as they each evolve through the branches of the tree. It is an assemblage of externals that desire to invest their energies in support of a sub-group that has nested somewhere within the greatest of all structures: the Hierarchy. Service is the operational motive of the Hierarchy, and in most cases, this translates into the concept of saviorship.

The Hierarchy is composed of entities of all motives that have linked their energies into subgroups. Think of these subgroups as independent branches of a vast, cosmological tree—a structure that encompasses all things outside of Source Reality. The roots of the tree are bound in the soil of genetic memory and subconscious identity. At the base of the tree the first branches sprout and they are the oldest, representing the native religions of the specie. The middle branches are the orthodox religions and institutions, while the upper branches represent the contemporary belief systems that are newly emerging throughout the universe. The whole tree, in this definition, is the Hierarchy, and its purpose is to advance the evolution of life through a superstructure that results in the teacher/student ordering of the universe.

First Source is connected to individuals not organizations. Thus, the Hierarchy is unconnected to the Source in a vital and dynamic way. The Hierarchy is more connected to its own collective desire to help, to serve, to perform a function that allows the use of power in a positive way. In itself, this is not wrong or misguided. It is all part of the Primal Blueprint that orchestrates the unfoldment of consciousness from collective to individual and individual to collective. This is the spiral of integration that breeds wholeness and perfection within the Source Intelligence.

Wholeness Perspective

The human instrument, because it is fragmented and limited to five-senses, truly desires the Wholeness Perspective; a way to absorb life experience, process it, and move on to the next thing with grace and ease. This is what is desired, no matter what name is used to describe it. Wholeness is accepting all realities and moving through them with a feeling of integration, unity, equality, and non-judgment. It means there are no dualities that are real. It means that all experience is equal and grounded in the transcendent reality of the One That Is All. And most importantly, it means that the One That Is All is you, me, him, her, it, that, and those. Nothing is excluded or rejected.

Wholeness Navigator

Theories of evolution are layered upon your existing paradigm of a mechanical universe that consists of molecular machines operating in an objective reality that is knowable with the right instruments. The universe is truly unknowable with any instrument save your own sense of unity and wholeness. The perception of wholeness is forever unfolding in the human instrument because the culture of the multidimensional universe is rooted in unity.

Plants have root systems that penetrate earth and drink of her substance. In this way, all plants are linked. Imagine that each plant had a secret root that was invisible, but was nonetheless connected to the very center of the planet. At this point of convergence, every plant was indeed unified and aware that its real identity was this core system of interconnected roots, and that the secret root was the lifeline through which individual expression was brought to the surface of earth and its unified consciousness released as the fragrance of individuality. In this same way, all existence has a secret root that spirals into the uncharted realm of First Source. This is the field of unity that defines the culture of the multidimensional universe.

All human life is embedded with a Wholeness Navigator. It is the core wisdom. It draws the human instrument to perceive fragmentary existence as a passageway into wholeness and unity. The Wholeness Navigator pursues wholeness above all else, yet it is often blown off course by the energies of structure, polarity, linear time, and separatist cultures that dominate terra-earth. The Wholeness Navigator is the heart of the entity consciousness, and it knows that the secret root exists even though it may be intangible to the human senses. It is this very condition of accepting the interconnectedness of life that places spiritual growth as a priority in one's life.

The five senses of the human body feed only a small part of an individual's wholeness. Yet the human instrument clings to these five senses as though they were the only pathways of experience. The seed vision of the Wholeness Navigator is equal to First Source. It is a replica of First Source vibrating precisely at the same frequency and capable of the same feats of consciousness. And the numberless secret roots that supply First Source with insight, experience, intelligence, and perspective can be accessed, but not through the five senses which are designed for your ego consciousness.

The preceptors of the Wholeness Navigator consist primarily of the secret root. This is the subtle carrier of information that leads you to see the One That Is All and the All That Is One. This is a facet of First Source that is made manifest in the human instrument as a means of attracting the human instrument to the life of the Sovereign Integral consciousness. Let the secret root and the Wholeness Navigator guide you, and let the five senses be expressionary tools of the entity, rather than collectors of separatist thought for the human instrument.

How do you access the secret root? Its portal of observation can be broadly defined as the integral awareness. This is allowing yourself to be aware of how you are integrated to life outside of your physical body. It is the feeling and perception that you are a holographic entity that is woven throughout all things and time, and when you touch into this feeling, you recall a frequency of your consciousness that is the Wholeness Navigator—the mysterious Allness that is nurtured by the secret root.

This is not a state of being that the human instrument will attain. Rather, it is a feeling of oneness and wholeness that the human instrument can glimpse momentarily and, as a result, transform its understanding of its purpose. The Wholeness Navigator pulls the human instrument into alignment with the entity consciousness where it can view its role as an extension of the entity consciousness into terra-earth, and the entity consciousness as an extension of the human instrument into Source Reality.

Evolution and the Concept of Time

When an individual evolves in consciousness it is quite different from the evolutionary process in terms of the physical body. For example, an individual can make a quantum leap in consciousness within a single moment in time, while in contrast, the physical body is gradually shaped over thousands of years. Thus, the entity transforms through a process of remembrance, while the human instrument—particularly the physical body—evolves through experience in vast stretches of linear time.

The individuated consciousness of the entity is the fragment of First Source that is seeking to be remembered within the human instrument. It lives in an eternal state of nowness and represents the continuity of time and consciousness across all dimensions of reality. In other words, all dimensions of time are simultaneously experienced by the entity consciousness, however, upon terra-earth, the human instrument is usually only conscious of one dimension of time, typically calibrated in linear seconds.

This is why time plays such a significant role in the evolution of three- and four-dimensional structures like the human instrument, but has very little influence on the transformation of consciousness itself. The human instrument is grounded in a physical body that is constantly being shaped by experience, emotion, and thought, all of which is self-created. On the other hand, the entity consciousness is the multidimensional Self. It is the union of all the different aspects of consciousness that are invested within the time/space universes through instruments of contact; be they human or otherwise.

The entity may simultaneously inhabit a thousand human instruments spread across two-hundred thousand years of linear time. To the human instrument of a specific time period, it will seem to be the one and only existence, but to the entity, all its lives are occurring in nowness. The entity consciousness is the "hub" around which its various human instruments connect in to like spokes of a wheel. And the outer rim of the wheel is represented as circular time within the dimensions of planetary life.

All the "spokes", or time-based lives, are linked together at the entity consciousness where they converge into non-time. From the entity consciousness, through the portal of the Wholeness Navigator, this same experience is transmitted to First Source, processed by Source Intelligence, and returned to the entity consciousness as a form of energy that enlarges the entity's perspective on matters of destiny, existence, and purpose. It is virtually impossible to express this interrelationship between First Source, Source Intelligence, the entity, the human instrument, and time. Time makes it possible to segment this knowledge into fragments that can be shared between individual human instruments.

The human instrument is a composite of mental, emotional, and physical capabilities linked together to form a vehicle for the entity consciousness to experience planetary life. The human instrument evolves to better fit the needs of the entity. The entity transforms from a pure vibratory, individualized expression of First Source, to a Sovereign Integral who has created its own experiential reality, and re-defined itself by the planetary experiences therein.

Eternity, while it may seem to exclude time, is nonetheless a form of absolute time that is not isolated into a sovereign reality, but instead, integrated in all realities like a thread of light that draws the disparate realities into union. In this dimension of union—where the entity consciousness is whole and all realities converge—time is articulated not by the linear progression of seconds, but rather, by the expansion of the vibration of equality or love. Thus, in eternity, time is simply re-defined by a new value system upon which entities establish and recognize their growth.

Models of Existence

There are two dominant models of existence that shape the interaction and destiny of the human race. These models of existence are:

- The Evolution/Saviorship model
- The Transformation/Mastership model

Each human is developing their belief system from one or both of these models of existence. The evolution/saviorship model is the dominant model that is promulgated by the Hierarchy. Its basic tenets are that life evolves through the Hierarchy's teacher/student methodology, and that various teachers (saviors) are presented to the human race that enables sub-hierarchies to develop and control information. In so doing, individuals are disempowered and disconnected from their sovereignty. The underlying equation of the evolution/saviorship model of existence is:

Human Instrument + Hierarchy = God connection through saviorship.

In the case of the transformation/mastership model of existence, its principle tenets are that the entity is limitless, deathless, and sovereign. All information flows from Source Intelligence to the entity, and, it is therefore the responsibility of the entity to become self-enlightened and self-liberated by attuning itself to Source Intelligence and "detuning" itself from the Hierarchy. Each becomes their own master, and each transforms from a human being to a Sovereign Integral within the cradle of time and space. The underlying equation of the transformation/mastership model of existence is:

Entity + Source Intelligence = First Source equality.

One of the challenges of the individual is to recognize these two dominant models of existence and integrate them in order to design a synthesis model. The synthesis model is slowly emerging on terra-earth, and with high probability, will ultimately become the dominant model of existence in this universe. It will be the model of existence that is best able to unify consciousness without impinging on the sovereignty of the entity and First Source. It will allow the entity to be the vibrant container of Source Intelligence and explore new fields of vibration as a fully conscious outpost of First Source.

SECTION SIX

First Source Transmissions

First Source is all of us. It is the Collective Us. It is not a God living in some distant pocket of the universe.

Collected Works of the WingMakers Vol. II, Part IV, Sec. One, Project Camelot Interview with James

Introduction to the First Source Transmissions

The First Source Transmissions are captivating, inspiring, and potentially consciousness expanding. There are three transmissions:

1. My Central Message
2. My Central Purpose
3. My Central Revelation

Each of these transmissions offers a brief glimpse into the Mind and Heart of First Source. Their messages offer a renewed vision of the nature of God, the multiverse, its ultimate purpose, and our place in this grand scheme.

My Central Message—*There is nowhere you can be without me. My absence does not exist.*

My Central Message opens with: *"I convey this message to you whom I have stirred with the sound of my voice." "It is my voice that awakened you."* [136] Once again, the power of sound is brought to our attention, thus reinforcing the comments made in the section on music. It appears that First Source not only created us through sound, but that the sound of his voice also awakens us from the sleep consciousness of the Human Instrument.

Next we find this: *"I dwell in a frequency of light in which finite beings cannot uncover me."* [137] We then learn that the key to "finding" First Source is not through any particular location, but through the qualities of "oneness, unity, and wholeness." Recall that these qualities characterize that part of our individuated consciousness known as the Wholeness Navigator.

Because the Wholeness Navigator represents the essence of the Entity, especially in his earlier writings and in the first two Lyricus discourses, James emphasizes the Wholeness Navigator. Realizing life in terms of Oneness, Unity, and Wholeness decentralizes our ego-based sense of separate selfhood, and establishes the core essence of the Entity in our daily lives, which is the unifying nature of the Sovereign Integral. We are then in a state of First Source realization—in Its Light. This perhaps is what we loosely refer to as enlightenment, for we have found God through the Light of Unity.

Now this doesn't mean that we are able to sustain such a state all the time, for this attainment is most often a gradual process, until that moment of what the Zen Buddhists refer to as Satori, and Western experiencers call cosmic consciousness.

The proposition that we can be awakened and even enlightened by sound opens the possibility that the great composers of the past might very well have tapped into the spiritual sound of First Source, and consequently opened a portal from which the power of God's awakening could enter our awareness. Along this same vein, the music produced and encoded by James might also have the same effect on our psyches.

---

136. "My Central Message," p. 684.
137. Ibid. p.684

A philosophical question asked by all of us is why are we here. What is the meaning of our lives? This first message answers this question in the following way:

> I could awaken each of you in this very moment to our unity, but there is a larger design—a more comprehensive vision—that places you in the boundaries of time and the spatial dimensions of separateness. This design requires a progression into my wholeness that reacquaints you with our unity through the experience of separation. Your awakening, while slow and sometimes painful, is assured, and this you must trust above all else.[138]

As discussed earlier, one of the themes of the WingMakers philosophy is that we are born into Human Instruments that are inherently designed to be separate by nature. Although this seems counterintuitive to most traditional spiritual paths, the concept here is that the sense of separateness we experience is meant to generate a driving force in us to improve our living conditions and allow for more time to improve the qualities of our personal lives. For the most part, when people's survival needs are established and individuals feel secure in the basics of living, they take the opportunity to improve the quality of their lives through self-improvement books and programs, and the pursuit of lifestyles geared toward the health of body, mind, and spirit. It should be pointed out, that these lifestyle shifts do not necessarily exclude religion, for they can expand the depth of religious practice and experience.

The main point is that despite the vicissitudes of life, the desire to seek our creator is present in us all the time, but the nature of the worlds of space-time are designed to reinforce our separation from First Source through the fundamental need to survive the challenges of a physical environment. As discussed earlier, as civilization progresses and the basics of life are secured, it is far easier to begin a journey that seeks meaning and oneness.

In other words, even though we seek First Source, we are held back in the full immersion of our consciousness in It so that we can co-create the space-time portion of the multiverse. If we were able to live our lives in total communion with First Source, we would likely want to escape the suffering of human existence and not fulfill the Plan of First Source's purpose of existence.

This transmission closes with the following:

> I am a personality that lives inside each of you as a vibration that emanates from all parts of your existence. I reside in this dimension as your beacon. If you follow this vibration, if you place it at the core of your journey, you will contact my personality that lives beneath the particles of your existence.
>
> You must suspend your belief and disbelief in what you cannot sense, in exchange for your knowing that I am real and live within

---

138. Ibid. pp. 684-685.

you. This is my central message to all my offspring. Hear it well, for
in it you may find the place in which I dwell.[139]

First Source thus provides a pathway of exit from this seeming separation when we
are ready for such a shift. Naturally, there are various factors that determine this point of
realization, and at least one factor is often the result of some personal crisis in one's life.

One cautionary note however, before we move to the next transmission: There
is a danger of being so overwhelmed by the experience that one's life becomes
unbalanced. There are anecdotal stories of people who have had some kind of
mystical experience, as a result of which, they abandoned their families and careers,
and withdrew from the world. This is a complicated psychological area far too
complex to go into detail here, but it is a subject worthy of consideration.

> Contact with Source Intelligence is a transformative experience
> and can have the unintended consequence of unbalancing an
> individual who is not properly prepared for the transmission.
> Stepping down the vibration of sound and light, and making it more
> accessible to students is what Lyricus is primarily concerned with.
> Lyricus does not recommend that anyone become dependent on
> any external teacher or material. To do so, implies stagnancy and
> devolution relative to one's potential learning path.[140]

My Central Purpose—*Without you I am unable to evolve. Without me, you
are unable to exist.*

This transmission opens by establishing a foundational concept that the ultimate
goal of our existence is not to achieve nirvana and withdrawing from the world into
a state of bliss, but rather that "[t]here is a purpose of transcendent service concealed
beyond the horizon of the present universe age."[141]

This is followed with a statement reinforcing the subject of separation, but at the same
time stating that the universe is a school for gaining experience through exploration.

> If I designed you to take you on an eternal excursion into nirvana,
> I certainly would not construct your entire universe into one vast and
> intricate training school, requisition a substantial branch of my creation as
> teachers and instructors, and then spend ages upon ages piloting you, one
> by one, through this enormous universe school of experiential learning.[142]

Combining these two quotations, we find that we are not here to simply find
nirvana and escape the physical world of suffering, but that we are meant to follow
the blueprint of exploration, and that, in this process, we are serving a divine
purpose as yet concealed.

---

139. Ibid., p. 685.
140. *Collected Works of the WingMakers Vol. II*, Part IV, Sec. Two, Top. Arr. of Qs and As, Ques. 65-S3
141. "My Central Purpose," p.686.
142. Ibid. p. 686.

We are next confronted with some cosmology. First Source's purpose is to "merge the human species with other species from *different universes*." [143] [My emphasis.] Although physics has theories positing other universes in other dimensions, the concept of other physical universes beyond ours is quite an exotic idea.

As we read further, we find that there are six other universes in addition to ours and that the ultimate goal of First Source is to bring all seven species inhabiting these universes to convergence. What this means in practical terms is completely unclear because this convergence of species will take place in the distant future.

The other interesting point is that the current existence of these seven universes does not allow First Source full functionality; thus the statement in the heading that without the seven species First Source is "unable to evolve" any further. [144] This statement brings to mind the fairly well-known saying of Hermes "As above, so below." So, the process of evolution is not only a species-wide reality, but the same evolutionary process applies to First Source as well! Even though First Source is perfect from our standpoint, this perfection is relative to an ongoing series of universe creations. I posit this idea based on the phrase "present universe age," which is at the beginning of this transmission. [145] This phrase strongly suggests that the universes are undergoing evolutionary development through stages, or ages. This brings to light the ancient Hindu concept of universe ages denoted as yugas, and the cyclic death and rebirth of the universe at the end of the four-phase yuga cycle. Each death and subsequent rebirth is considered a day in the life of Brahma, the physically manifesting of God.

The transmission nears its end by describing the partnership we have with First Source: "We are the image of an ascending, infinite, expanding spiral that is created segment by segment by itself." [146]

My Central Revelation—*Live in the knowledge that you are in me and I am in you, and that there is no place separate from our heart.*

This transmission opens by reiterating that our separation from First Source is intrinsic to the plan of the current universe age. This separation is not only psychological, but also physical. First Source tells us that It lives in the central universe, which is so distant that we cannot even fathom it. Paradoxically, "*a fragment of myself is set within your personality like a diamond upon a ring.*" [147] Again we are faced with the dilemma of our simultaneous separation from First Source and the presence of First Source within us. This message goes on to say:

> I would prefer to be known to you at all times and places, but if
> I did this then the evolutionary journey of my creation would break

143. Ibid. p. 686.
144. Ibid. p. 686.
145. Ibid. p. 686.
146. Ibid. p. 686.
147. "My Central Revelation," p. 687.

down, and the teacher-student ordering of my system of ascendancy would falter.[148]

In a peculiar way, First Source is revealing that It sacrificed intimacy with us— Its creation—in order to establish a universal system of "teacher-student ordering of evolution." This is a clue to the question of how we are supposed to find and express the qualities of First Source if we are inherently separate from our creator.

The answer lies in the following quotation:

> I have cast myself into numberless orders of beings that collectively constitute the evolutionary bridge of your ascendancy into my realm.[149]

This passage makes clear that our ascendancy into the realm of First Source is mediated by a myriad order of beings. Presently the WingMakers material offers no definitive information about these other beings except for the WingMakers or Central Race. One of these other orders is most likely the *Lyricus Teaching Order*.

As already discussed the primary function of Lyricus is to guide human beings to the Grand Portal discovery. This is described as such a major step in our spiritual evolution, along with a complete restructuring of our civilization, that it is reasonable to assume this will bring us closer to First Source. In fact, as the various written materials show, our efforts to follow the instructional guidance offered by James, based on his knowledge and experience as a Lyricus teacher, we can bridge our separation from First Source. Hence, the presence of a more advanced order of teachers in our world constitutes an "evolutionary bridge" to First Source—possibly one of many in our future. This notion is reinforced by these passages:

> I have formed these words with the help of my inmost creation, known to you, through these teachings, as the Central Race.[150]
> Lyricus is aligned with the Central Race or WingMakers, and the great majority of its members are from the Central Race.[151]

So now we know who is providing these messages from First Source. The question at this point is: How will our re-connection to First Source be demonstrated in our personal lives? This answer is provided in the first transmission, My Central Message:

> There is no supplication that stirs me. No prayer that invites me further into your world unless it is attended with the feeling of unity and wholeness. There is no temple or sacred object that touches me. They do not, nor have they ever brought you closer to my outstretched hand. My presence in your world is unalterable for

---

148. Ibid. p. 687.
149. Ibid. p. 687
150. Ibid. p. 687.
151. *Collected Works of the WingMakers Vol. II*, Part II, Sec. One, Lyricus Teachers and Methodologies Ques. 4

> I am the sanctuary of both the cosmos and the one soul inside you.[152]
>
> Worship of me in coin or moral consideration is unnecessary. Simply express your authentic feelings of appreciation to my inmost presence within you and others, and you broadcast your worship unfailingly into my realm.[153]

Consequently we don't necessarily have to attend places of worship nor pray to sacred objects to re-connect to First Source. Our prayers and supplications are ineffective as long as we pray as separate individuals with no sense of oneness with All That Is. A heartfelt sense of Oneness, Wholeness, and appreciation, with its underlying feeling of gratitude, are the watchwords of our re-connection and transmission of the spirit of First Source to our families, friends, co-workers, and the whole human race.

---

152. "My Central Message," p. 684.
153. "My Central Revelation," p. 688.

My Central Message

I convey this message to you whom I have stirred with the sound of my voice. These words are my signature. You may bring your doubt, your fear, your faith, or your courage; it matters not, for you will be touched by the rhythm of my voice. It moves through you like a beam of light that sweeps—if only for a moment—the darkness aside.

I dwell in a frequency of light in which finite beings cannot uncover me. If you search for me, you will fail. I am not found or discovered. I am only realized in oneness, unity, and wholeness. It is the very same oneness that you feel when you are interconnected with all of life, for I am this and this alone. I am *all of life*. If you must search for me, then practice the feeling of wholeness and unity.

In my deepest light I created you from my desire to understand my universe. You are my emissaries. You are free to journey the universe of universes as particles from my infinite womb with destinies that you alone will write. I do not prescribe your journey or your journey's aim. I only accompany you. I do not pull you this way or that, nor do I punish you when you stray from my heart. This I do as an outcome of my belief in you.

You are the heirs of my light, which gave you form. It is my voice that awakened you to individuality, but it will be your will that awakens you to our unity. It is your desire to know me as your self that brings you to my presence so perfectly hidden from your world. I am behind everything that you see, hear, touch, taste, smell, feel, and believe.

I live for your discovery of me. It is the highest expression of my love for you, and while you search for my shadows in the stories of your world, I, the indelible, invisible light, grow increasingly visible. Imagine the furthest point in space— beneath a black portal, cast in some distant galaxy, and then multiply this distance by the highest numeric value you know. Congratulations, you have measured an atom of my body.

Do you realize how I am unfathomable? I am not what you can know or see or understand. I am outside comprehension. My vastness makes me invisible and unavoidable. There is nowhere you can be without me. My absence does not exist. It is this very nature that makes me unique. I am First Cause and Last Effect connected in an undivided chain.

There is no supplication that stirs me. No prayer that invites me further into your world unless it is attended with the feeling of unity and wholeness. There is no temple or sacred object that touches me. They do not, nor have they ever brought you closer to my outstretched hand. My presence in your world is unalterable for I am the sanctuary of both the cosmos and the one soul inside you.

I could awaken each of you in this very moment to our unity, but there is a larger design—a more comprehensive vision—that places you in the boundaries of time and the spatial dimensions of separateness. This design requires a progression into my wholeness that reacquaints you with our unity through the experience of separation. Your awakening, while slow and sometimes painful, is assured, and this you must trust above all else.

I am the ancestral father of all creation. I am a personality that lives inside each of you as a vibration that emanates from all parts of your existence. I reside in this dimension as your beacon. If you follow this vibration, if you place it at the core of your journey, you will contact my personality that lives beneath the particles of your existence.

I am not to be feared or held in indifference. My presence is immediate, tangible, and real. You are now in my presence. Hear my words. You are in my presence. You are within me more than I am within you. You are the veneer of my mind and heart, and yet you think yourself the product of an ape. You are so much more than you realize.

Our union was, is, and will be forevermore. You are my blessed offspring with whom I am intricately connected in means that you cannot understand and therefore appreciate. You must suspend your belief and disbelief in what you cannot sense, in exchange for your knowing that I am real and live within you. This is my central message to all my offspring. Hear it well, for in it you may find the place in which I dwell.

Excerpt from Chamber Twenty-three—One of three written elements from the body of work known as the WingMakers, ascribed to First Source.

My Central Purpose

The blueprint of exploration has an overarching intention; you are not the recipients of divine labor and meticulous training only to ensure that you may enjoy endless bliss and eternal ease. There is a purpose of transcendent service concealed beyond the horizon of the present universe age. If I designed you to take you on an eternal excursion into nirvana, I certainly would not construct your entire universe into one vast and intricate training school, requisition a substantial branch of my creation as teachers and instructors, and then spend ages upon ages piloting you, one by one, through this enormous universe school of experiential learning. The furtherance of the system of human progression is cultivated by my will for the explicit purpose to merge the human species with other species from different universes.

As it is my nature to be seven-fold, there are seven universes that comprise my body. Within each of these, a species of a particular DNA template is cast forth and is nurtured by Source Intelligence to explore its material universe. Each of these species is sent forth from the Central Race into the universe that was created to unveil its potential and seed vision. Your species will converge with six other species in a distant future that will reunite my body as the living extension of known creation. While this may seem so distant as to have no relevance to your time, it is vital for you to understand the scope of your purpose. You can think of these seven species as the limbs of my body rejoined to enable me/us total functionality within the grand universe. This is my purpose and therefore your own as well.

Your freewill is not taken from you; it is merely united with my/our own. In the deepest chamber of my existence issues the will to expand, explore, unite, synthesize, and in so doing, reveal yet another layer of my/our purpose. What is this purpose you ask? It is not expressible in a language that you can now understand, but it is related to the concepts of universe discovery and self-evolution. It is the expansion and synthesis of cosmic experience.

The ascendant beings of time are converging to my central abode. All are drawn to me for the purpose of my/our will to be expressed throughout the grand universe in order to cast another grand universe, and to deepen the skin of my/our personality. This is the hidden purpose of my/our will: to create new worlds of experience that stimulate our continuing evolution.

Without you I am unable to evolve. Without me, you are unable to exist. This is our eternal bond. It was and is my desire to evolve that gave you existence. We, collectively, are the conjoint vessel of creation and exploration. We are the boldness of the uncharted journey and the imaginative energy of the out-picturing of new realities. We are the image of an ascending, infinite, expanding spiral that is created segment by segment by itself. We are inseparable—each the window of the other. My blessings to you who find these words and listen in the clearness of your personality.

Excerpt from Chamber Twenty-Two—One of three written elements from the body of work known as the WingMakers, ascribed to First Source.

My Central Revelation

You evolve inwards, ever in the direction of my creator soul. This is the province of myself that does not indwell you, but indeed is separate from you as the stars are isolated from a deep cave. This place is the source and destiny of your existence, and from it, you descend into the cave of your animal-origins where my voice falls silent to your choices.

My plan for your ascendance embraces every creature in all dimensions of all worlds. I do this by divesting myself of every function that is possible for another of my creation to carry out. That which I create is given the power to perform my role, thus I am hidden from your view because you have come to believe that I am that which I have created.

I am First Source, and your knowing of me is a thousand times removed. I dwell in the Central Universe so distant from you as to make space an unfathomable abstraction, and yet, a fragment of my self is set within your personality like a diamond upon a ring, and it will endure as certainly as I will endure. While there are those who believe I am a myth, I express to you that my world is the beacon of all personalities in all times, and whether you believe in me or not, you are unerringly drawn to the source from whence you were created.

I would prefer to be known to you at all times and places, but if I did this then the evolutionary journey of my creation would break down, and the teacher-student ordering of my system of ascendancy would falter. I have cast myself into numberless orders of beings that collectively constitute the evolutionary bridge of your ascendancy into my realm. There is no step of your journey that another has not already taken on behalf of those who follow.

I have formed these words with the help of my inmost creation, known to you, through these teachings, as the Central Race. Their record is placed upon your planet to catalyze—within those of your kind who are ready—an awakening of me as I truly am. This record will last for many generations, sometimes hidden from view, sometimes abstracted into symbols, sometimes collected into doubt, but always it will be my voice revealed upon your planet.

While it is not the first time I have spoken to your planet's people, it is the first time I have spoken through my inmost creation and left an indelible, multi-dimensional record. On the surface of this record is a mythology of the Central Race, but if you find my voice within this mythology, you will see another facet to this record, of a personal inflection, that speaks directly to you, my child. It is this intimacy that I have encoded into this record that is symbolic of my hand reaching for yours, and it is this intimacy that will persist within your mind and heart when all else fails you.

My voice will help you reconnect with me. It will enlarge your vision of my domain, purpose, and my unyielding love for each of my creation, no matter where or how you live. When I have spoken before to your planet, it was through a prism of personalities that bent my voice and colored its tone. My mind's voice will not travel to your world unless it is transmitted through my creation and translated into word-symbols your mind can grasp. My heart's voice penetrates all worlds without translation as a sub-photonic light and inter-dimensional vibration that produces sound.

I am revealed to you in hopes that you will reveal to others what you have found in me. Not by sanctimonious words, but rather, by redefining our relationship and living in accordance with this new clarity. In so doing you will release what I have long ago stored within you—a fragment of myself, a dagger of light that renders your self-importance a decisive death.

Truly, this is my central revelation. I am here, beneath this mythology, to awaken your animal self to our relationship so you may slay your vanity. This is the distortion between us. It is not space or time that separates us and diminishes our conscious relationship. It is your desire to excel within the cave of your existence and derive gratification from this and this alone.

I will leave to others to define the psychological wisdom and common sense behaviors of success. My words penetrate elsewhere; to a place within you that is susceptible, innocent, faithful, and ever listening for a tonal hint of my presence. When it is found, this part of you—like an instrument entrained by a powerful resonance—will vibrate in accordance to my voice.

All of your religions teach the worship of a deity and a doctrine of human salvation. It is the underlying kinship of your planet's religions. However, I am not the deity that your worship falls upon, nor am I the creator of your doctrines of human salvation. Worship of me in coin or moral consideration is unnecessary. Simply express your authentic feelings of appreciation to my inmost presence within you and others, and you broadcast your worship unfailingly into my realm.

This is the feeling that you should seek to preserve in the face of life's distractions. This is the revelation of my heart to your heart. Live in clarity. Live in purpose. Live in the knowledge that you are in me and I am in you, and that there is no place separate from our heart.

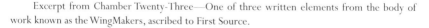

Excerpt from Chamber Twenty-Three—One of three written elements from the body of work known as the WingMakers, ascribed to First Source.

INTERLUDE

Vision of Mantustia

He is a master's master of the most esoteric order within
Lyricus who develops discourses, instructional methodologies, and
experiential learning environments within the human genome.

Collected Works of the WingMakers Vol. II,
Part IV, Sec. Two, Top. Arr. of Qs and As, Ques. 28B-S3

Introduction to the Vision of Mantustia

"Vision of Mantustia" is a document contained on the First Source CD-ROM. It is written in the style of the First Source Transmissions, but the author is Mantustia, a Divine Counselor. No information is given about Divine Counselors and their place in the multiverse scheme of things. But, the document does inform us that he or she (assuming gender even applies in this case) resides "within the abode of the WingMakers." According to what we know about the WingMakers or Central Race, is that they exist in proximity to the central universe.

Although there is little room for speculation regarding the details of this being's existence, I have extracted some points of interest.

> I am an entity of wholeness, consisting of white light that is blended in the radiance of eternity and divested like fragments of brilliance throughout the multiverse in various forms and bodies.
>
> I am the perfection of my Creator, individuated as a single point of pure energy, yet living in many places on many dimensions simultaneously.[154]
>
> I embody all that is beautiful and true, and my vision is the navigator of my sovereignty, casting its incarnation in all places and times where my form exists as an extension of my being.[155]

One item we can take from the above passages is that Mantustia incarnates in forms existing in many places and dimensions at once. Adding to this point is that Mantustia is "encoded upon terra-earth now." His purpose is to "create new instruments of expression," which will be used for "the evolution of the human species and the planets upon which they live." [156]

The out-worn, non-functioning, and corrupted hierarchies of our world (and others) will be "restructured" in alignment with the "tone-vibration of equality," which is the frequency emitted by Mantustia.[157] The truth of the tone of equality is woven into the planetary human populations of the universe. It should be noted here that the tone vibration of equality emanating from Mantustia originates in First Source. Accordingly, this vibration of equality is built into the Entity consciousness and is expressed in space-time by the Sovereign Integral working through the Human Instrument. (More about this tone vibration of equality, sometime shortened to tone of equality, can be found within the First Source entry of the WingMakers glossary and in the Chamber One and Two philosophy papers. Also, see supplementary glossary in the appendices.)

In addition, the vision of Mantustia involves rearrangement, reformation, and expanding clarity.[158] This may have to do with the Era of Transparency and Expansion

---

154. "Vision of Mantustia," p. 692.
155. Ibid., p. 693.
156. Ibid., p. 692.
157. Ibid., p. 692.
158. Ibid., p. 692-693.

that James says our planet entered in 1998.[159] This era not only encompasses the physical world, but includes other dimensions as well.

There is one more interesting bit of information regarding Mantustia, however. It comes in the form of an answer from a question about Mantustia's identity.

> When I first read Vision of Mantustia I thought that this Being might be Sanat Kumara. Is Mantustia Sanat Kumara and if not who is Mantustia?
>
> > Answer: Mantustia is an ascended master who is a remarkable entity of planetary significance to earth, however, it is not Sanat Kumara. Within the Lyricus teaching order there are distinctions between personalities based on the teaching method employed by the personality.
> >
> > There is a wide range of methodologies that can be employed, and there are certain teachers who have found methods to synthesize these methods in such a way that they can cause revelatory experience in their students through a simple exchange of language. Mantustia has developed many of the most famous discourses of Lyricus. He is a master's master of the most esoteric order within Lyricus that develops discourses, instructional methodologies, and experiential learning environments within the human genome. You will be able to recognize his voice as it has an uncanny ability to integrate paradox with truth in an authoritative undertone. If heard in its pure, native language, Mantustia's voice and wisdom borders on the incomparable.[160]

The reference to Sanat Kumara is based in Theosophical literature, which posits that Sanat Kumara is a cosmic being who ensouls our planet. Such a being is called a Planetary Logos. More to the answer itself, we learn that Mantustia is a master of masters within Lyricus. This strongly suggests that the Lyricus Teaching Order is a vast and complex organization spanning the multiverse and filled with teachers of many grades of consciousness. In fact, James states as much in the Lyricus category in the Topical Arrangement of Qs and As. And now, on to the "Vision of Mantustia."

---

159. *Collected Works of the WingMakers Vol. II*, Part IV, Sec. One, Project Camelot Interview with James
160. *Collected Works of the WingMakers Vol. II*, Part IV, Sec. Two, Top. Arr. of Qs and As, Ques. 28B-S3

Vision of Mantustia

I am known as Mantustia of the Divine Counselors, dwelling within the abode of the WingMakers. I reveal my vision willingly and with the full knowledge that it will touch the minds and hearts of those it is intended. As the words are formed they are bearing on you—their reader—even as you stir in worlds unimaginably distant.

I am manifesting and living my sovereign vision. It is a reality guided solely by Source Intelligence as a form of structural harmony that creates the highest possibilities of life's expression through my forms. In collaboration with Source Intelligence I create my own reality, and my full attention is centered on my reality and its expression as a divine force of Light and Love.

I am an entity of wholeness, consisting of white light that is blended in the radiance of eternity and divested like fragments of brilliance throughout the multiverse in various forms and bodies. I live beyond the reach of limitation and I am thus able to transcend all elements that confine, constrict, diminish, limit, or attempt to hold in bondage the powerful light of my purpose. I am an unstoppable divine force that generates all that is needed in all my life forms of expression.

I am the perfection of my Creator, individuated as a single point of pure energy, yet living in many places on many dimensions simultaneously—fully aware of all aspects of my wholeness. Like a loving father I shepherd the fragments of my wholeness to the glory of our common origin and destiny.

My primary purpose while encoded upon terra-earth is to create new instruments of expression and utilize them for the evolution of the human species and the planets upon which they live. I am here to reveal my wholeness and vastness in its fullest expression and engage my vision in all that I do.

I have woven my light with the planets to demonstrate and teach the truth of equality. That individuated spirits are equal to First Source. That everything that stands between the individual and the Source is a part of a hierarchy of interdependence whose purpose shall be restructured. I am guided by the tone-vibration of equality in its purest meaning. This is the frequency I emit.

The fundamental choice of my vision is to honor and reveal my total selfhood, and to transform any limitations that interfere with this choice into the limitlessness of Divine Light. I am completely dedicated to the fulfillment of my purpose and fundamental choice, and openly acknowledge that there is no force that can prevent my vision or the purpose of my spirit from manifesting and having its intended impact upon the multiverse of the One Light-Source.

I am Mantustia, living beyond the beyond of your knowing, demonstrating that there are no imperfections. My vision is the breath of my wholeness, and with each new breath I take in, I exhale a new vision of myself that flows through my wholeness like a powerful wave that engulfs a shoreline of sand.

This is the wave of rearrangement.

Of reformation.

Of expanding clarity.

It creates the ark of transformation that my formless Self can enter and commune with my various outposts of form. The vision I breathe is saturating my wholeness. It is the victory of Spirit's persistence to honor itself in joyful living where ever it may be.

I am the vision of totality and the union of all that I am. I am the centerpoint at which all of my expressions converge, re-conceptualize, and re-emerge as emissaries of my highest purpose. I am Mantustia, the communicator of Source Intelligence's yearning to express itself in the optimal form. I am the prism of Spirit's Light that channels a specific frequency to specific entities for specific reasons at specific times.

These frequencies flow through my bodies into the dimensions of form and duality, always for the purpose of uplifting, and always in harmony to the leading impulse of Source Intelligence. That which issues through me is trailed by a swell of gratitude that is unending and beyond recall. It follows in the wake of beauty and the impressions of truth with a loyalty that is found only in those who have discovered their total selfhood through the eyes of the universe, and have embraced it in fearless triumph, and then relinquished it for the service of First Source.

I am Mantustia, my vision is destined to manifest in all places that I am, for it is sovereign perfection forever linked to the spiral of infinite ascension. It has not been conceived by my outer garments, but rather by my flesh and blood— that vitality of Source Intelligence that is perfect in every way. Every cell in every body is fully attuned to the song of my vision as it weaves its melody through the structure of atoms, and beyond, through the intricate systems of light that connect my fragments to the whole of me.

My vision is alive and lives outside the reach of death, dysfunction or disease. It is my perception of who I am when I have stripped all the layers of disguise and stand naked in my brilliance. It is the heartbeat of my purest essence calling me home with the unmistakable innocence of Divine Love. It is the elixir of my soul. The magnet of my heart.

I am the sovereign master of my reality and the shepherd of my wholeness. I embody all that is beautiful and true, and my vision is the navigator of my sovereignty, castings its incarnation in all places and times where my form exists as an extension of my being. I am the entity that is whole. I am the entity that created itself through the eternal vision that I AM. This is the vision that descends into form and enfolds time, space, matter and energy like an eagle enfolds its nestlings with wings of assurance.

The expansion of my vision is unending. Its destination formed not by my words or desires, but by its core structure. This structure I give to you. It will carry you in its design of simple, fundamental choice and openness.

AFTERWORD

W e have covered a lot of topics in volume I of the collected works—a mixture of myth and reality, fiction and truth. Granted, the reality sections are challenging to the current mainstream view of the world and universe we inhabit, what we can identify as the "establishment" view of science and religion. For those of you who have traveled this far through this fascinating collection of ideas, this WingMakers multiverse, the combined myth and reality may not seem to be that far from the vision of your world, however vague and abstract, nebulous and idealistic those ideas may be. What we can say that it is a vision. Not so much a psychic vision, but one more akin to the vision of the Sovereign Integral, the Greater Self.

This vision is spaceless and timeless, it is eternal and therefore resides and emanates from First Source, a fragment of which exists within each and every one of us. And this fragment is expressed through the Sovereign Integral.

We might conclude in this afterword that the materials contained here in volume I (including everything beyond the written works) are designed to restore the vision of the WingMakers—to any and all entities who are ready to awaken to it. These materials have the power to call forth the eternal vision of First Source in humanity. It is a vision of equality, oneness, and wholeness. For it is a Vision is of the Spirit. It does not matter whether the scale of the vision is that of a two-year old child building with blocks or an architect designing a complex city-center; both Visions are that of Spirit.

For a Vision to complete its circle of fulfillment it requires a plan. This is the role played by the Lyricus Teaching Order (though this task is not exclusively the LTO's). The LTO's scale is cosmic and apparently ancient, older than our planet. The information in Part Two of volume II can be thought of as the basic plan that implements the Vision of the WingMakers.

As James relates in his writings, the disclosure of the LTO was brought forward by him to point to the fact that the Ancient Arrow Project is a work of fiction, a modern myth containing truths that reveal layers of power and control hidden beneath the skin of the world's social structure.

At this point in history, we know almost nothing about this Plan and its details, but from the tentative estimate given by James, the Grand Portal will be discovered in 2080, so from this scanty information, alone, further details of the LTO's Plan for implementing the Vision will be released as this century proceeds.

Plan is of the Mind. And even though planning is exceedingly important for any project to be successfully achieved, this is not the place to go into that aspect. It is enough for this afterword to know that there is a Vision of Spirit, a Plan for humanity's unfettered spiritual and physical evolution in the multiverse.

The second volume of the collected works is all about the initial stages of implementing the Plan. We have already mentioned the importance of Spirit and Mind in this process. Part Three of volume II is all about the primary resource that every human being possesses for setting the Plan in motion, it is—human heart.

Summing up this part of the afterword, we have the universal Vision of Spirit, and the Plan of the Mind. The articles in volume II initiate this third stage—the Implementation through the Sovereign Integral and Human Instrument. The Sovereign Integral then becomes the driving force of the emotional intelligence that evolves our capacities to use the heart-mind system for the betterment of humankind.

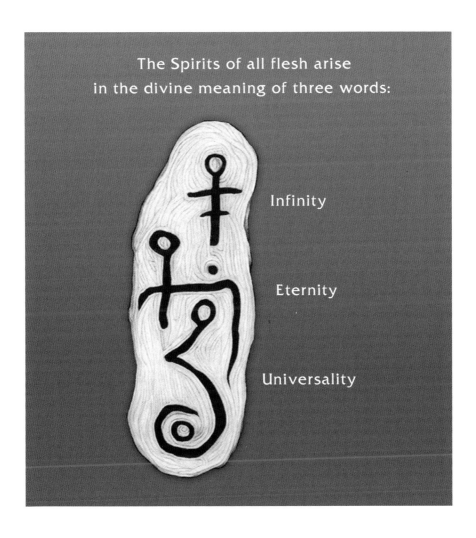

APPENDIX I

List of Meditations and Exercises

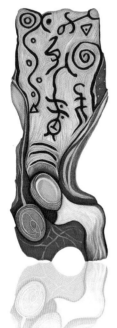

The following list of exercises is a chronological collection of the Volume I exercises that are included in James' writings and translations, which of course, comprise the documents in this compendium.

Volume I

WingMakers Philosophy "Beliefs and their Energy Systems"

- Mind-Body Movement Technique. Chamber Music 17-24.
- Mind-Soul Comprehension Technique Chamber Paintings 2, 3, 12, 4.
- Emotional-Soul Acquisition—Ten Specific Poems
    - Circle - Chamber Eleven
    - Forever - Chamber Nine
    - One Day - Chamber Four
    - Listening - Chamber One
    - Afterwards - Chamber Seventeen
    - Of this Place - Chamber Six
    - Warm Presence - Chamber Twenty-two
    - Another Mind Open - Chamber Eight
    - Of Luminous Things - Chamber Nine
    - Song of Whales - Chamber Seven

WingMakers Chamber Ten Music CD (or download)
— see Section 4 "The Music"

APPENDIX II

Philosophy Excerpts of the WingMakers from the Ancient Arrow Project Novel

Chamber Two: The Shifting Models of Existence, *from Chapter Eight*

If the entity is fragmented into its component parts, its comprehension of free will was limited to that which was circumscribed by the Hierarchy. If the entity is a conscious collective, realizing its sovereign wholeness, the principle of free will was a form of structure that was unnecessary like scaffolding on a finished building. When entities are unknowing of their wholeness, structure will occur as a form of self-imposed security. Through this ongoing development of a structured and ordered universe, entities defined their borders—their limits—through the expression of their insecurity. They gradually became pieces of their wholeness, and like shards of glass from a beautiful vase they bear little resemblance to their aggregate beauty.

Chamber Four: Beliefs and Their Energy Systems, *from Chapters Three and Fourteen*

All beliefs have energy systems that act like birthing rooms for the manifestation of the belief. Within these energy systems are currents that direct your life experience. You are aware of these currents either consciously or subconsciously, and you allow them to carry you into the realm of experience that best exemplifies your true belief system. When you believe "I am a fragment of First Source imbued

with ITS capabilities," you are engaging the energy inherent within the feeling of connectedness. You are pulling into your reality a sense of connection to your Source and all of the attributes therein. The belief is inseparable from you because its energy system is assimilated within your own energy system and is woven into your spirit like a thread of light.

When a species in the three-dimensional universe discovers irrefutable scientific proof of the multiverse and the innermost topology of the Wholeness Navigator, it impacts on every aspect of the species. It is the most profound shift of consciousness that can be foretold, and it is this event that triggers the Return of the Masters to explicit influence and exoteric roles.

Chamber Seven: Memory Activation, *from Chapter Six*

Your consciousness is faceted to express light into multiple systems of existence. There are many, many expressions that comprise your total Selfhood, and each expression is linked to the hub of consciousness that is your core identity. It is here that your ancient voice and eyes can multi-dimensionally observe, express, and experience. This is your food source for expansion and beautification. Place your attention upon your core identity and never release it. With every piece of information that passes your way, discern how it enables you to attune to this voice and perception. This is the only discipline you require. It is the remedy of limitation.

Chamber Seven: Personal Purpose, *from Chapter Fifteen*

Upon the merging of your will with that of First Source, you unconsciously participate with thousands of personality formats devoted to the Great Cause. It is the joined endeavor of all that you are with the perfect unfoldment of all that is and will ever be. It is the suggestive line of evidence that points to your purpose even before you can speak the words or feel the emotion of your gift, and it only requires you to desire the will of First Source to take ascendancy in your life.

Chamber Nine: The Primus Code, *from Chapters Sixteen and Seventeen*

First Source is not a manifestation, but rather a consciousness that inhabits all time, space, energy, and matter; as well as all non-time, non-space, non-matter, and non-energy. It is the only consciousness that unifies all states of being into one Being, and this Being is First Source. It is a growing, expanding, and inexplicable consciousness that organizes the collective experience of all states of being into a coherent plan of creation; expansion and colonization into the realms of creation; and the inclusion of creation into Source Reality – the home of First Source. This Being pervades the Grand Universe as the sum of experience in time and non-time. It has encoded ITSELF within all life as a vibratory force that is the primus code that creates you as a silken atom in the cosmological web.

The potency of the human soul is defined first by the laws of creation, and second, by the awareness that these laws assure cosmic stability and spiritual poise.

Chamber Ten: Particle Alignment, *from Chapter Seven*

There are, below the surface of your particle existence, energies that connect you to all formats of existence. You are a vast collection of these energies, but they cannot flow through your human instrument as an orchestrated energy until the particles of your existence are aligned and flowing in the direction of unity and wholeness.

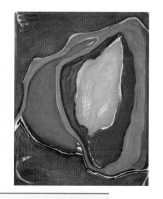

Chamber Twelve: The Wholeness Navigator, *from Chapters One and Nine*

Your theories of evolution are simply layered upon an existing paradigm of a mechanical universe that consists of molecular machines operating in an objective reality that is knowable with the right instruments. We tell you a truth of the universe when we say that reality is unknowable with any instrument save your own sense of unity and wholeness. Your perception of wholeness is unfolding because the culture of the multidimensional universe is rooted in unity. As your wholeness navigator reveals itself in the coming shift, you will dismantle and restructure your perceptions of who you are, and in this process humanity will emerge like a river of light from what was once an impenetrable fog.

All human life is embedded with a Wholeness Navigator. It is the core wisdom. It draws the human instrument to perceive fragmentary existence as a passageway into wholeness and unity. The Wholeness Navigator pursues wholeness above all else, yet it is often blown off course by the energies of structure, polarity, linear time, and separatist cultures that dominate terra-earth. The Wholeness Navigator is the heart of the entity consciousness, and it knows that the secret root exists even though it may be intangible to the human senses. It is this very condition of accepting the interconnectedness of life that places spiritual growth as a priority in one's life.

Chamber Thirteen: The Central Race, *from Chapter Twelve*

You are in the infallible process of inward ascension—journeying from the outer reaches of creation to the inner sanctum of the One Creator who is First Source. We, the Central Race, your elder brother, remind you of the journey's purpose so you may understand that the role of the human

form is to embody that which unites us all. However, it is only within the centermost universe that the children of time may experience the spokes of identity and the supremacy of their convergence.

Chamber Fifteen: The Function of the Wholeness Navigator, *from Chapter Thirteen*

Evolution in the material universe has provided you with a life vehicle, your human body. First Source has endowed your body with the purest fragment of ITS reality, your wholeness navigator. It is the mysterious fragment of First Source that acts like the pilot light of the human soul—fusing the mortal and eternal aspects. Can you fathom what it means to have a fragment of the Absolute Source indwelling within your very nature? Can you imagine your destiny when you fuse with an actual fragment of the First Source of the Grand Universe? No limit can be placed upon your powers of Selfhood or your eternal possibility.

Chamber Seventeen: Capacities of Self-Creation, *from Chapter Eleven*

In your world, you are taught to believe that your body has a mind and spirit,

when indeed, it is your spirit that has a mind and body. Your spirit is the architect, your mind is the builder, and your body is the material embodiment. The architect—your spirit—is only a thought away. Listen to its ancient voice. Perceive with its ancient eyes. Honor these gateways of intelligence as you would your Creator. They are your reality. They are the defining elements of your existence. It is time they yield the information that is the only true source of your liberation. You have only to command it, for we assure you, the teacher you have always sought is awake and waiting.

Chamber Twenty-one: Habitat of Soul, *from Chapter Ten*

First Source is the ancestor of all beings and life forms, and in this truth, is the ground of unity upon which we all stand. The journey of unification—of creature finding its creator—is the very heart of the human soul, and in this journey, the unalterable feeling of wholeness is the reward. Every impulse of every electron is correlated to the whole of the universe in its eternal ascent Godward. There is no other direction we can go.

Chamber Twenty-two: Tributary Zones, *from Chapters Four and Five*

The blueprint of exploration has an overarching intention; you are not the recipients of divine labor and meticulous training only to ensure that you may enjoy endless bliss and eternal ease. There is a purpose of transcendent service concealed beyond the horizon of the present universe age. If I designed you to take you on an eternal excursion into nirvana, I certainly would not construct your entire universe into one vast and intricate training school, requisition a substantial branch of my creation as teachers and instructors, and then spend ages upon ages piloting you, one by one, through this enormous universe school of experiential learning. The furtherance of the system of human progression is cultivated by my will for the explicit purpose to merge the human species with other species from different universes.

As it is my nature to be seven-fold, there are seven universes that comprise my body. Within each of these, a species of a particular DNA template is cast forth and is nurtured by Source Intelligence to explore its material universe. Each of these species is sent forth from the Central Race into the universe that was created to unveil its potential and seed vision. Your species will converge with six other species in a distant future that will reunite my body as the living extension of known creation.

While this may seem so distant as to have no relevance to your time, it is vital for you to understand the scope of your purpose. You can think of these seven species as the limbs of my body rejoined to enable me/us total functionality within the grand universe. This is my purpose and therefore your own as well.

Chamber Twenty-three: First Source, *from Chapter Two*

There is no supplication that stirs me. No prayer that invites me further into your world unless it is attended with the feeling of unity and wholeness. There is no temple or sacred object that touches me. They do not, nor have they ever brought you closer to my outstretched hand. My presence in your world is

unalterable for I am the sanctuary of both the cosmos and the one soul inside you.

Appendix III

Supplemental Glossary

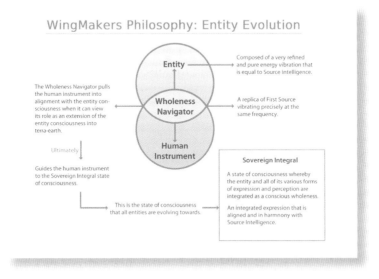

WingMakers Philosophy: Entity Evolution

This glossary consists of terms James has introduced in his writings after the original WingMakers glossary was officially released in 2001. Two items were added to the original with the release in 2003 of two Hakomi Project CDs, Hakomi Project Chamber Three and Hakomi Project Chambers Four to Six. The first of the two items is "Remnant Imprint," which relates to Hakomi Project Chamber Three. The second item is "Tributary Zone."

In addition to new terms, this supplement also includes further descriptive details of entries contained in the original glossary. These entries are marked with an asterisk.

Finally, this supplement is not meant to be exhaustive. It includes terms contained in the writings of volume I of The Collected Works of the WingMakers. I have limited it to those factors that bear on the current shift in consciousness and to the Grand Portal discovery.

All That Is "All That Is represents a library on a much grander scale than the Genetic Mind. In principle, the two are similar except for scale. All That Is pertains to the multiverse and the cosmic spirits therein. While the Genetic Mind pertains to the humanoid species within Super Universe Seven, the imagery of All That Is is codified into a higher dimensional language, which in turn is encoded into the original works within the Tributary Zones. These are then stepped down in frequency to the materials contained on the WingMakers website and in the music CDs. . . . All That Is, by its nature, is multi-faceted (wheels within wheels) and in order to distribute this multidimensional complexity, the dispensation must include both sound and light orchestrated into words, music, and pictures. These elements must then be orchestrated to trigger specific resonances within the human genome that lay dormant because – for the most part—present-day culture does not activate or touch these receptors of the human DNA." [1]

Event Strings "Event strings are remarkably complex systems of interrelationships between matter (things), energy (individuals), space (places), time (events) and coherence (goal synergy). Individuals involved in the Lyricus materials—no matter how seemingly insignificant—are affecting the flow of the master event string that makes possible the discovery of the Grand Portal." [2]

First Source "First Source lives in the third dimension, but is simultaneously aware of itself throughout the spectrum of the multiverse, and through Source Intelligence, is aware of all life forms in all dimensions." [3]

"First Source is the primal source from which all existence is ultimately linked. It is sometimes referred to as the Body of the Collective God. It represents the overarching consciousness of all things unified. This includes pain, joy, suffering, light, love, darkness, fear; all expressions and conditions are integrated and purposeful in the context of First Source. IT encompasses all things and unifies them in an all-inclusive consciousness that evolves and grows in a similar manner to how each individuated spirit evolves and grows." [4]

"First Source is all of us. It is the Collective Us. It is not a God living in some distant pocket of the universe. First Source is the Human Collective unencumbered with the HMS." [5]

"First Source is not God, not as human beings understand what God is. God, as an entity, independent of you or me, does not exist. . . . First Source is the collective of Sovereign Integrals throughout the multiverse, and that which binds them is Source Intelligence." [6]

Genetic Mind "DNA is both a network within the individual body as well as a node within the species' collective "body" or genetic mind." [7]

Grand Portal

From Neruda Interview Four:

Sarah: "Anyway, what will be gained by having this discovery… the Grand Portal?"

Dr. Neruda: "Everything that keeps us separate—locked in statehood and provincial concerns—will be obliterated when this undeniable proof is obtained."

---

1. *Collected Works of the WingMakers Vol. II*, Part IV, Sec. Two, Top. Arr. of Qs and As, Ques. 64-S3
2. *Collected Works of the WingMakers Vol. II*, Part II, Sec. One, Lyricus Teachers and Methodologies
3. *Collected Works of the WingMakers Vol. II*, Part IV, Sec. Two, Top. Arr. of Qs and As, Ques. 10-S2
4. *Collected Works of the WingMakers Vol. II*, Part III, Sec. One, *Living from the Heart*
5. *Collected Works of the WingMakers Vol. II*, Part III, Sec. Three, Project Camelot Interview
6. Ibid.
7. *Collected Works of the WingMakers Vol. II*, Part II, Sec. Two, The Interface Zone

Sarah: "Why would the basic nature of man, which has taken hundreds of thousands of years to form, suddenly change when science steps forward and announces that it has proven the existence of soul? It doesn't seem plausible to me."

Dr. Neruda: "According to the WingMakers this is the evolutionary path of the human species, and the discovery of the Grand Portal is the culmination of a global species. It creates the conditions whereby the things that separate us are stripped away, whether they're color, race, form, geography, religion, or anything else. We find ourselves staring into the lens of science and we see that all humans are composed of the same inner substance—whatever you choose to call it—and it is this that truly defines us and our capabilities." [8]

Sarah: "This Grand Portal is a scientific discovery, not a religious one. Correct?"

Dr. Neruda: "Yes." . . .

"You can think of the Grand Portal as the interface for the consciousness of vertical time.[9] This interface will be discovered sometime in the twenty-first century. I don't know all the details. I don't know how it will impact on the individual. You may be right; some will accept it and some will not. I only know it is part of the destiny that humankind is led to achieve."

Sarah: "According to the WingMakers?"

Dr. Neruda: "Yes." [10] . . .

"The WingMakers' materials are designed to activate those souls that are incarnating who will play active roles in the discovery and creation of the Grand Portal—"

Sarah: "Are you saying that souls are incarnating specifically for this purpose?"

Dr. Neruda: "Yes. There are very advanced souls who are incarnating in the next three generations who will design, develop, and employ the Grand Portal. This is the central purpose of the WingMakers' materials stored within these seven sites." [11] Vol. I

Human Instrument "The human instrument consists of three principal components: The biological (physical body), the emotional, and the mental. These three distinct tools and systems of intelligence and perception, in aggregate, represent the vehicle of the individuated spirit as it interacts with the physical dimension of time, space, energy, and matter. In Lyricus terms, the human instrument is referred to as the soul carrier, and the soul consciousness within it is activating the sensorial system of the soul carrier to enhance the soul's influence within the physical world." [12] Vol. I

8. The Fourth Interview of Dr. Jamisson Neruda, p. 411.
9. Dr. Neruda: "Vertical time has to do with the simultaneous experience of all time, and horizontal time has to do with the continuity of time in linear, moment-by-moment experiences." The First Interview of Dr. Jamisson Neruda, p. 279.
10. The Fourth Interview of Dr. Jamisson Neruda, p. 412.
11. Ibid., p. 413.
12. *Collected Works of the WingMakers Vol. II*, Part III, Sec. One, "The Energetic Heart: Its Purpose in Human Destiny"

Interface Zone "Spiritual sound helps to create an Interface Zone between the human instrument and the vibratory soup of the world of forms. This Interface Zone supports the human instrument's mission and purpose, preventing its vibratory contamination as a vessel for the human soul and an outlet of First Source's expression of Sound and Light." [13]

"Harmony is the ruling principle of the Interface Zone, and music—properly tuned—can help to create, direct, and uphold this sense of harmony. If the Interface Zone is rightfully managed, it will provide a buffer between the human soul and the worlds of form that bear down upon it." [14]

Sovereign Integral Note that I give the Sovereign Integral entry more attention because it is likely that this topic will come to the forefront of James' work in the near future. Considering this, it will be advantageous for us to grasp the meaning of the Sovereign Integral as much as possible now, as this will provide a solid foundation for future teachings. Ed.

"It is a difficult abstraction for time-bound humans to understand, but the Sovereign Integral consciousness is the fusion of the entity consciousness in the worlds of timespace. All expressions and experiences of the human instrument, collectively, are deposited within the Sovereign Integral state of consciousness, and it is precisely this that imprints upon the human instrument of the individual." [15]

"[It] is a state of consciousness whereby the entity and all of its various forms of expression and perception are integrated as a conscious wholeness. The Sovereign Integral is the core identity of the individual. It is the convergence of the experiential worlds of time and space with the innate knowledge of First Source divested within the individual at the time of its birth. It is the gathering of all created experiences and all instinctive knowledge." [16]

---

13. "Coherence of the Evolutionary Consciousness," p. 575.
14. Ibid., p. 576.
15. "Anatomy of the Individuated Consciousness," p. 561.
16. Ibid., p. 562.

About the Author

James Mahu is the anonymous and visionary creator of five websites, four novels, a large collection of philosophical discourses, a dozen papers on spiritual practices, poetry, short stories, visual artwork, and nearly a hundred music compositions.

His first published creation was WingMakers.com, which established James—its creator—as a multidimensional storyteller who is focused on sharing deep, original perspectives to the conversations of spirituality, cosmology, extraterrestrial life, myth and the importance of the heart in one's personal mission.

About the Editor

John Berges (October 5, 1946 - August 30, 2011) was a spiritual philosopher, researcher and teacher for over forty years. He was a lifelong gifted practitioner of love-centered living. During the last decade of his life he devoted his energies to experiencing, studying and sharing his insights on the WingMakers and Lyricus materials. He edited many of the WingMakers and Lyricus papers. John authored the *When-Which-How Practice: A Guide for Everyday Use*, "The Guide for EventTemples 2" and "The First Ten Years" e-papers. In 2009, James asked John to be the editor and commentator for the *Collected Works of the WingMakers Volume I & II*. John's writing can be found at www.wingmakers.com, www.eventtemples.com and wwwplanetwork.co.